Storms at Sealandings

Jonathan Grant is a doctor specialising in Tropical Medicine. Under his pseudonym of Jonathan Gash, he is the author of the ever popular *Lovejoy* novels

He lists his hobbies as antiques, his family and more antiques. Jonathan Grant is married with three daughters and lives near Colchester in Essex.

GW00542574

STORMS AT SEALANDINGS

Jonathan Grant

ARROW

First published 1992

1 3 5 7 9 10 8 6 4 2

Copyright © Jonathan Grant 1992

Jonathan Grant has asserted his
right under the Copyright, Designs and Patents Act, 1988
to be identified as the author of this work

First published in Great Britain by Century 1992

Arrow edition 1993
Random House, 20 Vauxhall Bridge Road, London SW1V 2SA

Random House Australia (Pty) Limited
20 Alfred Street, Milsons Point, Sydney,
New South Wales 2061, Australia

Random House New Zealand Limited
18 Poland Road, Glenfield
Auckland 10, New Zealand

Random House South Africa (Pty) Limited
PO Box 337, Bergvlei, South Africa

Random House UK Limited Reg. No. 954009

A CIP catalogue record for this book
is available from the British Library

ISBN 0 09 978720 2

Printed and bound in Great Britain by
Cox & Wyman Ltd, Reading, Berkshire

Dedications

For Matthew, Sarah, Jack, Charlotte.
And for Brian, the last gentleman.

Thanks

To Susan.

1

Hate.

How beautiful hate was!

The woman looked down at the distant figure stooping in the garden. She had been watching from the road for almost a quarter of an hour. It was only the beginning. Hate was now her cause. The woman Mehala could live a thousand years, serving her master at the decrepit old house called Shalamar, yet on her last hour find Judith Blaker there crowing *hate* at her bedside.

Then would be a time of rejoicing, pure ecstasy, for which Judith Blaker would thank whatever forces, good or evil, brought about the fall of Mehala. She found herself smiling at the delicious thought as the seaspray dampened her cheeks on the veering wind. She turned, swept her skirt from her shoes to walk the last mile down the slope, past the gaunt relic that was Doctor Carmichael's home, and into Sealandings.

The Flora's Dial was almost complete. Mehala rose, brushing a wisp of hair from her forehead, and moved back to judge the plants. Positioning flowers was not at all easy, when they were at different stages of development. It was the way of all living things, herself and Carmichael included. The Flora's Dial was love's living emblem: each hour of the twenty-four, one plant would close its blossom and the next smile open. Old lore promised that, where a woman grew a Flora's Dial, so flourished love, told by the sequence of opening blooms, hour and hour about.

For a second, she imagined she caught sight of somebody moving along the South Toll road, and stood on tiptoe to see. There was no one. Probably just some fox loping across from the De Foes' grand estate to seek easier pickings in the slipshod estate of their cousin, Sir Charles Golding. Wrong time for a badger. And such folk as took the walk from the neighbouring coastal village of Whitehanger came by the sea path. Only waggons and carts followed the South Toll, grudgingly paying the extortionate costs at the toll-bar. Why, even an unladen horse was charged a penny – a whole penny! For nothing! A score of sheep levied at five whole pence! It was nothing less than a scandal.

She listened. Had she heard the thin *seeeep!* of – what was it – the redwing? Surely not. Redwings arrived at night, flying in over the North Sea, to rest hereabouts in East Anglia for the autumn. No. Too soon, far too soon. No prettichaps, the garden warbler. Oh, let the summer wane slow, she prayed silently. She was happier now than she could ever remember. She shivered as the wind veered further, and bent to her task. The Doctor would love her arrangement even though, manlike, he'd be slow to see the flowers' meaning. She found herself smiling. The hussy's meaning, her old mother would have chided, bridling at so forward a daughter. He'd be home in an hour from the surgery he held in the little school by the market. It seemed too wonderful to be true, that he would come walking up the long slope, his old surtout as always flapping about his homemade galligaskin leggings, that his face would give its slow awkward smile when she stepped from the creaking doors to welcome him.

That hateful thought made her suddenly angry with herself. No! Life in Sealandings was *fact*. She had made it herself, for herself. It was her old, forgotten life that was too bad to be true. Life with Doctor Ven Carmichael was wondrous enough to *be* true. That was the way to see it. Let others try guessing about her early years. Ven never asked, sensing that she wanted the veil to remain.

She was Mehala of Sealandings now, and would remain so for ever and ever, housekeeper for the Doctor. Whether she was something more to him, or could become so, was for others to speculate. Let them gossip, tattling that old Mrs Trenchard was past noticing much these days and sniggering about possible goings-on between Mehala and Carmichael. Her life was well-nigh perfect. She had fought before to protect it and him, and would do so again.

'Get me the brandenburgs.'

Carradine's patience had gone. No mirror in this fleapit of a house, no servants now Carradine Manor estate was in the hands of the odious Prothero. All for a single disastrous bet. And, he told himself sardonically, hardly a mistress to speak of. The lady was scarcely proving her worth. It was a pity she clung so, but he'd be in a finer mess still if he discarded her.

From the bed Thalia De Foe eyed him warily. They had been lovers too long for her not to fear his moods. But fear was a woman's love.

'Can't you do without?'

He straightened, colouring at her tone, crossed to stand looking down at her for so long that his silence unnerved her.

'Without brandenburg cuffs, on a bright fawn pelisse coat? Show everybody that I lack money to match a mink collar, set them giggling that Carradine has lost his clothing as well as his estates?'

'You haven't yet lost Carradine Manor, darling. Come to some arrangement with Prothero – '

'*Prothero?*' She recoiled, half-raising an arm to protect herself from his rage. 'Go cap in hand to a bastard peasant who holds a handful of scrip on my lands?'

'Not to beg, darling. To lead him by the nose. Then to seize what's rightfully yours. And in the process venge yourself on the upstart.'

Thalia De Foe raised herself to a kneeling position and beckoned him, smiling. He sat for her to comb his dark hair. She recognised all the signs, his suppressed fury coming dangerously near the surface. That formed part of his attraction for her, even though now he was reduced in circumstances. Gambling, and worse, had brought him down. Nothing of course would keep him there. Not Carradine.

'Upstarts,' Carradine said. He was not mollified.

Thalia agreed. 'And Mehala can be dealt with any time.'

A purr entered her voice at the image. The woman deserved punishment. Chastisement delayed was chastisement ignored. Leniency was interpreted by the lower classes as weakness – and that was subversively close to upsetting the natural order of society, which must be maintained at all costs. Heaven appointed the gentry to rule, and others to serve. Position relinquished was duty failed.

'She's caught the eye of Squire Hunterfield, God damn him.'

'Henry Hunterfield's unmarried,' Thalia reminded, combing with gentle skill. 'I'm taking that small problem in hand. Then the

3

bitch Mehala can simper all she chooses. She's only a peasant. Hunterfield will slip her from mind once a wife takes command of Lorne House.'

Carradine turned. This woman was full of surprises. 'Who've you got? Some friend of your husband's?'

Thalia laughed, smacked him playfully with the comb. 'You think I should select some mare that Fellows uses on the sly in his London stews? No, darling. I've chosen closer to home. Let me keep it a surprise.'

A knock came on the door. 'Madam? The clock is on the hour.'

'Right, Meg. I shall be out presently.'

'The whisky is ready now, ma'am.'

Thalia cursed her personal maid under her breath, rose and caught up her clothes. 'These servants will be the masters of us all yet. My time's not been my own since Fellows came home.'

'When does he leave?'

'This week, thanks be to God.'

Carradine watched her dress, marvelling at the complications of her attire. He disliked the ninon, though the stout silk voile's transparent surface looked enticing. She would drive the whisky herself, taking Meg along. He caught the two brandenburgs Thalia flung mischievously at him, and pulled them into place, the loops on his cuffs over the buttons. She must have concealed them deliberately, to delay his departure. He stamped into his boots, caught up his beaver.

'You look beautiful, darling.' She came to embrace him but he pushed her away.

'Time you got a cheval glass in this wretched place.'

She choked back an angry retort. 'I shall, darling.'

She watched him leave, heard the outer door slam, listened a moment for the scuff of the horse hooves on the path, then shouted for Meg to come and insert the whalebone through her back lacings. This instant unlacing was a boon when disrobing, as when a hot lover came to seize his rights, a single movement lifted out the whalebone rib from between the shoulders, and all was ready for rapture. But it was a feat of engineering to restore.

Carradine's command about a looking glass was infuriating. Who had found this cottage, in the inland wilds near Maidborough? Who had plotted its hire through nominees, carefully considering *his* reputation? And who, damn it, still had reputation to lose? For the slightest breath of scandal would ruin her, her marriage to the powerful Fellows De Foe, and doom her ambitions for Carradine.

Carradine. She melted at the thought of him, though he had been gone a bare minute. Carradine was her religion, her life.

She disagreed with him on one point. Mehala *had* been instrumental in procuring his downfall. Ever since she had arrived, quite out of nowhere, the bitch Mehala had been trouble. Never quite prominent enough to blame for anything, oh dear no! But always there. It spoke of the girl's cleverness, her deep witch-like subterfuges, rather than revealed her innocence.

Thalia's experience was that women were more blameworthy than men, for men could be easily handled by a skilled and determined woman. No, it was Mehala who ought to suffer, ensconced with her penniless quack in Shalamar along the South Toll road. How was a slut like her proof against disapproval?

'Meg!' she called, angrily slamming the door ajar. Meg was just scurrying towards her from the small vestibule, where she had doubtless been ogling Carradine as he rode off.

Thalia slapped the girl's face, viciously using the back of her hand. Meg rode the blow by swinging with the force, so proving her insolence.

'I've been calling for you these ten minutes, and you failing in duty by gaping at your betters!'

'I'm sorry, ma'am. I was – '

'Get me dressed! Concentrate for once! As soon as I'm returned to Milton Hall I shall want Ennis to carry an urgent invitation to the Misses Astell at Arminell. No dawdling.'

'Yes, ma'am.'

Thalia smiled to herself. Meg knew which side her bread was buttered. Loyal, obedient, yet with that quality of silence which a personal maid had to have. Husbands were a danger. Even the complacent Fellows, eager to be gone to London's banks and coffee houses in the Strand and East Cheap, could be notoriously whimsical. One minute casual, not minding about country estates, and the next setting agents among the very foliage to act the spy on families and land stewards to trace every farthing. Yes, even a maid like Meg needed firm reins, and sometimes a harsher touch still, to keep her docile.

As Meg laced her into the corset, Thalia decided that enough time had elapsed since the trouble between Sir Henry Hunterfield and her lover. She should procure a wife for the senior magistrate, place him in her debt. As a lover, Hunterfield was never a patch on Carradine. She didn't want him back: she wanted him married. Then she must somehow scheme the repellent Prothero out of Carradine's family estates and, most pleasant of all, effect the ruin of the girl Mehala. That revenge would be like a sweet pepper cake after a deliciously heavy supper.

'Meg?' she said thoughtfully.

'I'm hurrying, ma'am!'

'Not that, dolt!' Thalia breathed in, trying to lift her breasts, for a narrower waist. You never knew who would ride the Sea-landings road. 'You recall the wench Mehala?'

'The girl *The Jaunty* fetched from the sea? Yes, ma'am. She does for Doctor Carmichael at Shalamar. A right old ramshackle pile it be, ma'am. Nigh to dereliction. Only kept together by bat droppings and ivy, they do say.'

'Has that dog-leech another housekeeper?'

'Mrs Trenchard, ma'am? Little good these days, her being poor by age. Her husband works your estate, ma'am.'

'Doing what?'

'He dogs rats and the like, in season, to earn a shilling or two. But of course he's of age also.'

'Does Mrs Trenchard ever, well, say anything about Mehala? Anything about her family, friends, relatives?'

'No, ma'am. The girl was wit free when she got drownded, and comes only slow into her mind. It is several months since Jervin's lugger brought her in.'

How odd, Thalia thought. How *very* odd. She knew of people rescued from drowning, of course. Here on the coast, who didn't? But all of them were fully recovered in a week, or else they remained witless for life. They never became capable, brisk and bright – yet selectively short on memory.

Clever Mehala, Thalia thought, smiling to herself. There's something she wants to hide, and what better way to hide a past than pretend a loss of memory? The sooner that snippet of

6

information was harvested into her trug, the sooner the utterly enjoyable task of punishing the bitch in the way she so richly deserved.

'Meg,' she said sweetly. 'When I'm home to Milton Hall, I want you to ask for details of Mehala. You understand?'

'Details, ma'am?'

'Nothing too pointed. Perhaps I might be able to help the poor creature to improve herself to better station than working for that impecunious leech.'

'Very well, ma'am,' Meg said. Poor Mehala, she thought. Help, from her sugary-voiced mistress, was perilous assistance for anyone.

Doctor Carmichael heard the scream over the travelling fair's music and bells, and pushed his way through the awestruck crowd to see a toothdrawer grappling to extract a man's tooth. Carmichael guessed the problem immediately, for it was one of the commonest causes of illness. A huge boil in the man's lower gum distended his whole face. His lips were brown-frosted with dried blood, rivulets of fresh blood running down his chin. His groans were drowned by the musician – the assistant who always accompanied wandering toothpullers. He capered, the bells sewn on to his clothes and cap tingling, blowing his fife and thrashing his tabor. The crowd watched in horror. Hardly a man or woman in Sealandings had white, regular teeth. Not even the gentry were free of hurtful gum and jaw disease; bad teeth killed almost as many inhabitants as plague and phthisis.

The small travelling fair was grander in title than reality. It had a dancing bear – mangy, old, handling its chains with weary familiarity – sellers of simples and gaudily coloured lotions, singers and tinkers and, receipt of all attention, the wandering blacksmith-dentist.

His skills were advertised: *Jno. Bellingham, Blacksmith-Cum-Toothdrawer to His Most Excellent Majesty the King of Naples Since Three Year*. The weathered board hung on an ineffectual tattered sacking screen draped on staves driven into the earth. Children were laughing, miming the patient's suffering.

'Here, you!' The blacksmith kept hold of the iron hook fixed into the man's mouth. 'Jem booy! Come and shift this man.'

The musician capered closer. Doctor Carmichael edged to face him. Such grinning buffoons were more like marauders, and some said cutpurses, than helpers. He pointed a finger at the man, keeping a wary eye on the toothpuller.

'I am the Sealandings surgeon,' he said. 'Careful, friend.'

The capering musician hesitated, looking at the crowd to gauge its sympathies.

'Stay, Jem booy!' The toothdrawer decided to seize advantage. 'D'you see, folks? This famous medical gentleman, from the London College of Surgeons, has come to learn Bellingham's superb medical art!'

Doctor Carmichael ignored this. The suffering man was middle-aged, smocked, and shod with homemade leather boots. A long stave and a small sack on a leather strap lay beside his feet, and a bonnet where it had fallen. A northern drover, by his look. He was drenched in sweat, almost fainting, swaying so badly he was like to fall from the stool. An everyday picture of agony, Ven Carmichael thought bitterly. If only the great painters would banish their expensive models, draped in allegorical costumery, and come here into the Eastern Hundreds! Then they would paint subjects to move men's stoniest hearts. No need to search – a walk down any lane would find them. Just follow the sounds of weeping.

'Friend.' He touched the swooning man on the shoulder. The eyes flickered, tears streaming. 'Has it been slow in coming?'

'Aaaah.' Assent.

'How long have you been trying, Bellingham?' Carmichael asked. The toothdrawer let go of the instrument with a shrug, causing the drover to howl in agony. Ven noticed a black D tattooed under the blacksmith's arm – the shaming insignia of a deserter from his ship or regiment.

'A few moments.'

It was a lie. The unfortunate man was almost prostrate, and these drovers were strong, who came afoot the length of the Kingdom. Doctor Carmichael looked at the faces in the crowd. None met his eye. Could he blame them? Give offence to a wandering strongman, you might be followed back to your cottage and . . .

'Here,' the blacksmith growled as Ven bent to examine the drover's mouth. 'He be my patient. To me goes the fee!'

'You're killing the man, for God's sake!' Ven's exasperation brought a gasp from the people, who backed away.

'Jem!' The huge blacksmith spat on his bloodstained hands. The musician dropped his tabor and fife, grinning at the prospect of inflicting a beating.

Carmichael stood his ground, then was conscious of a sudden quiet. He looked round. A young man had stepped forward to lean an elbow on a screen pole.

'Good day, Doctor. I finished making your flintlock.' He was carrying a slim mahogany box.

'Mr Hast.' Carmichael was about to deny having ordered any weapon, then understood. Bartholomew Hast, the harbour's gunsmith, was offering him protection.

The blacksmith inhaled slowly, looking at the newcomer. Ven nodded mute thanks to the gunmaker, and turned his attention to the drover.

An abscess was festering deep inside the gum, the turgescence shining dully, speckled with flecks of suppurating points. The breath stank. The tooth was almost hollow. Ven removed his glove and put his finger gently inside to feel along the gum. It was fluctuant, like a small play-bladder filled with water. The prong of the rusty iron hook was embedded in the man's jaw beneath, causing a seepage of pus from one loculus. The rest of the pus was still within. He examined the skin over the mandible, the neck. Lumpy, but no pointing there.

The weight of simple unknowing pressed dismay into his spirit. How paltry medicine's understanding. How ridiculous that the nation's teeth were craggy, erratically grown, blackened or discoloured, filthy, the breath fetid and the gums scarred, running with pus. There was no dentist in the entire Kingdom, not a single one; no training, no college to teach dentology. An occasional duchess had her own private surgeon responsible for her teeth, but the rest of the population suffered every day of their lives. Teeth were left to chance, and blacksmiths.

The drawer had simply guessed where the root would be, and jabbed the iron point in hard, hoping to loosen it. The Ancient Greeks at least had a semblance of expertise in dentology. The London Hospital, where he had trained, provided their students with no lectures on gum diseases, nor taught how to remove a bad tooth. Once, he had nearly been able to afford the entry fee to a lecture delivered by the redoubtable toothman L. S. Parmley – only to learn with horror that his private courses in the dentological art cost from 100 to 200 guineas! A sum beyond imagination. Could even a royal duke afford so much?

'Stay still, man,' he said to the drover, pressing the man's head close to his own side. With his right hand he took the end of the iron implement, and dragged it out of the jaw. The man heaved with the pain. Ven examined the rusty hook. None of its prong was left in, thank God. He let the man go, who sat with his hands against his face, moaning and dripping blood. The onlookers exclaimed like a theatre crowd suddenly released from tension.

'What instruments have you, Bellingham?'

'Those.' The toothdrawer sulkily indicated a rag lying on the grass, a small hammer, a bradawl and the iron hook.

Carmichael closed his eyes for a second. 'You keep a pelican instrument, or a toothkey?'

'Have you?' the man shot back instantly in aggrieved denial.

Ven asked the drover to open his mouth and probed along the jaw. The Ancients, he remembered from his Latin studies, sat the patient between the knees, and cut sharply down through the gum with a knife. Then they seized the offending tooth with anything handy and rocked it loose enough to be pulled out. That had been the only way for nigh on two, maybe three, thousand years. Now, all sorts of instruments were rumoured to exist on the Continent, in London, even the Americas, but only once had he ever seen either of the instruments he was asking for. He felt absurd, a charlatan. What right had he to blame a wandering blacksmith? The only difference between them was that Bellingham pretended he was highly skilled, with the help of a clowning musician and a painted notice whereas he, the doctor, pretended with some debased dog-Latin and a degree from a medical school that taught in suppositions.

He opened his case and drew out his one lancet. The abscess in the drover's mouth was fluctuant, turgid with pus. Carmichael kept the lancet hidden from the patient, palming it as he turned. Without a pause, he clasped the man's head firmly and told him to open his mouth.

The lancet slipped into the ugly swelling, deep into the tissues.

A spurt of yellow pus came out, the fetor almost making Carmichael gag. He bent the man forward.

'Spit all you can, friend. Spit out. Come *on*.'

He asked for some small beer, that being much cleaner than any available roadside water. Nobody offered any. Hast the gunsmith disappeared for a moment and returned with a stone jar.

'Borrowed from the actors,' he explained, smiling.

Carmichael let the man take a mouthful and spit it away. He pressed the gum gently, expelling still more festering matter and repeated the process while the tumblers came to grumble at the confiscation of their drink.

'Who'll pay for our small beer, Doctor?' one demanded.

'Here.' Carmichael threw the woman a penny. She caught it, her annoyance undiminished. 'At least it's not a shop token!' he told her, alluding to the common practice of minting copper pieces for local spending when the Royal Mint failed to keep pace with public need.

'That cost two whole pence!'

The drover gingerly felt his jaw. He would remain feverish for some time, but at least he would not be in utter agony, and the abscess might drain away. Or not. His survival lay in the lap of the gods.

'When the swelling lessens,' Carmichael told him, 'then seek a doctor or surgeon who will take away the tooth.'

He washed his lancet in a glug of the small beer, causing the actors to howl angrily at such waste, then dried it on his old surtout. Cleanliness was a foible of his. It always had been, causing him much derision at The London Hospital when a student in Whitechapel. He nodded his thanks to the smiling gunsmith, who left shaking his head ruefully. Ven walked off feeling ashamed at his crude surgery. The poor drover needed rest, clean water to wash away the pus, repeated examination to ensure the deep cut stayed patent so the matter could drain away, but he would have nothing. It was degradation, shaming the Doctor at Sealandings. Thank God for Mehala, his one help.

Mehala was cooking samphire when the thought struck her. *Mehala*. The strange name puzzled the market woman. Serving girls, tinkers, travelling mongers, seemed slightly intrigued.

11

Those who could write asked its spelling. Was it her real name? Or something dredged from the recesses of her mind as she floated in that dark North Sea?

The shiver took her so severely that she had to pause. Memories were profound when they came, their intensity making her queasy. Could recollections be figments? No. Take this samphire, a simple plant gathered on the seashore. Even that lost its innocence, measured by memory. For how exactly did she know it was so useful? Cooked rightly, it became almost a meal in itself, though it grew humble and wild along the sealands.

A strange sense enveloped her. What impulse had sent her out into harsh weather? She had gathered it, prepared it, all without conscious thought. She *knew* this virginal weed, and well. It lay there in a heap with its fleshy leaves, its stout rays made to withstand the cruel winds, its short stem no more than twelve inches. See how she had prepared it as a pot-herb! Her hands had expertly stripped off the corky fruits, made ready the extra mace for the vinegar with the samphire, and so created that elegant condiment known only to the indigenous coastal folk. Its spicy aromatic scent was familiar. Hadn't she gathered it in her little trug with old Abby Abraham, every childhood year? Some folk fried it on a low pan rubbed with beef dripping . . .

For a moment she went to sit down. The man she had married, madman Elijah Rebow, was drowned. A certainty . . . She must cling to that, as proof that it all was deep in the past. Macabre and mad, that dark swirling nightmare had become. Suppress the terror of that time, yes, but nurture the fact, the sureness. Already its grim power was lessening, like some receding thunderstorm. Dreams could always be recaptured entire, their meanings explored in idle hours, chatted about with friends who found giggles in the meaning. But fragments of memory were more elusive. Illusory and even sinister, they could not be tethered for scrutiny. Like those fleeting half-glimpses you saw from the corner of an eye, and on turning found no one there.

And now the man in her life was as far from Elijah Rebow as could be, that gross man with the fierce eyes, ferocious aggression and personal love-greed so much part of his nature. There was nothing in a woman to resist such vehemence, no depths to draw on. Mayhap a time would come when society would allow a woman to determine her own course – or was that simply a silent plea for Heaven to come now, not later?

Ven Carmichael was the opposite of her dead husband. Rebow had been vicious but Ven was mild, loth to speak for fear of hurting the listener, sombre in his broodings about the poor and ailing, and desolate nigh to tears when treatment failed and a soul was lost. Self-critical to a fault, he drove himself, sketching fanciful new instruments, returning time after time to see a sick child, always away in some future dream where terrible fevers could be allayed with wonderful medicines that might one day be made. Yet there were days when he laughed like a little boy, his face splitting in a great grin of delight when some little moppet uttered a childish incongruity. Then his hesitations vanished all of an instant, and his laugh would set all laughing with him, most not knowing what was causing the Doctor's merriment. Then it was a return to gravity and the next case. In his quiet moments, the ones she cherished more as the days drifted through Shalamar, he would quietly speak of his doubts. He saw himself as ineffectual, a drop of water to quench an inferno of disease. No, there could never have been two men more dis-alike, than the struggling Doctor Carmichael and her . . . she determined she would never use *that* term about Elijah Rebow. Never.

What a hateful word it was! *Hus-band*. A woman's house bond, was it, or some Old Tongue similar? But Ven Carmichael was nobody's husband. She knew from occasional remarks that he had visited Calling Farm as a boy, and that Mary Calling and he had been friends. She also knew he had once courted some London lady and been disappointed, though Mehala still did not know how far his hopes had taken him.

Of course, logick urged that she seek some knowledge of Red Hall, the home – home! – she had mistressed after leaving Virley church as Rebow's wife. She ought to make a journey south, through Colchester and then out to the sea marshes where Red Hall stood, and discover her possessions. Then Doctor Carmichael would have lamps of the new Argand type, perhaps even that new gaslighting piped through the house into his study! She had never seen it, but had once heard two abigails, personal serving maids of visiting mistresses, talking nose-in-air of the backward ways of the sealands and the lack of gaslight and mantles . . .

13

But what would be the effect on him, were she to disclose her past? Shock, that she was once married? Would he be able to come to terms with her ever again? Nothing spoils easier than a dream, and Ven Carmichael was a dreamer. He longed for a blissfully perfect world. Women knew the world better, Mehala acknowledged with inner candour. It was given to men to dream in the strange reserves of mind, and for women to face reality. This was apparent even in small things. As when an urgent medical call came. Ven would make to hurry out without his old coarse surtout even in the wildest weather. Or when some despond would cause him to pause so long during his evening meal that she feared he had fallen asleep. She always liked having to chide him so, though mildly, for he would give her a moving smile of apology.

'Look at me, sitting here with the work all undone!' she scolded herself, and returned to her samphire. Storm-gathered, sea folk called it, knowing samphire nourished best before a great Sir Roger storm whirled in from the sea.

No, she would make no journey south. No return to Red Hall. No more those stroods and salt sedges of the low sea marshes by the Blackwater and the Colne. No excursions into the past, for past she had none. She lived here, in Sealandings, an unknown sea-fetched girl. Mehala of Sealandings was housekeeper to a humble doctor, and as yet nothing more.

2

The implications of Mrs Mary Prothero's visit on the little school was not lost on the schoolteacher Miss Matilda Gould – but her visitor's timing was less than fortunate.

Miss Gould was dismayed somewhat by the presence of Doctor Carmichael, even though he was respectably out of the way in the tiny lean-to shed adjoining the schoolhouse's small kitchen. She explained to herself that propriety was satisfied. No parents could complain. Better still, Reverend Baring could not raise his voice and preach next Sunday of sinister threats to the schoolchildren's virtue. Miss Gould's advanced age – forty-five years this summer –made her long for peace and order, especially in this harbour where she had lived all her life.

'Good day, ma'am,' she managed at the second attempt, annoyed that her face was scarlet from the excitement of the occasion. 'Welcome to Sealandings School!'

Mary Prothero smiled, too diffidently Matilda Gould thought, seeing the lady's fortunes were soaring so splendidly.

'I had not far to come, Matilda.'

The schoolteacher was flurried by the lady's condescension. 'I only meant, ma'am, that it is indeed an honour for our little establishment!'

A line of tiny children was drawn up in the hallway, all smocked in white. The tallest could not have been more than six years old. Mary's expression mellowed as she stopped to touch the face of the shy tot nearest the door.

'Come, Matilda. Didn't you chide me through my first hornbook? Wasn't it you rescued my chalk from bullies, my first Lent in school?'

Matilda Gould was almost overcome. 'You remember, ma'am!' She beamed. 'This angel is Julia Temple, daughter of Harold Temple who did that terrible deed!'

'Hello, Julia.' Mary took the child's hand. 'I knew your daddy when he was a little boy. He and I were in the same class. Isn't that happy?'

'Yes, ma'am.' The child swung shyly on one foot.

Matilda observed Mary Prothero closely. It wasn't that Mrs Prothero was overly effusive with the children. There was something too diffident in her manner, making the children reserved. Too little encounter with them, perhaps, the schoolteacher guessed. Mary Calling had been a frail child. She was the one who hung back when sides were picked for skipping games, too timid to push brashly forward and claim a place. Yet she had been able, skilled at needlework, artistic in paints. She was quite the class decorator, fast to learn and apt with tables and language alike. Musically she was excellent, at the keyboard borrowed from the rectory. The very first truly able scholar Matilda Gould had discovered, when taking up her new appointment after Mr Fairnshaw's retirement.

Then had come the hesitant burgeoning of the young girl, the gentle powers emerging from the dainty girlchild. And Mary Calling, heiress to Calling Farm's large wooded acres and arable lands that formed the schoolhouse's skyline, was a perfect beauty. Not quite perfect now, for her frailty lingered on in the woman, as vestige of the child.

Until Jason Prothero, a mere herdsman. The unexpected deaths of Mary's parents, her lack of any brother to take control, the seeming lovelorn obsession of Jason Prothero with the silent withdrawn woman that Mary Calling became, all led only to one thing – the inevitability of the marriage between Prothero the farmhand and the heiress of Calling Farm.

From there it had been a sorry tale of increasing reticence on Mary's part, and swelling bumptiousness on Jason Prothero's. His attitude towards Mary became aggression, his obsequiousness nothing less than frank bullying. His herdsman's taciturn reserve was swapped for naked ambition. Gentrification was all. Prothero became noted for ostentation and greed for ever greater status in Sealandings.

The gambling coup whereby Prothero had gained control of Carradine's estates was still the subject for coastal gossip. Matilda Gould had no truck with gamblers of any kind, winners like Jason Prothero or losers like Carradine. Satan's games they played – and Mary Prothero's husband's increasing wealth seemed to have done evil rather than good. Mary's face was drawn, her hesitation worse than when she had acknowledged Miss Gould in Market Square two months previously.

'Children, say your welcomes.'

A little lad counted on Miss Gould's nod. 'One, two, three.' The children chanted together slowly, 'Please, ma'am. Welcome to Sealandings School and we hope your stay will be as happy as it proves gracious!'

'How delightful!' Mary Prothero clapped her hands.

The schoolteacher laughed. 'They've laboured at it.'

'Thank you, children, for your kindly welcome.'

The children curtseyed or bowed, and filed into the classroom where a monitor stood with a chalk and slate to record any child who made noise during the important visit.

'I had hoped, ma'am, that you would take tea with me.'

'Thank you, Miss Gould. I regret I shall not have time.' Mary Calling smiled to take the sting out of her declining. Tea was inordinately expensive. The schoolteacher's stipend could hardly be expected to run to Congou infusion. 'Though I have a definite purpose – indeed, two – to my call.'

'Do come, ma'am. The office is just as you'll remember.'

Miss Gould led the way through the corridor where the children's outer coats hung on wooden pegs, passing the four small lead-lined basins where hand-washing was ritualised before the precious spelling hornbooks were brought out.

Mary Prothero cried, 'Oh, how very small it seems!'

The schoolteacher smiled, standing while Mary looked about, finding astonishment that a blackboard's easel stood so short against the wall.

'It was a giant!' she enthused, colour in her features, her smile spontaneous and fresh.

Miss Gould warmed to her. So she was still the same, responding with such pleasure in details, her eyes shining as she turned to be seated in the low Windsor.

'I rejoice your memories are so pleasant, ma'am.'

'First, please be less formal when we are alone. After years at your knee, I count you as an acquaintance, and trust you will count me the same.'

'Oh, ma'am! Such condescension!'

'Please. Mary, when outwith the children's hearing. In company, what you will.'

Matilda Gould was touched, seeing the effort this familiarity called for. Mary Prothero had obviously rehearsed the little speech. It would be Mrs Prothero and Madam in public, but this was a delightful favour.

'How kind you are . . . Mary.'

'There! Not too difficult, was it?'

The schoolteacher laughed openly at Mary's joke. It was her own phrase, brought out when some child managed its letters after a period of daunt and doubt.

'Secondly, Matilda. A benefice from Mr Prothero.'

Matilda was so astonished she felt her mouth open, and had to restore her composure. Jason Prothero, distributing largesse?

He was a different man for two kinds of people, she thought. One, his workers, who had best slave until they had earned every copper paid in begrudged wages. And two, the rest of mankind, who were clearly undeserving. A louring, dour man with florid face, his eyes never smiled.

She remembered the small lad, an age or two above Mary, but she never recalled him smiling, except to ingratiate or to exploit. She had never reached him in all his five years – admittedly, farm labourers' children could only afford their schoolday penny once a week, or even less. He never joined in the schoolyard games. She had learned of Mary Calling's marriage to the man with dismay. Prothero's rumoured nocturnal visits to the notorious Two Cotts, out on the Norwich road before Quaker Bettany's windmill, were something not to be thought about.

The effort of not thinking of such terrible passions made her cheeks burn. She obfuscated quickly, for adult Mrs Mary Prothero might retain the silent astuteness of child Mary Calling.

'Oh, Mary! The school would be blessed by a contribution – '

'Matilda, you misunderstand.' Mary was taking huge delight in carrying such welcome news. 'My husband insists on increasing your stipend, plus a regular sum for school purchases.'

'To my stipend?' Miss Gould asked faintly.

'Three shillings and fourpence weekly, to yourself. Plus six and eightpence for buying materials and what-you-wills. To be paid from Calling Farm estate, commencing instantly. Holidays excepted, of course.'

It took some moments for Miss Gould to reply. 'Such generosity, Mary! I know full well to whom thanks be due, and I thank you and Mr Prothero for this benevolence.'

'No thanks are necessary, Matilda. Your devotion to the children is a legend.'

Matilda's mind swam. Three shillings and fourpence! A sixth of a whole pound! Forty pence extra a week, with a third of an entire sovereign weekly to help her teaching! More than a windfall, it was a wonder. If only she could feel unreserved joy. From the Calling estates held firm in Jason Prothero's hands, something was amiss. It was in Mary's nature to give, and generously, but in Prothero's only to buy, and begrudge payment. Since Prothero's new authority extended to Carradine Manor by reason of Carradine's gambling debts, was this money tainted by immorality? She concealed the agonising thought in smiling attention on her visitor.

'Matilda, could you see your way to allowing a portion of the latter sum to the benefit of the children's health?'

'Health?' The schoolteacher wondered for an instant what she had missed, in careless concentration. Then she understood. The Doctor was here to treat the injured Doadie Baines. She smoothed her expression. 'Of course, Mary. Nothing would give me greater satisfaction than to allocate a proportion for the physician's care. So far he has given his service freely, and the children have benefited.'

'Perhaps between a shilling to half a crown?' Mary suggested, far too casually. 'But I know your responsibilities to the children would reconcile any payment by your frankest opinion of what is most urgently required.'

Miss Gould rose with her, smiling thanks. Did veiled admonition lie in Mary's overtly polite words, to the effect that a small payment must go to Doctor Carmichael, *or else*? No. She dismissed the unworthy notion. Mary Calling was never so blunt, nor quite so calculating. And she was Mrs Prothero by reason of the sacrament of matrimony, wherein holiness reigned. Past affections were forbidden entry. Whatever little Mary Calling had felt for Ven Carmichael could nevermore be expressed by

Mrs Mary Prothero. Unthinkable. She moved with her to the corridor.

The visitor paused, as if taken by a sudden notion. 'I wonder if I could inspect the Doctor's arrangements, Matilda? Perhaps when Doctor Carmichael is here? I should not want to be an intrusion. Simply for the purpose of reporting to Mr Prothero, you understand, should I require to do so.'

'Doubly welcome! By happy coincidence Doctor Carmichael is here this very minute! His surgery is being held in the lean-to. Might I invite you to an immediate inspection?'

'Oh, I wouldn't want to interrupt – '

'Please,' the schoolteacher begged, now in no doubt as to her visitor's concealed purpose. 'Doctor remarks on charitable interest shown in the children's well-being.'

She ushered Mary outside, casting a quick glance into the classroom where the children sat silently mouthing from their hornbooks, overawed by an important guest. Most knew Mrs Prothero by sight, and knew of the consequences any transgression could bring upon their parents' chances of continuing employ in Sealandings.

'It is used now for better purpose, on occasion.' Matilda led the way round the rear of the narrow school building.

'I'm pleased to hear it!' Mary was smiling, for this weathered cabin with its earth floor and splaying planks was Miss Gould's punishment nook, where children were banished for misbehaving. The only chastisement Miss Gould resorted to was making a child miss a lesson, and telling its parents, who could then draw conclusions about how well the family's hard-earned lesson penny was spent. 'I twice passed a sorry hour in here.'

'How very unkind of you to remind me, Mrs Prothero!'

Matilda's raised voice warned the Doctor inside. She knocked and opened the door.

Inside, Carmichael was kneeling, dressing a little boy's knee with a coarse linen bandage. A girlchild sat by, holding a bowl. A sour stench filled the cabin. The lad was pale. His forehead shone with a clammy sweat.

'Good morning, Doctor Carmichael!' Mary said. 'I fear . . .' She faltered. The man did not rise.

'Stay still, Doadie. All done in half a minute more.'

20

'It hurts,' Doadie said.

'It will, for quite a while. You must not run about on it, nor play kickbat. Understand?'

Mary watched his hands bandage with deft slowness. The bowl held by the tiny girl held a purulent greenish matter and a stained lancet.

'Doadie's to the wharf tomorrow, please Doctor,' the girlchild said.

'Can't your big brother – Hal, isn't it? – do your work?'

'Please no,' Doadie said. 'I load fish on the tax cart.'

'Damn.'

The ladies gasped at the outrageous expletive.

'Doctor Carmichael!' Matilda Gould felt matters slip out of control. What had augured so well was now disaster, what with irreligious exclamations uttered by the Doctor in front of children. Word of this was sure to get about like marshfire. Oh, why on earth couldn't the physician have been simply holding a child who had sweetly fainted, something gracious and pleasant?

'Perhaps some other time, Mrs Prothero,' she said desperately.

'Now, if you please.'

And to Miss Gould's alarm, her august visitor stepped forward on to the very earth floor, and asked if there was anything she could do to help.

The Doctor's reply was dismissive. 'No, thank you, ma'am.'

It was all too much. Miss Gould felt weak from shame and dismay. How could he be so discourteous to a lady of such position in Sealandings? The whole town would hear of it, however much she threatened the children to silence. The Doctor ought to have left his work instantly, conversed for as long as Mrs Prothero desired, then escorted her to her new four-wheeled pilentum which stood so grandly before the school. Worse, it was as if Mary Prothero conspired in her own humiliation, so quickly did she stand away when rebuffed. And only moments ago, Miss Gould thought, she had been imagining all sorts of concealed affections!

'Tell your father, Doadie, that I beg he lets you stay home tomorrow. I shall call during the morn.'

'Please yes, Doctor.'

'Good lad.'

The man rose, straightened up and stretched without shame.

And Mary Prothero was actually half-smiling! Miss Gould felt giddy. She was suddenly aware of the two, standing there looking at each other, almost as if they had deliberately planned to make a distinct contrast.

Mary wore a full pelisse in russet cashmere, with a risky mauve silk showing beneath its white fur hem. The grey felt bonnet was trimmed with foreign feathers that curled to add height to her diminutive stature. Miss Gould was firm with herself, sternly putting aside the uncharitable idea that Mary's new attention to fashion was an indication of Jason Prothero's wish for exalted status. The lady was a delight to see, at once fetching and demure.

The Doctor on the other hand was dishevelled. His topcoat's hem was mud-stained, showing where he had crouched to attend to patients on damp earth floors. It was nothing more than an old Newmarket surtout, clearly some coachman's cast-off with its chamois-coloured cloth showing old rents. These were newly mended, some so skilfully as to be almost invisible. Though his six buttons did not match, they were neatly sewn. One had even been handmade with diminutive stitching across a coil of wire. His beaver hat was clean and brushed, but still an ancient thing. She shrewdly guessed that whoever's hand had restored his surtout was quite capable of keeping his tall hat in service. That Mehala had improved his appearance. Even his hard-wearing brogans were almost gone at the sole.

Their manner too was a stark contrast. Mary Prothero's was gentle but a little agitated, the Doctor's defensive and sharp. *They're a pair*, she realised with a shock, then had to struggle for equanimity.

'I apologise for distracting you, Doctor,' Mary said.

'Thank you, Mrs Prothero, but you did not. I am finished here.'

His expression eased into a smile as he took the metal bowl from the girlchild and shooed them both out.

'Doctor Carmichael,' Miss Gould cut in with desperate brightness. 'Mrs Prothero has been greatly generous.'

'It is little enough, Matilda.' Mary spoke breathlessly, as if fearing something might be said to upset the agreement. 'May I ask how you fare at Shalamar, Doctor? Well, I trust?' In the awkward pause, she spoke hurriedly on. 'I well remember Mrs Trenchard, how angry she was when we of younger years chased the pheasants through the lovely gardens. Is the old lady well?'

'Thank you, Mrs Prothero,' he said gravely. 'She suffers somewhat from her joints, but bravely faces up to each day.'

He came to Sealandings as a boychild, Miss Gould mutely recalled. *His father, in that old cape, clambering along the shoreline looking for plants and sketching birds. They stayed at Calling Farm* . . .

'Please to say I asked after Mrs Trenchard, and send wishes for her well-keeping. Good day, Doctor.'

'Thank you, I shall. And good day, Mrs Prothero.'

Miss Gould hurried after Mary, unable to resist giving Carmichael a sharp backward glance.

It was with relief that she stood to curtsey the carriage away. She waited until it vanished from view along the road to Whitehanger before scurrying impatiently inside. She hoped to catch Doctor Carmichael before he left, but was disappointed. The lean-to door was closed, and there was no sign of him. He must have gone northwards, across the livestock field towards the Norwich road. He was likely to have duties among those dreadful ladies of evil repute who inhabited Two Cotts. Their wretched occupation was the horror and shame of all godly folk in the entire district. She did not allow herself even to consider their sins.

Mrs Wren thought power, ate power. She loved the very concept. To any whoremistress it was as necessary as breath. It was, she instructed her girls in the sprawled confines of Two Cotts, the only code to live by. She ruled her girls with a rod of iron: other rods broke too easily.

Some might plead Law. Some might observe the tortuosity of religions, with all the cruelties for which the various competing sects were notorious. Still others, like the intemperate Sir Charles Golding, cousin of the vicious Lady Thalia De Foe, longed for political office. Others, as the grand magistrate Squire Henry Hunterfield of Lorne House, might seemingly desire only the peace of the realm . . . the more fool he!

For herself, and the bordello of Two Cotts, simple power had to rule, for the benefit of her clients and to resist the bigotry of the locals who hated her establishment.

She drank two glasses of Portugal at the same hour each morning, repeating the dose at four every afternoon the Good

Lord sent. She was quiet in herself, with stillness at her very centre, but not in quite the way Mr Bettany the windmiller preached in his lunatic Quakerism. No, her tranquility stemmed from the influence protecting her – which emanated from her clients. Oh, they were a mixture right enough! Not every footfall was pliant tanned Wellington leather or Cossack pleated kid. Why should it be so? Drovers from St Edmundsbury, stern broad-tongued men on the long march from Yorkshire's South Riding herding cattle nearer to hungry London's clamouring markets, travellers crossing the magistrates' line ten miles inland – all men deserved to have a woman. Why not? Here at Two Cotts, the concourse of men, from influential and titled down to the lowest stratum, came for solace.

She contemplated the dark Portugal bottle, egging herself on. Another small tot, Mrs Wren, just for sustenance. She was likely to be tasked severely before midnight struck from Reverend Baring's church tower. She surrendered easily, poured a generous glass, and thought with wonderment of the way men emerged from the girls.

High or low, herder or baron, a man rose from a woman's legs with a deep stillness in him. When first she'd started in the stew trade in Convent Garden off London's Strand, she had been worried. It was as if she milked them into a personal oblivion by her ineptitude. With years and experience, she knew it for what it was, a relief, a calm she had not before recognised. And she was glad, proud even. Of having taken a poor tormented creature from some campaign abroad, some ship long at sea, or simply some tired defeated waggoner who had dragged for days along England's rutted roads, and bled away his torment. Theirs was a surgeon's art, she lectured her girls. Better, indeed, for an apothecary could do nothing for the soul, and little enough, God knew, for the body. The prostitute's calling was to restore the souls of men, giving life back to the dying.

'Lucy?' she yelled through the hatch. 'Here a moment.'

The girl came so quickly Mrs Wren wondered suspiciously if she had been waiting, but dismissed the idea. No, Lucy was a bright ambitious girl. Of the six or seven lolling in the lounge nearby, she'd be the one to spring up whoever was summoned and come running.

Lucy entered, drawing the curtain across Mrs Wren's alcove. It was no more than a small nook off the main lounge, connecting with the hallway. Two small windows were draped, but gave sight into the lounge and hall, the better to control egress and inspect customers.

'Your special gentleman comes today?'

'Please ma'am, yes. He said six of the clock.'

'He'll meet somebody here? Or will he want service?'

'He didn't tell me, ma'am. I think he'll probably – '

'Stupid!' Mrs Wren kept her voice low. Her girls had mighty hearing, and mightier tongues to wag gossip to the wrong people. 'I always tell you – find out a gentleman's purposes. Three times you've told me nothing! Carradine – '

'Shhhh, ma'am, if you please!'

Mrs Wren calmed. The girl was right. Perhaps she'd been wrong to have that little extra, for Portugal was a gentleman's wine.

The girl was pretty, true. She could understand how even a high-born rake like Carradine, dueller, gambler and certainly no respecter of womankind, preferred a sharp-eyed comely lass like Lucy. She stood fairly tall, astonishingly undeformed by the dreaded rickets – that disease which twisted too many girls out of beauteous alignment, when they might be useful to an establishment like Two Cotts. Lucy was clever as she was shapely, had an unfailing memory for names and tattletales, and could count to well over a hundred, for Mrs Wren herself had tested her.

Carradine was a careful man, for all his wanton reputation. He'd need to be, having lost everything down to the gates of Carradine House.

'Prepare the best front room for him – tell Lizzie to help you. And Lucy . . .'

'Yes, Mrs Wren?'

The whoremistress considered her words. It would not do to antagonise a slut in favour with Carradine.

'Pay particular attention to anything he says, and report to me. I want names, dates, intentions, who'll still receive him as visitor, and who not. You understand?'

'Yes, Mrs Wren. But what if he says nothing?'

'You'll still report to me, after he's gone.'

'Very well, Mrs Wren.'

The girl went through into the lounge, calling Lizzie who, Mrs Wren observed with anger, answered Lucy's summons with a weary groan. That was all the thanks you got. Give them a lovely home in beautiful East Anglia, with money coming in regular as the church clock, and they groan.

She'd wait until some drunken sot oafed in from Southwold, stinking of fish scales and oily from the North Sea, and would take pleasure in allocating him to Lizzie. Let the idle bitch do her groaning then. It would delight the rest of the girls, and give some of the gentlemen clients a good laugh.

She eyed the dark bottle of Portugal wine, and decided to risk another drop. Laughter too was another aspect of power, for money flowed faster when smiles abounded.

Two Cotts could boast a couple more girls of Lucy's standard, but the one who'd really bring the men, high-born and low alike, panting at the doors, would be that girl Mehala. God, what money would flow then! And what power would be hers if Mehala came to Two Cotts! She was a whoremonger's dream. Not that the girl had shown the slightest inclination. The few times Mrs Wren had glimpsed her, driving the brewer's dray from the Donkey and Buskin to the livestock field on market days, she had been striking. Every man's gaze had latched on the girl and followed her from sight. Yes, Mehala was the local darling, even though she was mistrusted, being still unmemoried from drowning.

The trouble with being the Sealandings whoremistress was religion – or rather the maniacs who saw it as their Holy Writ to exterminate her brothel by Christian means or foul, bad cess to the lot of them. She sighed and sipped. The lot of a lady who dealt in 'country matters' – a euphemism for sex from time immemorial – was not a tranquil one.

On impulse she rose, with a slight difficulty, to peer through the front window. In the distance she could just see a figure striding determinedly this way, its chamois-coloured surtout flapping. Doctor Carmichael. She sighed with mingled annoyance and weariness. No do-gooder he, but trouble nonetheless. He stood against sickness as if by resolve he could wrestle death itself to an end. A man of vision, and therefore a sort of lunatic. As if mankind could ever conquer diseases! Didn't the Good Book say that we should suffer sickness for ever?

26

Worse, Doctor Carmichael never took his pay in kind. Any of the girls would happily have paid him the medical dues for Two Cotts, but he'd flown from the very suggestion. So it had to be hard-earned coin of the realm. Money out, rather than money in, was the road to ruin. It really and truly pained Mrs Wren to pay money for mere medical services.

A knock sounded. That would be young Doctor Carmichael, with his leech's bag and his lopsided beaver hat. He never used the bell, the prerogative of client callers. Purity, she thought sardonically. As if there was such a thing! Weren't all men sinners? She was sure God had said that, somewhere or other. She cuffed the girl who trotted past to answer the door.

3

Carradine saw the woman ahead on the path where it straightened to become the Norwich road. He admired a woman so confident of her own attractiveness that she is lovely to behold. It gave pleasure, her inner delight resonating in a man. Carradine slowly overhauled the woman. He did not hurry. Her gait altered, subtly changed from a stolid pace to a showy sinuousness. She knew she was being observed.

Yet there was danger in that full sureness a beautiful woman displays. It challenges all, women *and* men, for where a man is drawn by a bonny woman, finding himself fighting duels and losing wealth like water from an unplugged butt, a woman finds she suddenly has a rival and is passed over, having to see admiration shone on a prettier female while she herself goes neglected. A man who loses his heritage – like myself, Carradine thought in bitterness – might recover, but a woman eclipsed is forever dulled.

He let his mare's gait lengthen slightly. They were within a mile of Sealandings, and he wanted to see if she was worth his attention. For one moment he hoped she might be Mehala, that bitch who, if all was examined dispassionately, had been the instrument of his losing to that baseborn Prothero who now owned Carradine Manor.

The clever bitch had shortened her stride, he saw, amused. She was as desirous of discovering him as he her. So she had her core of natural cunning – but the woman wasn't yet made who could work round Carradine. Mehala had been simply fortunate.

'Morrow, mistress.'

'Good morrow, sir.'

She was what, twenty-three? Maybe a year or so older? She dropped a token curtsey as he came abreast, then resumed walking. Her manner announced that she was no mere country lass, to swoon and go giddy when addressed by a gentleman. Her clothes suggested that she had seen better days, perhaps been used more to carriage riding than trudging. She wore her shawl about

28

her shoulders, instead of gathered tight round her head. It was that palmyrene material Thalia De Foe raged about so tiresomely. Lately all the fashion, its quality lay between barege and poplin, and could carry silk embroidery, as here. He had told her roughly that he had nothing to buy with. Her husband Fellows could shoulder her bills. It was only right.

The woman's dress was kirtled up for the unmade road, but it was marquisette cotton, which spoke of a housewoman, not a labouring lass. The kirtling hid part of the bright patterns. Good attention to detail, this, proving her modesty to prying eyes.

'Name, woman?'

The face was somewhat more tanned than a lady's should be, for no lady wanted her complexion browned like a fishwife's, leathered by East Anglia's onshore winds. But it was comely, and her gaze unafraid.

'Judith Blaker. Of Sealandings lately, sir. I was housekeeper to the Honourable Charles Golding.'

'Were you, now.'

Carradine took the next few paces in silence. He knew of this woman. Golding was an inept drunkard, in spite of his claim to've mended his ways. This Judith Blaker could only be the same housekeeper who had installed her tribe of a family – brothers, uncles, cousins – into Golding's huge estate along the South Toll road, so incurring the displeasure of Thalia De Foe, Golding's cousin. Thalia had taken charge and bagged this wench, sending her and her load of miscreants off to be tried in St Edmundsbury's Quarter Sessions for deceit and fraud of a master.

'Who was gaoled? You move fast, to've escaped!'

'Thank you, sir.' To his amusement she was unabashed, answering calmly. It showed courage of a sort, for were he to take her by force on the roadside nobody would raise the law on her part. 'I was released, on consideration of payment.'

'Your fine was paid? By whom?'

'It was said a gentleman, sir. But I do not know.'

He approved of her wish to conceal the identity of her benefactor. Golding? This woman was more than mere house-keeper, according to Thalia's pillow whispers. Which had proved more galling still to her, for this Blaker was a meddler in family affairs.

'Who was the magistrate, Blaker?'

'Sir Philip Banks, sir. A kindly and honest gentleman.'

Indeed, Carradine thought wrily. An old fool, with too many fingers in too many political pies. It would be easy, but not without risk, to find out what underlay the girl's reticence.

'You were found guilty, then?' Thalia had sworn she should be transported for life, no less.

'In a manner of speaking, sir. But the lawyers found new witnesses after a time, and I was let go.'

Aye, they would, and milking every hour God sent for fat fees. 'Men of straw' – wastrels willing to swear any evidence – hung about law courts, a wisp of straw projecting from their shoes signifying their availability. Perjury was cheap.

They were coming in sight of Carradine Manor, which stood back from the Norwich road among high elms and mulberries. His chest tightened, his response catching the woman's attention. Too sharp for her own good, this one.

'I am in lack of a character, sir,' she admitted candidly. 'I go to seek a place, however humble, at Carradine Manor, sir. But I have no appointment with the servantry.'

He reined in. 'Why at Carradine's?'

Her gaze was level, frank, suddenly burning. 'I heard that one had misused the master there. That same female told tales against me when I housekept at Bures House. It was she condemned my character.'

Thalia said Blaker was a bitch with sticky fingers, no oppressed innocent.

'And so I was replaced, sir. By Mehala.' She spat the name. Venom, the woman's weapon, Carradine reflected.

They paused there, the woman with her head raised, not at all undaunted, and the silent mounted gentleman. Both were impoverished, and both saw their plight as brought about by a common enemy. Blaker had family, a crowd of near-vagabonds, true, but allies for all that. And he had none save Thalia De Foe, and he was rapidly tiring of her. Her efforts to extricate him from this mess had proved unavailing. What was the use of a wealthy mistress who failed to advance her lover's interests? This chance meeting might offer more.

'It is known that Carradine Manor is now taken by another.'

'If it is not presumptuous to say, I never serve the lowly who pretend to higher position.'

Not a Prothero, only a Carradine? He nodded slowly. 'You know that Carradine stays here only at the behest of Prothero? Yet you will serve only Carradine?'

'If I am fortunate enough to be given position, sir.'

A spy in the camp, Carradine thought: a true ally. It would be stupid to harbour any illusions about this woman, for once a thief, always a subtle-monger. Yet she offered advantages. Thalia would be furious if she recognised Blaker at Carradine Manor, but he could disclaim any knowledge of her hiring. And Thalia hated Prothero, so Blaker's employment would only strengthen that antagonism. Not only that, but this woman seemed to have had Charles Golding in the palm of her hand for quite a time. It would do no harm to have her reintroduced, perhaps clandestinely, to Golding at Bures House, for the man was weak though wealthy.

'What if the position was lowly? A housekeeper is a woman of good standing and high skill. Such a one does not . . .'

'Sink so low that she shall have less than her due, sir?' The woman's face was alive with eagerness now, naked ambition showing. The mask was off. She knew he was Carradine. 'Such a status would only be temporary, sir?'

They were speaking obliquely. Carradine revelled in it. Why had he never met her before?

'Indeed – assuming that the woman was keen to help her master in any and every way possible.'

'Gratitude is the spur to endeavour, sir. For a generous master, I should prove the ablest servant, honest, privy and true.'

'Then I shall see to it, Blaker.' He twisted in the saddle. A waggon was trundling up the slope towards Carradine Manor. It would have to go by the estate entrance, for it was nothing more than a common tax cart piled high with chairs. 'Come along tomorrow dawn, soonest, to the servants' door. Ask for Hobbes, my chief servant.'

'Thank you, sir.' She dropped a curtsey. 'You shall have my greatest endeavours.'

He flicked her a shilling. It caught against her shawl, and fell into the roadway. She neither scrabbled after it nor glanced down at the coin, though she was sure to snatch it up the instant he looked away. He was pleased. This bitter woman had a sort of perverse pride, and pride was costly attire. No harm to know that she had her Achilles heel.

'There's earnest money. You will earn my generosity, if I'm not mistaken.'

The waggon slowed, was hauled to a halt. Carradine morosely recognised the driver, the local chairmaker.

'Good day, sir!' the man called.

'Where the hell're you taking those, Brown?'

'Why, to Carradine Manor, sir! Twelve handsome Somersets, made withy on willow as ordered, for delivery this day.'

'No, Brown. The Manor spends no more for the whilst.'

The rotund driver shifted uncomfortably on the box seat, pulling the brake to a stand to ease the Welsh cob.

'Begging pardon, sir, but the order's already been paid for, sir. Against a bill of hand.' Brown glanced at the motionless woman as if asking help, and managed, 'Of Mr Prothero, sir.'

Carradine concealed his hatred, struggled to swallow this utter shame. He nodded briskly. 'Ah, yes. I forgot. I told him to place the order. A dozen, was it not? Drive on. See Hobbes, or Mistress Tyll.'

'Yes, sir. Good day, sir.'

Brown drove on, avoiding Carradine's eye while guiding his cob past along the lane. The tubby chairmaker was not deceived by Carradine's fiction. He had known Carradine Manor and family intimately since birth, as had most of the folk in Sealandings. Secrecy was well-nigh impossible, and ruination flew on gossip's fastest wings.

Carradine glanced at Blaker, who had moved out of harm's way on to the bank. The shilling had gone, right enough.

'Judith Blaker, sir.' The hireling's correct response, when accepting her earnest money, that coin which sealed the bond between master and servant. Her expression showed no recognition of the mortification he must have felt during the brief exchange.

'Very well, Judith.'

The mare walked on, but not before he caught a gleam of pleasure at the use of her Christian name. Perhaps this chance meeting bettered any amount of scheming and planning. If so, it was high time good fortune smiled his way instead of upon foes.

From Shalamar, a footpath traced inland. It ran erratically for a few hundred yards, twisting here and there through copses to dip towards several ponds, then rising to become a decent footway. Mehala loved it, and determined to use it as a short cut to meet Doctor Carmichael as he returned from his harbour visits. He had three domiciliary calls to make after the school surgery. She could carry his bag for him part of the way.

The footpath was substantial, which lent weight to the tale that it once had been an ancient marching road, built by the Romans after they had taken the British tribes' capital of Camulodonum and made it into Colchester. She shivered at the very name of that town, and put it from her mind. The less thought of it the better. Where memory failed, she encouraged its failing. Where memory recovered, she quickly forced it to abdicate, and felt herself blessed. Unhappiness was in the past, to the south, in Mersea Island, the sea marshes by the long strood across the tidal sea-sedge. She prayed she might never see them again.

The ancient people who had dwelled here even before the Roman Emperor rode in on his war elephants had been a rustic contented folk. Country people still had an innocence that tradesfolk and merchants never possessed. And the earthworks hereabouts stood proud from the low sealands, cattle enclosures and remnants of old flint dwellings, strange oblong tumuli that children believed were the longships of sea rovers buried along the shores.

As she walked, she searched the banks and glades to each side for some of the plants she lacked for her Flora's Dial. She had her list of names. The new fashion for Latin names was something she had never learned, but was eager to know. She told them off by the country names everybody knew.

The idea was to plant in two concentric circles, or four, those plants which opened in sequence through the twenty-four hours. It was a pretty conceit, much filled with lovers' symbolisms, therefore shameless on her part! But though too preoccupied to come out of himself, Ven had begun lately to smile more, converse the readier, and now looked forward to reading with her in the candle hours after dusk. Let others see what they chose, she told herself defiantly. This was happiness such as she had never known.

It would grow into greater happiness still, she was certain, as his confidence edged back into his soul. Her Flora's gardening was but an innocent thing to please him. Old Trenchard was willing, but hopelessly thumbed when it came to gentling the plants from the wild. 'Weeds all,' he grumbled when she read him the list of clock flowers.

'They'll prove a delight, Mr Trenchard,' she'd told the old man. His wife, custodian of Shalamar in exchange for a few inadequate household services, was also sceptical.

'Much labour, no harvest!' she'd scolded, starting one of her mild rambling reproaches.

Mehala smiled and said nothing. There were harvests and harvests, she told herself.

The common English Garden Lettuce opened at seven of the clock; the Scarlet Pimpernel at eight. If Mr Trenchard complained too much about the latter, why then she could easily substitute the Proliferous Pink for it. Nine o'clock was as easy, the Field Marigold. Ten the Red Sandwort – but how to grow this in the clayey soil of Shalamar? Washed sand, she decided.

At a stile, she paused. This was the boundary of the Milton Hall estate of De Foe. She could see it below in the valley, for here the ancient trackway gave quite a vantage point.

The vale showed a green wooded slope against pasture land, then the sweep of a drive and ordered trees, with a lake and arbours set near the great house. Distantly, she could see the roofs of Sealandings, the tower of Reverend Baring's church, St. Edmund the Martyr, the red trebled tiles so favoured in these parts, and the squat flat roof of the Corn Mart in Market Square. With a faint pang of nostalgia she picked out the three sloping roofs of the Donkey and Buskin, the tavern where John Weaver and his wife Sarah Ann had taken her in the night she was rescued from the sea. Lovely people, kind though strict. She hoped to visit them soon.

A horse snorted, scuffed impatiently. It was close. She moved away from the stile and saw Squire Hunterfield within a few yards, sitting his mare Betsy and staring morosely down into the vale. She hesitated, wondering whether to discover herself to him from politeness or whether to slip through the undergrowth and continue on until she came into the churchyard and thence Market Square and the schoolhouse.

34

But Hunterfield was countryman born and bred.

'Good day. Mehala, isn't it?'

'Yes, sir. Good day. I am going to meet Doctor Carmichael on his return from the schoolchildren's surgery at Miss Gould's.'

'Mmmh.' He was looking down at Milton Hall. 'You're at Shalamar, I gather, housekeeping for the sawbones?'

'Yes, sir. He is a boon to Sealandings, sir.'

'I know, Mehala,' he said frankly. 'I mind when he laboured to recover the child Clare, at John Darling the waggoner's in Whitehanger, thanks be to God.'

'Amen, sir.' It had been a famous triumph – over the lethal croup no less, a feat still spoken of in Sealandings, as much as in the rival harbour of Whitehanger down the coast.

She carefully did not notice that Squire Hunterfield avoided speaking of little eight-year-old Clare Darling as John Darling's daughter. Neither she nor Ven Carmichael had voiced their suspicions to each other, though Squire Hunterfield's gratitude after Clare's recovery had been heartfelt. Rumour touched the Darling family, and Hunterfield's concern for little Clare.

'You are content at Shalamar, Mehala?'

'Indeed, sir.' She found herself colouring.

'Do not make your satisfaction too apparent. A lack of common attention is a boon, to a degree not often appreciated.'

'Forgive me, sir, if I fail to understand.'

He looked seawards with a half-smile. 'You follow me well enough, Mehala. You choose to pretend otherwise. The quiet fox goes best fed, as people say. They're right.'

'Yes, sir. I shall remember. And thank you.'

'My compliments to that crocus of yours, Mehala.' He nodded dismissal, and she moved away with a murmured good day.

His gentle manner made the term of abuse for a doctor, 'crocus', but a mild jest. The jeers of others in Sealandings all too often made it offensive, though Carmichael took insults with a smile from farm youths, aye, and grown men who ought to know better. Until they needed him, she thought angrily, when they became all fawning placation.

As she resumed her journey, she was aware of a man standing silently among the trees within a handsbreadth of the track. She started in alarm, but relaxed almost immediately. Simple Tom was the Squire's mute groom. She should have expected him to be close by, for Hunterfield went hardly anywhere without him.

'Good day to you, Tom.'

He whistled twice, short quiet cheeps, as a dove makes at the day's turning. She smiled. It was his only way. He had said nothing from birth. She had once pulled him from the mudflats out in Whitehanger Bay, beyond Widow Maderley's watermill, and saw from Tom's eloquent gesture – smoothing down his groom's coarse smock coat as if brushing off grime – that he too remembered. She reached out and touched his arm as she passed, smiling, tilting her head to deprecate his implied obligation, and walked on.

Eleven o'clock, Star of Bethlehem. Twelve noon, the ice plant. Space between plants was as much a problem as the placing order round a simple circumference.

The trackway gradually bent round, winding now between the southern limit of Calling Farm where common land yet lay outside the Enclosures Acts, where Sealandings folk shared grazing rights from time immemorial. Not far.

A sound came, somewhere up ahead, a repeated light tapping which somehow afrighted her. She had reason to recognise that hideous regular hissing, ending as it did in a horrid abrupt noise. And something was squealing – some animal? It was certainly in pain, definitely being punished.

It was wrong to intrude, to risk the stern sanction of some landowner, but she was drawn towards the sound. A clattering was added to the din. She parted the leaves of a low scrubby elder, and looked into the flint-cobbled yard of Calling Farm's stockpen.

'Bastard!' somebody was yelling. 'Hold! Is'll teach the bastard to fault agin me!'

A young stallion was tethered to a wall, its back ribbed with bloodstains. Bright red dripped as it squealed in fright. It lunged, trying to escape from the whip the big man wielded.

He looked berserk. One arm hung straight down his side. In the other he held a team holly, the twelve-foot whip used for a driving team. He drew back, adjusted the thong with some difficulty and lashed the stallion, screaming abuse at the crazed animal.

To one side was a landau, a splendid vehicle of the very latest design, emblazoned with a newly painted coat-of-arms. A huge scar ran the entire length of the grand carriage, opening the paint down to bare wood. The creature must have been startled and kicked out, damaging the landau's finery.

The man was Prothero. Before she knew, she stepped out from the foliage on to the edge of the cobbling.

'Please, sirrah, spare the animal, I beg.'

Two stockmen were standing forlornly by the far side of the yard. Their employ was in jeopardy for having let the stallion damage their master's property, a cardinal offence. Neither moved.

Prothero paused, amazement in his dark features. 'Who in hell's name. . . ? I don't believe this!' He was thunderstruck. 'Trespass? Intrusion? Baulking a master of his God-given rights? And committing felony of challenge to rightful authority? Are you mad?'

'Please, sir. I beg you. A carriage may be mended, an animal only rarely.'

'You hear this madwoman, Perrigo?' Prothero called over his shoulder. 'Take her! Have her brought up!'

'Yes, sir.'

One man stepped reluctantly towards her. She thought to run, but her mischief was done now. The two would give evidence for their master on sworn oath.

'Please, Mr Prothero,' Mehala begged. 'I had no right to leave the footpath, but I feared somebody was in distress – '

'Dear God, if the madwoman doesn't give me the lie as well!' Prothero forgot the stallion, which was still starting and backing at its tether. 'You know I've the right to impose such sanction as I see fits your misdemeanour, girl?'

'Yes, sir. But I see your arm is bad hurt, and I came to render assistance – '

A shrill whistle pierced the wind, long and slowly rising. It grew in sound until the whole farmyard filled with it and Mehala's eardrums seemed like to break under the crescendo force. The horse froze, legs asplay as the shrillness expanded and rose to the clouds. Even Prothero remained motionless.

It ended abruptly, the silence more painful than the whistling. The stockman Perrigo pointed to the edge of the field. Some hundred yards away, Simple Tom was standing, one hand out behind himself, clutching on to some bough of a tree. That was adequate defence against the punitive landlaws; to be still hold of a branch of a wayside tree meant one was not yet trespassing against the landowner, not having truly left the ancient trackway.

'Coming, Tom!' Mehala called desperately, starting away.

'Take her, Perrigo!' Prothero called up. The stockman hesitated only an instant, then came at a run.

A horseman broke from the undergrowth on to the field and approached at a trot. Simple Tom released his hold on the branch and loped after. Mehala felt almost sick with relief as she recognised Squire Hunterfield on Betsy. She angled her walk to meet up with him. He nudged the mare past, not giving her a glance, taking in the scene and staring at the stricken stallion roped at the stable wall.

'Good day, Prothero. Are you hurt, then?'

'Aye, that I am, and learning the beast better manners.' Prothero glowered at Mehala. 'At least, so I was, until challenged by this trespasser. It's just and proper you came by, Squire. I give this woman in charge. Is'll want her gaoled, for the public good. What she might have done – or even stolen! My men here prevented a series of greater felonies – '

'Mr Prothero,' Hunterfield cut in with a slightly apologetic voice. 'I regret to inform you that the blame is mine, for I saw her coming this way and instructed my man Tom to follow and signal me if the maiden seemed to think there was something amiss.'

'*You* allowed her? *Allowed?*'

The word was chosen well, Mehala realised with relief. It could mean anything from a definite order to the absence of any. Now it was for Prothero to gainsay Hunterfield, something even he would never dare.

'I regret, Mr Prothero, if my action proved discomfiting. I perhaps should have come myself instead. I can see that an apology is called for, so I make one. I trust you will accept, in the spirit in which it is made?'

Prothero swallowed with a great effort. Then he nodded, but surly enough.

'Thank you, Squire. I accept the apology.' He strove to smile, ingratiatingly managing a semblance of grace. 'And thank you for considering the possibility of an accident on my property. In fact, I wonder if I might use this occasion to extend an invitation to you and yours to visit myself and Mrs Prothero?'

Squire Hunterfield was taken aback, but inclined his head courteously. 'I welcome the opportunity, Mr Prothero. I am sure my sisters will also look forward to visiting Calling Farm.'

'Ah, sir. I mean our new residence, Carradine Manor!' Prothero watched the Squire's expression for signs of astonishment, but was disappointed. 'I trust that address proves no problem?'

'Of course not, Mr Prothero. I would be delighted to meet you and Mrs Prothero in your new residence. I look forward to hearing from you, and bid you good day. Tom, Mehala.'

Mehala saw curtains part slightly in the big farmhouse which overlooked the yard. Mary Prothero was there, standing obliquely so she could instantly withdraw. She herself moved slowly away from the yard during the exchange of courtesies between Prothero and the Squire, placing herself with every step more under Hunterfield's protection.

'Good day to you, Squire, and thank you.'

Prothero was in pain, Mehala saw. His arm, she surmised, if not actually broken, must be ruptured internally as well as opened for part of its length. The wound was concealed by the sleeve of his spencer.

Here was another injured man who would for a moment cease to vilify Doctor Carmichael and come wanting treatment. After, his abuse would return stronger than before. She walked on Hunterfield's command towards the footpath. Hunterfield moved Betsy alongside. He waited until they were well out of earshot.

'I have sacrificed a great deal, Mehala,' he said. 'I consider the assistance you have given me in the past now amply repaid.'

'Sir, I am ever grateful for your kind protection. And no repayment was ever necessary, sir.'

Hunterfield sighed. 'I only wish the repayment was not so exacting, Mehala. To endure some caterwauling at a spinet murders a gentleman of my fine sensibility. Enjoying Mr Prothero's company is more punitive still.'

She strove not to laugh at his wit. Amusement would have been improper, she a servant, and he single and Lord of Sealandings. She had been fortunate in his solicitude. She could not always depend on such bon chancing. In fact, he was as good as telling her to look to herself in future.

'I shall remember your words, sir, and abide by them.'

'See you do, Mehala.'

He reined Betsy in by the trackway as she started down the long slope into Sealandings. She aimed for the stile which let the path into the churchyard between the tall yews. When she reached it, she glanced covertly uphill, and saw he was only then pulling the mare round to head back to Lorne House. A gentleman among the gentry. Thank God. Without him, Sealandings would be in dire straits, with only Protheros and Carradines.

On reaching the schoolhouse she was dismayed to find Doctor Carmichael had already made his way. She hurried out south, along the South Toll road, hoping to overtake him before Shalamar.

Home.

4

'The point of my story, Lydia,' Tabitha Hunterfield lectured her sister, 'is that a family divided by great oceans and half a world is not likely to prosper!'

The ladies were seated at embroidery in the newly completed annex to the Lorne House orangery. Tabitha hated sewing; it was devised solely for the purpose of sending one thoroughly mad. Sitting 'at leisure' was the most boring of pastimes, and Lydia was cruel to insist on it. Oh, how marvellous to wake one morning a man, able to do whatever entered one's mind!

Lydia took her younger sister's assault calmly. 'From what fund of experience in wifely affairs do you make this assertion, Tabitha?'

'Common sense! Letitia agrees, don't you, Letitia?'

'Mmmh? I'm sorry, Tabitha. I was reading.'

'Diplomatic absence, as usual!'

Tabitha found Letitia exasperating. Forever with her nose stuck in a book of bizarre poetry. *Writing* poems even! No conversation to speak of, presenting the appearance of fustiness when hardly into her twenties . . . It was all screamingly *dull*. Lorne House was *boring*.

Letitia closed her volume as Tabitha raced through a biased account of the argument. 'I positively *insist* that Lydia write *at once* to Captain Vallance and compel his return! For heaven's sake!'

'Language, Tabitha!' Lydia reprimanded.

'It's been several *years*! What good is a husband in India?'

'Next April tenth is his second year,' Letitia said mildly.

'Why, so it is!' Lydia was pleased Letitia remembered the date so exactly. Still waters did run deep. No stiller water – nor deeper – than a *poetic* sister.

'Letty puts it too kindly!' Tabitha put in tartly. 'She means the start of Captain Vallance's third year.'

Lydia sighed. This discussion was getting out of hand. Tabitha had the knack of spinning argument from conversation.

'We shall have to see what his regiment ordains, Tabitha. And please be a repecter of persons. Letitia, not *Letty*!'

Tabitha felt like exploding. 'Yes, ma'am,' she said with mock meekness, hoping to infuriate but only succeeding in making her sisters laugh.

'Pleasant sounds, Mrs Vallance!'

Their brother Henry entered and sprawled in a wicker chair opposite the garden view. He had chosen the aspect for the new orangery against his sisters' combined wishes. They had wanted it to be set at a distance from Lorne House, the better to provide spectacle for visitors. Henry had wanted something usable, that one could enter of a cold evening. His sisters joked that their brother was a bumpkin, for he was nothing but a countryman more interested in the sea dykes than society.

'Tabitha argues that I should force James home, Henry.'

'Force, eh?' Hunterfield was amused.

Tabitha bent over her embroidery, tangling the coloured wool in her temper until it snapped. Letitia quietly took the work from her sister and began to find ends to unravel.

'Our sister wants Lorne House less tranquil, Henry!'

'That so, Tabby?'

Tabitha darted a triumphant glance at Lydia at Henry's use of the diminutive. Lydia's lips thinned. Henry's manner was unfortunately sometimes too homely. She signalled to Tabitha, who rose and poured their brother a glass of thick green noyau, his preferred drink after riding. To please him, she used his favourite blue-tinted Cork glass.

'Thank you.' Henry sipped the opaque liquor. 'Who made this? Letitia, I think?'

'Yes, Henry.' Tabitha smiled as she took her seat. 'Mine is somewhat creamier than *Letty*'s, and perhaps a little more evenly textured, being not so . . . well, *bland*.'

'I look forward to it, Tabby. Letty, this is exactly right.'

'Thank you, sir.'

'I fear Lorne House is already on a way to being disturbed,' he said heavily. 'We have invitation to call – tea, or some damned thing – '

His sisters gasped at his expletive. He waved them to silence.

' – at Carradine Manor. I agreed you would receive the written invitation, Lydia. My sincere apologies.'

'Carradine Manor, Henry?' Lydia said faintly. Their silence told their astonishment.

Tabitha brightened. The antagonisms between the families was old standing. She had never expected it to end during her lifetime.

'No, ladies.' Already he was regretting his handling of events at Calling Farm. 'Mrs Prothero will entertain us. Of Carradine himself I have no knowledge.'

Lydia was sceptical. She could read Henry like a book. She suspected he still longed after that terrible Thalia De Foe, who was widely believed to be a special creature to Carradine when Fellows stayed in London and in ignorance.

'Is there a reason we should know, Henry?'

'Tabitha!' Lydia snapped. 'That will do, miss. Apologise at once to your brother, *if* you please. You shall *not* enquire as to the family's directions without express invitation to do so!'

'I apologise, sir.' Tabitha saw she had gone too far. 'I apologise, Mrs Vallance.'

'Thank you, miss!' Lydia raised her eyebrows to Henry. Tabitha was proving more difficult with every passing day. Something would have to be done very soon to avert a family disaster. Letitia on the other hand proved no problem, never had.

She recognised the faint lift of his chin as understanding and acknowledgement.

'I was about to say, Lydia, that my conversation at Calling Farm was the means of preventing charges laid against that Mehala girl. She had unwisely asked Prothero to spare some stallion he was thrashing.'

He gave them an account, ponderous and slow, hoping to allay further interrogation. He was disappointed.

'Should she not have been allowed her punishment, Henry? I mean, such unwarranted rudeness! And wasn't her trespass illegal?' Lydia saw Henry was in difficulties, though his interest in the girl was surely innocent. 'I am sure you acted in the very best interests of the landowner.'

'Thank you, my dear.' The vague irony was a gentle warning. 'Prothero was hurt. The girl is Carmichael's housekeeper. She acted with good intent. In any case, a magistrate would have difficulty, as she is still of unsound memory.'

The ladies considered this. Tabitha drew breath to speak, but was silenced by Lydia's glance.

'It was then that Mr Prothero extended the invitation,' Henry confessed. Heavy-handedly he tried to make a joke. 'We shall accept on condition his wife does not play music at us!'

Letitia smiled to lessen his unease. 'That is a pleasure I insist on giving you tonight, Henry, to make up for your disappointment!'

Henry was grateful for Letitia's wit. For all her faults – reticence, a mouse-like reserve which put off would-be suitors – Letty sometimes intervened in a most fortunate way, almost as if she understood more implications in conversation than was possible.

'How marvellous, Letty!' he said dolefully, laughing. He stood, placing his Cork on the sofa table Lydia favoured for the orangery.

His duty was done, the awkward business of warning his sisters achieved without too much trauma. He signed thanks to Lydia, received smiling acknowledgement, and went to change for the evening.

They waited until he was safely out of hearing before bursting into talk.

'Well!' Tabitha got in first, seeing Letitia make to speak. Her sister could scamander on, with so many veiled hints you could be lost in a trice. 'I've never heard the like! We are to accept to Carradine Manor! Will Carradine be there? Is Mrs Prothero now mistress there? Is Mr Prothero there as master? What of Carradine?'

'Tabitha!' sharply from Lydia. 'Henry has told us what we are to know, and there's an end to it.'

'Mehala,' Letitia said quietly. 'She must be grateful Henry happened by.'

Tabitha asked blankly, 'Do you mean. . . ?' Her wary glance gauged Lydia. 'Do you infer that our brother has some interest in the girl? More than that of courtesy?'

'No, but Doctor Carmichael saved little Clare Darling from diphtheritis, did he not? Whose father John Darling is Lorne's chief hired waggoner. Henry perhaps was discharging an implied obligation to Mehala. She helped greatly in the nursing.'

Lydia heard her out, marvelling. How *did* Letitia learn things? The way she presented it made it factual, when another woman would make it the merest gossip.

'The obligation is ended, then,' Lydia said comfortably.

'I *want* to go to Carradine Manor!' Tabitha announced. 'I shouldn't think many others will have accepted so far, do you?'

It was Letitia who answered for Lydia. 'They will, once word is about that Sir Henry Hunterfield will attend.'

Tabitha was delighted. 'So they will!' she cried, clapping her hands. 'So they will! Why, all Sealandings!'

'Possibly not Carradine himself,' Lydia commented.

She spent the rest of the hour wondering if she should somehow bring to Mary Prothero's notice that the Hunterfields would be pleased to remark the absence of Carradine at her gathering. It could be done quite tactfully, through some condign intermediary.

By tea-time she had developed a headache and was forced to retire early. Letitia presided over tea in her stead.

To his surprise, Henry found the interlude oddly pleasant, with Letitia's quiet conversation about Sealandings folk astonishingly well-informed and pertinent. Almost as if Lydia – an impossibly wrong thought, of course – was a restraint on the girl. It was something he'd noticed before, that Letitia was excellent company, once Lydia was out of the way. As if his sister grew in stature and capability, as well as in intellect, when deputing for her older sister.

Tabitha fumed throughout, bored to her very soul by the talk of shore, sea, country, mills and markets, and stupid people who were nothing better than peasants in this beknighted rurality. She could not endure Lorne House's peace much longer.

Ven Carmichael was relieved it was an emergency he could do something about, and a medical condition he almost understood.

The man was old, having difficulty in breathing. His abdomen was distended, the upward pressure on his diaphragm keeping his chest from expanding. He was puce, yet his lips had an unhealthy pallor. An old woman looked after him, but did not much care for the task.

'I'm his neighbour, y'see, Doctor,' she told Ven frankly.

'When he goes, I get his furniture, and his goat. I live two doors along.'

The sea cottages were the last line of dwellings on the Blakeney road. It skirted the harbour and ran north along the coast, passing through Carradine lands beyond the North Mole.

'Did he drink?'

'Some, Doctor. Old sailors of the King always are mortal 'bibers.'

Hydrops utricularius, he knew it as, called so from the bottle-shaped protruberance of the belly in the swelling of ascites. He had been taught that schirrous liver was the cause – though causation was near to fairy tale, in medicine. He knew a way to alleviate this old man's symptoms. No cure, but at least a way to keep the patient in breath.

'Could you give me an empty jug, please?'

He placed her earthenware container on the floor beside the bed.

'Now wait outside, ma'am, if you please.'

'Is'll wait in my own home, Doctor!' The old woman left, grousing at having to dodge the chill wind.

The device he had made himself. It consisted of a catheter tube of gum elastic, fixed into the end of a small piece of hollow cane, waxed and polished until it shone like some golden straw. He had bevelled it at the free end, and honed it carefully to a sharp point.

He uncovered the recumbent man's distended abdomen, and gently shook him.

'Listen, Sir. I am Doctor Carmichael. You know me?'

The old man was some time focusing but eventually gave attention. 'I can't breathe,' he managed to say.

'I know. Listen.' Ven leaned close, and detected the sweet odour in the old sailor's breath. 'I'm going to pierce the skin of your belly. Nothing too bad, just a short pain. Lie still.'

The old man was almost moribund, unable to say more. He breathed in short rapid snores, high-pitched. Ven rolled him on one side, and knelt by the bed. He spread the skin tight with the fingers of his left hand and took his lancet from his leather bag. The end of the catheter he trailed into the jug.

'Now, sir. Be still.'

He slit the skin with the lancet for a quarter of an inch. Blood

46

oozed immediately. He laid the lancet aside, and drove the sharpened cane deeply into the incision with a slight screwing motion. He felt the point give slightly. A hissing sound began. He looked down. Amber liquid was flowing freely along the tube into the jug. He sighed with relief, and held position.

It was a full quarter of an hour before the fluid draining from the old man's abdomen dwindled to almost nothing. Ven struggled to roll the recumbent form over a little more, hoping to drain a few last fluid ounces. The old man's breathing was steady, freer. His lips were less blue. He seemed simply at sleep now, instead of in a shallow stupor. Ven quickly withdrew the cane, and sewed a waxed linen stitch through the lancet's slit to hold the skin. He left it uncovered.

It took him a few moments to empty the jug into the open drain outside the cottages. He went to find the old woman, knocking at her door for quite some time. She did not appear. He returned to the old sailorman, made him as comfortable as he could, gathered up his things into his leather bag, and left. The fluid would return, and the paracentesis operation need doing again. And again. Until . . .

Shame was nothing new. That he felt shame after a modest success was unusual, he realised with surprise. Perhaps because any success was so scarce! The wry thought made him smile, but with bitterness. How marvellous it would be if, in some future ideal world, a doctor could operate, as he had just done, then leave a nurse in charge of the patient! But such foolish daydreams were impossible. He admonished himself. These absurd flights of fancy were coming more frequently these days. And him a grown man! He had best never admit to such imaginings, or folk would think him mad.

At least he could tell Mehala. She never seemed to mind. And indeed she was learning apace, absorbing practically everything he told her. Amazing. He wondered if, perhaps in his wonderful imaginary world of the future, a woman like Mehala could ever be admitted to the medical profession! A woman *doctor*? There I go again, he chided himself inwardly. More insane dreams. He must stop these lunatic thoughts. A windblown fragment of newspaper caught his attention. He snatched it up and read it as he hurried to the next case.

47

The Goat and Compass stood against the wharf at Sealandings. Its position was fortuitously good for, facing south-east as it did, it occupied the start of the sharpest incline of the entire waterfront. The taverner Ben Fowler liked to tell his cronies that it 'dominated' the harbour.

Across the bay, beyond the South Mole where the hard expended itself into muddy sea flats, there was no feature half so prominent as the Goat and Compass. The only distinction for that area opposite was Watermillock, the tidal seamill where Widow Maderley still hoped that her artist son William was going to prove a successful miller at last. The cottages ended at the small River Affon, on the inland bank of which stood the rival Donkey and Buskin.

That enemy hostelry, where John Weaver and Sarah Ann his wife held the inland coach terminus, and made a fortune from travellers' coppers, was nothing like as favoured as the Goat and Compass. For here was the place to be for night walkers to come calling, for receipt of the dark boat cargoes when all lanterns were dowsed. Neither Customs nor Excise, with their watching gunners at sea, could prevent black imports.

'Carradine's done for,' Ben told Martha.

'He can't be,' she protested. They were alone in their small parlour. Agatha, the head serving girl, was audible in the taproom loudly upbraiding some fisherman to roars of laughter. 'He's gentry. Been at Carradine Manor since – '

'Aye, aye. Tell me the tale.' Ben listened as a blow was struck and the laughter gave way to scuffling. He relaxed when the chatter resumed and Agatha's abuse was restored to normal. 'All is Prothero now. I heard it from Brown the joiner. Carradine backed down before Prothero's written order.'

'Backed down? Carradine?' Martha spoke in awe.

'Prothero's already hosting the gentry to Carradine Manor. He's like to take residence there soon.'

'What'll happen to Carradine?'

'I must ask.'

His wife caught him. 'Ask, Ben? Dear God! Don't meddle. We can't afford long memories. Only gentry have that luxury.'

He pulled his arm away. Sometimes a woman retarded a man

when she would help best by staying dumb. 'This is an opportunity, Martha! Can't you see? Carradine won't be kept down for long, not he. I want to stay in favour. But if Prothero pays half so well as Carradine, I want to be in his good standing. *Who* lords at Carradine Manor is nothing. Money's everything.'

Martha was still frightened. 'Who'll you speak with, Ben?'

He thought for a moment. 'Carradine first. Then Prothero.'

'Ben. Wait – see which way the cat jumps.'

'And let John Weaver take greater hold on Sealandings trade?' He cursed her away and stood, a florid man with huge girth. 'You'll have us in the poorhouse, Martha. I can play one off against the other. I must speak, pay respects.'

Martha tried to envisage her husband, a mere tavern-keeper, calling at a manor house to 'pay respects', and could only groan. He was driven by his hatred for the Weavers.

'Instead, Ben,' she said, going with him to the outer door, 'why not send word to Carradine, the way you always did?'

He paused, hand on the Suffolk latch. 'Why do that? There's no cargo in this night.'

'Then send word about the next incomers,' she pleaded eagerly. 'That would show Carradine you were loyal to him. It wouldn't stop you from complimenting Prothero.'

He looked hard at her. Maybe this was more cunning still. His hand fell, to her relief. 'And do what with Prothero?'

She smiled now. 'Bide, Ben. Simply bide. We know Prothero. He'll soon come knock.'

'By God, Martha. I think that's the thing to do.'

The uproar in the outer taproom rose. A beaker shattered. Ben swore under his breath and hurried to the fray.

Mehala thought she had started the evening well. Doctor Carmichael had entered excitedly, waving a scrap of newsprint.

'Look, Mehala! Read this – a charity bequest to the poor! We may write and ask help.'

'Like other charities?' She hated to quash his optimism, but was too experienced. He stood on the steps, too thrilled at his find to take off his coat.

He would not take caution. 'Listen. The late Mrs Susannah Hammant's charity is to be distributed to deserving paupers, at the behest of the Minister and churchwardens!' He showed her the fragment, smoothing it, his eyes shining, and quoted, ' "For the worthy poor"! I need only write to the Rector, listing any impoverished folk, for them to receive a bread allowance. In money!'

'Doctor,' she began, reluctant to spoil his innocent delight.

'You don't see, do you, Mehala?' He was all enthusiasm. 'We must start small, then grow – perhaps do as the City of York, establishing its Lunatick Hospital in 1772. Why mayn't Sealandings, with such munificence as this Hammant Charity? Oh, I know that York institution fell into abuse, as lately exposed by Magistrate Higgins, but we would rule ours with leniency and care. Think of it, Mehala!' His eyes radiated hope. 'I write directly this evening! Reverend Baring is too holy a man to let our past differences intervene . . .'

'Yes, Doctor.' Mehala went through into the kitchen. The poor man lived in a rosy world of kindliness and optimism. It was her task to protect him – but first to feed him, which meant doing battle with Mrs Trenchard.

Old Mrs Trenchard was pleased with the help she had given, preparing the evening meal. Mehala wasn't, for she wanted this evening to be specially momentous, and here was the old body still chatting when she ought to be on her way home. Mrs Trenchard was a serious impediment. At any time a patient could send for help, and then the quiet time Mehala specially hoped for this dusk would be gone.

'Yes, Mrs Trenchard,' Mehala said, trying to urge her out. 'I see you've done splendidly.' She meant nothing that couldn't be mended, providing she scampered before Carmichael came from his scrupulous washing in the outhouse.

'See, Mehala,' Mrs Trenchard preached, 'you young people don't really appreciate inland fish. I mind years ago when my old grandmam, God rest her, first showed me how to cook the jack pike. Freshwater wolf, we call it. All like Mr Walton the angler said, keep it complete as one, so the flavour – '

Mehala could have thrown her down the steps. At least the old dame had kept the fire going and made the panada, though she had wasted all but a few of yesterday's bread rolls.

'And thank you for making the love-apple sauce, Mrs Trenchard. Oh, how I wish I had your knack!'

Go! Mehala's mind screamed. She could hear Ven clattering the eshet against the well's crumbling brickwork. He'd be in any moment now, and her lovely planned supper nowhere near ready.

'Oh, you're welcome, m'dear. I mind well when I started. Heavens, the stories I could tell!' Mrs Trenchard creaked with laughter, ready for more reminiscences.

Mehala pulled the old lady's bertha round her. 'Mind you prevent chill, Mrs Trenchard. I'm sure Trenchard's waiting. I don't want him putting salt on my tail for making you late!'

Mrs Trenchard resisted. 'One thing, Mehala. It's unwise to make quenelles from jack pike. The old ways are best. Roast *whole* when a jack's over a three-pounder, as you got. Clean it, then mace, thyme and winter savoury in the belly, and spitroast him with lath binding.' She sighed, shaking her head. 'Though you'll know best for the worst, like all you modern girls. Talk-all-know-nils . . .'

Mehala almost threw her from the door, and flew back.

The daylight had already dwindled, so she had to waste time by finding one of the old lady's country candles of hog tallow. She hated the offensive smell and its irregular guttering, but reserved her two good tallows for when she and Carmichael were undisturbed and him able to listen to her plans for Shalamar.

Mrs Trenchard's grandiose scheme for the jack pike was hopeless, for pike could never be roasted with any success when less than a yard in length. Everyone knew that. Mehala had the fish skinned and boned, nutmegged, and the skin and bones pounded for sieving into her court-bouillon. White wine from France was impossibly expensive, so in went three glasses of her own pear wine. It had not yet reached its second ferment, when its parent tree burgeoned the following spring. That was beyond mending without money.

She started. A still figure was observing her from the hall doorway. Colour flooded her cheeks.

'Doctor! You gave me quite a start.'

'I was watching, Mehala. Do you mind?'

'Why no, sir.' She caught herself. Her plans for the evening did not include maid-and-master formality. 'Your house, my task. Watch as you please.'

'A pretty picture.' He was smiling. 'I wish I had William Maderley's skills with paintbrush and easel.'

'That would be Sealandings' loss, Doctor Carmichael.'

He nodded, something in her remark clouding his face as he stepped in and sank on to a chair, propping his chin on it so comically that Mehala had to smile.

'What is it?' he asked, puzzled.

'Like a little boy.' She set the bouillon boiling well and the sandglass running. 'Peering into a yard.'

'I ought to have some Lancashire chairs, or a few Cardiganshires about. Perhaps in time.'

'I meant you deserve better.'

'Deserve, Mehala?' His tone was bitter. She kept working the butter with the panada as the fish flesh became smoothed by the egg yolk. Cheap food. But rough country fare was how you fed innocents, as ordinary folk said, rough and enough. And this poor man was a true innocent, for all his learning. 'I receive more than I deserve.'

'More?' she said, stung. 'Less is the truth. No man in Sealandings is as conscientious. It's Sealandings as doesn't deserve, truth be known.'

He stared into the old range. The firelight reflected in his eyes. His hair fell like an untended thatch, still damp from the sousing with well water.

'Except I don't succeed, Mehala. Look at today. Those women at Two Cotts. Never a step forward, but two back. I hope for progress, children free from ailment, old folk spared pain, mothers saved derangement over babes, fathers going mad when infants die!'

The huge pan was hot and buttered, but his talk sent a shiver up her spine. She had to pause, the first quenelle moulded between her two largest spoons ready for poaching.

'Please. You must not speak so, I beg.'

'I mean it, Mehala,' he said morosely. 'That little Baines lad, for instance. His leg needs three days of rest – but I know they'll set him to labouring on the wharfside.'

'Hal Baines? Of *The Jaunty*?'

'His little brother. I saw him at Miss Gould's school.'

'I pray he recovers.' She resumed forming the quenelles and

placing them in the pan. 'That's what I meant. You do your school surgery coin free.'

'They're children, Mehala.' He sounded astonished.

She poured the boiling court-bouillon over the quenelles until they were just covered. A quarter hour, and all would be ready. But the time had come to talk.

'They're children, yes. But Sealandings folk expect that you live on air.' She tried to keep her voice mild, her manner light. He was easily affronted by medicine mixed with money. 'Some families can afford to pay something, Doctor.'

'Mankind has a right to be ill in peace, Mehala.' There was reproach in his voice.

She rested the sand-glass, judging half its bulk by eye, and lit her two special sheep-and-bullock tallows from the guttering hog, flooding the kitchen with a steady golden light. She extinguished the black smoker thankfully, and set the table with platters and knives. The pear wine had nothing grander than small ash cups.

'It must surely be the Almighty's intention for that happy time to come, sooner or later. I worry about the present.'

'Mehala. I was thinking about you on the way home.'

'About me?' She decanted the wine, seeing its amber pick up the candles, gilding. 'Have I done wrong?'

'No, Mehala. How could you?' He said it quite naturally. 'It's me. I've been very remiss. I've accepted your help, but haven't yet been able to pay. I see you in the garden, that herbal corner –'

'You need medicinals, Doctor. How else can you make simples? That apothecary in Maidborough's the greediest exploiter I ever did see, taking advantage of your unconcern for money – '

'I'm very abstemious, Mehala,' Carmichael said, surprised.

'Of course, she concurred quickly, coming to sit opposite. 'But you can't keep purchase prices in your head, to deal with tradesfolk, walk the leagues to Maidborough for remedies. No wonder they take advantage!'

Especially when you give the remedies away, she did not say. Then forget to bill even the rich, while I feed us with whatever John Weaver lets Sarah Ann send over. Why, if it wasn't for – hideous word – charity, from friends like Little Jane, assistant housekeeper at Bures House for Charles Golding, Shalamar would resound to clanking bones.

She put in as he made to speak, 'I know your aversion to raising fees on the sick.'

'It's like . . .' he ran his fingers through his hair helplessly. Her heart went out to him. 'It's taking advantage of the suffering poor.'

'Yes, Doctor.' She rose to check the poaching pan, to avoid reaching out to touch him.

Suffering poor, she blazed inwardly. Mrs Wren in Two Cotts demands his services, to make her gross living from the willing bodies of girls. Suffering poor! Like the stockman on Carradine's estate, whose pustular contagion needed treatment all hours of the day and night, and never a penny piece. Yes, it *should* be free, in some paradisical world. But here on earth this innocent man didn't have leather under foot, while the people he cared for rode by without a nod.

'I wonder if there is some way I could help.'

He stared. 'Help? Impossible, Mehala. Before you came, why, I . . .' he hesitated, only shrugged. 'It's been like sunshine, even in the lantern hours, having you in the house. Even flowers! It's a delight.'

'Thank you.'

He looked, shook his head uncomprehendingly. 'You could have gone to any of the great houses hereabouts. Why, I heard they asked for you at Arminell. Yes, the Astells! Yet you came here.'

'It was my wish.'

'I can understand your wish to escape the gentry,' he said seriously. 'I hope that Shalamar has served its purpose. I have no illusions, Mehala. This can't suit you forever. You have a great destiny. I can see it, as can others.'

Mehala smiled. If that was how far the poor man could see for the whilst, so be it. She had time on her side. She decided to postpone mentioning ownership of Shalamar. That would come later, and by then she'd have discovered about Shalamar herself.

'Doctor. Let me try, let me be your assistant!'

'Assistant?' He must have misheard. There was no such thing as a doctor's woman helper. 'Mehala. Some things are beyond reach.

54

For a woman to become an apothecary, a doctor, is . . .' Words failed.

'I assisted at Clare Darling's sickbed, Doctor,' Mehala reminded gently. 'I fetch, carry, assist without any grand title, don't I?'

'But even in London infirmaries the nurses are . . . women from the streets, Mehala. I couldn't subject you to that.'

'You – we – could not afford an apprentice, Doctor. Nor a fetch-all.'

'Mehala. You're not suggesting. . . ?'

'Yes, Doctor. I'd be your true apprentice.'

His voice was so quiet it was almost inaudible. 'No, Mehala. And have you ridiculed by the fishwives? The goosegirls stone you for an unnatural creature who seeks to emulate menkind?'

'No, Doctor. To be your walking servant. There's an old dog cart in the stables here. It could be restored.'

He reddened. 'That would set them a-laughing on the harbour wharfs, Mehala. They'd call me Dutchman, and worse!'

She rose, saw the quenelles had poached perfectly – more fortune than skill, the lack of attention she'd paid – drained and served them on the low dishes. Eight quenelles for him, four for herself. She cut bread, served the sauce with steamed mushrooms.

'I didn't know we had love-apples, Mehala.'

'Tomato, they now call them in grand circles,' she said with a lofty air. 'The old tumatle.' She did not say she had found them growing wild on the rubbish, where the haulms were cast.

'It's a marvellous meal. Thank you.'

'We lack truffles, though.' And a dariole mould for the quenelles, and proper dishes, and heaven-knew-what else.

'You'd be willing to be fetch-all for a quack, Mehala? And be called crocus? Sawbones? Peel-pox? Pus-monger? Pill-roller? Gut-wrench?' He could have gone on with the thousand abusive names.

He was close to agreeing. 'Think how much more work you could do,' she said. 'Time to read more, keep the records you execute in the new modern way you mention.'

'Why, so I could!' He was pleased. 'Old doctors scorn the new system, but I believe that writing down the symptoms, signs and progress of each disease – yes, even drawing maps of where each illness occurs – might show how diseases spread. Think of it!'

'More time,' Mehala prompted gently.

He was staring through her at a dazzling vision. 'I wondered the same thing today, Mehala, by curious chance. There never has been a woman medical apprentice.'

'You could teach me secretly, at Shalamar.'

'Teach medicine? Surgery?'

'It is done thus throughout the Kingdom.'

'And wholly disorganised, with medical schools going their own ways and country doctors as lost as all!'

'I do not know if I am equal to the task, Doctor – '

He smiled denial. 'Mehala, you can do anything, everything. It is within your capability.' His eyes widened. 'By God, Mehala, let's do it! I shall instruct you. You shall learn, and secretly become the world's first doctress!'

'A housekeeper with a little learning!' she corrected.

'No, Mehala. A doctor is all or none!' He raised his cup. 'Well, apprentice. Here's to your health, Mehala.'

'Health to you and all, Doctor.'

His expression sobered. 'I must warn you, Mehala. It's the most dangerous profession on earth. We die oftener than all. I make you a solemn promise. Knowledge is progress. I undertake to teach you, just as if you were my honest apprentice.'

'I thank you, Doctor.'

'On condition that you don't act as such, for your own protection among ignorant folk. They might accuse you of unnatural behaviour.'

'I promise.' In guarding herself, she would guard him.

'And call me Ven, Mehala.'

She said, colouring, 'But Mrs Trenchard might assume – '

'Let her. Let them. Here as now, Mehala.'

'Thank you.' She found him waiting, and said, 'Ven.'

'Rotten name,' he said unexpectedly with a grimace, and set her laughing. 'Come. Time to write to Reverend Baring.'

Nothing could stop her now. Her heart sang. Tomorrow she would set about the urgent task of seeing who could afford to pay for his services, and keep good records. She might even make a room draught-free, please God.

Then as time passed, she could discover who owned Shalamar, and on what terms it might be purchased, in Doctor Ven Carmichael's name.

And then . . .

She smiled at him through the candleglim. It had taken much ingenuity, and some charity. But that was tonight. Tomorrow she would change his world, and hers with his.

5

'How fared your enemy, Prothero?'

Carradine did not smile, but the other knew he was poking fun at his injured arm. Prothero was in no mood for banter, especially from a former gentleman who now danced to a landlord's tune.

The farmer could acknowledge the jibe without rancour as he took a seat in the taproom. He was Carradine's master now. His arm was giving him hell, though he'd treated it properly with horse dung, and bound a tight wadding over. That stallion had deserved every lash. The beast was so damaged that he had this very morning ordered the stockmen to dress it as best as they could, and sell it at the Suffolk horse fair. Perrigo and the men had been sullen. He'd had to bate their wage threepence apiece. Times were a-changing round Calling Farm. They'd have to learn, like this fallen gentleman opposite.

The Goat and Compass was thinly occupied this morning. A few drovers were in early, among fishermen wanting their boat. Two of the fishwives were complaining about the prices offered by Martha Fowler for their produce, but Agatha was giving back all their abuse and more. Ben Fowler was setting up casks for the day.

'No fight I couldn't cope with, Carradine,' Prothero said easily. 'I'll have small beer.'

Carradine's stillness was typical of the man. Prothero's insult was studied and timely. Time was when Prothero had stood barefooted and tugged his forelock as Carradine's family had ridden in their grand carriages to Evensong. Not now.

He watched Carradine signal to Fowler for ale, and said smugly, 'I need a word by reason of your impending move.'

'Move?' A dusky red patch showed on Carradine's cheek. 'I intend no move, Prothero.'

Once more, no courtesy title. Prothero scored its absence as a studied offence. Carradine was behaving as he always had behaved, as a high-born manorial family scion with any merchant or tenant. It fuelled Prothero's anger.

'Oh, but you do, Carradine. And soon.'

The tavern servant set the pewters down. Prothero let his gaze follow Agatha across the taproom. Rough fare, but worthy of her hire.

'I need your house, Carradine. So vacate it. I'll allow you a few days, of course, but don't tarry.' He drew on the ale, grimacing to Ben Fowler in disapproval. The taverner looked across anxiously. The small ale was sound – it had better be – but it would do no harm for Fowler to know which of his customers paid the piper.

Carradine was still, a hunting heron. For a moment Prothero wondered if he had gone too far, knowing Carradine's fearsome reputation. The law was on his side, however. Carradine owed Prothero his all, except perhaps a ruin here and there and stretches of worthless coast, mere samphire and water sedge.

'You want my house?'

Prothero saw with delight that the grand gentleman had paled. '*Your* house? Get through your thick skull that the Manor is mine. I have the deeds. Your gambling debts are honoured in full. I return your notes.'

Prothero felt replete, as after making love, or a gargantuan feast. He observed Carradine's expression with relish. Revenge is all the sweeter for remembering the slights of all those years. It was pleasant to see a man try to come to terms with the new order.

'I don't think there's anything else, Carradine.' Carradine had not touched his drink, he said nothing. 'I shall start Mrs Prothero making arrangements regarding the servantry at Carradine.'

The farmer spoke as if it was all too much bother. Languid, that was the way to be. Offhand, effete. His smile was constant.

The other drinkers had left, he saw with grim humour, wisely realising that all was not sugar and spice. Fear of Carradine, or awe of the new gentry? Surely the latter, for the man opposite was finished. Prothero could not conceal his scorn. Take away his fine M-cut collar, his elegant spencer in Chine silk, the crisp Wellington hat, ignore his square-cut pantaloons, the Spitalfields velvet he affected, the claw-tailed riding coat – and what did you have? A creature of appetite, who had started life with everything and thrown it away by stupidity. And him still far from his thirtieth year!

Well, let the gentleman live as the ruffian.

'That will be all, Carradine,' he said in dismissal.

Carradine rose, adjusted his coat, and strode slowly away. Prothero let him take a few paces before calling him to a halt.

'Oh, Carradine. Don't forget the taverner's coin, eh? And I want your – *my* – coaches left in prime condition, mind!'

The man stood motionless for so long that Prothero's unease returned. Then he walked from the room. He made no payment, gave no acknowledgement to the words everyone must have heard.

Cowed! Prothero crowed to himself. One cowed, another proud. Life was superb! He, Jason Prothero, was master of Carradine Manor *and* Calling Farm. Wealth was the maker and breaker of gentlemen, no matter what grovelling countryfolk thought. It only took a real man to grasp all he wanted. He beckoned Fowler, who came at a run.

'Sir?'

Prothero nodded towards the open door. Through the stone-flagged corridor the sea horizon was visible.

'That's what ship? It's tacked a time or two.'

Fowler inclined his head and pursed his lips, the coast man's sign of regret.

'It's the Revenue cutter, sir. The *Hunter*.'

'You're certain?'

'Absolutely, sir. Of the Preventive Service. She carries galleys and gigs hoisted almost on every sheet, sir.' The taverner added, 'Her small white boats are for boarding and ashoring, sir, when they inspect night passages.'

'Didn't she victual in Sealandings some weeks back?'

'Yes, sir. Can't mistake *Hunter*, sir. Painted black overall, damn her, with red bulwarks. Red lasts at sea when other colours don't. She victuals at Harwich or Lowestoft, though she's made chases as far north as the Yare and Gorleston.'

'Bastards,' Prothero said, quietening his voice.

Ben Fowler nodded with feeling. His unease was evident. Carradine was lost to Sealandings, and was replaced. No mistaking by whom.

'Not like in the old days, when gin come in regular at twenty-five shillings the tub, Holland geneva the same rate.'

'And segars?'

Fowler scanned the room, closed a serving hatch, returned to speak softly. He made to sit, then changed his mind at Prothero's look and remained standing.

'Cigars they call them now, sir, when fetched in. They're casked in false bottoms and margins.' He hesitated, unwilling to disclose too much. 'Or so I hear. I'm honest as the day is long, sir!'

'I'm sure of it, Fowler.'

'Even Giffler's not doing much – they say, sir.'

'Giffler?'

The big farmer occasionally felt the gap between landsman and sea folk. He'd never been one for water. His world was farming, earth and all its progeny. These illiterate seamen were beyond him, never at peace lest they trod oceans, their land a set of boards beneath the feet, moving and churning. It might be a profitable world, for the right man.

'Yes, sir. Giffler's a fisherman. Wanders more than most, hence the name he goes by.'

Giffler in local speech was a restless beast, easily startled. A night-walker, then, this Giffler. The name might be worth remembering. But Ben Fowler had been Carradine's man. It was important to teach him a new allegiance.

'Pity.' He let the word hang for a moment. 'Such a man would be invaluable, properly financed.'

'Indeed, sir.' Fowler's tone was respectful at the implications of wealth. Funding a night run was expensive to a degree. 'But it's a sore risk to them as sail.'

'That would be taken into account, by the right backer.'

'That's a difficulty, times being so hazardous.'

'Are they so dangerous?' Prothero asked calmly. He was under no misapprehension. They were now debating terms. 'Look at your own trade, Fowler.'

'Mine, sir? Hostelry's different from taking any sea wind God sends, sir.'

'Not really, Fowler.' He watched the man's face as he said, 'Look at the Donkey and Buskin. The coach stands there. The post. Your rival is highly favoured.'

Fowler nodded. 'I'm aware of John Weaver's good fortune, sir. He's luckily placed. The South Toll road is easier for wheeled waggonry and carriages.'

'But you have the drovers, Fowler,' Prothero said with innocence. 'The Norwich road is as sound as the South Toll.'

'Much I make from goosegirls, sir. And the cattle droves from the Ridings aren't what they used to be.'

Prothero was glad to have dug down to Fowler's bitterness so quickly. He said idly, 'Influence could possibly change, say, the coaches' stand.'

'Get the coaches for the Goat and Compass, sir?' Fowler's belly churned with greed.

'If the right people could be persuaded, Fowler.'

'I'd be eternally grateful, sir.'

The man fawned like a patted dog. Prothero felt nothing but contempt. These lowlifes who depended on their betters for advancement were nothing but peasants. Like Carradine, now that fine gentleman stood unmasked.

Prothero stood, despising the man. He strolled out, confident the publican wouldn't dare call him back for the ale money, and was right. He walked along the wharf, occasionally glancing out between the harbour moles to where the *Hunter* showed on the horizon. So the great days of contrabranding were done. But what forbade their return, to the greater benefit of all? Only that single ship trying to govern an entire coastline. Yes, Jason Prothero could easily finance the profitable night voyages Carradine and Ben Fowler had for so long enjoyed. Gold bred gold, folk said. How true.

Thalia De Foe's heart leapt as she caught sight of him. Oddly, he moved at a slow walk, his hunter on a careless rein.

She called to her coachman, 'Ferrars, pass by that gentleman. He will particularly want to greet me.'

'Yes, m'm,'

The old man was deft with the pair of greys, his favourites, and rounded the huddle of tinkers in Market Square with yards to spare. He drew the phaeton to a crawl opposite the Corn Mart building, so the rider would cross at the junction with the Blakeney road. It was improper for a lady in her carriage to extend first greeting to a gentleman, so propriety would be served.

Thalia watched Carradine come. He was handsome enough to set any woman stirring. In spite of their last parting, a thing of near-acrimony, the glimpse of her lover melted her. His nature was so brilliant, his power so intense, he surely must resurge. Until a little ago, Carradine was admired, even feared, by almost all in Sealandings. Even London too knew of the firebrand Carradine.

Thalia adjusted her dress, conscious that she made a pretty picture. Her imbecile sleeves were full as full, tight-gathered at the wrists, and showing daringly from beneath her pelerine. The French hood she wore was accidentally falling from her hair, showing its lining of green worsted-silk tamine. Carradine always admired style.

He rode on.

She stared, appalled. Ferrars quickly geed his greys without instruction, having practically staled them to permit the exchange. Nobody was near enough to have seen the outrage except tinkers watering donkeys and a packhorse at the water trough beside the Corn Mart step.

Thalia flushed red, then paled. She felt her face prickle at the unforgivable slight. It was an insult, a degradation. It was beyond belief. She sat bolt upright as the phaeton rolled on out of Market Square and turned right down the Blakeney road.

She was faint at the implications. Ferrars had seen, but was a true servant. He would say nothing. If he did, he'd not eat another meal in the Eastern Hundreds. But it was impossible to pretend. Sealandings saw more than it had eyes to see. This scandalous occurrence would be into the great houses by nightfall.

The Goat and Compass lay to the left of the wharfside, within its yard, and walking out like King George himself was Prothero. Full of himself, raising his hat quite as if he was entitled to be acknowledged. She hated the odious stoat who had disgraded her lover.

'May I bid good day to you, ma'am?'

On impulse laden with suspicion she inclined her head. 'Good day, sir.' She allowed him a glacial smile.

'I trust you had as pleasant an expedition?'

She leant forward to tap the Salisbury box, and Ferrars drew the greys to a stand. It might be nothing, or it might offer some explanation for Carradine's white, set face as he had ridden past her carriage. He had been coming from this direction. Tact was called for.

'My expedition is not for a gentleman's ears,' she said. 'And yours might not warrant a lady's attention.'

'I'm still sober, ma'am. The tavern served respectable purpose.'

'Impossible, sir!' She could see the fool was thrilled to be conversing with a grand lady before all eyes.

'I assure you, ma'am!' He preened. 'I was giving notice that I shall move to Carradine Manor.'

'To Carradine Manor?' She was stunned. 'But how can that be, sir? Is Mr Carradine about to depart Sealandings?'

'That's for him to decide and me to observe, ma'am. However, I hope I may be permitted to send our invitation to Milton Hall?'

'How very precipitate you are, sir! Ferrars.'

Prothero raised his hat as the phaeton moved off. She almost forgot to acknowledge his gesture in her turmoil. Carradine could be forgiven, of course. For Peasant Prothero to reside at Carradine Manor was unthinkable. It made the blood run cold. Imagine, apes and villeins usurping the very homes of manorial titled families! How marvellous it must have been in the days of absolute power, when rulers had no need to consult babbling jackanapes fresh-lifted from the gutter on to horseback!

The idiot had the effrontery to imply that he was now good enough to issue invitations! For her to visit the very house so deceitfully stolen from her own lover . . . Her mind swam in the magnitude of the catastrophe. The whole world shifted, all points of reference gone.

She did not hear Ferrars call for permission to stop. The phaeton drove on along the shore road, past the cottage where she met Carradine. It was a mile further on before she came to and lashed at the coachman's nape with her ridicule.

'What, are you abducting me, fool? Turn about!'

'Yes, m'm.' The old man reined the greys, started them aback. 'Where to m'lady?'

'Carradine Manor. No dawdling! I've urgent matters!'

Ferrars had the phaeton rolling gently down the slope to the Sealandings wharf in less than ten minutes, but was still soundly abused. He said nothing. The ways of the gentry were simply the ways of the gentry. He was more concerned for his lovely horses, anxious to protect them by making their effort seem a deal greater than was the case. From his lady's furious silence, he'd have plenty of time for them to recoup from this needless haste once in the great drive at Carradine Manor. But God help all within.

The convex lens was homemade, ground between local flintstones from a fragment of crude bottle glass. To polish it, when finally it was bi-convex, Ven carried it in a pouch of calfskin filled with fine sand, thus abrading it in his surtout pocket with each step. Now, the glass was almost transparent. The candle burned steadily.

Rumours abounded, in London's medical schools and hospitals, of surgeons who had somehow managed to see directly – imagine it! – right *to the inside of the ear*! Down to the very drum! 'Aural speculum' was the instrument's name, though Ven, like many medical students, had no reason to believe such an instrument in fact existed. But how, then, did Sir Astley Cooper manage to perforate a patient's eardrum for relief of agonising deep-seated inflammation? By guess? Excellent judgement? Measurement of the ear canal of a corpse?

He tried a roll of paper thin as a pencil, to simulate the ear canal. Then a hollowed reed. Then goose quills, that Mehala prepared for pens. Then a narrow tube of baked clay. He tried the lens to read characters on paper, guessing distances down the small tubes. He tried in daylight, in darkness. Hopeless.

But one day . . . He thought of the scores of children screaming the nights through with earache, some even dying of the brain fever that sometimes followed. Discharging pus seemed to restore the child, at the cost of partial deafness for life. Could it be that perforating the drum was a means of preventing the brain fever? He sighed and put aside his lens, blew out his candle. One day . . .

He found himself humming a tune. Mehala was singing it only this morning: *Pleasure it is, To hear, I wis, The birdes sing* . . . And smiled, recognising Cornysshe's old Harvest Carol.

How wonderful, he thought wistfully, to have Mehala about his home, singing. For Mehala would sing the year round. Soon, it would be the Advent Carol, *Shepherds, shake off your drowsy sleep; Rise and leave your silly sheep*. Then *The Holly and The Ivy*; the Candlemas Carol, for dark February; the Flower Carol of Spring; the May Carol; then the Furry Day Carol; to Chaucer's gay Summer Carol, one of his favourites.

> *'Saint Valentine that art full high on loft . . .*
> *Thus singen smalle fowles for thy sake . . .'*

And round again to blackest midwinter's Welsh *Nos Galan* that the entire Kingdom sang to spin the world through New Year's Eve into the next's first bright dawn.

One day.

'Tyll?' Carradine called.

His usual homecoming was a whirlwind of shouts and noise, a slapping of behinds and clattering of feet as servants scampered for Portugal or hot Geneva.

The maidservant's expectant smile faded into alarm. 'Sir?'

Carradine stood in the vast hall. His expression was one she had never seen before. It terrified her.

'Who is it?' He roused, glanced at her as if he had never seen her before.

'Please sir, it's me, sir. Dee.'

'Get Tyll.'

'Sir.' The maid-of-all flew, clutching skirts for speed.

Carradine remained motionless, taking in the great staircase, the portraits, furniture.

This was home. It had resounded to laughter of huntsmen before drinking stirrup cups from the silvers, before the whip got the hounds moving. It was here his father, his grandfathers, had held balls, masques, entertained royalty. In this very hall, as a little boy, he had bent the knee to the Prince of Wales himself, and been praised afterwards in Father's study for creating a fine impression on the future King.

It was there, under the banisters, that he had taken his first girl – from below stairs, but the sweeter for all that – and been caught by old Hobbes. Who had not informed on him, though the old dunderhead esteemed religion and Deity, but who had been the more loyal ever since, while despairing for the young master's morals.

And here on this very stair he had taken the housekeeper Barbara Tyll of a dark homecoming, forcing her all unwilling, and so bruising her into acceptance that now was their regular custom and, on her woman's part, perhaps something even more than that.

66

'Sir?' Tyll emerged from the west corridor. He shed his coat on to a hall chair. 'Are you ill, sir? You've had an accident! Let me call – '

'Shush, woman. Get to my withdrawing room upstairs. I shall need Hobbes in an hour. Have a meal an hour after that.'

'Sir.'

She hurried to obey. Carradine slowly climbed the stairs. Each rise was an effort. He avoided looking at the familiar portraits. It wasn't reproach. It was shame, hatred. Prothero, bumptious prig that he was, *owned* all of this. For a while he had deluded himself, imagining that nobody would ever call in his gambling notes, or keep the chests of money he had lodged as surety.

This was reality. His room, where he'd seen himself perpetuating family, adding sons and daughters to run the estates and take their places in the growing empire which spun on Great Britain's hub.

Now, nothing.

He sprawled on the chaise longue, was suddenly irritated when his sleeve caught in the chenille. He started up, then paused. Usually he would have ripped the ornamental silk cord from its stitching in temper. This time he dislodged his cuff, and examined the decoration. Small incidentals went unnoticed. Now, he saw it for the first time. He looked about the room, saw the great bed with its red velvet canopy and valance, the half-cheval mirror, the occasional painting, the oval carpet where the maids-of-all brought his bath.

'Sir? You did not answer. I did knock.'

He almost laughed, but it would have sounded wrong. 'You women are incredible, Tyll. Close the door.'

She obeyed, came to stand before him. He pulled her gently down. She sank, glancing apprehensively towards the landing door. He smiled openly.

'We rut almost every day, Tyll, yet still you – '

'Sir!' She tried to rise, colouring quickly in offence, but he kept her pressed down. 'I will not be spoken – '

'Shush, Tyll.' He touched a finger to her mouth. She stilled. 'It's all pretence, isn't it? You are outraged because I put it into words. We rut. Regularly as our Tompion clock, we make the two-backed beast. I'm pleased and you're pleasured, yet we cannot say the words. Isn't that odd, Tyll?'

She stared, her eyes large. She had never heard him speak this way. He could be crude, yes, and in the throes of love howl out corrupt words that even rough fisherfolk refrained from. But that was only a man's passion overcoming the fair side of his nature. A man cannot keep control like a woman can, ought, must, does. Also, men – especially one like him, with heat generated in him like a furnace – had some inner ferocity that women had simply to accept.

'I'm frightened when you talk so, sir.'

He gave a short laugh. 'You see, Tyll? *Sir*. You sir me even when you're sweating under me and I'm spending seed like a forest animal raping its mare.'

Tears started. 'Please, sir. I mislike this.'

'Stay, Tyll. You have to know.' He looked at the fire the maids-of-all had laid.

'You're not going back to London, sir?'

He shook his head, but not in denial. 'You're aware I lost heavily at the prizefighters' match between Rendell and Goring?'

'Yes, sir. To the book agent Mr Quilter.'

'Through him to Prothero. My notes-of-hand left Quilter at fourteen shillings and elevenpence on the pound.'

She was pale with worry. 'What does it mean, sir?'

He flung away and went before the fire. Usually, he would stand astride looking into the flames, palms outstretched to protect his eyes, but not now. 'I have to go, Tyll. From Carradine Manor. Prothero will take up residence.'

'Go, sir?' Her voice was almost inaudible. For a moment it seemed one of his mad jokes, that tormented then made her laugh with relief as he revealed the trick beneath. But he stayed glaring into the fire as if he could see Prothero burning among the sea coals. 'But where?'

He swung away. 'Away, you stupid bitch. Are you deaf? I'm dispossessed.'

She rose, angry, urging him. 'He can't do this! He can't make you leave! You must tell Squire Hunterfield. He won't permit – !'

He struck her then. She retreated a step, hands to her face. It was nothing new, but this time her world was crumbling.

'It can't be changed, Tyll.' He sank on to the chaise, suddenly drained. 'I leave forthwith.' He beckoned her.

'Will you take me, sir? You said you might have me to your London house.'

'That's gone too, Tyll.' He was looking at the fire, a picture of sorrow. 'Strip us, Tyll. Lock the door.'

'I have, sir.' She bent her head, ashamed at her admission, took his head between her hands a moment, then started to gentle his clothes away.

'What happened at Shalamar, Mrs Weaver?'

Sarah Ann smiled, pouring hot water on to camomile leaves. 'Oh, Mehala! You don't want to be thinking of past things, dear. Good heavens! To dwell on doings long gone?'

'It can't simply have been built a ruin, Mrs Weaver!'

'Of course it couldn't. I remember when it shone into the sky with lights and fireworks. Great parties they used to have, once upon a time.'

'Who? Who held parties there?'

'Who on earth can recollect that, girl?' Sarah Ann kept up the evasions, smilingly asking how Mehala was getting along with the Doctor for master. 'And Mrs Trenchard? Still managing, in spite of her agues and pains?'

'Yes, thank you. She sends her compliments.'

Sarah Ann sat comfortably on the kitchen bench. Nellie the chief servant was in and out, and Mrs Nelson the tavern cook was busy at the long cutting board. Two minute under-skivvies scuttled about, laughing at some prank.

'Is the garden full planted, Mehala? I remember the plans you had for that, even before you lived there!'

Mehala blushed at her teasing. 'It's coming. The Flora's Dial is all but done. I only lack the Night-Blooming Catch-Fly, for to open the eleventh hour before midnight, and the Dark Crane's Bill, for six o'clock eve.'

'We'll find for you, Mehala!' Nellie called, hurtling through with lidded tankards and a stoneware jorum.

'The water lily might prove difficult to place.' Mehala was conscious of Sarah Ann's reluctance to speak of Shalamar. She knew something, and was not telling.

'You could have a small falling waterflow.' Sarah Ann stirred the leaves and let them settle before pouring. 'The Misses Astell have such a wonder at Arminell Hall.'

'Mrs Weaver, if one might wish to purchase Shalamar, to whom would he apply?'

'Buy?' Sarah Ann's fingers found her throat. 'That's preposterous, Mehala! I mean . . . well, Shalamar!'

'It stands derelict. No great family takes notice. Houses do change hands, like farms and fields.'

'Mehala! You're not hoping . . . It's unthinkable!'

'I'm thinking nothing, Mrs Weaver. Only enquiring.'

They sipped, weighing their next words. Outside, coach passengers were arguing that the enormous cost should be reduced, there being heavy talk of an increase on the mail-coach fares, halfpenny a mile more, a giddy rise.

'Does Mrs Trenchard not know?' Sarah Ann suggested.

So Mehala knew Mrs Trenchard was safely ignorant.

'She only knows that an agent in Maidborough gave them permission to stay, as means of guarding the pile from intruders.'

'Be careful, Mehala.' Sarah Ann reached out to touch the girl. 'Ever since you were brought in by Jervin and *The Jaunty*, I feel responsible for you. Look to yourself. Be warned.'

'I shall, Sarah Ann. I thank you.'

They parted amicably enough, but it was unsatisfactory. Mehala paused as somebody called her name. Nellie came into the yard, casting a nervous backward glance.

'Here.' She beckoned. They went to stand by the stable where the water piped into a trough all the way from the Bures House estate.

'You know something about Shalamar, Nellie?'

They had been enemies once, when Mehala had recovered enough to start earning her keep at the Donkey and Buskin. Then they became firm allies. Nellie kept glancing furtively at the tavern.

'I heard you ask. Shalamar's in the gift of the De Foes.'

Mehala stared, her heart sinking. 'Are you sure?'

'Men talked of some row between Carradine and Prothero at the Goat and Compass. Terrible it was, with Carradine walking out white as a sheet and Prothero jeering.'

'What's this to Shalamar and me, Nellie?'

'It started talk of other houses. Carradine's had to sign over his London place, and two small farms elsewhere on the coast, one towards Whitehanger. They mentioned Shalamar as Fellows De Foe's, and rightly belonging to Milton Hall estate.'

'Any more, Nellie? They're calling you.'

'Mrs Nelson,' Nellie grinned toothily. 'It was her as sent me after you. Her way of warning me Mrs Weaver's noticed my absence. Is'll say I was to the privy.'

Mehala detained her. 'Nellie, did anyone mention the Darlings, John Darling from Whitehanger?'

'The waggoner? As the Doctor brought his daughter alive? No. Shall I ask?'

'No, Nellie. Thank you. You are invaluable.'

Nellie darted inside, leaving Mehala to walk on towards the Market Square. Fellows De Foe, owner of Shalamar? Best if she expressed no interest, for fear of rousing a wasps' nest.

6

Cowpox had been rumoured for several weeks before it was found in Sealandings. Ven Carmichael was overjoyed when Mehala brought word of this valuable medical happening.

'On a tenant farm of Calling,' Mehala told Ven, proud of her news. 'Three cows fallen with the sickness.'

'Marvellous news, Mehala! We'll go immediately. You must see how I select beasts for our vaccination.'

He was so animated, and she excited by the prospect. 'Will the farmer allow me, for that I am female?'

Ven paused, drawing on his boots, so sad of a sudden. 'He will take the money, Mehala. Principles, right or wrong, vanish when Soho sings its song. Tuppence a child, that's been agreed.'

Coinage. She nodded. He meant copper coinage, minted in the Bolton and Watt foundry in the Soho which stood near Birmingham, under licence from the Royal Mint in London's Tower.

She ran to fetch his surtout and hat, and her outdoor straw cottage bonnet. He set out briskly, she running after fastening the chin stays and trying to latch her cloak against the wind.

'Call on those who have expressed their willingness to suffer vaccination, Mehala,' he reminded her. 'You must remember the names of those who undergo the cut.'

'I have brought your lead pencil.' She trotted to keep up.

'We make no notes, Mehala. People distrust the act of writing. List them from memory later. The keeping of written statistics is going to become the greatest asset to medicine, you'll see! We are in modern times!'

'Yes, sir,' she said meekly.

He shot her a sharp glance and grinned. Her light jibing was her quiet way of bringing him down to earth when his interest fired into overwhelming enthusiasm.

They struck down the South Toll road into Sealandings. The winds were onshore now, rain spattering in the road pools and tapping leaves above them. He walked preoccupied, occasionally speaking disjoined sentences as they bubbled into his mind.

'Temple will possibly not be vulnerable to the small pox, you see . . .'

Temple the blacksmith had been one of the first to agree to two of his six children being vaccinated when the chance came; his other four had already suffered cowpox, so were safe. Mehala occasionally glanced at Ven's intent face as they hurried, thinking of the opposition he had had to endure. She had heard of the religious fervour excited against his attempts to give the protective cowpox to the populace.

'. . . Blacksmiths, farriers, grooms and their families all know . . . Country lore, Mehala.' He caught himself, grinned again shamefacedly. 'Here am I extolling the old folkways, when you know ten times more!'

'You told me of Doctor Jenner,' she prompted, not wishing to break his train of thought. Much of her growing knowledge was culled from these incidental mutterings. She would ask more at the evenings.

Ven sighed. 'Yes. God, the obstinate opposition! How many have we lost to the small pox, from ignorance? Time is against us, Mehala. Health is a terrible race, and time the fleeter runner.'

'Perhaps Mr Temple's action persuades others?'

'I fear hardly, Mehala. People take a stance against or for an issue, for no reason. Reverend Baring preaches against cowpoxing children, as contrary to Holy Writ.' He gave a rueful smile. 'That particular battle I lost before we . . . met, Mehala.'

Her cheeks felt hot. Their first meeting was hardly dignified, herself dragged from the dark North Sea and brought to life half-naked on a taproom table.

'I tried persuasion through stewards and masters,' he went on wistfully, 'ship masters in the harbour – anyone who might be persuaded. Miss Gould the schoolmistress has tried to be of help, but she is in an invidious position and her voice small.'

'A kindly lady,' Mehala praised.

Whose wages depend on such parents as can afford to pay their offspring's learning penny, Mehala thought. Should parents take offence and refuse their coppers, Miss Matilda would be on the next Edmundsbury coach in search of a new post.

73

'Did you ask Squire Hunterfield?'

'He demurred, after much thought. Miss Letitia was minded to seek my opinion on the subject, but Mistress Vallance forbade.'

Lydia Vallance running true to form, Mehala noted candidly in the new racing vernacular. That lady would think highly of an esteemed London physician, but would be demeaned by the attentions of a country doctor. Mehala felt anger rise, coming to only when she had missed some of Ven's thoughts.

'. . . Of course, it was anciently known that innocent pox, passed to man by a lancet wound from cows and horses, protected against the lethal small pox. India, China, the mediaeval doctors in Salerno . . .'

'The farm is here. Andrew Nelmes', tenant of Prothero.'

The Church of St Edmund the Martyr was rimmed with hedges, along one of which a footpath ran, skirting the glebeland and Prothero's acres to emerge a mile beyond the church in a wide heath. Then Ven smiled.

'An omen, Mehala! The milkmaid Doctor Jenner took his first pustular lymph from was one Sarah Nelmes!'

'Brave gentleman.' Mehala followed on the path.

The church was still, the rectory garden showing no sign of anyone. She adopted the country trick of walking with a slightly splayed gait, the better to find purchase on untrodden grass along the muddy path's margins.

'Braver yet, Mehala,' Ven's voice floated back, 'for Doctor Jenner tested the lymph on his own eldest son!'

Mehala exclaimed, but wished Ven would keep his voice down. The rectory stood close to the path.

'Jenner was not a poor man, having the money to publish the book . . . Made a deal of difference . . .'

'So he had influence?' Mehala tried, seeing movement by the postern in the churchyard walling beyond the hawthorns.

'Jenner *was* fashionable. Studied at St George's Hospital in London, with so notable a teacher as Doctor John Hunter . . .'

Mehala's heart sank, recognising ahead the figure of Reverend Baring. He was walking slowly towards the church, presumably returning from a parish visit.

Ven went on, oblivious. 'He was made Fellow of the Royal Society, though that was for an article on the cuckoo . . .'

'The cuckoo!' Mehala said brightly, to no avail.

He talked contentedly. 'How marvellous Gloucester must have been, back then, Mehala! Over fifty years since, yet they had their laudable Medico-Convivial Society . . . Edward Jenner took advantage of it most ably. He'd spoken frequently of passing the cowpox directly from cows' udders to children, as we shall do today . . .'

Mehala saw the figure ahead pause attentively and remain still while they passed. It was the Rector, without mistake, and he must have overheard every word. And no blame to the wretched man, for he was in his own churchyard.

' . . . The dispute should be left to people themselves, without religious interference. Don't you agree, Mehala? *Variola vaccina* – the cowpox – knows no theology! Why ought a terrible disease like Variola, small pox, be subject to religious divines? Surely the Lord meant us to use our brains for good? He said so often enough!'

Oh, Ven! Mehala thought in worry. He could not have said anything worse, for Reverend Baring's ears. Wildly she tried to think of some casual remark to turn the subject, but failed from anxiety. Ven chatted on.

'The Americans have also had their indecisions,' he said loudly, over his shoulder. 'The first Boston doctor to practise it was threatened by hanging. But their Puritans were early persuaded by a loquacious gentleman called Increase Mather, who used ingenious arguments to confound opposing orthodoxies . . .'

The damage was done. As the footpath rose slightly Mehala glanced back, to see Reverend Baring in plain view gazing after them. Too far to perceive his expression, she yet knew his sense of outrage at such appalling public expression of opinion. To many, the words would be tantamount to blasphemy, and even disloyalty. Ven was still happily going on about the London Vaccination Institute, founded as long ago as 1802 only to close after four short years. The Government should pass a Vaccine Law . . .

'We're not far,' she called as they made the heathland. 'We can enquire at the farmhouse yonder.'

' . . . Jenner gained from his success. Imagine receiving thirty thousand pounds from Parliament!' He paused as she caught up and they struck across the heath. His eyes were brightly animated, even twinkling. 'His influence was such that Tyrant Napoleon set free his friend Doctor Wickham, a prisoner-in-war, on Jenner's request . . .'

'How marvellous,' Mehala said nervously.

Carmichael took her hand. 'Mehala? You look quite pale.'

'Thank you. I am well.'

'Have I walked too fast?' He was concerned. 'I'm a fool, prattling on like a fishwife and you trying to keep up.'

Her thanks were acknowledged with a bare nod. They set off as quickly as before in spite of his intentions. She had a heaviness in her. Trouble would come from St Edmund's. This dear man was going to be more difficult to protect than she had imagined.

'Ven,' she asked, thinking of the task ahead, 'how can we pay Nelmes for the use of his sick cow, if some folk receive vaccination and will not pay?'

'Ah,' Ven said after an uncomfortable moment. 'That is difficult. Unless I have a coin or two spare in my pocket, why, the child must go unlanceted. Which of course would be a tragedy . . .'

She waited for him to amend his lame conclusion, but he said no more. It was as she feared, that he himself paid. He was a wonderment – so serious in mind, yet capable of such evasion that even the stupidest woman would think him a blockhead. Listen to him, going on!

'. . . Should be the Exchequer who pays for each vaccination, don't you think? Since variolation – the passing of a mild small-pox to a healthy person – has ended, on account of occasional failures and deaths, we could easily keep in store some pustular lymph fluid, or even maintain poxed cows, don't you think?'

Then he turned and grinned at her. She cast out all her forebodings, and found herself smiling back.

'Yes, Ven,' she said. 'I think exactly the same.'

Reverend Baring could hardly control his anger. He entered his study without answering the maid Bridget's offer to bring some hot Congou. He sat in his chair and stared at nothing.

Of course, quacks could only follow pagan instincts, that much was clear. Uneducated, they taught ghoulish practices, without rhyme or reason. Yet they believed they had the right – *right*, if you please! – to foist their wishes on society as a code of behaviour to be followed blindly by all! It was madness.

To regulate the social order without the Church? Why, that was tantamount to ordaining their own bizarre priesthoods, for their own lunatic moralities! Medicine was a pagan ritual of blisterings, simples and potions! Should he preach a sermon against Carmichael, this time by name? He brightened. One could make use of amusing tales of the mad inmates of Bedlam, that Bethelehem Hospital formerly of London's Moorfields, now moved to St George's Fields, where Londoners went on outings, to poke sticks in the lunatics' cages and laugh at their antics. Yes, it would prove an enlightening sermon, one Sealandings folk would talk of for weeks! The Church was not too holy to provide clean, innocent amusement.

But Carmichael, banned from attending St Edmund's services –a necessary proscription, after Euterpe showed interest in that tradesman – would not hear the sermon. Direct action was needed.

He sat, tipping his fingers together as his former tutor at Trinity College used to when pondering grave theological issues.

Yes, barring Doctor Carmichael from attending church services had successfully nipped Euterpe's leanings in the bud. Her duty lay here, as rectory housekeeper, until the attentions of a gentleman – *gentleman*, note, not an ignorant quack – were approved of by the Rector, her brother. Baring sighed. It was a responsible position, being guardian and vicar to one's sister, but duties must be accepted, not shirked. Doctor Carmichael had been a threat, now fortunately fought off. But the wretch, with the tenacity of the heretic, persisted, threatening the morality of Sealandings with his damning opinions against Church and State.

Disloyalty was subversive to Crown, nation, the entire Kingdom. Wasn't it disloyal to spread heresy? And to teach those heresies to an innocent girl, under the guise of medical instruction? For that was clearly what he had heard, as the man walked outrageously along hallowed ground! He groaned aloud. Oh, God, he prayed, is there no end to the effontery of unrepentant sinners?

Yes, stern action was needed. Carmichael had to be banished, not only from St Edmund's services, but from Sealandings itself. And he had allies. Lady Thalia De Foe had promised to support the Church – if he would write to the Bishop, nominating her cousin Charles Golding for advancement to Parliament. He had obediently written to His Lordship proposing Church support for Golding's candidacy.

He now had the clear duty to point out – it must be a sad, reflective letter – to the Sealandings gentry the sorry state of local morality, under the pernicious influence of such heretics as Doctor Carmichael.

With satisfaction he went to his writing desk. He inspected the goose quill's point, and was gratified to find that Euterpe had sharpened it admirably. And the ink was fresh. The sand-shaker was still warm from drying. He smiled approval. Yes, Euterpe was proving an admirable asset at St Edmund's rectory. He would write the letter then, having dispatched it, tell her its contents and test her on its merits. She would like that.

'Mehala, I believe that the fluid from the vesicle on the cow's udders is Nature's fountain of the virus.'

Ven spoke as the children assembled in the farm shippon. There were eight, plus one grey-faced adult whose nervousness was adding to the children's. Andrew Nelmes walked in from the rain to watch.

'What is the virus?' Mehala asked. She laid a cloth on Ven's homemade leather case, and placed his lancet thereon.

'A word we coined from antiquity.' Ven lowered his voice. It would not do to advertise ignorance. 'To mean the living principle, that imparts the disease. We suppose it to be some humour in the fluid.'

'Shall I stand with the children, Doctor?'

'If you will, Mehala.'

'And the gentleman?'

Ven recognized the agitated man. Bartholomew Hast was now only half so assured as he had been when coming to the rescue at the travelling fair. He was an unmarried tradesman, and a cousin of the famous Colchester gunsmith of that name. Normally cheerful, today he paced fretfully and coughed anxiously, for no reason.

'I shall ask him first, as example to the children.'

A herdsman brought the cow forward into the shippon. Ven asked him to pause while he examined the udders.

'One day, Mehala,' he said, quietly kneeling, 'we might have the active principle perhaps even in glass phials, and send it to doctors without a source of poxed cattle!'

Mehala stooped to see over his shoulder. He held the udder gently. It was blotched with small bluish patches, though a livid red.

'You see the vesicles, Mehala? Raised edges, depressed at the centre? The redness surrounding we call inflammation, a modern word.' He looked about for the herdsman. 'The beast's milk flow has lessened?'

'Yes, sir. Her'm sickened these seven days.'

'Keep the animal still, if you please.' He looked at Mehala. 'I shall take fresh fluid from one pox for each person. Several vesicles are exactly right.'

He rose and went to the children, Mehala following.

'I bid you a good day, children. This will not inconvenience you. Mr Hast will come first, to show all is well.'

The gunsmith swallowed, and slowly approached the tethered cow. Mehala talked a moment with the children, as Ven signed for Hast to remove his spencer and roll up his shirt-sleeve. The gunmaker complied, with a shaky apology to Mehala for such state of undress.

'As you are a technical gentleman, Mr Hast,' Ven told him, for Mehala's sake, 'I shall explain what I do. I follow Doctor Hooper's procedure, which is to take vesicle fluid from the teat . . . so!'

Ven held the teat, and made a small incision into the clearest part of the pock which everted against his knuckle. Fluid expressed quickly. He scraped the minute drop up on the lancet blade, and grasped Hast's arm. Mehala watched attentively. He made a small cut into the gunsmith's skin.

'Is it atter, Doctor?' the gunsmith asked nervously. Hast was almost fainting, but trying to appear casual.

'No, not pus. The clear fluid is used. We choose the insertion of the deltoid muscle, Mr Hast, because it causes the most rapid result, and the mildest attack of cowpox to you, while protecting against the small pox. Stay still.'

The shallow cut hardly showed. Ven bent to take a second bleb of the cowpox and ran the drop into the scarified line on Hast's arm.

'There – done! And so quickly!'

Hast was reeling. Ven firmly walked him to a low wooden tether rail. It was curious how some men, often the staunchest, were susceptible to the slightest medical event. Here was a strong young man almost overcome. Why, the gentleman was white as a sheet.

'Now, children,' he heard Mehala saying with great cheerfulness. 'As you see, Mr Hast kindly agreed to remain, to show us just how quickly it is all over! And Cushy says we can all have some of her special milk – but only a drop, because it's very precious . . .'

Ven stood observing Mehala, smiling at the name Cushy, East Anglia's favourite country name for a cow. She was heartwarming to watch. In moments she had developed a game, calling the children in order of age, then letting them argue. She brought the queue in, clapping and chanting the childhood rhyme, *'Cushy cow, bonny, let down thy milk,'* to which the children sang in response, *'And I will give thee a gown of silk; a gown of silk and a silver tee . . .'* which Mehala capped with, *'If thou wilt let down thy dabby for me!'* They all laughed, excitedly pointing out her error.

'It's *milk*, Mehala! Milk! You said dabby!'

She shook her head, pretending to admonish them. 'Oh, no! Today Cushy gives us a little dabby, for Doctor.'

Dabby, the local word for something moist sticking on the skin. So clever and so lovely.

It was sheer delight to hear her laughing with them. Perhaps she was of a large family? Or, the thought suddenly struck him, did she in fact have a child of her own? Was she indeed a spinster? He put the thought from his mind as Mehala approached. She caught his look, quickly hiding her response by bustlingly uncovering the children's arms.

'The Queen of the Russias was also called Catherine,' Mehala told the first little girl, one of the blacksmith's daughters. 'She too had this done. Arm from out your smicket!'

Ven smiled. Mehala had learned well from his reminiscences.

'Come, Catherine,' he said. 'First and best. Like Mr Hast!'

'Will it hurt, Mehala?' the little girl asked.

'Hardly at all. It makes but a tiny rove!' Ven thought ruefully, if only everybody in the Kingdom could be given this miraculously protective 'tiny scab'.

The gunsmith wiped his damp forehead with a kerchief, but managed a wan smile for Catherine. He caught Mehala's eye, and shrugged with mock heroism. A pleasant man, Ven thought. Then noticed Mehala smiling back, and wondered if Hast was quite so pleasant after all. The man had already been scarified, so why didn't he up and away to his work?

Worse was to come, for the gunmaker paid not only his own tuppence, but also paid for three children who had no money. This caused Mehala to enlarge on Hast's kindness all the way from Nelmes' Farm to Market Square once they were done. It was an unpleasant experience, Ven found. He was at a loss to explain it. He had always found the lone gunsmith friendly, and knew no reason to revise his opinion.

All the way home to Shalamar he talked of the need to select the youngest vesicles. Mehala seemed to wish to talk of something else, but he overrode her, telling her to visit the families concerned and record the first sign of infection on each vaccinated arm by the third day.

'The areola is extensive on the ninth day after vaccination,' he lectured absently, 'declining fully by the twelfth, whereafter it desiccates. It is detected easily, for a small brown spot appears in the centre. I shall show you the first, then you will observe the same sequences in all.'

'Very well, Ven.'

'You understand what we have done so far?'

'Yes,' she said, hiding her amusement. 'I quite understand.'

He shot her a suspicious glance, but her gaze was serious and downcast. She wondered at the simplicity of the male creature. Bartholomew Hast was personable, yes, and reputedly a gunsmith of profound skill, but that was all. She sighed, listening obediently as Ven mumbled on about the vaccinations that showed no areolar flare at all.

'Yes, Ven,' she said. Yes, Ven, a millionth time.

Old Abby Abraham, who had taught her about the sea estuaries by Mersea Island as a girl, often exclaimed, 'The cleverer the man, the more babe he!' cackling at his paradox. Looking at Ven's intent face, Mehala wondered if there wasn't a grain of truth in old Abby's saying.

The churchyard was deserted as they passed the glebeland this time. She thanked Heaven.

7

'I'm not at all sure, Golding,' Sir Fellows De Foe told his neighbour bluntly. A dogman was parading the hounds around Milton Hall's stableyard. Selection was proving unexpectedly difficult. 'I'm setting up a new cry, not starting a breeding kennels.'

De Foe was impatient. It was hardly noon, and the Right Honourable Charles Golding was three sheets to the wind from toping.

'I insist, Fellows,' Golding said, absently kicking a hound away, to the other's annoyance. 'Southerns breed south, northerns north.'

Fellows restrained himself. This was his wife's favourite cousin, God help them all. Why a personable noble should sunder his mind by tippling, was beyond his guess. He himself drank his share, but Golding was a sot.

'This wine is uncommon good, Fellows.' A manservant came at a resigned gesture from the master and poured a refill. 'They say Spanish Montillado's secret lies in their white albariza soil. D'you think that's true?'

Fellows wished to discuss his problem of the new pack of hounds. Golding's obsession with alcohol was maddening. He persevered.

'Hunterfield tells me the modern notion is that the northern beagle is unequalled when the scent is fresh and straight, but the long-trunked southern hound has better smell sense – their extraordinarily moist muzzles and lips, so say.'

'D'you know, Fellows,' Golding interrupted. 'In Queen Anne's day the Kingdom drank a gallon of wine per person? And now not two pints apiece?' He shook his head dolefully while Fellows gestured impatience to the beagle servant. 'It follows exactly the decrease in Portugal wines, and the rise of the Spanish!'

Fellows for once was relieved to see his wife's carriage approaching the front steps. She could entertain her sottish cousin, thanks be to God. He spoke over the toper.

'My father's old *Sportsman's Dictionary* says the cat beagle, the northern hound I mention, is essential, but the southern lacks concentration when bred on alone. It goes after a mouse, weasel, rabbit – anything instead of its lawful intent.'

'Fellows!' Golding exclaimed, as if struck by a brilliant idea. 'Let's try some of your excellent Malmsey wine. It yields nearly thirteen per cent alcohol by weight, compared to London porter's little over five, when four months bottled!'

'Might they be like hackneys, best got from coupling thoroughbred sires with half-bred mares?' Fellows wondered aloud, but Golding babbled on about some drink or other. He surrendered in disgust.

'Roundell,' he told his dogman resignedly. 'Run perhaps the beasts late this afternoon. Not now.'

'As you'll, sir.'

The beagleman was as disappointed as his master, and led the hounds away. The two gentlemen strolled towards the house, Golding lecturing his host on the astonishing virtues of Madeira wine which, long in the cask in the East Indies, was only one hundredth part by weight weaker than White Port's fifteen per cent . . .

'Fascinating,' Fellows said, bored to death, desperate to escape this yawnsome drunkard. Not long ago Golding was on the mend from his addiction but now he was worse than ever, an embarrassment to all. Fellows hurried him indoors with almost indecent haste. 'I'll send for a bottle or two of the, ah, what was it?'

'I shall lay down a finer cellar, Fellows.' Golding needed De Foe's assistance on the corridor steps. 'Every gentleman's first obligation! But Carradine's default on his vintners beggars my ambition.'

'What was that?' Fellows stopped, astonished. Golding swayed tipsily on, blundering into the main front hall.

'Didn't you know? Prothero's taken up Carradine's notes-of-hand, to save the man.'

'I'd no idea it was so serious.'

'Indeed.' Golding beamed as Thalia swept in, her maid Meg scurrying to gather the curricle pelisse her mistress flung off. 'It's a sour business when county succumbs to farmer.'

'Good day, Thalia.' Fellows stood there supporting Golding.

'Charles here tells me of Carradine's misfortune.' He paused before continuing innocently, 'It seems he's gone in utter default. Perhaps I should ask after his hounds, Charles? Or will Prothero take them on?'

'Good day, sirs.' Thalia stepped easily into position as hostess and wife. 'How pleasant! Has my husband been entertaining you, Charles?'

Fellows tutted in mock annoyance. 'I am myself in default.' He cast about for a servant, called the head footman. 'Ennis. Malmsey, in the withdrawing room.'

'Meg, see that tea is brought also.' Thalia smiled sweetly at Golding, angrily noting his inebriated state. 'The sumlo – its violet scent clears the most befuddled head.'

Fellows acted out a charade of forgetfulness.

'Look, Thalia dear, would you excuse me? Charles, would you mind? I quite forgot to instruct Roundell. That rascal's hopeless. I shall rejoin you presently . . .'

They murmured compliance. Fellows made to return to the yards while his wife ushered her cousin to the withdrawing room.

De Foe paused in the long passageway to pick a riding whip from the walnut stand. He considered it, then examined the rest one by one. He could not be seen from the main hall. He whistled absently, finally decided randomly and strolled towards the outer door. A figure was standing there.

'Meg.'

'Sir.' She spoke quietly, bobbed acknowledgement. 'Ennis is with Mrs Thornton and Mrs Randon, the maids-of-all at duty. The footmen are at board. None saw me, sir.'

He dropped his casual manner. 'I want you after dark, Meg. Anything urgent?'

'She's asked me to discover Mehala, sir. I've only heard one thing: Mehala's asking who owns Shalamar. I've told her this.'

The spite with which Meg spoke of his wife as *she* and *her* interested Fellows as much as the news. Odd that Thalia was concerned about a girl dragged a-drowning, nothing more than a leech's maid-of-all. Fellows didn't know whether to be amused.

'This Mehala looks to nest Carmichael at Shalamar?'

'I can't be sure, sir.'

'Ought else?' He knew the answer before asking. 'Carradine?'

85

'She sees him still, sir. The coast cottage.' Meg hesitated. She knew not to underestimate this seemingly genteel master. Behind his mask he was a man of intense power. She knew him better than any woman in Sealandings. 'The gentleman did not meet her, though she begged. He had been banished from Carradine Manor by Mr Prothero, who boasted to m'lady on the Blakeney road.'

'He would.' De Foe eyed Meg in silence until she became uncomfortable.

'Did I do well, sir?'

'Very well, Meg. Go. Two hours after lanterns.'

He stepped out into the stableyard, unsmiling. So Thalia's infidelity with Carradine continued. Pretending ignorance of the affair served his purposes. Carradine was a receding problem, but this Prothero might well prove worse.

He called for Roundell. Thalia was not stupid. Indeed, her astuteness was profound – he had proof enough of that. But here she was, still clawing her way after a reprobate who had defaulted – no greater crime for gentry – and who now was dispossessed of his lands, home and Manor. And by a farmer greedy for advancement. As if anybody could buy that rare commodity! And that 'begged' hurt, in spite of his loathing for Thalia's betrayal.

Oh, Thalia, he thought. Some women were ruined by ambition. Some pushed sons, daughters, husbands, lovers – but the ones who ruined themselves most thoroughly were those who betrayed their station in life by using all their cunning and fortune to further a wastrel. Carradine was a notorious gambler, wencher, rake, dueller. What *was* it that afflicted Thalia, he wondered. Some craving for risk, that her normal life lacked? They still acted out marital intimacy, but the façade was maintained by consort with others. On Thalia's part, no need to look further than Carradine; on his, the pleasures of London served during his lengthy sojourns there and in Sealandings Meg sufficed, serving him more fully than a quiet reporter.

'Sir?' Roundell was before him, puzzled by his silence.

De Foe cleared his throat, trying to find words. 'Ah, Roundell. An equal mixture, north and south beagles. Breed for service-ability.'

'Yes, sir.' Roundell had already received this instruction. He spoke guardedly, waiting for more.

'You'll doubtless hear rumours of Carradine Manor. I shall hire no men from there. Your post is secure. Purchase no dogs from there.'

'Yes, sir.'

Roundell watched the master return to the house, mystified. This was none of his business; it was for agents to execute. Maybe the Golding gentleman had driven the master to distraction. It happened. He shrugged and went back to the hounds. They were saner, more loyal and indeed, had greater sense.

The note came by a child while Carmichael was in the garden admiring Mehala's handiwork. He opened it immediately. It was a summons to wait on Reverend Baring at the rectory. He passed the note to Mehala, who rewarded the little boy with an apple.

'What do you think, Mehala? Perhaps he responds to my letter! Remember? The Hammant Bequest for the parish poor!'

She read it at a glance. She now clerked his correspondence, and was learning the system of records that concerned him so. Carefully, she waited until the boy had gone.

'Its tone is peremptory, Ven. I mislike it.'

'Surely it is to discuss how to distribute the bread money!' Carmichael smiled his hope. 'Even though he barred me the church.'

'Because he feared you were about to entice Miss Euterpe away to housekeep here.' She smiled at his astonishment, and spoke on as he started an indignant denial. 'I know, Ven. But Reverend Baring suspected it, and moved to thwart what he imagined were your intentions.'

'That's preposterous!'

'Of course.' She spoke kindly. He was baffled by matters like this. 'But he pursues his enmity still.'

'Enmity?' Ven sighed. It was all beyond him. 'You know, Mehala, I sometimes wonder what folk are . . . well, up to. I mean, just look at Sealandings.' He swept his arm to show the countryside, the trees, the pale gleaming sea. 'Lovely, yet love-lorn. Paradise, corrupted with hatreds.'

He started to walk up the path, as if seeking better vantage. She went with him. Absently, he slipped his arm through hers. She moved step for step lest some unequal pace break the mood.

'I long for a time when health will precede all religious squabbles. And even before political powers – '

He often spoke this way, dreamily, as if describing a vista before his very eyes. But it made her fearful. These turbulent days, all the country was discontented, labourers restless and artisans reaching uproar. In the north, new factories were pillaged and burnt. Militia regiments camped in the big cities. England was no longer the peaceful nation poets sang of. She was spawning new ideas, starting trains of fire, creating a million startling advances that threatened to shake the very world. There were more regiments standing to arms in England than overseas in the vast expanding empire. In this broilsome climate, politics were dangerous ground, for the rich and powerful. For humbler folk like Ven and herself, obscurity was safety.

'Is it too much to hope for, Mehala?' His eyes were shining as he looked from the garden knoll out to the North Sea. 'We can move mountains, change whole countryscapes. Why not work as hard for the sick?'

'Why not, Ven?' she agreed quietly, but with sorrow.

His dream was hopeless, for how could his imaginary world ever become reality? The poor, shielded from their poverty? The sick, cared for until they were well and whole? Pay lip-service, she thought, but don't let such absurd fantasies enter everyday life.

'Reverend Baring,' she reminded him.

He hesitated. 'I suppose if it were a medical reason, he would have said?'

'Doubtless, yes.'

The sky had assumed a strange pallor far out on the horizon. Mehala reluctantly let him relinquish her arm.

He shaded his eyes. 'Storm?'

'Yes, Ven. Reaching the coast before night.'

He smiled as they went towards the house. 'I trust your weather lore, Mehala, as I do your other attributes.'

'You should take your case. I have made it ready.'

'I shall. Thank you.'

She stood to watch him leave from the gates. Trenchard was clearing the weeds around the house itself, his inept dog sitting by. She stepped into the rutted track to watch Ven trudge down the curve of road into Sealandings. She had reminded him about his case of simples and instruments only so that the peremptory summons would seem to have been interpreted as a medical call, and not the response of someone inferior to Reverend Baring.

'Dear man,' she quietly told his dwindling figure, 'I shall have you in your own dwelling, 'thout fear or favour. Your reading shall be bright lit with Argand lamps. Your fare will be goodly. You shall ride, not march in all weathers. Servants shall answer your beck. I promise.'

One thing she knew: the Reverend's summons was not the result of Euterpe Baring's machinations. That lady was back under her brother's oppressive thumb, and a good thing too. Mehala sensed a rival. She eyed the louring skies anxiously as she returned indoors.

'You are quite the historianess, Thalia!'

Golding's attempt at humour only maddened Thalia. She observed the terrified maid-of-all coldly.

'Where's Mrs Randon? Too busy to wait on her mistress?'

'No, ma'am. I think she's at other duties.'

The wretched girl fumbled placing the tray. The silver waterpot dribbled. 'Think? You don't *think*, girl! Look at the mess! Get *out*!'

The maid fled in tears. Golding sighed, cheering as Ennis brought a butler's voider stand and tray. Thalia stared venomously as the footman uneasily unfolded the voider before the wine fountain.

'What do you think you're doing, Ennis?'

'If it please, m'lady, bringing the wine as directed.'

'Then I *un*direct, sir!' Thalia's sudden scream startled the servant so he almost dropped the tray. 'Out! With that slut!'

Ennis retreated. Thalia rounded on her cousin, slouched unhappily in his comfortable twiggen chair.

'Historianess, you call me, Charles? Because I am of the same exalted family which you now disgrace, in your besotted state of carousing?'

'Look here, Thalia,' he tried, but she glared him down.

'No, sir! You look *here*! To *me*! Your cousin, who now has the unenviable responsibility of rescuing you from your appalling decrepitude!'

Charles had weathered this tirade numerous times, each worse than the last. Now he hated visiting Milton Hall. Hardly worth the bother of having the grooms saddle up. He'd not had a decent drink since he got here.

Miserably he watched Thalia spoon out the sumlo leaf and set the silver over the flame. He'd have to drink the stuff.

'Can't believe that whole wars are fought over tea leaves,' he muttered morosely. And he was uncomfortable. Thalia put him in this infernal chair simply to see him squirm in the damned thing. Why couldn't she get reasonable conjoined-back settees, where a man could spread himself, for God's sake? 'Like this opium business in the East Indies. Can't see what's wrong with wine and Maryland tobacco.'

Thalia let him stew in a pained silence as the sumlo infused. She judged its scent right, and locked the tea caddy. She distrusted the maids-of-all. Stealthy weighings of the tea were called for, to alarm honest old Mrs Randon into greater vigilance, if nothing else.

'Charles, I have an important matter to discuss.'

Charles sipped the tea. Dreadful. 'Ah, well, Cousin, I'm not up to serious talk at the moment.'

'You shall listen, sirrah,' she told him, 'while I refresh your memory and point to a new direction. You were recently sober, were you not?'

'I'm always sober, Thalia. I take the odd evening glass.'

She glanced at the Vulliamy ticking deeply in its long case, and threw away pretence. 'Early eve today, Charles! And you so tipsy you clutch Fellows to stay erect!' She gave a harsh laugh. 'Erect, God save us! You can hardly *sit* upright, so imbibed are you. Worse than any sloven tinkering at the roadside!'

'Thalia, that's unfair – '

'Listen to me, Charles Golding!' Her hissing voice, he registered with dismay, so no escape now. 'You shall mend, sir! I promise you. I set you two tasks to complete forthwith – without dissembling. D'you hear?'

'This is unseemly, Thally – '

'*Don't you Thally me, sir!*' Her shrill words cut him. He shrank. She was too enraged to notice his saucer dripping on to the carpet. 'My first command: you shall drink *less* than one bottle daily.'

90

'Good God, Thalia! How can a gentleman survive – ?'

She coursed on. 'The second command, Charles, is that you allocate a small estate some distance away, for Carradine.'

His befuddled brain tried to see reason behind this.

'Why should I find for Carradine? Let the oaf look to his own laurels, I say.'

'You are too stupid to think. This is a closet secret, *sub rosa*.'

'Why does Fellows want this? He dislikes Carradine – '

'This is between you and I, Charles. Family bred, not family wooed.' She poured herself more tea, wondering how much longer before Fellows came in. 'Your ambitions were ruined by your squalid life at Bures House. I aim to restore them.'

'Using Carradine? A defaulter?'

'An ally, Charles.' She moderated her tone. Charles might be tipsy, but he was no fool. 'You need one, besides myself. I shall procure the assistance of Philip.'

Her cousin groaned. 'That boring old dullard? Sir Philip Banks should stay where he will, and let me be.'

'Sir Philip is our cousin. A friend to the Astells, at Arminell Hall. You are too pickled in brandy to observe that Sir Edward Astell and Philip are thick as thieves in their horse breedery and falconry. And that bitch Brillianta Astell hunts altogether different game.'

'Carradine?'

Thalia collected herself before continuing. The thought of Brillianta Astell setting her poke at Carradine was intolerable. 'Not probable, Charles. I shall soon find out what that mare has in her clever little mind.'

'Nothing to do with Carradine, yet I must lodge him?'

Thalia sipped, steeled herself. 'Remember the hustings, Charles? When Carradine aimed to enter Parliament?'

Golding nodded, stung. 'Bastard tried to get me to stand in his stead, and be his creature.'

Thalia nodded. Charles was alert still. 'If Henry Hunterfield were to leave Sealandings – as, suppose, to London for Parliament – why, then the Eastern Hundreds would need a new senior magistrate. A trustee for the roads, the commerce, the Preventive Service, and even something perhaps much greater in due course.'

'Me?' Golding breathed.

'Who else, Charles?'

'Not Carradine? I often thought you and Carradine were a deal too friendly, Thalia.'

She bit back a retort at his effrontery. 'Why wouldn't I be friendly to a close neighbour? Especially one whose family traditionally nominates magistrates these three centuries past!'

Golding slowly worked his way through her plan. 'I see. Carradine would nominate me as magistrate for the Eastern Hundreds, when Hunterfield is elected off the coast?'

At last, Thalia thought in relief. She smiled fondly at him. 'That's the scheme, Charles! Not a word to Fellows. We've been so close, Charles, you and I, ever since we played together as children. I trust you. I want you to assume your full position in life.'

'That's right, Thalia,' he agreed. She was always coldly logical. She had sometimes frighted him as a little boy. She pulled the servant cord.

'Now you shall have a small glass, in celebration. Remember your first step is to find a small manor somewhere for Carradine. In greatest secrecy, Charles. We shall make the next moves openly.'

'Splendid, Thalia.' It was perfectly true, of course. He was the longest blood on the coast, the Hunterfields excepted. Therefore he deserved a superior position, not be hanging on everyone's else's words. It was only natural that he should displace Hunterfield. He had the right connections, influence, the wealth.

'Tell me, Charles,' Thalia asked innocently as her cousin's eyes lit up at the mention of wine. 'How is that new housekeeper at Bures House? Reliable? Sound?'

'Hardly see her,' he admitted. 'Could do with somebody . . .'

'Yes,' she interrupted quickly. 'The Blaker woman was a serious mistake, Charles, and one I shall not allow repeated. That Mehala slut managed to correct your abysmal behaviour – while she bothered to stay.'

She smiled as Fellows entered and a maid-of-all tremulously glided after.

'Our problem, dear husband, is a satisfactory housekeeper to Bures House. It requires solving without delay. Send for Ennis,' she ordered the girl. 'Our guest is ready for the wine now.'

Fellows took a chair, casually smiling.

The meeting was to be a trial, Carmichael saw immediately.

He was admitted by Bridget. The maidservant did not look at him directly, a bad sign. He received nothing except a furtive attempt at a smile before he was in the presence of the stern Rector of Sealandings.

'Good day,' Josiah Baring said, in the dry reedy monotone Carmichael knew so well.

'Good day. You asked me to call?'

'You know these other gentlemen, I trust?'

Carmichael nodded to the miller who sat beside the desk. 'How do you do, Mr Bettany?' And then to the heavily built man by the window, Parker, of the public stables on the Norwich road. 'How do you do, sir?'

The men returned greetings, but distantly. Parker was somewhat edgy. Bettany was the local Quaker leader, whose mill served himself best and others second, and who toured the Eastern Hundreds assiduously in the cause of his sect. Robert Parker was a Methodist elder. Neither rose or extended his hand. The Reverend sat at his desk, leaving Carmichael standing. A triumvirate, with a criminal come to be tried.

'Carmichael. It has come to general notice – not to say public scandal – that you are in breach of your Hippocratic Oath. We intend, sir, to correct your attitude.'

Carmichael heard the words with disbelief. He stared, said nothing.

'I'm sure you understand to what we refer,' Baring continued, annoyed by his silence. 'Your misdemeanour is twofold. You administer treatments to the . . . to Two Cotts on the one hand, and free service to the children at Miss Gould's school on the other. It will not do, sir!'

Carmichael breathed slightly faster as anger slowly entered him. He had not felt so enraged for months, years. Mehala had advised him to keep his composure. He struggled to stay mute.

'Mr Bettany?'

Reverend Baring was now pleased. Carmichael's silence testified to his wrong-doing, that much was plain. A frank apology, and the matter could be closed satisfactorily.

'We've never met, Doctor,' the miller chanted sonorously. Carmichael listened. His chest felt tight, his temples tapping warning of the coming fight. 'But I've heard quite good reports of you. I have every reason to expect a sensible response.'

Parker spoke up. 'This isn't an inquisition, Doctor. Merely an attempt – '

'Thank you, Parker,' Bettany said correctively without a glance. 'Carmichael. We can resolve your abberations. You have, as Reverend Baring states, given offence – '

'Serious offence,' Baring interposed.

'Sadly, serious offence,' the Quaker nodded with profundity, 'to the good folk of Sealandings. You shall cease this school surgery forthwith.'

'Why?' Carmichael asked. His first attempt to speak failed. He made a second, a voiceless whisper.

'Because it is improper, sir!' Baring thundered, rising in rage. 'You cannot treat the children *and* the . . . the prostitutes. That condones their profane practices, sir! It degrades the sanctity of childhood, the essence of family life!'

Bettany shook his head. 'Regrettably, it has come to our ears that you spend an inordinate amount of time at Two Cotts among the, ah, the ladies of that establishment. We impute nothing, Carmichael. Guided by our Christian faith, we have no doubt that your medical attentions lend scandal.'

'Where there is already scandal enough!' Baring cried. He subsided, tapping his waistcoat, swinging his hunter chain, arranging quills on his desk with trembling fingers.

'Indeed.' Parker gained confidence from Carmichael's stillness.

'You see, Carmichael, we are reasonable men,' Bettany intoned. 'You're educated, after a fashion. We have deliberated, and will permit you to apologise to the devout of Sealandings, and beg forgiveness for transgressing. We are not uncharitable. We can forgive. You can expect a return to your trade once it is free from these errors, though the stain on your reputation will be hard to eradicate.'

'That is for Heaven to decide,' from Reverend Baring.

'Is there anything else?' Carmichael felt hot and cold. He wanted to smash these men, ruin this tidy roomful of hypocrisy.

'No. That will be all.' Bettany looked for concurrence at his partners. 'Questions?'

'I'm satisfied,' Parker said, every passing minute swelling his self-importance.

'Anything to say, Carmichael?' Reverend Baring was reluctant to let the gratifying moment go.

Carmichael turned on his heel. He did not hurry, opened the door indolently and leaving it ajar after him.

'Carmichael!' He heard the parson's angry call.

He went through into the vestibule, was let out by the silent Bridget. On the rectory path, he felt white with rage, almost choking in fury.

Sealandings lay before him, the Market Square, the streets of small crouched houses under their red trebled tiles, leading down to the harbour where the boats were bucking at the moorings.

He stood by the ancient churchyard's lych-gate. Here, biers carrying the coffins of the dead sheltered before the deceased were carried in for the last rites. Here, fishergirls and their beaux met illictly on rainy nights for moments of fumbled love. Here in summer the goosegirls dozed, having driven their flocks miles to the Sealandings market.

'Day to you, Doctor!'

'Mmmh?' Carmichael stirred from his reverie. It was Hal Baines, the young deckhand from *The Jaunty*, the Yorkshire lugger that had rescued Mehala. Hal recoiled a moment at the Doctor's expression: the eyes were blank, rage-hot. But as he stepped away in alarm the anger drained, leaving the same slightly injured countenance he knew.

'Good day, Hal. The sea is getting up, I think.'

'True, Doctor. A real Sir Roger be coming, that's sure.'

Doctor Carmichael shivered. The East Coast sirocco, as Sealandings folk called the terrible onshore storm, always brought disaster.

'God save them at sea. How is the lad?'

'Doadie's leg festers. Would you come, if you please?'

Ven drew breath, nodded. 'I'll come, Hal.'

He heard rapid footfalls on the gravel path from the church, guessed it might be Miss Euterpe, did not glance back and hurried resolutely towards the last row of cottages by the hard.

8

The room was one of the smallest in Carradine Manor.

Carradine entered with something approaching awe. How many years was it since he'd been whipped by Father in here? Nineteen? His smile did not reach his eyes. Peeping into a maid's bedroom, drawn by the sound of grunts and whimpers, he had found Father pumping into some maid-of-all amid a naked tangle.

'Gentlemen never pry on another at flesh,' Father had grandly stated afterwards.

'Yes, Father.'

His laughter bubbled even as Father spoke, for which he'd received a second thrashing. And very right too, Carradine thought. I must have been a little bastard.

No. That was the trouble. Not a bastard. Legitimate, in the true family line, the core stirps of which must be perpetuated, in and because of Carradine Manor. Were he simply an opportunist – as Prothero – there would be no problem. Carradine Manor would simply be a place to be bought or sold for mere expediency. Carradine Manor, a farm villein's . . . *commodity*.

But he was Howard Carradine, of Carradine Manor. Centuries of Carradines had ruled and despoiled here. Blind events, conspiring against him, had caused this loss. Even now he could not fathom how. He could not even work out how much he had left, now the vandals were in.

'Who is it?'

The noise in the corridor stilled instantly. A light step. A woman, who must have climbed the twisting stair that led from the third floor.

'I, sir.' Judith Blaker stood in the doorway.

The woman from the road, that day Brown delivered chairs against his instructions. He vaguely recalled having spoken about her to old Hobbes, then mislaid her in this harrowing business.

'What do you do here?' he demanded, but listlessly. He was less entitled to roam Carradine Manor than she.

'I followed you, sir. To report, and ask for instruction.'

'Hobbes asked your religion?' Carradine said, with bitter humour. 'I trust you answered with devotion.'

'I attend services regular, sir, and worship as my forefathers.' Her unsmiling gaze was undaunted. 'Mr Hobbes was pleased at my devout character. So was I, by his appointing me chambermaid. I did not want to disappoint you, sir. In need.'

'Need? Me?' He listened a moment as the rising winds huthered in the chimneys of the great house.

'Yes, sir.' Her voice raised, to be heard over the onshore gusts' clamour. 'You are leaving Carradine. You have nobody here, sir. Except me.'

'Yesterday, I would have thrashed you for saying that.'

'I offer assistance, sir.'

'What assistance?' A tile clattered above them. He smiled before his face clouded. The times he had heard that sound, knowing that he would clamber up next morning to watch the tilers at their mending.

'I have a large family, sir. They be wheelwrights, coopers, blacksmiths, tawners, tanners, and horsemen to spare, sir.'

Gypsies, perhaps, judging her colouring. Dark, but not jet. She was pert, zestful as any roadmonger, but somewhat paler than the vagabondage. Her eyes were not even dark brown. Her skin was spared much of the sun's cruel tanning that great ladies dreaded.

'I have nothing to offer you, Judith.'

He found himself looking from the small dormer light. The familiar view covered the north road's entry into Sealandings, the cluster of cottages by the Corn Mart, a sliver of the South Mole with its lighthouse, and the sloping wooded hill which shouldered the coast road to Whitehanger.

'That is so today, sir. The new master of Carradine Manor will stay only while the house offers welcome, and his fortunes benefit.'

'What do you mean?'

She had approached silently to within arm's reach. 'A great mansion knows its destiny, sir. This house speaks, would we hear.'

A shiver prickled his shoulders. He stirred with unease. This was witch-talk.

'Your foolery's beyond me, Blaker. Go now.'

She stayed her ground. 'Please, sir.' Her face glowed with fervour. She moved even closer. He felt her intensity like warmth. 'I expect nothing in return, sir, nothing. Only to serve your interests. That woman Tyll, sir, the housekeeper, might have pleased you – '

Carradine listened, astonished. Was his habit with Tyll so well-known? More likely, was this creature, now making her case, so astute that she had already discovered all?

'So you heard.'

'Quickly enough, sir, but not a word have I uttered. It is war, sir, now loots your treasures. You do not require a genteel lady as your quiet woman. Why, any tavern wench'd do for that. You need a woman who can fight, do battle by your side.'

'And who'd that be, Blaker?' he asked thickly.

'Me, sir.' Her face was almost gleaming in exaltation. 'Anything for your cause. I shall be here for your bidding. Every word I hear shall be yours, my every act yours.'

'For nothing?'

'For nothing, sir. Save the hope of future advancement.'

He moved, conscious of the effect she was having on him. He had to go. 'A bird in the hand, Blaker, from Prothero. Is that not preferable?'

'No, sir.' She spoke with scorn. 'I know my own kind, sir. He is a peasant farmer. He would not be even that, but for the pathetic lady who fell into his pocket when her parents died.'

He had to laugh at her disgust. 'Yes, that's Prothero! Climbs on those he trips.'

'Say yes, sir, and you shall be back in Carradine Manor by the year's turning. I promise.'

'Back here?' He pursed his lips. Undoubtedly this woman had a compelling force almost as powerful as . . . *as Mehala*. The contrast between the two was extreme, in appearance, manner, beauty even. Yet their impact on a man was profoundly disturbing in exactly the same degree. Almost. 'You *promise*? Singularly hard to fulfil, Blaker.'

'I shall install my relatives as hirelings for your estates. They shall work as never before.'

The woman spoke as mistress of Carradine Manor. 'For Prothero?' he cut in bitterly. 'His fortunes wax enough. I must look to my own.'

'I am your own, sir,' she said quietly. 'Try me. You shall be pleased.'

What could he lose, he asked himself. Barbara Tyll had served well, but timidly, as a servant should of course. He was not displeased with her, either as housekeeper or bedder, but her morals prevented her acting the spy while Prothero ruled Carradine Manor. In spite of Tyll's tearful supplication to leave Sealandings with him, she was married, to the toll-farmer on the shore road's tollgate. Making a pretty penny on the carts and herds that could afford to travel the rutted track, Carradine didn't doubt.

No. Loyal Tyll laboured under morality's sombre cross. This one travelled light of any such burden.

'Very well. I shall send you word where I abide.'

'You need not, sir.' Judith smiled at his surprise. 'I shall know within the day where you stop. If you need me, ask any drover or pedlar for Bellin. I shall come as soon as I can get leave.'

'Bellin? Another relative?'

'Just so, sir.' He saw she had nudged his door to. 'It would be wrong of you to leave Carradine Manor without a taste of your eventual welcome, sir. You told the grooms one hour?'

Yes, he thought, as she came closer still. Her woman's power was as potent as any he had experienced since Thalia De Foe first showed her heart. He slipped her mob cap, in ire snapped the bridles with a curse when it would not let her hair fall quickly enough. She laughed, her breath on his cheek as he pulled her to him.

Doctor Carmichael was opposite the church when the woman caught up.

He was preoccupied, bent low against the whippy wind. She had an old grey capouch latched about her, the hood gathered close. Her hem trailed on the ground, so low was she having to stoop to stay on her feet in the strong gusts.

'Doctor. It's the master. He's severe taken. The mistress begs you attend.'

He recognised the Calling Farm housekeeper. 'Prothero? I'll come, Mrs Perrigo.'

A figure stepped from the rectory path as they passed.

Carmichael recognised Parker, the public stabler. The man should have turned left for home, but fell in.

'Doctor, if I may.'

Carmichael did not pause. 'Please. Some other time, Mr Parker.'

They were practically bawling, the wind catching their words off the lips. Spots of rain slapped the ground now, presaging the coming downpour.

'Doctor, I wish to say I do not fully agree with the sentiments expressed by Reverend Baring.'

'Indeed? You convinced me otherwise,' Carmichael shouted back. He wished no more of the man.

'I have responsibilities to the congregation, you see.'

'You Methodists share more with Baring and Bettany than I supposed. I must obey all three, when you sing in harmony?'

'If you would give me a moment, Doctor – '

Carmichael had to yell. 'Mr Parker. When your famous Mr Wesley was but a boy, he was trapped in a house afire. His father knelt blubbering prayers; less holy neighbours climbed up to save the child. There lies the difference between you religionists and myself. Good day!'

They left him standing in the Market Square, calling after, 'I trust you understand why I must concur with the learned gentlemen . . .'

Mrs Perrigo's husband was waiting by Calling Farm's gateway with a donkey cart. He helped his wife in and took Carmichael's case.

'Thank heavens you've come, Doctor,' the stockman said. 'The mistress is almost out of her mind.'

'I'm here now, Perrigo. Drive on.'

The hood gave some protection from the storm's rush ashore, though Mrs Perrigo still had to shout to be heard as the donkey cart jolted forward towards the main house.

'The master's arm it is, Doctor. He's in fearsome pain. He was against sending, but the mistress prevailed.'

'How long has he been so, Mrs Perrigo?'

'Since a horse kicked against him, Doctor.' The housekeeper glanced at her husband's back. He wore the familiar wrap-rascal of the country driver against the howling wind, and a battered beaver cobbled with thick cord to stay on in all weathers. 'Might I seek your advice, when occasion arises?'

Perrigo glanced over his shoulder in warning. Doctor Carmichael recognised the look. The man was against making any approach, the woman desperately for it.

'If you wish, Mrs Perrigo,' Carmichael said.

'Thank you, Doctor. I beg you to say nothing indoors.'

'Of course.'

They alighted from the donkey cart at the front entrance of Calling Farm, almost mocking the style of visiting gentry. A manservant hurried them inside, taking Carmichael's surtout and Mrs Perrigo's capouch.

'Thank you for coming, Doctor.' Mary Prothero hurried to meet him, as he stood trying to wipe his boots. 'Please not to care about your half-jacks. Mr Prothero is in the withdrawing room.'

He was conscious of the faint stink of fish from his clothes – the visit to Doadie Baines in the fisher cottages. He was still apologising when they were beside Prothero.

The farmer's face was flushed, his fast breathing shallow. Never pale, he was now a deep ruddy hue, and feverish.

'I don't want you meddling, dog-leech,' Prothero growled. 'It'll get better on its own.'

'Am I to look, or not?' Carmichael had not put down his case. He had no illusions. Little Doadie, worsening, forced to labour at the wharf – and this rich scoundrel. The contrast could not be greater.

'Ar, then.' Prothero's surliness did not disguise his dislike. 'But mind you're careful.'

The arm was wrapped in wide linen bandages, tied with riband below the wrist. Carmichael took scissors and cut the tie. The forearm was distended, puffy and swollen. The whole had begun to fester.

'I need to touch it, Mr Prothero,' he said. 'Where the arm is roundest and most swollen.'

'He will permit that, Doctor,' Mary said quickly.

Carmichael gently placed the pulps of his fingers on the distended area, and pressed. The man groaned, but did not move. Carmichael had to acknowledge Prothero's character. Strong, but detestable.

The flesh beneath was turgid, but fluctuated under pressure. He repeated the touch along the arm as far as the elbow, then down to the wrist.

'There is pus deep in your arm, Mr Prothero. It needs out.'

'Cut? That's all you leeches think of! Well, you'll not cut me. Sure as God made trees.'

'You decide, Mr Prothero. I can only advise.'

Carmichael was suddenly tired. Mistrust was perennial, and there were many who hated doctors. God knows, he thought wearily, the poor patients had reason enough. No wonder they abuse physicians, surgeons, for we are creatures of enormous ignorance. A slight knowledge and a trace of experience were not much to combat mortality.

'Let me explain, Mr Prothero.' He made sure Mary was in earshot. 'This pus is a sac of matter which, if left confined, will spread up your arm. Unless it points through the skin and discharges through a spontaneous ulcer – '

'Then what?'

'If it points? Well and good. The pus can escape. If not, it will spread – by a means we know not – through you, possibly killing you in the process.'

'Ha!' Prothero exclaimed triumphantly, glaring at Mary. 'What did I tell you, woman? The man admits his own ignorance!'

'What should he do, Doctor?' Mary asked.

Carmichael said emphatically, 'I would incise, to let the pus flow free.'

'He'll not cut me!' Prothero cried, feverishly twisting his head on the cushion. His eyes were unnaturally bright, almost delirious. 'He's nought but a rape-and-scrape loon.'

'I'm sorry, Doctor,' Mary said pleadingly.

Carmichael shook his head, in mute signal that he would stay despite her husband's insults.

'Mr Prothero. Either you hope on unaided, or I cut and you probably recover. Your choice, sir.'

Mary sank beside the improvised bed while Mrs Perrigo watched beside the drawn curtains.

'Jason, my dear. Listen to what Doctor says. The pus will spread inwards, and you may lose your life. Or he will cure you.'

Carmichael coughed into his fist, to warn that it might not be so easy, but Mary was oblivious.

'I beg of you, let him operate.' She looked up imploringly at Carmichael. 'It won't take more than a moment, will it, Doctor?'

'I'm afraid it would take more than that.'

'You see?' Prothero threshed in an attempt to rise. 'You hear him? Bent on torture! Don't think I don't know what's going on, your simpering talk with this crocus! You'd trust me to him? For why, madam? For what motive?'

He sank back, exhausted by the outburst. Mary was distressed, trying to rouse him. Carmichael filled with pity for her. He murmured his regrets and left the sickroom.

Mrs Perrigo quietly followed, ostensibly hurrying to see him out. At the outer porch she hesitated, glancing back to where the door stood ajar and Prothero's mutterings could be heard with his wife's faint protestations.

'Doctor Ven, may I speak?' She was beside herself with anxiety. 'It is the mistress. The master's cruelty is so unrelenting that I fear for her.'

'So bad?' Carmichael was appalled. The storm outside had intensified, the winds now sounding fiendish.

'Terrible, sir. In solitude, she often speaks of the times you came here as a youth with your father. That memory seems her only happiness. His cruelty knows no bounds, sir. She talks of leaving Calling Farm, only she has no relatives.'

The words rushed out so frantically that Carmichael shushed her. Inside, Prothero was shouting incomprehensibly.

'I want to help, Mrs Perrigo, but I am sent away. What can I do?'

'Please, Doctor.' She stayed him. 'Were I to arrange a meeting, would you come?'

He was shocked. 'Mrs Perrigo! I cannot agree to an assignation with a married lady!'

'You were such friends once, Doctor. I truly hoped . . .'

'That will do, Mrs Perrigo! I must take my leave.' Carmichael gathered his surtout about him, checked its buttons, and nodded for the outer door to be opened.

'I shall persuade the mistress to see you privately,' Mrs Perrigo said firmly close to his ear.

'Please don't summon the donkey cart.'

He pressed the Suffolk latch himself. There seemed more safety out in the wild evening.

Charles Golding was almost drunk, but not quite. 'That will do, Lazell, I think.'

'Very well, sir.' Lazell was the Bures House land agent, a calm, middle-aged man who had seen most of Golding's tribulations. He often had to exceed his given authority, but kept excellent records to present a lucid account of the estates whenever the master came briefly to his senses and demanded a reckoning.

'How much does it bring?'

'You have the accounts there, sir, with your pardon.' Lazell reached over the table dormant. Golding showily assumed his late father's posture when discussing accounts, the wine decanter filled for the occasion. 'It yields four hundred and twelve pounds, sir, without the rents for two six-acre fields. Payable each Lady Day, with a small come-back of a half-guinea – '

Charles Golding was bored. 'Thank you, Lazell. An excellent summary.'

Golding filled his glass, not offering any. Lazell had tried to teach Charles about estate matters, but progress had proved as disappointing in youth as in seniority.

'One small problem, Sir Charles, if I may.'

'Always "one small problem" with you, Lazell, isn't it?' Golding said testily. 'One small problem – concerning waggons, game, taxes, horses, Government taxes on menservants. What now, sirrah?'

'The income, sir. From Hoddinott.'

'Why, it must accrue here, for sure!'

'Very good, Sir Charles. And the expenses?'

'What are they?' Golding was pleased with himself. He had to lodge Carradine – but *pay* for the privilege he would not! Power over neighbours did not come often; authority over maids and flunkeys was of no account.

'For the arable land, sir. Keepers. Stockman, three Maidborough lads hired payday-or-play. A riverman for the weir, sir, shared with the Astell estates, Arminell Hall.'

'Really?' Golding let his surprise show, to Lazell's chagrin. He had been over the Hoddinott ledger only three weeks since, and still the master was in ignorance.

'Sir Edward Astell suggested the riverman be shared, sir. Hoddinott abuts on the Arminell land but a small stretch – '

'Very well, Lazell. Brook no alteration from the guest who will soon reside at Hoddinott. You understand? All revenues and expenditures must come through Bures House, as for any . . . *tenant-farmer!*'

It was unusual, but obviously some arrangement best not enquired into. Lazell courteously collected his ledgers, the Hoddinott documents, and withdrew, leaving Golding contemplating the fire and smiling to himself as if he had begun a great and successful game.

9

The battle to make her brother agree to sit for his portrait was long and attritive, but Lydia Vallance knew her duty. She faced Hunterfield with every wile a woman possessed. She was astonished to find herself using all the phrases Mother and even Grandmother had, in support of her cause. Finance: 'The artist has been commissioned, Henry dear; should Hunterfield himself be omitted from the portraitures?' The appeal to lineage: 'Father had his likeness fashioned; is it not therefore proper. . . ?' *et cetera*.

Henry grumbled, of course. 'I'd feel a fool. And don't call that dolt an *artist*, Lyd. The London Academy has artists; William Maderley's the incompetent son of the Watermillock tidemill widow, nought else!'

She finally brought in Henry's honour – tactfully, for her brother, poor innocent that he was, was stern on *that* little matter.

'You see, Henry, dear,' she said at breakfast, 'the effects on Sealandings cannot go unnoticed. That the Lord of Sealandings leaves his own likeness to the last is an exquisite politeness. But for the Squire then not to sit for the . . . the *painter* might be taken as too haughty.'

She saw her brother pause before starting on his seventh course, French forcemeat quenelles which she had herself prepared at the cost of a day's suppressed temper from the cook. Mrs Kitchiner always wanted to substitute butter for the cow's udder, properly sieved after a thorough pounding – no slut's cuts in Lorne House, thank you, Mrs Kitchiner – and her panada was always seriously under-flavoured. Henry loved her – *not* Mrs Kitchiner's – quenelles.

'May I draw to your attention that Mr Maderley might not be available one day?' she continued. 'Who knows? And then, to complete the family likenesses, you might have to hire some London fashioneer.'

'Is there Herodotus, Lyd?' Henry asked, still in doubt.

'Certainly, my dear.' She felt relief. More evidence of her

superiority over Mrs Kitchiner, who had tried insisting (*insisting* – a servant!) that Herodotus should only be served at supper with a white-wine sauce. The cold fig-and-egg pudding was one of the Hunterfields' breakfast traditions, though inferiors could hardly be expected to understand. An occasional suppression did Mrs Kitchiner good.

'It is a nice point, Lyd.'

The fond diminutive she accepted only from Henry, though his use of it in front of the breakfast maids was too familiar. Lydia drove home. 'I cannot ask, of course; only bring these thoughts to your notice – '

Hunterfield sighed, then reluctantly conceded. Lydia was gratified rather than pleased, for Letitia's sake. Maderley's attendance at Lorne House would give opportunity to assess Letitia's fondness for the artist. Not long since, Letitia had harboured affection for William Maderley – indeed, that was the very reason she had persuaded Henry to hire a local artist to paint the family likenesses in the first place. But Letitia's hopes foundered when Maderley became overwhelmed by Mehala, that maid fished from the sea. Her own choice for Letitia was Charles Golding, or one of Henry's London friends. Her sister had borne the disappointment seemingly with equanimity, but Lydia suspected the wound was deep and enduring. Lydia meanwhile continued a protracted correspondence with several eligible Home Counties friends, with both her sisters in mind.

She pressed Henry to honey cakes and a selection of breakfast breads, to encourage his appetite for the tenth course, a particularly excellent mutton hodge-podge she considered her speciality. It was a dish Mrs Kitchiner consistently managed to get wrong.

The artist arrived an hour before the appointed time. This caused problems, for Mrs Vallance was giving afternoon audience to Robert Parker, owner of the common stables and leader of the local Methodist sect. He wished to persuade the Squire to allow the building of a small chapel on Hunterfield land abutting the Whitehanger track. Lydia kept the artist waiting, sending Crane to see if the Squire was still engaged in legal hearings. She finally sent Parker off, promising to pass on his request to the Squire, but the coolness of her manner left Parker in no doubt as to her inclinations. Privately, she thought the Methodist's approach a downright impertinence. Those of a persuasion who wished to build, let them build, but not at others' expense. Religious impertinence equated with greed.

She called on Letitia, reading in the orangery, to conduct Maderley to Henry's study when he was sent for.

'I would perform that service, Letty,' Lydia announced innocently, 'only I am positively *tormented* by religionists today. I must caution Henry to beware. Why *do* they see Our Saviour's intentions as an excuse for extortion?'

Letitia smiled, laying aside her Byron. 'I am pleased to deputise, Lydia. How long has Henry agreed to sit?'

Lydia grimaced. 'I have not arranged that, Letty. Gaining Henry's approval was wearing enough!'

The younger sister accompanied Lydia as far as the west corridor, enquiring after her husband's well-being, for a letter had arrived that morning from India. Lydia was delighted, and became quite lyrical on James' chances of promotion. A regimental majority was not far off, with the privileges of leave that entailed.

Lydia parted sweetly from Letitia by the hall, but was profoundly irritated. Letitia was far too *close*, she thought, making her way to the withdrawing room. There was such a thing as being so indrawn that not even a sister could see beneath the calm exterior. It was very wrong of Letty. How could Lydia judge the help she might need? She almost stamped her foot, so enraged was she at these sisters. Letitia had always been quiet, reticent to the point of causing their parents consternation. Tabitha was almost incontrollably wayward. Equally hopeless. It was high time she had something definite to tell Henry about *one* of them, for heaven's sake! He was beginning to hint blame, she thought crossly. Were there not suitors a-plenty? What more could she do?

Letitia entered the study's ante-chamber without pause. There was no door, otherwise it would have been impossible to enter, both she and Mr Maderley being unmarried and of an age. The artist was sitting by the window, and stood with an eager smile.

'Good afternoon, Miss Hunterfield!' He dropped a small fascicle of brushes and stooped to retrieve them. 'I am delighted. And quite ready to start!' He indicated a canvas leaning against the wall, and his folded easel. 'You will notice I have a fine wooden case for my pigments and vehicles, as used by the finest Academy artists. And I have admirable new badger-hair brushes, which give excellent results. I conducted trials, using all manner of . . .' His rushed phrases became disjointed. She smiled to ease him.

'Please, Mr Maderley. I do not really understand art. I am to bring you to Sir Henry when he is at liberty.'

She positioned herself facing him across the ante-chamber. An unexpected meeting was preferable to one planned. It gave her an advantage, amplified by its taking place in Lorne House. William had not changed.

Standard courtesies had to suffice – how was his sister Olivia, how fared Watermillock with these threatened high tides, the stormy weather . . .

His spirits seemed to sink at the mention. 'Miss Hunterfield, permit me to say that I am a man of few exertions in that regard. Our fore men are of the highest quality, but half of their duties I simply cannot comprehend.'

'Surely that is not true, Mr Maderley?'

'It is, Miss Hunterfield. Or I am lost in thought when they make report. Yet,' he rushed on, anxious to make a better impression, 'I have recently been favoured with a success at the Academy – in London! One of my countryside works has been accepted for exhibition!'

Letitia felt her colour heighten with pleasure for him. 'How splendid, Mr Maderley!'

'A triumph, Miss Letitia, which I hope to dedicate to . . .' He looked aside, quickly resumed, 'My paintings have been condemned, being only of country and the sealands. Insufficient historical content. Classical allusion is paramount.'

'I only wish I painted with a tithe of your ability, sir.'

'You sketch, paint, Miss Hunterfield? I had no idea.'

'Only to fail, sir.' To her relief Letitia heard the door of Henry's study open. She quickly rose.

'Fail, Miss Hunterfield?' William cried. 'There is no such *thing* in art! Please allow me to offer my services as instructor, Miss Hunterfield! I have no teaching experience, but am willing – '

'Excuse me, Miss Letitia.' Crane the elderly butler appeared.

'The Squire has concluded the Poor Law hearings and proceeds to the conservatory.'

'Thank you, Crane. I shall conduct Mr Maderley there.'

'The conservatory is quite wrong!' the artist burst out in dismay. 'The light is southerly. I need a northern aspect – '.

'Please, Mr Maderley.' Letitia's evident distress quelled him. 'The Squire has many serious matters weighing on him. I require that you work within the stringencies imposed by his duties.'

Maderley fell silent. A maid came to gather his materials but he shook his head and clasped everything to him.

'My apologies, Miss Hunterfield. I, of course, will obey.'

She so wanted him to succeed. Her ache for him was almost pain. William blundered after as she glided down the west corridor to the conservatory. Twice on the journey she demurred about her talents, saying how impoverished was her knowledge of pigments and canvases, how she would be a hopelessly inept scholar, yet implying how she longed to study art . . .

By the time she admitted him to the conservatory and sent Crane to inform Henry, she knew the artist was sufficiently fired to make a definite approach. She only prayed he would have the sense not to raise the question of tutelage to her brother immediately. Henry considered all artists lunatic. Discussion so soon after making Poor Law ratings would be damned to fail. She hinted that tact was the day's policy, but William managed to fall over the edge of the carpet scattering his brushes. The head maid Rebecca was still trying to restore order when Hunterfield himself came along the corridor. He raised his eyebrows to Letitia, and paused.

'See how I love my sisters, Letty,' he whispered, making her blush with pleasure. 'I waste an hour staring into space with a madman, all for your purposes!'

'Thank you, Henry.'

He raised his voice. 'One hour, if you please, sister. I shall trouble you to come for me yourself.'

'Certainly, Henry.'

She was almost back at the orangery when she thought of his words *'your purposes . . .'* Surely there was no double meaning? That would mean Henry understood far more than a gentleman, even an older brother, ever should about a sister's innermost wishes. Yet he had instructed that she should come to announce the end of the sitting herself, an order nobody dare gainsay. No. It was fortunate convenience, she decided.

Yet she now felt far less anxious about what William Maderley might say to Henry during the next hour.

By the candle's light Mehala watched Ven examine the piece of glass. He had been struggling with it for some time.

She was seated by the fire's dying embers. The draughty room was far too large, but at least it was dry. Very few rooms at Shalamar were intact, let alone free from the draughts that blew like gales through missing window panes. She had stuffed some with rags and reed matting, and tried filling cracks in the walls with clay and dry grass, in the old country manner.

Their one candle was fine tallow, not the humbler reed and mixed fat that she managed with for herself. Ven was using the more valuable light, but grumbling at his bits of glass.

'What do you, Ven?' she asked finally. He cast the pieces from him in disgust.

'It's the principle of micro-scoping, Mehala.' He seized on her interest to resume his fiddling. 'See? A lens shows things in great detail, so we see it better.'

He held a fragment of a spectacle lens. She could hardly see the white morsel on the flat piece of glass on the table.

'Well,' she said encouragingly, 'not really.'

'No, Mehala!' His delight in having to explain made her hide a smile. He was like a child, so excited by experiment. 'That is with *one* lens. See here? I have a different lens. The white grub is made bigger still. It is called magnification.'

She bent to look through the two fragments he was holding, and leapt back with a cry, sending the chair crashing. He hurried to help her up, soothing.

'Do not be alarmed. I should have warned you – '

'It is a monster!' He held her in an embrace to calm her fright. 'A great thing!'

'No, Mehala. It is a minute grub, from a leaf. See!'

She would not approach the table until he went and held the white speck in his hand.

'Where has it gone?'

111

'It is here. Just as small as before.' His eyes were gleaming, imagining some glorious triumph. 'A small insect, hardly visible to the naked eye. By micro-scoping, we see it made huge! Think how wondrous it would be if doctors were taught this device – and if each doctor owned one! To study diseases, and so help . . .'

His shoulders drooped. Dejectedly he stood looking down. She came beside him. The two lens fragments were from broken spectacles, quite uncommon instruments though now seen more often than in her girlhood. She had only seen three wearers of them before her life in Sealandings.

'How hopeless, Mehala.' He sounded so despondent she wanted to embrace him, offer any consolation. 'These lens pieces I've harboured for a year.' Reality drained his enthusiasm. 'And you need bright light. A steady holding tube of some sort, perhaps more than two lenses, even.'

'Where do these glasses come from, Ven?'

'Instrument makers.' He took her hand quite unconsciously and drew her to the fire. He slumped on to her chair, staring into the embers and putting an arm round her waist as she stood. 'I'm told the micro-scope principle acts as Galileo's telescope, such as sailors use.' He smiled up at her shamefacedly. 'Though I never saw one close, except through an anatomist's window when a medical student.' He sighed. 'Micro-scopes were first made by a Dutchman, van Leeuwenhoek, in 1683, by means of a compound system, one lens upon another. The image – that which we see, nothing tangible – is multiplied in size. It is wonderful.'

She was reluctant to break the spell. 'Can we acquire one, Ven?'

'How far that hope, Mehala! The special glass must be *made*, then ground into lenses, by techniques I have never even seen. Then those lenses are assembled in tubes, with complex mirrors and other lenses to gather the weak light of our inefficient lanthorns.' He raised a haggard countenance. 'Don't you see? It always remains a dream.'

'Are there differing sorts?' She meant cheaper versions.

'Yes.' He spoke dully. 'John Marshall of London made great double micro-scopes. A student friend's father saw one once, and described it to me most beautifully. Then Edmund Culpeper brought in mirrors. The scopes were made all of brass! Can you imagine it?' His smile was back, his eyes shining with admiration. '*Brass!* For stability!'

'It is frightening,' Mehala said quietly, looking down at him, then over to where the candle guttered.

'No, Mehala.' His arm tightened, and shook her slightly. 'No. It is a window into a new world! Think! We could study miasmata, by which diseases may be spread. We could perhaps even . . . *see* the cause!' To her disappointment he released her, and shot to his feet to pace the room. 'God! What I would give!'

'Is it only instruments, Ven?'

'Good God, no, Mehala!' He rushed to her, seized her hands and stared with the brilliant eyes of the mystic. 'Don't you see, dearest? It is everything we doctors do. Instruments, yes, but also the drugs we use! The food, each mouthful we advise, for babes and all! We only need look at tomorrow.' He resumed his pacing. 'Look! Once upon a time, back in the distant past, ancient doctors had knowledge of soporifics, draughts which put patients to sleep for surgical operations. Without pain! *We can't do it now,* Mehala! Yet *they* knew how!'

'Without pain? That is against Holy Writ!'

He was stung. 'How so? Why, the ancient church fathers Hilary and Origon used sleeping draughts! Literature tells that Nicholas of Salerno used *anaesthetic sponges!* Patients inhaled the vapour, and slept for their surgical operations until all was painlessly done. Then he wakened them with drops of fennel juice in each nostril! It was an entire discipline of medicine, all now lost to us.'

'What can we do?'

'One day people will see, Mehala. I know it.' He was on fire with conviction. 'I can see it, dearest. We need someone who will catch the attention of all folk, common people and royalty alike. From the stews of London, perhaps, to tell moving tales of orphans and workhouses! Rouse us to the cruelties of schools where children are starved and blinded, to our ignorance of the poor, the old. Until he comes to light the way, we ignorant doctors are all people have. At least,' he caught himself and gave an embarrassed laugh, 'at least, we two, plus any person with compassion. There *are* some in Sealandings!'

'Tell me, Ven.'

She sank into the chair, and listened as he started to speak of his hopes for the sick if only there was money, instruments, learning.

10

The storm swept in low across the night sea. For the last hour before midnight it seemed about to pass southwards, gathering force as the whole moiling front moved. Then it was pulled inland, and the world maddened itself to destroy and spoil.

From the Wash to the Colne mouth, life halted as the winds struck. The work of seasons was ripped and tumbled, pulled apart and flung across fields scagged by blown trees. Lowestoft boats foundered even at the wharfside. Further north a Morbihan lugger was savaged in sight of Brancaster, its two tall sails and its legendary speed unable to save its three Breton crew. Before such ferocity even ships of the line ran for harbours from the Orwell to the Humber as, behind the turbulent front of gales and slashing rain, the seas grew huge and ran upon the low coastline.

Inland, waterways were ravaged even before the following rainstorm fell on the shallow vales. The Gipping Navigation flooded between Stowmarket and the estuary, two men drowning as banks subsided under the onrush. Farms across the Eastern Hundreds were devastated. The fairs at Orford and Yarmouth were ruined, with heavy injuries suffered by those assembling. Livestock perished, inland Norfolk wherries were cast abank. Coaches and carts alike were mired in mudslides as roads instantly became impassible. The raised seacliffs at Hunstanton and by Cromer were almost unaffected, but the marshy lands of the west and the low cliffs near Hunstanton were battered worse than within memory.

Through the night the storm raged on, tearing buildings, scattering tiles and ripping roof trusses, breaking down the sea dykes. Whole herds, caught bewildered between their tumbled shippons and submerged pastures, were covered and drowned in the downpour. Uncannily, no lightning cracked, and no thunder rolled. The sea gale became a living devil through the long dark hours, seeming intent to spare no place and nothing within, creating a world solely of itself, drenching wetness, floods and winds.

It was not yet five, the gloaming hardly showing through the house. Mrs Trenchard had not yet reached Shalamar from her cottage. Mehala had roused early after a fitful sleep to make breakfast for them both. She carried up an eshet of warm water to fill Ven's ewer on the wall table, and shook him awake country style, by tapping his foot gently until he stirred.

'The storm's abating, but's still rare fierce. The water's off hot, but will serve.'

He rolled his head on the pillow to look at her. It was one she had feathered and stitched herself, made from an old linen sheet. He seemed so young to her in that waking moment. But that was ever men's trouble, a lack of age, Mehala thought, whereas we women suffer a perennial excess of it.

'The hour's bare five, Ven. I'll have breakfast on the board.' She placed the low tallow candle by the broken piece of mirror.

'Thank you, Mehala.'

His half-shirt she had washed after his arrival, dishevelled and windblown, in the rising storm the previous night. His surtout was still heavy with damp, on the clothes mane by the kitchen range. To help drying she had everted the canonicals – his linen pouch for carrying medicaments, twines and small instruments. His half-jack boots were another story; worn to the soles and irreparably slit. She glanced round the bedroom, a veritable barn with lath-and-plaster walls crumbling and the windows leaking rainwater from the sloping roof's drindles. As uncomfortable as any bedroom could be. Add that to Ven's instinctive reticence, his liking for solitude, and his life was a monk's rather than a busy doctor's. It would have to change, in every respect. He would be the happier.

Unsmiling, she went downstairs. Time was flying – no way to retard that familiar enemy. Speed was needed on her part, for she wore the only wary pair of eyes at Shalamar.

Lighting candles before dawn was said to be a spendthrift's habit, if not a slut's, so Mehala habitually left the tallows unlit until evening. Candles for night, daylight for dawns, Mother had corrected her one morning on Ray Island when she had heedlessly tinder-lit a candle stump.

The fire was banked to save wood – no costly sea coals at Shalamar. She broke it with the long poker from the fire tiger. Logs a-plenty after a storm, she told herself, though storm wood took an unconscionable time to reach dryth. Birch was best; no tree nurtured heat in its bole like birchwood. That horrid wet willow never forgot its love of wetlands, and spat hatred at the very flames that consumed it. Trenchard must collect birch quickly wherever it fell.

Breakfast would be sparse today. She was desperately short of provisions. Mrs Trenchard took some, which was her entitlement. Her husband foraged in the free wooded land on the Shalamar side of the South Toll. In fact, Mehala depended on the old country-man's skill. She knew Ven rued not being able to pay the elderly couple.

Half an hour later, she heard Ven come in from the lavatory and felt the faint tremor as he stamped off the old boots he kept for the muddy yards. He carried his ewer and basin.

'It will stay you, Ven, but I fear it isn't much.'

He nodded thanks and sat on the bench. Trenchard had made it from old planking. She noticed that Ven avoided her look, the same as the previous night. She had then put it down to fatigue.

'The two brill are small, but I've lemoned them to keep white. The porridge is without milk, I'm afraid. There's tea, with honey. Your breakfast cake is toasted, as it staled yesterday. I would have baked, but the storm curdled the quarter-pint of milk. An ounce of soured milk tastes through a peck of bread.'

'I'll survive, Mehala.' He caught her hand and held it. She gave an involuntary cry of surprise. He held firm. 'But I doubt Sealandings will, for my work.'

'What do you mean? What's happened?'

He relinquished her hand. She sank on to her stool. 'Last night, I was ordered to cease surgeries at the school, and Two Cotts.'

'By whom? Was that the summons to the rectory?'

'Yes.' He told of the sanction, the meeting afterwards with Parker the stabler. 'They were implacable.'

'Or what?' She served his meal and gestured him to start.

'My penalty? They didn't say, but they could make me leave Sealandings by simply forbidding their congregations to speak to me.'

'Can they do such a thing?' Her pallor became a fixed mask. Two blows; learning that the De Foes of Milton Hall owned Shalamar, now this.

He spooned carefully, blowing on the porridge. 'You know they can, Mehala. They represent all sects save the Romans, who are few but as intolerant.'

Mehala curbed her anger, slowly tasted her food. She chose her words.

'Do they not know your work, Ven? Have they never seen the sick children? Have they themselves never – ?'

'I will receive a donation to support the children's surgery, though. Mrs Prothero at Calling now pays a small stipend to Miss Gould for school materials, and to us.'

'Do the religionists resent that?'

'It was not mentioned.'

Her face felt white-hot. 'That only means they have not yet heard, or they would cry that you exploit children!'

'Please, Mehala.' His mild voice made her angrier still.

'No, Ven!' Her control broke. 'What right have they? You treat their children free, and they whine morality? Is that right? Is it fair?' She was standing of a sudden, clutching her arms about her. 'The prostitutes at Two Cotts – I ask you, Ven – who uses those women? Were it not for the money they earn in their beds – '

He held his head. 'That doesn't alter – '

'It *does* alter, Ven!' she cried. 'It alters everything! It shows the argument to be hypocrisy! We must get back at them, fight them, show them we won't be treated – '

'Mehala.' He waited for her to quieten. 'Do you know what hopes I had for Sealandings?' He gave a bitter laugh at his own stupidity. 'I foresaw a bright new future. Not for me – for the people. I knew a family, stayed with them in Sealandings, with my father.'

'The Callings?'

'Yes.' He was surprised she knew. 'It was a community of folk so deserving of medical help. They had no doctor among them. They depended on wandering apothecaries, quacksalvers, roaming surgeons. They *were* glad I came.'

'Their change of mind isn't your doing, Ven.' She had learned from her outburst. He could be won over, by quietude.

'Perhaps it is, Mehala.' He looked away, distressed. 'If I conformed and perhaps tried to be pleasanter, this might not have occurred. Maybe they would be willing to compromise.'

Her eyes filled as she listened. The poor deluded man. 'People aren't like that, Ven. They are thoughtless, self-seeking, vengeful. Was it compassion that sent little Doadie Baines back to the wharf when his leg was so? A mere child, carrying two stone of fish from the luggers? Or Christian charity that traps a gaggle of girls to serve every sordid whim in Mrs Wren's brothel? Is it kindness that makes bigots enforce their cruel policies?'

'We agree, Mehala.' He gave a wan smile. 'With no solution.'

'Ven. Dear.' She cursed herself for allowing him to see her stupid tears fall, aware that the endearment too was a mistake. 'Please believe me. You wrong yourself, trying to accommodate Reverend Baring, Quaker Bettany, Methody Parker. Can't you see? They have combined for no other reason save to punish you, make you come to heel like a cur.'

'Would they, when there's vital medical work to do?'

She was distraught. 'Of *course*! Their standard is planted on the high ground of dogma, Ven! They can't shift! You are different. You find some treatment that's better, why, you change your surgical practice. Look at little Clare Darling's diphtheritis. Shall you forget your new operation, the next time a child starts a-dying?'

'Certainly not!' He was aghast. 'It's now part of the treatment!'

'*That's* the difference, Ven. We must fight them!'

'How?'

She had not thought of an answer before a loud knocking sounded at the door: the first summons for help.

'Hurry breakfast down,' she urged, wiping her eyes and rising to answer. 'You'll not leave before it's eaten, whatever the urgency.'

Carradine had ridden as far as the cottage, and sheltered there as the storm savaged the Hundreds.

He awakened to a cold bed, a colder hearth, and was quick to discover that his horse had lamed herself kicking the shed door in terror. As far as the eye could see, the countryside was ruined, as if giants had gambolled everywhere. Trees were uprooted, crops flattened and sullen slow-moving sheets of grey floodwaters occupied the sealands.

He laughed aloud, at the upstairs window. Carradine Manor, Calling Farm, all the great estates would have suffered immeasurably.

'Good fortune, Hunterfield!' he crowed exultantly. 'This Sir Roger will cost you a pretty shilling!'

Hunterfield it was who, practically alone of the noble families, maintained the sea dykes and land drainage. Lorne House, too, pushed the Turnpike Trusts to provide parish roads – often nothing more than rutted cart tracks whose traffic was exploited by the toll-houses worse than any bandits. And Hunterfield it also was, who urged rebuilding shattered pavements broken by cattle and the huge broad-wheeled waggons called 'road-rollers', with their metal fourteen-inch tyres.

'The more fool thee, Hunterfield!' Carradine inspected the devastation with delight.

And Hunterfield's ludicrous scheme for parish dung-carts would be destroyed! The man was mad, striving for cleanliness, cautioning that only low two-wheel carts were safe along the narrow streets. The idiot Squire even argued amalgamation of parish workhouses into a single large Corporation of the Poor, as at Sudbury, and the building of a House of Industry for all the Sealandings Hundred, as Colneis had done.

'Money out, 'stead of money in, Hunterfield!'

The storm was a huge joke at Hunterfield's expense. All the Squire's lunatic 'advancements to progress' dragged money from participants. Even the Hunterfields' inordinate wealth could not go on sustaining unlimited mills, sea dykes, tollgates and turnpikes. The senior magistrate was even suspected of harbouring sympathies for the hovels covered by The Workhouse Test Act of 1722, and the Houses of Correction. The storm's levelling was fit punishment for a secret *leveller*!

Hunterfield's sympathies were intolerable. Class was synonymous with status, privilege and rights. Low class was synonymous with duties, obligation and labour. Blend the two at your peril. Mules did not breed. It was God's divine way. Where would a country be without its leader class, ordained by inheritance?

Carradine believed, as his father, that the scandalous Act of 1601, which levied rates to give 'out-relief' to the poor and provided them with work, was the only mistake Good Queen Bess ever made.

'You'd have us wiping the arses of widows and orphans, Hunterfield!' he crowed, jubilant. 'Not now!'

Then Carradine's smile faded. Why laugh? Hunterfield could shell off these responsibilities any time. Why, even this morning, Hunterfield and his three sisters – including the delectable Tabitha – could wake to a shattered world, and say, 'To hell with it. I've done enough.' And walk away, sport with his hounds, live aloof, ignore Sealandings and its carnage, and let somebody else fork out.

But Carradine of Carradine Manor? Dispossessed, without means of support.

He remained motionless, thinking of that earlier image which flitted across his mind. Hunterfield's sisters, *including the delectable Tabitha!*

Not *penniless* Tabitha Hunterfield. Heiress Tabitha, no less! Who would inherit Hunterfield land, coin in abundance. A lively, empty-headed girl, admittedly, whose wilful insolence seemed never far beneath her surface. Willing, if he guessed right.

He leant indolently on the window jamb. It bore thinking about. The other sisters were not 'in the running' – the Prince of Wales' liking for horse meets had popularised sportsmen's slang. Lydia, the eldest, had stupidly married Captain James Vallance of the Indian militaries, which left Letitia, who was too silent for a man of his proclivities. No, a woman with fire was more desirable.

What of Thalia De Foe? Married, though pliant and accommodating in any sense of the words. Fellows De Foe was astute, for he too wagered at the same catastrophic prize fight. The swine had walked away laughing.

Forget Thalia. Tabitha on the other hand was worth remembering.

As were Hunterfield's misgivings, for the Squire even had him taken in charge – that bitch Mehala again using her malign influence on matters that should never have concerned her, a servant slut.

Yes, it would have to be Tabitha. Marriage? Wedding, or bedding? The risk of crossing Sir Henry Hunterfield . . .

He was still mulling over possibilities when he saw a rider

walking a hack breast-deep through the flood. He recognised Ennis, the De Foe footman, and smiled. Thalia's promise, filled at last? A home, thank God! Knowing Thalia De Foe, it would be one deserving of a gentleman, not a serf's cottage.

He examined his reflection in the window. He didn't want to look less than affluent when arriving at his new abode. The residence Thalia arranged had better prove worthy, or he would punish the selfish bitch. A mistress' duty to her lover must come before all, when that lover was Carradine.

11

He hurried to the harbour, drenched through and mud-stained. Often he fell to his knees, clutching at wayside grass to haul himself upright.

The scene down on the hard was unimaginable. The ugly ochrous pallor of the dawn sky made the picture all the more frightening.

The seas were running high. The wind had only abated a little when he finally reached the hard. The South Mole was obscured in a thick hoary line of spray. The light on the harbour's northern arm was extinguished, an ominous sign. Men were assembled on the foreshore, but even as Carmichael peered, shading his eyes as if into a rising sun, a wave almost swept one man away. It was only by an astute linking of arms that the rest kept him from being dragged away. They scrambled in ungainly retreat further up the hard. One saw Ven and came across. He had to shout to make himself heard over the pounding seas and the wind.

'You know me, Doctor. Churcher. It's *Dander*, Doctor.'

'*Dander*? A vessel?'

'Ar. Mine.' The man saw the difficulty Ven had in seeing through the weird light, and pointed. 'Yonder, Doctor. We've a line on her, but the last man off was young Diss. We clung him back ashore.'

'Where is he?'

'He's sound, Doctor.' The man was leaning into the onshore gale. 'It's Raffin. He's all but done for. He's aboard, and caught sore.'

Ven was quite lost. 'Where?'

'There, man.'

Ven failed to see the stricken vessel at first, so high was the spray and the light so sour. He followed Churcher's arm, holding the fisherman's oiled cape for support, and saw her.

It seemed small, a dark shape partly sunk in mid-harbour. She was swamped every few moments and obscured in the spray that blew like a cloud rising from the turbulent sea.

Raffin. Ven recalled him, a laughing man with seven or eight children, a regular drinker at the Donkey and Buskin, a teller of jokes.

'Caught how?' he yelled.

'He's steersman, Doctor,' Churcher shouted back. Two other men joined them, both at a crouch from the wind. Churcher lost patience. '*Dander* be a ketch, Doctor.'

One of the newcomers bawled, 'The mizzen mast be stern fallen. The mizzen's for'ard of the steering, see? Hol Raffin's trapped beneath.'

'I reckon he be drownded by now,' the other put in. 'She's rolled like a log a time or two.'

'Is the line serviceable, Churcher?'

'For the whilst, Doctor.'

Ven stepped away, floundering as he lost his footing on the shingle. Between flurries of spray he managed to make out the state of the *Dander*.

She was lost, of course. Only one line, forlornly held at the bows. Even as he screwed his eyes against the stinging spray-borne sand, he could see the ketch shake herself, quite like an enormous hound worrying a leash to tug free. The stern seemed almost under water.

He beckoned to Churcher. 'You were aboard?'

'Me, these two, Raffin. Ran for harbour when the storm caught. We're fortunate to be here, no hope of reaching the Orwell mouth.'

'Tell me how Hol Raffin lies.'

'The sternmost mast, the mizzen, you see trailing over the stern, Doctor. Hol was at the tiller in the steering well when we struck. *Dander* went aback. The mizzen lifted, pinned Hol.'

Ven shouted, 'Can we go out, cut him free?'

Churcher held the edge of his oiled hood away from his face to look at Carmichael.

'It's possible. I doubt the return. Raffin might be gone.'

'Let me take a net, on a rope, to hold the man.'

Churcher nodded, crouched and bawled to the men through cupped hands. Three more joined them as they went down to stand by the rope. They seemed nonplussed, dumbly holding the line.

'Will this lessen?' Ven indicated the weather.

'No. The Sir Roger allus come round twice. He'll come ashore in another hour.'

'Twice? You mean the storm?'

'Aye.' The man nodded. He was old, wrinkled, with a mariner's wiriness. 'Southwold gets him once, Sealandings twice. It be allus so. *Dander* is lost. She'll founder.'

Ven tried to look along the line. It was perhaps a hundred yards from shore to *Dander*, but a hundred yards of churning sea that hurled repeatedly on to the hard. Each time, it sucked back with a hideous rasping of shingle only to gather itself for a renewed onrush.

'Move back, men!' The old man seemed in command. The men shuffled away a further yard or two. 'She's rising.'

The sea was trying for the land, the wind strengthening. The low hush between gusts had gone, in the constant shrill keening. He sought the old man, shouted his question.

'Will it be as bad as last night?'

'Aye, Doctor. But he'll come faster.'

Churcher was beside him, a length of line in his hands attached to a ball of netting.

'Thank you, Churcher. Who will accompany me?'

The man said nothing. The nearby men looked away. Ven nodded, took the end of the line in his hands. It seemed inordinately thick and heavy.

'How do I hold it? And the net?'

'The net's corked, Doctor.' Churcher's relief at being exempted showed in his shout. 'You trail it floating. We bind the line about you, for us to recover you should you lose the line to *Dander*.'

'Then do it. How long before she goes?'

'Not long, not long!'

Ven shed his surtout, now impossibly heavy from wet. He was chilled, but fear would see to that. He retained his trousers and shirt, but removed his boots. As Churcher lashed the line about him, Ven sorted his instruments.

He was almost ashamed to do so under the gaze of the men. On a kitchen table they looked appallingly crude. Here, it was even clearer how inadequate they were. Fashionable London doctors had all kinds of new instruments, some already in use, others still

125

evolving. He settled for a knife, some sutures, and his only saw. Country implements, simply mounted on slits in pieces of wood. He had hatched the saw's handle himself, using a carpenter's borrowed file. His attempts to manufacture a guard for the saw's untoothed edge had failed miserably, from inability to drill a pivot through the blade.

'We'm ready, Doctor.'

The shout startled him. For a moment he was miles away, in the surgery of old Doctor Arbuthnot, whom he had served after his surgical apprenticeship. The old drunk had talked of fancy new serrations cut high into amputation saw blades, to prevent the teeth clogging during operations. 'See how we doctors and surgeons benefit humanity, young man?' the old cynic had wheezed, chuckling. 'We invent instruments solely to our purses' benefit! The modern saw will soon be available to any doctor who can buy one – thereby saving ourselves the expense of using three saws per sawn-off limb!' And the fat old doctor had laughed until he'd almost –

'I'm ready.'

He tucked the saw into his belt, tying a suture round its handle with a quick surgical knot, and slipping the knife into his stocking.

'What must I do, Churcher?'

'Tie the line on to the mast, or the tiller. Anything to hold fast.'

'How will Raffin be pulled in?' Ven had never seen it done, but knew that the shore men's line ran through a pulley block to a stricken ship. 'A pulley? A turn-rope?'

'There will be none possible, Doctor.' Churcher averted his face, evidently from the gale.

Ven hesitated, nodded. 'Very well. Wish me Godspeed.'

Ven put his right arm over the shore-line, and stepped into the sea.

The icy cold shocked him in spite of his chilled state. He forced himself to exhale, to restart his breathing. The sea's power was impossible, dragging him forwards then shoving him back on to the sand. Twice he was suddenly cast back on to the hard before he got himself beyond his depth. There, he panicked himself into imagining that he had lost hold of the line, but it was there under his arm.

The simplest way, floating free, was to wrap his right arm along the line as if entwining it, and reaching his left forward to grab hold, and haul himself along.

The difficulty was the amount of slack that threatened his twined arm. He held on with both hands, chin high, gasping for air, never loosing grip until the slack was behind him. A yard at a time, he pulled himself out.

It was there, a few yards afloat, that the riotous sea really took him. Before, it was mostly spray spumed at him from the crests of the waves. Now it seemed the water took on a new solidity, slamming at him, shooting pain up his arms and making his palms sting. But he held on, learning to contain his breath as the waves struck, seize more breath and wriggle along the line before the next sea crushed down.

Odd that confidence was as much danger as terror. A sequence of six heavy seas fell on him, each with a brief pause before the next wave, which made him once risk trying a double grab for quickness. The sea's treachery almost proved fatal. An oblique wave thumped sideways against him, nearly dislodging him from the line. He recovered, choking, clinging on. But thereafter he moved one arm's length at a time, but weakened fast at the exertion needed to move at all. He tried counting, five pulls, ten, twenty. Lost count, guessed, pulled himself on. From fatigue, he paused and simply held on, but felt less secure, and instead struggled on.

The looming bulk of the *Dander* suddenly rose from the sea and hit him, startling him into a cry of fright. It was immense. For a moment he instinctively tried to flail away from the rolling black mound. The line he clutched sloped up out of the sea to something like four feet above his head. He held on, coughing sea from his lungs.

The deck lay at an angle. The *Dander* rolled as if trying to come upright but failing with each wave. To climb the bowline he would have to unwind his right arm and use both hands, his feet on the hull.

He took hold two-handed and pulled forward, suddenly finding the hull rush at him, buffeting his shoulder. He struggled, feet foremost, trying to leave the sea. The effort of it daunted him. He remembered the line round his chest, the men paying it out. He was having to overcome the net's weight.

Suspended, the sea welling up to cover him before falling away beneath, he spun several times before he could drag himself free of the heaving water. He clung with one hand to the gunwale for a moment's respite, then crawled clumsily up the hull's rolling side and flopped over, lying gasping, amazed at being still in the centre of a world gone mad. The deck canted, shifted. He was suddenly disorientated, tried to gather breath and look about. The shore-line was in his hand, and he was sprawling on the *Dander*, the wind whistling and the sea rushing and retreating along the tilted boards.

In the weird light he could see the broken main mast, its stump mercifully free of spars, one of the main hazards of shipwreck. To go towards the stern meant letting go of the precious shore-line along which he had swum. What had Churcher said? Tie his lifeline to the mast, then . . .

He clawed along the angled deck, keeping grip on the line. Some sort of signal was vital, to make the men slacken his line so he could move more freely, but what? He waited, judging the sea, let go of the bowline and slithered towards the stump of mast, then clung to it in relief with a monkey's embrace as the next sea crashed down, dragging at him with appalling force as the ship rolled beneath.

He saw Raffin.

Astonishingly close, the man lay propped up on one elbow, in crazy semblance of one reading by candlelight when abed. The man was conscious, but seemed shocked, observing Ven with hopeless eyes. As Ven tried to inhale to shout, another wave lifted the ship and roughly dropped her, the hull crunching the seabed and swinging her stern to the sea.

Raffin lay aslant in a recess, his hands on a tiller, trying with each shift to keep it from crushing his chest. A mast's free jagged end projected from the well, but the mast itself seemed immovable, jammed somehow in the ship's interior. Raffin's leg lay beneath. Each new wave flooded the well, which explained the man's strange posture – trying to keep his head out of the wave long enough to take a breath.

Ven gauged the distance to the steering wheel. What, three yards, four – more? He fumbled with the line, managed to loop it over the mast stump. Two turns, then he drew twenty feet free before attempting to tie it fast. His hands were too cold to obey. Every few moments the seas heaved over, pushing him so he almost lost his grasp. The ship groaned, chewed the seabed. Gravel, no longer merely sand beneath the hull. The *Dander* was moving. He tried to see the bowline. It was no longer visible.

He found the corked net on the loop about his chest. As the sea sucked away to gather itself, he scrabbled across the hatches, and tumbled down into the steerage well on to Raffin. The man screamed, frightening him so much he almost let the line go, but caught it and hauled until it was taut between himself and the mainmast. He expanded the loop, put it about Raffin's chest and his own.

He leaned close to the man, and between waves shouted, 'I'm going to try to free you, Hol. I cannot hope to shift the mast, for it is held by the *Dander* herself. She's like to go under soon.'

The man nodded. His eyes followed Ven's, but the hopelessness stayed, as if the end of his world had begun. Ven felt for his knife, and stuck it into the mast which pinned the seaman. His saw was more of a problem, tied as it was to his belt. Finally he cut it free, and tried to steady himself in a kneeling position.

The leg was caught at the knee. An above-knee amputation it would have to be. For a fleeting instant he thought of Robert Liston, practically the same age as himself but now the most fashionable London surgeon, reputedly able to perform this amputation in twenty-eight seconds. He tugged off his stocking and shoved it into the man's mouth to bite on. The man turned his head to look away. A heavy sea crashed down into the well, and took longer flooding away. The ship was rolling worse, perhaps surrendering now.

The knife was in his right hand, the saw in his belt. Should he do three successive circular cuts, as the exalted Doctor Larrey advocated throughout Tyrant Napoleon's wars? That at least gave a deep conical wound, easy to close. Yet, what of Robert Wiseman's dictum of 1676: *more creditable to save one limb than amputate many*? Or a simple blunt severance, as the Prussian and Russian surgeons did? But the skin afterwards needed stretching to a tight agony over the raw bone. Or the French flap method, so hopeful, if the amputation was through a joint. . . ?

He was wandering. He admonished himself, and ripped the

man's trouser, exposing the thigh. He cut downwards at once, despairing at not being able to use the circular movement round the femur as recommended by his old teachers. The leg was crushed to the deck. A clumsy downwards hacking throughout.

Raffin whined, his platysma muscle straining and his neck taut as he bit hard on the wad. Ven cut across, taken with fear as another wave flooded the well and Raffin coughed explosively, straining for air. Blood flowed, was washed instantly in the draining sea.

The rectus femoris muscle parted at the first transverse cut, the thick vastus lateralis and bulky medial muscle taking longer. The thin strap-like sartorius, the 'cross-legged tailor's muscle', flapped free, the white femur beneath. He desperately wanted to preserve the great blood vessels until he had sawn through the bone. They lay in the subsartorial canal, he remembered – which must be this gleaming pale line running towards the knee. He felt lost. His anatomy had always been poor, from never having seen the internal actual structures. In common with other medical students, he recited names parrot-fashion, rarely being privileged to examine real anatomical structures, to gain some idea of shape, depth, how the tissues actually felt.

He shouldered a sea aside almost impatiently, found himself toppling, and got back into position. The saw in his right hand, he began sawing frantically, every few strokes stopping to wipe away the bone clogging the saw's teeth. The sea washed and slammed, but he clung to the fallen mast, working deeper and deeper. The sea flooded the operation site time and again. He kept going.

The arteries and veins gave. Blood spurted. He took a suture, holding the saw handle in his teeth as taught, while he shoved the knife beneath the great artery's canal. The suture took four attempts before he was able to tie it. He repeated the process, managing a double tie. It was dangerous to make the threads too tight, or they might cut through the vessels and start bleeding anew. The bone.

Frantically he sawed through the femur, clumsily falling over as the ship rolled even further. The deck was at a steeper angle than ever now, *Dander* failing to recover her earlier tilt as she dragged slowly away from the shore with each wave. The bone gave.

The saw was superfluous. He cast it away, took the knife and cut savagely down through the great adductor muscle. The glistening sciatic nerve was transected. More bleeding, but even less time. *Dander* was going. No intervals now between that frightening crunching of the seabed. Had the bowline gone? The femoral biceps were tough, the fascial planes inordinately resistant to his blunt blade. But he felt the knife stick in the planking beneath Raffin's leg. The thigh was suddenly through. He was so astonished. It moved, flexed up almost against the man's belly, its raw stump flailing bloodily. He pressed it down, using all his weight, while he stabbed the muscle hopefully beneath the position of popliteal blood vessels, and used his fingers to drag a suture through.

The tie took longer than the rest of the operation. He felt *Dander* go, trundle a few feet inshore under the slamming press of a huge slow wave, then roll almost over as she was drawn back, her heel scraping the seabed with an ugly moaning sound.

He let the knife go, pulled the line round himself and Raffin, bagged the man's shoulders in the net, cursing as the corks fouled his intent, and crabwise dragged himself and the seaman up and across towards the mizzen mast.

The ship keeled as he reached it, starting to glide as if starting a long silent voyage. He slithered down the sloping deck, unlooped the line and flung himself and Raffin together into the water.

They were hurled back, hitting the bulwark as it slanted into the sea, then were rushed aside. For one second he glimpsed the ship's deck, standing vertically as if *Dander* wanted to prove she had no further cargo, then it was only the plunging sea and the waves, all vision blinded.

The sudden tautening of the line about his chest crushed out breath for a moment, between two huge waves. Raffin's face was buried in his neck. He almost drowned himself in the struggle to free the man so he could breathe. The compression of his chest went on, steadying and loosing, until he could no longer see or think or even feel, and the water entering his lungs seemed to be there of right for hour upon hour, almost a lifetime. He speculated quite idly on the definition of Time. It had always fascinated him, that Time lay beyond all man's attempts to define it . . . He rose and fell, rose and fell, a vertically oscillating pendulum.

He could see sky, as through mottled glass spoiled in the firing, too thick for any apothecary's phials, and opacities that could only surely be heads of people bending over between himself and the sky. People asking if he be dead or no. The cold so intense he began to shiver until his teeth chattered and his whole frame shook.

Fire? There was a fire, dancing somewhere before his eyes, and something wrapped around him. He struggled to get free, with people talking and somebody saying two more ships were down along the coast, and the wind was howling now like no wind he had ever heard before. And the rain slashing down on to tiles, and some old woman's voice saying there'd never been storms like it, all due to modern wickedness, and like to worsen afore it bettered.

And some woman with her arms about him, and her cheek on his brow. He thought of Harriet, who'd written him a letter refusing her hand when he'd proposed, but it couldn't be Harriet, for she was far above him in station and he a mere tradesman without prospects of advancement, so it couldn't be she, not now. And it did not matter, for this woman meant something more than any.

It was his woman's cheek upon his brow, and his own woman's arms about him holding him at peace before that curious gleaming fire. And he had lost his valuable surgical instruments, without prospects of procuring any more. His livelihood was gone. And he knew himself alive, and in Heaven.

12

'Please, Mr Greyburn, sir!'

Judith Blaker had her chin stays fetchingly tightened beneath her poke, and smiled as she tripped down the steps to the new estate bailiff.

'Yes, child?'

Greyburn was a taciturn Midlands man, almost a gentleman, appointed to replace Lennon the disloyal former bailiff. Prothero had accepted a Norwich testator's recommendation.

'A workman called, sir. Left this note-of-hand, sir. Name of Foley.'

'Thank you.'

Greyburn undid the note immediately, perused the words. 'Is he here now?'

'Indeed, sir. I bade him wait outside the gates, sir. Not knowing his character, you see.'

Greyburn nodded. 'Excellent, child! It does not do to have strangers in. I shall see this Foley man presently.'

Judith curtseyed and left, pleased. She had written the letter herself, in the style of a workman's rough penmanship but with a hint of learning above that of a mere travelling joiner.

With the damage sustained by Carradine Manor's home estate in the recent storm, a trustworthy skilled joiner was most valuable. Too many great houses would rue their lack of such a handyman, for wood should never be allowed to go to waste, a risk with so many huge oaks, beeches and elms down. For weeks to come the entire countryside would resound to the crack of axes. Only the charcoal-burners would relish the bounty of savage Nature.

She undressed her hair, placing the poke bonnet aside near the kitchen porch – Hobbes' standing order – and shed her rough woollen cape with its horrid pattiswax lining. Everything cadged, begged, borrowed, she told herself angrily. Well, my girl, not much longer.

By permission of Mrs Chandler the cook, she sought out Mr Hobbes, and found him doing a meticulous count in the wine cellar.

'A man calling himself Bone attended, sir,' she said with becoming meekness before the grand old chief servant. 'I sent him away, as I knew you were busy. Did I do right?'

Hobbes peered down at the girl from his ladder, and adjusted his spectacles.

'What did he want, child?'

'Please, sir, he petitions paid employ, here at Carradine Manor. A carter and wheelwright, sir.'

'A travelling workman, then?'

'Please sir, I do not know. He spoke true rough, sir. His manner led me to believe he might not be the right God-fearing sort for Carradine Manor.'

Hobbes descended, and patted her hand. 'There, child. Do not worry yourself so. I shall see him if he returns. The estate might require his skills. The storm damage will be soon fully assessed.'

'Oh, sir!' Judith lowered her head, and wept copiously. 'Did I do wrong to send him off, sir? Only, I feared you too busy. He seemed unfamiliar to local speech, sir.'

'Never mind,' the old servant consoled. 'You can't be expected to plan such things ahead. Let me be informed when this – Bone, you say? – returns.'

'Thank you, sir.'

'And your religious sentiments do you credit, child.'

'Thank you, sir,' Judith sniffed, curtseying her way out of that scenario and recovering the instant she'd climbed the cellar steps. The old fool would carry out her next plan, and hire her Cousin Bone as carter-cum-wheelwright at Carradine Manor.

Judith hurried to the kitchen, to offer willing help to Mrs Chandler. Deception always required a seeming joy, Judith believed. It was so important to appear briskly eager to please whoever one wished to deceive, whether a prayerful old dolt like Hobbes, a hard-working cook like Mrs Chandler, or an elderly bailiff like the stoical Greyburn. Or, she smiled to herself, when pleasing a great gentleman like Carradine, as he flailed into her compliant body to reach that little death men were desperate for. Yes, compliance was bedfellow to complicity, a lesson a woman never dared forget.

By nightfall she would have three relatives in employ at

134

Carradine: Bone the wheelwright and cartmaker, Foley the joiner and Prettiance, who had better get herself taken on as scullery-maid, or she'd scratch her eyes out. Judith had chosen cleverly, for Prettiance was exactly the right age for a scullion, fifteen. Prettiance was so deadly plain that any housekeeper, such as that grand snobbiness Mrs Barbara Tyll, so clearly bedazzled by Carradine, would hire her instantly.

With three allies on the estate, she could make a start on undoing Prothero and his meek mouse of a wife, and getting Carradine back where he belonged. But he wouldn't return alone. He would come with a woman able to cope. She only knew of one: herself. Judith Carradine? It sounded absolutely perfect. Tyll would have to go, of course.

She composed her features and meekly entered the kitchen.

'Please may I be of assistance, Mrs Chandler, ma'am?' she asked brightly.

'This?' Carradine reined his mount angrily to a stand. 'The bloody place is derelict!'

'Sir, begging your pardon. Sir Charles' keeper of the grounds is shared, at the river by Arminell's boundary; there's an oldly housekeeper. And two men are – '

'Silence!'

In a blind fury, Carradine thought of Thalia's words. He had instructed her to provide him with a new place. Clearly, something akin to Carradine Manor. Very well, then, not quite as imposing as that, but not a mere *farm*. God's blood. This was less offer than insult.

'Arminell?' The name was familiar.

'Yes, sir.' Ennis stood in the stirrups to point. 'That tree-line marks the Hoddinott bound, sir. Mr Lazell was most detailed. Arminell Hall abuts on the river's far bank, Hoddinott this.'

'The Astells' place.' Floods obscured the river-line, marked only by a rim of willows.

Carradine remained quiet for a moment. Ennis had already given him documents. It was Carradine's conviction that one sheet of paper was mostly acceptable – a lady's protestations, a wager, a coming prize-fight, but documents in legal binding, leather casing with a sombre ribbon, were portents of doom.

If it was Drunkard Golding's intent to force him into paying for Hoddinott, he was sorely wrong. However Golding used his agent Lazell to confine him, he'd best them – by the simple expedient of squeezing Thalia De Foe for funds to return to civilised society. She'd pay up. She'd love to. In fact – he started to smile slowly – it would do her no harm at all to hear of his meeting that lush bird Brillianta Astell while out riding. He could imagine the conversation, Thalia erupting in one of her jealous rages.

He would deny it, of course, claim that only necessity drove him to make up to Brillianta. Really, he would tell dear Thalia, poverty made him everybody's creature. A reasonable income would make him independent, free to turn his attention upon his own darling, Thalia, whom he really truly loved . . .

'Let's have a look, Ennis,' he said curtly, and spurred through the gate into Hoddinott.

By late that second afternoon the storm abated, gradually expending itself over a wide inland area between the Thames and Cambridgeshire. In Sealandings, two had died under fallen trees. A child was perilously rescued by Whitehanger charcoal-burners from drowning in the River Affon, when the frail wooden bridge was swept downstream.

Ven decided to start teaching Mehala his whole art immediately he resumed work. Already he had been to see Raffin, in his small cottage along the hard. They discussed the patient on the fish wharf, near the Goat and Compass.

'Amputations, Mehala.' He smiled. 'Your first practical surgery lesson.'

'Thank you, kind sir.' She tried for levity, but the sight of his poor hands almost made her weep.

His palms were almost skinned, though sea-bleached and wrinkled from immersion. The land-line had been thick tarred rope. She had left his hands uncovered, which he said was the best thing to do, as healing would occur faster. But it pained her to see him, hands stiffly before him, as if about to clutch his stomach. Placing a final suture over Raffin's amputation stump had hurt him badly and set his hand bleeding anew. He had sent for an eshet of seawater and soaked it before leaving the cottages.

'Old surgeons covered amputations with a pig's bladder, or a

136

beef carcase bladder, drawn tight upon the stump,' he told her. 'Not satisfactory.'

'How was it held?' She had no idea she would be so fascinated.

'By thongs, strips of linen, latchets. Never sutures, for they tend to inflame. Celsius, an ancient doctor of Rome before the Saviour, has left a description. I never could afford the book.' He spoke wistfully, looking out at the wrecked *Dander* lying near the South Mole. 'I heard Celsius' account read out in the medical school. I went hungry to pay my entry fee. It was worth it.'

'You smiled when passing the last suture, Ven. Why?'

He smiled again, almost embarrassed. 'I was pleased at the amputation, Mehala. Even as Raffin lay, I did the essential thing. You've seen a butcher cut a ham? Well, think of cutting so the bone was left protruding: the terrible spreading fermentation that kills so many would be inevitable.'

'You cut the bone higher than the flesh?'

'Pressure, Mehala. Shove it upwards with one hand, and saw the bone. I did it quite reflexly. Luck!'

'Devotion, Ven,' she said quietly. Unpaid, she did not add.

'So I was able to draw one suture through the skin as a great flap, with minimal exposure of the flesh.'

'The *Hunter* is entering harbour.' Mehala pointed. The Revenue cutter was gliding in, stark as ever, but significantly lacking several of her white boats.

'The night-runners have had rare profit,' she said thoughtfully. '*Hunter*'s boats will be along the creeks after them. Hopeless, after such a storm.'

Ven could not avoid looking at her, her face to the sea, hair blowing back, skin pale and smooth. He was tempted to ask how she knew such lore, but forbore. She was a secluded woman, keeping a life apart. It was she whose arms had comforted him when rousing from his cold immersion. She must have been on the life-line as he was dragged ashore. He fervently prayed he had not uttered his thoughts aloud.

'Nobody injured, please God,' he exclaimed.

'No, Ven. They would have lowered a lighter to hurry casualties ashore at the Mole, and signalled for cartage.' She became aware of his scrutiny. 'Will Raffin live, Ven?'

'He has a strong chance, Mehala. Sea surgeons say the sea

137

favours wounds, shore does not. Amputees survive aboard ship. Those in farms and towns mostly die of inflammation.'

'Why?'

He shrugged. They started homeward. He thrust his hands into his pockets, while Mehala carried his case.

'We don't know. Sea air? Sailors' food? I follow the practice of a certain French doctor, Dominique Larrey. One of Tyrant Napoleon's field surgeons, he made astute observations. He has long advocated cutting high on the bone by retracting the muscles from the amputation site.'

His enthusiasm was fired. 'Oh, Mehala! If only I had instruments – they're called retractors – made for the purpose! Some doctors use leather ones, but metal serves best.'

'Perhaps one day, Ven.' They progressed in silence before Mehala asked the question uppermost in her mind. 'What of Raffin now? The man, his family, children.' There were several, and a wife who worked on the wharf.

'Lameness serves hard for the man.' Ven was deep in thought. 'I often wonder at our folly, Mehala. How wrong it seems, for us to treat a child so it recovers, then send it straight back to its misfortunate life where it succumbs instantly to something worse.'

'Could we approach some gentry for charity?'

'Who?' He was at a loss. 'We would do nothing else save beseech charity from every passerby. All of Sealandings would need charity. Then the religionists, the moralists – they would preach that we fostered idleness. They are the enemy, Mehala, I truly believe. They control the purses.'

'Those who forbade you the surgeries?'

'The same.' They turned right, leaving the harbour to walk slowly up the sloping street to Market Square. 'Their literal versions of Holy Writ condemn us all to perdition. It's criminally wrong.'

'Shhhh,' she cautioned urgently, smiling at the women who stood at their cottage doors. 'Speak softly, Ven, until we are on the South Toll.'

He moderated his voice, but persisted. 'I can't for the life of me see what's wrong in using our brains. God gave us legs to move, explore. Why is it blasphemy to explore through thought? If we can discover a better way of treating illnesses, what contradicts Divine Law?'

'Shhhh.' She was now really anxious, asking loudly to change the subject. 'Doctor, you lost instruments in bringing the man ashore. Can we replace them?'

He gave her a quizzical glance, aware of her tactics. 'I shall try making some, Mehala. I made the ones you are kindly carrying for me.'

'Make?' That startled her. '*Make?* Of metal and horn?'

'I shall do the best I can.' He was tempted to tease her by arguing that Divine Law should have provided Man with metal arms, but saw her worry and desisted.

Instead, he asked about the *Hunter*, how a ship managed to survive a storm as fearsome as the one just past. She answered at length, delighting to tell of some storms she had seen 'to the south'. One when she had been crossing a wide estuary, and barely managed to save herself on a falling tide.

He marvelled. Her expertise made him realise she was a creature of sea, and he of land. He was fortunate she bothered to share his meagre life at Shalamar. She could fittingly seek employ at, say, Carradine Manor, with its own fleet of small coastal boats, even a pilot schooner, and three Norfolk wherries. Or Lorne House, where Squire Hunterfield had interests in coastal vessels. He did not deserve her.

13

The argument could not properly be called such, not to Reverend Baring. It was a 'corrective discussion'. He loved the term, having first heard it when he was at school. *Discussion* occurred over trivial things, where dogma did not apply. In matters moral and social, inflexible propriety ruled. It had to. It was his proper duty to expound. Others had the duty of hearkening to his moral imperatives. He saw himself as a translator, a medium of exchange between the Almighty and members of the human race. Those who differed were in serious error, their souls condemned to hellfire for all eternity.

Listening to his sister Euterpe, he was disturbed, then appalled.

'Yours are but opinions, Euterpe.'

It should have been the final word. Christian teaching could not tolerate mere personal opinion on doctrinal matters. Yet his sister's expression did not change.

'The Almighty gave us brains to reason, I believe, Josiah,' she said calmly. 'What else are we to do with them? Should we also stand with our arms hanging, in case we provoke criticisms that we are wrong to work?'

His face darkened. 'I thank you not to foil words with me, Euterpe. You understand clearly. Carmichael is a mere quack, who has transgressed.'

'Our Saviour assisted the sick irrespective of – '

'That will do, Euterpe Baring!' her brother thundered.

He was standing in his favourite pose, arms behind, tailcoat lifted before the fire. His study was a sacrosanct place for issuing directives and composing sermons. Euterpe was pleased to be the docile housekeeper, smilingly keen to take on good works as he suggested them, to listen to his sermons and practise sacred music.

Unfortunately, Euterpe now betrayed herself, since he had forbidden her association with Doctor Carmichael. His ban was reasonable, just, proper. It also excluded the man from attending St Edmund the Martyr.

'Am I to say nothing further, brother?'

She sat primly without her usual embroidery, hands folded, the amadis sleeves of her plain pelisse tightly cuffed at the wrist. This fanciful dress irritated him, for it was nothing more than a sop to new convention. What was that but deplorable slavery, to sinful *fashion*?

'Your duty is plain, Euterpe!' he said. 'I suggest an instantaneous course of action. Confer with the parish ladies. Issue a Christian statement against the Doctor. That reprobate gives not the slightest sign of obedience! We instructed him in a truly charitable manner.'

'And he made what reply?' She had gone pale.

He smiled tightly – now his facts were striking home. This interview showed the benefit of a theological education over the common mind, leaving aside the male's natural superiority.

'The wastrel didn't even have the grace to reply!'

'Was he given opportunity?'

'He was given every chance, Euterpe!' Baring shouted, losing composure. 'He stood there with that scrawny pale visage of his, without a word of apology!'

You would wait some time, brother, Euterpe told him inwardly. 'Have you thought of the consequences?'

'Of forbidding his surgery at . . . at that sinners' den?' He wagged a finger. 'Why, decency might rise again in Sealandings, Euterpe! Can't you see? This man enters respectable houses! The gentry, pillars of our community! And the cottages of decent fisherfolk, foresters, millers! The decent suffer by contagion from the ungodliest!'

'And the diseases he treats, Josiah?'

At least she had the modesty to lower her eyes while the evil subject was discussed! He swelled with importance, though not too much. Best never to seem boastful, when one's argument prevailed. The work of the Lord, he thought piously.

'Diseases? Why, those are sent as punishment for, ah, the sinful of, well, *those* places, Euterpe. Divine retribution!'

'Those fallen women might seem a *source* of diseases to those who associate with them, Josiah. They need treatment to reduce that risk.'

He shifted uncomfortably. This was taking an unpleasantly

141

practical turn. The very thought of fornication made sweat trickle down his nape. He cleared his throat. 'We wander from the religious question, Euterpe.'

'Perhaps Doctor Carmichael tries to protect Sealandings from the prostitutes' diseases, brother.'

He sank into his chair, aghast at her frankness. 'Sister! What are you *saying*? Have you no decency left? Such a word, in this rectory?'

She faced him. She could never remember feeling so sad.

'Brother, dear. Josiah. If I can't speak my thoughts to you here, where may I? I am not joining the forces of perdition. I simply ask: why stop Doctor Carmichael treating these poor females at Two Cotts? All Sealandings – all the Eastern Hundreds, indeed – know what trade they ply. Is it not incumbent on us to give Doctor Carmichael help, rather than hindrance?'

'Biblical authority forbids – '

'Forgive me, Josiah.' Her quietness cut through his hectoring. 'Argument brought against Ven Carmichael's work at Two Cotts must apply equally to his surgery at Miss Gould's school.'

Her brother considered, eventually rising to resume his posture.

'Euterpe, I have shown you your proper Christian duty. It is to summon the parish ladies and urge them to exclude this sinister tradesman from their homes. In that way, we can keep Sealandings clean of this filth besmirching our society.'

'We have not yet – '

He erupted, 'Yes, sister! I have deliberated! Stand aside from God's work if you must – but do not represent your wayward opinions as coming from any source except your own backsliding soul!'

'Brother, I beg you to reconsider – '

'I am Rector of Sealandings, Miss Baring!' he shouted angrily. 'I do not *need* to reconsider. Mine is the authority of the Almighty. You have merely fond whimsy, and your absurd preference for that despoiling sinner. Leave the study!'

She rose, gave a bob and retired, eyes moist. This was by far the gravest breach between them. Before, she had always managed to get round him somehow, relinquishing some small sector for advantage in a greater. Now, though, he seemed implacable. His hatred for Carmichael had grown rather than dwindled.

Bridget the maid-of-all was dusting the hall furniture as Euterpe emerged. She made to speak, but Euterpe shook her lowered head and hurried past into the withdrawing room.

'The hand is a beautiful structure, Mehala,' Ven was saying as she tried to remember the drawings he had made to show her the bones, tendons, and where the arteries and veins ran. He smiled ruefully. 'Some consider we are the work of the Creator. I'm not so sure, when I see the messes the hand can get into.'

Mehala glanced about, worried he was being overheard. The parlour was subdued, apart from the unconscious man's stertorous breathing.

Mary Prothero knelt by the chaise longue. Prothero had been all but stripped, and was covered by a sheet. Libby the chief housemaid stood by her mistress. Mrs Perrigo was in the kitchen procuring hot water.

'This is my aim, Mehala.' Carmichael listened to the patient's harsh rasping. 'To cut into the pus, at the point of greatest fluctuance.'

He took her arm to show her. 'You test for pus by sight, of course – red turgidity, swelling, heat, sight of yellow matter beneath. Then you test for fluctuation. Press two fingers gently into the skin, then with a finger of the other hand, press nearby. Remember the children's game, when farm boys blew up a pig's bladder for a balloon, and you could twist it into many smaller balloons? And how each fluctuated to finger pressure? This is exactly the same.'

'But where to cut, Ven?'

They spoke softly. The others were standing apart.

'Recall our drawings, Mehala, the flexor sheaths for the tendons, and how they relate to the digits. You recall, I likened them to scabbards? The large central one has an extension along the small finger. The other three fingers have separate sheaths. The thumb – ' he drew his finger from above his wrist to the nail ' – the thumb has an individual sheath, starting above the wrist's retinaculum.'

'Must you cut into each?'

'In those containing purulent matter, yes. But the problem here is pus lying deep in the forearm. New spaces may be created, we

143

believe, in fascial planes lying deeper than the tendons – the "leads" butchers speak of. These seem altogether different from the "compartments" of the anatomist.'

'The pus causes them?'

'We don't know. It's actually as if the pus is able to dissolve parts of the flesh somehow, cleave a silent way through the body's planes and so spread.' He turned her hand palm upwards. 'For deep pus within the forearm, spreading up the front, as with Prothero, we find the lowest part of the radius bone, and cut along the anterior border.'

He nodded his readiness, and approached the chaise longue. 'We shall know success, pus coming from within.' He stood a moment. Mary seemed oblivious.

'Mary?' he said. 'I'm ready now. Can I begin?'

'Yes, Ven.'

The sound was almost inaudible. Mary Prothero's face was streaked with tears, long since dried. She stirred, made way and beckoned Libby to come closer.

Mehala brought up a small table. Ven rested Prothero's arm on the surface, turning the palm up and telling Mehala to take hold of the hand firmly at the fingers.

The arm was huge now, an ugly dark carmine, magenta in the middle of the forearm, putrescent and turgid.

'Is it gangrene, Ven?' Mary asked.

Mehala looked at the lady's use of Carmichael's first name.

'Not yet, Mrs Prothero,' Ven replied formally. 'I believe it is purulence, which may be relieved by incision. I do not know.'

She raised wide eyes. 'You don't know? Then why risk surgery?'

'To leave him is to let him die. I believe it.'

She withdrew slightly. Ven took a lancet. His remaining instruments were piteously few, numbering a pair of scissors, a probe, a needle honed down from a large housewife's bodkin, a lancet and a pair of homemade forceps.

'It is fortunate your husband is unconscious, Mrs Prothero. This operation inflicts great pain. Say when I may proceed.'

Mary closed her eyes. 'Yes. Now.'

Ven gauged the long line of the flexor carpi radialis, prominent along the distended forearm towards the palpable prominence of the scaphoid bone. It was difficult to feel in the swollen flesh. He glanced at Mehala as he tested the skin for fluctuation. He nodded imperceptibly, and pointedly indicated the line marking the radius bone's lower third.

He quickly cut down. The tissues bulged, oozing dark blood as the muscles everted like huge fleshy lips. He cursed himself for the paucity of his instruments. He needed small delicate retractors, like some the surgical instrument-makers were reputedly selling in London. Instead he had mere strips of boiled leather.

Prothero groaned, jerked, tried to pull his arm away. The strength of the recumbent man was prodigious. Mehala tried hard to force the arm down by pressure, but it took all of them including Libby to stop Prothero from clawing at his arm.

Eventually he quietened, but Ven had lost time. He reversed the lancet's point, and with blade upwards slit slowly along the forearm, trying to guess where the radial artery lay. One slip would mean the artery would gush, and might prove impossible to stop.

Mehala's gasp surprised him as much as the fetid stink that arose as, from the glistening fascia which he incised, there welled a dirty cream exudate of pus, in part bloodstained, in part yellowish grey. Its stench filled the room as the pus flowed like a hideous lava, out of the forearm, over the skin, and on to Ven's hands and over Mehala's.

She gagged. He reached up, over the elbow's flexure, and squeezed gently: no increase in the flow of pus. Perhaps it had not yet reached that far? He swabbed the pus aside, trying vainly to see the tissues beneath.

'Light, Libby, if you please.' He smiled at Mary with pretended confidence. 'One day, maybe we shall have that new wonderful gas invention. I saw one such mantle in a London hospital. Brighter than a star! You could read by its glow in every corner of the room!'

The flow of pus was lessening. He tried a gentle squeezing, wrist upwards this time, and partly succeeded. The erythema, the evil redness, of the swollen palm showed where pus was forming locules in the large flexor sheath. He asked Mehala to pull hard on the fingers and, blade downwards, cut through the thickened palmar skin.

145

This time the pus flowed with astonishing fluidity, almost like stagnant yellowish marsh water. The swollen palm collapsed. Ven was able to ease pus from the wound by gentle pressure.

He laid the lancet aside and took up a thread.

'We tend to call pincers by the grand word *forceps* now,' he said, trying to lessen the anxiety, 'though it is stupid to invent terms that sound more select. In Ancient Greece, the old surgeons first made them in imitation of thumb and forefinger!'

He pushed waxed thread into the wound along the flexor sheath. He repeated the procedure, trying to insert threads into each deep tissue cavern where pus might still lurk.

'Mrs Prothero,' he said, straightening up stiffly as he inserted the last. 'These threads will serve as small canals, along which remaining pus might flow out. They prevent a deep abscess.'

'What happens to them?'

'I shall pull them out eventually, if all goes well.'

'And if not?'

'If not, there is nothing more I can do. I am ignorant of the causes of inflammation. We think it a ferment, but do not know. And we cannot treat it, when it assumes its spreading manner. We can only sometimes drain pus, as in this case.'

'Will he recover, Ven?'

'That too depends. I hope so, Mrs Prothero.'

In the background, Mrs Perrigo stood with her mouth set in a grim line as Mary Prothero and Libby murmured a thanks-be.

On the chaise longue, the patient stirred and opened his eyes. His face was flushed and red, his eyes unnaturally bright, but he asked for a drink of water and seemed to recognise his wife as she hurried to comply. Ven turned away.

On the walk home, Mehala asked Ven about his training. So far, her lessons had been in anatomy and the theory of blood circulation.

He told her, but concluded, smiling, 'Look at us, Mehala, at what we have just done. It embarrasses me.'

'Saving a life? Even one as repellent as Prothero?'

He thought how to convince. 'You see my training in a glow of magic and mystery. I see it from within, as a few untrustworthy facts cloaked in mystique which serves only to hide the ignorance

146

of us doctors. How many drugs are we sure of? Opium from the poppy, digitalis taken from the foxglove for the dropsy, perhaps belladonna from *Atropa belladonna* for some eye problems, and Dr Jenner's cowpox for prevention of the small pox. Those.'

'But you understand so many other simples, unguents, tinctures!'

'Their effects we know little, Mehala, and can explain even less.'

They were into the curve of the South Toll road. Ahead, Mehala saw a horseman at a stand by the gate to Shalamar. The mount was still, the posture of the rider unperturbed, as if waiting for them to make the long slow climb up from Sealandings. Mehala felt a thrill of worry. A messenger? Or perhaps, she thought in a flood of hope, somebody needing help for someone sick in his family. Somebody who could pay . . .

'. . . the possibility of transmitting infections,' Ven was saying. 'I mean, look at this hedgerow.'

'Hedgerow?' she repeated, eyes on the distant figure.

'Yes.' Ven paused, pulled up a small floret. 'This flower – is it periwinkle? Who is to say it doesn't hold more pharmacy than the drugs we know?' He indicated the countryside with a sweep of his arm. 'Think of the ponds, streams, herbs, flowers, even animals, and us ignorant of them all!'

'To know all these, Ven, is beyond comprehension.'

'You remember the other day, Mehala?' He was laughing as they resumed. 'You found a round egg, spherical as a child's alabaster! I asked, would it be as tasty as the rest. Remember?'

'No,' Mehala said severely, but smiling.

'You do, my lady! You said, "We shall see at breakfast". Then, thinking me preoccupied, you took it in your apron, and *threw* it over the outhouse roof. I heard it smash!'

'You were dreaming, sir!' she cried in reproof.

'I'm sure you are superstitious! The old lore, Mehala – a round egg is Friday lain, and brings ill-fortune! Am I right, ma'am?'

She said with asperity, 'It's an old wives' tale, Ven. Such silly talk! Why, fisherfolk won't even say the word *egg*! They speak of a "roundabout", or "roundmeat". Lore is absurd!'

Her face clouded. He only laughed.

'You see, Mehala? We don't *know* if that little snippet is true or

147

false! Is a round egg tainted, a proper oval one not? We don't know, because nobody has ever tasted one. They cast it over the house from superstition, and that's an end to it.'

'Harmless story-telling, Ven,' she said, more to ease her own anxieties. The horseman had not moved. 'Why, everything has lore in it. Along the Blackwater, there's no marrying until after the fishing's done – they believe marriages bring stormy weather! And they never buy colts born in May, believing they lie down in water and never ride on through!' It was only when she saw him smiling, looking directly at her without shyness, that she caught herself. 'All the harmless nonsense of children!' she finished lamely.

'You've never spoken so before, Mehala. Not directly.'

'I forget most of it, Ven. It returns in glimpses.'

'That happens,' he conceded gently. It was none of his business. What right did he have to ask? To cover the awkwardness he started telling her of great London surgeons, who strolled to their hospitals in surcoats stiff with dried blood and pus, living proof of how fashionable and successful they were.

'Only poor new surgeons wear clean coats, you see Mehala. Cleanliness means inexperience . . .'

The attempt at levity failed. They grew silent as they walked up the rutted slope towards the horseman. A goosegirl passed them, driving her noisy charges downhill, her willow wand swishing in the air. She cried her birds' praises to Mehala, who regretfully shook her head. How lovely to afford a goose. Mrs Trenchard would speak another fine lecture, telling how skilfully the women of her day prepared a goose for table, and how badly young women managed in these gaudy, over-busy days, cooking with disregard of flavour. And how modern kitchens were filled to bursting with girls unable to stir a stockpot without running crying for instruction . . .

The rider was cloaked, wearing an old tricorne. He had the steady weathered appearance of a traveller. The horse was a cob, not large but sound, ponderous even, just the sort to plough loyally through the deepest rain-filled ruts of East Anglia's roads. He was expressionless.

'Sir?' Carmichael called as they came within earshot.

'Sir.' The rider touched his hat, but did not move from the gate. 'Do I address Doctor Carmichael, of Shalamar?'

'You do, sir.'

148

'And Mehala, from Sealandings?'

'That is I, sir.' Mehala's foreboding returned. She felt numb as the messenger spoke the words she knew were inevitable.

'I bring eviction notice to you both, from Willoughby, agent for Milton Hall, to which this house belongs.'

Ven glanced at Mehala, then back to the horseman. 'Us? To leave Shalamar?'

'Within one hour, sir. I wait on your going.'

His voice was disinterested. Mehala felt dulled as Ven started to ask for explanation, reasons. Her heart bled for him. She wanted to console, cry that all would be well, that they would manage somehow. He stood stricken as the rider repeated his message tonelessly.

'One hour, sir. I take possession on the minute.'

'Then there's still time!' Ven cried eagerly. 'I must go straight away. Sir Fellows, isn't it? I've never met the gentleman, but I'm sure he would rectify this mistake – '

'The order's signed, crocus,' the man said rudely.

'Who is this Mr Willoughby, then?' Ven asked. 'I'm certain that if we were to speak – '

Mehala drew him aside, spoke under her breath. 'Ven, dear, we have no hope of staying. I know. It will be by order of Thalia De Foe, not her husband. He probably knows nothing of this.'

Ven looked at her, uncomprehending. 'But why, Mehala? What have I ever done to her?'

'You took me as housekeeper.' Mehala prevented herself from holding him. 'She wished me to serve her cousin, Charles Golding at Bures House, but I came here instead. She is not a woman to forget scorn, even from a servant such as I.'

He stared. It was beyond him. 'You don't understand, Mehala,' he said patiently, as if explaining to a child. 'I have no other place to go. Where else can I take you?'

'Leech,' the rider called. 'You've had five minutes. I have you on the watch. Fifty-five more, and I shall forbid you entry!'

Mehala drew Ven along after her. 'Come, Ven,' she said gently. 'We'd best find our things, lest we be on the road without them.'

'My books.' He started to stammer slightly under stress of emotion. She had noticed this before. It endeared him to her more than ever. 'And my notes.'

'Yes, dear. All that we can carry, we shall.'

Ven glanced back at the rider. 'But where to, Mehala?'

'I do not know, Ven.' She felt such a burning protectiveness she could hardly speak. It was all-consuming, a furnace whose heat stripped her senses. 'But I promise you, dear. This shall never happen again.'

His face was even more gaunt than usual, drained of everything save exhaustion. They stood together as her fierce words penetrated his shocked state.

'Do you hear, Ven? This will never happen to you ever again. I promise, as God's my judge.'

'My books,' he said quietly, recovering. 'Come, love. We've not much time.' He patted her arm consolingly as they went to Shalamar for the last time.

14

Brillianta Astell watched the horseman take the leap in the valley below. Happily, her dear sister Lorela, older and more gorgeous –you did not dare think of mere prettiness for Lorela – was in London, and unlikely to return before three days.

He was a gentleman she recognised, surely? The very image of that bestial Carradine, of Sealandings. But Carradine was unlikely to be out riding the Maidborough district, except for sordid reasons, and Maidborough was the most staid of places. Her father Sir Edward saw to that.

She rode Jamestown this morning, he being docile and in any case a dark chestnut colour which complemented her. Ever since dear sister Lorela's awful remark at the great ball in Milton Hall ('*Such* a pity that dear sister Brillianta's rather plain . . .') in the hearing of that ghastly bitch Thalia De Foe and Squire Henry Hunterfield's gruesome trio of unutterably dull sisters, Brillianta had never let herself think of Lorela in any other way than *dear* sister Lorela.

And since that glittering evening she had turned to fashion in a way that astonished everyone at Arminell. Even dear sister Lorela observed her clothes. She never rode out, not even to vestry almsgivings, but what she was exquisitely attired. Style is as style does, she had learned, and not a moment too soon.

Today she wore a six-guinea riding habit, with two riding hoops – a breathtaking forty shillings the pair from Blundell's in London. The material was princetta, plum colour, offset by the Regency furred hat. She chose the latter because of its daring gold hatband, not because it signified a more staid, less fashion-conscious epoch. The safeguard offered to her by the maids this morning – the weather was hardly high summer – she rejected. 'I'm no farmer's wife heading for market,' she told them, 'to need accessory skirts against the mud.' Also, the rough outer protector would spoil her figure, even if her object was no one more interesting than Cas Deeping, in Maidborough. A bachelor too intent on mercantile pursuits, he was nonetheless a young man of good family. And *dear* sister Lorela had twice singled Mr Deeping out for attention lately – all the more reason to exploit a particular absence.

She had seen the horseman, and reined in, intrigued. The horseman reversed, took the larger leap into the great field they called Long Tom, and cantered easily down to the river, making for the tumulus on the far bank.

She smiled, clicked Jamestown to a walk, and headed him towards the low weir by the mill. Cas Deeping could wait, and for quite some time too, if she happened to encounter Carradine – accidently, of course.

Carradine saw her come. He had been riding almost half an hour before the Astell girl showed against the dark wood's outline. He was pleased, for he might otherwise have been obliged to ride over during the afternoon and leave his calling card. That would mean a delay of three whole days, at the end of which the Astells would send over their card to Hoddinott. Then would ensue the tiresome ritual of announced arrivals, a returned greeting, then the invitation to afternoon tea a week ahead . . . three weeks! Who could endure propriety, when life burned so fast?

For show, he could not resist taking a couple of leaps, then moved down the bank and headed upstream to the vantage point of the old tumulus. From there the eye could see half the Maidborough Hundred, including the grounds of Arminell.

He was there, silhouetted against the light, when Brillianta rode up and made the modest turn to avoid him, predictably taking the lower path. She gave Carradine the opportunity of recognising her presence by putting Jamestown through low brush. The noise made Carradine look down. Brillianta could have wished for somewhat better light.

'Good morning, m'lady,' Carradine called, putting his mount slowly at the slope. 'Do I have the good fortune of meeting my neighbour and acquaintance Miss Astell?'

'Forgive me, sir, but I . . .' She paused, letting her hauteur ease as he approached. 'Carradine? Where on earth do you journey so early, and through here?'

He noted her surprise. So she had not heard of his misfortune, anyway not all. He reined alongside, and fell in with her walking pace.

152

'I am temporarily at Hoddinott, Miss Brillianta, by courtesy of Golding. I have left Carradine Manor for a month or so.'

'Why, sir! I had no idea you were afflicted by the sea vapours! How ever do you manage when your vessels require your inspection?'

He looked hard at her, but she was all innocence. Depths to this one, unlike that Lorela, who was shallow as a pilgrim's shell.

'I have too few ships to bother me, Miss Brillianta. I was eager to pay my attentions to your father. This happy meeting serves my purpose faster, and if I may say, more pleasingly.'

'Sir Edward would be delighted to receive you at Arminell,' she gave back. Words remembered were foes, never friends. 'And even though the road to Maidborough lies through Arminell, I am grateful for your protection.'

He breathed easier. To have offered his company as protection might have given offence, implying that Sir Edward was unduly lax. Her assumption that his company served a gentlemanly purpose suited his aim.

'And I for yours, Miss Astell.'

'Mine, sir?' She laughed, moving Jamestown more confidently as the path left the muddy riverbank. 'A lady protect a gentleman?'

She favoured his riding coat, though it was hardly the most fashionable, being free of cut-ins and made of stout russet worsted. But his dark colouring, his cream buckskin breeches, his curt manner, made her wonder about possibilities. There must surely be a way to have him meet Father almost immediately, to ensure further company.

'Seeing that I trespass on your province, m'lady.' They were on Arminell property, and he the interloper.

'I shall guard you against all comers, sir,' she quipped, and instantly remembered. All comers – the cry of pugilists before barefisted fights. The prize-fights, for a purse of money, were held illegally near some magistracy boundary, the quicker to move the contest and continue with impunity should authorities intervene. The crowds had recently come through Maidborough for one such – where some fighter called Rendell had won against fantastic odds . . . *and lost some gentleman a fortune!* She gave no sign. Did dear sister Lorela know of this?

153

'Your generosity does you great credit, Miss Brillianta. I hope to trespass even further. I hear Sir Edward has new stable stock.'

She smiled inwardly, but showed offence. 'Is that how you please a lady, Carradine? Say that you admire her father's horses?'

'It is all I am permitted to say, to my deep regret.'

Promising, she told herself, and they rode on towards Maidborough. She was quite put out when the spire of its great wool church rose from the treetops and the smoke showed they were nearing the town. In spite of urgent reflection she was unable to think of a way of substituting Carradine for the ineffably dull Castor Deeping. She managed the next best thing, which was to promise to mention Carradine's wish to visit the Astell stablery to Sir Edward.

By the time he delivered her at the residence of Mr Deeping's sister, Brillianta had already decided on the Bavarian pelisse robe, the one with the double blush pink trimming *en tablier* from shoulder to skirt hem, with the most extravagant feather adornment to a velvet beret . . .

Carradine rode on, satisfied for the moment. One more day in the wretched hovel of Hoddinott, and he might resume the life he deserved.

Ven Carmichael wakened stiff and aching. He had been sorely bitten during the night and roused without his usual sense of expectancy.

The shed was familiar, with its floor of beaten earth and warped planking. Mehala had called him, knocking gently and leaving hot shaving water outside. He shaved clumsily with his lancet, honing the instrument on its stone. He was brought a bowl of oats and milk, bread and a piece of cheese, with a dish of tea to which milk and sugar was added in the growing fashion.

He made himself as presentable as he could, and went to knock at the schoolhouse. Miss Gould came, flustered.

'Good morning, Doctor. I . . . I . . .' She glanced for help. Mehala joined her.

'Good morning, Ven. I think it would be wisest if we talked in the classroom, rather than in Miss Gould's house.'

'Thank you,' he concurred gravely. 'I shall go round.'

They admitted him through the main door, conscious that the ceremony was visible from Market Square. People were already gathering.

Miss Gould sat. Ven perched awkwardly on one of the small desks, Mehala by the window.

'I can't thank you enough, Miss Gould, for your kindness in taking us in last night. Without you, I fear it would have been the stars and hedgerows.'

Miss Gould pinked at his gratitude. 'I could do no less, Doctor. I am dismayed by your ill-fortune . . .' She failed to continue.

Mehala came to her rescue. 'It would be injudicious for Miss Gould's charity to extend to a second night, Ven. She has already compromised herself by favouring us as it is.'

'I acknowledge that, Miss Gould, and thank you.'

'But what will you do?'

Matilda Gould was in her fifth decade. These were two young people at the start of life, crossed lovers even, should she dare to think that far. And the prospect of Doctor Carmichael's leaving Sealandings was truly terrible.

'There seems no staying in Sealandings, Miss Gould. I have no money. Mehala gave up the chance of a secure position at – '

'We are not destitute yet, Matilda,' Mehala interrupted, reluctant to have her past offers revealed even to the schoolmistress. 'Many Sealandings folk owe Doctor Carmichael. They might be glad to see him leave. Their debts and guilt would vanish at one blow!'

'There's the money from Mrs Prothero!' Miss Gould remembered eagerly. 'I was urged most particularly to pay you half a crown, Doctor!'

Mehala felt herself pulled apart. To accept money from Mary Prothero, Ven's childhood friend, was nothing more than subjection. To be a vassal, of Mary Prothero? With Ven the fief? Yet Ven had operated on Prothero's arm. She recalled angrily how Ven had not been offered so much as a drink of water, let alone been paid a farthing. Mary Prothero owed him. Wasn't this school money simply part of his fee rendered by different route?

'Thank you, but no, Miss Gould,' she heard Ven say calmly. 'The money was meant to assist the children. I would be wrong to take any. I should have told you my opinion on the matter earlier.'

155

'But perhaps – ' The schoolmistress searched Mehala's face, guessing how wrong this would seem. 'Perhaps it is acceptable as payment due for your past services to the children? I see not the slightest moral objection, Doctor.'

'I'm afraid I do, Miss Gould. I thank you.'

She was almost in tears. 'Then where shall you go?'

He thought a moment. 'I have patients to see in Sealandings. Then I suppose I shall head away, perhaps to St Edmundsbury, or Norwich, Southwold, I don't know. Find some temporary work as an assistant to some busy doctor.'

'And you, Mehala?' Miss Gould asked, frantic with worry. 'I might be able to offer lodging – '

'Why, Mehala shall come with me, of course,' Ven answered, surprised. Then he coloured, realising the extent of his assumption, and began to stammer. 'That is, I intend to ask Mehala if she would oblige me by accepting my present adversity in hopes . . .'

'There is no question, Matilda.' Mehala was smiling. Here was her answer, plainer than his words. 'I thank you sincerely, but shall go.'

They left then, Ven listing patients he had yet to see in Sealandings, and Mehala waving to Matilda Gould and thinking hard about where next they might lay a head.

Thalia De Foe swept into Shalamar like an empress, and paused in horror. Mrs Trenchard, curtseying before the great lady, was terrified at the calamity that had come so swiftly. Outside, Trenchard stood forlornly with his old dog.

'This?' Thalia demanded. 'This *ruin* is Shalamar?'

'So it is, m'lady.'

Willoughby was already exhausted by the unwonted business. The Doctor's eviction should have been the end of the matter. Instead, this troublesome lady, his master's demanding spouse, kept on and on. He had ridden in from Maidborough after a four o'clock start, the day after the greatest of storms, to please her. And she insultingly kept him waiting three hours.

'Are you responsible?' Her eyes glittered with malice.

'Firm orders from Sir Fellows, m'lady, to the effect that – '

'*To the effect,* sir?' Thalia screeched in sudden fury. 'To *what* effect, sir?'

'To leave it alone, m'lady,' Willoughby said bluntly.

Willoughby was an old man who had served the De Foes most of his life. All was not smooth between master and lady, but experience reminded him it would be highly dangerous to express any bias. Later, in his quiet house in Maidborough's Wyre Lane, he would rest with a drop of Portugal and forget this traumatic episode. Why she interfered, when common sense was best served by leaving the Doctor and his doxy strictly alone, Heaven alone knew.

'Why, sir?' Thalia fumed at the old fool's impertinence in leaving her nothing to aim at save her husband's impotence. The realisation that the ancient idiot was unswervingly loyal to Fellows worsened her temper still more.

'That is not for me to enquire, m'lady.'

She entered the hall, and rounded on him in rage. 'Was it not your duty to *enquire* whether to stir your stumps, sir? And work to your master's benefit? Or are you and your ignorant lackeys too busy wining and dining on your unearned commission to bother at all?'

'M'lady, every instruction I execute to the letter – '

'Look at the place! Cobwebbed, dank! Mould everywhere! Holes in every wall! Dust! Utterly derelict!'

She stood on the bottom stair of the once-grand staircase. 'Just *look*, idiot! Broken windows! Did it not enter your stupid head to procure workmen to redecorate? Mend gutters? Deal with the windows?'

'I was instructed to the contrary, ma'am.'

'You abrogate all responsibility! I see!' Her gaze fell on the old lady trembling a few yards away. 'You?'

'Please, m'lady, I'm Mrs Trenchard. That yonder's my husband. I keep here for the Doctor and Miss Mehala.'

Thalia De Foe was silent a moment. Mehala, the sea witch who had created such a stir. Doctor Carmichael, who was so well regarded – only by the ignorant, of course, who knew no better than to trust a young country sawbones.

'Show me the house, Trenchard. Follow, Willoughby.'

With the old lady wheezing ahead with a Norfolk lantern, Willoughby carrying a pig's-fat candle burning smokily, Thalia began a tour of Shalamar. She held a silk handkerchief to her face against the dust which rose in clouds as they passed from room to room and along corridors. Several times Thalia halted, calling Mrs Trenchard back to explain what use certain rooms and closets once had, but it proved hard for the servant to remember.

'That was in the old times, m'lady,' Mrs Trenchard gasped, breathless at the pace. 'I fear I recall little of who lived here between the time of the old master and Doctor. They sailed oversea. I served only the old master, God rest his soul. It was beautiful then, a score or more servants.' Even in tribulation Mrs Trenchard managed a reminiscent smile. 'Filled with sunlight, m'lady! Night seemed day!'

'These rooms have been inhabited, Trenchard.'

The old lady shuffled through the doorway into a decaying panelled room. Its plaster flaked badly. Rainwater had seeped in, stained the sills and adjacent walls. Mould grew in a ceiling corner. A ramshackle truckle bed, tidily made, stood against one wall away from the window's draught. A screen of old sewn blankets had been erected by it on a wooden frame to offer seclusion and stem the chill. This part was clean, the sheet bright linen. A cracked pot stood on a red brick, holding a few fresh flowers.

'The Doctor's room, m'lady. Mehala is – was – down the wing.'

They made their way along the threadbare carpet, the light flickering. Drapes and tapestries sagged on the walls, though here and there a start had been made to clean and align the hangings. One, in the corridor opposite the Doctor's shoddy room, had been beaten and was partly restored, its colours startlingly bright even in the dour light. The old housekeeper opened a door at the end of the corridor.

'This is Mehala's room, m'lady. It was a maid-of-all's, in the old master's time.'

Willoughby discreetly remained outside, passing his candlestick to Mrs Trenchard for Thalia to have more illumination.

The room was small, swept, the walls washed free of grime to hand height. A simple pallet lay on the floor along one wall. The window was begrimed on the outside, but the interior was clean and the panes showed a glimpse of the sea and the harbour's South Mole.

'A pallet? No bed?'

'There's but the Doctor's truckle, m'lady. Mehala said the pallet sufficed.'

Thalia looked about. Sparse, not to say spartan. Well, well. Had morality made a brief appearance in Sealandings, flourished here against all odds? Or was this Mehala stranger than she seemed? Surely not. No woman casts her reputation on the waters of rude opinion, taking up residence to serve some penniless surgeon in a gaunt ruin like Shalamar, unless she has some scheme. Or unless she was driven by desire. Yet Mehala slept with only a thin pallet between her and unyielding draughty surfaces, while the Doctor had the truckle. The girl had a view of the sea. The Doctor's room had view only of meadowland, and part of the garden.

An intriguing mystery. Certainly, it was impossible for a man to harbour a woman under his roof without tumbling her. Morality or no morality, Nature went her own way. Life proved that. They must surely have . . . Her mind closed the subject. There would be time to think that over at Milton Hall. For now, Carradine was her problem. He would look grand at Shalamar, once it was restored. And it was nearer to Milton Hall than Carradine Manor. She would convince Fellows of the need to refurbish and, if need be, rebuild.

'Willoughby. Outside.'

'Yes, ma'am.'

The garden dazzled as they left the gloom. Thalia walked to a position commanding a view of the front façade, and turned to inspect it.

'The vermin here is indescribable, Willoughby.'

'Indeed, ma'am. I did draw the master's attention –'

She cut him short. 'If I want comment from you, Willoughby, be sure I shall demand it! Until then, stay silent.' She stood looking. 'Rats in every nook. Gales through every wall. Plaster crumbling, boards rotten. Windows sag, everywhere open to the elements. The stonework leans, the brickwork powdered almost as it stands.' She waited, then rounded on the agent, blazing. 'Well, sir? Have you nothing to say? No excuses for your incompetence? I tell you now, sir, I shall not endure this insufferable penalty you have imposed on my family's possessions one minute longer!'

'Yes, ma'am. What is it you wish me to do?'

'On pain of instant dismissal, you will restore the building!'

The old man stared at her, appalled. 'Restore, ma'am? But the expense, the very magnitude – '

'Work daunts a bungler, Willoughby! No task daunts a doer. Start immediately. How soon might it be completed? A week? A month?'

Willoughby was thunderstruck. The Trenchards stood apart, awaiting their fate. The agent gaped at the façade, the grounds. His voice trembled.

'Ma'am, Shalamar cannot be restored within a twelvemonth. To establish one wing, with kitchen services and rooms for family habitation, would take two seasons. There's the paint barrels, stone-workers, carpenters, shipments of materials . . .' he petered out under her glacial stare.

'You confess to yet more incompetence than you have so far revealed, Willoughby?'

'Any builder in the Kingdom would say the same. It is – was – a great mansion, m'lady. Its immensity means it will require time, labour and enormous expenditure, always assuming – '

'Willoughby,' Thalia De Foe halted him, pointing imperiously. 'Look there – the new flowerbed. Its circular form is at once dainty, and most skilfully executed. This old couple, in spite of their decrepitude, have embellished this overgrown garden with a rondel of beauty. So work *can* be done, as long as there's will!'

'Please, m'lady.' Mrs Trenchard stepped forward, eager to please. 'That was Mehala's.'

'The flowerbed?' Thalia gazed at the flowers encircling the central rose cuttings.

'Yes, m'lady. She worked mortal hard, almost before any other duty.'

'Did she, indeed!'

Thalia walked slowly round the bed, the servants following. Concentric rings, each small group of plants different, species by species, as if marking out . . . Her brow cleared. A Flora's Dial, each plant opening at each succeeding hour. The lovers' clock, an eternity ring in blossom. She stepped aside, to look up at the house. The window directly above the flowerbed was the bedroom with the truckle, the Doctor's. So. Mehala ran even deeper than she had supposed.

'Thank you, Trenchard. Willoughby, report to Milton Hall with

160

a full estimate for the immediate restoration of Shalamar by late afternoon.'

The agent drew breath to advise her of the impossibility of the task, and thought better of it.

'And Willoughby.' She indicated the flowerbed with a sharp glance. 'Get rid of that hideous monstrosity forthwith. Set these two dotards about it.'

'Yes, ma'am.'

She nodded for the agent to summon her barouche, and stood waiting impatiently for its approach. Carradine would be thrilled at her decision to repossess Shalamar and install him within. She grew weak at the thought of his forcible expressions of pleasure. She allowed herself to be driven from the grounds in a gratifying silence that worried the coachman all the way to Milton Hall.

15

Hunterfield's mare Betsy was the most reliable phenomenon in the Eastern Hundreds, he sometimes thought. Today she would need be.

He rode out in a harsh dawn along the rough road towards Sealandings from Lorne House as far as the bridge over the River Affon. There he turned seaward along the devastated riverbank and headed for the hard. The bridge was mostly swept away downstream. Simple Tom accompanied, following behind at a chain distance, the safe gap between trailing riders. Hunterfield rode slowly, grimly inspecting the damage as he went. He was an hour reaching the harbour within the South Mole, and reined Betsy in.

'God save us, Tom. Would you see that mess?'

Several houses were damaged. He could see at least three roofs tumbled in. The storm's swathe of destruction had started upon the harbourside cottages, haphazardly smashing walls, chimneys and roofs as it went.

'Isn't that *Dander*, Tom?'

A vessel lay partly submerged. Full settled, it no longer rose and fell with the waves. Hunterfield had received word earlier of two shipwrecks, but had envisaged them farther from shore.

'God, the sea's innocent as a maid. I expected the storm to be still busy, somehow. How far, Tom?'

The dumb groom stood in his stirrups. He weighed the distance, and spread his hands quickly, four times. Hunterfield nodded. Simple Tom was coast and country, and used only old measures. Both hands four times, forty. But goads, each one a yard and a half. So *Dander* lay forty goads, sixty yards, from the hard. The ketch was done for, he guessed, though Whitehanger shipyard might effect a mend – if, for once, both townships could share a firkin of friendship's ale instead of dislike. He sighed. As if life wasn't difficult enough.

'Squire, sir, if it please.' A youth ran up, breathing hard.

'Yes?'

'I bring word from Watermillock, Squire. The Widow Maderley says as the sea dykes be broached a mile from the tide-mill.'

'What has been done?'

'Her men, and some charcoal-burners, be there. The tide be fast turning, Squire.'

'How wide the pierce?'

'Please, Squire, two chains in one place, and one chain in a second. The mill meadow is under sea, sir.'

'Very well. Return, saying I shall come.'

The lad set off towards Watermillock. *Very well!* He should have said *More calamity!* Hunterfield stirred Betsy into a walk northwards to the harbour proper. A fisherman approached.

'Squire, sir. Good morning. Churcher, of *Dander*.'

'Good morning, Churcher. A sorry piece of weather. What other vessel was lost?'

'A Revenue vessel, sir, nobbut a hoy, single master she.'

'Whereabouts?'

'Off Whitehanger, sir. From the *Hunter*. 'Tis said two souls were lost.'

'God rest them, then.'

'Amen.' Churcher glanced up at the rider. 'Squire, sir. It seems *Dander* be wholly done. I went out to her at early low water, sir. Her back be broken, and her foundered.'

'How many men will suffer, Churcher, besides yourself?'

'Me and three, Squire. One's Hol Raffin, whose limb went in the saving, sir.'

'Raffin? Who dances the morris fool?'

'Verily. Doctor went out in the storm, cut him.'

The Squire reined in. They were alongside the Donkey and Buskin, by the alleyway where flint cobbles led up to the tavern yard where the coaches turned. He gazed at men collecting fallen debris, pantiles, sections of guttering and plaster.

More mouths to feed in the Raffin family cast upon the parish. He could not recall whether Raffin owned his cottage, or if he owed weekly rent.

'You got the Doctor safe? I commend you, Churcher.'

The man avoided the Squire's eyes, and spat expertly downwind. 'I were ashore, loike, sir.'

'Carmichael went aboard alone?'

Churcher's attitude was story enough. 'It were mortal rough, Squire, the worst tempest in memory. The Sir Roger, he come up a-sudden from easterly . . .'

Hunterfield sat Betsy, thinking. Some reward might be in order, though it would be improper to take a direct hand. Seafarers could be counted on to see justice done, even to a leech who was doing no more than trying to make his mark among these dour Sealandings folk. He dismissed the problem from his mind, and nudged the mare on.

'I'm inspecting damage, Churcher,' he said by way of dismissal. 'See my agents in perhaps three days. I will endeavour to assist you. Mark that I cannot replace your vessel, mind.'

'No, Squire. Thank you, Squire.'

Hunterfield reached the harbour centre, and swung in among the houses, Simple Tom behind. This was his township ride, first the northern aspect as far as the cattle market's broad field, working back seawards towards the Goat and Compass, then south among the fisher cottages until he had cornered the square, finishing at the church. It would be expected that he call in and pray a thankful deliverance.

'Who comes here, from Sealandings?' Carradine asked Lucy.

The prostitute made a moue as she dressed. His hour was gone, the sandglass showed.

'Whore, I asked you a question.'

She was in a sulk, though God alone knew why. Hadn't he been considerate? Hadn't he promised to give her extra, next time? And hadn't he sent for her by name, the supreme accolade that any strumpet prized? The bitch always had been temperamental, ever since he started singling her out. He'd been too kind, as always.

He propped himself up on one elbow to watch her dress.

'You can be replaced. Shall I supplant you by Phoebe?'

'She still has a merkin!' Lucy shot back in temper. 'No gentleman demeans himself using a whore with a belly wig from the small pox, that I do know!'

He laughed in spite of himself. Women always settled on the smallest significance, however large the problem.

'Who comes here, Lucy?'

'You think nothing of me, Rad.' She had extorted the right to use his name, in sexual heat once. In privacy, she held to this right however tumultuous their coupling and whatever the consequences. A gentleman could not withdraw a permission once given. 'Yet I serve you better than any woman.'

He lay back and thought, reaching for his glass and sipping it so his tongue smarted. What allies had he, when all was said and done? He listed them, seeing the face of each in his mind's eye.

Thalia De Foe, of course, she of the furious temper and long plans. Where the hell her husband Fellows De Foe – no mean name, with London connections and his new banker friends of Threadneedle Street – figured in her ambitions, God knew. But she had paled lately. Too demanding, entwining him like an octopus, never leaving save with petulance and fits of jealous rage.

There was Barbara Tyll, the housekeeper at Carradine Manor. Steady, warm. He found himself smiling. Women gave pleasure, yes. The one he always came back to, especially during troubles, was Tyll. Young still, and married – her husband had bid as toll-farmer some moons since. Another smile was Tyll's strict propriety. With her, it was the locked door, the desperate pleas for silence as his orgasm shuddered them both and rattled the bedstead, her hot palm capping his mouth as he expended in her. And afterwards, her meticulous search of the bedroom for the slightest trace of evidence, the lotions to conceal her bruises, the high bertha to hide his teethmarks on her neck. Yes, Tyll was the still lagoon within the reef. Always discreet, sure, trustworthy. And, with her woman's perversity, always refusing to admit her craving for him. With Tyll, lust had to be cloaked in primness, never admitting that it was sheer naked passion, savage gratifying of a carnal appetite.

Judith Blaker? New of course, without much to commend her except a giddy ambition. He had had women like her before, all schemes for taking command to the exclusion of all other females. They never lasted – though this one did seem to have a brain, a kind of strong reticence that made her stand out.

Then, to complete the list, there was that star of Georgian London, heroine of a hundred supper tables, salons and gaming tables, Mrs Isabella Worthington. Who, from being his mainstay at every address between Blackfriars and Shepherd's Market, had railed worse than any tempest, simply because he had ravished that Hussar's wife from the cavalry barracks. God, he couldn't even remember the incident! Who ever could? You'd need a secretary to keep track of every shirt you changed, every bawd tossed, every plate consumed. The truth was, women were impossible creatures.

Lucy? He'd not forgotten her. She was standing gazing down at him. Pleasing, a real little worker at the giggling trade, as capable of flaunting dominance as whimpering in subjection. For Lucy, no passion was too exulting, no abasement too degrading. She gave sexual satisfaction, utter repletion. Jealous of the rest of her sisters, but that was only usual. She was a blessing, if that thought was not blasphemous.

'What are you thinking, Rad? Of some grand mare you ride on silken saddles?' She meant the 'venus gloves', contraceptives used by fashionable ladies; woven silk inside a piece of gut. Supposedly impervious to a man's seed, each one needed prolonged soaking before use. Whores scorned such aids.

'You, Lucy.' The lie came without conscious thought. 'Remembering how first I had you.'

She smiled, swinging her dress slowly. 'I remember. You in your cups, surprised to see me still there next morning.' She laughed, throwing her head back. 'I lied to Mistress Wren. I told her you insisted I sleep with you until dawn, but you hadn't.'

'Minx!' He laughed. One old lie always earned two afresh. 'So I paid twice for half work?'

'I've repaid you since!' she shot back, mood changing swiftly to anger.

'Then pay me anew, Lucy. Who comes here, from Sealandings?'

'You'll ask for me again, as always?'

'Would I seek any other girl in Two Cotts?'

'Thomas Parker,' Lucy said. 'Brother of the common stabler. But concealed always, for fear of his brother the Methody. Drovers, who sojourn at Sealandings. Lack, the old fisherman – a real pest he be . . .'

'No tiddlers, Lucy. *Names*, silly bitch.'

'Quilter, the gentleman from London, the gamester. Once, Sir

166

Jeremy Pacton, a lovely lad he, two yards long, smells sweet as a May Meadow. Codgie the longshoreman.'

'Prothero?' Carradine asked suddenly. 'Temple, the blacksmith? Reverend Baring? Hunterfield? Maderley of Watermillock? Charles Golding? Fellows De Foe?'

He ran through the list of best-known people in Sealandings, getting denials. Except for Ben Fowler, landlord of the Goat and Compass. Little surprise.

'There's Doctor Carmichael,' she finished hopefully. 'He examines us, despite the religionists who tell him no.'

She told her gossip. 'Mr Bettany the Quaker, Reverend Baring and Robert Parker combine against Carmichael, to stay his attendance here and at the school.'

This was the only news she could give. Of no importance, however it seemed to stick in his mind.

He commanded her to bring his clothes. She watched him dress, replenishing his glass twice before his Anglesea hat was in place, his feet stamped into the half-Bluchers, burrail collar exactly adjusted.

'I have a task, Lucy.' He usually slipped a half-sovereign into her hand at this point, but not now, to her disappointment.

'Yes, Rad?'

'Keep observation on Carradine Manor, in any way you can. Anything – movement, hirings, any baggings of servants, rumours, talk or trade. Understand?'

'Yes, Rad.' She was thrilled by the charge. It was a responsibility, in a part of his life she had never before been allowed to enter. 'Where shall I send word of it, darling?'

He swallowed his pride at her presumption. The Devil drove, so needs must.

'If it seems important, send to Hoddinott, by any means you may. If not, keep it. I shall come every few days.'

He ignored her glint of triumph. Pride was the costliest of all commodities. He had no coin for any these days.

'Kiss me a good day, Rad.'

He hesitated. The tiresome request had a hint of command. Paid servants worked sweeter, it was said. In the circumstances, he bent and placed his mouth upon hers for a breath, then shoved her roughly aside and flung from the door leaving her smiling breathlessly in the room.

'*Meklis!*'

Judith Blaker was furious at the man who stood before her in the lane. He was carrying a pedlar's ped a-back. To a casual observer, it was a blameless meeting of a wandering street hawker trying to sell to a serving woman.

'I repeat, hold your tongue!' She lapsed into English, seeing no one was within earshot. 'I have chance of an excellent position at Carradine Manor, with the *guero*, the gentry. You will obey me exactly!'

'*Ava*,' the man agreed sullenly.

'Give me no *chingaro*, Bellin, no fight back. You hear?'

'*Ava chiricli*,' the pedlar muttered.

'Don't you little-henbird me, *cooroboshno*!' Judith spat the word for fighting cock with spite, making the pedlar flinch. 'You will *luvvo* and *luripen* for the family.'

'*Ava, Chovahani*.' The man's eyes glittered at the mention of money and loot.

Judith lowered her voice in anger. 'Don't call me witch! Ever!'

'*Ava*, Judith.'

'Very well. Stay ready for signs. Go now, *chal*.'

'*Ja Develehi*.' He gave the ancient parting courtesy, to go with God.

'And you stay with God. *Az Develhi*.' Judith saw his dejection and added kindly, '*Mang, prala, mang*,' calling him brother, jokingly telling him to beg on.

The man brightened. Judith made to go on, thinking that men were children, mischievous but easily subdued with firmness. After which a little flirtation worked wonders.

'*Kushto, chiricli*,' the pedlar said. '*Kusho si for manqui*. I am content.'

And you had better be, Judith thought, gesturing him away. For I am now on my way to riches and power. Help, or be crushed. She walked with becoming modesty, and gave a pious curtsey at St Edmund's lych-gate, earning Reverend Baring's approval as he stood eyeing the weather from the rectory porch.

16

Perrigo stared at the dead animal, gripped by a fear he had only known once before.

'What is it, Pel?' the herdsman asked. He was a youngster, fen country born and bred, but inexperienced.

'You touched him, booy?'

'No, Pel.' The youth became scared too, backing away. The stockman fidgeted nervously, staring. 'Be it same as the others, Pel?'

'It seems so.' Perrigo looked along the ditch where the cow lay. It had struggled in blind bewilderment, slavering its last as it reached the hawthorn and sloe hedge, tried to blunder through, then succumbed in its terminal sickness. It had died either of the disease, or from drowning as the torrential rains swelled the brook. 'Have you seen the others?'

The young herdsman was puzzled. 'You saw them yourself, Pel,' he said. 'When we drove them from the shippons into Short Bob.'

Perrigo rounded on him, yelling, 'I know, you ninny! And I told you which field, dolt! Answer me straight, booy, or Is'll have you bagged straight off!'

'No, Pel, not since we put them to pasture,' the youth stammered. He had never seen Pel Perrigo so fazed before. And the beast lying in the ditch was somehow different from the others. Many were drowned in the flood waters. This lay unnatural, neck extended, head back raised as if under terrible tension, eyes a weird mustard colour, feverish even in death.

'Go over to Short Bob field, booy. Don't enter. Tell me if any lie thus. Come at a run.'

'Roit, Pel.' The youth set off at a lumbering trot.

Perrigo thought a moment, called after him, 'An' booy! Call in the men, y'hear?'

The young herdsman raised an arm to acknowledge, gathered his frock-smock with his other hand, and leaped the ditch. Perrigo stifled a further shout. He realised he ought to have sent the lad round by the path. Worse, some of the farmhands were loth to drink small beer, saving the allowance as money. Which set them drinking from ditches, the cattle troughs, or even sharing the cattle water from the carts he dispatched on dry days from Calling Farm.

Though what did he know of the sickness vapours, or miasmas, all those invisible powers that were magic itself, which laid waste worse than in any Bible story? Even educated men knew nothing about cattle plagues, how they came, whether or not they were spread by some demon that stalked the countryside unseen.

He shivered, staring down at the poor animal. It was a prime Suffolk. The Polled Suffolk was the prize of all England, famed for its short leg, its broad round body, its speed in fattening for the butcher's shambles, and renowned for its quick weight gain compared to the dull polled cattle of Norfolk, which had lately begun to supersede the middle-horned breed.

The beast had died bravely, struggling to regain its herd. The Suffolk was supposed to be descended from the Galloway, though its 'snake head' was a distinctive feature highly prized among estate breeders. Heavy of belly, narrow of loin, with its peculiar squarish udder so crowded with knotted puffs of milk veins. At once beautiful and wondrous, Perrigo loved the Suffolk more than any waggoner his horses. This one he recognised. A special favourite, red and white, with a tail he'd often pulled in play. This lovely animal would smile when he twisted her tail gently, joking that he'd soon put her under the bull . . . Calamity never came alone, for the master was ill, with his arm all of a swell since leathering that young stallion, Doctor Carmichael bleeding him or whatever. He came to, hearing a distant shout, and saw the herdsman. He'd climbed a stile for view, and was waving his cloth hat slowly to and fro.

Pel Perrigo's heart fell even further. More calamity, out in Short Bob field where the Suffolks had been herded this dawn. Resignedly he flourished his own hat in acknowledgement and carried the bad news to the big house.

Prothero glowered at Carmichael. His mood was not lightened by the girl Mehala. That she came at all was infuriating. Even in his debilitated condition – that idiot sawbones well-nigh fetched him to death's door – he felt the familiar hunger for her. The bitch knew it, too, flaunting herself with that cunning windswept air.

'What, crocus?'

'Shhh, dear!' Mary Prothero smiled weakly, hoping to disarm offence at her husband's abuse. 'Doctor has come to see how you are!'

'A brief call, I trust, Mrs Prothero.'

'I'm so thankful you did visit. Mr Prothero felt a night pain along his arm.'

'He kept cool, less feverish?'

'Why, yes! Is that all right?'

'Very good, Mrs Prothero.' Carmichael explained to Mehala, 'Patients who have had suppurations lanced to draw pus sometimes experience a pain, almost as if the swelling had not diminished. We don't know why. You remember Hol Raffin? He soon will feel a pain in his absent limb. It is as if the amputated limb still remained, as a kind of phantom. That is indeed what we call – '

'Here, leech,' Prothero growled. 'No talk of amputation!'

'No reason to fear. Your arm seems to be bettering well enough.'

'Thank goodness!' Mary exclaimed. 'Please to leave instructions about the dressings. Are there lotions, poultices, perhaps, that I might – ?'

Carmichael glanced askance at Mehala, back to Mary, then examined the incision lines and the drains from Prothero's arm. The yellow pus was seeping still. The bandaging was thoroughly stained. He moved aside with Mehala and Mary.

'Here, quack!' Prothero called after them. 'No whispering in corners, either! Not in this house, while I live and breathe!'

Mehala drew a sharp breath, but Ven's mouth set, and she said nothing. Mary flushed slightly. Mehala was close to retorting that but for Carmichael Prothero would be attending his burial instead of shouting abuse.

'I'm sorry, Ven,' Mary said quietly. 'As you see, he is gaunt, bone weary. He isn't himself.'

'Two days, Mary, or three if he seems too tired by his first exertions. Not too much food. Keep him to broths, fish, a few

171

vegetables. No alcoholic drink. What does he normally have for breakfast?'

'Mr Prothero is a creature of habit, Ven. Always breakfast cakes, collared meat, spiced potted meat – his favourite – a cold joint and whitened bread, broiled kidneys, poached eggs. He isn't one for breakfast fruits, saying those are for infants. He has several breakfast breads, and a few fried tansies.'

'That is excessive, Mary, for his present condition. Give but a single broth, and perhaps tea. You can raise him towards the end of the day, but no work.'

'He has pressing mercantile matters, Ven,' Mary said anxiously. 'Can he see those through? Carradine comes later, to arrange the transfer of Carradine Manor and our entry there.'

Carmichael tried to conceal his surprise, nodding gravely. 'I should try to postpone that Mary. Slow for three days, is the rule.' He smiled at Mehala. 'You see now why old doctors called the discharged matter "laudable pus", since its effluence begins recovery.'

He opened his bag, and took out some capsules.

'I shall leave these for you, Mary. I'm afraid I cannot give you more, for I . . . I run short, unfortunately. But you may keep what I have. The travelling apothecary can make up more. You have an apothecary box, I trust?'

'Certainly, Ven!' Mary ushered them to a tall court cupboard on which stood a mahogany box, polished to a gleam. She opened the lid, showing compartments each containing a rectangular stoppered bottle. 'It is stocked very well, I hope, from Gascoyne's at Maidborough. He calls every Lady Day.'

'These tablets are valerian, with two other compounds. I shall write the prescription for you.'

He took out his travelling inkhorn and quilled slowly. He smiled, shook sand from the shaker when the paper threatened to scroll, and blew until the writing dried.

'One day those famed metal-tipped quills will eventually reach us, as the iron-masters of the Midlands keep promising. Imagine –pens that need neither goose nor sand!'

He put away his accoutrements and nodded a goodbye to Prothero.

'Please, Ven,' Mary asked, reluctant to see him go. 'Might I send for you if need be? Only, one hears of so many people suffering relapse after surgical operations . . .'

Ven hesitated, made as if to speak, but instead only nodded and took his leave. Mrs Perrigo glided ahead through the hall. Mehala hung back to speak with Mary.

'Mrs Prothero, might I trouble you for the fee, please?'

She spoke softly, and only when the door had closed behind them. Ven Carmichael was talking with the housekeeper, indicating the boxes and chests ranked along the length of the hall, presumably for the expected move into Carradine Manor.

'The fee?' Mary Prothero looked blankly at Mehala, then coloured slowly. 'Money?'

'If you please, Mistress.' Mehala had to strengthen her resolve. It sounded shameful to demand money this way, but a service was a service. In better times, money could wait. For herself, she would not care, but the day was already into its allotted span. Evening would come, and rain again threatened. Tonight there would be no resting place, unless they had the wherewithall. Her temper flared at the woman's startled look.

'It might have escaped your notice, Mrs Prothero, but Doctor Carmichael wrote not with a fine goose quill, but a crow quill I foraged from the undergrowth. His ink I make from hedgerow berries and oak galls, without alum, for he can afford none. I collect his medicaments, from such plants as he instructs. He concocts them himself, late of a night, as long as there is taper enough to see by.'

Mary Prothero's gaze searched Mehala's intent expression as if looking for answer to an unspoken question. Mehala's voice whispered on.

'You see his hands, skinned and sore? He went to the *Dander*, sinking offshore in the tempest – even its owner deserted – to rescue the man Raffin. He escaped with his life but narrowly. Yet he came to succour your husband when every move causes him pain. He expects no reward, and demands none too.'

'I heard of his bravery,' Mary said, speaking with difficulty. 'Believe me, Miss Mehala, there is none in Sealandings more appreciative of his worthiness than this household.'

'Then pay him, Mistress Prothero,' Mehala said with low vehemence. 'For Sealandings, your splendid township, has rewarded him by turning him out of doors. He slept on bare earth in the schoolyard closet last night. Tonight he is less fortunate still.'

'He . . .' Mary Prothero paused, suddenly seeing in Mehala's features the answer to her unspoken question, and nodded slowly. 'I see. And you too were made vagabond with him? Or did you choose that particular destiny?'

Mehala felt her own colour rise at the implication. 'I'm aware that Doctor Carmichael used to be a friend of your esteemed family, Mistress Prothero. I shall speak frankly on account of it. Yes, I left Shalamar with him.'

'But you were sought after by the Golding household – and by Reverend Baring at the rectory.'

And your husband at Calling Farm, Mehala thought, but did not say so.

'The worst servants follow the best masters,' she quoted, to conceal her dislike of the direction the conversation was taking. 'All I ask now is that he is paid what he has earned. I do not seek charity. He would never allow me to beg, no matter how low fortune sinks. He would disapprove were he to learn that I made even this natural request.'

'Very well.' Mary glanced across to where the Doctor and Mrs Perrigo were talking by the vestibule, and gathered her dress. 'I shall make enquiry.'

She went inside, leaving the door slightly ajar. In the quiet, Mehala perceived Mrs Perrigo's low fervour and almost secretive words. She became aware of Mehala, and managed a quick smile across the hall.

'Your mistress has gone to see your master, Mrs Perrigo,' Mehala called in explanation.

The housekeeper resumed, with the Doctor listening carefully. Mehala also heard Prothero's voice, thick and angry.

'You think I'm made of money, wife? What the hell do you mean, when I'm still suffering from that quack's cuts and slicing?'

Mary Prothero's words were indistinct. Mehala made to move away from the door lest she be accused of eavesdropping, then stayed in growing anger.

'Money, for him and his slut? Not until I'm well – you tell him that! Then he can have his money, if I'm pleased to pay!'

174

More pleading from his wife made Mehala seethe in outrage at the indignity. For herself, she would not have cared. For Ven it was insufferable. The rich might rob from the poor with impunity, it seemed, while those who gave faithful service had to starve in hopeful expectation.

'You think I care, you stupid bitch?' Prothero was shouting. 'Didn't you hear what the stockmen just reported? That my animals are down with sickness, that I've lost three valuable breeding creatures? The fever spreading? Money flowing out of my herds with every hour that passes? And the storm damage, the floods! Yet you have the stupidity to come soliciting coppers for a pill pedlar? Get out, woman!'

Mehala composed herself, and walked to the vestibule. Mrs Perrigo saw her approach, and bobbed a farewell curtsey to the Doctor. She spoke no more when Mehala joined them, simply ushered them both quickly to the outer door and onto the driveway.

They made a formal goodbye, without undue haste. Carmichael and Mehala left side by side. Mehala said nothing about Calling Farm's failure to pay his fee, nor about Mrs Prothero, not daring to risk losing complete control at the injustice. Inwardly she was in a savage rage. She felt almost capable of killing to obtain justice. When they had gone some way and were almost among the cottages, and Ven remarked how well Prothero was recovering, she perversely began to laugh from anguish.

'I fail to see . . .' he said, worried he was being foolish.

She had to sit by the horse trough to recover, dabbing her eyes.

'I know you do, Ven dear,' she said, regaining control and straightening her skirt. 'Where next?'

'Two Cotts, Mehala.' He hesitated, looking across to where a group of drovers were strolling down towards the Goat and Compass. 'I would be greatly obliged if you were to wait, perhaps at the Donkey and Buskin, in the care of John Weaver, until I have completed my medical duties.'

'I must accompany you, Ven.'

'No, Mehala. Once seen in the vicinity, your reputation would be wholly lost. I can go with impunity. All know my position in Sealandings.'

The trace of bitterness was the first intimation of how deeply he felt. It was a revelation, and made her acquiesce, against her better judgement.

'You will be careful, Ven?' she asked, worried. 'I don't trust those holy gentleman who impugned your motives.'

'It's only words, Mehala. People are good, deep in their hearts. It is only circumstance that makes them forget.' He had recovered from that small despond, and now was his old self as he bade her a smiling goodbye.

'I shall be at Sarah Ann Weaver's,' she called anxiously.

With misgiving she watched him cross the square in front of the school, leaving the cottages and striding up the Norwich road. A woman in a cottage bonnet, quilted petticoat and a simple pelisse passed by Mehala. Mehala had often seen her at St Edmund's evensong. Mehala gave her an absent curtsey, and was astonished when the woman rounded on her.

'Harlot!' she cried. 'We don't want your sort!'

Mehala drew breath to retort, but thought better of it and hastened towards the Corn Mart, the short cut to the Weavers' tavern. Too late now to rush after Ven, but he had been quite firm. When antagonisms towards them both ran so high, she must do as he said. The feeling of foreboding grew, as if suddenly everything had gone worse awry and both were now at serious risk. Please God he had few duties at Two Cotts, and would come quickly. She headed for the Donkey and Buskin, praying that they meet soon, and safe.

17

The dull sheen of water could be seen almost a mile off, even before Hunterfield heard the shouts of the Watermillock men. Simple Tom, with his acuter hearing, had given his low whistle two furlongs earlier, alerting his master to danger ahead.

Hunterfield reined Betsy in on a low rise and stood in his stirrups. Immediately he cursed.

'The stupidity of this God-damned Kingdom, Tom! The folly of it all!'

The seas, under the press of the storm, had dashed against the low sea dykes, finally overwhelming them. Debris lay in black ridges beyond the tide-mill of Watermillock, reaching inland as far as the wooded slopes that shouldered seaward to form the boundary proper between Sealandings and Whitehanger.

He nudged Betsy to a steady walk. The metalled roadway gave out alongside his own Lorne House estate. It became a rutted track of potholes and sharp flints, dangerous to horses and mules alike.

'These are the times we should have stuck to oxen, Tom,' he called back irritably. 'Those beasts can do less in a day than horses, but they're surer of foot in these conditions.'

The old argument. Simple Tom knew it all too well. Hunterfield, asked by his inquisitive younger sister Tabitha how he and Simple Tom managed to discuss anything, usually replied that with Tom's boon of silence the master of Lorne was able to talk without fear of contradiction. Now, he spoke angrily as the mare picked her way carefully towards the spread of rippling sea which covered the coastal plain. Betsy mistrusted the strange aromas, of seas admixed with the scent of tilled land and pasture.

'Seven fields, for God's sweet sake! You count, Tom!'

Tom whistled, six sharp peeps and one longer trill.

'Six fields, one breach in the dykes? Christ Almighty!' He heeled the mare, leaning on the right rein to avoid a hollow where the sea encroached. 'All produce lost. Land to be drained, restored. It'll take a fortune – mine, of course,' he shouted bitterly. 'As usual, the government pays nothing, taxes everything. My idle neighbours stare down their long noses until calamity strikes. Then they petition me, to keep the North Sea in its place!'

He kept up his grumbling all the way round the limits of the flood. Some twenty or thirty men were busily employed ineffectually trying to drop shoring into a breach. Nearer, he estimated the gap far wider than the message had said. Two chains and a half and two chains, more like, and the sea's inrush was still working sinisterly below the surface. The import was woefully true; the whole mill meadow was submerged.

He urged Betsy up on to the sea dyke itself. It was a broad structure, made of earth and flint, with great piles driven in to stay the whole mass. Granite was sorely lacking in East Anglia, unlike the northern counties which had it in surfeit. A dyke in these parts depended on wood, and on soil and gravels that a rumbustious sea could erode.

'Who is in charge?' he called ahead to the men labouring at the gap. A man detached himself from the crowd and came slithering along the dyke crest.

'Good day, Squire. I'm Kettle, Watermillock fore man for Mistress Maderley.'

'How many men have you, Kettle?'

'Twenty-four, Squire, from Watermillock and your own of Lorne House. There's said to be more on the way, from the charcoal-burners in the hanger.'

Hanger, the wooded hillside that rose from the sea meadows. Hunterfield suppressed his anger. Hopeless, far too few. But even these were not being used to their uttermost. He would have to take charge.

'What vessels do you have, Kettle?'

'Boats, sir?' The uncomprehending man looked about.

'Boats, man, for God's sake! This is land no longer. It is a sea come ashore! Thereby we need boats! And what are those mules doing, I beg? In God's name, stop them floundering on the dykes. They're causing more damage than they're mending. Who's your helper?'

'Ayrton, Squire.' Kettle yelled out, and a stout elderly man strode over, touching his forehead.

'Ayrton, sir. Tide-mill waterman.' He pointed, quiet and decisive. 'I've men floating boards across from Watermillock, that I use to course the tide waters. But they'll be another hour, and I fear the tide'll be on the turn.'

Hunterfield bent low from the saddle to speak to the mud-splashed pair. 'Do I recognise the gentleman on the dryfland mark?'

Kettle gave an angry shake of his head. Ayrton answered calmly for them both.

'William Maderley, Squire. Millmaster. Widow Maderley's son.'

The man in question was busy at a canvas. In the midst of disaster, the bloody man was painting! Unbelievable. His easel was set where the meadow started its rise into Whitehanger's hill. He was painting with total abandonment, ignoring the need to repair the sea damage. His box of paints was beside him, and he held a palette, thumb crooked to hold the wooden plate almost as high as his shoulder. Kettle was furious with the artist. Ayrton was merely resigned, regarding Maderley as a simpleton best ignored.

'You want him summoned, Squire?'

'No,' Hunterfield said drily. 'I know well what assistance he would give.'

Several of the men were frantically trying to drag mud on to the sea wall, but even as Hunterfield looked another section gave way. Two breaches to heal now. They immediately started trying to shovel part of the remaining sea well into the new gap. Two men slipped, falling in as the weakened dyke started to crumble even more. 'Odds gods, Kettle. This is wanton! Call a halt this instant!'

Kettle nodded, but it was Ayrton who drew breath, bellowing for work to cease. The men halted, looked round with relief when recognising Hunterfield.

'Why so few men, Kettle?' Betsy chaffed, recovering from Ayrton's sudden bellow. 'I expected a dozen from Calling Farm, and twice that from Bures House.' He scanned the far side of the dyke. 'Do I see any from Milton Hall? Or Carradine?'

'I sent word, Squire. The Honourable Charles Golding promises some, but we await them. There's some plight at Mr Prothero's lands. Milton Hall made no response.'

No response? Hunterfield deliberated in silence. This was unprecedented. A sea wall was like the Sword of Damocles, calamity ever impending. Here now was nightmare suddenly made reality – with the gentry and great estates ignoring it. It was beyond belief. Of course, they might claim that he was responsible, as hereditary Lord of the Manor of Sealandings, its Squire and virtual ruler. It was to Lorne House that dryfland was paid. This ancient fee was passage money, given by those who annually drove cattle through his manorial lands to fairs and markets.

Anger choked him. He alone kept much of Sealandings viable. Why, these ancient sea walls were of his own rebuilding. Without his weekly inspections, there would be no sea meadows, nothing more than an expanse of mud at low tide, and uncontrollable seas at high.

'Plight? What plight?'

'There's sickness, Squire. Among cattle. Among horses too, I hear tell. People whisper it's a cattle plague, the gargle murrain. The drovers from Elperstone are afeared, and have left before the market gathering. Some Polled Suffolks are dead of it.'

Hunterfield swivelled in the saddle to glance at Simple Tom. The mute groom sat his hack in attentive silence, his gaze meeting his master's in swift understanding.

'Milton Hall also?'

'We don't know, sir. They send no man nor draught-horse.'

Dear God, Hunterfield thought, almost despairingly. Tragedy and calamity, partners coming to share the spoils of depradation.

'Then do you send to the hard. Rouse any seamen. Get them to bring the low dredger to stand offshore. With expedition, one hour.' Hunterfield glared hard at Kettle to show his firm intention. 'Send also to Bures House, giving the master there my compliments and thanks for the men already promised. Demand in my name the duck punts The Honourable Charles keeps, and the dozen punts used last Lammas Day for the fireworks on the River Affon. Say Squire Hunterfield requests them with all speed.'

'Begging the Squire's pardon,' Kettle said diffidently, 'but the punts are too light to carry earth for the broached dykes. They would sink – '

'God damn you, sir!' Hunterfield's anger gave. 'Do as I say! Get messengers off, or Is'll bar you the Eastern Hundreds!'

Kettle paled at the threat. 'Yes, Squire. This very moment.' He lumbered off at a run calling the youngest men from the group above the gap.

Hunterfield calmed. Ayrton was the sounder fore man. 'Ayrton. The charcoal-burners – how many?'

'Eight, Squire. Others are working the slopes at Lornhanger, but are a-coming once they've banked their fires.'

'I understand.' Hunterfield's anger abated. Kettle was the senior by tradition, being fore man of the tide-mill's machinery with special mysteries in his hands, but this Ayrton was coast born and bred, raised on the ways of tides, water, plants. His was an innate skill, deep with ancient knowledge guided as much by instinct as reason. In a way, very like his own. He, like Ayrton, could make allowances even in this peril for the need of the charcoal-burners to maintain their fires in the forests. Scores of livelihoods depended on supplies of charcoal. 'Right, Ayrton. Leave but two men at each of the dyke breachings to tally the changes in width. Then get the rest across to the dryland markers – '

'Squire Hunterfield!' A muddy figure came wading through the flood, arms raised.

'Easy, Betsy, easy!' The mare skittered. 'God damn you too, Mr Maderley!' Hunterfield gazed down at the artist who now stood in the field, waist-deep in the water. The man glared angrily up at the Squire.

'I want those men working, Sir Henry!' Maderley was beside himself. 'You've stopped them!'

Hunterfield sighed. Broached sea walls, an outbreak of cattle plague, panic among visiting drovers which might ruin Sea-landings for a generation, eroding dykes, floods that could ruin the township's vital tide-mill, and God sends a lunatic.

'Indeed, Maderley! Work unreasoned is work cast for nought.'

'Don't you see, sir?' the artist cried, waving the brushes he still held in his agitation. 'It's heaven-sent! It's magnificent! The scudding skies, sir! Don't you see them? The rising wind whipping at the sea! The gaping holes in the dykes – '

'Ayrton.' Hunterfield ignored Maderley. 'Move the men as I command. Have you a Gunter's Chain?'

'At Watermillock, sir.'

The Gunter's Chain was an attempt to standardise the chain, the most useful measure of farm and country distances; it had a hundred links, totalling sixty-six feet. Counties varied, but Gunter's measure was used everywhere locally at Hunterfield's insistence.

'Then bring it, Ayrton. Make several ropes of lengths equal to three times the breach, every rope being flagged out in chains with any colours you might obtain – '

'Squire Hunterfield!' the artist begged, trying to steady himself as the tide swirled about him. 'Please, sir! Let the men work just one more hour! Thirty minutes, Squire! I beg!'

Hunterfield checked Ayrton with a raised gauntlet. 'Wait, Ayrton. I shall save a man if my groom goes. Tom – you heard the instruction. Carry it to Widow Maderley at Watermillock. And say I demand also all small ropes.'

Simple Tom whistled in response, and rode off at a trot. Hunterfield looked down at the artist.

'Mr Maderley. To your several requests no, no, and no. Kindly neither impede nor trouble me, nor make any further demands on my attention.'

He nodded to Ayrton. 'Your men to the dryfland markers, taking any and all implements. See that they go along the stetches for safety.'

'And the watchers, Squire?'

'Two, asplay each broach.'

'I have but one who can swim, sir, plus myself.' Ayrton looked ashamed. This superstition testified to primitive belief, that learning to swim was to invite death by drowning. Few had the skill, mostly got accidentally, as mischievous children in the River Affon when absconding from school. Otherwise, the art was virtually unknown.

Hunterfield nodded wrily. 'You at the larger, the other man at the farther, then, if you please. Get me a nimble youth. I shall want mules and horses summoned from Milton Hall and Calling Farm.'

'I'm sorry, Squire. Mr Kettle did send for that assistance early this dawn. Bures House has sent nought, sir, neither mules nor drivers.'

'Then call out the old oxen teams held at Bures House. This work is theirs, ideally so.'

Ayrton looked askance. 'They too, Squire.'

Impossible. It was utterly impossible. Hunterfield felt a splash of rain on his face, and examined the sky. News and portents conspired against Sealandings. Why the hell did Golding not send the oxen? Out of proper use these days, but here they would be invaluable. He felt the first twinge of true fear, though did not dare allow it to show. The men gathered on the dyke watched him in silence. He gave a reassuring touch to his Wellington riding hat, and stood high in his stirrups to address them.

'You have done very well, men. I am very pleased. New materials and assistance are coming to aid us. I require that you repair to the dryland line of markers. You all know them, yonder where the wood rises. I shall remain on the dyke here to make inspection by riding its length. Go now.'

'Squire!' Maderley called, splashing alongside and looking up.

Hunterfield ignored him still. That Maderley was enamoured of his quiet sister was irrelevant. Letitia's feelings he could only guess at. There were no clear hints of attachment on Letitia's part recently. She had withdrawn into her usual shell. Perhaps it was just as well, for he suspected that in Letitia there was a great fund of loving passion that all her stately gentleness somehow masked to reveal. This artist might prove incapable of coping – he was proving his ineptitude when tide and tempest called him to duty.

'Ayrton,' Hunterfield said. 'The weather. Predict it for me.'

'Worsening fast, Squire.' Ayrton had to protect his eyes to examine the sea. 'The wind's onshore. Rain'll set in steady for the day.'

'Gale, or less?'

'Twenty knots, sir. Nightfall.'

Hunterfield smiled to show confidence for the sake of the men in spite of the grim news, and straightened up. Simple Tom would bring the necessary cordage within the hour. The punts from Charles would be a heavensend. Thank God Golding's father had been addicted to meres and decorative ponds, and to taking pretty ladies punting among the water lilies. But carting them here would be well-nigh impossible. The harbour dredger was an ancient craft unused for a past decade. He had little hope it would be of much benefit now. But it was a vessel, and could come close inshore to drop gravel and so possibly raise the seabed a little near the sea dyke gaps.

He watched the men take up their tools and splash down into the flooded fields. He greeted those he recognised from Lorne, speaking each man's name when possible, and raising a hand to acknowledge those he did not know. He too would soon be well wetted, riding the sea walls south towards Whitehanger to assess the dyke's reliability. That would mean dismounting, getting Betsy down into the water and leading her until he could regain the opposite side of the far breach.

Gathering his cloak about him, he slid from the saddle and caught Betsy's reins.

'Take care, Squire,' Ayrton called. Hunterfield started cautiously into the water. He was a tall man, but even so the sea rose almost to his waist, the cold making him gasp. Betsy whinnied anxiously but floundered after him.

'Squire! Squire!'

'Dear God, Maderley. Can't you simply depart, man?'

The artist was wading along with him, his expression one of eager excitement as he tried to keep out of the way of Betsy's hooves.

'The colours, Sir Henry! The ones on the ropes! Can you order them red, like neckerchiefs? Only, I'd like to try a combination of hues – '

Hunterfield closed the madman from his mind, and pressed forward hauling the mare's reins as the rain came down in a steady hiss.

18

'I'm afraid it is, Mistress Wren.'

Doctor Carmichael was at his unhappiest imparting bad news. He stood as a child before a threatening teacher, as if he was the sufferer instead of the girl he had left weeping upstairs. The whoremistress was torn with mixed emotions, her face suffused with anger.

'You realise what this means, Doctor! How much I lose if she stops working.'

'That is not the issue.'

'You stupid man! What else does she do, but exercise her slattern's body for my gain?'

His expression clouded. 'There is the child herself.'

'Bella? You say *child*? God's sweet mercy!' The mistress of Two Cotts threw back her head, screeching with laughter. 'She's sixteen, you fool! Four years she's lain in every position! Been used, abused, every way the mind can imagine! She's had two, three, aye, four at a time! She's used every orifice God saw fit to endow!'

He winced at her frankness, but pressed doggedly on. 'That is all the more reason, now she suffers from the French affliction, for you to keep her until mercuries can be purchased from a good inland apothecary. A cure can be attempted. I need not remind you, Mistress Wren, that the consequences are serious.'

The woman's face became ugly. 'I remind you, leech, that the consequences for *you* would be serious, were you to leak tattle-tales in Sealandings! My establishment is renowned in the Eastern Hundreds. Titled gentry come – aye, and their ladies too, for sweeteners! Influence, my penny sawbones, that's what I have! You'll not spread rumour about my girls, as God's my judge!'

Offence mingled with outrage in him as he spoke. 'Any word of Bella's condition will not come from me, Mistress Wren. I obtained the girl's permission to tell you, else I should not have told you she has pox rossals on her skin.'

185

She saw she had injured him, at a time when she had need not to, and smiled ingratiatingly.

'Please, Doctor. Don't take umbrage! I only want common ground for mutual assurance. You can depend on me. I shall act in a proper Christian fashion.' She wheedled, smiling with gruesome reminiscence, 'Oh, many's the happy moment I've had, talking with the girls of how to act for the best! We follow your instructions to the letter, sir, I assure you.'

He accepted her seeming earnestness at face value for the girl's sake. 'You make sure the girls use the Venus gloves, I take it, when coupling with, ah, clients?'

'Of course we do, Doctor!' she cooed, finally giving him a chair and rushing to pour him a glass of tent. 'Genuine tentish wine, Doctor! Seeing the weather turns inclement once more – they say the storm's like to return. Just the drop to warm away the chill.' She trilled a discordant laugh. 'Hark to me! Teaching the physician his trade!'

He would not be diverted. 'I fail to find evidence that some girls use them during, ah, conversation with clients.'

She carried the brimming glass to him, smiling with a show of sweet honesty.

'I assure you, Doctor – do drink up, dear man. The expense! Our lovers' hoods are made by the best glove-maker in all East Anglia! It well-nigh cripples me!'

'I'm aware of their cost, Mistress Wren. Is each one properly soaked, before, ah, making love? They protect both client and whore from some diseases. Indeed, from the woman's natural consequences of sexual ingress.'

'Just so, Doctor! No girl at Two Cotts ever falls pregnant. Does that not prove my assertion? You should see the expenses, listed in my ledger books! For heaven's sake! How costly it is, to bring hot water and lavender oil to every bedside, that the girls might soak the tubelets well, making them supple and pliant!' She spoke with feeling. Ven tried hard to convince himself that she spoke at least some truth. 'It's the clients who are unwilling, Doctor. But my girls *insist*! The weeks of meticulous training, inordinate discipline, to ensure the new girls become nimble-fingered at the art!' She sighed sorrowfully. 'Don't look to me for blame, Doctor.

Look instead at the mischievous, thankless, disobedient Bella who cast my incessant warnings to the winds.'

'She seems most biddable, Mistress Wren.'

The whoremistress sniffed. 'Does she! All I have to say to *that* little deception, is that the face a girl turns to a young man – for *any* purpose – is very different from the one she shows me when I'm checking her performance.'

'I don't quite follow.'

She smiled, friendship gushing from her eyes. He recoiled slightly as she laid a heavy hand on his arm.

'You see, Doctor, it's like this: a girl will try to cheat. Sad, but true! Wants a shilling more than her prick price. Understand? A client thinks to ride her bareback, promises her a sly half-crown, and she complies. She keeps the money, see?' Thought of such treachery momentarily contorted her features. She sensed his aversion and restored her winsome smile. 'What happens then? Why, the client goes away happy that he's not had to use a Venus cap, enjoyed raw meat, and the girl is that little bit richer.' She snorted, unable to suppress her anger. 'And she keeps any other memento he has left her, to boot! Bitches, all of them!'

Carmichael stirred unhappily. 'The question is the girl's well-being, Mistress Wren. The other girls are clear of signs of disease, but the French affliction is injurious and permanent. Even with treatment, it may stay in the girl and pass covertly to a, ah, sexual partner.'

'She must go, that's clear.'

'But where?'

'That is not for me to say, Doctor. She has broken my house rules.' Righteousness sugared her voice. 'It's your own advice I apply, Doctor. Were I to keep this girl here after her indecency, why, what effect do you think that would have?'

Agitation sent her to the decanter. 'Only a little light distilled Geneva spirit, Doctor, mixed with a herbal cordial. For my chest and the rheum. I get it sent from the new distillery in Maidstone, to save the ruinous import duty, though the Kentish are worse than cutpurses, the prices they charge.'

He nodded politely, though the aroma of juniper and turpentine gave her away. In the most expensive Geneva, that common folk were now abbreviating to 'gin' in emulation of the Fancy's slang, Scotch spirits were distilled and juniper berries steeped in the fluid. But mostly the cheaper Holland liquor was substituted, and damaging oil of turpentine dripped in to provide the tang which drinkers seemed to crave. It did untold harm, to children given the poisonous drink by dissipated parents, and to adults themselves, though the true thanatology was yet unknown. Was it any wonder that working folk of the industrial north were banding themselves together in hatred of strong liquor? They were even signing pledges of total abstinence, since Church and chapel temperance movements had failed utterly.

'I'm not wholly in agreement, Mistress Wren.'

'Not with your own rulings, Doctor?' she chided roguishly.

He managed to suppress his rage. Her archness was grotesque. The odious woman should speak frankly of some practical arrangements for the girl. They could settle this in half an hour. 'With those, yes, of course. I'm thinking of Bella. You know the risks, for a soul turned out of doors. No address or character. No food, nowhere to lay her head. She becomes a wanderer, stoned away from every parish boundary in our fair nation. Why even lepers get stale bread thrown to them!'

'Please, Doctor! No agitation!' She opened the door and yelled for Bella. 'Your emotions do you credit. Gentleman in your profession! Sentiments of highest approbation . . .'

The woman's claptrap was almost insulting. She went on trying to oil the waters. He only half-listened, waiting for Bella's footsteps in the hallway, her knock on the door.

'Come in, Bella. Doctor and me wants a word, dear.'

Ven found it hard to meet Bella's fearful gaze. A gloom settled on him. She clearly looked to him for defence, and he was able to offer none. It must have showed, for she turned even paler.

Mrs Wren sipped at her drink. 'It's your problem, dear. Brought upon yourself, of course,' she added quickly to disclaim responsibility. 'But never mind, dear. We'll solve it somehow.'

'Tell me, Bella,' Ven cut in to silence the woman. 'Your people, family. Have you any?'

'No, Doctor. I'm Cambridgeshire, without family.'

'Her father died, Doctor.' The whoremistress blinked back tears. Her glass was empty. She tutted, refilled it. Ven observed that the decanter was now by her elbow. 'She was fortunate I found her, brought her in from kindness.'

'Is there anybody you can go to, Bella?' Ven asked desperately. 'Who might give you employ?'

'No, Doctor. Nobody.'

Her mouth was set. He felt more dispirited than ever. She would follow the ages-old path to degradation on the wet roads of East Anglia, an animal moving by instinct. As he himself would be by today's dusk, he realised with a shock. She would fall prey to any ruffian, be mauled by any wandering lout. It was the common tale. Reputation slew with the speed of gunfire in this fair Kingdom of Church and lip-service charity.

'Wait outside, Bella, if you please.'

He waited in silence for the whoremistress to speak, but the woman was pretending to weep, eyeing him obliquely. He gave up.

'What disposition will you make, Mistress Wren?'

'Disposition?' the woman asked blankly. 'For who, pray? The girl's made her bed, and now must lie!'

'You can't mean to turn her out?'

'Doctor, do I look that cruel of heart? Haven't I the most wholesome reputation in my profession? Our professions, after all, the two oldest, Doctor! That counts for something!' She gauged him calculatingly. 'I don't suppose you'd practise what's preached? I mean, in Shalamar you have many a room would welcome a hard-working girl, who could earn her keep while setting aside pennies for your mercury treatment.'

'I regret to inform you, Mistress Wren, that this will be my last visit. I have been dispossessed of Shalamar, and am myself without lodging.'

She stared, aghast. 'I'd heard tales, but gave it no countenance. You mean it's *true*? You are cast out?'

Shame was never far from the surface. He was scarlet with embarrassment. 'I am presently to St Albans. My father had a cousin there.'

'Leaving Sealandings?' She stood in tipsy outrage, glaring down at him. 'And you have the impudence to sit drinking my best Spanish tent wine, that I reserve for paying customers? Get out, sir! Get *out*!'

He fled, glimpsing the stricken face of Bella in the hallway, not even managing a despairing word as he was showed through the vestibule into the open. The door slammed, but even so he could hear the whoremistress' shrill abuse as she raved about duplicity, tricksters, leeches and their kind. He retrieved his beaver which had been thrown out after him, and dusted it down.

The wind was rising. Perhaps the storm veering? Or maybe it was one of these twindled Sir Rogers that, famously along the coast, had a double eye, deceiving mariners and country folk alike by a false pass, returning even more savagely than before.

He headed for the Norwich road, stooping into the gusts. Father's cousin in St Albans was possibly nothing more than a figment of childhood imagination. He was as deprived as Bella. No address, only a vague memory of a lady with iron-grey hair and a caged bird that sang to order, in a cobbled street sparsely remembered. How old had he been – eleven, twelve? Needle in a haystack. Possibly she was long since deceased. Not only that, but she might even be no true relative. That was the manner of families, to adopt 'uncles' and 'cousins' from among friends, only to lose them as time and circumstance undid the bonds of familiarity. London would be the last resort, for without money he would possibly not reach there. His old teacher Doctor Arbuthnot, he'd heard by chance a year since, had been stricken with a serious ailment requiring surgery at The London Hospital, in Whitechapel's sordid slums.

At the edge of the road, he paused. He felt already tired. Despond made a man lose energies quicker than labour. He heard a distant argument, smiled wrily as he recognised the cause – some traveller wanting to evade the tollgate's levy. The toll-farmer, one Tyll, whose wife was Carradine Manor's housekeeper, was hectoring while receiving abuse in return. Even grand carriages were not above 'charging the pike', in an attempt to force the gate-keeper to raise the barrier, so saving mending costs after horses smashed through. Such scapegraces as Carradine, of course, paid neither coin nor respect, galloping and clearing the obstructions with impunity, a deplorable example.

To despair was absurd. He forced himself to think of blessings he possessed. Mehala. Resolute, talented beyond any measure in his experience. And – the ultimate for any man – she was willing to stay with him, share his misfortune with a good humour beyond comprehension. It wasn't as if they were . . . well, promised, though God knows there were moments when he felt the most fundamental emotions. In this way, Shalamar had been a peculiar hell, having to resist the urge to speak out. She was a creature of such perfection, for all her acceptance of his poverty, that he shied away, fearing to startle her into flight and so lose her for good. Once, he had been precipitate, and suffered as no man ought ever to suffer, losing Harriet Ferlane by sheer stupidity. Losing Mehala would be unbearable anguish. His need of her, admixed as it was with carnal desire, made reason impossible. He would have to declare his feelings soon, but clearly that must wait until he had managed to set himself up, in a decent home. She deserved the best. Somehow he would obtain it. Then, with care, he would consider how best to tell her of his . . . He baulked at the word . . . feelings. As long as Mehala stayed by his side, the world could do its worst.

The argument at the tollgate seemed to have come to fisticuffs. He gathered his old surtout as the wind strengthened, and stepped out downslope towards Sealandings. One further blessing was that travellers afoot paid no gate toll, thus it would be a cheap journey to St Albans, if he and Mehala decided that there lay their only prospect.

19

Charles Golding attempted a confident laugh. His visitor stood in stern silence, having refused a chair with an irate gesture.

'It isn't me, Henry,' Golding apologised. 'It's Lazard.' He shook his head at the vagaries of servants. 'Bloody agents rule us more than our parents ever did.'

Hunterfield replied mildly, concealing his anger at Golding's effrontery, 'Your parents I well remember, Golding. Your father rode with mine to mend the sea dykes more than once. Aye, and took every ploughman to see to the land's safety! Will you do less?'

Golding hid his impulse to smile. 'I honestly wish I saw things clearly as you, Henry: everything for the sealands, eh? Black and white? Preservation of the coast pure white, and everything that impedes you an unspeakable black? Agents are not easily mollified. Were I to change Lazard's orders, I'd be sore pressed to please him for months afterwards.'

'Bend him to *your* will, for God's sake. You're the master, he the man!'

Charles Golding sighed. 'Would it were so simple, Henry. He might resign – then where should I be?'

'Managing like a man, God damn it, sir!'

'Henry, Henry,' Golding pacified. He still did not offer the Lord of Sealandings a chair. 'It was easy for Father, bred like you and yours in the ways of country and fen. But for me? I've been raised to a higher order of life. There are us – you and I, Henry – who are of the nobility. Mundane folk *do*, while we reign in our small spheres. Just imagine what we would be without them!'

'Clothes maketh man, Golding? That's contemptible!'

'As garments do not hinder truth, Henry,' Golding countered easily. 'And the truth is plain. The great storm has caused untold damage along the coast. Estates are ravaged. The land itself is sick and sore. We *need* our agents and farm managers, to put things to rights.'

'As the seas break in? As Sealandings itself awaits another tempest that might bring total devastation?'

'Henry, Lazard says that to risk the beasts now would be to throw them away.'

'To *risk*? You only keep your oxen for nostalgia, Golding! They are badly needed! To do work they know best!' Hunterfield was mud-spattered. Simple Tom stood in the doorway behind, having ridden with news of Golding's refusal of draught animals, carts, men already promised.

'Indeed, Henry.' Golding avoided his visitor's glare. 'I couldn't lose Lazard. Nor my herds, or horses.'

Hunterfield was having difficulty keeping his temper. Outside, the rain intensified, lashing now at the windows. Thunder rumbled. A single flash of lightning cast the room into a ghostly brilliance for an instant.

'Charles. Listen to plain facts, I beg. I speak of the work a beast can do. Coach-horses run one stage a day only – eight miles, at ten miles an hour. Cart-horses pull waggons at two miles an hour, working nine hours a day, and pull a twenty-four hundredweight load, excluding the cart's eight. Six days a week.'

Golding sampled a new carafe of wine. 'I really must get a Rodney decanter, Henry. Flavour is affected by the crystal, don't you think?'

Hunterfield spoke on, toneless. 'The conditions out on the dykes preclude good work performance from the horses I have. The tracks are quagmired, almost impassable. My own ploughing-horses can work an eight-hour day. That is fourteen miles. Work it out, Charles. It's a simple sum. Even with good weather, we shall fail. The sea dykes will vanish, the sea fields submerge. Watermillock will wash away, a quarter of the town's prosperity.'

Charles pretended exasperation. 'Stop complaining about your nags, Hunterfield! I've my own beasts to consider.'

'For God's sake, Golding! Then forget the draught-horses! You have *three* teams of finest oxen! Archaic, yes – except in these conditions. The urgency is mortal.'

'Urgency, Henry? The tempest has been and gone –'

'It has been, sir. I assure you it has yet to depart. Sealandings is at hazard. Any casement fool can see there's more to come. Ships

193

are scurrying back into harbour afore the nor'-easterly! The wind's veering like a mad thing – '

'Henry, old friend.' Golding was trying not to allow his old indecision to return. It had proved his constant enemy. It was inconsiderate of Hunterfield to come barging in, wild of eye and mad of mien, demanding anything that took his fancy simply to splash about the shores like an idiot. 'I cannot risk my men or my animals in some cause that, frankly, seems far less disturbing – '

'Animals? Men?' Hunterfield was puzzled for a moment at the other's turn of phrase. Then his brow cleared, and he stood in still fury. He needed several moments. 'I see. You promised a token of men, to appear a responsible gentleman. Now you have heard the rumours of the cattle sickness at Calling Farm.'

Golding heard somebody arrive, but did not allow himself to be distracted. There were voices in the outer hallway, and the sound of a servant running.

'Something to that effect, Henry. It is highly responsible of me to refuse your request. Everybody knows the way to confine outbreaks is to keep stationary. Maintain order by example. Pray. Let the disease take its course over the months. Contagion afrights communities more than anything. Plagues are worse than mere drops of rain, Henry. I'll not fuel your panic by sending men and beasts on wild goose-chases down the coast.'

'For Christ's sake, Golding, *there will be no coast!*'

Golding drew himself up. This was his finest moment. Hunterfield had played right into his hands, losing control in such an ungentlemanly way.

'Your loss of demeanour, sir, does you no credit. I see my duty plain. It is to revoke my promise, and contribute nothing to your mudplay on the sea dykes. Go. Make sandpies with my blessing. Expect nothing from Bures House, or my tenant estates.'

Hunterfield was white. His voice was almost a whisper. 'I've always known you for a worm, Golding. You've calculated with Agent Lazard that, should the sea flood all the coast between Whitehanger and Watermillock, you will lose only a dozen or so acres. That would increase the value of Bures House immeasurably, and any animal and pair of hands you muster.'

Golding paled to a greater degree, and shook as he countered, 'That's the sort of prattle I've come to expect from a country bumpkin like you, Hunterfield! Don't think I've been unaware of your sly rutting with my Cousin Thalia – and don't think I ever condoned it, not for one second! I rejoice that she rejected you as contemptible! You'll get no help from me, sir, not if you stand there begging for your stupid sea dykes for ever!'

Hunterfield stood as frozen for so long that Golding thought he had been struck dumb. When he spoke at last it was in words so quiet that Golding had to struggle to hear.

'Then, sir, allow me to add to your profit. Would you oblige me, the town, and all Sealandings Hundred, by selling me the oxen teams at any price?'

'Certainly not!' Golding crowed, exulting. God, but this triumph called for a celebratory drink! He'd make sure that talk of this reached St Edmundsbury by weekend, Cambridgeshire soon after. Hunterfield was doomed! Inland and anonymity! That he, Golding, once stood in awe of this muddied reject!

'Hire?' He actually laughed aloud, feeling freer than he had ever done. It was bliss. He had come into his own at last!

'*Hire*, sir? What, are you the tradesman you've just accused me of being?' He laughed, astonished that he had ever felt the lesser man. Hunterfield was nothing more than a jack a-horseback. Take away the trappings of greatness, and what do you find but a silent oaf shaking in impotent rage, a spoiled brat denied a sweetmeat!

'For Sealandings, sir. For land, harbour, country. I beg you.'

'Go, Hunterfield!' Golding wondered why the activity in the outer hall had ceased. He'd perhaps stroll out after a drink or two, and command his servants to explain the meaning of such pandemonium. 'Go. Make mudcastles with your peasant friends.'

The Squire was some moments replying, long enough for Golding to start wondering uneasily if he had gone too far.

'Good night, Golding.' Hunterfield turned on his heel.

'Good *night*, sir? With the day not half-waned? You take leave of your senses, Hunterfield!'

Hunterfield strode out, his spurred riding boots striking the marble flooring as he went. Faint echoes came as of a distant ringing chime with each step. Golding noticed that, in strange contrast, Simple Tom's footfalls were silent, that the man made no curtain waft as he passed, and managed not to make the large double door creak as he touched it to. Golding shivered. That mute idiot made his flesh creep, with his silent staring and immediate understanding of Hunterfield's intentions. It was uncanny, warlock and familiar, witches and cats.

He gave Hunterfield time to depart, resolved to impose himself on the household instantly. He strode manfully to the door.

He yelled into the hall, 'Clark! Where the hell are you, Clark? Bring that idleback Lazard! And fetch along a new bottle of Portugal! I'm celebrating!'

There was silence. Angrily he repeated his shout. Then became aware of a lone figure seated at the far end of the hallway, on one of the tallback chairs.

'Who the hell is that?' Golding shouted. 'Come into the light, damn you!'

The figure rose, and the woman glided into the window light. Two maids had appeared in response to his summons, and stood petrified by the banisters.

'Good day, Cousin Charles,' Thalia De Foe said evenly. 'Might I have few moments of your valuable time?'

Old Clark came creaking up the cellar steps bearing a bottle of Portugal wine, wiping cobwebs from it as he wheezed into view.

'Begging your pardon, sir,' he croaked. 'Is this the vintage you require?'

'Thank you, Clark.' Mrs De Foe did not move her gaze from her cousin. 'Your master has decided not to partake of wines and spiritous liquors. Lock the wine cellars. Charles?'

She swept into the withdrawing room and stood waiting, hands clasped in her travelling Berlins. Golding licked his lips, hesitantly followed. She said nothing until the door closed.

'Henry Hunterfield passed me in the hallway without a word, Charles. A man who greets even a stray cat. Why?'

'Is that all?' Golding grinned, eyeing the decanter of Holland Geneva. 'I refused his petition. Sent him off with a flea in his ear. I knew you'd be pleased.'

Slowly she sat to listen to her cousin's embellished account of the interview. Foreboding grew with every word, until she was still as stone, and as cold. The prattling fool did not understand. Hunterfield was not a spiteful man, but even he could not endure beyond his limit. Now, certainty grew within her that, sooner or later, Hunterfield would ruin Charles Golding. Her cousin was doomed. It might come in a year, or a month. But come it would, as night followed day. The question was, could she salvage any part of Charles Golding's position and status before it happened?

'No, Charles,' she said as he reached for the decanter. 'I wish to hear again exactly what was said. Word for word.'

20

They were waiting by the edge of the cattle field, where livestock were sold on market days. Sixteen of them, mostly women but with several men from the farms and sea cottages. Only rarely was opinion resolute as well as shared. They held sticks, one a battledore, another a short stave used for May dancing. Several women had gathered small flintstones in their aprons.

'We ought to pray, Jeckel,' a woman said. 'This is the Lord's work.'

'It's prayer enough, woman.' Jeckel was a burly man from the common stables, in Parker's employ. Given tacit clearance from his employer, he needed no women's scolding at this juncture. He was impatient to get on with it, excited and breathing hard.

'We'm gathered in His Name. 'Tis fitting to pray.'

'Then do it, but silent,' Jeckel told them. 'Too loud and we'll scare him away. It's deserving that he suffers, encouraging sin so.'

They stood, heads bowed, until Jeckel began to fear Carmichael might slip past unseen, and called them back to vigil.

They were beside the hedgerow bordering the Norwich road. Across, looking eastwards, stood a scatter of three or four cottages, fortunately set back from the thoroughfare, with scrubland where pigs snuffled and a few goats foraged. To the left, a furlong off, the entrance to Two Cotts showed its discreet gateway, a flint wall with a small lanthorn set atop, and dense hedges allowed to flourish untended. To the north side of the livestock field, the perimeter hedgerows gave way to thickets and unenclosed terrain that marked the limits of the township. It was ideal. Sealandings territory was vague at best, and land disputes always uncertain in law. The parish boundary was walked through the cattle field's midline, another help.

'The nigget's a-coming, Jeck booy,' somebody called softly. The jibe caused subdued chuckles, a nigget being an unlearned village midwife, usually a drunken old slattern.

'Quiet! You see him?'

'Carrying his case.' A woman's voice rose, eager. 'He's done his sinfulness! Acted against God's holy law with his evil ways.'

'Hush one, hush all,' Jeckel commanded angrily. 'Talk sillinesses, you'll frighten him off from justice!'

'Silence. He's here.'

They watched through the foliage as Carmichael trudged down the slope towards them. There was no pavement. According to practice, he used the grassy verges which, though awkward and cambered from the hedge roots, were drier and less rutted than the trackway. He would pass within easy reach. Several nodded, pleasure shining in their eyes at this sign that the Almighty was aiding their sacred work of punishment.

'*Now!*'

Jeckel was the first out of the space, confronting the startled man. A woman keened in a high crazed whine as she rushed out after the big groom, and flung the first stone. It thudded against Carmichael's surtout. In alarm he retreated a step, exclaiming at the mob who poured out onto the road, blocking his path.

More stones flew. One struck him on the side of his head, knocking his beaver. He used his free hand to try to deflect the flints, backing up the road.

'What is this?' he called. 'I'm Doctor Carmichael. Don't you recognise me? I'm – '

'You'm about Satan's work!' the first woman called. Others began shrilling, ululating as they threw. Some cast about for more missiles.

The men were advancing, brandishing their sticks.

'We know you, Carmichael!' Jeckel boomed, thrilling to the excitement of inflicting a just sanction. 'The Devil's helper!'

Carmichael stared, retreating as they advanced on him. It could not be happening. It was unreal, a nightmare from which he surely must wake any moment.

'Jeckel? It's me. I delivered your second babe but two months gone. What wrong have I done?'

Two stones caught him simultaneously, one high on his cheek, the other thumping into his chest and drawing an involuntary groan of pain from him. It served as a spur. They rushed forward, throwing and hitting, impeding each other but driving him along the road. He raised his hand, his case, trying to ward off the blows

199

and protect his head, but it was unavailing. They battered him down into the mire. They fell on him with knuckles, stones and swinging sticks.

He tried to crawl away among the feet, with no thought of trying to fight back, only to escape and think of reasons, find explanations, ask what they intended and why. Blows rained down on him.

There were shouts, curses shocked of a sudden into cries of alarm, but no longer from himself alone. A horse's hoof splashed frighteningly near his head. He tried to roll away from the hooves. A horseman? One arm would no longer obey him, and his legs seemed paralysed. He thought, Dear God, am I done, by a mob that mistakes their doctor for some footpad? Yet as he put that thought away, sickened by the truth that they had surely identified him, talked without seeming mistaken, he lay and retched alone by the hedge. People were running, scattering, and two horsemen whipping them, men and women alike, screams and imprecations borne on the wind.

'Who is it, Ryde?' a voice called. 'Does he live?'

'He does, sir! A leech, by his attire.'

'What was the occasion of the assault, then?'

'I don't yet know, Sir Edward, I'm sure!'

'Get him up if you're able.' A sigh. 'This is becoming a trial of a journey, Ryde. I swear I've travelled further from the Sealandings boundary stone than all the way from Arminell, as God'll judge.'

'Here, master. Up you come!'

A hand lifted Ven. Dazed as he was, he tried to express thanks, and stood leaning heavily on the groom who held him. His legs were shivering in the most extraordinary manner. His chest stabbed pain with every breath, probably a rib fracture. He tried to cough experimentally, testing for a punctured lung, but the pain was too great. He almost fainted at the hurt.

'Stand still, sir,' the rough voice said. 'Lean on me. We're Sir Edward's company, Arminell Hall at Maidborough.'

'My case, sir, if you will. It's all I have.' Ven could not quite see, except a vaguely grey world of swimming shadows. He felt retchingly sick. Blood was in his mouth.

'My fellow has it, Doctor. Get your breath.'

Ven tried to push himself away and stand alone, but dizziness toppled him. Even as the groom strove to keep him up, he slipped into a deep water-filled rut with a splash.

'Get particulars, will you, Ryde?' a voice commanded. 'I can't delay more than a little. Look sharp, now!'

'Yes, Sir Edward.'

The groom hauled Ven across to the grass verge and lodged him down against the trunk of a small beech. He mopped with brisk clumsiness at Ven's face with a kerchief, making him wince.

'There, Doctor. You're good as new. Well, almost.'

Ven's vision cleared slightly as the groom turned and called up at a coach which stood some ten yards away. A fine vehicle with four matching chestnuts and an elderly coachman in a thick wrap-rascal. A coat-of-arms showed in glowing colours on the box and on the coach itself.

'Sir Edward. The leech is sore injured. His arm's gone, I think.'

'Bring him.'

A liveried postillion dismounted to join them. Together they helped Ven to make his way towards the coach.

An older gentleman looked down. 'Your name, sir?'

'Doctor Carmichael, Sir Edward, from Shalamar. At least, lately.'

'Shalamar?' The gentleman seemed surprised. 'Are you related to the people who used to dwell there?'

'No, sir. I had it at a peppercorn, while I established myself in Sealandings.'

Sir Edward appraised him with an ironic glance. 'Judging from the townsfolk's response, you have failed, sir. I have to inform you that you make enemies with great facility. Why the assault?'

'I'm in ignorance, Sir Edward, except . . .'

'Come. I need to know, else how may I judge?'

Ven hesitated. 'I make no complaint against anyone, sir. My assailants spoke against my character, saying I did my work against the Almighty, and for Satan.'

The second groom gave a sharp breath and would have stepped away, but Ryde curtly signed him to stand fast.

'Against Satan?' Sir Edward seemed amused. 'Not at any great profit, Doctor. I'd heard that sin is much to the sinner's pecuniary advantage! Where do you carry out this gainsome labour of yours?'

'I tend the bawds at Two Cotts, sir. The nugging-house yonder, standing back from the road. Mistress Wren's the whoremistress.'

'Tend for what gain, Doctor? Personal or coin?'

'As it happens, neither, Sir Edward. She refuses my help, now she knows I am expelled from Shalamar.'

'Cast out? Isn't it of Sir Fellows De Foe, Milton Hall?'

'I believe so, sir. The agent evicted us. I plan to walk to relatives at St Albans.'

'Quite a journey, Doctor. Ryde, help him aid to a dwelling hereabouts.' Sir Edward's eyes wrinkled in humour. 'A different address than the one he lately, ah, visited. Yonder windmill house, I think. Give them my compliments. Have him cleaned and fed, rested until he can continue. Then see him safely on the inland road as best you may.'

'Yes, Sir Edward.' Ryde was displeased by the orders.

'Rejoin my service at Lorne House, before nightfall.' Ven heard the Baron's ironic chuckle. 'Take care, Ryde, to protect him from these good Christian folk of Sealandings.'

'Yes, Sir Edward.'

Ryde tethered his mount to the hedge, and signalled to the coachman. Ven tried to express his thanks as the other outrider mounted and the coach sprang forward. Ryde waited as the vehicle splashed past, then smiled down at Ven.

'Well, Doctor Carmichael. You're a fine ruin and no mistake. We'm do as Sir Edward says, else it'll be my hide and not yours.'

'Perhaps the Donkey and Buskin, Mr Ryde.' Mehala would be waiting.

'Is it far?' The groom eyed Ven's condition with mistrust. 'Sir Edward said the millhouse yonder.'

'That's the Quaker household, Mr Ryde,' Ven said quickly. His giddiness was returning. Blood was running into his eye. 'I have reason to believe my attackers were among the religious.'

Ryde snorted. 'Holy mouths and sinners' hands make hypocrites. But Sir Edward said there, so there it is. Let them turn us away first, before we think again, eh?'

Ven wiped the blood away with a sleeve. He could see the groom's face. A large bearded man, bluff and decisive from years in charge of beasts and coaches. He had been lucky in his rescuers. He was only thankful that he had insisted that Mehala wait safely among her friends at the Donkey and Buskin. For once, he had done the right thing. Relief weakened him at the thought of what could have happened to her among that crowd of thugs.

'I'm grateful for your kindness, Mr Ryde, and to your master.'

'Don't be too grateful, Doctor. Sir Edward is hard when it's called for. He's the Justice at Maidborough, so couldn't ride past a public affray on the King's highway, even in Squire Hunterfield's district.' The groom deliberated, weighing up Ven's deplorable condition. I'd best horse you, and lead. Give me due warning should you decide to take tumble!'

With difficulty the groom lifted Ven into the saddle and took the reins. 'She's a quiet old mare this one, thank God. You'll be safe.' He clicked his tongue and the mount started along the road. 'Did you hear my row at that tollgate? The keeper asked us tuppence more than he ought, just because of our coats-of-arms and emblazons. Well, he picked a wrong one, I'll tell you. The master knows the charges on every road trusteed between Brancaster and Lizard Point. So there we were, me offside outrider, as is my rightful position, young Billie second postillion, when the toll-farmer calls out . . .'

They moved at a slow walk, the groom talking all the while. Ven clung to the saddle pommel, his gaze fixed on the mare's mane, as if fearing the beast would vanish from under him and he would be back among the hating mob who had beaten him into the mud. As they passed the gate of Two Cotts Mrs Wren emerged to stand in the porch, glaring as the groom led his mount into the grounds of Bettany's mill.

The running boy overtook Mehala just before she reached the hard. The mud on him was streaked white by sweat rivulets.

'What is it, booy?' she called as he paused.

'The sealands be mortal breached beyond 'Millock,' the boy gasped. 'Squire calls out any and all.'

'Stay, booy.' She caught at him. 'Where be's Squire now?'

'Bures House, gal. For the oxen teams.'

Mehala thought swiftly. She had driven oxen, six to a waggon, over Mersea Island's tidal marshes. Here in Sealandings they were almost obsolescent. She remembered Charles Golding's old oxherd, Pilgrim, the one remaining ox-team driver. She had play-mocked him for his beasts' newfound idleness, now all turned to cobs, shires and dray-horses. Imagine the gratitude of Hunterfield – and all Sealandings – if she drove an ox-team to rescue the flooded sealands . . . It was heaven-sent. Here was a means of restoring Ven Carmichael's fortune throughout the Eastern Hundreds!

'Run on, then. When you reach the Donkey and Buskin, seek out Doctor Carmichael. Tell him Mehala goes to the floods. Promise!'

'Promise!' the lad breathed, and ran on.

Mehala gave a last searching glance for a sight of Ven, then turned back and hurried through the cottage lanes, southward, where the Bures House estates lay.

21

The rain fell aslant the breaches in the long sea-walls. Hunterfield rode slowly along the highest points of the dykes guiding Betsy to the driest footing. She was tiring. She was no longer young, but had wisdom to lean expertly against the chilling sea wind and pause to test the firmness of each doubtful patch of the path along the crest.

He saw another part of the wall give way, up ahead, tumbling into the fields under the press of sea. It was impossible, almost hopeless. He reined Betsy in and turned, holding his Wellington to protect his face from the gale and so enabling a detailed inspection.

Along the dryland markers the assembled men were standing, their implements impotently stacked on the wooden slopes. A cluster of smoke-blackened men stood somewhat apart; the charcoal-burners from above Whitehanger.

'Ayrton?'

The stoutish older man was sitting, breathing hard, on the earthen wall above the first breach. Sea was still flooding in. Ayrton was soaked, muddied, now hardly recognisable.

'Here, Squire sir.' The man seemed exhausted. 'I've been down, sir. It's broached bad, and the sea working away yet.'

'The gap shelves beneath, or not?'

'Undercut, Squire, I'm afraid. That far side'll go soon without shoring. Perhaps another hour.'

Hunterfield nodded, trying to appear optimistic. This was the worst news possible.

'I've some assistance coming, Ayrton, but people are slow from Sealandings itself, I fear. We'll not have the assistance I'd hoped from the estates.'

'We've the cordage from Watermillock, Squire. It's ashore there.'

'Good!' *Ashore*, Hunterfield thought in dismay. In the hour he'd been away, wasting time pleading for that namby pamby

Golding's oxen and punts, 'shore' had depressingly moved from the sea breakwaters on to the dryland line. This morning, the low-lying fields were 'inland'. Now, indisputably the sea had reclaimed all. The whole meadow had abruptly reverted in Ayrton's consiousness to its ancient title of sealands. Anger swelled in him. It would not happen. It must not.

'How many charcoalers? The Lornhanger burners too?'

'Kettle tells me nigh on two dozen, Squire, all able. No swimmers among them.'

There came a sudden cry and a splash as the man on the far breach slipped into the flooded field, the dyke dissolving beneath him. He surfaced gasping, standing with his head just above water, waved tiredly to show he was safe, and started to wade back to clamber on the dyke again. It was Ayrton's other swimmer, Jourd. Ominously, Hunterfield saw that the man was neck-deep. That madman Maderley had, not long since, waded easily across the sea meadows. In this first gap, he himself had been waist-deep. So the flood had deepened more than half a yard in the lapse.

'I've taken the first measure, Squire.' Ayrton sounded almost apologetic saying it. 'The spans of the first two openings, by Gunter's Chain. I'll do the new one now, with Jourd. I've sent to open the tide-mill's locks, much good though that'll do.'

'Excellent, Ayrton!'

Hunterfield rebuked himself silently. It should have been the first thing to ask, that his orders had been obeyed about gauging the breaches. He was stupidly letting himself be overawed by the magnitude of the calamity. Thank God this artisan prompted him to common sense. Opening Watermillock's sea gates was sound practice, for a flooded tide pool would support the mill's inland perimeter dyke and lend strength there.

'That's a risk to Watermillock, Ayrton,' he said with a smile. 'Your inland dyke's built for a pond, not an ocean.'

Ayrton answered soberly, 'Without this land Watermillock loses its own footing, sir.'

'As long as you take the blame from Widow Maderley, Ayrton,'

Hunterfield's heavy attempt at humour was met with silence. Among the men standing ashore, Kettle the fore man was prominent, standing on one of the dryland stones, head tilted, watching for orders.

'Get the carboneers to work, then, Ayrton. Cut piles, some eight or nine feet in length. We shall drive them first into the broaching to form a palisade against which we shall drop flints, stones.'

'Right, Squire sir.' Ayrton sounded none too sure of this plan. 'That will throw more risk to the undercut dyke, sir, which is next along.' Ayrton looked at the sea swirling through the gap. 'We've not time, sir, begging your pardon. Cutting the timber, floating it over, infilling without landcraft, takes us to nightfall. An ebbtide cuts a broached dyke faster than a rising sea, sir.'

'I know, Ayrton,' the Lord of Lorne said wearily, thankful that the men were out of earshot. 'But we must do something.'

Ayrton almost staggered as a gust shoved at him. He recovered his footing, watching the foam rise with each incoming wave. 'Squire, my father rebuilt part of these walls, as my Grandfather did for your father, the old Squire sir. They brined and tarred piles vertical every ten links, wattled between with alderwood.'

Hunterfield looked down at the man in surprise. There were depths to this folk tradition, everything according to an ancient wisdom these labouring people knew so well. Golding, for all his wealth and position, had only shown his ignorance in deriding these people.

'It gives best support, Squire, with the materials we have, sir. I've already set charcoalers hard at the brattlings.'

Brattlings, the loppings of felled trees, were a ready supply of thin pliable timber after a storm. Hunterfield smiled his approval, and steeled himself to speak.

'We must manage with ourselves, Ayrton. If we lose the race the sea meadows are lost for a generation. I've sent Tom to raise every able man from Lorne House and anywhere. Call Jourd. For Christ's sweet sake stay together.'

'Yes, Squire.' The order was an admission that they would be without any floating craft at all, and Ayrton knew it.

'Rig a jury rope and a pulley on the dyke to float logs across the flood to here, where we stand.'

Ayrton glanced shrewdly across to Kettle and his men, wiped his face free of rain. The man's opinion was crucial.

'I can, sir. But it'll weaken the dyke.'

'Then strengthen the dyke inland and seaward where the pulley is set.' The Lord of Sealandings felt bone tired. His every decision was countered by yet more difficulty, though Ayrton was right to speak the truth.

'With so few men, it must be one or the other, sir, before night comes. We can work through the darkness, but even so . . .'

Hunterfield stared out to sea. 'What of Carradine's two vessels? They can work inshore.'

'No, Squire. They embarked from the north wharf soon after I sent word. Neither's to be seen. The man Giffler embarked as temporary pilot, Squire.'

Merchants, Hunterfield thought in fury, merchants all. Families of lineage, some of blood royal if whisper be believed, yet they think pence instead of protecting their own shores. Barbarians, who seize the opportunity to send their vessels to bring contraband ashore when the King's Excise ships were busy along the stricken coast. Mention of Giffler was most revealing: the night boatman, smuggler. So Prothero, not content with Carradine Manor, betrays Sealandings for yet more silver. The list of gentry willing to give assistance to their own fief dwindled to none.

'I have sent Simple Tom to fetch small craft,' Hunterfield told Ayrton. 'They may take time, coming all the way from Sealandings hard.'

'Just so, Squire.' Ayrton was not deceived. Nobody could sail small boats across with such a sea running. 'I have a boy haltering the Watermillock dinghy with the mule. He should be here betimes.'

'Good man.'

A boy, and a mule pulling a dinghy across the mudflats. An act of despair. Betimes, Hunterfield thought dejectedly, meant any day.

'My own horses will be on the road from Lorne, so set the men to work, Ayrton.' Hunterfield caught himself in time. He had almost said, in default of carts and beasts from Bures House and Milton Hall and Prothero's Calling Farm. He would never again be tricked by reputation, not after this disaster. For too long he had let Lorne become a sporting retreat, ignoring all but the most essential farming activities.

'Right off, sir.'

'Never think I shall forget your endeavours this day, Ayrton. Let us pray for success.'

'Thank you, Squire, and amen.'

Hunterfield slid from the saddle and took Betsy's bridle to lead her back along the dyke. He walked on the landward side of her for shelter as Ayrton started shouting the despairing instructions to the men on the dryfland. As he went, he roundly cursed the idlebacks and cowards of the district. Where were the farmers and other menfolk of Sealandings? Or the fishermen who could work small inshore craft round headlands? And the gentry, with their work forces from the estates? Why, he remembered well when Father had the church bells pealed for breaches in these very same dykes, and over two hundred had come within the hour, bringing more boats than he had imagined Sealandings could claim. Aye, and four score horses, mules, farm waggons and drovers' carts and gentlemen's punts and cordage . . . Now, he had only a scatter of ragtaggles, plus his own estate men – and they more able to serve sportsmen's shotguns and tend racing stock than wade through floods to drive stakes into crumbling sea dykes. Why, he realised with a shock, all his heavy waggonage was done by hire, and half of those from Whitehanger. He almost groaned aloud. How Father would have chided, were he here to make comparison with Sealandings of twenty years ago!

It had been a wondrous sight, all Sealandings rushing to the rescue. And in a raging storm, too. He heard a call from the shoulder of the hill, and saw that idiot William Maderley standing on a stile madly waving, the men all looking. He ignored the shouts, bloody madman and his colour mania, and plodded along round the curved crest of the dyke, desperately wondering where he could get help, now there was none to be had.

'Hold your team a-line, gal,' Pilgrim Fleet shouted at Mehala, hitting the oxen with his reed wand. 'You've done this afore, I see!'

'Once or twice, Pilgrim,' Mehala said, trying to seem calm though she was almost shaking with apprehension. 'Have you?'

He cackled. 'Ox are flatland folk, see?'

'Let's get on, Pilgrim.'

'As the Lord wills,' he chanted. 'Proceed only at a shug-trot, my girl – the butterwoman's pace to market!'

In spite of her worry Mehala had to laugh at Pilgrim Fleet's local witticism. 'I hear, Pilgrim. Nothing rumbustical until we reach the gulsh!'

'Easy with my beasts, young lady, even on the mud. My oxen are as the Lord's oxen, as mentioned in Holy Writ.'

The old man's scrawny neck showed as he lifted his stubbled chin and laughed. Mehala couldn't help liking the old oxherd, for all his religious sayings and chantings. He wore the old smock, decorated with thick wool stitching about his shoulder yoke. He insisted his beasts were children.

As Mehala had hurried towards Bures House, women had been shouting the sorry tidings of the flood from the windows. In the worsening downpour she had seen Simple Tom cantering down towards the hard. She had called out after him, catching up as he reined within sight of the harbour's South Mole, and been told in mime of Hunterfield's need of the lowly ox spans from Golding's estates. She could still see Simple Tom's eloquent mime of the oxen – arms curved out ahead, swaying in the saddle to copy the oxen's slow trundling walk. Then his arms stretched, head between and staring in swift display of the silent punt gunners floating upon the duck mere.

She had found Pilgrim brushing his oxens' hides, singing and bullying them in their stalls. There were three ox spans, each six, with their long-bedded road carts. The old saint had relished the bad news, quoting biblical doomsaying prophesies with delight as he rushed to harness the creatures to their old waggons.

'I knowed they'd be needed, see, gal?' he'd laughed, showing his two brown teeth and cackling gummy derision. 'Modern ways can do without my beauties, just as long as things go bootiful. But let the heavenly blast trumpet forth the Lord's wrath on this ungodly land, and no fancy prancing tits are needed. Oh, no! For the Lord is terrible: a great king over all the earth – Psalm forty-six, verse three.'

As Mehala hurried to aid the old oxherd, she remembered the ox-team she had driven before, across the strood from Mersea Island, to the shores facing the low Ray Isle at low water. They were Elijah Rebow's teams, before the bizarre, mad marriage and his swirling drowning death when he had dragged her down into the sea in the low mist, floating, drifting, until hands had reached down and . . .

'Here, gal!' Pilgrim was shaking her arm. 'You didn't say your amen! You ain't one of they heathens? For I shalln't let you touch my beasts!'

'Amen, amen, Pilgrim.' She shook her head, tied her bonnet tighter. 'A silent prayer, that's all.'

Pilgrim scanned her harness, nodding with reluctant approval. 'You harness roit well, gal. What other orders from Sir Charles, afore we start?'

'The punts are needed, Pilgrim. Simple Tom gave me the message.'

It was another hour before all were ready and laden. The three ox-teams were in line, with their low-slung carts. Pilgrim climbed on to the first, Mehala the second, the third team loosely tied to the tail of the second cart. Donno, Pilgrim's seven-year-old grandson, stood alongside the last team to switch them on. He was too small to use reins. Mehala knew Pilgrim would want the lad out of harm's way for the long downhill slide to the flood. Pilgrim's waggon and hers were fully loaded with punts, tied down but uncovered. The rear cart was only half-loaded, for lack of an able driver, which meant three sporting punts had to be left behind. The loading had been done by Golding's gamekeepers and their rivermen, at work along the Affon mending the bridge.

'Ready, gal?' The old oxherd raised his goad erect, and gave the cry 'Coop-coop-coop,' yodelled in a surprisingly melodious tenor voice, cracking his sixteen-foot lash above the lead oxen.

'Coop-coop-coop!' Mehala shrilled in imitation, Donno echoing her. She earned a glance of appreciation from Pilgrim when she cracked her long ox-whip over her own lead pair. The teams trundled forward slowly into the worsening rain, their long straight backs rocking slowly from side to side in characteristic motion as they heaved forward on their split hoofs, soled in leather but splaying on the muddy ground.

As the three waggons moved from the ox compound, Mehala thought of Ven. He would understand, when he heard. They had often talked in the lantern hours, she of her love for the sealands and he of his for the folk. He would know she must go to help. Her ache to be used, to protect the coast from the terrible sea, was as compelling as his. Most delightful was the realisation that each complemented the other. Together they were one, in a bond as yet undefined but no less permanent. Ven would wait at the tavern for her. In fact, she guessed with a tingle of pleasure, he would probably come after her to help. He was a man with a great capacity to love. It would be for her, when time was opportune, to release that love. And that time was fast coming, even though they were wanderers.

'Keep in line, gal!' Pilgrim was shouting back. Mehala hauled to correct the offside lead ox gently into the centre of the trackway that climbed the wooded hillside, the higher boundary of Lorne's manor.

'Mind your own path, Pilgrim Fleet!' she shouted, tugging her bonnet so it fell back on its brides. 'And Is'll mind mine!'

His cackle of amusement came to her through the hiss of rain. 'I loike you, gal,' he called. ''Tis pity you're gentry!'

''Tis pity your daggly weather doesn't treat me according, then!' she gave back, cracking the nearside ox a sharp reminder as it showed too much interest in the hanging foliage. She glanced at little Donno. At seven, he was already the veteran, keeping upslope and offside of his lead pair.

Pilgrim almost fell from his box laughing at her use of the local dialect. 'You bain't blaming the Good Book, Mehala? *Neither shall there any more be a flood to destroy the earth.*'

'Genesis nine, verse eleven,' Mehala shouted, breathless with her effort.

The old man made no reply. He was standing, coaxing his team up through the storm. His was the most difficult task. They were heading for a point high on the hillside's broad shoulder so they would emerge above the sea fields. Managed right, Pilgrim would fall his team down upon the dryland line, so the teams could be used to maximum advantage on the driest part, on the promontory's rise. She concentrated, wishing she had asked Pilgrim for a double tether on the front yoke, but now too frightened to call and stop him for this purpose.

Had he been asked, Emanuel Bettany the Quaker would have denied that he was a sombre man. A man's self lay inward, except the acts called forth by religion – of the right kind, of course, for many religions were contaminated by perdition.

The injured man, partly cleaned and dozing restlessly on the couch in the parlour at the millhouse, was such a contamination.

'Cast forth from his own religious community,' Bettany rumbled in his deep, unforgiving voice. 'Into the outer darkness.'

Bettany's son Richard, all of fourteen, was heartily sick of sonorous pronouncements. He gazed with concealed admiration at the recumbent figure of Doctor Carmichael, and wore his most innocent expression to ask, 'Why, Father?'

Helen Bettany was suspicious of her son's disingenuous questioning. Since the lad was apprenticed to the Sealandings clockmaker, Horatio Veriker, admittedly a respectable craftsman of the London guilds and a regular nonconformist attender, Richard's eyes were mischievous, almost playful – a horrendous development. She looked at her son. God-fearing parents had to exterminate every trace of levity from their offspring. Correcting illicit merriment was her holy duty. She had laboured long and hard with the lad, as had Emanuel her husband.

'Why? Matters of the flesh, son,' Bettany intoned. 'Josiah Baring had the decency to debar this man from attendance at their wretched misguided steeple-house rituals.'

'What has he done, Father?' Richard asked with a frown. He had long since learnt that frowning passed for grim fervour in this pious household.

'You are too young to know, son,' Helen interposed quickly.

'I accept, Mother,' Richard answered, hands joined. Carmichael was the best diversion Bettany's windmill had experienced. He was thrilled, and gave his gravest frown. 'I wonder only, is it my solemn duty to enquire about his sin, to be forewarned against similar temptation?'

Helen Bettany wavered at the moral dilemma. A proper request, indeed. But her son had never lacked for wit, that cue to devilment. His expression showed only devout simplicity, yet still a hint . . .

'The boy's correct, Helen,' Emanuel decided, to Richard's hidden delight. When Father pronounced, he seemed to swell to an immense size. His words came ponderously one by one, until you could doze off waiting, finally making no sense of what was said because you'd forgotten the beginning.

Bettany closed his eyes, accepting divine inspiration. Richard did likewise. Helen Bettany bowed her head.

'This man showed signs of emotional attachment to Miss Euterpe Baring, Reverend Josiah's sister.'

Richard was astonished. What about Mehala? Horatio Veriker's workshop, for all that master clockmaster's dedication to timekeeps and mechanical regulators, was a hive of joviality well concealed from customers. Indeed, Richard believed that Veriker merely maintained his God-fearing sobriety as a sop while thinking exactly what he pleased. Richard had learned a great deal at Veriker's, including how to turn a blind eye when Horatio Veriker and Mol the maid-of-all slipped upstairs in breathtaking silence at midday. Richard also knew how to disarm customers with glib excuses during Veriker's absence.

He knew Mehala lived at Shalamar with Doctor Carmichael, though old Mrs Trenchard's cottage was there. He once ran an errand for Mehala, and had been smitten in a way he could not quite understand. It was probably sinful. So many things seemed to be sinful. The injured man groaned in fitful sleep. His lips were swollen, cracked and caked with blood. Mother had washed his face with warm water, but kept the flannel at arm's length. More contamination?

'Yes, that startles you.' Bettany misjudged Richard's silence, adding with relish, 'Sin's guises tempt souls from paths of righteousness.'

'Reverand Baring stopped it at the outset,' Helen Bettany announced with firmness. 'Very properly.'

'Is this God's punishment, Father?' Richard asked gravely.

'Probably, son,' Helen Bettany replied. Her husband stayed uncharacteristically silent. 'This man was told to restrain from visiting houses of sin in Sealandings, and heeded not the warnings of good Christian folk.'

'Who, though?'

'The instruments of the Lord, son,' Bettany answered in his sombre bass. 'God works in mysterious ways, His wonders to perform.'

'True, true.' Helen Bettany was pleased at Richard's acceptance of the lesson. 'The Almighty sent this as a sign to instruct you, son. Actually smote him!'

'It was Jeckel, Mother,' Richard said candidly. 'I saw him and the farm people when I was counting tally marks for paying the carters. They had staves and cudgels. I called out, but they ran on into the cattle field.'

'Anyone can be a chosen instrument, son, however lowly.'

'Thank you, Father,' Richard said, frowning. 'I shall reflect on it. Will I be needed here, Mother?'

'No, son. I shall manage.'

'Will Sir Edward's groom come back for him?'

'No, Richard,' his father said with a sigh. 'The man's request was to take Carmichael in, and care for him until he can depart. It goes against my principles. Were it a lesser personage than Sir Edward Astell, I should not have accepted.'

Richard's brow cleared. 'I think I see, Father. The parable of the Samaritan. Sir Edward being the Good Samaritan, while others pass by on the other side?'

Bettany glared at his son. Helen said nothing. This whole event was making her uneasy. She remembered Emanuel's meeting at St Edmund's rectory.

'And we, Father, are perhaps the innkeepers who for a coin cared for – '

'Erroneous, son!' Bettany gave out, rotating towards the recumbent figure. 'We represent religious charity, accepting even the fallen sinner. Remember that.'

'Thank you, Father. I shall.'

The intensity with which Richard spoke was suddenly too revealing. He checked quickly as both parents looked sharply at him.

'How soon can we send him from here?' he asked.

Bettany nodded approval. The boy was right to feel disturbed by the presence of this sinner at the mill.

'We can hardly keep him less than an hour, son. But the quicker he goes the better.'

'I shall go to watch the mill-sails, Father, if I may be excused. The wind rises anew, and is backing fast.'

'Good, son. Work and wait on the Lord.'

Richard left the room, then hurried into the millyard. The windmill was in lock, its four slabbed wooden sails fixed against the louring sky. The wind made an eerie whistling as it cut through. He felt an instant's pride at the spectacle of such a grand ancient machine ready to harness the air's power at the pull of a lever, then thought of the injured man indoors.

An hour? He had heard from Mol that the Doctor and Mehala were moving out, but exactly where nobody knew. So where was she? Doctor Carmichael had mumbled something when Sir Edward's man had hauled him unceremoniously in and delivered his ultimatum. One thing was certain: Carmichael would soon be sped on his way from Bettany's mill whether he was in a fit state to walk a furlong in the returning storm or not, though doubtless with many a holy thought to lend him crutch.

He looked back at the millhouse. All was still. He crossed the millyard where the grain was fetched on the waggons, paused to glance furtively round, then started briskly towards the road into Sealandings.

22

The shouts finally made Hunterfield pause, Betsy halting with a tired shiver as the gale gusted.

'Stay, girl,' Hunterfield consoled. 'You'll be resting soon.'

It wasn't true. Yet was there excitement in the cries from the dryfland? Had that drunkard Golding finally relented? Or Carradine, Prothero, the De Foes, the townspeople . . . were they coming at last to aid the men cutting and sawing? He peered across the intervening flood, but could see nothing. That idiot artist Maderley was waving madly, shouting himself hoarse, but so? Men were pointing up into the woods. The only arrivals expected from that direction were the handful of carboneers from beyond Whitehanger.

'Soon, soon, girl,' he crooned gently to the mare, ducking under her head to squint seaward. Nothing there either, no boats, no ship scudding before the driving rain. The sinister white-topped waves were atop an ominous heaving which preceded another onrush against the weakening dykes.

'Squire!'

He looked down into the flooded fen. Ayrton was still near enough for Hunterfield to see his delighted expression. He was holding on to some submerged fencepost, and gesturing.

And Hunterfield saw the men running and guiding . . . what? He stared, wiped rain from his face, looked the harder.

'Well, God bless you, Golding!' he muttered in disbelief. For a team of six beautiful, glorious oxen was swaying slowly downhill, legs splayed to slow the descent, coming from the trees towards the floodline. An old besmocked driver was hauling hard on his reins even as the men took hold to lead the beasts down. They were slithering and coming slow, having difficulty restraining the heavy waggon with its load of . . . its load of some layered things. Could they be pallets, cradles? Or the punts he had begged for?

Relief weakened Hunterfield. 'And bless you again, Charles,' he said wonderingly.

Another team was slowly trundling after, making the descent seemingly on a long tie, driven by a slighter, bonneted figure, a girl who leaned and strained to hold her team. And both carts were loaded.

'The punts, Squire!' Ayrton shouted in delight. 'From Bures House!'

Hunterfield cupped a hand at his mouth to direct his reply. It would not do for relief to show.

'About time! Very well, Ayrton. Get wattles and cradles made with all speed. Put flintstone into punts, as much as they can bear without sinking. We still need the logs and pulley.'

'Will do, Squire!'

Jourd was wading out of the flooded fields, almost up to the dryland marker-posts. The girl was being helped down, Hunterfield saw. But what was she doing, beckoning men into the trees? The old oxherd was also clambering down, and starting upwards with her. The sound of axes resumed. Men scrambled over the flat-bed waggons to start unloading.

'One last ride, Betsy,' Hunterfield apologised, remounting and nudging the mare along the dyke. The floods were now too deep for a horse to wade. She responded patiently, but would not last much longer.

'At least this saves us beating the bounds of that miserable town, Bets,' he said bitterly. 'We can make a fist of plugging the broaches, boats or no boats.'

He kept glancing towards the dryland as he moved north along the dyke. How many punts could an ox cart carry? Eight? Ten possibly? Had Golding that many? His river-beaters used small ones for duck farming. He himself had seen four longish punts on the mere which the River Affon fed. He reached firm land, and came on the working men.

Kettle's indecision had evaporated. Hunterfield could hardly believe that circumstance could change a man so quickly. The fore man was everywhere, cheerful and grinning, chastening the charcoal-burners and gabbing with his own Watermillock men. As Hunterfield rode up and dismounted he saw Kettle stoop to help up a carboneer's lad, ruffle his head and cuff him amiably back to his work of dragging alder staves.

'A better day now, Squire sir!' Kettle called, touching his

218

hat in salute. 'Thirteen punts, Squire. Four more coming down.'

'More?' Hunterfield counted them. They lay on the trampled grass, several already holding cradles of interwoven willow, ash and alder wands. 'There are more?'

'Another ox cart, sir. The oxherd and the girl bring a third team. It's tied. They had no other driver.'

'I understand.' Uphill driving with ox-teams in train was comparatively simple. Downhill was impossible, for a led team would slide down unchecked and bring disaster to the leaders. 'Ayrton?'

'Here, sir!' Ayrton arrived soaked, almost indistinguishable from mud.

'Your plan, if you please?'

'Float piles out, using a dyke pulley. Drive them a fathom to landward of the broaches. Then position the cradles in a vee, with gaps between.'

'Gaps?' Hunterfield asked, startled.

'To let the ebbtide, Squire. Silth we can cope with, once the sea's abated a good stound.'

'Of course.'

Ridiculous that he had not seen the obvious. Mud was manageable, after a time. Seal the dykes, and you would be left with a flooded plain of seawater, requiring pumping out. Let the sea do part of the work.

'Nobbut a sprink, Squire, to serve as a gully-hole.'

'Very well, Ayrton.' Only a crack, as the mouth of a drain.

The Watermillock men were invaluable: reason to call on Widow Maderley to express thanks, even if her tide-mill would benefit immeasurably from the land's recovery. He noticed Bartholomew Hast and Horatio Veriker walk up together and set to work without a word. So Sealandings was not wholly lost to honour.

'Come, if you please.'

Hunterfield stepped away out of the path of his Lorne House men who were heaving a cradle towards the punts. The two fore men accompanied him away from the industry.

'The ox waggons,' he asked bluntly. 'Can they be floated?'

'Floated, Squire?' Kettle looked his surprise, nodded to Ayrton to make the judgement.

219

The man was slow answering. 'Yes, Squire. But to what purpose, now we have the flatboats? We'll ferry enough cradles and smallstone to infill.'

'How soon?' Hunterfield remembered Ayrton's warning.

'By dawn we'll have broken it. Seal as the tide turns.'

'With what margin?'

Ayrton paused. He knew well what the Squire of Sealandings was asking. As long as the ebbtide helped, by draining the flood, the men's desperate work would make progress. But if the repaired breaches were too weakly underpinned, a brashly turning sea could undo it all in minutes.

'With none, Squire,' Ayrton said soberly. 'It's a race against the hour. And every minute the breaches widen.'

'The delay is against us?'

'Indeed, Squire.'

'Then we float across two ox waggons, just as they are, and sink them. In the breach, to seaward of what stout piles you can, in the time God allows.'

'Sink the waggons?' Both fore men were appalled.

'And the punts, too, when they've served their purpose,' Hunterfield said bluntly. 'It's my responsibility, and so I order. Can it be done?'

'Wheels and all, Squire?' from Kettle. To a fore man of mill machinery a crafted wheel was sacrosanct.

Hunterfield stifled his exasperation. Each was as obsessive as that mad Watermillock artist, seeing nothing but his own craft.

'If they serve our purpose submerged in the North Sea, Kettle, then dammit sink them.'

Ayrton had been staring across the flood to where another sliver of sea wall crumbled and slid into the water.

'Floated across, Squire, without the wheels. But we'd like them wheeled to help us stave them in.'

'Would they show above water?'

'Just below, Squire.'

'Then up-end them in the breach,' Hunterfield said harshly. 'Or fasten posts to them to serve as tethers, whereby they'll lie set in the dyke's topmost edge.'

'We have no such posts, Squire,' Kettle said.

Hunterfield gestured. 'Use the dryland posts, Kettle,' he said, ignoring their gasps of horror. The posts were huge and ancient, sanctified by custom and touched under peril of the law.

'They posts be set for all time, Squire,' Ayrton reminded him. 'They be placed under the King's order.'

'The Sovereign's law set the posts,' Hunterfield agreed. 'But God sent us the flood. Let us obey Heaven.'

Men were shouting as a third ox-team edged from among the trees. The thin old oxherd was driving, shouting ribald challenges at the woodcutters' lack of progress, and receiving crudities in reply. The girl Mehala was with him, her shawl cast back from her shoulders as she strove to hold the cart brake's long lever. The wheels were skidding, but with each slip she released slightly to let the wheels take new grip before resuming the pull. It was an expert display.

'Four more flatboats,' Ayrton said with relish. 'Had we more men, we could – '

'Squire. Your man.'

Hunterfield turned at Kettle's words to see Simple Tom approaching from Sealandings on his blowing hack. He went to meet him, surprised by the astonishment on Tom's face.

'Tom! The ox-teams and punts. Did. . .?'

Tom slipped from the saddle, quickly taking in the scene. He shook his head.

'What word from Bures House? Some messenger?'

Tom denied this, pointing to Mehala, and making a mimed bonnet. His hands opened. Surprise.

'She asked you what had transpired?'

A nod. Tom patted his chest, his hand describing a donation, then a palm held up in denial.

'You explained I was refused assistance,' Hunterfield translated. 'Whereupon what, Tom?'

Two fists shaken together, a nod to the north. The bonnet, a lifted palm.

'You went on to Sealandings, and Mehala went off somewhere?' Hunterfield returned to Kettle and Ayrton. 'Sink the waggons. And send me Mehala.'

He was sitting on a stile when she approached. The rain was easing slightly, but the onshore wind had freshened. Rivulets of mud were coursing faster from the wooded slopes everywhere.

Only the oxen kept footing slowly on, hauling the freshly cut logs. The men were cursing and slithering as underfoot the mud thickened. He appraised her for a few moments.

'You did well, Mehala,' he said evenly. 'I am indebted, as must be Sealandings, if we succeed in avoiding total loss.'

'Thank you, Squire. I only did my plain duty.'

Not long since, Hunterfield remembered, he had come upon the girl near this very spot. She had saved Simple Tom from drowning.

'You drive an ox-team, Mehala, as well as you find careless grooms a-drowning.'

Simple Tom was nearby. Hunterfield jerked his head, ordering Tom to lend the charcoalers help dragging wattles on to the punts. The groom went, smiling. Mehala flushed at being reminded.

'I could do no less, sir.'

He eyed her. 'Tell me, miss. Was there message for me from The Honourable Charles Golding? Or perhaps from Agent Lazard?'

'No, Squire. I saw neither of the gentlemen.'

Hunterfield waited. She stood in silence, levelly returning his gaze.

'You obtained permission from his gamekeepers? Or Bures House stewards?'

She showed mild surprise. 'No, sir. Only Tom's indications.'

'Indications? What indications?'

'His gestures, sir. To say he had made plea at the manors, sir.'

'So you took it upon yourself to. . .?

'I hastened to lend aid, sir.' She was speaking as if making a rehearsed speech. 'I guessed the oxen would be needed for the flood work, with waggons and flatbedders. So I called on Pilgrim Fleet.'

'I see.' To give himself time to digest this surprising girl's scheme, Hunterfield watched two punts being poled towards the dyke. A third punt was in tow, containing two boys and a heap of pulley ropes. 'You did not offer to help with horse waggons?'

'Any man here can manage horse-drawns, sir. I bethought myself of Pilgrim, the only oxherd left, since all be horses these days.'

'Almost, Mehala.'

'If it please you, sir, I knew there'd be sore need of flatbedder boats, and shulves to dig gripples for releasing the floodwaters.'

222

Indeed, digging tools would be needed for narrow trenches. Hunterfield gave her his frank attention, this girl who used coastal folk words, evidently by accident in unguarded moments, as now. Who had inordinate skill in the ancient art of driving man's oldest animal help, the ox, when it was all but extinct. Whose mind was nimble and clever. Whose fetching brightness would please any man – and set any woman brooding on rivalry. Who was less pretty than beautiful, once you looked, took trouble to see the sheer allure that lay within.

She said something about harness. He came to.

'The harness is so simple, sir, compared to that for horses. That is how I managed to help Pilgrim.'

'Very well.' If that was how she wanted her deed registered, so be it. For the moment he would let her words mask explanation. He knew the difficulties of driving animals. Getting the ox-teams across the shoulder of Whitehanger woods had been a feat for the old oxherd; it was no less a triumph for this girl. And it might save the sealands.

He pointed. 'Who drives the ox-teams now, miss?'

'Please you, Squire, Pilgrim the one, I the other, and a charcoaler from your Lornhanger has some skill for the third.' She halted, in the trap Hunterfield had set, and finished lamely, 'All the men want to try, it being a simplicity, sir.'

'Mehala. The Honourable Charles Golding refused me these same oxen, waggons, punts.'

Her eyes opened wide in astonishment. 'Sir? But I understood . . . Oh, sir! What have I done?'

He eyed her response. Her alarm was well-executed, but a shade too practised. He did not smile. She had done the right thing. He was in no doubt: Mehala had seen Simple Tom's meaning, but in spite of it had gone to find Pilgrim Fleet with the wrong message, knowing the grave need.

'Theft, Mehala. That's how the law might see it.'

'Oh, sir! I would never, never, sir! Whatever will become of this?'

Her response was still short of emotion, a fraction too calculated. Another man might be taken in, but he had three sisters, all eternally asking him to judge the rightfulness of their disparate causes. He was a veteran, of half-revelations cunningly construed to lead an unwary brother towards a desired decision, of planned oh-so-sudden displays of temperament intended to eradicate doubt or deflect anger. He cynically accepted the possibility that Mehala was showing only part of her acting skill.

'Less than you *seem* to fear, miss,' he said, his eyes holding hers. She must be left in no doubt. 'I accept your account, and take responsibility for what transpires hereon.'

'Oh, thank you, sir! I am so grateful! I would never have – '

'Your oxen wait, miss. Go to your duty.'

'I shall, sir. This instant, sir!'

He watched her move back. Within a few yards she was tilting her head in mock rebuke to the men who called and teased.

The girl was an enigma, obscure in origin and destiny. For a moment tiredness made him wander. He had a strange vision of Mehala presiding at dinner, laughing, in a jewelled necklace of rubies with diamonds splendidly setting her off, hair piled naturally, without the absurdities of wig and unfetching fashion. A lady for candlelight, graceful as breath, yet with a depth of sincerity to belie all modern whims. Fleeting affections were the norm in these insane days. She would converse with guests of all ranks, and – for so seemed the truth of this creature – be more knowledgeable than they. Not for her the modern manias, like those enthusiasms that caused women – like his mother, God rest her soul – to stalk in the deformed posture he recalled from his boyhood, the Grecian bend, in which ladies perambulated with their head carried turtled before them. No. A woman could be vivacious, yet a source of human wisdom and kindness.

He brought himself to heel. This would never do. Weariness was making him slip from awareness of the moment into dreams that would never come.

A man was calling for attention. Slack, one of his own gamekeepers, as muddied as the rest. He had the wheels off one side of the first waggon, but was questioning whether that was right. A good thought, for surely four wheels could not stand proud of the water. Hunterfield cursed himself for stupidity. Slack had been the cleverer. He rose and strode towards the man, trying for an attitude of calm purpose. He passed Mehala, and saw her quickly avert her face.

23

The land about Arminell was renowned for its prettiness. Even after so great a storm its appearance was less one of dishevelment than of countryside discreetly disarrayed.

Brillianta Astell told this to Carradine, and was rewarded by a laugh. A groom followed a furlong off as they rode at a walk through the valley.

'That only proves countryside is a lady, Brillianta.'

She decided to take mild offence. 'Sir! We ladies are not so cynical that all is design and nothing mere chance!'

'Chance is a wanton.'

Brillianta was delighted at the bitterness in his voice. Even in so short a time, she had managed to discover almost all of Carradine's sorry circumstances.

'Not to everyone, surely? And not on every occasion, otherwise Lady Chance would become Lady Certainty!'

Carradine shot her a glance, but she was blithely paying attention to the riverbank and reining in at a secluded spot. He pulled his horse in beside her.

'*Dear* sister Lorela returns today, Rad,' she said after a moment's pause. 'When we were little girls, this was our favourite spot in all Arminell. We used to sketch bold knights and dragons here.'

Carradine shifted uncomfortably in the saddle. Her whimsy disturbed him. Life was ferocious, at times bestial, unadorned with florets and sweet imaginings and children's drawing books. He was interested in the dislike which crept into Brillianta's voice when she mentioned Lorela.

'Do you have dragons, Rad?' she teased. 'Fair ladies?'

'Both,' he said sourly, wanting only to know why her father had so suddenly decided to leave Arminell for the coast. 'I have no skill to sketch any.'

'You shall tell me about them in plain words, sir!'

'I do not betray any lady's confidence, to friend or foe.'

225

She pretended horror. 'You do not say which of the two I am!'

'Why, foe, my lady, of course.'

She was surprised. 'Foe? For why, sir?'

He was a long time replying. 'Everybody is foe, Brillianta, until proved otherwise.'

'How can a lady know where proof lies?' she punned, striving to lift his humour.

'A lady always knows, but pretends ignorance.'

As Brillianta tutted reproof at the riposte he planned his next remark. He had to know the whereabouts of Sir Edward.

'Brillianta. May I ask a question?'

He was aware of her interest. Trammelled by the absurd conventions between the sexes, he was experienced enough to detect the signs. Were she living in London he would have already seized the delights she promised, but here in the remote provinces, it sometimes seemed that every blade of grass watched courtships—and cruder approaches, too – and spread the news with alacrity.

She for her part knew his reputation. Under no misapprehension about Carradine's appetites, she knew his affairs in the capital, his fiery temper, the duels, his unspeakable appetite for base indulgence. Against these was his handsomeness, youth, restlessness, that sullen quick anger which a woman could ignite by even the most innocent flippancy. And the sensation of danger, even fear, which he excited in her.

'Since when did a gentleman require permission to make an enquiry of a lady?'

'Since I met you riding this vale, Brillianta.'

She remained outwardly tranquil, but felt her breast tighten. No woman had captured Carradine, it was said, though rumour whispered of clandestine liaisons, the most threatening one with a married lady at Sealandings.

'Met me, Rad? I could have been anyone out riding past Hoddinotts.'

'About your sister.'

Swift annoyance coloured her throat. '*Dear* sister Lorela, sir? Have you renewed acquaintanceship with her? Met her accidentally in London?'

'I do not ask of her, Brillianta. Only of Miss Lorela in relation to you. Is there agreed preferment?'

Seniority of children was sometimes made a condition of proposals for engagement. When that rule was laid down, usually at the instigation of a vigilant mother, the older offspring were obliged to betroth before any younger child. Preferment was a difficulty, especially among sisters, and often caused seething resentment. Brillianta being the younger of the two Astell daughters, it was the first thing to be considered when a gentleman became enamoured of a lady of a titled family.

'Sir?' She pretended not to understand.

'I would have approached Sir Edward,' Carradine said, looking straight ahead, 'but he left late yesterday. I would have followed, but knew no direction. I trust it was not bad news?'

'No, sir. An important concern in Sealandings.'

Carradine nodded to himself. Lorela Astell's name had once been linked with Henry Hunterfield's. That was a sufficiently sound explanation. Maybe Hunterfield had at last given up hope of resuming his ridiculous affair with Thalia De Foe – God knows she'd played him for fool long enough – and was surrendering to Lorela Astell? Yet Brillianta spoke with disinterest of her father's journey. Had it been an affair of the heart, she would have made some cutting remark about her bothersome sister. And Sir Edward was the Justice in Maidborough, just as Hunterfield was the law in Sealandings.

'It is presumptuous to ask whether a preferment would be imposed,' Carradine continued, cautiously. He wanted to provoke revelations, yet vaguely hint at a proposal.

'Should it be a concern of yours, sir?'

'I hesitate to speak in the way I wish, my lady. I am very inexpert.'

'Is the occasion unsuitable, or the location?'

'Perhaps it is that, Brillianta,' he said, breaking off his seriousness and inclining his head in invitation to continue the ride downstream. 'My lack of expertise is a handicap. I shall rehearse, and do better next time.'

'I wish you success.' She entered into the spirit of his sudden light-heartedness, though she was annoyed at the new turn in their conversation. 'I should hate the great Carradine to fail.'

'So should I,' he said, having got the necessary information. He had to reach Sealandings quickly, and discover what her father, the crafty old fool, was up to. 'Rest assured, Brillianta. I do not lose easily.'

Her sudden dejection went as quickly as it had come. So he was addressing her availability for proposal. It could only be that. She wondered how far she could go, before Father returned from Sealandings, and was about to speak when she saw dear sister Lorela and a companion, trailed by a vigilant groom, riding towards them at a canter from the low wooden bridge. They came hallooing.

'Good heavens!' Brillianta exclaimed brightly. 'See who arrives home to Arminell! How very nice!'

24

'I'm as fit as ever I was,' Jason Prothero boasted to Mary, flexing his arm before the half-cheval glass.

Her attitude irritated him. Look what he had accomplished, despite the limitations of this indrawn wife! The conquest of Carradine Manor – it could not be described in any other terms – against all odds of birth! It showed a skill above circumstance. He grinned, pleased at his reflection.

'You are rising too early, Jason. Doctor Carmichael distinctly said – '

'That crocus!' he spat, rounding on her so furiously that she stepped back in alarm. 'What the hell does he know?'

'He was at pains to warn of relapse – '

'Listen to me!' His voice had an ugly intensity she recognised only too well. 'That quack fancied aggrandisement when he came a-visiting years ago. He has no right to dictate what goes on in Calling Farm! Remember that, my good lady!'

She was driven to protest at the slur. 'Jason! How can you say such a thing! Doctor Carmichael was no more than a boy when he and his father, an acquaintance, came expeditioning hereabouts.'

'Acquaintance!' he mimicked in cruel falsetto, then growled, 'I recognise a climber, woman. What idiot becomes a leech, save a fool unable to earn an honest living! They qualify by Fleet papers, and live thereafter on myth and dog-Latin! Your penny pillmaster comes here no more, d'you hear?'

Her timidity forced her to keep silent, though she felt the unjustness of the accusations. Ven Carmichael was no 'Fleet' doctor. He had studied his full years at The London Hospital, unlike the shams and quacks who simply bought their paper degrees for a few sovereigns in the alleyways of London's Fleet district. Prothero calmed, appraising himself. He had always been big in stature. Henceforth, he would be great in status. Triumph came to the deserving, not to ignorant dreamers like his stupid wife's girlhood friend. Her pathetic handwringing exasperated him beyond measure. No wonder he had to solace himself at Two Cotts. Whores knew where women's duties lay.

'You don't see what I have achieved, do you? We – I – now own Carradine Manor. *Own!* I will occupy the seat of a Lord of the Manor! Entitled to wear a coat-of-arms! Have liveried servants! I'm gentry.'

He examined his clothes. He caught sight of the woman's reflection, so agitated, so anxious. And so damned . . . *feeble!* Enough to make him spew with rage. He eyed her witheringly in the seeing glass. Was ever a woman so dull, so ineffectual? He'd done wrong in marrying the hopeless bitch, he could see that now. She was a burden to ambition. The old saying was true: ambition breeds itself a-plenty. How true!

'These garments won't do,' he told Mary roughly. 'I need completely new. London fashions, new weaves. See to it. I shall find time more pressing. Move yourself.'

'What new things, Jason?'

He erupted. 'God's sake, woman! Do I have to tell you everything? Other women know about fashions, styles, what's worn in the capital! And isn't the North's manufactories turning out novel materials every single hour?'

'Yes, Jason. I shall write off this morning, instantly.'

He glowered, not trying to conceal his contempt, and went downstairs to see Perrigo. The man had importuned him every second, practically on his deathbed after that ignorant sawbones had almost done for him with his cackhanded mangling.

Mary desultorily started to replace his linen, hearing him stomp down calling to Libby the maid-of-all for his riding coat. Even to that harmless girl he shouted abuse about his thick surtout, though it had been waterproofed by Mrs Perrigo and herself with beeswax and oils of turpentine only two days previously.

She sat on the edge of the bed, tears starting. So desperate was her torment that she wondered if the whole world itself had changed. Were men and women the creatures they once were? In her parents' days, the world had seemed secure, for all that all Europe, indeed this very Kingdom, had been in upheaval. But this was something different.

As a little girl, she indeed admired the quiet, amused boy who had come to Calling Farm. Mr Carmichael was a botanically-minded gentleman, with a fund of slight stories that somehow never ended. His profound knowledge of herbs and seashells much excited Father's admiration. And Ven had liked her company, a blessing. She had no siblings, and suffered from the fatal indecisions of the lone child. Then had come a time when the Carmichaels stopped coming. Youth was ended. Apart from rare courtesy letters, communication was somehow lost in the press of adulthood. The very worst happened when Father and Mother passed away. The dearth of close relatives truly wounded her, with the realisation that she was alone. No advice or aid, yet possessing lands and wide influence. But she had the supporting hand of Jason Prothero, herdsman, then chief herdsman, assistant agent, estate steward. Then suitor. It seemed so natural a transition, almost inevitable. His large, decisive presence took the place of the authority Father had exercised so naturally. Jason Prothero's proposal had come as a blessing, an enormous relief. She simply placed in his capable hands all the responsibilities of Calling Farm. From that very moment, wedlock's instant, her staid, tranquil world had started to crumple, though she was only now realising how seriously her life was distressed. She refused to acknowledge the source of her anguish.

Seeing Ven enter her house, the changes in him, the drawn haggard features, his helplessness and his worry, had drawn her heart in a way that could only be sinful. She knew that mistakes were features of life's landscape for every woman, as rocks and cliffs were for the traveller. They were marks to go by, to remember their location should one ever journey along that same road a second time. Chances do not recur. Marriage was a onceship. As you wedded so you bedded, she recalled her grandmother saying.

She went to the window to look out. A grey, importuning sort of day with the weather at its rumbustious worst. From here she could not clearly see the roadway through the screed of trees. She often looked out hoping to glimpse Ven. Were he a fashionable doctor, she thought wistfully, he would ride a grand hack or drive a whisky. Then he would appear above the hedgerows at the end of the South Toll road, and perhaps smile and maybe doff his old beaver hat knowing she'd be there. Perhaps she would wave, as when he used to come running across the sands by the mouth of the River Affon, smiling, always smiling . . .

Perrigo was out in the Short Dog pasture where, Prothero remembered with satisfaction, he himself had tended the cows in all weathers. Not any more! That was for serfs. He felt the same glow of gratification when, riding the boundary hawthorns, he saw Perrigo catch sight of him and come instantly to intercept.

'Well, man?' he called out as he approached. 'All in order, eh? I expect it!'

The herdsman looked askance at his master. 'I have a report, sir, and serious thing to ask.'

'Ask of me?' Prothero swelled with pride, even though this was but a labourer, and deeply beholden to his owner who gave him wage, hearth and home.

He almost laughed in triumph. Naturally he should have expected this grovelling admission of his exalted status. Word must have got round Sealandings like a fire, of Mr Prothero's swift advancement! The Quality must be swiftly reconsidering their acquaintanceship with Prothero of Calling Farm, hoping he wouldn't remember the slights they'd inflicted on him! Well, he just might make a few hides smart! Like he had subdued that now not-so-grand Carradine.

'What is it, Perrigo? Out with it, man!'

'It's the herds, sir. The murrain's mortal bad, and – '

'That tale again?' Prothero exclaimed impatiently. 'Are you bereft of sense, Perrigo, that you can't cope. . . ?'

His exasperation faded. He saw cords wound round the black-thorns, staves carrying strips of cloth dyed with autumn crocus, the ominous meadow saffron that indicated the most feared of afflications, the cattle plague. Perrigo's men had driven one stave every eleventh perimeter yard. The lines stretched into the adjacent field called Turn Sickle. The same hideous colour flickered distantly on the third pasture, upland from where he was, across his greatest and hitherto safest pasture Thin Den. The brightly hued cloths, flapping at their staves in the wind, constituted the horrid stigmata of an outbreak of disease. His mind chilled.

'What's this, Perrigo? All herds?'

'I tried to tell 'ee, sir, but you were afflicted.'

'Don't you know not to raise that meadow saffron unless whole herds sicken?'

Perrigo looked across the Short Dog pasture, saying nothing more. Prothero stood in his stirrups to see. A score of corpses lay strewn over the grass by the far hedges. Smoke was rising distantly. The herdsman nodded.

'We'm burning, masther,' he admitted laconically. 'But there's too many of them to keep pace.'

Prothero stared down at the man, stared round his acreage. No cattle moved. A trio of herders was standing immobile at the entrance of the Hook pasture, two furlongs off. He made to speak, could not, tried again and failed. This was outrageous, an imposition. It could not be happening. It was . . . it was simply *wrong*. His plan had different components – advancement, gain, acquisition and power. It included no failure, epidemics, setbacks so severe that he might be brought under. He recovered, gazed imperiously round. It could not be as bad as this incompetent man said. It was not as it seemed: it was all carelessness. He saw that with instant clarity. This calamity was the direct result of Perrigo's gross lack of discipline. He should never have been sick, that was the trouble. The moronic quack's ineptitude had kept him delirious far too long. This was not, could not be, cattle plague. It was simply some chance transitory malady that Perrigo had allowed to get out of hand. While the cat's away, mice will play. He glared down at the chief herdsman.

'How many afflicted, Perrigo?' he demanded.

'All herds, sir,' Perrigo answered after a moment. 'Thirteen, all tainted. Provinder neither in nor out, nor cattle to be sold or moved, since it became known.'

'I see,' Prothero said, nodding knowingly. 'I see.'

So the gentry's resentment was such that now he himself, Prothero of Calling Farm and Carradine Manor, was to be persecuted! Soon it would be by additional means – the law, petty magistracies, legalities, any that the Quality could bring to bear! Each coughing cow, each calf limping on a swollen hoof, was a plague! And they would lay their costs at his door! Snivelling wretches, is all they really were. He should have guessed. The gentry was closing ranks against him, a threat to their élite society. They didn't dare do it to his face, oh, no! They had to wait for him to fall sick. He smiled, recognising the neatness of their nefarious plan. No sooner was he laid low than they plotted against his rise.

In fact, thinking of how he came to be stricken in the first place, was it not clearer still? That bitch Mehala had carried out orders given her by Hunterfield and his Quality brigands! And why Mehala? Why, she – whose interruption had caused him injury so he was temporarily removed from his proper position of authority – she was selected *because she was no mere serving wench*! All too often she gave herself away. Her wide knowledge of purchasing, weapons, beasts, accounts, her carriage even, her allure, all betokened status which proved only too clearly she was no mere ordinary creature. She was in league with Hunterfield, Lord of Sealandings. His whore, doubtless.

Hitherto, his ascent had been a negotiated brawl. Henceforth it would be war, the one thing at which he excelled. It was a challenge, the gauntlet cast for him to pick up. Who knows, he wondered frankly, but what this was their refined way of initiating him by test, like the knights of old tried novitiates by exotic trials of character!

Perrigo gaped to see Prothero smiling. 'Your orders, masther?'

'Orders?' Prothero exuded confidence. 'First, Perrigo, have the cow doctor from Maidborough, to prove that this is merely a three-dayer.'

The herdsman drew a sharp breath. A three-day ailment was a quick-come quick-go cough from which coastland cattle suffered in these months. It caused no loss, though it was known to move from one herd to the next.

'Three-dayer, sir?'

'You heard me, man!' Prothero shouted, making his mount shy so he had to wrestle with the beast to regain control. 'Get him! Show me the latest beast down with it.'

Perrigo led the way a hundred yards further along the hedge and stood several yards off, merely pointing.

The dying animal lay on its side, flies already settled on its head and eyes. A gumaceous secretion, thick as a man's finger, lined the poor beast's eyelids. Its tongue lolled out so far that it touched the grass, not furred but ominously shining. The cow's chest heaved in short spasms. The head was swollen, the throat rattling even when the animal was still. Prothero tried not to recoil: all were the signs of cattle murrain, the feared animal plague. But surely many potions, extracts from plants, galenicals and tinctures known to

234

gypsies and cowmen, could produce this gruesome appearance? And just as certainly some poisons – *perhaps even introduced of a night by enemies?* – could cause these effects. His early years as a herdsman had taught him how to deceive cattle buyers at market.

'As I thought, Perrigo. It's simple bellyblow.'

'But, sir!'

'Sir me nothing!' Prothero yelled down at the dolt in fury. 'I have the evidence of my own eyes, man! You've let these cattle wander into forbidden pasture, where they may graze on any wild plant they care to! Where they may lick dead badgers, contract any ailment. It's clear negligence! I'll have your hide for this, Perrigo! You and your lazy idlebacks have ruined the most valuable herds in the Eastern Hundreds! You'll pay, Perrigo!'

'Sir! By my life I swear – '

'The cattle have been neglected,' Prothero shouted. 'Don't deny it! Is'll have those saffron markers out for a start!'

'Sir? The magistracy's orders – '

Prothero's wintry smile silenced the herdsman.

'You don't understand, do you, Perrigo?'

The farmer scanned the pasture, nodding in satisfaction at the disaster. How hopeless to explain to folk whose destiny was to remain villeins, peasants for all eternity. Some were lodged by the Almighty in lowly niches, to serve and obey, to pay homage. Those, like Perrigo, remained hewers of wood and drawers of water, humbled and humble. Then there were those like himself, selected for higher things, raised above the common lot into positions of authority. To combat the envy which such exaltation provoked, was at once challenge and duty. It was the Law of God.

'No, sir.'

'All right, Perrigo, all right.'

Prothero's resolve was complete. Every detail was in place. That Doctor Carmichael had come here with the bitch Mehala, had he not? Ostensibly to attend at a sickbed. But it was ample opportunity to whisper messages, from Carmichael to his childhood sweetheart Mary, of how to execute the downfall of Jason Prothero! He should have guessed from the outset. Who better than his own wife, influenced by Carmichael, to undermine his new position by prolonging his illness? The interval they gained was enough to allow the murrain to spread through Calling

Farm's valuable herds. That in itself was sure proof of conspiracy.

Was Carradine himself the instigator, and Hunterfield fed false information? He almost laughed aloud. False! Even that possibility was falsity! Mary Prothero by all rules of logick was proved deceiver, preferring a wandering quackster to her own spouse.

Very well, Mary Prothero, he thought grimly. Betrayer, you must take your chances with opponents, having swapped fidelity for illusion.

'Do as I order, Perrigo. Remove all signs within two hours. And get these cadavers buried.'

'The newly sick, sir? The produce?'

'Compound the animals, but bury them too as they die. The produce?' Prothero thought hard. Sealandings would be averse to taking any produce from Calling. Stupid superstition, of course, but that's how ignorant folk behaved. 'Our produce is the best. They need my barley for brewing, as well as corn, beef, hides. They'll buy.'

'But drawing it takes horses, masther, and they'll be shunned for fear – '

Prothero grinned. Perrigo started back in alarm. Nobody grinned at calamity, save the mad.

'For fear of putrefaction of the air to other herds outside my acreage, Perrigo?' Prothero chuckled. This dolt still couldn't see the obvious. The perpetrators of this evil hoped that Calling Farm's produce would fall in price, that barley would be omitted from brewers' buying-ins, that Calling corn would cheapen, that fatting cattle and stock beef would be begged away at the selling stumps, that Calling wool would be left for gypsies' night-stealing.

His mind examined charts of selling, buying, shortages. Ever since Gregory King, the famed 'farmer of reason' nigh two centuries agone, people as eminent as Doctor D'Avenant had tried to logick rules of profitable farming for times of shortages. Most common belief in the Eastern Hundreds was the one-to-three rule – that a defect of one-tenth raised prices by a third of that tenth, but that a deficiency of five-tenths increased the price of a commodity by four-and-a-half tenths. Lately, modern savants were arguing the inconsistency of such 'rules', but what had served country farming for centuries would serve Jason Prothero. Let them go short a day, two days, a week, even. They'd soon realise that deficiency damns, and come begging for his produce. He would increase Calling prices to make up for cattle losses. A singular pleasure! He'd charge most to those he suspected most. Fair is as fair does. Prothero lands now were nearly the largest in Sealandings. Power was wealth.

'Perrigo? If we lose ten per cent of cattle, pass word to my tenant-farmers that rents increase fifteen per cent.' He smiled, in expectation of trouble. 'Should my grains be refused at market, rents shall be regulated by a new scale. My average wheat price is thirty-six shillings, so the average price to regulate rents will be two guineas. And for every wheat-price shilling, vary the rents by eighteen pence. Remember that example, if you please.'

'Two guineas, sir?' The herdsman gaped in bewilderment, wondering if he was hearing right. He knew that corn rent was the money value of land converted into quarters of wheat. The increase was an impossible imposition on the small renters – and Calling Farm had many.

'That's so, Perrigo. Carry out my instructions immediately.'

The chief herdsman stood watching the master canter from the field towards the main house. Behind him, the poor beast gave a last shudder, and died.

25

'Who the devil are you?' Carradine had seen the man loitering – at the main front gate, mark you – of Hoddinott. A gross impertinence.

He strode out with his whip in hand and waited. The man approached him with the right amount of deference. Indeed, the oaf was almost ingratiating as he came, grinning with uneven teeth. He doffed his ridiculous old fantail tricorne in deference, and plucked with seeming nervousness at his smock frock, the drover's garb. Carradine watched. There had been too much awry in the region lately, robbers having lately set upon a gentleman at Wheatfen, and robbed a barouche and two ladies therein near Falldyke, less than fifteen miles off. For all the vagrant's show of deference, the man could not be trusted.

'Saving your presence, sir, might I ask who you might be?'

'Your damned impudence has earned you a flogging.' Carradine advanced with his whip raised.

The drover did not flinch. 'An you please, sir. The gentleman I have message for might be cross.'

An unpleasing man, Carradine saw instantly. A jack-in-office, a beggar a-mount, of the sort all too common these days. A reformationer, that now littered the North's mad mills and undermined society at every turn. And succeeded, when gentry were too weak to suppress such perfidy. Ideas above his allotted station.

Carradine smiled grimly. 'Name that gentleman, and I'll see.'

'One lately come to Hoddinott.' The drover was unfazed, stood his ground, cocksure.

'From where in particular?' Carradine asked, suddenly realising.

Judith Blaker had said one of her relatives would come, should anything of importance transpire in Sealandings. What the hell was his name? Bellin came to mind, but she seemed to have relatives abounding.

'From Sealandings, sir. Not far from the Norwich road.'

'Bellin, is it?'

'Myself, sir. Do I address Howard Carradine?'

'You do, sir.' Carradine's sarcasm was lost on the drover. 'You have word?'

'From a lady acquaintance in common, sir.'

Ten minutes later, Carradine was standing before the fire in the hall. The drover was drinking with relish from a pewter cup which the maid-of-all, an elderly Maidborough woman, had provided with downturned mouth at this intrusion by a mere turnpike drover. Until she departed, Carradine pretended to question Bellin on the condition of the coast roads. The drover glibly fell in with the deception, only coming to the point when they were alone.

'Mistress Judith sends her compliments, sir, with assurances that she remains devoted – '

'Get on, for God's sake.'

The man nodded. 'Three messages. One, Mr Prothero is ill, but recovered under ministrations of Doctor Carmichael. Two, the sea dykes be broached, flooding the sealands between White-hanger and Watermillock. Three, estates and small farms alike be mortal afflicted by the storm.'

'Very well.' Carradine was unperturbed. Nothing new, not really. He already had in his pocket a note, penned by the whore Lucy in a surprisingly firm hand, telling of Prothero's illness. He had not yet taken possession of Carradine Manor in person, though he had removed to Calling Farm the barouches, the whisky and two of the larger carriages. 'How manages Mistress Blaker?'

'Very well, an you please. Her position strengthens daily. The South Toll turnpike is on tender again.'

Carradine took stock of the drover. The man was holding something back. He nodded in mute recognition of the problem.

'I am going to reward you, Bellin. I appreciate loyalty, both in you and in your . . .'

'Cousin, sir,' Bellin said affably. 'My mother's side. The stronger.'

Gypsy, then, Carradine noted. At last he knew the play. Judith Blaker, gypsy to her stem, could call on a host of readymakers, artisans skilled in waggons, wheelwrights, roadmending, forestry,

239

horse breeding, aye, and thieving; night-runners all. Never a gypsy but lurked a score of cousins round the next bend. However, Judith Blaker was learned, with talents to charm any man. He had only used her on one occasion, but it had proved memorable. An ally indeed.

'Bellin, I want you to take a message back.' He passed over three gold sovereigns. Bellin's hand hardly seemed to move, but they were gone.

'Thank you, sir. Oh, there was one other message. I forgot.' Bellin poured himself another draught uninvited. Carradine waited. There was a danger, he knew, of getting in too deeply with these people. But danger he never shirked. It was exhilaration – if coped with in the right way. And Judith Blaker was enticing danger, all the more delightful.

'Written, or unwritten?'

'It's more . . . shall I say rumour, sir.' Bellin rose, hitched his smock to sit well on his shoulders prior to leaving. 'There's tale of a murrain in Sealandings.'

'Murrain?' Please let it not be at Carradine's tributary farms, or the main estate. 'Cattle plague?'

'Itself, sir, sure as God groos acorns. So far only Calling Farm, main and tenancies.'

'Prothero's place.' Carradine studied the drover for signs of scurrilous humour, decided he was speaking the truth. 'Can that be? Prothero's is supposedly the most agricultural farm in the Sealandings Hundred.' The man was obsessed with every thatch on his tenant-farmers' roofs, each thoroughfare to Sealandings market. But it was high time Dame Fortune lent the Carradine purse largesse from Prothero. 'Mr Prothero's far too meticulous to let an epidemic take hold.'

'I spoke with Judith a day agone, sir,' Bellin said comfortably. 'She tells of tea invitations to Carradine Manor being cancelled. And Mr Prothero and his lady's move into Carradine is postponed on account of it.'

'I can check your veracity, Bellin. I ride soon to Sealandings.'

'Then Godspeed, sir,' Bellin said with composure, making slowly for the door. 'I trust you'll wish the same to Sir Edward Astell, should you overtake him.'

Carradine thought swiftly. This man knew more than he was

telling. His words seemed worthy of half an ear, especially as the three sovereigns had already been paid. 'Sir Edward, you say?'

'He's also to Sealandings, sir,' Bellin replied calmly. 'He will avoid the Wheatfen road and take the Opshall fork. The turnpike twixt here and Wheatfen be mortal flooded.'

Carradine swallowed his pride. 'Do you know why Sir Edward journeyed to the coast in the first place, in these inclement weathers?'

'I'm not sure, sir, but a magistracy which announces public warning of murrained cattle consults neighbouring magistracies.'

'So.' Carradine nodded, feeling excitement grow. This was fantastic, almost wondrous news. Prothero's estates murrained – and his cattle so badly afflicted that magistrates conferred to establish procedures! And Carradine Manor was not yet affected, it seemed. Judith Blaker was now vitally important, a spy ensconced in the Manor itself. Sir Edward Astell was the seniormost Justice of the Peace inland. Sir Philip Banks ruled to the north in Wheatfen, Opshall, Fenham. And on the coast Sir Henry Hunterfield, Squire of Sealandings, at Lorne House – which was exactly the place Sir Edward had gone in such early haste, according to his own beloved daughter Brillianta! It all fitted, close as a Priapus hood on a Saturday night paramour's joystick in Covent Garden's busy brothels.

'How fares Mr Prothero's health, Bellin?'

Bellin laughed through two scagged rows of bad teeth. 'Well enough, sir. His wife had Doctor Carmichael operate, then refused to pay when that leech came palm out!'

That too fitted – a nice touch of truth establishing what could well have been an unfathomable mystery.

'Here, Bellin. Another two sovereigns for your tidings.'

'Thank you, sir.' Bellin took the coins. 'I'd have liked these with the King's head doffing his laurels, sir.'

Carradine had the sense to smile at the insolence. The laureated royal head on the recently minted pound golds was distinctive, but not nearly so distinct as the large bare unlaureated King's head of the two-pound gold coins.

'Be gone, Drover Bellin!' he said. 'Next time say double, and I shall pay double!'

Bellin left, grinning, having done well for the day. Carradine wondered how much Judith Blaker received of the sum he had paid over. Probably nothing, if he guessed aright. She was stalking larger game.

He sat in silence for a long hour, thinking of new possibilities opening up. It was time to execute the plan he had been harbouring since his ruinous crash of fortune. He would ride to Sealandings, yes, by the Opshall fork, and take great pleasure in doffing his riding Wellington to Sir Edward Astell – with the appropriate exclamations at so fortuitous a greeting, of course. Then take Sealandings by storm.

The girl sat by the harbour, wet and chilled, waves almost reaching her as they dashed upon the Mole.

There was nothing now. Meals were a thing of the past. Clothes, money, converse with others, the same. Home was a distant nothing, a place for rejection. Warmth was draining from her disastrously wronged mortal frame.

Ruin came in many guises. Some were sudden and overwhelming, like those of the Bible, like in the parson's sermons in the Sunday church of girlhood. Or they crept up, drifting like a miasma into breath, skin, bone, blood, making mockery of life and blighting the future so it became a vast nothingness. Perhaps it was in that great void that souls flew to live again in Heaven's kind care? Her mind offered nothing to this idea except denial. It was too good to be so, too blissful to suppose that ending life like this would bring peace, a mystic happiness in some delightful Heaven.

She had seen them set upon the Doctor, as she had run after him out of the door, fleeing Two Cotts to go with him. She knew that as long as he had a crumb to share she would not starve. And she could serve. She had been quite good at helping, cooking even, doing menial tasks about a house, keeping hearths in a semblance of order. Even if he had nowhere, as the girls were saying at Two Cotts, she would have gone beside him. He was another person, Bella told herself. One who would speak. Maybe say nothing sometimes but be there. She could accept the occasional buffet if he got into a temper – she'd already learned to accept those, God knew.

They had set on him, Jeckel and his great gang of holies, the church folk who so loved their evil God that they'd even slay a kindly soul like Doctor Carmichael, all for nothing. She'd seen the beating they gave the poor man. He'd tried to shield his head as their blows rained down. Nobody could have survived such assault. Her guardian was gone, that was plain. Nobody would take her now Mrs Wren had cast her out. It was done. All done.

She said a prayer, a short singsong incantation she'd learned at the church school, waited until the next wave hit, and slipped forward off the Mole into the dragging waters as they lifted, halted, and withdrew from the shore, carrying her form with the outrush of sea.

26

'Good of you to come out, Sir Edward.'

Hunterfield was a little embarrassed, not to say ashamed, of the dishevelled crews who made up his workforce. This was the trouble: inland guests visited *down*, while coastals going inland felt visiting *up*. It was discommoding. Fortunately, Sir Edward Astell was well aware of the responsibilities of authority, and Sir Henry was at ease whenever their concerns coincided, as now.

The sea dykes had almost been stopped, all three. Four score men laboured, some drawing wood downhill to the dryfland, but most employed hauling baskets of smallstone to the edge of the morass. Everyone was covered in slimy seamud, their clothes unrecognisable and their faces a greyish patch atop a blur of sombre blacks and umbers.

'I apologize, Sir Edward, for my early departure from Lorne House this morning.' Hunterfield had returned immediately to the flooded sealands once his host had been absorbed into the household, having merely ridden swiftly home for a quick breakfast and to give Lydia instructions concerning their guest.

Sir Edward Astell was not deceived by the kindly fiction. He knew Hunterfield would pay less heed to a guest than to the sea defences.

'Henry, no offence. I missed you at a lengthy breakfasting – almost as much as I missed Captain Vallance!'

The two men laughed at the joke; the vivacious Lydia's husband was in India. Hunterfield respected the older knight, had no qualms about his conduct. Indeed, he suspected that Astell, in hurrying from Arminell through such tempestuous weathers and over East Anglia's notoriously quagged trackways and turnpikes, had two purposes in mind. One of course was their coterminous judiciaries, the other possibly concerning his daughter Lorela Astell and himself.

Henry, so decisive about urgent matters of Excise and Customs, harbour controls, regulations for roads, commerce and everything from land drainage to the tax on windows, carts and tinkers, was apprehensive about more personal concerns. He knew that, even if Sir Edward Astell had not been driven by urgent circumstance, Lydia was due to visit the Astells. She had raised the issue several times lately, recently with little regard for circumspection. Why, only a week ago he had almost rebuked her for making a direct remark on the elder Miss Astell's admirable qualities! Much correspondence had taken place between Lydia and Lorela Astell. Why, these days even Tabitha – so young, for heaven's sake! – had taken an uncommon interest in the goings-on at Arminell, repeatedly urging Lydia to arrange a fortnight's stay for them all there. Letitia said nothing to little, as ever.

'How came the news to you, Henry?' Sir Edward asked finally, watching an ox-team slide with that ungainly downhill spread-legged gait, dragging bundles of oaken staves to be woven with split larch, birch and alder brattlings.

'I heard accidentally, Sir Edward.' Hunterfield gestured at the flood. 'But for the storm damage, I should not have gone seeking assistance from my peers.' His voice became bitter at the thought of his many rejections from the Sealandings gentry. 'I found myself crying alms from pillar to post, almost begging for hands, waggons, beasts of burthen, any assistance at all.'

''Tis a sorry state, Henry, when a nation must collect coppers in a squire's hat to mend sea defences.'

'Like a dancing-bear's master,' Hunterfield complained. 'It's the same with the poor. To take but one instance: we've a seaman suffered an amputation, from a ship aground. He has no support, living in a cottage rented from the Carradine estate. What can the man do, but trust to fortune? I'm hearing for parish support, as soon as the sea's made safe.'

Sir Edward chuckled at the choice of words. 'Brave Henry. There's cause for few smiles. You noticed cattle sick at Calling Farm yourself, then?'

'No. I'd just come from Golding's – you visit Bures House occasionally, I believe – and was directing myself to Milton Hall. I sent my groom Simple Tom – there he stands – to Calling Farm, only to find him riding hard to come up with me. He'd seen the sick cattle, some dead even then.'

'So no report was made directly to you?'

245

'Nor to anyone else, Sir Edward.' Hunterfield's dislike for Jason Prothero fought for an instant with rectitude. He added with some reluctance, 'Admittedly, Prothero is afflicted with a festering arm, occasioned by an injury. Our local leech was treating him. I hear he has recovered, thanks be.'

'Amen. Good God! What on earth. . .?'

Hunterfield hid a smile. 'I've been watching her ever since the raised paths between the fields showed. Isn't it remarkable?'

'I've never seen the like, Hunterfield!'

Sir Edward walked to the edge of the dryland and stood close to a marker-post where the ground rose slightly.

A kirtled girl was gliding along at incredible speed across the mud, almost as fast as anyone could run. Lines of thick glutinous mud, coal-brown, showed in flat strips between the flooded fields. The paths between were first to show as the flood level started to fall.

'Dammit, but she skates, Henry! D'you see, sir? Actually glides!'

'The men tried it too, but failed.'

Sir Edward Astell was hardly able to restrain his amusement and interest.

'Her name's Mehala,' Hunterfield told him. 'A drowned girl, taken from the North Sea by a Yorkshire lugger. Her mind is not yet recovered, but she seems well enough, as you see!'

The girl had rough oval boards tied to her feet. The boards were nothing remarkable, being rounded into a broad curve at the fore, and blunt-pointed behind. They served for shoes, she being otherwise unshod, leather thongs holding them firmly to her feet. She moved with an indolent grace Sir Edward found amazing. It looked so simple, almost like swimming without the need to enter the water.

'Here, Henry. Wherever did she learn that trick? People inland would never believe my account!'

'Somewhere in her background, I surmise.'

The girl was skimming smoothly towards the dryland, where she slid to a halt against a marker-post two chains off. She took up a rope from a man and, without waiting, turned again towards the sea dykes. She started off but this time slower, towing a punt laden with washed smallstone. The grey-painted punt moved with slow jerks as she pulled at each step, until gradually it too settled into a steady glide. She had a clear road along the raised stetch. Further along, an ox-team hauled three filled punts along on a parallel course, but slower.

'It was her idea, Sir Edward,' Hunterfield informed his astonished guest. 'One of my men cut a backboard from yonder waggon, and she was off like a . . . like a . . .'

'Skater!' Sir Edward exclaimed. 'I saw this when I was but a boy. London's Thames froze: people built fires on the ice, and held games and feasts with stalls. But such accomplishment here – no offence intended, Henry – on sealands mud!'

'She does the work of a third of an ox-team,' Hunterfield said. He was unsure whether to allow his feeling of pride to show, or whether to remain disparaging. 'The punts bear the weight, going alongside the stetch paths where the flood's fallen away. The men say they have seen it somewhere.'

'See how she manages the towing rope?'

'Yes. It conforms to all logick, once you've seen it. But try to do it without advisement, and even the strongest man comes a cropper. Several tried!'

The two main breaches in the sea walls were closed now. The last was being filled as the ebbtide reached its lowest level. The great art was to staunch the flows simultaneously, but as Hunterfield pointed out to his visistor, there were too few men to operate three closures simultaneously.

'I've put a dozen men, with an oxen-team each, strengthening the pledgets. You'll notice the nether one? Preparing a plug almost immediately.'

Thirty men were at the breach, several wading about the gap, holding the wattles floating on the water. Two great cairns of stones surmounted the dyke, one each side of the opening. The sea could be seen beyond, shifting and white-topped, reminding the teams of its power every so often by a chance inrush, making the men shout warnings as they tried to stay linked across the space.

'What desperate labour, Hunterfield! We inlanders ne'er think of this, when we come to your stands and pick fish for a tasty supper in an Arcadian setting!'

'It's good of you to come, Sir Edward.'

'At least you had some assistance from our rank.' The Maidborough gentleman eyed the oxen. 'Pleasant to see those ancient beasts working so gaily, under these sorry skies. I think I noticed Golding's flatboats, did I not?'

A voice behind exclaimed. Charles Golding came riding from the Sealandings coast road. The two turned in surprise. Golding's face was flushed with anger. He shook his gauntlet towards the sea dykes, wrenching his gelding's mouth savagely.

'Indeed you did, sir!' Golding's voice was a loud rasp, though they stood within easy earshot. 'I demand an explanation of that frank transgression!'

'Transgression, sir?' Astell glanced in surprise at his host. 'Sir Henry, party to a transgression? That cannot be, Golding – '

'Those, Sir Edward! Those!' Golding rose in his stirrups, pointing with his riding whip. '*My* punts. *My* waggons. *My* ox spans, sir. Removed from my lands!'

'But – '

'Ye gods! *No!*' He waved and yelled. 'Stop! See what they're doing!'

'Sir?' Kettle called, standing beside Ayrton on the dyke's rim, signalling with a neckerchief. 'Ready for the drop, Squire!'

'Go ahead!' Hunterfield called, and raised his hat.

Mehala's final puntload of smallstone had been lifted in simple trugs and added to the mounds. The punt itself was being tilted, and placed on end projecting from the water. Men on each side of the gap held taut double ropes in tug-o'-war positions, eight to a side, three punts projecting end-on from the water, gripped between the ropes.

'They're not going to – ' Golding's voice choked. Sir Edward's eyes raked the man, took in Hunterfield's pallor at the accusation, and ahemed casually.

'This reflects excellently on your reputation, Golding. Your sainted father would be proud of you. I know of nothing so generous, as your surrendering your favourite sporting implements to save the sea dykes. Most warming, sir.'

Golding looked down at the magistrate, bewildered. 'My punts, sir! I had them especially constructed for the sole purpose of entertaining my guests!'

'Please, Golding, do not try to lessen your sacrifice. I know full well in what affection you hold your sport, sir! Very like your father in every way! I heartily approve, sir!'

The first punt slipped sideways on Ayrton's cry. It splashed into the gap. A second followed, the men shouting last-moment adjustments to direction. Those in the water did the bulk of the work, floundering as they tried to keep footholds in the mud. The third was simplest, falling like a card slotted into its pack between the first two, end on. Their gunwales could just be seen level with the surface of the water in the breach.

'All done, you see, Sir Edward?' Hunterfield spoke quietly. 'The punts will be piled – supported by stout baulks of timber. Between them will be similarly placed wattles – rafts of interwoven oak staves and split hazels. The sails and shores are different lengths –'

'Sails? Shores?'

'Sails are sticks left pointed but short, as along the wattled hurdle's length. The shores are end staves, pointed and cut long enough to be driven into the mud below. Each is riven neatly – mostly by charcoal-burners from Whitehanger and my own men.'

'All this achieved thanks to you, Golding,' Sir Edward said, smiling as if with admiration.

'Well,' Golding swallowed. 'Well, Sir Edward, I had originally little intention of . . .'

'Ah, rank imposes obligation, sirrah!' Sir Edward wagged his head knowingly. 'I saw through your masquerade of petulance immediately! Trying to disguise your gratification, exactly as old Sir Charles would have done! It touched me quite, sir, I'll not deny.'

'I only . . . It's actually . . .' Golding lamely took refuge in a furious silence, glaring at the dykes where the men had started to shovel the flintstones into the gaps in a series of rhythmical splashes.

'Very heartwarming, Golding. I'm proud to know you.'

Hunterfield could almost see Golding's mind working: political aspirations meant hostages given to fortune. And one principal decider of political fortunes in the Eastern Hundreds was the powerful Sir Edward Astell, sage of the Whig party. Golding could not afford to offend him. Sir Edward's approval meant a vital step forward for ambition.

How far Golding's train of thought carried him was immediately apparent when he turned with a forced smile to Hunterfield.

'I must have seemed out of countenance, Sir Henry, coming upon you so rudely. I hope and trust that nothing in my speech or manner gave injury?'

'Mmmmh?' Hunterfield murmured. He was not going to let Golding's rudeness go quite so easily. He guessed that Charles Golding was reading into Sir Edward's visit exactly what Lydia did, namely a possible union between the Astells and Hunterfields.

'It was simply that . . .' Golding dabbed at his mouth with a monogrammed cremyle. 'Simply that I imagined for a moment that the men were acting contrary to my, ah, wishes, ah, out there.'

'Such a mistake is easily made, Golding,' Sir Edward said affably, not deceived.

'Indeed it is,' Hunterfield remarked drily.

'Ought we to go along the sea wall now, Henry?' Golding asked conversationally. 'Or do you think they have made sufficient progress?'

'They seem to be managing, Golding,' Hunterfield said. 'I must say, your beasts have proved their worth. Perhaps you can offer them again, in support work. What do you say?'

'Oh, ah, why not?' Golding stifled his anger at being made to pay such a price for Hunterfield's resolution of the argument.

Sir Edward concealed a smile. 'What will be done with these fields, Henry?' he asked.

The expanse of water was sliced with parallel stetch paths where the mud now showed.

'It's a problem, Sir Edward. This is all sea water, you see. Dutchmen in their polders have a sequence of draining steps to free the land of the sea's taint. Of course, they use windmills, as in Lancashire's Fylde.'

'Is that. . . ?' Golding was trying to interrupt, pointing.

Mehala was returning in that sinuous glide on her mud boards. He spoke on.

'Our east coast technics are different. I shall divert the freshwater brooks, especially those falling through Whitehanger, into this sealand, hoping for a successive dilution of the sea salt. Arrangements will be needed for proper use of the small streams. I aim to dilute by catchment, releasing the excess waters at low tide.'

'Might I speak with the girl, Henry, an you please?'

'Why, of a certain, Sir Edward.' Hunterfield signed to Simple Tom, who strode across to meet Mehala as she skimmed to a halt on the dryland line.

'That's the girl Mehala!' Golding exclaimed. 'The sea waif.'

'True, Golding.' Hunterfield darted the man a sardonic glance. 'You must recall. She assumed your permission to procure the oxen and carts by the Affon, and had your men load up the punts to come hither. I do believe she took word – of a silent kind! – from Simple Tom, my mute. In error.'

'Did she now?' Golding was nodding, accepting the inevitable as the picture was completed.

Sir Edward looked wrily from one to the other, then said heartily, 'As long as the outcome is as you wished, Charles, then all's well and the King's shores are held, what?'

'Indeed, Sir Edward.' Golding watched Mehala approach.

Hunterfield had to smile at her muddy appearance, still mindful of the astonishing beauty she had revealed when he had seen her properly for the first time.

'Good day to you, Mehala. I either find you covered in Sealandings mud, or attired to best all ladies in the Kingdom.'

She bobbed a curtsey. Even in dishevelment there was nothing comical about her.

'I apologise for my bruckled condition, Squire.'

'No need, Mehala. All here will be as begrimed before this work's done. Sir Edward?'

'Mehala, I've been mazing at your inordinate grace on those . . . what, shovels? Wherever did you learn this?'

The girl spoke with perfect calm. 'Spuffling, sir? I do not know,' she answered directly to the magistrate. 'I am sea-fetched, and not mindful of my past. I thought it was sensible, sir, in these conditions.'

'You speak as if the sealands were a life, girl.'

'Living, sir, yes. That is so.' She thought a moment, then spoke on with quiet assurance. 'I do believe our land is blessed by Heaven, sir, if that is not presuming so to say. Any gentleman apprized of its sorry plight must be moved to rush to its assistance.'

'You infer we are stewards only?' Sir Edward asked keenly.

She turned to look over the flooded fields. 'It does not appear much, sir. Poor fields, on a windswept coast. Class Three pasture, if that. Yet with a beauty as deserving of protection as any living thing made by the Almighty.'

Hunterfield shifted from one foot to the other. The girl was at her most confounding, speaking in ambiguities that made him wonder if she was poking wry humour, or slyly striking at Golding, who had reddened slightly as her barb struck home.

'What's your place, girl?'

'I have no place, sir.' Mehala hesitated, then took a resolute step forward. 'I am housekeeper until now, for Doctor Carmichael of Shalamar House, Sealandings. He is evicted, by order of Milton Hall, and is leaving for inland.'

Hunterfield stared. Golding frowned so ostentatiously that the Squire wondered if he had already heard of Carmichael's eviction.

'You will accompany him?' Sir Edward enquired.

'Of course, sir, for so I am instructed.'

Sir Edward smiled. 'A pity you leave the coast, girl. I'm sure Squire Hunterfield would want your accomplishments in curing the sealands. You seem wondrously adapted.'

'You are very condescending, sir. I thank you. But Squire Hunterfield, saving his presence, has no need of my services. Squire has his own genius – and the Watermillock men can set up a sailed screw.'

'A what?' Sir Edward glanced at Hunterfield.

'An Archimedean screw, sir,' Mehala continued. 'A device ancients used to lift water from land. A wooden engine is operated by wind. Placed ashosh on dykes, it turns a wooden screw which, enclosed, pipes the water by night and day over the dykes into the sea.'

'Does it, now!' He cocked an eye enquiringly at his host.

'Ashosh is at an angle, aslant'ards, Sir Edward.'

Mehala put in, 'They are used in the Fen country. Some have canvas sails, of hemp instead of wood like the great windmill of Masther Bettany here.' There was a silence. Mehala felt obliged to speak into it. 'Boys wet the sails on gale days, for the screw's swifter turning.'

'How much pay?' Astell was frankly enjoying this conversation. 'Penny a day?'

Mehala's level gaze did not waver. 'A lion penny, for an honest day, sir.'

Sir Edward burst out laughing. The silver sixpence of 1826 bore a lion surmounting the crown, but no copper penny. 'Your oratory outdoes your memory, Mistress Mehala! I pray one recovers to match the other!'

'I thank you, sir, for your kind courtesy.' She bobbed a curtsey and withdrew at Hunterfield's nod of dismissal.

'Remarkable girl, Hunterfield. Surprised you are willing to let her go to us inlanders. And we have leeches a-plenty, though God knows not all are much use!'

'I shall make enquiry, Sir Edward,' Hunterfield said thoughtfully, not wanting to admit he was uninformed about Carmichael's eviction. 'Should we persuade Carmichael to remain, Golding?'

'Oh, indeed, indeed,' Golding said hurriedly.

There was a sudden cheer from the sea dyke as the pile drivers started up with their hammering. Golding swallowed hard. The men had set one of his remaining punts atop the improvised pledget in the broach. The two strongest men were swinging five-pounder hammers to drive timber piles into the mud on the landward side. No sea ran now. The gap was sealed.

'Success, it seems!' Hunterfield called over to Ayrton and Kettle, who were both clapping the achievement. They doffed their hats and waved acknowledgement. 'Right! Now to make repair of ourselves, Sir Edward. Tom? Do you ride Mehala back to meet with Doctor Carmichael in Sealandings. Take the small brougham.'

'A triumph, Henry,' Sir Edward complimented. 'Might I be bold enough to ask, did you know of this wondrous Greek engine?'

'I had heard of them,' Hunterfield said equably.

'Mehala implies she comes from Norfolk, or the Fens.'

So she did, Hunterfield thought. Which raises the interesting question of why a girl without memory cleverly suggests her origins might lie in a direction other than evidence indicates. It was time he made enquiries of officials near the Blackwater, or the Colne and Stour estuaries to the south.

He walked with Sir Edward towards the horses, not quite excluding Golding from the conversation but demonstrably less

253

condign towards him, talking of the various ways in which a salted marsh might be recovered for arable work. Golding eagerly agreed with every point of view expressed, conscripting of the powerful Astells for his political ambitions. It was time Thalia pressed their relative Sir Philip Banks to propose an appointment as magistrate. Golding felt he deserved it, after the costly contribution he had just made to public works.

On the slow jolting ride back to Sealandings Mehala learned of another disaster. She looked out to see what obstructed the brougham when it rocked to a halt near the gateway of Lorne House. Simple Tom was ahead, listening to the gatekeeper, glancing back at the carriage.

'What's amiss, Tom?' she called, suddenly filled with fore-boding.

He pulled his mount round. It splashed the few paces to the vehicle. Mehala felt her heart constrict, her breath halt.

'What?' she said faintly, thinking, Please God, not Ven. Please, no. Not now.

27

Memory was uncontrollable.

Old Doctor Arbuthnot used to laugh, taking snuff the way he did on the hour with his famous groan and volcanic sneeze.

'One day, mark me, Carmichael, they'll know the intimate workings of the mind. It is a wondrous engine.' The old man shuddered as he inspired the snuff inserted into a nostril. 'Though why to God we would want to, when we can't even set a fractured limb without killing a third of our patients, Heaven only knows!'

Ven had asked, intrigued, 'How can the mind be explored, sir?' which set Arbuthnot roaring and slapping his thighs in merriment.

'Our future colleagues in this esteemed profession'll find ways, boy. There's gold in it! And you know what'll earn them most coin then? The extirpation of memory. Mark me well, boy!'

To rid oneself of ill memories? Yes, it would be a benison, when memory was of lying in a muddy road while a crowd bayed for his blood and kicked, punched, cudgelled . . .

Ven came to in a world of pain. His face was swollen, his jaw ached – oh, how it ached! Every muscle screeched as he tried to move. He was alone, in a plain room. Nearby a rhythmic creaking sounded so loud that he could feel the vibrations through the building. He vaguely remembered a heavily built groom dragging him along a path, up steps.

'You are wakened, sir, praise be.'

The woman stood by the doorway. He must have dozed. He could hardly see through his swollen eyes. Everything was a blur.

'Amen,' he croaked, and moaned as the effort stabbed sharp pain into his ribs. 'Is it Mistress Bettany? I cannot quite see.'

'It is, Doctor. You were set upon close by.'

'Is it late? How long ago?'

'It is five of the afternoon, sir. I shall send the maid Praisewell with a mending drink.' She paused. He tried to estimate time. Mehala would be wondering. 'Sir, I trust you have but a short way to go?'

He understood immediately. Mrs Bettany wanted nothing to do with contumely. To her, he was simply a man who fought in public. He was being expelled. For an instant he worried if the crowd was still out there. There was still time to reach the Donkey and Buskin; Mehala would be waiting faithfully. In spite of this setback, he had to stay loyal in turn. She was become the central point in his life, even if he had nothing to offer.

'Thank you, Mistress Bettany. Yes, but a step. I must express my gratitude for your Christian charity in extending the protection of your house.' She coloured slightly, which he did not see. 'I must leave.'

'Very well, as you will.' Her relief was transparent. 'My husband wishes you his godspeeds.'

'Please thank him, mistress.'

The maid-of-all was a slight dark-haired girl from Wheatfen, her manner embarrassed. She brought a cup of warm whey a few moments after Helen Bettany left, her quick arrival a clear encouragement to leave. She knelt solicitously and helped him to drink.

''ee be too hurt to go a-walking, masther,' she told him softly, glancing guiltily at the door. 'I wanted to make a proper posset, but the mistress forbad. This whey's been got up with runnet.'

'It'll do, Praisewell.' He found he was sweating heavily and starting to shiver. 'I'm only to the Donkey and Buskin.'

'Shall I ask if Master Richard be free to walk with thee, masther? He's a kindly young gentleman. I saw the onset. It were fearsome, and the crowd very partial against.'

He tried to smile, wincing. He ought to feel along his gum, test if his jaw was unbroken, but even that simple act would drain his strength. He felt ridiculous. That he should be grateful for rescue by a stranger, for protection from a reluctant miller, and to this lowly servant for sympathy.

'My company would count sore against Richard, Praisewell. Let him be. Who brought me here?'

She saw the whey between his swollen lips with practised concern, and laid the cup aside to help him up.

'Sir Edward Astell's man, masther. By his order.'

Ven struggled erect, almost fainting at the hurt and astonished at his feebleness. He managed to get upright, though breathless.

He stood dizzily, leaning heavily on Praisewell. Bettany had given succour only because he was ordered to by a passing Justice of the King's Peace. Good fortune, if a savage beating from a mob was such.

There was no sign of the Bettanys. Slowly he made his way out with Praisewell's help, downstairs, as far as the outer door. There he tried to say his goodbye, but the maid insisted on walking with him as far as the road. He recognised her solicitude. A mob would be deterred from assault by the presence of a witness. He thanked her, saying he hoped she would not be punished for leaving the household without permission.

'Maids have been bagged for less, Praisewell.' He warned her to hurry back.

'If Mistress Bettany gives me the bag for doing my duty I shall repair to my father in Dedham Vale.' She was not at all subdued.

'Dedham Vale? So far from home?'

Ven was only spinning out his departure. Both were scanning the Norwich road. Nobody seemed to be there.

'They're gone, masther.'

He smiled, placing his beaver on his head with a grimace. 'I wish you could extend your protection all the way to the Donkey and Buskin, Praisewell! I am sore shamed to be passed from the guardianship of one lady to that of another, quite like an infant! Mehala will scold!'

'Mehala?' the maid said eagerly. 'The girl saved by *The Jaunty*? She awaits you? I mind her, from the Colchester meeting!'

He wondered if he had heard her right. 'Colchester meeting? Mehala?'

'Not *in*, masther. She was never a Friend. I saw her in her carriage one Sabbath, bound for St Peter's. I asked particular of my parents, admiring her comportment.'

He stared, almost disbelieving. 'You had Mehala's acquaintance, Praisewell?'

She smiled shyly. 'I have not, sir. I glimpsed her but once here. In the market, and could not speak.'

Of course not. Servants of different households were fiercer rivals even than the families they served. It was all different from past times, when an entire household, lord and servant, would dine at one board and converse in general.

'It is a pity, Praisewell, for . . .' He caught himself. Better say nothing about Mehala to Praisewell. The Bettanys, being Quakers, and millers to boot, while not quite ostracized stood somewhat apart in Sealandings. They merchandised among their own, held separate religious services, educated their children differently. Indeed, he thought, this was probably the most eventful occurrence in Praisewell's life for many a week. 'For,' he concluded lamely, 'I well know how you women like to chatter.'

She smiled. 'I do love to speak, Doctor. It is for this reason I am here, having uncles who are still Puritant.'

She must have a kindly father, then, Ven registered, taking his leave and slowly setting out to walk to Sealandings. The Puritans who ruled during the Commonwealth and Protectorate were not yet altogether vanished, especially in East Anglia. They held rigorously to solemnity in their grim households. For an innocent smile Praisewell could be threatened with hellfire. Incessant prayer warped the spirit. No dancing, no Christmas, no wine, no smiling, no holidays, no Thanksgiving or Harvest Home, nothing save downcast looks worse than in any nunnery.

He found he kept tapping his pockets fretfully, then realised it was on account of not carrying anything. His case with its few instruments was lost, then. And his invaluable silver watch? He felt in his spencer pocket. Gone. It had been given him by Hunterfield himself, after treating the child Clare Darling at Whitehanger, with Mehala's help. Hunterfield's generosity at the recovery of a little maiden belonging to a humble carter's family was a mystery best left unexamined.

Mehala, though . . . in a *carriage*? And in Colchester, that important hilltop town just south of Suffolk? Not any carriage, either; Praisewell had said *her* carriage. She was a lady, then, in her own equipage. So notable that a Quaker girl was able to enquire among her family about the passing lady's striking beauty and receive explanation. The implications were there, in what Praisewell had said.

He felt suddenly exhausted. His legs were trembling, as if he had run miles. He was still some distance from the first houses, and the road a quagmire. The rain had returned. He had no stick, and without a knife was unable to cut one from the hedgerow. But Mehala would be waiting faithfully, as eager to welcome him as he

258

to see her. He stood a moment, and struggled slowly on, trying to place his feet on level parts to avoid slipping in the wet.

Dedham Vale was north of Colchester, by some miles. And on the River Stour, not the Colne. Along both those rivers Father and he had hunted plants and insects. His mind worried restlessly at the mystery, though conjecture seemed almost disloyal to Mehala. Her memory, and the amount of it she wished revealed to Sealandings, was surely her own right. A question nagged at him as he struggled on: did *he* count as simply one more person in Sealandings? Or was he something more? But that sly, unfair question was fully answered by Mehala's loyalty. Time after time, she stood by him. When he sent to Sealandings asking for help to nurse the Darling child, who came? Mehala. When he was alone in the cold Shalamar, who came to make the place live? Mehala. And who amazed him by bringing flowers, and making a room free of draughts? And in final proof, at the ninth hour, who firmly stepped into vagrancy with him, into a future of almost certain poverty? Yes, Mehala stood firm by her convictions . . . Or was it something more dangerous, like a desire to conceal a threat in her past?

He tried to avoid a wide pool by pulling himself close to the hedge. His hands were pierced by the haw and blackthorn. He finally gave up the attempt and plashed slowly through the shallowest part. He was in sight of Miss Gould's school now and the tower of St Edmund's among the yews.

The last thought was unworthy, and he erased it from his mind, only to find it recurring with every painful step. A grand lady, accidentally lost at sea and presumed drowned, rescued by a fishing lugger returning early by reason of a poor catch, was miraculous indeed. She would have every reason to regain her status at the earliest opportunity, unless there was some pressing cause to remain anonymous in a newfound existence.

'This is unworthy, Carmichael,' he mumbled to himself, turning into the Square. 'Mehala has suffered by losing her past life. She is desperately trying to find herself. It befits, Carmichael, to play fair.'

His anxiety was born of solicitude. Or admiration. Or more? He steadied himself against the Corn Mart building, and stepped for a moment under the shelter of the covered space. The walk had seemed inordinate, the effort prodigious. He would have to come to terms with his feelings for Mehala, and take a resolute step. But how? And when? Answer: the instant he gained a position, with prospects. Then, as Mehala's memory returned, together they would rejoin her family . . .

A carriage rattled by, a brougham with two double seats. As it passed, the windows caught the last of the true daylight, showing the interior. Mehala was within.

The brougham was adapted for double seats. The driver was on his box seat, protected against the rain by a thick wrap-rascal. It was gone in an instant, splashing by with the two horses evidently glad to be on the move.

He watched it out of sight. Nobody was about, save a farm girl hurrying towards the harbour cottages below. In that direction lay the Donkey and Buskin. The brougham had been travelling away. Had Mehala assumed him gone somewhere? Or, impossibly, that he had given up waiting? The carriage bore the emblazons of Hunterfield, the coachman one of Hunterfield's own Lorne House men. Surely Mehala could not have abandoned her wait? For that catastrophe would mean he truly was alone, without the woman he relied upon, trusted and needed . . .

Laboriously he sat himself on the dusty floor, under the protecting canopy of the Corn Mart. He leant aslant against the wall, to ease his breathing and let the gathering dusk enfold him, the Square and the desolate drenched town.

St Edmund's rectory study was lined with books. To one side of the fireplace, where seacoals burned summer and winter, stood the carved eagle lectern on which Reverend Baring habitually wrote, standing as if preaching to a congregation. It helped in his deliberations, and style – that neglected instruction – could by indoctrination develop to a degree. Never a bored congregation, he thought with satisfaction, with Josiah Baring in the pulpit!

He eyed his visitors gravely. They were not quite enemies, one could not go that far, but they were certainly misguided people, however much they shared his precepts, in a world of sloth and insolent disregard for morality.

'I trust, gentlemen, that you accept the presence of Miss Baring?' He smiled fondly to disarm opposition. 'Should we *brawl*, ha-ha-ha, Miss Baring can serve as peacemaker!'

'It is always a pleasure to see Miss Euterpe,' Parker said soberly. 'She may mislike our talk of fisticuffs.'

Euterpe was discreetly seated to one side of the room, occupying a curricle chair. She had heard of a fight on the Norwich road from Bridget, but the maid had irritatingly failed to learn details. Euterpe considered that her time would be better spent by finding Doctor Carmichael. She had been badly shocked to learn this morning of his eviction. Here again her only source was Bridget, the careless girl imprecise.

She served the three gentlemen with whipped Italian creams, those being most convenient to eat as well as refreshing, with a selection of two draughts of ginger and lemon. The flummery, which she had made the day previous – always wise to have those to hand – met with a mixed reception, for Mr Bettany had demanded to know its ingredients. On learning that raisin wine (of *course*!) was incorporated, he had refused with a sternness quite uncalled for. He could have taken the gentlemanly course, merely declined with proper appreciation. Was there ever a flummery made without a pint of raisin wine to a quart mould? Parker had accepted a glass of Jerez, as had her brother, the former from anxiety, the latter from ebullience.

'Fisticuffs!' Josiah Baring chuckled. He alone remained standing, the others seated on bended-back single chairs as if in serious conference. 'I have one of the men, ah involved, reporting here for interrogation. The rectory tonight will be no mere salutatorium, gentlemen, I promise!' He chuckled. 'But fisticuffs? Storm in a teacup, sir!'

Euterpe listened to Josiah's opening remarks. She had seen his tactics too often to be deceived. To others, he might seem at ease, but tonight there was something profoundly disturbing in his manner. She had felt foreboding all day. Since noon, the sense had worsened. She had quite wantonly sent Bridget on a false shopping expedition in hopes of gleaning more news of Doctor Carmichael's whereabouts after leaving Shalamar. No doubt he was safe, being so valuable to Sealandings, but what was his destination? The stupid girl returned with the wrong potatoes anyway, bringing only stories of the excitements down on the sea dykes which had evidently broken. And all afternoon Josiah's attempts to conceal his unease had communicated themselves to her.

'Carmichael's sore injured, sir.'

It was Bettany's policy to avoid calling Baring by any orthodox title. Not for him the hypocritical 'Reverend', implying a grade of piety above all homo sapiens. He was affronted by visiting this place of 'vain repetition', as he called it, where ritual replaced prayers and a steeple-house supplanted a congress of souls. He rose ponderously and crossed to where Euterpe's pencil and notebook had fallen from her lap. He politely retrieved them for her.

'These things happen, Mr Bettany,' Baring said, consoling. 'A few take umbrage, a few blows are exchanged. Is that a crime?'

'Yes,' Bettany replied bluntly. 'It is sinful, criminal.'

'One of my servants was nearby when the mob attacked the leech,' Parker said candidly. 'I brought him because the questions will be asked: Is there a witness? Is there just cause? Magistrates take a dim view of contumely.'

Euterpe was writing, as instructed, but she knew not what. Her pencil flew of its own accord. She was curiously breathless. Carmichael? *Attacked?* Surely he could not have been the target on the Norwich road? A doctor, going to the sick?

'And the instigators,' Bettany added. 'Whoever they be.'

'Instigators?' Baring cried with a laugh of incredulity. 'Mr Bettany, you make it sound a conspiracy, sir! As if some gathering had put the mob up to it!'

Hadn't they? Euterpe asked silently. She was shaking with a rage she had never before experienced. Oddly, her pencil had steadied, and wrote meticulously. Could rage be cold? No, she realised. It could only pretend to be.

'I won't be party to this.' Parker said. Twice he had glanced across the room at the Rector's sister.

'This, Parker? What's *this*?'

'This suggestion of a concerted act, Reverend. When we interviewed the sawbones about surgeries we disapproved of, we did not mention threats.'

'Yet your stable hands were close to the mob, sir,' Bettany said heavily.

'You live close by!' Parker shot back tersely. 'And was none your customer, Bettany? Was none a member of St Edmund's congregation, Reverend? Was none a decent law-abiding inhabitant of Sealandings?'

262

'Gentlemen, gentlemen!' Reverend Baring cried. 'Let us take stock. It is a simple matter – an accidental brawl involving a tradesman!' He smiled, ingratiating himself by nodding and opening his palms. It was an act Euterpe had witnessed many times. Indeed, she had oftimes seen her brother practising these very gestures. 'Has this never happened before? In a thousand other *law-abiding* hamlets, towns – cities even?'

'Could Carmichael make out a case for its being accidental, Reverend?'

'Look, Mr Parker.' The Rector's voice soothed. 'Could anyone make a single accusation that would stand in court?'

He twinkled benignly around at them, not omitting Euterpe. He had been wise to bring her to the meeting. Prove to her, once and for all, that life was a serious matter, not a mere game of affections played at whim. No; life was one long clarion call to duty. All else was sham, fustian, a shirking of moral tasks set from On High for our improvement. Turn aside from that, and one became as nothing in the sight of worthy-minded people everywhere.

'May I remind you of one small point? *Carmichael was warned!* His conduct had given us grave doubts about his propriety. Was he not told, in a truly Christian manner, of his transgressions?' He stared at Euterpe and stated solemnly, 'Becomingness is a behaviour which needs be laboured at. Those of falsest rectitude are precisely those with an outward show of delicacy!'

'The man is under my roof, sir,' Bettany put in. 'That is at the heart of this.'

Parker was impatient, on edge. 'Where the man lies is irrelevant, Bettany. What's more to the point is that our congregations were the attackers.'

'You are wrong, sir!' the millmaster said coldly. 'We Friends do not assault, cudgel, batter. We are for peace. Secondly, your public stables and my mill grounds well-nigh conjoin. This leech was in no state to carry himself anywhere.'

'Then how came he to you?'

Bettany answered the Rector directly, ignoring Parker, whose stables were in any event a hideous nuisance, where ostlers and grooms caroused until the early hours practically every night, in the way of their roisterous kind.

'Sir Edward Astell's man carried him in. That gentleman's coach stopped further injury.'

'Why, then there's an end to it!' Reverend Baring cried, beaming. 'Things could not resolve better. A magistrate for witness, no less!'

'Except that magistrate will report to Sir Henry at Lorne House, where he was bound.'

The room fell silent. Reverend Baring thought quickly. For a moment he was startled by Euterpe's expression as she raised her head and stared at him. Her face was quite pale, white even. Perhaps it had been indelicate to bring her into this after all. She was bound to be affected. But only he knew how necessary it was for Euterpe to be told the facts about Doctor Carmichael. This was beneficial instruction for her. He looked away. The intensity of her gaze was disturbing. He would have a word with her later.

'Exactly!' Baring decided. 'Just what we need! A legal summary of the man's misdemeanours laid before Hunterfield. And let's not be deceived. No wallowing in pity for him. His sins are proven. His reprehensible activities form a sorry life story entire of itself. The magistracy will not fail us!'

'Are you sure, Reverend?' Parker queried in growing unease. 'What if the Doctor, well, dies of his injuries?' He glanced at Bettany. 'Did he look so badly hurt?'

'Serious. He was mindshot, rambling.'

'Then we must speak with your man, Parker,' the Rector said. 'Admit him please, Euterpe.'

'Jeckel does work for me, Reverend,' Parker interposed quickly, 'But that does not mean he acted under my orders at the time.'

'Of course. Nobody implied so.'

Reverend Baring watched his sister glide slowly to the study door and open it. For an instant she stood motionless as the man outside approached. It was almost a tableau as she confronted him. Then she stepped aside.

'You see, gentlemen,' he continued, 'these events were set in train by Carmichael himself. They were beyond our control as Christians. Sinners reap as they sow.'

'This is Jeckel, gentlemen.' Parker nodded for the man to come forward into the light.

Jeckel held his hat in his hand. He wore a loose smock and trouser ties, and stood in a deferential stoop.

'Tell Reverend what you saw, Jeckel.'

'If you please, reverend sirs.' Jeckel spoke hoarsely in an unpleasant wheedling voice. 'I was out a-walking, and saw a mob of folks – you are acquainted with the cattle field, that Squire set aside for fairs? I thought at first they was gypsies, but saw no horses. They were by the hedgerows.'

'You recognised any, Jeckel?' Parker asked.

'No, masther. No call to, y'see, not knowing what they was about.'

'How many?' Bettany asked.

Jeckel gave a sheepish grin. 'I'd say about sixteen, sir. About the same as your maid-of-all would say, sir. For she stood by the gate's turning.'

Parker looked sharply at Bettany, who stared at the carpet with sudden intensity.

'You saw the attack?'

'Yes, sir. They set on poor Doctor terrible, sir. Gave un a right ainting, they did. Dunshin' and poultin' him they was, sirs.'

'Did they try to, ah, rob him, Jeckel?'

'No, Rector.' Jeckel glanced from one face to the next, licked his lips. 'Though I saw two of them trying to open the duffel wadmul he wore.'

'His greatcoat,' Parker translated to Reverend Baring. 'You raised the alarm, Jeckel?'

'No, sir, I'm ashamed to say.' Jeckel looked downcast a moment. 'I saw the coach a-coming, sir. The outrider took his crop to the mob and called on his groom and postillion, sir. The mob fled.'

'In which direction?'

'Every way, sir. Across the fields, along the hedges.'

Reverend Baring nodded with satisfaction. 'Thank you, Jeckel. You may go. Gentlemen, vagrants are clearly responsible. Nobody in Sealandings can be blamed, certainly not our congregations. It's Carmichael's own fault. Let us hope he is affected deeply enough to mend his ways hereon.'

He was about to enlarge on these happenings as moral guidance when he noticed to his surprise that Euterpe's curricle was empty.

His sister was gone. He was astonished. She had not asked permission to go. Had she returned to the study once she had admitted Jeckel, or left immediately? That was impossible. She had probably slipped out unnoticed, to provide the gentlemen with refreshment, or to see about his supper, which tonight would be woefully overdue. He returned with gusto to the subject, and struck his pose. 'Gentlemen,' he said portentously, 'let us consider the moral lessons which these events elucidate . . .'

Euterpe shamelessly drew on her Adelaide boots while perched on a landing chair, calling in a frantic stage whisper for Bridget. The maid-of-all came running up the stairs, astonished to see her mistress in such a scandalous position, her ankles visible for all the world to see.

'Bridget! My capote, if you please!'

'But mistress! The gentlemen are yet with the Reverend – '

'*My bonnet this instant! And cloak! Hurry!*'

The maid flew, her face averted lest the study door open and the Rector's visitors disgorge to discover the mistress in apparent flight, and herself abetting. A minute later she was opening the front door on to the rainy dusk.

'What when Reverend sends for you, Miss Euterpe?' she asked nervously.

'Say . . .' Euterpe tied her brides firmly beneath her chin. The advantage of the capote bonnet was its rigid brim close about the face though the crown was pliantly soft. 'Say I visit the sick, Bridget.'

'I shall be asked where, Miss Euterpe!' Bridget wailed, but the Rector's sister had already rushed into the fading light.

Euterpe kept her gathered cloak tight about her as she went down the rectory path towards the Square. A boy was standing by the gate, and stepped forward, raising his hat. She halted with some trepidation, for Miss Gould's evening lanthorn was the only nearby light. He wore the short cloak of an apprentice, and a fearnothing.

'Miss Baring? Please do not take alarm. I am Richard Bettany.'

'Richard!' Euterpe exclaimed in relief. 'The miller's son. I regret the Rector is presently engaged, while I am on an urgent errand.'

The boy stood his ground. 'My message is vital, Miss Baring. Twice I have waited by the church, hoping to see you.'

'For why? A message, Richard?'

'No message – news. Doctor Carmichael was attacked – '

She cried, 'I know! I know! How fares he? Is he – ?'

'He left my home, Miss Baring.' The boy sounded ashamed. 'Our maid Praisewell said he intended to meet Mehala at the Donkey and Buskin. I ran to the sea dykes, where I heard Mehala was aiding the breach. She had already gone. So I sought you.'

'Where is he?' Euterpe asked faintly.

'A fisherlad told me he sheltered in the Corn Mart, then went towards the hard.'

'How long since?'

'Minutes, an hour.' The lad hesitated. 'He did not cross the Square southerly, Miss Baring.'

She saw Richard's meaning. This did not accord with Praisewell's account. The Donkey and Buskin, where presumably Mehala waited, lay in a different direction. Ven Carmichael was making for the sea cottages, or the Goat and Compass. Her hope lifted. He was alive, able to walk. Had he abandoned the idea of meeting Mehala?

Involuntarily she cried out, 'Why did you not stop him, Richard! Bring him to me at the rectory! Or tell me earlier?'

He faced her with candour. 'My father's displeasure, should I be seen in Doctor Carmichael's company, answers your first, Miss Baring. Concern that I would earn Mr Baring's anger for one other, answers your second.'

She felt colour rush into her face despite the cold. This youth was wiser than his years. He was protecting her.

'Thank you, Master Richard,' she said formally. 'Do you have any firm idea where the Doctor was going?'

'Praisewell said he spoke of Mehala, whom Praisewell knew elsewhere. He expressed intention of visiting his patients in Sealandings before leaving for St Albans.'

Raffin, Euterpe told herself. The seaman saved from the ketch wrecked in the great storm. The sea cottages by the hard.

'Thank you,' she said. 'Will you do me the service of accompanying me?'

'Honoured, Miss Baring.'

They set out across the deserted Square. The covered Corn Mart, where townsfolk could shelter from rain, Euterpe saw now empty. It was maddening that he had been there only recently, that circumstances had conspired against her finding him. As they left, hurried downhill towards the sound of the sea, a light carriage passed them heading northwards. Euterpe glimpsed a pale oval at the central window, a woman's face perhaps, but in the dusk could not make out the features. If only she herself had a whisky, or a small gig. She would overtake him in minutes! But Ven Carmichael surely could not have gone at speed, considering his injuries. She felt him close, and took hold of Richard's arm for security as they gained the flint cobbles of the Blakeney road that ran by the wharf, the inn and the sea cottages.

28

Sealandings was enveloped in rainy darkness by the time the small brougham drew up at Two Cotts. The coachman descended and knocked, conversed a few moments with the lady who answered. Mehala peered without showing herself, but the twin lanthorns at the porch were feeble.

The coachman returned, climbed on to the box seat and adjusted his wrap-rascal. He wheeled the vehicle out of the gate, and drew to a halt, the light carriage tilting on the rutted surface.

'Miss? The, erm, person said as Doctor Carmichael was injured by here, but denies knowledge of who, and where he is.'

Mehala was distraught. She signalled Underwood to drive down into Sealandings.

She was less muddied, having dried herself in the kitchen of the Donkey and Buskin. She and Simple Tom had discovered that Ven Carmichael had not reached there. And the Weavers had given her some provisions – a little mutton and bread, some cheese – in muslin to stay Ven and herself during the start of their journey inland. But where was he? She was beside herself with anxiety. Fearing the worst, she had urged Simple Tom to take her to Shalamar, thinking Ven might have returned there. Then she had taken the brougham under her own charge, and told Tom to make a separate search.

The patients at whose cottages she had called so far knew little. It was the same tale everywhere – people had attacked the Doctor, and Sir Edward Astell's man had taken him to Bettany's. The Quakers' maid-of-all had told Underwood that the Doctor had insisted on going townwards, alone. Twice so far the coachman had driven to the Market Square without success. She made him clamber down and help her to search the hedgerows by means of the brougham's two lanthorns. Fear was thickening in her breast. A mob can as soon reassemble under cover of darkness as disperse.

'Where now, Miss?'

The vehicle had drawn to a stand by the Corn Mart's pillars.

'Let me think.' Across and to the right stood St Edmund's Church, its rectory behind the tall yews, trees that botanical gentlemen called the oldest ones in the world. For a fleeting instant her head sank in weariness, and she drifted into another St Edmund's, as old as this, with a squat grey tower just as square. On the wall by the canopied wooden pulpit hung the oblong gilt, red and grey commemoration board for *Collonell Edward Bellamie, obit. 1656.* Obliquely across stood the baptismal font, of pale incised stone, octagonal top on an octagonal pillar on an octagonal pedestal base. The times she had traced, as a maidchild, the gothic letters cut into the incised brass plaque set in the flagged flooring before the altar! The lettering so marvellously pretty, the gleaming brass so vast and bright. Only when she was grown did she notice, with a shock, that the brass rectangle was a mere foot wide by fifteen inches. And read the sad Old English poetry recording the passing of one Mistress Mawdltn Owtred on 8 December, 1572, wife of the East Mersea Rector Reverend Marcellinus Owtred, 1562–1572. Had he too died that year, deprived of his lady? Or did her death send him fleeing from the island in despair?

> *'Thy soule is fled to heaven right,*
> *Of this I am certaine . . .'*

that Rector had inscribed. Had he been as stout, as ferociously opinionated, as Reverend Stamford Stane who terrified the island children with his sermons? And who had once caught her swinging on the arched half-door to set its three iron hinges squeaking and its wooden peg-lock clicking!

'Miss Mehala?' Underwood called her back. She came to.

'A moment, if you please.' The one thing Ven would do, however badly injured, was reach his sick, give them what treatment he could before leaving. He must still be here somewhere.

She had called on the Cants, whose boychild had been injured in a fall from the wharf. Not there. And the babe born to swell ploughman Densell's vast brood. Babe fine, no Ven. The hugely poulticed carbuncle which immobilized Anne Cotton's shoulder was resolving; Ven had called there.

There were others, down the harbour.

'Head for the Goat and Compass, if you please. We shall call on Doctor Carmichael's sick on the way. Hurry.'

The bandage was up to the job, Ven saw. The man Raffin was healthy, though worried by the Doctor's alarming appearance. Ven tried to pass off his dishevelled state, and his lack of instruments, but had to admit he had been attacked.

'If I may perform my examination while seated,' he begged. The children stood in awe within the light of the rush taper. The family had only a hog's tallow taper for him to examine the amputation stump. The better quality – half bullock's, half sheep's tallow, with a good cotton wick – were too expensive for a fisherman's purse. Ven usually carried a candle and a tinder-box, but they had gone with his lost instruments.

Raffin was perched on a rough country-made stool, his stump supported on a box that stank of fish.

'I've been in the open air, Doctor, as you said. Every daylight hour, and half the night, too.'

'Good. That's essential, Raffin. Remember to avoid letting rain wet the stump.'

His old sense of helplessness was stealing back over him. The quiet, the warmth and dryness of the cottage was making him drowsy. A small fire of seacoals burned itself to red ash, but even so it gave the room a pleasant familiar feel. His childhood, he was startled to realise – that's what it evoked, this sense of one-ness with others. Cosiness and certainty, with all doubts and fears shut outside in the wet night.

But he sorely needed his small bottle of vinegared lead solution, to dampen this bandaged stump.

Among his few medical beliefs was this one treatment, of amputations being done by the three-cut method popularized by Larrey the Frenchman. The bandage was linen, the scultetus, a many-tailed wide piece that was fenestrated, cut with holes to allow inevitable discharges. It should be first soaked for a day in camphorated wine, but seawater was supposed to be just as effective in lessening the chances of fatal gangrene. He remembered adding ten drops of the precious phial of vinegared solution of lead, urged by that Napoleonic surgeon across the

271

Channel. What he would not give for a copy of Doctor Larrey's book!

'Did you wipe away the matter that came out?' he asked Raffin's wife.

She nodded eagerly. 'Yes, Doctor. Every hour, as you instructed.'

'Did much pus come forth?'

'Some, Doctor. Not thick or stinking, just thin.'

Thanks God, he prayed in silent fervour. The cut 'windows' in the linen were intended to leak the discharges – serous fluid, any pus forming over the raw severed muscles and bone, and the liquefying of caked blood. The terrible mistake some surgeons made was to transect the limb in one plane, simply shear it away as if with a beheading axe. But that left the bone protruding, as the sectioned muscles drew back in Nature's retraction. The skin withdrawing further still, there was nothing left save a pointed end to a limb, unprotected and raw. Continental surgeons dragged the skin taut over the projecting bone, stitching it agonisingly tight. As the tissues swelled with fluid, the bag of skin glistened, became increasingly turgid, trying to discharge its purulent necrosing horror while the poor patient was racked by fever and excruciating pain. No, amputations had to be done speedily after the injury, the way he had been lucky enough to do. Most good medical fortune rode on luck's wayward steed.

'The press of the bandage on the wound, you see, Mistress Raffin, is uniform wherever it touches. Do you see the openings? Wipe those, if you please, with seawater fetched from outside the harbour mouth. Take a clean pot. Leave it in the seawater pail for half a day, together with the linen you will use. You understand?'

'Can I use my own linen cloth, Doctor?'

Ven thought a moment, trying to concentrate. Who knew the answer? He only had a handful of half-truths, knowing no more than this uneducated woman.

'No, Mistress. New linen, if you can. If not, stand it in a pail of sea-water as long as possible.'

He ought to be able to provide her with a small quantity of the valuable lead solution, for it served best. In fact, he thought drowsily, it was almost as if some putrefying essence, flying unseen through the air to vulnerable wounds, was opposed by seawater or plumbic solutions. Could it be that simple?

'I have none of the solution,' he confessed.

Sea air, seawater, a sure method of amputation and this style of bandaging, was all he knew. It was humiliating. So much of his medical education was nothing more than dog-Latin shrouded in mystiquery.

'Doctor?'

Mrs Raffin was offering him a cup of whey and water, hearth-warm. He sipped gratefully, aware that he was slipping slowly into a sleep, the children talking in whispers and the rush-light giving out its guttering light. Through his somnolence he heard a familiar voice.

'Doctor Carmichael? How do you, sir?'

Euterpe Baring stood before him, her covering shining with rain.

'Miss Baring!' He struggled to rouse himself, conscious of the terrible appearance he must present. She demurred and insisted he remain in his chair.

'I came as soon as I heard, Doctor.'

'Your charity is appreciated, Miss Baring.'

The women talked together. He could not concentrate on what was being said, something mundane, housekeeping trivia. A little girlchild came close, and leant with the casual familiarity of the moppet against his knee, swinging her leg and humming absently. The rocking motion was decidedly soporific. He drifted away from the room, Raffin's cottage and Sealandings altogether.

The women talked in undertones, both keeping their gaze fixed on the sleeping Doctor. Euterpe by her quiet gestures intimated to Raffin that he shared the conversation.

'My question is of Doctor's disposal, Mistress Raffin.'

'I do not understand, Miss Baring.'

'He is evicted from Shalamar. Rumour says he departs Sealandings as soon as he is able.'

'Leave Sealandings?' The implication made the seaman's wife gape in alarm. 'What will become of my man?'

'And the others ailing in the place!' Euterpe added. 'Indeed.' She hesitated, unwilling to let her personal interest give rise to scandal. She went on firmly, 'My consideration is the reputation of

273

this parish. We do not lack charity. Reverend Baring decided that the Church cannot support one who has incurred the displeasure of our religious communities.'

'Displeasure?' Mrs Raffin's hand went to her throat.

Euterpe thought, hang it all. The woman will know soon. Her response might be nothing more than a respectful pretence.

'Displeasure, yes,' she said bluntly. 'Doctor Carmichael, as is well known, often risks public disapproval in order to treat the sick.'

'I see,' the woman said slowly, glancing at the Doctor.

'Just as,' Euterpe added for good measure, 'he did for your husband.'

'Yes, yes, Miss Baring.'

'We know what cruel reputation this poor gentleman's banishment would confer on Sealandings, and how we would fare without his assistance.'

'Oh, indeed!'

'I propose that he stay with some cottager,' Euterpe pressed, 'until he recovers from his injuries.'

Mrs Raffin glanced at her husband. He looked away then back at his wife.

'We ourselves might not be able to remain here, Miss,' Raffin said gruffly. 'I bring no wage. I hope for a settlement.'

'Settlement?' Euterpe said blankly. Then she understood. The law allowed for a Justice to make a charge upon a community, to maintain somebody disabled and deprived of livelihood. The sums were paltry, and the payments erratic. 'What if you are not settled?'

'We don't know,' the man said miserably. 'I was hoping for Doctor Carmichael to speak before the magistrates for settlement under the Poors' Rate.'

'We have no close family, Mistress, saving my sister. She married into a family at Wheatfen, and lives in a tied cottage, her husband a farm labourer.'

'Then the course seems clear,' Euterpe said, with assurance she did not feel. 'Doctor Carmichael must stay with you.'

'Here? In this cottage?' Mrs Raffin slowly went to stand by her husband.

'Here.' Euterpe surprised herself at her firmness. 'A small

recompense for Doctor Carmichael's lodging will be paid over. You need not declare it, when your Poors' Rate petition comes before Squire Hunterfield. I shall imburse.'

'But . . .' Raffin looked at the Doctor, whose head was now lolling. 'What of the displeasure you spoke of, Mistress?'

'That will not affect you, as long as you stay silent about Doctor Carmichael's presence here.'

Mrs Raffin looked doubtfully at her children. 'What if his presence here becomes known?'

'It won't.' Euterpe looked about the room. 'You have two rooms, Mistress Raffin?'

'Yes, with a yard petty. One room upstairs, the cottage being on a steep slope, y'see.'

'Would it be only a day or two?' Raffin asked, eagerness showing for the first time.

'Yes,' Euterpe invented. 'Not one moment longer.' In two days hence, she thought, looking across at Ven, I can surely come up with some other plan.

He looked battered, his mouth swollen and eyes bruised. His clothes were a mess, and his inexpressibles and boots muddy and soaking. Even his knuckles were grazed and blood-caked. His hair was thatched, falling over his forehead. She felt a sudden impulse to cross the room and tidy it, even if only by means of a 'German comb', as folk called the four fingers, for lack of an expensive horn comb. No wonder the Raffins had looked thunderstruck when she had arrived. Her heart went out to him.

'I have certain administrations to make,' she said confidentially. 'They concern Doctor Carmichael's relatives in St Albans. I shall send them word to make expeditious arrangements for his departure.'

'Very well, Mistress,' Raffin said, though with a reluctance that started Euterpe's anger. 'For two days.'

Euterpe kept calm, though she could have struck Raffin where he sat. The people of Sealandings wreaked their fury on Ven Carmichael, then treated him as a liability. They stole his instruments and books, then needed bribes to shelter him.

'I shall pay you a shilling a day, Mistress Raffin,' she said coldly. 'Twelve pence each morning – assuming no word has got to anyone about the Doctor's presence here.'

'You have our word, Mistress!' Mrs Raffin said eagerly.

'Then I thank you, on his behalf,' Euterpe said, concealing her relief. She wanted to stay, but that would have been improper. She retied her chin stays, and made for the door.

'Please try to give him a little food,' she asked.

'I shall do as you say, Mistress.'

Euterpe managed to leave without a backward glance. The outside shadows separated as the door closed and only the faint sheen of the sea showed her direction.

'Thank you for waiting, Richard. Will you please accompany me as far as the Square?'

'My pleasure, Miss Baring.'

They walked together, Euterpe taking the youth's arm for steadiness, and trying to judge how best to beg for secrecy about Doctor Carmichael's lodging. He could easily construe some tale that would satisfy both conscience and parents, just as she could compose a modest litany for Josiah. With this youth bluntness would pay best, she decided.

'Could I rely on your discretion about tonight's events, Richard? I have reasons, chief being the disregard with which our religious leaders hold Doctor Carmichael. I feel he needs a day or two's respite from trouble. It would be most Christian if – '

'It would simply be sensible, Miss Baring,' the youth interrupted candidly. 'Once Doctor Carmichael has had sufficient rest, there will be time for theology.'

She was surprised, but delighted. His apprenticeship at the clockmaker Veriker's workshop was proving an asset, especially in view of his upbringing.

'Excellently put, Richard,' she concurred gravely. Richard's complicity having been assured, she had now only to concoct a story for Josiah's consumption. This could be something to the effect that she pitied the plight of the Raffins, cast on the Poors' Rate, separated in the workhouse or wholly dispossessed and scattered. Well, it was true, was it not? In this youth Richard it seemed she had discovered an able ally.

29

Lorne House had withstood the great storm. The home estate, its grounds, and the walled rose garden laid out in a series of curved paths and beds to signify an elegant and symbolic knot, had suffered little. Already the gardeners were labouring to clear felled wood and paths on to which branches had been shredded.

Charles Golding alighted from his carrige, feeling pale from tension within. This was the most significant move he had ever undertaken alone. That is, he acknowledged bitterly to himself as he nodded dismissal to his coachman, without Cousin Thalia De Foe. Bad cess to the damned woman. This step would realise his ambitions. Or break them. Miss Tabitha would be as astonished, but none more astounded than Hunterfield himself.

As he sat waiting in the great hall, he wondered at the curiously perverse certainty that had set him on this course. Sleep had eluded him for so long he felt a somnambulist, everything in view at some enormous distance. He had retired to bed the previous night not befuddled from drink. He knew he had overstepped all boundaries of sense and decency when booting Hunterfield out of Bures House – at least, that would be the judgement of all who heard of the episode. Unsavoury, unworthy. He hadn't needed any vitriolic cousin to come flinging her temper around to know that, thank you.

It would do no harm for the other two Hunterfield ladies to be present when he made his overtures to Tabitha, through the intermediary of her elder brother. Hunterfield was the one with the power. And Sir Edward Astell was just the sort of audience to see how modestly Charles Golding could behave, which would allay any doubts which the astute Astell might have, after that episode by the flooded sealands. Fine, he acknowledged with suppressed anger as the Lorne House servants wafted about their work with discreet glances at such an august visitor before mid-morning. Yes, fine that he had allowed himself to be tricked into sanctioning that bitch Mehala's illicit use of his oxen. But after this visit, if all went as planned, he would be the gainer. In serving their respective ambitions, they would serve his.

He gazed at a portrait of Tabitha Hunterfield on the far wall. As if waiting patiently, he slowly crossed to it. This must be one of the family portraits Hunterfield had commissioned from that idiot William Maderley of Watermillock. It was unfashionable to have a local dauber make likenesses, when gentry strove to hire London painters, but there was no doubt about Maderley's skill. He had caught Tabitha's gaiety without infringing the rules of propriety. She was positioned at a window – that one across by the main door, facing the gallery – wearing a close-fitting dress with Donna Maria sleeves. A Bermuda hat was cast on the seat beside her, and the tip of her brodequin footwear showed beneath the hem. Risky indeed to depict a lady so young in such about-to-depart attire, but effective with the light blue of the curricle pelisse adding a hint of sobriety.

Her smile, though, was the masterpiece. It suggested nothing, or everything. Describe the features and the subject's comport-ment, and you spoke only of a mundane painting, the like of which hung in every great house in the Eastern Hundreds. But see the smile for yourself, and you found yourself wondering what emotions actually lay beneath. The smile was at once obedient, diffident, compliant to a degree. Indeed, Tabitha's meekness was portrayed further by the vague picture – no more than a faint impression of one – shown on the wall behind to her left, of an older lady in a sombre attire, her dress exhibiting the 'frisk', that French bustle obsolete nigh on ten years. Take all at face value, and you had a docile maiden primly seated before a picture of an adored elderly relative. As allegory, Tabitha was sweetly stationed ready to uphold the traditional family values passed down from Grandmother. Look longer, and her expression was almost suggestive in its implied secrecy, as if something wanton compelled the artist's hand to reveal more than he intended . . .

A door opened, and the grave figure of Crane emerged.

'Good day, sir,' he intoned. 'The master is in receipt of your card early this morning, and is pleased to receive you in the orangery ante-room presently.'

'Thank you, Crane.' Golding waited the proper instant, then allowed himself to be ushered from the hall. The time for his proposal had come. It would be a master stroke, refusal or acceptance, and rescue him from the tyranny of Thalia De Foe.

In the breakfast room, Sir Edward Astell was speaking of his difficulties as the father of two imperious daughters, to the amusement of the three Hunterfield ladies. Henry disagreed.

'Even with the assistance of Mrs Vallance,' Henry was countering, 'a brother has not half the moral imperative of the father. See how mischievously these three manage me!'

Sir Edward laughed. 'We're all in the same boat, Henry! Lately I have suffered two blows to my position. Two days ago, my daughter blithely informs me that Carradine – from your area, Henry, not mine! – called to leave his card at Arminell, having asked for – *and provisionally been granted!* – permission to accompany one of my wanton moppets on a journey to Maidborough.'

'What a splendid gesture, though!' Tabitha recklessly interposed, to Lydia Vallance's hidden consternation. 'To save a father's natural concern, knowing how anxious he would be for Miss Brillianta's safety!'

'That is one way of telling the facts,' the older man conceded. 'But it can also be regarded as manipulating my concurrence – before it has even been sought!' As Tabitha laughed delightedly, Lydia and Letitia smiled, the latter acknowledging Tabitha's skill at these conversations. Tabitha's taunt was a clever ploy to discover if it was Brillianta, not Lorela, who had ridden in Carradine's company.

'For the best of all possible reasons, Sir Edward,' Tabitha added. 'To rescue a father from worries! Might I ask if the journey went safely?'

Lydia darted Tabitha a sharp glance. The girl was becoming altogether too forward, quizzing such a distinguished visitor. Were he to divulge details of his own accord, a pleasant interest should be proffered. And if he decided to enlarge on his first remarks, well and good. But for Tabitha – youngest sister, at that – to cut swathes through protocol needed correction. Surprisingly, Letitia came to her rescue as Sir Edward hesitated.

'I think my sister means that of Lorela, Sir Edward. Was she not in London? I remember having correspondence two months ago, when London was mentioned.'

Lydia caught Henry's relaxation. He too was conscious of Tabitha's bold impropriety. Lydia suddenly wished the breakfast over. The clock had yet to strike ten, and already she was tense. Her brother's manner was an additional secret cause of concern. He was showing an increasing preoccupation with the estates. When first she had arrived back at Lorne House to take over the housekeeping, on the departure of James for India, Henry was frank and outgoing. Now increasingly he seemed burdened, almost distant. It might be to do with the estrangement between himself and that horrid Thalia De Foe. A happy event, she thought, to part from a detestable married and unscrupulously ambitious lady. Marriage was a pious duty, being Heaven's Contract. But her brother had been sorely hurt, and now rarely seemed as enlivened as before.

'Lorela is now home in Arminell, Letitia,' Sir Edward was replying, accepting a fricassee of skate with puff-pastry croutons. 'I thank you. Her sojourn in London was successful. She made several pleasing word sketches for her journal.'

'What accomplishment!' Letitia complimented. 'I always admired Lorela's talents with the quill. Her letters are a godsend, even on the brightest days.'

'She had the company of Mistress Carmady and her brother Percy Carmady. They proceed to Sealandings, I believe, though they were so unkind as to decline our hospitality!'

'To Sealandings!' Tabitha exclaimed brightly. 'Is it their intention to call – ?'

'Is that not the same Lieutenant Carmady we know, Sir Edward?' Letitia interposed swiftly. 'Oh, forgive my interruption, Tabitha!'

'Forgiven of course, sister!' Tabitha replied with a winsome smile of apology to the visitor, but thinking, that's the last you ever see of your rose pendant earrings, Letitia, seek hard as you may. Lost they will be, and ever shall remain.

'Yes, Letitia, the same, I think. He has left the King's Navy, and seeks a residence.'

'Seafaring men settle near the sea,' Henry put in. 'Pleasant fellow. Stayed with us when the De Foes held their great ball.'

Astell prophesied, 'Oh, it will be Sealandings. His interests are the coast and all things maritime. He will enjoy your fish victuals as much as I, Mrs Vallance!'

'Mistress Glasse's white fricassee, Sir Edward, not mine,' Lydia confessed. 'My apricot tansy is one of Henry's favourites for breakfast. Do try the apple tansy also.'

'I will! I admire your special flavours.'

Lydia coloured with pleasure at the compliment. 'I add walnut buds instead of herb tansy, which is a little too bitter.'

'You vie with my Lorela, Mrs Vallance. She admires your pain perdy, calling it the best egg dish ever.'

'My panperdy is also stolen, Sir Edward! It is the old receipt of Gervase Markham for the English hus-wife. I would not fly under false colours, but please thank Miss Lorela.'

Lydia was gratified. Breakfast was a notorious difficulty in country houses, for gentlemen were all too easily bored by the same routines of potted meats, broiled mackerel, sliced mutton, rump chops, bacon rashers plain or fat, poached egg dishes, muffins, various toasts, broiled kidneys, dishes of hot dried haddock, and the several breakfast breads and preserves, with marmalades and jams to supplement the fruit dishes. Naturally, she had provided all of these on the two horseshoe tables where the serving maids officiated, but a lady was always at her wit's end thinking how to vary the meal. Collared meats a-plenty, of course, and Henry's favourite breakfast cakes made with equal proportions of butter and sugar, two ounces of each to the pound of dough, plus the new American breakfast cakes served hot with butter. She had remembered her mother's predilection for tansies – especially Mr Walton's minnow tansies, with primroses and cowslips – but unfortunately it was the wrong season, they being a spring countryman's dish. The sweet ones were popular, she saw with ill-concealed pleasure. Sir Edward asked for more. It was astonishing how the gentlemen loved fried foods. How on earth did those Continentals manage, with plain foods of a morning?

'Please do have more, Sir Edward,' Letitia surprised Lydia by urging their visitor gently. 'Or we shall believe our brother quite wore you out, keeping you down on the sea dykes for so long.'

'Thank you, my dear.'

'Especially as you had scarcely recovered from your daughters' oppression at Arminell,' Letitia smiled. 'Were I the senior lady, Sir Edward, I should insist that Henry detain you, to ensure a sound recovery.'

'Ah, the kindness of the lady!' Astell said, dealing with the fricassee. 'I almost forgot my second oppression. It was occasioned by Lorela's return, in that she now seeks to visit Sealandings, perhaps with a view to our residing here for the summer!'

'Really?' Letitia said, with pleasure. 'Please, may I ask our brother if you might stay here?'

'Wouldn't dream of it, my dear.' Sir Edward found Letitia's conversation most agreeable. He'd had no idea that this quiet, rather grave young woman could be so interesting. She took after her mother, of course, always reading poetry given half the chance. 'I fear matters are already too far gone! I shall be told my sailing orders presently!'

Lydia was delighted at the effect Letitia was having on Sir Edward, and could see that Henry admired the way her sister had turned the conversation round from a risky affront to a benevolent complicity.

'As long as your voyage harbours in Lorne House, Sir Edward,' Letitia finished neatly, causing laughter.

Crane quietly interrupted, murmuring the compliments of a gentleman come to visit.

Hunterfield explained to the gathering that the visitor was Charles Golding. 'It is a matter of some urgency, I understand.'

He exchanged significant glances with Sir Edward. Lydia did not need prompting to effect a swift withdrawal of the ladies. Leaving, she managed to catch Henry's eye and remind him that he had asked for coffee to be sent him at eleven-thirty. It was her convenient fiction, scope for tiresome visitors.

'Golding?' Sir Edward said ruminatively once they entered Hunterfield's study. 'Toujours perdrix!'

Henry laughed at the notion of being sickened by a surfeit of refinement. 'Always partridge, indeed!'

'Actually I wonder about him, Henry. Has he the stability of his ancestors, d'you think?'

Hunterfield thought a moment. 'He varies, Sir Edward. I know he wants to inveigle the authorities into appointing him a Justice.'

Sir Edward stood appreciatively before the fire, warming his hands. 'His response to your request for help at the floods was less than enthusiastic?'

'Downright rejection! And with the cattle sickness none of the great families or their tenants was inclined to offer. Getting help from Golding is always trying to wash white the Blackamoor.'

'That girl Mehala saved the day, eh, Henry?'

'Indeed. Strange creature, she.' Henry found himself at the window observing the slackening weather. 'I thought she was a mere drifter, when she was fetched from the sea. Then she seemed a Marplot, a troubling interferer.'

'And now?' The astute older man cocked his head, inspecting Henry. He saw in the young Hunterfield the mannerisms of his father, especially when profoundly disturbed by something too deep for open examination.

'Now, Sir Edward!' Henry turned, smiling. 'Now I have encountered her on less than half-a-dozen occasions, each so remarkable that I have learned only to be baffled. Muddy as she was, skating on those filthy boards more bedraggled than any workman, she yet seemed some strange exotic bird.'

'Who leaves Sealandings with her dog-doctor?' Sir Edward provokingly used the common abuse.

'Oh, he's more capable than many, Sir Edward. Saved a child of the croup in Whitehanger not long since. Extraordinary. I should regret to see them leave. That's why I sent my personal groom with her, partly in thanks, partly to retard Carmichael's departure.'

'Very wise, Henry,' Sir Edward smiled. 'Perhaps she is one of those women who, thrown into new circumstances by a quirk of Fate, becomes wholly different from what her past would allow!'

'I had the same thought, Sir Edward. Would you care to accompany me in receiving my visitor?'

'Thank you, no. I shall avail myself of Mrs Vallance's kind invitation to examine the paintings recently executed by your famous William Maderley.'

Henry paused. 'Famous, Sir Edward?'

'Yes. His name is broadcast as far as Maidborough and Wheatfen, for his country scenes.'

Good heavens, Henry thought, taking his leave. A lunatic? Famous? He sighed as he walked briskly towards the orangery, an abigail scurrying ahead to open the doors. It was a weird world.

'Sir Henry.'

Charles Golding rose to greet the Lord of the Manor of Sealandings with a slight bow. He was nervous now the moment had come.

Hunterfield stood somewhat taller than Golding, and often affected a stillness of manner that could disarm anyone, friend or antagonist. Also, advantage always lay with the host. The matter of their past encounter at Bures House had yet to be settled.

'Golding,' Hunterfield acknowledged. 'Please be seated. May I offer you refreshment? Tobacco? I have some excellent Russian tabak, which I assure you is not adulterated with the usual walnut leaf or hops.'

'Thank you, no.' Golding drew a breath, and plunged in. 'Sir Henry, I have come for a two-fold purpose. On a certain night recently, I behaved towards you in a reprehensible manner, that even my sainted parents would find hard to forgive. I have come to acknowledge that offence. Further, I give my assurance that such woeful conduct shall never be repeated. I am gratified that you accepted the use of my beasts and carts in the sea breaches, and will gladly make any contribution towards the sea walls' upkeep you might suggest.'

'I accept the apology,' Henry said. He was unpersuaded. How many times had he seen this same gentleman drunk, blaspheming, offensive to a crudity? How could this reformed character, standing before him, frowning with concentration, suddenly declare himself true as touch?

'Please, Sir Henry.' Golding swallowed. This was harder than he had guessed. 'I know my past demeanour gives offence. I ask only the condescension you would show any felon who comes before you in court. You have every right, so often have you seen me in drink, to suppose this visit Thessalian, one of deceit. I honestly avoid soft sawder. I intend no scheming flattery. I apologize unreservedly.'

'Then the matter is finished.' Hunterfield rose, trying to show himself mollified. 'We shall meet as plain acquaintances in future.'

'One thing more, if I may, Sir Henry.' Golding scrutinized Hunterfield's face for signs of reserve. 'I have long admired a certain lady, but for months now have not allowed myself the privilege of expressing that admiration.'

Hunterfield stared at him without a word. Golding gathered himself, ploughed on.

'Sir Henry, I am obliged to inform you of this admiration in general terms, hoping that you will not be averse to my eventually waiting on you to express my respect more precisely.'

'I acknowledge what you say, Golding.'

'Further, Sir Henry, I have maintained the greatest secrecy with regard to this. No breath of it has been communicated in any manner to another save yourself. I hope you will see my circumspection as a commendation.'

'I acknowledge that too, Golding.'

Golding bowed to make his leave. 'I had considered the wisdom of asking a lady to be my intermediary in this matter – not as a Blackfoot, a surreptitious go-between. That act, considering the circumstances of the offence I gave you, would have lacked courage. Hence, I came myself.'

'Very well, Golding.' *But which?* Hunterfield queried, as he held out his hand for the other to take. *Letitia or Tabitha? Has Lydia any inkling?* 'Pax, then.'

'Thank you, Sir Henry, most fervently!' Golding's relief seemed genuine, as they left the orangery talking of dispositions yet to be made for the sea dykes. Hunterfield saw his visitor off with a show of casual calm, but as soon as the Bures House carriage was out of sight he sent a maid-of-all to seek Lydia, who surely to God must have known something of this beforehand. If not, why not? It was her duty, for God's sake, as lady of his household. Some eminent gentleman sees the Squire's sister as his blue bonnet, unattainable object of his heart's desire, and the Squire is not forewarned? It was absurd!

He lost patience waiting for the servants to discover Lydia, and set out to find her for himself.

Codgie the longshoreman was almost drunk again, almost unable to find his feet and almost defiant when coming from the Goat and Compass. He was almost fit for work, almost able to find his dinghy, so he did nothing except stand tipsily in the dwindling rain and wish for a pint or two of honest ale that put a man's soul back in his chest. Warmth, that's what ale gave, warmth against the terrible North Sea.

285

In despair he reeled along to the wharf where the Yorkshire luggers berthed. *The Jaunty* was there, Master Jervin and young Hal Baines readying for sea as soon as the last of the storm abated.

'Need any hands, masther?' he shouted at the vessel.

'Who's there, then?'

'Codgie, Masther. Ready and willing!'

'Aye, come if'n you be sober.'

'I'm that, masther, for sure!'

'Haul the lines over the side, and the nets the same, with Hal here, Codgie.' Jervin eyed the drunken old longshoreman. He was well known for staying sober until the last measure was drunk, and for his knack of retaining strength in spite of ale. 'I never did trust nets that dried full. They forget the sea.'

'As y'say, masther, as y'say!'

Codgie was overjoyed. Too many of the young fools stayed indoors these times, forgetting that bad weather fetched good work. Foul sky, fair penny, he crowed to himself, shoving young Baines aside and reaching out to haul the net from the harbour.

He touched the girl's dead eyes that stared up from the water, screeched in terror and was violently sick.

30

Mehala was beside herself. The atmosphere in the Donkey and Buskin felt so wrong, and there was no news of Ven anywhere.

She passed the night at the tavern helping in Mrs Nelson's kitchen, anxious not to take undue advantage of the Weavers' charity. She was still in favour, she felt, but Little Jane was gone to Bures House, in the grand situation of under-housekeeper, wearing the chatelaine of Sir Charles Golding's household. Little Jane had been Mehala's especial friend at the tavern, right from the first.

She worked well, making scores of bottle birds, country apples baked in substantial crusts. Mrs Nelson wanted them on account of their popularity with coachmen and outside travellers for, well heated, they retained warmth. Charcoal stomach-braziers were sold in the taproom, with burning charcoals in the covered metal cage, but folk on long journeys had enough to pay – an horrendous fare of tuppence-halfpenny, or even three pence, a mile! For a single outside passenger! And an unbelievable five pence a mile, no less, for the sheltered inside position! No wonder charcoal stomach-warmers went often unsold. Mrs Nelson wisely said, 'Once a bottle bird cools the traveller may eat it to gain inner warmth. You can't do that with a charcoal engine!'

She met Mehala slitting salmon lengthways and tape-trussing the fish for spit-roasting. Mehala's culinary skills were well known, though the cook still watched her closely for transgressions.

'You'll know your task when the roast is finished, Mehala?' she prompted.

'I shall have the orange-peel and wine ready, Mrs Nelson. Shall I use up any excess butter after stirring the former into the fish juice and butter?'

'You had better, my girl!' Mrs Nelson threatened, only half in pretence. 'But before that – '

'Ten minutes before, I shall remove the tapes, that the pale bands they would leave may be browned and so will not show.'

'Carry on, and look sharp. Don't forget the orange garnish.'

'Yes, Mrs Nelson.'

Nellie the head waiting-maid gave her a wink as the cook returned to the chopping table. Then, seeing Mrs Nelson was preoccupied, Nellie shrugged to show that she had still learned nothing of Doctor Carmichael's whereabouts from taproom talk. Nellie had been Mehala's implacable foe at first. Now, their terrible fight, hands and claws, was forgotten. They were firm friends. Mehala tried a smile in reply, but could not concentrate. Even that skirmish with the friendly Mrs Nelson taxed her almost to the limit, so distracted was she about Ven. Surely he would not have quitted Sealandings without waiting for her, as they had agreed? She had spent an inordinate time down at the flooded sealands. Perhaps he had misbelieved her intentions. . . ? No, never. Why, she was sure – *sure* – that he felt far more for her than even he imagined.

She knew he was still here, somewhere. She had asked Sarah Ann Weaver if Doctor Carmichael had called, even paused to dry himself before the taproom fire. Nobody had seen him. And there was an air of withdrawal from her. Word had got out that she and Ven were evicted. Vagrancy was an horrendous accusation, for vagrants were punishable by law. Lack of employ was as bad. She felt shunned. Oh, the Weavers were kindly still, and John Weaver himself had found cause to exchange a friendly word. And the two under-scullions joked as always. But she would have to find Ven today. She could not outstay her welcome, a truly dreadful thought. Yet the consequences of leaving the Donkey and Buskin were so grim she could hardly bear to think of them. No money, no home. Any accuser could bring her before the magistrates as a wastrel going about the countryside Thomasing, a begging idler. Vagrants were cast into the town prison, the bocardo. How could she then stand by Ven, when he needed her more than ever?

Today was kill or cure. As soon as she had worked enough to pay for her stay, which at five pence a day meant somewhere towards noon, she would venture out into Sealandings, and find him. Then all problems would vanish. If she failed, she would have to get herself into the protective circle of the gentry. Or perhaps throw herself on the mercy of Miss Matilda at the school? Or to Lorne House, and seek Squire Hunterfield's help – though to reach him she would have to run the fearsome gauntlet of Mrs Lydia Vallance and her two sisters. No. Everything depended on finding Ven, her Ven.

She tied her mob cap more tightly, to keep back her hair while getting the salmon secure on the roasting spits, and set to. The mundane task of finding ingredients for the salamagundy would keep her occupied, especially as anchovies seemed in short supply. The merry jingle of the scullerymaids came as she went to gauge the oven's heat:

> *'Solomon Grundy,*
> *Born on Monday,*
> *Christened on Tuesday,*
> *Married . . .'*

From thereon the rhyme lost its merriment. It always had, even when she was a little girl. Resolutely she put it out of her head. Whatever today brought, she would fight as never before to find Ven and bring them both to haven. She had come too far, from that madman Elijah Rebow, whom she had been compelled to marry at Virley on that worst of all days. But that was in her old life. Her new life was at a low ebb, but she could *make* it turn and grow better, given half a chance. That half-chance would start with a painstaking retracing of Doctor Carmichael's steps.

Strangely, she found herself singing the children's rhyme she used to as a child.

> *'There were two blackbirds*
> *Sitting on a hill,*
> *One was called Jack*
> *And the other called Gill;*
> *Fly away Jack bird,*
> *Fly away Gill . . .'*

She looked across the kitchen and found Mrs Nelson staring, singing being forbidden without her express permission.

'No Greek ease here, miss!' Mrs Nelson reprimanded.

'Very well, Mrs Nelson!'

Mehala returned to her work, but finished in silent defiance.

> *'Come back Jack bird,*
> *Come back Gill.'*

The coachman drew to a stand outside the wide ornate gates at the entrance to Carradine Manor. Jason Prothero leaned from the phaeton, his eyes glittering with the thrill of possession.

'Just look, Mrs Prothero!'

'I see, my dear.'

'You don't! I mean look *out*, woman!' He was even more impatient with her than usual. 'It is surely not improper to set eyes on your husband's new home!'

Mary Prothero inclined her head and looked at the driveway, the gatehouse. A servant stood with his head uncovered beside the gate pillar. For a moment the coat-of-arms, seemingly so permanent, carved into the stone, took her attention. This whole move was a travesty, somehow an infringement of propriety. But Jason was driven. He was a man beyond all control, ever since his recovery.

Her husband's new home. Not hers. A cruel exclusion. Not the politer 'ours', nor yet the generous compliment 'yours'. His alone. No endearments now, only considerations of acreage, wealth, status and advancement into the ranks of the aristocracy. She stared at Carradine's coat-of-arms. Not all was nobility nowadays, not any more. Hadn't it been a humble vicar's son from Norfolk, the beloved Horatio Nelson, who had sailed the Kingdom to safety in the late wars? And a poor clerk, Robert Clive, who conquered the empires of India? And wasn't burgeoning industry created by the hands of artisans, of whatever family, inventors of genius? The North and Midlands were said to be already black with soot from fires, furnaces and mills. And yet Jason was behaving as if crazed by a few emblazons. It was hateful, hateful.

'There, Mrs Prothero!' His cry was the exulting glee of a small child, or would have seemed so if she could envisage him thus. Once, he had appeared a great gentle giant of a man, harsh and even thrilling, feral, theriac, powerful. But that was the power of a man's innocent strength, not this new malevolence.

Or was it new? Had it not merely been concealed? That thought was treachery. Her bounded duty was loyalty to her husband.

Marriage was the forging of two into one, by God's moral fires. Disunderment was forbidden by all religious rules. She sighed.

'It is beautiful, my dear.'

'Look, see, inspect, Mrs Prothero! Prothero Manor!'

'I have never seen it so lovely.'

The quiet remark sobered him. He glanced at her composed expression. Of course – she must have known this great pile ever since she could remember. Not so he, who could recall this place only when, as a lad, he tried to ingratiate himself perhaps by holding a tit's head while a child of some great Sealandings family dismounted at St Edmund's.

'Did you know Carradine Manor well?' The question was barbed, as all his questions.

'Once upon a time,' she answered, too wistfully. 'Papa and Mama took me occasionally to parties here. The ornamental ponds were stocked with golden fish, an astonishment then. Here I saw the new Pine Apple fruit. The lovely flowerbeds! And the new gravel walks that were laid out. It was Howard's grandfather, mostly. He loved a garden.'

Her tone was one of longing. The drive rose from the ornamental gateway, losing itself for a space among laid trees. A gleam of water showed to one side, then the drive recovered from the greenery before the manor house. A Queen Anne building, its modern façade was red brick with stone dressing. No false windows for adornment; many of the families used those to save on the pernicious window taxes. The lawns were close cut, and showed their stencilled margins between balustrades near the wide stone steps that climbed to the great portico.

'You knew them well?' he demanded, harsh.

'Not really. Howard was away, schooling somewhere. His relatives even in those days were never much in evidence.'

Prothero eyed her keenly. This wife of his, so highly bred and so self-contained, could prove a readier source of information than he had supposed. Every piece of gossip is useful. She ought to be eager to supply information about possible enemies among the gentry, make his advancement easier. Instead, here she was, a parasite on his endeavour, reaping the rewards that he alone had earned by right of conquest. Wasn't it always her way, to be indolent, playing the meek incapable, instead of buckling to and working to further her man's ambitions? Why, the stupid woman had needed telling twice that her hat was wholly wrong for a visit to the new Prothero abode! Brainless. And even now, at the third try, her Bermuda hat with its tight straw weave looked miserable instead of adorning, though she had claimed it was returning to London fashion.

For a fleeting instant he saw the face of Mehala in his mind. There was a woman! Younger, a little, than Mary perhaps; having no possessions, no fine birth, no family to speak for her. But who could take a man by storm, with her skills, her curious strengths, her – brightness. And who maddened a worthy man, such as himself, who was exactly the hard forceful mate she surely sought. Why, in a few short months she had risen from a penniless sea-taken to become Golding's housekeeper at Bures House, only to cast her position away on that cheap quack at Shalamar. Served the perverse bitch right, to get thrown out with him! Though if she were to come a-begging, should her newfound poverty bring her to her senses, he would take her on – only for board wages, to teach her a lesson. Cot and consumables, but no coin. That would quell any rebellion left in her.

'You shall conduct me round, then, my dear,' Prothero announced, commanding her to recover her appearance in the phaeton. He found her dreamy expression most irritating. She was always off into some reverie these days, as if finding refuge in fantasy. 'Seeing you are fully acquainted with every aspect of Carradine Manor!'

Alarm leapt to her eyes. He tapped on the coach side. 'Wake up, Plowden! Drive on!'

'Yes, masther.'

Prothero settled back with a grunt of satisfaction. Mary noticed the slight pause before the coachman had replied. She made to raise her hand in customary acknowledgement to the gate-keeper – she had known Danson since a little girl – but desisted at her husband's quick frown. She thought of Ven Carmichael, an increasing fault. Oh, for a chance to regress the sundial! How wonderful her life could have been! There again was her terrible treachery, just when she ought to be standing firmly by her husband. She was after all his property and possession, as true religion taught. Duty was duty.

31

Drunkenness was its own hazard, yet its own bliss. It encouraged in man a power to punish by simple reason of its own infuriating headache next morning. It lifted a man to daftness and laughter, and a woman to bleary maudlin. It sank the world to a poisonous obscenity.

'The last thing I want, Clark, is interruption!' he shouted. And the elderly head servant had the audacity to continue approaching across the breakfast room!

Charles Golding eyed the old gargoyle balefully, feeling like death. 'Yet I'm pestered by fools of Gotham!' The Nottingham-shire village had for centuries been a byword for stupidity, and the accusation was a studied insult. Last night's sexual adventure had been hideous, a total failure. He felt cheated. Nobody defrauded Charles Golding of Bures House and got away scotage free. He'd see to that! She would suffer for his lack of sexual satisfaction, by God! And anyone else who crossed his path this morning, like this stupid old peasant.

It had been ridiculous. The maid-of-all he had selected had proved ignorant, stupid and frightened during last night's bout – or so he thought. Instead of ecstasy it became a series of undignified fumbles, in consequence of which he had spent himself will-he nil-he over the bedclothes, and the wench virtually untouched. Worse had happened – she instantly became petulant, even cross, and had made him feel ineffectual. All along her protestations had been nothing more than a hair to make a tether of –an excuse for fuss. She was as innocent as the girls at Two Cotts, he thought bitterly. Her genteel squeaks and meek posturings were a mask to exploit his carnal desire. The slut knew only too well how generous a master was after enjoying the charms of an innocent girl. She was an expert, false brisle dice in a house of gamesters. And as well used, begod!

So he was in no mood to be courteous when sundry ancient idiots came interrupting his breakfast.

'What, Gothamite?'

'A letter, sir.'

'You interrupt me for a miserable letter, you doddering old fool?'

The elderly servant proffered a silver tray. 'I beg forgiveness, sir. It comes from London, at high charge to the post, and the seal is crested. Two shillings and four pence the one letter, sir.'

The breakfast maid standing by the hot table drew a sharp intake of breath – such giddy expense, to move a few words! Golding gazed at the letter, folded, sealed with red stamped sealing wax. The letter was a sparsely written one, not cross-written as many, to save paper and postage.

He took it ungraciously, bade Clark to leave, and shakily cracked the seal with a thumb.

For a moment the words seemed in a strange language. Then he got the sense, his eyes raking the lines, and inhaled slowly. He looked up, round the room, at the food before him, at the ceiling, in utter rapture. His headache was suddenly trifling.

'Sir?' she said nervously.

Only a few moments ago, and he had been wondering if the slut knew about his tussle with last night's maid-of-all! He knew how women chattered below stairs and in markets and the lanes of Sealandings. Now, it didn't matter a damn. For his family cousin Sir Philip Banks had achieved a great thing, news that would turn the course of his ambition.

'. . . *you will be apprized of this by other means,*' Sir Philip had written in his quivering hand. '*Suffice it for me to inform you that you have with immediate effect been appointed Justice of the Peace, with all the duties and powers conferred by stat. 16 Geo. 2.c.18, and 60 Geo.3 and 1 Geo.4.c.14 . . .*'

His mind settled. He rose and strode straight to the study, where he scanned the law books accumulated by his father. He grabbed one and read feverishly. Then another and a third, almost in delirium as excitement grew within and the magic golden – *golden* indeed! – words of authority leapt off the pages, one after another. He flung books aside, dragged others from the shelves in a cascade of dust and crumbling leather, cursing at the inconvenience of the heavy volumes.

. . . every Justice may do and execute all things appertaining . . .

he read, glowing. *For passing and punishing vagrants; for repair of highways; or to any other laws concerning parochial taxes, levies, or rates.*

It was a gift from God, he breathed silently, scanning the thick pages of *The Magistrate's Manual*. King of Sealandings!

. . . shall have full power at discretion to commit any person charged before them . . . to nominate any number of persons to act as special constables . . .

He found himself sitting on the wooden flooring, gaping, leaning back in a sweat against the shelving. He had had power before this, yes, but to such a degree? Royal authority, no less! In his hands! Restricted to Sealandings and its environs, of course, but nonetheless power he had never dreamt of. For the first time, his authority extended outside his own gates, on to the roads of the country at large, governing the people who lived and worked all about. His sudden grin was vulpine. He caught up the book he had let fall.

. . . It shall be lawful for every constable, headborough, &c. or other peace officer, for every parish, &c. to execute any warrant of any Justice of the Peace . . . within any parish . . .

Wasn't it Heaven? Wasn't it Christmas? His birthday, come daily?

A phrase caught his gaze and he paused, reading it over and over with a growing sense of vengeance.

. . . Every Justice has the power of committing any person guilty of insolent behaviour to him in the execution of his office instanter . . .

There were bound to be limitations, after all. The saving grace came next:

. . . If a Justice exceed his authority in granting a warrant, yet the officer must execute it . . . And the best wine at the last: *Justices cannot be proceeded against both criminally and civilly . . .*

Total power! Right or wrong, he would be declared right!

A final sentence caught his eye in the old print, so strange that he had to carry the tome to the window for adequate lighting. There he read:

By 43 Geo.3.c.141, in actions against Justices for an improper conviction, the plaintiff . . . shall not recover more than two pence . . .

295

He laughed and laughed, so much that Clark came hurrying to see what was ailing the master. He amusedly came to, and told him to bring a new breakfast.

'Not your miserable seven dishes, either, and two barely warm,' he said with disturbingly new affability. 'Make it a round dozen like I used to, six of them hot. And for once give me enough broiled kidneys, steaks, collared fish and potted meats with your veal-and-ham pies. You've starved me to death long enough. Serious work from now on, y'hear?'

The breakfast maid flew, while Clark dithered in wonderment at the master's unbelievably good humour before retreating to supervise the relaying of breakfast.

The homecoming was different. Barbara Tyll was almost sickened by the heartbreak as Carradine dismounted before the great steps and waited, smouldering, for Prothero to welcome him.

She stood, pale and almost visibly trembling, as Hobbes the chief servant stood respectfully beside the main entrance. The maids were absent. Normally they would formally line the portico. Now, they were mercifully out of sight, as indeed she herself ought to have been. She wanted no part in this. Carradine was clearly a gentleman visiting an acquaintance, and no longer a master returning to his ancestors' manorial hall.

'Are you all right, Mrs Tyll?'

Judith Blaker startled the housekeeper. This new assistant-housekeeper had an infuriating habit of suddenly appearing. Barbara Tyll restrained her irritation with difficulty.

'I am well, thank you, Blaker. Carry on with your duties.'

'I was instructed to see to the hall furnishings, ma'am.'

Doubly hard now to suppress a retort admonishing the girl, for she herself had issued that instruction only an hour before, far too brief a time to polish furniture and beat carpets, see to curtains, clean windows.

'Wait by the west corridor, Blaker.'

'Very well, ma'am.'

Barbara Tyll's attention returned to Carradine. He looked rested and well, though he had ridden all the way from Hoddinotts this morning. He was expected two days ago, then yesterday. Normally he would have flung himself up the staircases, dashed along corridors, talking and hallooing and shouting, teasing her – though she never approved of his alarmingly frank and dangerous displays of bear-like friendliness in public. Then it would have been the summons to his suite, after his bath waters had been heated and carried there by the three upper-landing maids. Then he would have locked the door, and . . .

Blaker was looking at her across the great hall. She gestured sharply for the irritating girl to pay attention and not to stand gaping. She must remind herself continually that sharp eyes abounded, and not reveal a thing about herself and the master. Master, Carradine would always remain to her, notwithstanding his rough seizure of ancient masters' sinful rights over her person.

Carradine and Prothero were slowly moving across the fore-court, making to stroll up the steps.

Judith Blaker also watched them, but was more conscious of Mrs Tyll's attitude. Well, well, she thought with astonishment. Imagine! Who'd have thought! Old Barbara Tyll a secret Guinevere, a wanton, maring under Carradine! The daft woman nigh on thirty years old if she was a day! Married, the austere and morally strict housekeeper of Carradine Manor was almost going to pieces before her very eyes at the sight of Carradine. It was not all mere sentimental bleating, either. Judith could tell. This was a transparent craving any woman would recognise. As the common saying had it, prim Mrs Barbara Tyll longed for the blue rose, an unattainable object of heart's desire, or her name wasn't Judith Blaker!

Clearly old Tyll was blinkered by strict ideas of obedience, as dray-horses in London's Cornhill. Judith sneered openly at the absurdity of it. An older woman, drooling! It was all but obscene, except it was so laughable. The silly old crow was no backfish, as folk called a girl of sweet sixteen ripe for the plucking. It was instantly clear as day: Carradine returning home well in his cups one night being carried to bed; Tyll sternly banishing the giggling young maids for shame of the master being seen in such a state. Then staying to get herself ravished by a Carradine briefly recovering from his drunken stupor. The usual process, as all maids knew. And – who could tell? – maybe it had happened once or twice more. She could imagine that too, the housekeeper staying up, beautifying herself as best she might against the master's return, and setting her cap at him. Well, wine blunts sight and sword. Who could say where Carradine's sword had blundered when he was stupefied with drink? Mayhap Barbara Tyll had proved herself, but the silly cow was hunting a pie's nest if she hoped for more, now Judith Blaker was here!

The gentry walked through the hall, Carradine nodding casually to Mrs Tyll but not noticing any other servants, except giving Hobbes a brief word. She observed Carradine's manner as Mrs Tyll followed the two gentlemen, her gown swishing on the marble flooring, her hands soberly clasped. No sign of affection there, she saw with immense satisfaction. Yes, mare Tyll was not the first woman to have a month's mind for an unattainable lord, when she should be sweating her own husband to that wrestling oblivion all men craved.

'Come – Mrs Prothero waits the withdrawing room, Carradine,' Prothero said airily.

'Very pleasant, Mr Prothero.' Carradine spoke with quiet urbanity as he followed the burly farmer through the double doors. *Followed*, he thought, suppressing his fury at the man's insolence. Once a peasant, always so. 'I am pleased to be so well received.' Carradine managed a smile at Prothero.

The oaf was mincing, imagining he was behaving like a scion of some great county family. A jack-a'horse if ever there was one.

Mary Prothero remained seated on a courting chair, looking somewhat pale. She inclined her head in welcome and like Carradine managed a smile as Prothero strode forward.

'You are welcome, of course, Mr Carradine.' Mary said the words stiffly, as if they gave her distress.

Her husband looked sharply at her, but Carradine stepped forward to play the guest. The courting chair was the only item of furniture in the room that had not been his own. Trust Mary Calling, the guarded little girl who always hung back at games, watching the boys' raucous play with timidity. For a fleeting instant something passed through his mind, of chances past. Then he was into his act.

'Obliged, ma'am. I do not have words to tell the joy my visit gives.'

'Please, Mr Carradine. You do us the honour. Won't you take tea? Or coffee?' For a moment animation showed through. 'I shall not offer you Arabica coffee, made in a hydrostatic urn in the new fashion! Do not fret!'

He was puzzled, but smiled and perched on a seat opposite. It sickened him to see Prothero thrust his feet up on a low drum table. It had once been Father's, for letters of the day. Carradine swallowed. One day he would have to kill this upstart villein. God's truth. But it would need to be done with refinement, not a mere swing of an axe. No pleasure in that.

'Arabica is most acceptable, Mrs Prothero. Thank you.'

Prothero interjected, 'Our visitor has worn the green bonnet for quite some time, Mary. He'll rejoice to taste some lively liquid!'

Mary could not disguise her sharp intake of breath at the studied insult. To wear the green bonnet, to fail utterly in some mercantile business, was a common saying in coffee houses about the London Exchange. Prothero saw his barb had struck home, and beamed at Carradine's sudden tautness.

'Come, come, madam,' he said jocularly. 'This fellow is able to laugh! Hey, Carradine?'

Carradine swallowed, but kept his smile. Everything here was a reminder and reproach. He had lost the portraits on the walls, the carpets, the windows and the lawns on which they opened. All. To this pig who scraped his heel on Father's table.

'I have that reputation, sir. I trust I maintain it!'

One more *sir* for which you'll pay, Prothero, Carradine registered, perversely overdoing his courtesies to suffer grievance all the more.

'And why not?' Prothero demanded, enjoying himself hugely. 'Just because *you* had to cross the Irtish ferry is no reason to sulk like some ignorant brat, eh?'

'Indeed no,' Carradine said quietly.

Mary, instructing the serving maid how to make the coffee, turned in consternation.

'The Irtish ferry, Mr Prothero? Surely to suggest that Mr Carradine had taken himself into exile is too extreme a remark? For Hoddinotts is neighbour to Sir Edward Astell's Arminell, and beautifully situate in Maidborough vale.'

'I didn't have your early affluence, madam,' Prothero said tersely. The woman was insufferable, putting on her airs with him who had saved her grand estate from falling to rack and ruin. Her glance when he had rested his heels on this table had not escaped him, either. Whose table was it, for God's sake? 'So I was unable to form an exact opinion of the great houses in the Eastern Hundreds in the same way as your good self.'

'Of course, Mr Prothero.'

Carradine was angry enough, without wasting time listening to two bores savage each other. He was here for a reason.

'I heard about your injury, and how well you have recovered, sir,' he said, taking the first step.

'No thanks to that dog-doctor Carmichael. He damned near killed me. It's fortunate I'm a healthy man and withstood his butchery.'

'How goes your move into Carradine, if I might ask without intrusion? Pleasantly, I trust?'

'Indeed, Carradine. I pride myself on being a supreme organizer, all manner of estates and chattels. I had it done in an afternoon!'

'The staff proved helpful, I hope?'

'They had better!' Prothero grinned. 'I was fortunate, in that several stout skilled artisans came wanting employ, just as the storm's damage became apparent.'

'Did you, indeed?' Judith Blaker's many 'cousins', Carradine thought. The more the merrier, for the while. 'That surprises me, for all the Eastern Hundreds suffered heavy damage, to carts and buildings alike. And go in lack of such men.'

'Ah, there's a difference betwixt older gentry and me,' Prothero exclaimed. 'They don't understand workers. I do. A skilled man trusts a gentleman who knows how to rule him, not like the degenerates who have lorded it hereabouts for so long. Decayed folk are effete. Mere shams. Copper captains, all.'

Mary was now almost waxen as the insults grew. She deflected the spate by referring to Carradine's coffee.

'They say the French coffee is much better,' she put in gently. 'Mocha is excellent. Do you suppose the government will allow French imports less tax duty than before, Mr Carradine? Or will we always be burdened by high revenues?'

'Y'see, Carradine,' Prothero surged on brashly, 'I make them work caution money here, like at Calling Farm. Caution money's sureity for good conduct. Never did any booy harm!'

300

Carradine nodded smiling. Here was Judith Blaker's hand for sure, for the journeyman artisan didn't exist who would work a month for nought, when his services were eagerly sought over the next hedge. No; the new men were here by her arrangement. For the first time since stepping in through the great hall's double doors, he felt a touch of confidence.

'I think I do remember, Mrs Prothero!' he exclaimed suddenly. Mary's remark had niggled. 'Your first attempt at making Arabica – you watered the carpet with it! And Lord Lothammer your father's guest!'

Mary turned bright pink. 'It was a most difficult engine, Mr Carradine, and I but ten years of age! Such a troublesome device! In exoneration, I hear it is not even yet perfected!'

Prothero smouldered at her interruption. He had generously welcomed this newmade peasant in order to rub his nose in the dirt. Then his fool of a wife spoils it by recalling her Halcyon days, their kingfisher times when the masters romped royally on greenswards –times when he had laboured like a madman for eleven pence a day in every weather God sent. He would grind this man down hab or nab. And punish Mary for her idiocy.

'How did Hoddinotts suit you, Carradine?' he asked bluntly. 'Your landlord make you comfortable?'

Carradine would have hesitated, but this was no time to bate his ace.

'I had neither landlord nor host, sir,' he said, under tight control. 'I was alone but for two elderly servants. However, I found the Astells most neighbourly.'

'The Astells!' Prothero echoed. The aristocracy stick to their own. But he was now among them, as they would know before long. 'Tell me, Carradine. Did they make any suggestions towards your maintenance? Or was their company merely poker talk?'

'I saw little of them, sir.'

Carradine accepted the cup from Mary, aware of her distress but as angry at her as he was at the odious Prothero. A wife ought to keep her husband in bounds, instead of listening to her dolt's moonshine. A woman should be a fighter, a veritable Female Marine as everybody now said, like Hannah Snell who fought with bayonet and sword at Pondicherry beside her man. His women's faces flitted past for an instant: Lucy, the whore at Two Cotts;

Judith the gypsy who had stood in the great hall's shadows watching his arrival just now; the composed, pale features of Barbara Tyll his housekeeper, staple bedfare when more exotic provinder was lacking; and, oddly because he had never yet had her, Mehala who once actually had the gall to turn from him to go with that impecunious quack. But all would fight for their man, whoever or whatever he was.

He found himself searching Mary Prothero's anguished expression for clues. Surely she could no longer love this toad Prothero? Duty, that was it. Women's curse since the dawn of time, their bizarre addiction to duties come what may, and playing Harpocrates all the while, mutely enduring all like that god of silence.

'I hope to see more of them, in due course. In response, sir, might I enquire after your fortunes at Calling Farm? I made it my solemn duty to send good wishes, on learning of your illness, but unfortunately the messenger bearing my letter was turned from the gate.' Carradine smiled openly for the first time. 'Some misunderstanding. I was distressed by not having managed to convey my sentiments.'

Prothero hesitated. This bastard had learned of the murrain at Calling. He must have. No country messenger ever returned but with a bigger tale than ever he set out with.

'There's a rumour, Carradine,' he answered, offhand. 'You know how they grow. Some mild coughing sickness, two or three cows. Illiterates spread alarm and despond at any opportunity. Why,' Prothero laughed, he thought convincingly, 'there was even some silly gossip that my occupancy of Carradine would be postponed!'

'I rejoice to see you in place, sir,' Carradine said, exulting inwardly but keeping composure. 'For that will surely give the lie to one and all!

'So I trust, Carradine.'

'And even the lawyers – bad cess to them, begging your pardon, Mrs Prothero – will have to accept that all is healthy at Calling! I am pleased, sir.' Carradine laid aside his cup, smiled his thanks at Mary. 'For, imagine! If accounts of the cattle plague were true, what a colossal expense would fall upon the Calling estates! And imagine what costs would fall upon Sealandings, district and all, if the denials proved a cruel deception! Which, sir, I hasten to state, is happily impossible!'

'Indeed,' Prothero said, feeling a sudden chill.

'A fortunate escape! The estate might then have to bear costs proportionate to the loss incurred by the whole area, including restitution to the markets of the Eastern Hundreds! Sir,' Carradine said with sincerity, 'I swear it. I rejoice at your happy position.'

'Your kindness does you credit, Carradine.'

'Madam, I shall now take my leave, if you will allow, with gratitude for your kindness in receiving me here.'

Mary bowed, not meeting his eyes. 'You will always be welcome at my husband's home, Mr Carradine.'

Well, well, Carradine thought, registering her careful words. A fighter after all, then? However, one of little account.

He walked with Prothero through the hall, where Judith Blaker was arranging the curtains over the great windows. He paused.

'Tell me, sir,' he asked Prothero. 'Do you not find the window tax inordinate in an establishment as large as Carradine? My former estate bailiff Lennon said the annual window taxes alone were sixty pounds and nine shillings, for one hundred and twenty-eight windows. Is it really that much? Never having had the fortune of a labouring education, I was quite unaware of those costs . . .'

Judith Blaker smiled to herself. Mention of any numbers in her hearing was the sign that he wanted to see her urgently, for so the message from Prettiance had been. And such numbers! she thought delightedly. She would be by the small boat dock, against the rising shore, before the tenth night hour.

32

The days were drawing in, Mehala saw as she walked through Sealandings. Autumn was advancing. It seemed there of a sudden, not coming imperceptibly as in some years but effecting swift changes of hues among trees and fields. It was uncanny. Or was it her awareness of her loss?

Along the lanes children were playing their autumn games. She paused by St Edmund's to watch, partly from weariness of her fruitless search, partly to allay her terrible sense of loneliness. Her lips moved as the line of children trotted forward and chanted: *'Mother buy the milk pail, mother, dear mother of mine.'*

Mehala found herself watching the little moppet who sat on a cottage step as she sang reply and the children opposite danced in retreat: *'Where's the money to come from, children, dear children of mine?'*

The tiny 'mother' did her part creditably, scolding the troublesome line of her play-children with such vigour that in spite of her despair Mehala found herself smiling. How often had she herself, as a little girl, plumped herself down on one of the Red Hills, supposed graves of ancient Mystery Kings, that rose along her marshy homeland shores to the south, and tensed, ready for the final rush after the rebellious infants with which the game ended.

'Mistress Mehala! You know the game, I'm thinking!'

'I recognise it. From where I cannot say.'

As an impromptu response it sufficed. Mehala smiled, showing more confidence than she felt. Whatever else, her appearance must be that of a woman employed, busying herself about her duties. To appear wandering in search of her employer would invite the vagrancy charge. A cottager's wife stood at a doorway in the narrow lane observing her. Mrs Shapley, Mehala remembered; she was barely twenty-four with six children and a seventh rising for its Christmas welcome.

'You poor girl!' the fisherman's wife exclaimed. 'What a pity

Doctor Carmichael cannot return your memory, with all his simples and potions!'

Mehala smiled. 'My memory is in God's hands, Mrs Shapley. He may see fit to bless me.'

The children were nearing the conclusion now. Mehala moved a step out of their way for the scattering dash which followed the last chant, then tutted inwardly at her foolishness. Mrs Shapley's eyes gleamed.

'You know it very well, it seems, Mehala!'

'I am puzzled.' Mehala frowned, hoping to turn the conversation to advantage. 'Like now. I am instructed to follow Doctor's visits, but am forgetful.'

'Doctor Carmichael was down by the harbour, my Benedick said. He looked sore hurt, beset by vagabonds on the Norwich road, 'tis said.'

'I heard, Mrs Shapley. Where by the harbour?'

'Far past the Goat and Compass, walking nor'ards.'

'Thank you, Mrs Shapley. I shall hurry on.'

The harbour! So Ven was heading for the last of the sea cottages. Probably to Raffin, the seaman taken from the sunken *Dander*. She walked down the steep lane of cottages. Behind her the children's voices rose eagerly: '*Oh then we should all of us be at an end!*'

And with screams they scattered, the 'mother' chasing them while they tried to sit on the steps for safety. Mehala did not look back.

From the end of the lane she could see the harbour below. She crossed the cobbled street and cut through a narrow back alleyway to shorten the journey.

Absurdly, she realised she was inwardly singing her favourite children's rhyme as she hurried, so apt for her present plight:

> '*Go round and round the village,*
> *Go round and round the village,*
> *As we have done before . . .*'

The choices before her were contradictory. Trying to retrace Ven's course by herself had seemed so sensible when setting out. The lack of news at the tavern, and of success when touring

Sealandings in the Squire's grand emblazoned carriage, had shown her the only way: go on foot, alone, and people would instantly tell her any news.

She sang silently:

> *'Come in and face your lover,*
> *Come in and face your lover,*
> *As we have done before . . .'*

If any one person so much as pointed the road he had taken, she would fly after him without any regard of her own safety. But there had been this strange silence – not lack of friendliness, no. The folk were as welcoming, or at least as accepting, as usual, but they were closing up, not revealing all. She was becoming frightened. The day was wearing on. It was now four of the clock, and darkness fell by seven. What if she had not managed to find him by then? What could she do? Compromise Miss Gould a second time? Hiding in some barn would be fearsomely risky, to be hallmarked as a vagrant . . .

'I kneel because I love you,' her mind went. She banished the ridiculous childish melody from her mind, to concentrate on her task.

The cottage was one of the terrace that ended the town, standing between the Blakeney road and the sea. Some disturbance was going on by the South Mole, where several ships were wharfed, one being *The Jaunty*. But Ven was nearby. She actually felt his presence as she knocked.

'Mistress?'

Mrs Raffin appeared at the door almost instantly, as if she was there waiting, her expression without surprise. Mehala thought, *She knew I would come.*

'I have called to see Raffin,' Mehala said, trying for composure. 'Doctor Carmichael cannot come, for he is injured. He instructed me to attend your husband.'

The woman's face showed relief. She opened the door. 'My husband sleeps, Mehala. Do come, but be quiet. Doctor was most insistent – '

A fire of seacoals burned in the grate, giving enough light for Mehala to see the sleeping man's amputation stump was unaffected by any change. It did not stink, and showed none of the sinister signs Ven Carmichael had taught her to look for. It seemed dry, the bandages not tautened and the thigh's skin not reddened or puffy. Raffin himself sat aslant a chair before the fire, his head flopped back upon the rest and his sound leg up on a stool. The man's face was pale, his breathing regular.

'He eats, Mrs Raffin?' Mehala whispered.

'Yes, Mehala. Doctor . . .'

Is very pleased? Mehala mutely finished for her. She tiptoed to the door and smiled a silent goodbye. The woman came to fasten the Suffolk latch in transparent relief as Mehala went down the steps and turned quickly towards the centre of Sealandings. She set out with brisk, quick steps, her heart lighter than it had been since Ven had vanished, for now she knew – she *knew* – that her man was lodged here, in one of the fisher cottages, or was actually in Raffin's home, and for some incomprehensible reason Mrs Raffin was keeping her from him. Rage rose in her as she walked, almost ran, from the terrace and headed for the Corn Mart. What right had that woman to keep silent? Nobody had more right to know his whereabouts than Mehala herself. Hadn't all events proved it to one, to all? How *could* the fisherfolk side with Ven against her? Such wanton stupidity! She was shocked at the savagery of her thoughts, and the seething abuse she was subjecting the folk of Sealandings to. She had been kindly long enough. Hours counted now, not days or months, and she would not be baulked.

She raced past the Corn Mart unheeding, though somebody called a good afternoon, and was almost breathless when finally she knocked on the door of Bartholomew Hast's gunsmithy at the south corner of the Square.

Carradine felt the exultation of repossession. He dismounted behind the larger of the two barns at Two Cotts. Both buildings were merged into Mistress Wren's bawdy house, but served the purpose of being places where selected personages could meet their chosen girls unseen from the Norwich road. Traffic as always was pestilential along that thoroughfare, Carradine observed with chagrin. His absence had meant nothing to Sealandings. He tied up his mount, then paused as a thought suddenly struck him.

Was that quite true? Late afternoon, five of the clock, yet the Mail post-chaise had not passed him in its dash from the town. It was never late. And should the goosegirls not already be making their hectic and noisy way downhill towards market, ready for the morrow? And wasn't this exactly the time that the great Suffolk farm waggons should go trundling through? He felt excitement, and went to have Lucy summoned by the yard ostler.

She came at a breathless run, almost flinging herself into his arms, so joyous was she to see him. He let her prattle and question him, kissing his face and generally behaving like a puppy. The large barn was sparsely furnished, not exactly the sort of place a gentleman should have to meet a favoured whore, but one side loft had been got out as a comfortable ledge, with a small aumbry holding a few wines and spirits. It had a livery cupboard, relict from former times and therefore of no intrinsic value, being such ancient furniture. It held a few victuals. There was also a shut-bed, its curtains made of old frayed atlas of which the cotton warp was almost completely decayed to leave only the silk weft showing satiny patches. Lucy all but hauled him up the steep steps into the loft.

'It's not so sweet here, my darling Rad!'

'It suffices.'

'Dearest!' She turned to meet him as he made the loft space and glanced about. 'Couldn't we go into my room at Two Cotts, instead?'

'No. I want here.'

'But darling.' She started to unlatch his coat buttons on his American coat, openly admiring it as the first she had ever seen. 'You know your little Lucy loves to please her Rad. She can do that much more prettily if she's allowed to play like she wants to.'

'Is this place full of ears?'

'It's safe, darling!' she exclaimed, shocked that he should doubt. 'Mistress Wren orders that the barns be only for one gentleman caller at a time! And two outer guards by the doors! You know that!'

'Then shut you up, girl, and get on.'

'Yes, dearest. I love your grand new coat! Is this the London fashion now? So long in its skirt! Such broadness in the collar, yet so narrow the lapel! What strange folk them American colonials must be! Wide skirt flaps, too!'

He let her chatter, dragged aside the atlas curtaining and sprawled on the bed while she straddled his legs in turn to struggle his Blucher half-boots off. He said nothing as she bustled to bring him drink and three plates of prepared meats and a few sweet puddings.

'Time you got some hearths here,' he grumbled, sipping the Oporto wine. 'Cold fare's not what I come for.'

'You'll get no cold fare from Lucy, darling, well you know.'

The food was on a trestled table-board within reach of the bed, so she had time, while he started to eat hungrily, to undress and slip in beside him. She lay propped up on one elbow, astonished at his voracious appetite. It was rare to see a gentleman eat so, like a starving cowherd wolfing victuals at harvest-time. Then she noticed his whiskers, quite untrimmed, stubble on his cheek-bones. His hair was almost matted, quite as if he had done his morning toilet unassisted. His clothes were of the finest material, of course – yet any gentleman in the Kingdom could walk into a tailor's shop and run up a billed debt for as long as six months without being dunned.

And here he was, back in Sealandings. In full spirits, to judge from the reception he gave her. This was no indecisive Carradine, her lost gambler facing ruination, scheming and ferreting for points of advantage. No; this was the Carradine she had first known, who walked as if he owned the countryside. Which he did! Rough and unkempt he might now be, but not for long if she read all the signs aright.

'Lucy.' He lay back on the covers, weighing her down, eating fast. 'Get these clothes off me, for Christ's sake, 'stead of lying idle. Why is Sealandings so quiet?'

She started to pull off his cossacks. 'Rumours abound of some murrain among Calling Farm's estate. Some say it's the pox, others a cattle plague.'

'Business diminished?'

'Lord love us, sir, indeed it is! The cheaper girls are mortal complaining. The mistress is fair driven to distraction. Since the week's start three of the ground-floor girls have only had seven shags among them! Can you believe it?'

Carradine's sudden intense stare made her uncomfortable. She paused. 'Do I offend, sir?'

'No, Lucy. How many would they usually have?'

'At least five apiece, sir.' She undid his full shirt, ruffling its chitterlings with pleasure. Good linen always warmed a woman's interest. This was especially fine material, pure linen: another indication that Carradine lived in appearances lately rather than solid solvency. 'More, on holy days. People are not moving through Sealandings like they should, all for a stupid rumour!'

'Is it rumour alone?' He remembered the drover Bellin.

'Why, ships turn aside from the harbour! And the King's ship victuals at Lowestoft! Ridiculous!'

'Has Prothero moved cattle, Lucy?' Carradine grimaced, spat out the brandy. 'God! Portugal spirit? You want to poison me?'

'I'm sorry, Rad. Mrs Wren orders it laid in the aumbry for the large barn. There's Madeira, and some Jerez.'

'Brown sugar the one. Brown pepper the other. Sherry, then.'

With ill grace he let her serve him a glass of Jerez. 'No, darling. Prothero wanted to move a herd through the market to Carradine Manor, but Sir Henry forbade.'

'You sure?'

'So 'tis said by the drovers. And the naval captain – '

'You've already told me about the *Hornet*, girl.'

'Not from a ship. Coaching from inland, with his sister, uncertain whether to remain or pass by Sealandings. Carmady, his name. I served his groom.' She blushed with genteel embarrassment. 'That is, I lay with the groom only once, during one of his earlier stays here. Not now.'

'Lieutenant Percy Carmady?' Carradine came on to an elbow to peer at her as she replied, flustered.

'Why, yes. I told you, sir! Coached from Wheatfen and Maidborough. They say he has no ship, Tyrant Napoleon's wars being long ended. He wants to settle as a coastal family.'

Indeed, Carradine thought. Percy Carmady was an acquaintance. A young, personable and well-connected naval officer would be in no great danger of finding a lack of ladies in Sealandings, that was for sure.

'Where has he alighted?'

'Milton Hall, darling. Staying with Fellows De Foe and his lady wife.'

She darted Carradine a sly glance. His liaison with Thalia De

310

Foe was well-known in the pantries of the Eastern Hundreds. He made no sign, which pleased her immeasurably.

'For how long?' This was all essential news, which Judith Blaker would confirm or correct when he saw her this evening.

'As long as his sister pleases, 'tis said. He dotes on her, meek little thing that she be! Seeking closer kinship with Sir Henry Hunterfield than a maid has a right to say outright, too!'

For a while he was silent, finishing his meal and drinking the distasteful wine. Lucy stroked his chest, riffling the hairs with her hand, thinking what strange folk men were. He felt brimful of questions, schemes, plots, yet there he lay gazing up at the rafters and not a word out of him. A woman, now, she'd be talking nineteen to the dozen, demanding this or that, never time to draw breath. That was normal. It was men that were oddities, as if they lived here with a fraction of their lives, and the rest away in some mysterious land nobody knew except themselves. But she knew them, and was gratified when he looked sharply at her, and smiled slowly.

'You are a good girl, Lucy. I am pleased.'

She took hold of him in the oldest caress. 'No, Rad. A good Lucy's a bad girl, for her darling. Say I'm your Lucy.'

'Get to work.' His voice thickened as her hand moved.

'No. Rad must obey his Lucy, or his Lucy'll get cross.'

'My Lucy, then, you bitch.'

Lucy laughed, head back in delight as he fetched her a buffet and bit into her shoulder. Now she was certain. Her Carradine was back, exactly as if his misfortune had never happened. And with Carradine in the saddle Sealandings would ride a wildly different course than it had these last few tranquil weeks, that was for sure. She worked herself under him, welcoming him as the man's power started to churn.

Bartholomew Hast was in the small foundry at the rear of his dwelling when Mehala called. Old Mrs Gomme hurried to find the gunsmith. Hast hurriedly draped a smock shirt over his shoulder and invited the lady through.

'Apologies, mistress! I am in my small-clothes.'

'Thank you, Mr Hast.' Mehala appeared in the doorway of the foundry, and waited his attention.

311

The young gunmaker stood at a furnace, heating a piece of metal on tongs, spinning the handles expertly. The fire shone on his sweating arms, sparks flying from the coals unheeded as he worked.

'This is the very devil, if you would pardon the word, Mehala!' Hast was a fine figure, strong and slender, sure of his strength and knowing his work. 'Especially as I'm helped with Master No-Help here!' A young boy was by the furnace, out of direct heat, working bellows.

'Jed, isn't it?' Mehala recognised the youngster, the only one of the seafaring family to shun the boats and opt for land.

The boy grinned, reddening with pleasure at being noticed. 'Yes, Mehala. My brother is . . .'

'Hal Baines. As rescued me from the waters. Yes. Doctor treated your burns two months agone.'

'I'm better now, Mehala.'

'Only time he got near to work, he set himself afire. Useless!' Bartholomew Hast was grinning widely to give himself the lie, and young Jed laughed openly. 'Who'd have an apprentice? I've a mind to send him to a London gunmaker, maybe those high-nosed Eggs of Hanover Square. No Blue Mondays for you then, Jed!'

Mehala tried to laugh at Bartholomew's exuberance, but managed no more than a wan smile. Blue Monday, the last before Lent, most workmen spent in idle dissipation. The gunsmith nodded for the youth to keep the bellows going, and laid the tongs aside.

'Go ahead, Mehala, if you will. Earn your keep, Jed. I trust Is'll be but a minute.'

Old Mrs Gomme was pleased to have a lady arrive, and unbidden was preparing tea in the back parlour. Her husband served as Hast's general labourer, and could be seen in an adjacent alcove planing the blocks of walnut wood from which gunstocks were fashioned. The whole place was scented with oils, wood resins, that tang of the smithy she recalled so vividly from childhood. The old man called a greeting. Bartholomew Hast replied with a mock corrective, which set them all grinning. A happy house, hard but friendly. The feeling set Mehala's eyes pricking.

'Close the doors between us all, you two old idlers!' the young gunsmith commanded. 'Miss Mehala's here to look at my arm, and Is'll not have the world and his wife ogling!'

They complied, amused and bantering, while Hast made a great show of rolling up his smock-shirt sleeve. Only when the door closed did his grin fade. He seated himself on the remaining chair by the window. Mehala was by the fireplace, regaining her composure.

'What is it, Mehala? Is Doctor Carmichael. . .?'

'I don't really know how he is. I've lost him, you see.'

She explained how she had searched and left messages, all to no avail.

'I feel he is still here, in Sealandings. I can't quite explain it. I know he would not leave of his own free will, lest he was . . . to . . .'

'Right.' Hast looked from the window as a waggon clumped past, its two Suffolk punches straining as they drew their cart inland across the Square. 'There is not much of the day left, Mehala. What do you wish me to do?'

'There is a cottage down among the fisherfolk.' Hesitatingly she told of her visit, and how Mrs Raffin had seemed almost on the point of making some revelation then maintained a relieved silence.

He sat in deep tonight. Mehala's plight was obviously serious. No abode, no work, no employer to speak for her, hers was all too common a danger for somebody unattached. Then he started to ask questions, slowly at first but gathering momentum. He wanted names, addresses of the homes she had visited, whom she had seen, where Carmichael might have gone. The daylight was bleaching from the windows when finally he had done. He rose, trying to show a confidence he did not feel.

'Very well, Mehala. I shall try the Raffin cottage, then the Donkey and Buskin. I shall try among the homes where Carmichael was *not* known to have sick patients.'

'Not?' Mehala asked, startled.

Bartholomew Hast grinned, fastening his sleeve, finding his leather spencer and looking about for his short cloak.

'You're talking to a gunsmith, Mehala. No highflown theories here. Do you know what we did when Spanish barrels were supposed to best our English ones, owing to the warmer Spanish clime?'

313

'No,' she said blankly.

'Why, we gunsmiths sent some of our number to Spain, to manufacture our barrels there, and test them with gunpower of all kinds. It showed that the Spaniards' barrels were indeed sounder, but it was due to their manufacture from the nails of horses' hooves, and similar well-beaten metals.'

'So, sir?'

'So we gunsmiths are direct men, Mehala. We waste no time in theories. Or beliefs!' He made apology, and drew off his bagging boots for stout leather half-boots. 'Ever since, we too use waste steel, and get gun barrels as excellent as Toledo. We trust results.'

He stood, solid, dependable, and found a new beaver hat. Mehala lowered her head. He turned away.

'I shall say I search for Doctor Carmichael, being in need of his assistance, Mehala. That should allay any suspicions. Meanwhile, send young Jed Baines on any errand you require.'

He left, bawling instructions to Mrs Gomme to stir herself and bring some tea for the lady guest.

Bartholomew Hast moved quickly through the small cottage gardens, calling out a cheerful greeting when he was seen from indoors. This way, he was soon walking along the wharf, planning what excuses to make to Mrs Raffin.

It was tragic to be the emissary for Mehala, when he would rather she was without attachment. He was no man to throw good time after bad. Mehala might look at him – or indeed at other men, too – but it was clear from her eyes, her mien, that she was Carmichael's woman. Was Carmichael her man, though? There was something missing when they were together, as the time at Nelmes' Farm when the Doctor vaccinated him and those children. They did not seem like lovers, nor yet like betrothed. It was a kind of reserve, a beguiling certainty on Mehala's part but a kind of wondrous innocence on Ven Carmichael's. How could a doctor, so long learning about mankind's illnesses and foibles, actually be so incredulous that he looked straight past so lovely a woman as Mehala? Or was there something too injurious in Doctor Carmichael's past, that he was unable to believe the evidence of his own eyes?

There was consternation down on the wharf, he could see. The light was fading apace. Folk were bringing lanterns from the cottages. A small tax cart had been got from somewhere. A heavy bundle was being lifted up from the stone wharf. There were shouts, children running and being banished not to see.

He hurried toward the cart, and shoved his way through. The body of a young woman lay on the cart, her face wax white and her hair streaked across the skin.

'It's the cot-quean, God rest her soul!' somebody said.

'I'faith, 'tis that Bella from Two Cotts!'

'A whore. She died unshriven, too! God save her.'

Bartholomew made to back from the press, hardly hearing the phrases. A lanthorn was passed forward. Being tall, he reached out and hung it on the tax cart board by the driver. As he did so, he caught sight of a face at an upstairs window of one of the cottages. A candle was lit within. Whoever it was, was in the act of cupping his hands about his eyes, to see the scene below. It was Carmichael. Bartholomew left the tax cart and began to walk away as fast as he decently could. There was no question. It was Doctor Carmichael, and the cottage Raffin's. Mehala had been right.

33

He heard the cries, echoing, resonant. The girl was dead, sea-taken, drownded as they said along the shores. Years ago, as a boy, he used to play the game of all country children, leaning down to a straight ditch and calling faint whispers along the surface of the still water, for the words to be heard at a distance clearer than words shouted in open air. They had a ghostly quality, as if some water sprite spoke from the depths.

His head was drenched with sweat, the hairs stiff. His chest ached, sore from the bruising. He had been lying half-dozing, wondering what to do, where to go, when the shouts began. He stared out, had seen them take her from the harbour and knew instantly it was Mehala. The past and present merged. The words re-echoed in his mind. Mehala. There was no doubt. So it had been a dream, these months lived at Shalamar with the girl who had made him smile. He should have known it was all some monstrous joke.

She had never really been. He slept fitfully, woke to know the terrible plight of reality. Oblivion would have been a great solace for this distress. Chalices of grief were not to be tipped away, or begged off. That was for God. Mortals simply had to endure agonies, come what may. Deaths of loved ones, sorrows of loves unrealised, longings unblessed, and Time the great thief, at the behest of a cruel and cunning Almighty.

He lay for what seemed hours, staring at the plaster ceiling of the small room. It receded, pressed down on his eyes, flew away into darkness, then pressed back and down so he cried out with the pain. But there was a worse agony. Mehala had kept him sane and whole all the while she had walked the sealands. Now she was gone. He had known it would be this way, that she would be taken from him with both their lives unfulfilled. If she was but a dream, he was cruelly wakened. If she was not, she was now drowned.

As he tried to rise he felt the room swirl. Outside, lanterns were moving and he leant over to see the tax cart once more as Mehala was carried away. A great lanthorn hung by the driver. It was Hal Baines, the very same youth who had come at a gallop for him to Shalamar, calling him to come and save Mehala when *The Jaunty* had brought her ashore. Hal Baines, with old Lack and Master Jervin, ship's master, walking sorrowfully behind as the cart rattled off along the cobbles. The North Sea never let go. Once a soul belonged, the sea would always reclaim.

As he dozed in his delirium an illogical question surfaced. Why had she not come to the tavern of John Weaver? She had never defaulted before. So why now, this one last time? Or was she deliberately kept from coming to meet him? Or, most terrible of all, did she realise his growing attachment to her, and resent it? His sick mind swam in its fever. Words formed senseless patterns to tease and torment. Once, he woke shouting out her name, only to find Mrs Raffin cowering at the bedroom door pleading him to silence, and he fell back into his babbling.

Few things he could remember. Once, dreaming no doubt, he imagined Mehala actually being there. She had leant over him, her long tresses unbridled, touching his face while she murmured that all would now be well, that he was safe and must not worry. She promised to make his life sound and wholesome, a life anew. He believed her – or the figment, or ghost. Did she mean her coming death in the sea, that he would be able to choose a new life unencumbered by her? Absurd, for he had found a completeness in her so thrilling, that he could not comprehend its extraordinary power.

No. Life without Mehala was incomplete, and ever would be. Even to stay in Sealandings without her compelling grace was unendurable. He wiped a sleeve across his eyes. The room was still moving uncontrollably, the window dancing in lessening light. He dragged himself erect, trying to think straight.

One point bothered, that they had taken so long getting Mehala on the tax cart. So many men, surely they could have lifted in concert? Indecent to take so long. They must have taken, what, three hours, for he had slept at least that long. It was a clear message from Heaven. He was to leave Sealandings immediately. His love was to be unrequited. First Harriet, whom he had loved, or thought he had, and to whom he had been stupid enough to propose marriage, only to be scorned as beneath her station. Then

317

Mehala, far above any woman, amazing all by her presence and beauty. Of course. He should have seen it at once, as clearly as he saw it now. Mehala had been sent to show him the unattainable. He had simply been too stupid to understand.

The clothes he wore were his own, thank God. He could not be accused of stealing, a common vagrant's cause of arrest. He moved with difficulty, falling over but finally righting himself to stand weakly against the wall. His mind slowly cleared. He sat, and with great effort slowly managed to drag his boots on. Lucky they were old and well-worn, slipping easily over his feet. The latchings he left undone, too complicated. His surtout was laid across the bed for additional warmth. An earthenware cup stood on the floor. With an effort he picked it up and drained it. A thin gruel only, but any strength rather than none.

Experimentally he walked a pace, rested to let the room settle, then stepped to the door. The house was in silence. It would not do to rouse the Raffins, who were probably dozing or tending to children. Or perhaps Mrs Raffin was with the fisherwomen out on the wharf talking about the drowning tragedy, Mehala's death.

Her name stabbed through him so painfully that he almost cried out. He waited, put his hand on the wall by the stairs and slowly started down. He would leave by the back door, and start inland. It was beyond dusk, and he would not be seen. He could not bear hearing the terrible news, that Mehala had drowned after all. He saw Raffin sprawled before the fire. A little girlchild was dozing, leaning on her daddy. Both snored gently, a lacuna of peace and rest. His eyes blurred for a moment, then he went to the back door and let himself out into the dusk.

34

The assembly at Milton Hall proved diverting for the Misses Hunterfield, knowing their brother Henry's aversion to music. Lydia Vallance was obliged to correct her sisters, going so far as to rebuke them both in the presence of Lieutenant Carmady and his sister Mercy, not to mention their host and hostess. The company was much amused.

Fellows De Foe admitted to doubts about Hunterfield. 'Is the Lord of Sealandings joking when he confesses to hating music so?'

The professional musicians had received their Boniface's cup, and were departing below stairs. The company was disposed round the withdrawing room, liqueurs, coffee and ratafias being served. Everybody smiled at Hunterfield's expense. He was unabashed.

'My dislike, Fellows, I suppress for the sake of our new inhabitants!'

'Suppressed, Henry?' Lydia put in. 'You fretted through the entire performance! I should not care to see your hatred fully revealed, sir!'

Percy Carmady laughed, knowing Hunterfield's pretended tone deafness.

'It always is!' he joked. 'I well remember the night of your great ball, not long since, when – '

'If I may interrupt, Percy,' Mercy interrupted smoothly, having seen the flicker of worry cross Thalia De Foe's countenance. 'I am intrigued to know why our esteemed host harbours such doubts about a lifelong friend.'

Fellows leaned forward confidentially. 'Not too long ago I saw a certain gentleman leaning against the fence of the livestock market listening with enjoyment to the wandering pipers! I swear it! Playing country airs, they were, on the smallpipes!'

'Then he is a secret romantic!' Mercy said in delight.

Hunterfield frowned in mock sternness. 'I am nothing of the kind, Miss Carmady. I encourage the lower classes by expressing interest.'

'I suspect you of duplicity, Henry,' De Foe said mildly. 'Don't you, Thalia?'

Thalia De Foe smiled brilliantly to cover her apprehension. Her husband affected this light bantering tone, but sometimes his words struck too close for comfort. How much did he know? The theme of duplicity had recurred too frequently lately, though she was certain Fellows still knew nothing of her past affair with Hunterfield. Past, since Henry discovered she was merely manipulating him in order to advance Carradine's ambitions. Hell hath no fury . . . A man scorned was somehow worse, for a woman may change her mind. Men were the stubbornest creatures alive, and had a horrid knack of simply closing some mental door to shut a woman out. During the performance of the string instruments and songstresses she had tried, quite accidentally of course, to catch Hunterfield's eye. A locked glance could rekindle former intimacy. But his returning gaze had been simply bland and well, dead. She was furious, at being almost invisible to him. She was beyond a door which he had slammed shut. How unfair! What were gentlemen's minds like inside, for Heaven's sake?

What made matters worse was that, when the same cunning trick of glances had been exercised by that hideous bitch Mercy Carmady, ugly as a crow and all a-flutter, obviously trying to ape a real living woman's animation with her clever I-know-London talk, Henry Hunterfield had responded with an engaging smile. It infuriated beyond endurance. But, no. Fellows could not know of the affair so finally ended. She would allay his suspicions, if they existed, long before he rode off to his gaming and banking boredom in the City of London. Thank God he was always content to receive the gift of her wifely duty. This she never refused, bearing its excruciating boredom for Carradine's sake. Her lover needed her support now as never before. She had lost Hunterfield's immense local power through carelessness, but would not lose that of her husband in Carradine's cause. She might lose Carradine himself, if she did. The thought made her ache.

Her immediate aim was to subdue this hag Mercy Carmady, the last creature she wanted queening it in Lorne House. As if the woman's presence were insufficient offence, the bitch had the effrontery to wear a peridot green dress with demi-gigot sleeves, full at the shoulder and tight from elbow to wrist – not as fashionable or as fetching as her own amadis sleeves, but quite acceptable. The effrontery! This drab Carmady whore, trying to compete! Thalia knew she looked her best, in a shaped Caroline corsage with its slender tumble of lace and light tartarian-cachmere material blessing her figure with its vee *en pelerine*. The ugly cow's brother Percy was a different matter. He was present-able, lively, eligible, having a spark in his depths. And interesting. Why had the Carmadys come to seek abode in Sealandings? Percy looked at her with pure desire. The explanation was plain, and truly interesting. She deserved a diversion.

'Why, I doubt him always, dearest!' Thalia responded brightly, darting a mischievous look at Hunterfield. But the Squire was tasting some green liquid reflectively and nodding approval to Letitia and Tabitha. 'Could any gentleman be trusted by *any* lady?'

Lydia Vallance smiled and cried a 'Bravo!'. Mercy Carmady laughed, rounded on her brother.

'Indeed, Thalia! I doubt the urgency with which Percy ordered our movements!'

Two birds with one stone, Thalia De Foe thought with satisfaction, and took advantage by raising her eyebrows as if scandalized.

'Lieutenant Carmady! I hope you are not treating your lovely sister shamefully!'

Carmady pretended a hang-dog air. 'Indeed I am, Mistress Thalia. I surrendered to her wishes years ago. Since leaving the naval service, I have been driven pillar to post. No place suits my sister and her friend. I live in hopes of reaching some new home – as the Tweed reaches Melrose!'

The old saying about the tortuous river amused the company. Hunterfield urged Carmady to try the green liqueur.

'This might convince you to settle here, Percy. It is a liquor made by Letitia and Tabitha. Green noyau, some old country receipt.'

The two young sisters smiled as Carmady tasted a glass and expressed approval.

'Why, Mercy! It is every bit as splendid as the noyau made at Ventris, where we . . . '

The ladies erupted into laughter, Tabitha clapping her hands animatedly and Letitia hiding a blush. Mercy joined in with Lydia. Thalia, not seeing the source of amusement, was further angered by Fellows' knowing smile. Letitia was swift to explain.

'Tabitha and I made the potable, Mistress Thalia, but to a receipt provided by a clever correspondent – Mercy Carmady!'

'I think it far superior to yours, Mercy,' Carmady insisted, causing a chorus of denials.

Hunterfield's pleasure showed, and he inclined his head in approval of his young sisters' skill. Tabitha was already telling Percy Carmady how she and her sister gathered beechmast, taking proper care to see the spiritous liquor used was highest quality Geneva . . . His smiling gaze met Letitia's. For a moment he was disconcerted. In her eyes he saw revealed something so warm, such deep generosity and even love for him that he was moved, knowing suddenly that she was the instigatrix of this little success. His fondness for things of the countryside, the coast and its dialect language, the skills of trade and farm, and the long learning he pursued in this direction, was the subject of much uncomprehending animosity from the local gentry. But she was always ready to listen. She would even discuss these mundanities. He was suddenly aware of how little he had availed himself of the friendship she personified.

'Then have we not a joint enterprise?' Thalia cut through brightly, hating the way the evening was going. 'To discover for Lieutenant Carmady an appropriate residence?'

'Thalia, take no trouble on my account!' Carmady was smiling, though. The gathering immediately began making suggestions.

'It is no trouble, Lieutenant!'

'Not my former naval rank, if I may ask. I am left the navy service, and landed for ever.'

For Thalia there were more important questions. 'Might I enquire as to the identity of the other lady whose opinions must be considered?'

'Ah, that is a most engaging lady! Mrs Treggan, wife to Rodney Treggan, an estimable London family. She expresses a keen interest in the Eastern Hundreds.'

His sister was amused. 'I am afraid my brother is circuitous about a certain lady. Must we ladies pretend we do not see through you, Percy? You always invoke my assistance in bringing Harriet Ferlane into discussion, the better to hide her influence over you!'

'How outrageous sisters are!' Percy groaned. 'How do you manage, Hunterfield?'

'Why, Henry manages by obeying his lovely sisters implicitly!' Thalia gushed, her mind active at possibilities. 'Our duty is clear, ladies. We must find a place for the Carmadys, hoping it will please Harriet Treggan also!'

Fellows accepted Madeira from Crane. 'I fear there may be cause for delay.'

'I have heard, Fellows. You refer to the murrain at Calling Farm?'

The talk dwindled. Everyone looked to Hunterfield, who drew breath soberly.

'It is becoming hourly more serious, I regret to say. Prothero admits to no sickness, and has occupied Carradine Manor.' His look scanned Thalia with indifference, but Carmady with warning. 'The town is already suffering. To the people, any malady becomes a plague, then *the* plague, the Black Death.'

'Those ignorant peasants!' Thalia De Foe burst out. 'You should command them to banish their fear, and act as normal.'

'I should, Thalia?' Hunterfield asked mildly. 'Why so?'

'Because you are the authority in Sealandings. You are its Squire – our chief magistrate! Set over the peasants by the Almighty, to rule these dumb brute beasts!'

'Madam,' Fellows said gravely into the silence, 'I will thank you to leave the subject.'

Hunterfield gave a drawn smile of appreciation to his host, but quietly started to speak. As he did, Letitia was struck by how tired her brother was. His features were taut, his expression seemingly affable but only concealing deep anxieties beneath. The breaches in the sea dykes, financing the maintenance of the sea walls, the atrocious conditions of the roads, the levying of the forthcoming Poors' Rate, all took their toll. Not to mention the present company's shifting tensions and anxieties. Everything seemed unfairly centred on her brother.

'No, Fellows. It needs to be said openly. Everybody else in the Eastern Hundreds is saying the same – that I should somehow seize all suzerainty, and torrefy Sealandings.'

323

'And why not, sir?'

Thalia's voice was querulous and shrill. Her husband shot her a rebuking glance. She stared challengingly at her former lover. She had schemed like a Fury to effect Carradine's return to the coast, yet all was obstacle. The longer Carradine stayed at Hoddinotts the more likely he was to fall into the clutches of Brillianta Astell, or that mare of a sister Lorela. And here was this dullard – a bore horizontal as vertical, as she alone could testify – actually still thwarting her. Was there no justice? These men kept a woman in chains.

'Who speaks of the general good is but a rogue and a scoundrel,' Hunterfield said quietly. 'All good starts with the particular.'

Letitia's head rose in surprise. Henry's remark was almost exactly one of her favourite passages from Mr Blake, a poet lately deceased. She had not realised he listened, when she read to entertain of an evening. How little we all know of each other, she thought wonderingly. Each believing we are friends, siblings, spouses even, and all mysteriously alone.

'You see, Thalia,' Henry went on gravely, 'we do not understand what causes cattle sickness. Nor do farmers. The government the same. It is easy to cry that the murrain ought to be stopped, before people start a-dying like the herds of Calling Farm, but how? We don't know. I too profess ignorance.'

'You have the power to keep the market open!'

'To command drovers from the North to drive their cattle into Sealandings? When they have, to a man, turned inland? Not a goosegirl or shepherd will come within two leagues of the Sealandings toll. Every pedlar is on the Cambridge turnpike by now.'

'So serious, Henry?' Fellows asked soberly.

'Worse! All Eastern Hundreds will suffer.' Hunterfield looked sadly round the silent company. 'To command folk to disbelieve rumour would be absurd.' He smiled at Carmady and Mercy in an attempt to lighten the moment. 'In the circumstances it is brave of our visitors to come!'

'Your cattle problems mean little to me, Henry.' Carmady tried to respond in like vein, but was made uncomfortable by Thalia's obvious agitation. 'Having been a-sea so long, I'm nonplussed by your landward difficulties.'

'Ticklish times pass, Percy,' Fellows said, relieved the awkwardness was over. 'And all shall be as usual!'

Crane managed to capture his master's attention as the talk widened. The ladies were particularly upset at the slowness of the letter posts, which were now almost impossible to rely on. Every excuse was made to delay riding letter-bags into the district. Fellows was pleased to announce the arrival of an unexpected guest, a relief and a diversion.

'Your cousin honours us, my dear!' He rose to welcome Charles Golding as the company made proper exclamations of delight when Crane announced the newcomer.

Charles Golding strode forward exuding a new confidence. He was pleased to see so many gentry there, including the Hunter-fields and the Carmadys. He deserved an audience, after so long being dismissed as somebody beneath notice. The introductions were carried out with stately observance of ritual, for Mercy Carmady had never previously met him. All eyes were on their first encounter.

The master of Bures House was eminently presentable, and to Thalia's vigilant eye preening himself. He had entered the room showing a hint of aggressiveness. His manner alerted the two men who knew him.

'Thank you, Crane.' Golding accepted the proffered drink and sat on a harewood drawing-roomer, gazing indolently round. 'I came not intending to interrupt your evening, Thalia, but to see Squire Hunterfield on an urgent matter.'

Hunterfield raised a hand to Fellows in mute request to be allowed to hear the visitor out.

'If you please, Fellows,' Golding announced bluntly, 'I am made Justice of the Peace for Sealandings, and assume post immediately. It is my duty to inform the senior-most authority.'

'Thank you,' Hunterfield responded. He showed his knowledge of the appointment by his lack of surprise. 'Have you any immediate intentions?'

'I have. I shall take in hand this business at Calling Farm. It has been allowed to let slide far too long.' He grinned at Hunterfield. 'I give you one of your country yokel sayings, Hunterfield: ale brewed too long needs go round again!'

He was the only one present who laughed, though some smiled.

Thalia De Foe was exultant, trying to conceal her relish of the moment. This would clip Henry Hunterfield's feathers indeed! Charles, a new Justice of the King's Peace! It was what she had schemed for. She remembered Carradine. He could soon be back in Sealandings! No power on earth could now prevent his return! She smiled at Hunterfield, at his detestable sister Lydia Vallance. The Carmadys and the two ignorant Hunterfield mice could be safely ignored, but it was difficult not to show malice. They would feel her claws soon enough.

'May I offer my congratulations, Charles?'

'Thank you, Fellows.' Golding sighed, eyeing Mercy and smiling at Thalia. 'I only wish my first burden was not so heavy. I have heard from our cousin Sir Philip Banks that a Justice's duty lies mostly in clearing up the messes left by others.'

Percy Carmady stiffened and glanced quickly at Hunterfield, who showed no sign that he had heard the implied rebuke.

'I admire your selflessness, sir,' Carmady told Golding, 'to exert yourself for society's good. You have able exemplars in the present company, I think.'

It was a decent attempt at peacemaking, for which Letitia gave Carmady a warm smile.

'Somebody has to take up the cudgels, sir.' Golding held out his glass insolently. Crane moved to refill it. 'I do think we have allowed our coasts to settle into a laziness that does the country little good.'

Hunterfield said casually, 'We were just debating the selfsame problem!'

'What will you do that has not already been done, sir?' Tabitha Hunterfield was aware of her reticence until now. She had been closely observing Percy Carmady, and now was torn between that gentleman and the newcomer. She had never thought of Charles Golding as anything other than one sunk into drink and looseness. Yet here he was, looking handsome, young, dominant.

'I shall appoint two special constables immediately, from among my own tenants, to apprehend that felon Carmichael. He has been allowed to foment this sickness at Calling Farm. In fact,' Golding coursed on over the ladies' shocked gasps, 'I fear that ruffian has no means to make restitution, once apprehended. He shall soon kiss the blacksmith's daughter, or I shall know the reason!'

'Oh, no!' Letitia's exclamation made the others stare. The blacksmith's daughter was the nickname for the key of the expunging house, the first-step prison. The thought of incarceration horrified her. 'Please. I am sure he is a goodly gentleman. If he attended at Calling Farm, was it not to treat Mr Prothero?'

'So rumour has it, Miss Letitia.' Golding was already on his fourth glass, and pointedly told Crane to supply brandy instead of the milder wine. He was delighted at the look in Thalia's eye. She was enjoying Henry Hunterfield's discomfiture enormously. He had achieved the most signal advance of any in their family for two generations. Her political ambitions for him were now within sight – election to Parliament, a seat in government, all the fortune that privilege would bring. What if her paramour, that sexually depraved gambler-cum-dolt Carradine, edged back into Carradine Manor in the process? Some of the gentry were born to make the Gregorian Tree, swing by the neck on the gallows sooner or later. He swelled even more at the thought: he had the power to initiate *that* process, too! Life was beautiful. 'Ladies should understand that a criminal may use his trade as a cloak to disguise his evil machinations.'

'What possible motive could Doctor Carmichael have for starting a disease?'

Golding said airily, 'We legal authorities do not have to prove *motive*, Miss Letitia. Evidence against the felon is already accumulating. I have made it my business to discover a few facts: Carmichael is a vagrant. He is penniless. He wanders abroad – doing who knows what harm! He was involved in an affray – possibly even disloyalty against the Crown! It seems fortunate that a few loyal subjects managed to restrain him, though he made good his escape.'

'How terrible!' Thalia's eyes were shining.

'It is, my dear cousin!' Golding paused. 'I am making enquiries about his debts. Has he, for example, lately vacated his place of residence, leaving it in sorry disrepair, thereby casting expenses on to the owner? Such tricks condemn a man more than open theft.'

'What will happen to him?'

'Prison, of course, unless he pays off his debts. Under the Insolvent Debtors Act he is allowed to keep his clothes, etcetera, to twenty pounds. But that refers only to *honest* debts, not the fraud of scoundrels.'

'What terrible times!' Letitia was in obvious distress.

Tabitha tutted at her sister. 'Oh, Letitia, such sentiment! It is justice! The law!'

'The offender will be punished, Miss Tabitha, I promise you. It is quite possible,' Golding added, speaking directly to Thalia as he brought out his trump card, 'that Carmichael was in league with another, perhaps even Prothero himself! The fortunes made from spreading rumours of murrains, sickness, diseases on farms, are incalculable!'

'On his own estates?'

'His *smaller* estate, Thalia! Which borders your own extensive property! Notice that Carradine Manor lies astraddle the northern limits of Sealandings, is on the coastal aspect *and* possesses ships of its own . . . I may malign that esteemed gentleman, but it does cross the mind that Carradine Manor, now owned by Prothero, will profit immeasurably by the rumoured sickness. *And Prothero will profit alone!* No other estate – those owned from ancient times by gentlemen of lineage – will profit. Many may not even survive intact. But Carradine Manor will. And, note, the very day that the rumours first appeared Prothero moved into Carradine!'

'Is this evidence, Charles?' Henry asked casually. He alone seemed unaffected by Golding's vehemence, even bored.

'It is, if a Justice of the Peace says it is, Hunterfield!'

'Are you sure you ought to send after Carmichael?'

Golding's voice was rough, accusatory. 'Are you questioning my decision?'

'Wouldn't dream of it, Charles,' Hunterfield said with indifference.

'Henry . . .' Letitia's hand was at her necklace, her features quite pale. 'Doctor Carmichael seems quite benign. All speak well of him. Can nothing be done to aid him?'

To her horror Henry seemed affably unconcerned. He declined another glass of wine, nodding amiably for Crane to serve Golding instead. He addressed his sister kindly enough, but avoided her eyes.

'A man in his position has aid enough, Letitia. Don't you think so, Percy? And duties enough, I should say.'

'Responsibilities must take their proper course,' Tabitha put in.

She could not take her eyes off Golding, so ebullient, so commanding. The transformation almost dazzled. His air of, almost, insolence was thrilling. Letitia on the other hand felt something awry in Henry's manner. And his words were not quite – well, disloyal to even think it – but not quite sensible. It was so out of character. Henry never acted irresponsibly, or so casually. He never spoke out of character, however much her elder sister Lydia mistrusted Henry's past infatuation with Thalia De Foe.

'You have no reason I should postpone the arrest, Hunterfield?' Golding asked, gulping the brandy and crooking a finger at Crane to be busy.

'Me, Charles?'

'Yes.' Golding relished the moment. All the gentry of Sealandings knew of Hunterfield's special concern with a girlchild who was passed off as the daughter of one of Hunterfield's waggoners in neighbouring Whitehanger. And how, it was whispered, that child was raised at Hunterfield's clandestine expense. It had been Doctor Carmichael who had seen that moppet through a terrible sickness. 'I mean, any personal debt of gratitude I should take into consideration before doing my sworn duty?'

Hunterfield smiled. Thalia rejoiced to see Lydia Vallance straighten agitatedly.

'Good heavens, Charles! Me? Seek protection from the law for a wanted felon? That would make a fine story, eh?' He tilted his glass for Crane to add more wine, though Letitia noticed her brother had hardly drunk at all. 'Fellows, would it be inopportune to suggest a toast, for Charles' success?'

'Splendid idea, Henry! Could I ask you to do the honours?'

'Charmed.' Hunterfield rose, and raised his glass. 'This is rather serious, ladies and gentlemen. You are all my friends, relatives. I propose the health and good fortune of Sir Charles Golding, now a Justice of the King's Peace.'

Golding sat, grinning. Thalia bridled, not wanting him to drink any more. He must learn how essential it was to create a good impression, especially on the two important visitors soon to come and live nearabouts. She would have a long talk with him on the morrow. However, it was a useful scheme to imprison

Carmichael. She could help immediately, as Charles had hinted, by commanding Lazard to list all Shalamar's defects, and lay blame on Carmichael. The thought thrilled her. To see him and his deep-water bitch Mehala suffer was almost an ecstasy in itself. And it brought a practical bonus too, for it struck at Hunterfield, showed the Squire the measure of Golding's new power, and opened up possibilities for Carradine. With Prothero arraigned, it would be impossible for that rich peasant to remain in Sea-landings. And he would suffer financially, which might let Carradine resume . . . She felt almost weak at the prospect of having him back. She craved to find him, tell him how superbly she had managed his ambitions, and reclaim him body and soul.

'To Charles!' she cried, and led the applause.

35

'He's gone, Mistress!'

Mrs Raffin was not dissembling. She was truly shocked, Mehala saw. There was more reason than charity for Ven's lodgement here. She suppressed a cry of distress in her throat and turned helplessly to Bartholomew Hast.

'Mr Hast. You are sure it was he?'

'I am, Mehala. He was clear in view at the window when the body of the dead girl was brought from the harbour.'

Mrs Raffin was upset, weeping. 'Please, Mistress, I only left for a moment, to walk with the cart a little way for decency's sake. He must have gone in that instant.'

'It cannot be long since, Mehala.' Hast was glancing about the darkening wharf and cottages, weighing the chances of catching Carmichael.

'How was he, Mrs Raffin?'

'Sore hurt, but mending with rest. He had gruel and tea an hour since.'

Mehala's mind flew at the possibilities. It was now dark. Had he seen in the dead girl a reminder of herself, as she had first come to him? Was his own mind deranged from injuries? Or had he simply given up hope of her ever coming to find him, and like some lost child gone to find a haven less cruel than the world of Sealandings?

'Can we search, Mr Hast?' she asked quietly.

The gunsmith pursed his lips, looked at the stones. 'Darkness is unsafe. Even drovers and waggoners go in company. Precious few folk travel near Sealandings, since the murrain began.'

'He has relatives at St Albans.'

'Good evening, Mehala. Mr Hast.'

Euterpe Baring was standing beside the cottage steps, her approach unnoticed.

'Miss Baring.' Mehala saw and immediately understood. She glanced from the vicar's sister to Mrs Raffin, and realised the source of the latter's agitation. It wasn't charity after all: the cottager was being paid to harbour Ven Carmichael, and by Miss Baring. She felt an unreasoning anger towards the lady from St Edmund's rectory, and an increased rage at her own self for not having stayed with him on the Norwich road. Suffering his beating for him would have been easier to bear than this.

'What has happened, Mrs Raffin?' Euterpe Baring demanded.

The fisherman's wife was stricken, wringing her hands as she explained Carmichael's absence. Euterpe was silent for a moment.

'You are not altogether to blame, Mrs Raffin. Mehala, might we converse a moment? No, Mrs Raffin. The wharf will suit our purpose.'

Bartholomew Hast withdrew to a respectful distance and stood looking at the harbour lights through the evening mists. Mrs Raffin stood by the open door as the two ladies moved aside and faced each other.

'You came across Doctor Carmichael suffering from his injuries, and moved him here, against payment to Mrs Raffin?'

'Yes, Mehala. Charity could do no less.'

Mehala was still wary, not trusting the other's polished reply. Formality hid oceans of feeling. She spoke as frankly as propriety allowed.

'My obligation is to find him, Miss Baring. For his sake.'

'Of course. I attended to his injuries, and saw him to a rest here, but he was suffering. Does Mr Hast think he can have got far?'

Mehala felt a spurt of anger at the other's assumption that she also had a right to see to Ven, but quelled her feeling. 'Half an hour, we suppose. Not much more.'

Euterpe Baring glanced across the wharf to the young gun-smith. She considered the man's presence, obviously in support of Mehala, and wondered why so busy a tradesman would put himself out so. Mehala decided to scotch Miss Baring's thoughts.

'I was making examination of Mr Hast's vaccination wound, and enlisted his assistance. We were uncertain of Ven's direction.'

'May he have gone blindly to Shalamar?' Euterpe suggested.

Mehala had thought of this, but as quickly dismissed the idea. Ven *felt* gone from Sealandings. Each passing minute increased her certainty. Which way was St Albans? And night was drawing in fast, the boats already showing riding lights, the North Mole an indistinct black blur.

'I believe he has gone, Miss Baring.' She hesitated, hating the very thought of asking for help from this woman, now surely her secret opponent, whatever her protestations of charity. But she had to find Ven at any cost, after which she would face the problem of Euterpe Baring. 'St Albans is the only possibility. It was there we were bound, but the floods delayed that enterprise.'

'I heard so.' Euterpe Baring was under no misapprehension. Mehala had the status of incumbency, as it were, having lived at Shalamar with Ven Carmichael, kept house, and helped in a million small ways that bound people more than any vow. And Mehala was bristling at the thought of another woman usurping her position, succouring him. But differences had to be put aside until he was found. 'I suggest we jointly consider what help we might obtain.'

A truce, then. Mehala agreed, with reservations. 'Very well, Miss Baring. There are two possibilities. One is Squire Hunterfield, who is most condign. He gave me a groom to aid my search, and a carriage. If I asked, he might renew that offer. I do know he will be agreeable to Doctor Carmichael's staying in Sealandings.'

'And the second?'

Mehala hesitated. 'There is a carter, one Jake Darling, at Whitehanger. His child Clare was saved from a mortal illness by Doctor Carmichael. And their cousins are the Overtons, charcoal-burners. They have speedier communication than any postal delivery. Ven might have gone to Whitehanger along the coast path.'

Euterpe signified approval. She adjusted her brides while she thought. The affair of the Darling children she remembered well. Little Harry Darling had died of the malady from which his sister had been saved. Rumours had abounded in Sealandings about Sir Henry Hunterfield's joy at Clare's recovery, to silent speculation. Mehala was clever, to couple the two most valuable means of establishing a search.

'For my part, Mehala, I shall send a letter to Mistress Prothero, seeking her cooperation.'

Mehala was startled. 'Miss Baring! The Protheros – '

'Permit me. I know of Mr Prothero. Carradine Manor's housekeeper is Mrs Tyll, whose husband is the tollgate keeper, is he not? Mrs Tyll once was employed at Calling Farm. Toll-farmers

333

have the readiest means of communication of any, each to the other, and so to us. We could enlist Mrs Tyll's husband's help through Mary Prothero.'

'Without her husband's knowledge?' Mehala completed.

Euterpe reddened at such frankness, thankful for the gathering dark. Surreptitious use of a wife's willingness against her spouse's wishes was wrongful interference in holy matrimony. Josiah Baring would be outraged. But surely the Almighty would condone this, in the desperate circumstances?

Euterpe said firmly, 'It is for Mrs Prothero to make her decision.'

'Thank you for your kindness in all this, Miss Baring.'

Euterpe drew herself up. She was not helping Mehala, but Carmichael.

'There is no need to express gratitude, Mehala,' she said with more asperity than she intended. 'It must be, for Doctor Carmichael's sake.'

'As you say, Miss Baring. We are agreed. I shall enlist Mr Hast's help to reach the Darlings' cottage at Whitehanger, if he will, after making my request of Squire Hunterfield.'

'And I shall ask for news through my servants and acquaintances. Don't worry, Mehala. I shall be circumspect. Injuring Doctor Carmichael's reputation is the last thing I want.'

It was as blunt a statement as any woman could make. Mehala acknowledged that it ended the conversation by calling for the gunmaker to rejoin them. Together they bade Mrs Raffin a goodnight, and made their way along the harbour terrace.

36

The night was heavy with drizzle. Ven found his surtout's weight wearing him down. His impervious beaver hat – he hated rain on his head – was his mainstay as darkness pressed on Sealandings and he plashed out on the Norwich road, between the small-holdings of tenant-farmers. It was opposite the livestock field where he had been battered. Now, hardly anything stirred. A dog barked, hens fluttered. A man shouted to his sons about setting traps for the night against predators. The night was not quite pitch. A few glims from cottages gave him direction.

Plodding northwards, he stumbled into the deep ruts, and twice fell as coaches floundered past outside the gates of Two Cotts. After that it was the tall gateway of Bettany's Mill, fortunately lit by an oil lanthorn. Then the common stables of Parker, Methodist leader. To the left, the looming ornamental gates of Carradine Manor and its round gatehouse with twin lamps at the windows. Beyond that, the Norwich road tollgate of Mr Tyll, and beyond that the empty unseen road winding north-west toward its forking to Norwich and St Edmundsbury.

'Who goes?' a voice shouted up ahead.

'No beast nor cart,' Ven called mechanically, the usual response of the pedestrian.

Oddly, his eyes could not focus on the lanthorn raised by the toll-farmer. It wavered, wore a great shimmering halo of golden light yet shed little illumination. It was most odd, the sort of symptom he had often sought when folk suffered *concussio cerebri* from sudden head injury. Surely it must simply be some trick of the flame? For his mind had never been so clear.

'Approach slow,' the man called warily.

Chance to sprint would be a fine thing, Ven thought with a mad urge to chuckle. He restrained his strange quirk of humour and advanced, keeping his feet. Walking was making him weirdly dizzy.

'It is I, Tyll,' he called. Toll-farmers were always on the watch for people, even gentry, who drove carriages at the gate and smashed their way through to avoid payment to the pike-keeper.

'Doctor Carmichael, is it? Come, booy. I heard you be stounded mortal bad.'

Again Ven felt that extraordinary impulse to chuckle, even though he had lost Mehala for ever and his world had ended. 'I'm fine, thank you, Tyll.'

The man had hold of him, easily keeping him upright with one hand. A taciturn, stocky man, not given much to converse, who stoically bore the injuries from fights with waggoners and drovers trying to defraud the parish, and the toll-keeper, of the lawful fee.

'Whither boun', Doctor?'

'Out of Sealandings, Tyll, for the whilst.'

'Come.' Tyll pulled him into the porch, a crude homemade shelter from where the toll-keeper could keep an eye open for approaching herds and vehicles. 'Wait here, Doctor. Is'll give thee a mouthful.'

'Thank you, Tyll.' It would be improper to refuse. 'Don't neglect your duties.'

'Precious few duties lately, what with the Calling Farm sickness.'

Tyll offered a drink of warm small beer. Ven took it and drank, though much spilled down his surtout. His blurring vision cleared momentarily. He had to chuckle at the sign hanging in the lamplight.

'*For Every Ass Not Drawing, 1d*. So a walker is worth less than a penny donkey, eh?' It seemed so funny he laughed outright.

'You'd be astonished. Even fine gentry hate to pay, Doctor.'

'They ought to support the turnpikes. Fifteen thousand parishes, a thousand Trusts, to maintain our abominable roads! One day some change, let's pray.'

'Indeed, Doctor,' Tyll said quietly, uncomfortable at Ven's words. 'Are you hale, booy? Stay and rest.'

'No, thank you, Tyll. I want to escape Sealandings. To stay will do for me.'

The toll-farmer watched Ven rise and make his stumbling way into the darkness on the far side of the barrier, calling farewell. He returned to his perch under the shelter, watching the road.

It was five hours later that the first of the special constables came through asking if he had seen Doctor Carmichael pass by on the inland road.

'You look a picture, sister,' Hunterfield announced, the pleasure in his voice so revealing that Lydia coloured. She tutted in pretended annoyance.

'Such foolishness, sir!'

'A pole screen?' Henry came to examine the work in progress.

'Beads, to concentrate the dusk's glim when you read. I hope you will enjoy the floral design.'

'A variety of hedge roses! Very pretty, Lydia. You have the touch of the Hunterfield ladies to excess!'

They were in the orangery, recently built at inordinate expense, but already proving valuable as an additional evening space which could be warmed by a coals stove. The section which opened from the yellow withdrawing room was furnished to please any member of the family wanting a few moments of peace. Beyond, the young orange trees flourished in their heated partitions.

Hunterfield stood for a moment looking out. Light from the exterior lanthorns fell into dark nothingness a few feet from the huge windows.

'We all three have those excellences, in different measure, Henry.'

Lydia laid down her beadwork. She was using a flash, a glass globe filled with slightly blued water to concentrate the light from a standing oil-lamp, but as the evening wore on she had to rest more frequently. She glanced at the darkness beyond the panes.

'I find it satisfying, Henry, that gamekeepers take turns at vigilancing the grounds.' She sighed. 'Our lovely country is the most blessed of any, yet seems always threatened by disorders, vagabondage.'

Hunterfield murmured agreement. He knew his sister's acute awareness of his moods, that she would have sensed his visit had a purpose.

He walked slowly along the long expanse of windows, pausing here and there to inspect some small detail of fixture. 'Were I less fond of Sealandings, Lydia, life would be easier. I should do what the Carradines have always done, Golding, the De Foes, and let the world go its way.' He suddenly turned and smiled at her, his trick to catch her expression ever since a boy. 'Think how simple life would be! No responsibility, save that which the estate stewards and bailiffs could cope with! All day reading, riding, going a-field for parties!'

'You love Sealandings, and its burdens.' Lydia had to speak to his back, for he had resumed his strolling. 'Your emotions are your captors. I only wish, Henry, that you were more stern. Your punishments of miscreants are notoriously milder than those of, say, Sir Philip Banks inland, or Sir Edward Astell at Maidborough.'

'Who loves, gives hostage to fortune,' her brother paraphrased casually. 'Legal decisions are easy, Lydia – though they do betray my lack of direction within the family's problems.'

'Family, Henry?' Lydia laid aside her work. Two beads rolled unheeded on to the carpet. Here was his reason.

He returned slowly. 'I was approached by Charles Golding, sister. No, not at the De Foes', in consequence of his advancement to Justice. An intimate matter: he professes a personal attachment. One of our sisters.'

'Golding?' Her mind raced, dashing at possibilities until her head reeled, all in an instant. She felt breathless. Bures House, the Golding family, Thalia De Foe, the magistracies, Tabitha or Letitia, Sealandings, its hierarchies –

'He demanded, and I allowed, the right to declare his affection without naming its focus, until such time as he had established himself as a proper suitor.'

'I see.' Was this the reason, then, for Golding's remark about any personal reason for delaying sending special constables after Carmichael? No, that was separate. Except, she remembered, the girl Mehala had once been housekeeper at Bures House, and in a few brief days had made Golding sober, and presentable – and enabled him to shake off the malign influence of his cousin Thalia De Foe. Only when Mehala left Bures House to serve the indigent at Shalamar had Golding gone to pieces again. She quelled her mind's tumult. 'Are Tabitha and Letitia to be told, Henry?'

'I seek your advice, Lydia.' He picked up the fallen beads, and pulled across a wicker basket chair to sit beside her. They fell into a reflective silence.

They had always been close, so akin in fact that his younger sisters often seemed incomprehensible. They were all so dissimilar. Extraordinary how different sisters could be! While Lydia had been, as a child, filled with innocent and spontaneous merriment, and had matured into a lady able to carry herself in any company and through any domestic entanglements, Tabitha and Letitia were strikingly disparate. The former – why did Tabitha always come first, when she had hardly emerged from her 'teens? – was spirited, even wayward, a source of anxiety to him. At times Tabitha's behaviour was so exuberant that she required correcting even in company. Yes, Tabitha could be a problem. Too often lately she had asked after Carradine, seemingly enthralled by stories of him, ominous conversation for one so young. But she was so vivacious that a brother had to love her, trouble or no. Her moods, that so irritated Lydia, seemed to Henry nothing more than the emotional swings women displayed. She could always bring a smile to his face, and had the gift of making him forget the responsibilities Sealandings imposed. Yes, a jewel, so pretty it was no wonder Golding had fallen for her.

Letitia? The quiet one, always reading, gentle of soul and manner. Her nature was such that a family could easily forget she was there at all. Yet as time passed Henry felt himself appreciating her company more and more. He remembered a single moment one evening not long ago, when the Prothero-Carradine Manor debts needed to be adjudged. The road Trust was in conflict with all and sundry. Vagabonds were causing such mayhem that no trackway of Sealandings or Whitehanger was safe. Worst, he had just realised the extent of Thalia De Foe's betrayal with Carradine. He was distraught that evening, and had gone straight into his library. There he slumped in Father's old chair, head in his hands. Daylight faded on the most dismaying evening of his life. The whole household had left him alone, fearing his response were he disturbed. He may even have slept. Then, in the stillness of the sombre room, he gradually became aware of a scent, and a faint gleam of light, and raised his head from Father's old desk to look up. There was Letitia. She was unafraid, had come silently in, seated herself on a French stool. She was reading by the light of a solitary taper fastened to a pricket. The aroma was that of the taper mingled with her perfume.

He found himself silently watching her as she read, her book leaning on the scrolled ends of the French. Her face was sweetly illuminated, yet partly in shadow from the single glim. He had studied her for what seemed a moment but was surely much longer, for when he finally came to, the taper was almost guttering. Her features were classical, so gentle, her presence so restoring. He found himself wondering about her, this most self-effacing of his sisters. How, for instance, had she managed to come in without rousing him? The few times he himself had tried to fasten the old-fashioned taper – no longer used for a master's library in this modern day of ingenious Argand oil lamps – to a standing pricket he had ended cursing, laughing at his clumsiness. Yet she had managed it easily. She knew everything but spoke hardly at all. She alone never took him to task for his love of the sealands. He remembered the time when she astonished him by respectfully offering an alternative meaning to some local word, some tale he was telling of fisherfolk dialect. But that picture of her there, seated in silent company with him in the library when he was in such a pit of despond, was endearing and beautiful. It stayed with him, for its charm and simplicity. It had taught him much about her. Others might have exotic beauty, yes. And be so captivating that one was made prisoner to their wit and charm, yes indeed. But Letitia had pure grace. That she never complained, when her affection for that lunatic painter William Maderley came to nought after his head was turned by a glimpse of Mehala, only confirmed her worth.

'I resolve the matter into one query, Lyd: is Golding a sound prospect for marriage to either of the girls?'

Lydia composed herself to deliver an unwelcome reply. 'I mistrust Charles Golding's recent . . . conversion, Henry. His one episode of stability was woefully brief. If you recall, Henry, it coincided with the sojourn of that sea girl Mehala as his temporary housekeeper. Once she departed to Shalamar to serve Carmichael, he reverted to a drunkard.'

'But him as he now is?'

'Forgive me, Henry. As he now *seems*.' She hesitated, knowing how much assistance the Golding estate had provided, at the last minute, to Henry's effort at the sea dykes. 'Were his contributions to the flood control willingly given? Or was it again that Mehala woman, who took it upon herself to enact Golding's generosity for him?'

340

'The latter seems the case, Lydia.' His sister had learned this from the supper table when entertaining Sir Edward. 'Which brings me to my problem.'

Lydia had expected this. Henry's solitary questions had a habit of compounding.

'Does either Tabitha or Letitia harbour any affection for Golding?' he asked bluntly.

This was the core. Tabitha had said little, most unlike her, but had seemed mesmerised when Golding called on the De Foes. For herself, Lydia disliked the man, putting on airs the instant he was advanced, trying to bluster her brother. What amazed her was the meekness with which Henry accepted Golding's decisions. It was most unlike him.

'I believe Letitia still thinks kindly of Mr Maderley,' she said finally. 'She confides little.'

Yes, Hunterfield thought. And Letitia would say nothing to Tabitha. It would be like giving a scroll to the town-crier.

'Tabitha seemed very taken with Golding, however, don't you think, Lyd?'

She nodded once. Her brother's perspicacity occasionally took her by surprise, as now. She had supposed him oblivious.

'Such dazzles are momentary to a girl, Henry, and easily forgot.'

'In this case I wonder, Lyd. I harboured thoughts of Sir Trev Bunyan, Captain Bussell, or Alex Waite – all friends of the family. Or, perhaps, Percy Carmady.'

'For Tabitha?'

Strange that the wayward, even fiery, sister should be the one they both thought easier guided. The implication was that the seemingly tranquil Letitia was far less biddable.

He smiled. 'Let us have tea, Lydia. Enough anguish. Dwell on the question, but find a resolution soon, if you please. Very soon.'

'Certainly, Henry.' Lydia rang the table bell, and smiled as Henry went to parade the windows. But her spirit was despondent. She now had her orders, and a list of possible gentlemen suitors. She was commanded to solve the problem of her two sisters forthwith.

Henry was right in one way, of course. Tabitha's growing resentments urgently needed a focus for her desires and interests.

And Letitia must not be allowed to withdraw further into her books. Youth passed so fleetingly. Lydia sighed. She would have to concentrate, perhaps add to the list of eligible suitors, and move at speed. She knew her brother. Once committed, he would never withdraw. As if all these complications were not enough, she had a further problem: Henry himself, the most eligible gentleman in the Eastern Hundreds. Twice lately, her husband James' letters had expressed anxieties about Hunterfield's bachelorhood, reminding her of all the natural concerns for Lorne House and the Hunterfield estates.

So on the one hand, James wanted her to magick the Lord of Sealandings into wedlock with any brilliant high-born lady. On the other, Henry had ordered her to prospect marriage for her two sisters with eligible gentry. I need Merlin's wand, she thought in distress. The issues would have to be faced 'very soon' – Henry's own words. She smiled brilliantly as the maids entered with the four tea trays, and gracefully rose to pour for her brother.

37

The small boat dock was ill-lit of a night-time, usually with one storm lanthorn hung by the jetty. Tonight, Carradine was surprised to see no light at all. This most unusual occurrence puzzled him. For a full quarter after the tenth hour he remained on his mount by the side of the path which led down from the Carradine estates towards the sea, wondering.

Here he was to meet Judith Blaker. Had she extinguished the flame? That in itself was a hanging offence, for it imperilled inshore boats. No magistrate would accept as excuse that a girl wanted to meet her lover by owl light. More likely, the estate keepers were gone slipshod for lack of a true master. He rather liked that idea. But there was no such thing as loyalty. Treachery flew in, when riches flew out; loyalty followed lucre. Surely the light could not remain unlit by Prothero's direct order? Unthinkable.

There was no sound except the sea's shushing. It was like some great monster breathing out there in the darkness. Carradine knew every stone on the beaches, and the footholds on the steeper parts of the shore. And the track to the Carradine jetty. He finally decided to go, dismounted and led the mare slowly down. The faint non-darkness of the sky was all the guidance he had, or needed.

He was almost on her, startled and cursing silently, when he heard her laugh.

'Sir?' It was a whisper. He controlled the mount's sudden backing by a sharp command and clouted the brute across the neck with his riding crop.

'You bitch!' He would have lashed out at the woman if he had been sure where she was, from anger at the stupidity of her sly stillness. A gypsy's trick. 'You could have had me fallen, were I riding!'

'You, sir?' Her voice wheedled with exaggerated awe, another goading trick. 'So grand a master, to tumble from his mare?'

Carradine did strike out in rage, but the crop only whistled in air. The woman had moved, unheard. He controlled himself. There would be another time. She would learn.

'Where's the glim, woman? I've always left strict orders – '

'Your orders, sir? Alas, they are un-ordered. There's a new master, sir!'

She was needling him still more. It was suddenly of secondary importance as the significance struck him. 'You mean Prothero ordered the sea-light unlit?'

A hand caught his arm, pulling gently. He followed, still not seeing her, but realising she was leading him towards the boathouse.

'For tonight and one more night.'

'Tomorrow?'

'Shhhh, sir. There are two men on the water, making time nor'ards. A pram, rowing hard. You hear them?'

He paused, listening, heard nothing. She could be deceiving him, having dowsed the light herself. There might be no men at all, or two in league with her. Pure rage boiled within him at his plight. Carradine, of Carradine Manor, to be stumbling behind some common woman, like a night-stealing thief, on land that once had been his.

The reins were taken from his hand, and the mare tethered. They were at the small boathouse now. He felt his way forward into the deeper dark. The place smelled musty, but wholesomely so, oil and tar mingling with the thin sharp scent of boat tackle. A more pungent aroma drew his attention. Its cause was revealed when a leather carapace was lifted from a string ball contained in a pierced glass cone. The string's end was smouldering red, giving a feeble glow that in other conditions would have gone unnoticed. Here, it was astonishingly bright. He saw Judith's face, dark and alive, smiling, and cuffed her from displeasure.

'Now, master!' she chided, laughing at him gently. 'No time for indulgences!'

She indicated a thick layer of canvas sailwork, and led him to it. A bottle of Portugal and some drop cakes in a small basket stood on a stool. She poured him a glass and took first sip.

'Time for what, bitch?' He still had not forgiven her the trick of silence on the shore path. She must have night eyes, like a witch.

344

'Details, master.' She was pretty, beautiful in fact, by the smouldering light of the glowing string, and knew it. 'Yes. Mr Prothero ordered the sea glim to be unlit two nights running – or so Giffler the smuggler will testify. And yes, Mr Prothero has announced his residence is permanent.' She went on over Carradine's sharp intake of breath, 'And yes, he has denied the murrain at Calling Farm. Yes, he has been taken to task by the Squire. And yes, has rebuffed Hunterfield's advices as impertinence.'

'The bastard!' Carradine breathed. 'He'll drag Carradine Manor down with Calling Farm! Does the peasant not know the power of the great families? Annoy any but Hunterfield!'

'There is a way out, master. Here, drink. You seem a cadator, from your attire and condition.'

He growled in anger at her insult but she caught his hand to her breast.

'Easy, master. That is the road home to Carradine. Keep control, and you will again sit in your father's great chair. The first to lose temper will fall to beggary. It is you or Prothero. Remember Judith's advice, and Carradine is yours.'

Carradine drank thirstily. 'It *is* mine, you cow!'

'Then resume your place,' Judith said calmly, conscious of her power. If she could install him successfully in Carradine, who knows what position she might attain? 'Listen to me.'

He lay back on the canvas. Ignominious, admittedly, for one of his lineage to sink so low that he was glad to lie on a heap of old sails, trespassing on land once his own, falling greedily on a few victuals stolen by a serving woman, hiding like a vagabond.

'Stop thinking that,' Judith was saying, pouring another glass, 'You would not have been better off at Hoddinotts, chancing encounters with Brillianta Astell or her sister Lorela!'

He eyed her, wondering at her perception. At least at Hoddinotts he had the semblance of a residence, even if it was at Charles Golding's behest.

'Your cousin, the drover?' he guessed.

'Listen, master.' She was not addicted to intimate names, like the whore Lucy. Did she see herself as forever separate, unlike Lucy with her silly grandiose hopes? 'Golding has been advanced to a Magistrate of the Peace for Sealandings,' she said casually.

'He's *what*? But the man's an – '

'Hear me.' Her voice was abruptly harsh. 'He has sworn out two special constables, to seek for Carmichael, the *dravengro*.' She quickly corrected herself. 'That's the vagabonds' word for a poison-monger, doctor, apothecary. Carmichael has fled north-west. He passed the tollgate.'

'With Mehala?' The question was out unthought, to his irritation. Judith was displeased.

'Alone, master. His woman seeks him in Sealandings. The stupid bitch is without home or coin. A pheasant.'

'A wanton? Prostitute?' Carradine gave a mirthless laugh. 'Not she! There's plenty in Sealandings would like to see her so, though.' He thought of the possibilities in Judith's news. 'So Golding's a Justice! And Hunterfield allowed this?'

'It's done, master. And Hunterfield with nothing to say.'

'Hunterfield is no cacafuego, Blaker.' Carradine uttered the crudity harshly. 'He's no shitfire braggart, not him. The Squire of Sealandings' silence costs its price. I have cause to know. What else have you for me?'

'Some maid, and one herdboy, lie sick at Calling Farm, and one other adjoining.'

Carradine felt a thrill of horror. 'From the same malady?'

'Nobody knows, with the Doctor gone. The headman Perrigo sent word to Prothero yester eve. The master does nothing but complain he is schemed against – '

'*Don't call him master at Carradine!*'

'There, master, there!' Judith soothed. Quite like a child, this great brash profligate. In cant speech he was worth only 'the Jew's compliment', meaning great of pricklust but gutted of pence. 'Jason Prothero is no man's master, nor woman's either. Rumour says that more go down with the sickness, seven together at Calling, not counting Nelmes' one farmboy.'

'What does the. . . ?'

Judith spoke into his sudden silence. She was holding him now, soothing.

'. . . the Doctor say? He's wandering the road inland. One of my cousins was setting snares by the tollpike, and heard him speak with the toll-farmer Tyll. He is bound for St Albans, I suppose to some relative.'

346

'The constables will take him before dawn.'

'Is'll hear soon, master. He's in for the monkey's allowance once took in Sealandings, that's for sure.'

Carradine smiled. The monkey's allowance, more kicks than ha'pence. A pleasant image, though Carmichael ought not to be too damaged in case this murrain got plaguey.

'That all you have for me, woman?'

'No, master,' she said evenly, quietly. 'I have solace better than from that whorehouse.'

So she knew. 'I have a whore there who tells me of the gentry. She means nothing.'

'She had better not, master.' The words were gently spoken, but he felt an incipient shiver. This woman must not be crossed. In future, he would stay clear of Two Cotts, in spite of the pang that thought gave him. 'You've only tonight to face the tasks of the morrow.'

'What are those?' He was furious with himself, almost asking this bitch for orders.

'Tomorrow you must see Lady De Foe, and become her man. Like before.' He listened almost in amaze. How much did this woman know, for God's sake? 'She will send to you, for I shall see her abigail Meg learns of your presence here. Be in one of the taverns to receive word. Agree to meet her.'

'In this state?'

'I bring clothes, master. Your own, from Carradine. Razor, soaps. Come dawn, you will emerge like a butterfly.'

'And Mistress De Foe? Her husband is at home.'

She laughed. 'Tell her to make Golding to invite you to stay at Bures House, anything. It is vital for you to be in Sealandings. Prothero's ship will *not* come home, master.'

'Ship?' Did she mean a literal ship? Carradine remembered the conversation he had had with Prothero about Excise ships, and he thought of Ben Fowler, landlord of the Goat and Compass. And the unlit light on the jetty, and Prothero's sudden move into Carradine Manor when by all tradition he ought to remain at Calling Farm and restore that estate to health. And Judith had mentioned Giffler.

He felt jubilation rise within. Success was beckoning as of old. Christ, if he had known the benefit a cattle plague would bring, he would have started one himself! He looked at her with a sudden thought. Could it be that this woman, so darkly secretive, was in fact the perpetrator. . . ? Impossible.

She undid her bodice, cast off her soprano cape, loosened her chin brides, and pulled at his clothes. All conscious thought vanished.

'See, master?' she whispered, smiling. 'See? Details are what count. For life, master. Yours and mine.'

He suddenly reached for her, clawing and grunting and sinking his teeth into her neck. She laughed quietly, and urged him down into the folds of canvas.

38

The discovery that his sister Letitia had *grace*, that rare character, in a degree at once disturbing and profound, caused Hunterfield to reflect on the conversation he had overheard that very morning between Tabitha and Letitia. Their words in fact decided the party which eventually rode out to visit Watermillock. It took place when Hunterfield was laboriously writing an addendum to one of Lydia's letters to Aunt Faith in Gloucester. He expressly indicated that her proposed visit to Sealandings, along with an entourage of relations that would engulf Lorne House, was too precipitate. He ought to have written a curt, *'Sealandings has had floods enough this autumn,'* and left it at that, but courtesy was the cornerstone of civilization, so he had to ponder and embellish while adding a Cromwellian refusal to Lydia's hints and preambles.

Crane had brought writing implements from the study, making sure the Squire's favourite quill-holder was cleaned of ink stains. The old servant sniffed his displeasure when assuring the Squire of this. Henry acknowledged Crane's disapproval without a smile – the ancient disliked Aleppo ink galls, on the grounds that good English oak galls stained with greater tenacity. Absurd. Everybody knew that boiled Aleppo galls made the best black ink, as Brazilwood raspings in vinegar made the best red. Why argue? Still, as long as mere trivia preoccupied the head servant, Henry thought, settling in one of the window alcoves of the west corridor. From there he could see carriages arrive. He wished to get this wretched visit to Watermillock over with. The arrangement was that Mercy Carmady would tour Milton Hall with Thalia De Foe, and appraise that lady's plans for some vacant manor house or other. Letitia was to provide company for Percy Carmady, while Hunterfield's portrait was inched nearer completion by that madman.

It was then that he overheard Tabitha's approach. He could tell his sisters' footfalls, but had not realised Letitia was nearby. She was reading in the next window alcove, one of her favourite places. Henry wrote, deliberated, frowning with concentration. These silly roundabout messages were more difficult than any legal decisions, and those were damnable. It was quite five minutes before he became aware of a tension in his sisters' voices. Or was it the pauses? For women mostly converse overlapping, catching the skirts of each others' sentences and taking up before friends had finished. Now, occasional silences punctuated their talk. His name had been mentioned.

'You see, Letty,' Tabitha said wheedlingly after one such halt, 'Mercy Carmady is of a rather *outward* disposition. Her mood might be difficult on this ride to Mistress Maderley's.'

'Is that a reason to change arrangements, Tabby?' Letitia's quiet voice asked.

'I should think it is, Letty!' Tabitha laughed as if disbelieving. 'Imagine the effect on the Carmadys, if the journey to Watermillock, and Henry's prolonged sitting for Mr Maderley, were conducted in total silence!'

Henry listened attentively. Tabitha could be almost stabbingly cruel, as now. Letitia could leave Tabitha smouldering in incomprehension if she ever had a mind, but never did. She was always first to guide conversations to give Tabitha a chance to shine.

'You wish to go in my place, Tabby?'

'Not *in your place*, Letty! Heavens, what an idea! I am only thinking how hospitable the Hunterfields would seem if we neglected to provide the Carmadys with the *best* available company, that is all.'

A pause, the sound of a book closing with gentle finality.

'Very well, if you wish.'

'Good heavens, Letty! If I *wish*? It is only a ride to a draughty old tide-mill house! I am saving you *bother*! You can stay and read to your heart's content!'

'Thank you, Tabitha.' There was a mild irony in Letitia's words. A rustle of skirts was audible, presumably Tabitha rising to make good her withdrawal after having got her way.

'Shall you inform Henry, Letty? It would be better. Plead a headache. I really ought to make myself ready, for when the coach returns.'

'Of course, Tabby.'

350

Tabitha tutted. 'I hope your tone does not signify a misplaint, Letty. Because if you feel I am in *any* way trying to supplant you, then I shall be only too happy to . . .'

'No, Tabby. You go.' Letitia's voice was hesitant. 'Will you please let me know how . . . how the visit goes? I . . . I hope Henry is not too bothered by it. He has so much on his mind lately.'

'Of course I shall!' Tabitha gushed, but her voice was already receding. After that, only silence.

Henry left the letter unfinished, to his eventual annoyance. But what he had overheard was too serious to bother with the Aunt Faiths of the world. Letitia was still deeply affected by mention of Watermillock and William Maderley: he had always suspected it.

The return of the carriage from Milton Hall bearing Percy Carmady and the hurry to welcome him – and Letitia's apologies to her brother when she found him in the first reception room with Percy Carmady – prevented him from finding a way to rescue Letitia. He even considered postponement, but reluctantly had to accept Letitia's withdrawal. Lydia sent to summon Tabitha, whose instantaneous appearance surprised the company in view of the sudden notice. She descended the stair in a new purple curricle pelisse with a cape cleverly opened to reveal Moravian work on the shoulder. Henry looked for Letitia to say goodbye, but she had already retired.

The party of four drove out in the golden autumn morning, with Percy Carmady seeming charmed by Tabitha Hunterfield, who was looking her best and knew it.

'The view from your window is quite splendid, Maderley,' Carmady said. He was not looking from the artist's studio, however, but amiably drifting, peering quizzically at the canvases strewn haphazardly round the place while William Maderley concentrated on his subject.

Hunterfield laughed, his change in position causing the artist to grunt in annoyance.

'Mr Maderley's lamps of an evening are said to have saved more vessels in Sealandings Bay than all the coastal lights, Percy! Isn't that true, Maderley?'

'Mmhhh.' The painter did not look at the speaker, except in that

351

curiously opaque way artists scanned their sitters. Maderley avoided Hunterfield's eyes. The Squire's gaze today had an unusually direct intensity he had never seen before. It worried him.

'Isn't this that girl, Henry?' Carmady asked. 'The one I thought I recognised, before that pugilist defeated Battling Goring. When Carradine . . .' He glanced at the artist, resumed, '. . . suffered.'

'Girl?' Hunterfield peered round the easel. Carmady took a painting up and held it. It was unframed, the canvas edges frayed slightly. There was no mistaking the portrait. It was Mehala. For the first time Hunterfield began to feel understanding creep into his mind. He glanced at the artist. 'Mehala.'

'Mehala! That's her name!' Carmady spoke as Maderley remained silent. 'Wasn't she the same one who. . . ?'

'Yes, Percy?' Hunterfield prompted, resuming his awkward position. He felt ridiculous, cloaked, in this infernally hot room, told to sit still as a heron while a madman daubed pigments on a stretched rag. Idiotic.

His friend hesitated, finally decided to say nothing. There was a mood in the studio he could not quite understand, as if he was spectator to some travelling play without a plot. He replaced the painting, but found his eyes drawn to it.

The portrait showed more than the usual. It depicted the girl standing looking out to sea – what she saw was not shown. She seemed on a hostile and deserted shore. Yet she was at home, belonging. Her clothes were inelegant, of rough material. She carried an ordinary fisherwoman's basket. The wind tugged at her hair. Beyond, the sealands and salt marshes stretched into a green-russet desolation. On the receding North Sea a lone lugger leaned in towards shore. Her complexion was not that of a lady of leisure, pale and wan, potioned to oblivion. It was honest, alive, natural. And the expression was, yes, extraordinarily . . . joyous.

Hunterfield prompted, 'She was fetched in by one of our fishing boats. Capable girl, works for Doctor Carmichael. I hear he has lately gone from Sealandings. Temporarily, I trust.'

'Sir?' William Maderley's concentration vanished. 'Forgive me, Squire. Carmichael? Left the coast?'

'Had you not heard? Mehala seeks him. Simple Tom, my groom, reports her at the Darlings in Whitehanger.'

William glanced towards the windows. He could see anyone walking the coastal track towards Whitehanger, along the dryland marks past the draining sealand floods, or along the restored sea dykes. He said nothing, recommenced his work. The Squire was almost done. Close to, his face was younger than Maderley had supposed. This was the benefit of portraiture. It revealed characters far more tellingly than any narrative. And some aspects proved disturbing. Only last evening, studying Hunterfield's countenance on canvas, he had been struck by a similarity between Hunterfield's gaze and that of Mehala. Not one borne of relationship, no. One from within. He had puzzled over this, until his sister Olivia had ascended the stairs in search, to remind him that supper was ready. Perhaps it was that he was continually sketching Mehala, seeking understanding. She was unsettling. He had several Mehala paintings, started and abandoned, but clearly this was no time to mention the fact.

'I am unhappy to think Doctor Carmichael is leaving the Eastern Hundreds against his will.'

Hunterfield ignored the implied question. 'How long?' he asked instead. 'This business is unconscionably drawn out.'

Carmady chuckled at the pun. William was immediately on the defensive.

'Art is not an instant's whim, Squire. Why, people study all their lives and yet remain unlearned.'

'That's what worries me, Maderley,' Hunterfield said drily. 'Your letter offering lessons in persective, pigments, all that. Isn't it a means of disguising children's daubing as something grander?'

'Sir!' Maderley almost spilled an ounce of valuable rose madder powder. 'Sir! Art is the highest expression of human genius! That is attested by royalty, and civilizations of the highest reputation!'

'The question is, can it be *taught*, Maderley,' Hunterfield mused. 'You see my problem? An artist such as yourself, well, I accept you have a certain skill, but that is a quirk of birth. I mean, in your letter you seemed to believe anybody, gifted or not, could be shown – '

The artist was beside himself, agitated. 'Sir, I beg of you! Art is its own understanding, its own creativity! That is acknowledged by the greatest masters. Wherever that love exists, please God let it flourish!'

Hunterfield frowned. 'That textbook you artists all use – isn't it writ by some ancient Jesuit? I shouldn't want anything subversive –'

'Sir, that is only one text of many!' William cried desperately. 'I should submit any books of instruction to you for approval before –'

'Well,' Hunterfield interrupted with reluctance. 'All right, then, Maderley. Your vehemence persuades me, if your logicking does not! You may discuss lessons with Miss Hunterfield. Make arrangements through Mrs Vallance. I shall expect rapid progress, mind!'

'Thank you, Squire.' The artist beamed, feeling he had struck a blow for his calling. 'You will never regret this!'

'That remains to be seen,' Hunterfield said sourly. 'Let Miss Tabitha's progress be a measure of your theories, then!'

'Miss. . . ?' William stopped, licked his lips, nodded.

'Yes, Maderley?' Hunterfield said innocently. 'I trust *one* pupil will suffice? Or do you intend I should order the whole population of Sealandings to your lessons?'

Maderley smiled weakly, resumed mixing umber to intensify the background.

Percy chuckled. 'Then I reside elsewhere, Henry!'

The gentlemen conversed idly while William Maderley concentrated on adding more drops of cold-drawn linseed oil to his burnt sienna powder, to minimise the chances of its appearing like Indian red, always a terrible danger. He was already desperately anxious about the Naples yellow, having risen early to mix more of that wantonly fickle colour. Last night, in preparation for today's sitting, he had absently stirred the powder using a steel spatula, and so created a hideously muddy green. Of course he should have used a horn spatula, so the yellow would stay pure. A stupid mistake. These were the fascinating imperatives of art, but how to convince disbelievers of their importance? Only Miss Letitia would understand. And somehow, instead of Letitia, he had landed Miss Tabitha for a pupil. He felt a strange longing for Letitia's gentle quietness, and savagely attacked the mixing with so much oil he had to apologise for a new delay and start again.

The special constables came upon the lonely figure just as the sun

354

broke through the clouds, for the first time in weeks. Ven was rousing himself from a sluggish doze, unrefreshed and finding difficulty in standing. He was in a small thicket by the roadside. His surtout was soaked, and his boots paled in streaks where water had leached the blacking. He had tried to keep his beaver on his head while sitting to sleep against a tree trunk, but it had tipped off. He was mopping the brim free of moisture when the constables came at him.

They arrested him by order of a Justice of the Peace. He tried explaining that he was merely walking to St Albans, where he had relatives. He was not able to remember the exact address. Nor could he move as quickly as the constables wanted. He fell during the climb to the road, and was struck several corrective blows for resisting arrest. He was finally driven, limping before them towards Sealandings, any tardiness being punished by prods from the constables' staves.

The journey was not much more than one and a half leagues. On arrival, he was incarcerated in a stinking out-privy behind the Goat and Compass, by arrangement with the landlord Benjamin Fowler. Nothing was said about the identity of the prisoner. One constable remained on guard outside the enclosed box, while the other set off to inform Sir Charles Golding of the felon's successful capture. The Fowlers and their servants were warned of the need for strictest silence, by the Justice's command. The sternest penalties would be enforced for non-compliance.

Mrs Maderley's coffee party had a celebratory air, so pleased did the Squire seem at the ending of the painting fiasco. He was so relieved that it became a joke.

Tabitha had enjoyed the outing, even though she was lodged in Olivia Maderley's boring company. The ladies' stroll in the garden did little to please, when Percy Carmady was ensconced upstairs with Henry. Even William, strange man, would have been better company than his sister. Olivia was pleasant enough, but a woman's company was purposeless when all was said and done. And dull. And feeble. Even though there were some slight amusements to be had, such as Olivia's Adelaide boots, and bottle-green velvet walking cloak. Quite wrong, of course, as any woman with half an eye could see. The poor thing was trying to make the best of herself. She had doted on Henry for years, though putting up a woman's usual show of indifference. Ridiculous. Olivia's station in life was absurdly out of line with the Hunterfield family's. Still, her hair was not quite such a mess, thank heavens, though no gentleman worth his salt would look at her twice. Odd that Percy Carmady seemed quite taken with her, though here again it was well-known that men were innocents, silly as magpies. All that glistered was not gold.

They conversed of nothing, and returned thankfully to the house when the painting was over.

'If I live to be a hundred, Mistress Maderley,' Henry announced with a show of relief as they settled, 'I should never wish to repeat the suffering your wretched son has inflicted.'

'Come, sir,' Mrs Maderley said in a mock scold. 'William is the kindest of souls.'

She was under no illusion. All Sealandings was scandalized by William Maderley's neglect of the tide-mill in his madness to paint. This response was the best she could make.

'I regard his efforts as pure extortion, ma'am.'

The room stilled. Olivia Maderley, supervising the serving of Scotch snow cake, froze in horror at the Squire's words. Even Carmady, who knew Hunterfield's wit well, raised his eyebrows in alarm at the mention of financial matters in the company of ladies.

'Pure moral extortion. He refused to let me shift until I had been forced to agree to let him teach Miss Tabitha here the rudiments of his colour daubing.'

The company laughed with relief. Tabitha looked from her brother to William, appalled.

'To instruct *me*, sir? In art?'

Henry sighed, taking one of Olivia's offerings with a smile of thanks. 'This is the trouble with acquaintances like the Maderleys,' he explained to Percy, who was smiling openly now. 'They take advantage of benevolence. You'll find it so, Percy, when you settle in. I only thank Heaven I was not persuaded into so useless an exercise myself! At least I have a sister on hand to perform that sacrifice for me!'

Olivia was amused, but managed to shoot her brother a glance warning him not to respond to the mild jibe with one of his

356

interminable lectures on art. William controlled his impulse, just, and smiled weakly.

'But me, sir?' Tabitha appealed to her brother, to Percy Carmady, to Olivia. 'While I have no wish to go against your command, I do feel I would not gain half so much benefit from Mr Maderley's lessons as – '

'See what I am up against, Carmady?' Hunterfield groaned. 'Sisters who gainsay? Who oppose my every plan?' He rounded heavily on Tabitha. 'I have agreed teaching, Tabitha, so you will please comply. I'm sure Miss Olivia here would gladly act as your substitute, but for the fact that she has obviously endured enough painting to last a lifetime!'

'I am proud to obey, sir,' Tabitha said dismally, racking her brains. Somehow she was being forced to exchange Percy Carmady for William Maderley. 'I only hope Letitia will not feel at all disadvantaged by my happy fortune.'

Hunterfield frowned. 'Disadvantaged? Your sister? Explain, miss!'

'I am certain Letitia would delight in such an enterprise, sir, were she so blessed as to be offered it.'

'You think so?' Hunterfield pondered. 'She found a ready excuse not to accompany us this morning. This painting thing is probably not to her liking.'

Tabitha clutched at the straw. 'Oh, I'm sure it is, Henry!' she burst out, frantic. 'She often confides how much she enjoyed seeing Mr Maderley's skills!'

'Well,' her brother said doubtfully. 'If you are sure Letitia would not find it an intrusion, then you may share your lessons.'

'Share, sir?' Tabitha said glumly, her dejection barely concealed. 'Are we to learn jointly? I think Mr Maderley could hardly instruct *two* pupils together, could you, sir? Especially in so difficult a subject. I would be content to forego my own lessons, so that Letitia could benefit from Mr Maderley's concentrated instruction!'

'Good heavens, Miss Tabitha!' William cried, to his sister's inward dismay. 'Of course I could! Why, there are studios on the Continent where as many as a dozen young artists study at one time! It would be my great pleasure to instruct two elegant ladies in concert!'

357

Olivia sensed Henry Hunterfield's irritation at her brother's dense compliance, but showed only a smiling delight as the arrangements were made. Mrs Maderley started calculating who was to chaperone the lessons. It was only when Olivia found herself being called upon that she coloured slightly and began to wonder quite how matters had turned this way.

Tabitha tried to find some way of putting a stop to Olivia's proposed visits to Lorne, but could think of nothing. It was most infuriating. She planned to approach Lydia urgently to devise some means of rescue: herself free from this silly teaching, and Olivia from accompanying William. Obviously, Olivia had schemed with the cunning of the vixen. The woman was smitten. If Olivia Maderley hoped to set her cap at Sir Henry Hunterfield, Squire and Lord of Sealandings, the ignorant bitch was mistaken. She should stay in her muddy waters in the tide-mill, and leave gentlemen of breeding alone. Tabitha smiled beatifically when Percy Carmady made some light-hearted challenge to William on teaching perspective as a practical rather than artistic necessity, as was the case in Navy ships, and exchanged confiding glances with Mrs Maderley. The widow was overcome with the honour of entertaining such prestigious guests. As well she might be, Tabitha thought sourly, wondering at the widow's age. What was she, forty-four or five? Considerable, in any event.

'So ends my excursion into the field of art!' Hunterfield exclaimed as his party took its leave of the Maderleys. 'I am uncommonly grateful!'

Olivia found herself on the Squire's arm, while Carmady escorted her mother and Tabitha came after, petulantly receiving William's enthusiastic account of the first lessons.

'Your seas are back to proper behaviour, Miss Olivia,' Hunterfield observed, pointing to the dykes. 'Your Watermillock men acquitted themselves well.'

'Mehala played a major part in the rescue of the flooded sealands, sir?'

'Indeed she did. Most timely. She has capabilities beyond her station.'

'What a pity she is unable to discover her memory, and know her origins!' Olivia was following the direction of Hunterfield's gaze, her remark apparently innocent.

'I wonder if the painting your brother showed us in his studio is not nearer the mark than any speculation.' He smiled at her, and the company made their farewells.

The carriage departed with William calling after it how he would finish the portrait by applying copal varnish after some seven months . . .

On arrival at Lorne House, the reason for Hunterfield's faint preoccupation was finally revealed. The two gentlemen conducted Tabitha in, then stood talking at the head of the steps, ostensibly to discuss alterations to the gardens.

'Mehala, Percy,' Hunterfield said without preamble. 'Where was it you saw her?'

For a moment the image of Mehala's portrait flashed into Carmady's mind, a picture of serenity against the desolation of a wild shore. He remembered her as he had seen her, in elegant company, richly presented. But her countenance had then seemed distraught, drawn, wearing the expression of one at the end of her tether.

'She is the Lady of Red Hall,' he said.

39

The church of St Edmund the Martyr was ancient beyond anyone's knowledge. Reverend Baring had constructed an ornate wooden board announcing the incumbents through the centuries to long before the Conquest. The names were in gold and black gothic lettering. Mehala stood observing the roll, and shivered at the sight.

'Good morning, Mehala. You are cold?' Euterpe Baring's soft voice made her start. The great door closed with a quiet echoing boom.

'No, Miss Baring. Good morning. It was just that . . . some recollections seemed stirred by these rectors, so long dead. An angel walked over my grave, that is all.'

It had been the same in East Mersea, with a similar board hung in the west, nearby the base of the squat tower; whereas at St Mary the Virgin at Virley, where she had been married, the decaying interior displayed hardly any adornment, except the . . . Euterpe Baring came on her, moving slowly through the church to the end of the rearmost pew.

'Is your memory returning, then?' When Mehala shook her head, Euterpe did not pursue the subject. 'We ought to complete our arrangments, Mehala. Reverend Baring will be calling for me. An urgent meeting is called tonight at Bures House. Charles Golding has summoned the religious leaders.'

Mehala found her hand moving to her throat. 'Is it to do with Doctor Carmichael?'

'I do not know. Did you discover any news?'

'No. He was not at Whitehanger. The Darlings know nothing.'

'So he did not head south.' Euterpe drew her cloak round her. The church was dank and chill in the autumn morning. Mehala's attire showed a distinct lack of grooming now, for she had been some days without respite. Yet she seemed in control, her steady gaze filled with resolve. She had rubbed her cloak free of the worst stains, and the colours seemed all the brighter. 'I have carried out my tasks. Written and made enquiry. Miss Gould has also made what attempts she may, without success.'

She saw Mehala's shoulders droop, then straighten. 'Have you any hopes, then, Miss Baring?'

'None, I am afraid. Unless I hire some pedlar to journey to St Albans.'

'Sealandings has no pedlars, no tinkers, no drovers.' Mehala spoke dully. 'None comes through any more. The post does, but only intermittently. They say the coaches will not travel coastwards beyond Maidborough. All on account of the cattle plague.'

'Then we must ask the great families,' Euterpe said firmly. 'Squire Hunterfield?'

'We are forced to.'

'And Mr Hast?' Euterpe suggested, watching Mehala's face as she spoke. 'He was most obliging yesterday.'

Mehala felt an enormous reluctance to ask Bartholomew Hast for more help. That Euterpe Baring suggested making this plea was all the more reason.

'What could Mr Hast do? He has his business to conduct. And he is as tied to Sealandings as . . .'

'As you and I, Mehala?'

Mehala remained silent. She was tied to Sealandings, yes, but less than Euterpe Baring. She had no family here. The other was the Rector's housekeeper, with responsibilities and position. She herself had no abode. Euterpe had the rectory. She had no money, whereas Miss Baring –

'I shall go to St Albans, Miss Euterpe.' Mehala's mind cleared in relief even as she heard herself say the words. She felt a lightness she had not experienced since helping Pilgrim with the oxen, and was elated.

It was suddenly so simple. Why hadn't she seen it before? Tiredness, probably, and worry for Ven. All the duties instilled since childhood, keeping to your allotted station in life. The whole ponderous mass of indoctrinations suffered by children, all had weighed on her soul, deciding her actions. The way she wanted to go lay before her. It was muddy and long. But so? It was *her* road. Ven was already on it, trudging alone, probably still sick. He was on the inland road to Hertfordshire, which made it her road. That was enough.

'Alone?' Euterpe was startled, abruptly jealous for no reason.

'Yes. Saving your presence, Miss Euterpe, I am wasting time. I could be beyond the tollgate in less than an hour. And the weather clears.'

'How will you travel?' It seemed important for Euterpe to dissuade Mehala from the journey. She was already moving towards the church door. 'You have no money.'

'I shall not walk as fast as he, perhaps, but I shall not pause. He must rest, on account of his hurt.'

That was a rebuke, for Euterpe had been less than forthcoming about Carmichael's injuries. She coloured, and accompanied Mehala, out and through the churchyard as far as the lychgate. She volunteered to Mehala all the details she could remember, Ven's belief that his ribs were broken, the wounds he had sustained on his head, his limbs. Mehala was pale as Euterpe finished.

'Please allow me to lend you some money, Mehala.'

'Thank you but no, mistress.' Mehala almost smiled. 'I can go faster unencumbered.'

'Please, Mehala,' Euterpe urged. 'Should you be accused of vagrancy, a few coins would exonerate you. And Doctor Carmichael also – think of his carency. You must afford him victuals once you find him. And mayhap a night's rest at an inn.'

Mehala hesitated, then conceded. The two retired to a position behind the line of churchyard yews as precaution against prying eyes. There Euterpe Baring gave Mehala all the money her household purse carried, nine shillings and elevenpence half-penny. She apologised for its paucity.

'Travel safely, Mehala. And success attend.'

'*Deo favente*,' Mehala replied quietly, and departed.

Euterpe stood by the lychgate, watching Mehala strike left towards the uphill Norwich road. A curious expression. *With God's favour*, instead of the more usual *Deo volente*, in common use. Some phrase that perhaps Mehala herself did not understand, picked up from Doctor Carmichael? The girl was moving slowly, but steadily and with an elegance of motion Euterpe could not help admiring. She felt grudging envy. Mehala had had no need to think. The journey way was no sooner in her mind than she was already taking the first step, the difficulties ahead as nothing. Why had the same course not occurred to herself? She could have sought him last evening, if not quite so boldly as Mehala then by perhaps hiring some ostler from Parker's public stables to conduct the search by proxy. Why hadn't she, then? She felt an unreasoning anger at the woman now gliding away from Sealandings.

Carradine's hunter was left at Parker's public stables to be groomed and rested. He hired a common gelding, using the last of the money provided by Judith Blaker. She had attended to his attire very well, providing him with his riding greatcoat with a high burrail collar, a tall Angelsea beaver and a light riding cloak of shiny everlasting, the double warps stoutly proving its worth in the wind. He felt excellent, expecially after Judith Blaker's sustenance. The clothes had seen a smoothing iron, thank God, though being obliged to a thieving servant for his own – his *own*, for Christ's sake! – clothes rankled. As he rode to Milton Hall he added the anger to the store of hatred building within.

The De Foes were in residence. He presented himself at the main porch without a card. He would no longer suffer the indignity of offering cards printed with his obsolete address. If they declined to receive him, then bad cess to the lot of them. But Thalia De Foe was at home, and fortunately her husband Fellows was accompanying Miss Carmady on her way to meet her brother and the Squire. Thalia emerged alone but radiant to greet him in the great hall. He declined refreshment. Together they walked through to the rear of Milton and stood conversing while Thalia's maid Meg rushed to bring her mistress a capote for her head and a warm cloak of bright blue vigonia with matching gloves.

The maid took far too long about it. Meg recognised the punitive look in Thalia's eye. She had to discover what Carradine's sudden reappearance meant, or she would have nothing to tell the master Fellows on his return. She was sent away with a sharp rebuke, though it was most improper for a lady alone to don even the slightest article in a visiting gentleman's presence. It was forward, a vulgar practice, unless he was a relative.

'That maid is getting above her station,' Thalia breathed as she indicated the rose garden. 'I shall whip the bitch into better obedience. Let us use the rose garden, darling. We can be seen – and see who approaches.'

'News of Sealandings,' Carradine ordered bluntly. 'I don't want to hear your domestic strifes.'

She appraised her lover, relishing his roughness and his imperious manner. It was wrong of course, meeting like this in full view of every maid and scullion. All Milton's servants would be ogling, speculating about Carradine. Let them! They were born to scour, not to gossip.

'Darling, I executed your wishes superbly. I have the very best news you could imagine. Cousin Charles is made Justice of the Peace. His constables seek Doctor Carmichael, whom I evicted from Shalamar. I am having the place refurbished, at speed, for you, though Fellows has yet to be told. And there's more, darling.'

He gazed down into her misty eyes. And felt nothing. She was his for . . . how long? Some months, maybe a year? It did not matter. Maybe he needed more earthy fare. Or more vigorous. Or more wanton. No woman could best Thalia De Foe's sheetwork, yet Lucy, and Judith, gave something more than this perfumed exotic woman, so affluent and submissive. Was it their determined independence, their withholding of some small fraction of themselves, a secret ambition to be gained by using him? It gave him a sense of danger he found thrilling.

'What more?'

'Prothero's cattle plague, at Calling. It proves disastrous. Fellows is always particular about his herds and horses. Already our tenant-farmers that lie between Calling Farm and Milton Hall's acres – you know some abut – suffer. It seems the same illness. Fellows last night confided he will seek legal redress from Prothero. Others are bound to follow suit.'

Carradine inhaled. The air was nectar. This was marvellous news. Prothero could never withstand a legal assault from De Foe. It was not simply a question of 'thirteenth juryman', a biased judge in favour of the established gentry. It was simple fact.

'Fellows is already at Lorne House, on the pretext of escorting Miss Carmady. In reality, to see Hunterfield in privacy, to fine Prothero.'

A joyous certainty filled him. Prothero was doomed, if this was managed well. He would have to sell Carradine Manor, the estate, the jetties and north shore, or accept Carradine to operate it – not as estate manager; that was unthinkable. As Carradine of Carradine.

'How long ago did Fellows leave?' he asked harshly.

Thalia began to say, 'Well, darling, less than a few minutes . . .' Then her eyes widened in horror as she realised his intention. 'No, darling, no! The servants! The gardeners' boys are at the mulberry trees – '

'Across to the summerhouse, bitch. Shut your noise.'

She pleaded. 'You cannot! Fellows may be home any moment – '

'Either I test your hair, milady, or you walk.'

He was already moving to the summerhouse, with its stone shoulders and ornamental margins and climbing roses. She had to step quickly, a matter of shame.

'Please, Rad, darling – '

'Quiet, woman.'

He was furious with that lust-anger she knew was never far below his surface. No sooner was she in the small space, its floor bare but for a stray leaf blowing in as Carradine shouldered the door ajar, than he spun round and wrenched her bodice. She begged, trying to keep him from disarranging her apparel further.

'The gardeners, darling! Please be quiet when you . . . They are but a few paces.'

His hand caught her across the cheek. She tried to help, then. There was no other way. Speed made her desperate, the possibility of Fellows coming home, Percy Carmady calling having missed his sister on the road, perhaps Hunterfield himself, oh God – haste was the only way. It exhilarated and appalled her.

The frenzy with which Carradine took her flung her into a vortex she had never before experienced. His abandon, his feral greed almost bestial, the mindless grunting, the sudden vicious clubbing he inflicted when she adjusted her position beneath him, sent her into a mindless pleasure new to her. The delirium of physical ecstasy banished the summerhouse, the gardens, as Carradine dissolved into her.

After, lying sprawled in sweat, breathless, sore from his thrusts, bruised, she floated in a dream state. The few moments had seemed to last an eternity. She soared, saw Sealandings far below. No wind, nothing material, yet she was there, intoxicated by the vision of greens and browns, the shore snaking its pale line into the distance, and the sea's small rims of waves whitening and fading into the dark green. Suspended in space, clouds brushing across her sight, she realised that love was no mere figment, nothing transient. Love is *long*. Love stayed. Permanent, indelible in the spirit. It usurped the soul, for ever and always. It was beyond debate, thought; reason was an enemy. It imparted a knowledge such that a woman who possessed it was elevated above her sisters to a superior plane of being. It brooked no discussion. An absolute. Was it worth killing for? An absurd question. *Of course it was*. The numbers of deaths necessary was also an irrelevant stupidity. Love was for ever. It had to be. By Nature, it could not leave.

Carefully, inchwise, she strove to move, give herself breath – her head was swimming from lack of it – and felt him slip out of her. She groaned, felt him stir, sink heavily down upon her again, crushing her so she was imprisoned more firmly than before. She gazed up at the ceiling, foolishly ornate for a summerhouse, and wondered how she now knew these essentials of love. They seemed familiar. Where from? How? Who among her scatter-brained acquaintances, the circuits of coffee parties and tea gatherings, who was the elegant lady in whose eyes she had seen this same new certainty? They were all too vapid, too insipid, to know the throes of sexual ravishment so ethereal yet so ferocious as to approach death or birth, the two absolutes . . . Then she remembered the eyes which knew what she herself had only just learned. Mehala. In Mehala, that girl born of the North Sea.

The revelation shocked and intrigued her. What was it Mehala possessed? She was but a girl still. Yet she was annointed, Thalia was suddenly convinced, by *owning* this brilliant, dazzling sureness. Annointed? Yes, a special sanctity that elevated and blessed, however sordid the circumstances of its coming. Such was sainthood, so martyrdom, so the perfection of a mystic. Love so simple, yet the lifelong commitment indissoluble and utter.

Tears came to her eyes. She found herself weeping, copious and joyous, dishevelled and spread in the ungainliest of positions, inelegant to say the least, pinned beneath Carradine. He was away in the man's little death, she hardly able to breathe beneath his weight. Yet the tears confirmed her new religion, devotion to her love in and through Carradine. She moved, trying to embrace him, come who may. Even failing in this simple act brought a renewal of that joy. Before, she had hedonistically played with fire, loving the danger in illicit sexual encounters, taking night loves as transitory as those of any nightgowner in Two Cotts. And she had dignified her pleasure by calling it divine. Now she saw her behaviour as crude, shameful, nothing more than the haystack gropings of a farmgirl. Paradise comes through love, sexual repletion through rutting.

That was the distinction, understood by Mehala, and visible in her eyes. That time when she had inveigled – or thought she had – Mehala into being housekeeper for Cousin Charles? And on that market day, seeing her walk through the fair, when Maderley had started Mehala's portrait in the churchyard? And. . . ? Any time at all, Thalia conceded. Once the love-knowledge was there, it was like breathing, never forgot. Because it was life. Hence many saw Mehala as the rival they most feared, even though they did not even know her. For she *was* an enemy. Thalia had no doubt that the penniless quack, now apprehended vagrant, held Mehala by love. Was the bitch capable of transferring her love to someone else, someone like Carradine? For Mehala alone was woman enough, whatever her youth, to cope with this rough beast she herself loved and must keep.

'Milady?'

The word made Thalia start, and set her heart pounding. She almost fainted at being discovered so, until her mind took over and told her it was only Meg. Her personal maid knocked gently on the door jamb.

'It is time, ma'am.' Meg's voice whispered, sounding far away. 'The master's carriage is by the South Toll road corner. I see Ennis making preparation.'

'Go. Make excuses. Tell the master I walk the grounds with a guest.'

'Yes, milady.'

Thalia heard her maid's light steps recede, and reluctantly started to push gently against Carradine's face.

'Darling? It's time to wake up. Darling. . . ?'

40

The triumphant special constable was pompously giving evidence. Moat was a smallholder, eleven acres held on a tenancy of Bures House. Beholden he might be to Golding, but now he was noteworthy. Barely thirty, strong and rustic. This was the first time he had ever entered the great manor, and gazed round at the assembled dignitaries. All hung on his sworn testimony.

'Are you sure this felon actually spoke those words, constable?' Golding demanded.

'Positive, sir. Swear on the Good Book.'

'Tyll reported that Doctor Carmichael was not certain where he was heading?'

'Yes, sir.'

'And Carmichael laughed – actually laughed at – the list of toll charges? The ones set by law?'

'Yes, sir. Tyll remembered his very words, sir. *One day some change, let's pray!*'

The gathering shuffled feet, ahemed, drew breath. *Change* was the code word of reformers, agitators all, a pestilence on the Kingdom. They were even infiltrating Parliament, in spite of the prayers of honest folk. Parker glanced at Reverend Baring, whose lips were thinned in disapproval.

'Was there some other statement? About his plight?'

'Yes, sir. Most damaging it was, too.'

Golding stirred impatiently. The oaf had been too well drilled. Fine time to put on airs.

'Give it at your own pace, Moat.'

Golding took in the faces before him. The large hall was rightly chosen as the venue for the preliminary hearing. He was not quite sure of the protocol, but had perused Toone's *Manual*. Whatever he decided was acceptable to law, as long as some veneer of legality could be applied. Whatever a magistrate argued in the interests of political stability was approvable.

Reverend Baring would be no problem. Every vicar a Vicar of

Bray, Golding told himself. He felt only scorn, whatever others thought of the Church and its toads. Robert Parker, Methodist leader, evoked the same derision, though at least he did proper work. Emanuel Bettany the Quaker elder was the same as all his kind: grasping by nature while preaching God, hated as all millers were while fawningly serving any ruling political power. How extraordinary it was, that religious dissenters dissented only from other religions, never about anything that mattered like power, war, authority. Not quite so extraordinary, for that way they feathered their own nests while convincing themselves they were true to some self-coined cause. Among the faces were other holy hangers-on, a few smallholders, tenants of his own, and a few shopkeepers. All he could safely disregard.

There was one man, some Wandsworthian maniac, probably Presbyterian or some such, living beyond even the Sealandings tollgate, whom he knew vaguely as Endercotte, staring of eye and sombre of mien. He wore black, affecting the white Geneva collar of Puritans and old-fashioned knee-buttoned black breeches, quite as if attending a funeral. His wife accompanied him, and stood at the rear. She was in unrelieved black, even to her cottage bonnet and shawl. Golding was satisfied. They would drink in any evidence, real or imaginary, straight or bottled, and call it justice.

In the second before Moat spoke, Golding caught sight of Bartholomew Hast's face. He had noticed the gunsmith, of course, but an artisan is only an artisan and nought else. What did he know of law? The gunmaker had no dealings with Carmichael, Golding felt sure, and was powerless to assist the miscreant even if he had. But the man's steady gaze was irritating. Coachmakers did not have the same steady implacability. In fact it was only such men who seemed confident. He found himself idly wondering who else among the local tradesmen showed the same taciturn character, and failed to find any. Not Veriker the clocksmith, whose exuberant tempers and bellicose laughs were famous. Not Bettany, or any of his holy lot. No, it must be in the item Hast created. Sure of his custom, whichever monarchs ruled, local or capital. An interesting thought. But the fool Moat was now drawling out his pronouncements, the longest sentences the peasant had ever spoken in his life.

'Doctor Carmichael said, *I want nothing more than to escape from Sealandings. To stay will do for me, I promise you.*'

'Condemnation!' Endercotte cried out, standing up and quivering.

'Silence in court!' Golding called imperiously, feeling the exhilaration of authority. He had no gavel. His own agent Lazard was serving as clerk. It was not good enough. He would have to see Hunterfield about obtaining appropriate staff, paid for by the Exchequer, of course.

'Condemnation! From the evil one's own mouth!' The religionist was shaking with passion, raising his arm. 'Let vengeance fall upon their heads, who speak against the righteous!'

'Silence!' Golding called. 'One more outburst, and I shall be obliged to close these proceedings forthwith!'

The muttering which accompanied Endercotte's cry subsided, but Golding enjoyed seeing the nods and head-wags. He had started the morning wondering about ample witnesses, and now had almost two dozen, all respectable rate-payers and voters.

'I shall have the felon charged and deliver sentence on him later today,' Golding announced. He really should have a gavel made, to some imposing design. 'Stand down, Constable Moat. I accord you the thanks of the Law for the prompt execution of your duty.'

Moat withdrew, beaming.

'Gentlemen of Sealandings,' Golding said portentously. 'I summoned you to bear witness of the evidence against Doctor Ven Carmichael. He has been nurtured, even favoured, by your good selves. Lived among you. He has enjoyed your favour, been blessed by your companionship.

'Did he deserve your trust? Did he prove reliable? One who could be given access to your homes, with confidence that he would be loyal to all you hold dear? Or did he betray that trust you so freely gave? He spread disease – by means we know not. Immediately, an epidemic of cattle plague started, destroying the affluence of Sealandings. Such an anarchic act must not go unpunished. His own words condemn him. He was apprehended while escaping. Though in hiding, he was captured by two vigilant constables. He tried to resist arrest, in itself an act proving his guilt.'

Golding felt extraordinary power. It came not from within, like the authority he had always known as one of the families ruling the Eastern Hundreds. This new power came from *them*, the people he addressed. Strange. Was this politics, or something novel he alone had discovered?

'He must suffer the harshest penalties of the law – ' he continued.

A man stood. Heads turned in surprise. It was the gunmaker, Bartholomew Hast.

'An you please, sir,' Hast said into the astonished silence. 'I ask if the miscreant himself be here.'

'No. He is confined, guarded by a special constable.' Golding was angered by this intrusion, a gross impertinence. 'By what right do you question this court?'

'No right, sir, I do acknowledge. I hear Moat's evidence passed from Mr Tyll the toll-farmer – '

'Evidence substantiated by Tyll himself, should you care to walk the Norwich road, Hast!'

'Might I humbly ask if Squire Hunterfield's will be the court where sentence will be pronounced?'

'No, Hast. This court will decide that, within the day.' Golding was fuming. Why, here was a Justice of the King's Peace being questioned by a mere tradesman! Let him step one word beyond the bounds of propriety –

'Only, I fear the felon might escape, sir, begging pardon.'

'Escape, Hast?'

Everyone was looking at the gunsmith now, a few murmuring. Golding felt his lips prickle from tension.

Hast said with humility, 'Sir, I know nothing of the law, sir. But I've heard of prisoners arguing against court rulings. And Carmichael is a London-taught man, sir. Some snakes wriggle mortal quick, faster than a pony, even!'

The murmurs of agreement grew. Golding commanded all to silence. A 'pony' was properly a bailiff, one who accompanied a debtor on brief liberty. Hast's metaphor seemed to strike a chord. Golding saw several nods. He swallowed his anger. If he was to have their votes when he stood at hustings, he must conform. Was Hast as innocent as he seemed? Or was there something deeper here? He had spoken to him only twice, and then only when ordering the conversion of out-dated Forsyth percussion fowling pieces to new style copper-cap locks.

He saw Endercotte start to rise, his expression one of Biblical thunder, and cut in.

'I promise you all. This spreader of plagues, this sinner against public morality, will not escape. He shall be sentenced. And with the sanction of the Lord of Sealandings!'

The murmurs now were of approval. Golding nodded for Lazard to dismiss the company, and strode commandingly from the hall. He was angry with Hast, but it could just be that the gunsmith had shown him how to assume greater authority still. The delay was not all loss. He had done what was necessary. Thalia would be as delighted as he himself.

As the gathering began to disperse, the gunsmith went to shake the hand of Moat in congratulation. He knew the tenant-farmer, who used a worn Manton double-barrelled fowling piece. He was a regular customer for black powder, shot and, each late summer, a half-pound of prime Suffolk flints from Grime's Graves.

'You and your nimble partner did well, Mr Moat.' He smiled at his own joke, for whispers had gone round the company that the corpulent Rodway was the second constable.

'Nimble, Mr Hast?' Moat preened in the approval. 'All he be good for is minding!'

'Somewhere secure, I trust!'

'Cannot get more secure than a tavern privy!'

The gunmaker left immediately, walking quickly. It would be the Goat and Compass, for Mehala's former services to John Weaver ruled out the Donkey and Buskin. He would risk leaving a note for Miss Baring at the rectory, then hurry to see how Doctor Carmichael fared in his temporary prison.

41

The guard by the petty was called Rodway. Ven heard him joking with the tavern maids, deep belly laughs.

It was getting on for afternoon of a brightish day, when Ven was roused by somebody knocking on the petty door. The place was cramped. Ven was crouched down, the least noisesome place with a waft of air coming beneath. The privy was nothing but a largish box over a cesspit, across which loose boards were lodged. The wattle-and-daub roof, thickly thatched, was oppressive and kept the stench in. He occasionally stood to peer out and stretch his limbs. His pains had dwindled to a constant deep ache, with occasional sharp stabs to remind him of the punishment he had undergone.

He had read once that the dejection of imprisonment was the worst, not the privation. True. Dejection from not knowing where Mehala was, his bright but vanished star. If only she would send word that she was safe, that she was not caught up in this. As long as she was spared the hatred of the Sealandings bigots . . .

Confinement's one benefit was that his crippled mind was slowly clearing. He realised with astonishment that he really must have suffered concussion. Stillness, rest, small frequent doses of nourishing fluids by mouth were all he knew for that injury. His lower lip split when involuntarily he grinned at the irony, and made him cry out. He had not had a drink since being fastened in, but rest he was getting a-plenty.

Memory was helping, strangely. The memories of Sealandings, when he and Father had walked the shores and seen the ships in the harbour. Visiting little Mary Calling, so pretty and quiet . . . who once brought a flask of small beer one hot day, skipping lightly along the shingle and shyly waving as she came. Memory, of The London Hospital's grim blackened exterior, the long bottle-green wards, the crude surgery, the deaths by gangrene, the shrieking, deformities, tumult of the lying-in rooms, fitful cries of the suffering children, the relatives blundering in the shabby wards, the ill lighting from dim lamps. The sickly stench there, too. The pathetic prayers to an ignorant and punitive God . . . And, over it all, the influence of wealth, which alone alleviated suffering, admittedly to some paltry degree. For himself, a young medical student 'walking the wards' as a surgical dresser, the repellent odour of soiled bandages. He did extra hours of duty, standing in for friends, to earn a few pence in hopes of being able to afford the entry tickets to the surgical lectures. A stout custodian stood at the lecture theatre door – was it Sparrow? – ticking off names and collecting gate money. That same servant would, for a silver sixpence, score an absent medical student as 'present' though drinking across the road at the Grave Maurice; personal attendance records gained the examining surgeons' approval, who notoriously favoured those who could prove they had been to the right lectures . . .

Ven shifted position with a groan. There had been one man, who had died. Almost his first patient. His name was Stanley, and he was dying of osteomyelitis. Stanley had tried to console Ven, whose distress was stupidly evident, to the extent of trying to recommend him a pie shop at Aldgate where, by mention of Stanley's name, Ven would get cheaper meals. A humble man, who in death tried to ease the lot of an impoverished student. That was holy. Ven felt the same ache of helplessness and ignorance now as then. So many people, children, babes, old folk, dying unaided in utter squalor, and the nose-in-air medical profession divided by bitter wrangles about precedence and privilege. And the political powers-that-be preoccupied with grandiose delusions and personal advancement. And the nation worked on burdened and oppressed by an ancient Poors' Rate system whose letter read fair but whose impact crushed . . .

'Go inside, Rodway. Is'll stand for you, booy. Has he said anything?'

'Muttered about people suffering in hospitals from the Poors' Rate, and twice asked me for water.'

'Tell Aggie the head servant to give you a quart of ale. An hour.'

'Thank you, sir! Most Christian, Masther Fowler!'

Rodway must be the short fat aggressive man, Ven thought, hearing the exchange. He sounded as breathless now as he had when dragging his prisoner back to Sealandings. Moat was the taller, both as brutal . . .

'Doctor?' It was the publican, Ben Fowler, conspiratorially close.

'Yes.' Ven's throat was dry, felt new and unused. He did not move, disqualified the hope that wanted to rise within. He stayed slumped against the wall, his boots on the soiled boards.

'I want advice, Doctor. It's my beer.'

'Your beer?' The irony was so surd he was in danger of grinning, making his cracked lip bleed all the more.

'You once mended John Weaver's beer of a souring. Mine's wrong this brewing, Doctor.'

'I mended. . . ?' Ven wearily tried to riddle his brain, but could not call the incident to mind.

'Yes, Doctor. One mash. Don't you remember? It was the talk of Sealandings. It soured fast, the sweetness all gone. You mended Weaver's yest with some fluid.'

Ven considered. His plight was hopeless, imprisoned for God-knew-what crime, facing coined punishments from a deranged and random legal system. Heartache dulled his senses, made him indolent, soporific, the sorrow eating into his spirit like a cankrous growth. What if Mehala was somehow in the same plight, incarcerated, suffering just as he? Should he not at least try to use this turn of events to some advantage, however slight? That in itself would be release of a sort.

'Listen, Doctor.' Fowler seemed almost near to panic. 'You understand local folk. Ale sickness at the Goat and Compass would bring ruination. You know that. Just tell me what's to be done.'

Bargain, Ven thought dully. That's what Mehala would say. Stand firm.

'Water, Mr Fowler. Bring me fresh water, a drink of mulled small beer, cheese and bread.' Ven felt ashamed saying the words. He had never bargained for a fee in his life, not even when wealthy patients like Prothero defaulted. And here he was, his voice thick and harsh, demanding morsels like any coachman.

'What? But . . .' *But you have never talked like this before*, Ven completed for him, and felt a small surge of power. Fowler was speaking the truth. He would be literally thrashed from the town, were he to sell spoiled ale. Fear would wield the flails, as ever. No wonder Fowler had sent the special constable off, in a show of kindness. Victuals for the gaoler, but a stinking pit for the prisoner wrongfully taken. Hate for the arbitrary system of things rose in him. He stayed calm.

'I want news of Mehala,' Ven said, astonished at his cold, precise voice. Was this what hatred did, gave power to reason ice-cold? 'Her precise whereabouts.'

'That's impossible! You don't understand! Listen, Doctor,' Fowler wheedled. 'I've not long. They could send for you any time. My chance'd be lost, see?'

'Go away, Fowler.' Ven put disgust into his tone. 'Get back to your rotting beer.'

'Please. I beg of you, sir!'

Sir, now. 'The solution is in your hands, publican,' Ven said loudly while the desperate man tried to hush him.

'Sir! Is'll strike a bargain, an you please. Give me what to do, and I promise on my mother's grave – '

'*Mehala!*' Longing and heartache to this degree was unmanly. Why then so compelling? Ven no longer cared.

'Doctor, Is'll be a broken man if word says I helped you.'

'Tit for tat, Fowler. Is'll tell Constable Rodway to cancel my pleas for a drink. I'd rather thirst than sup spoilage.'

'Doctor!' The man was sweating hard, agitated, angry. 'Listen. Promise you'll say nothing, and Is'll tell what I know.'

'Promises, is it?' Ven tried to sound mirthful, but failed. 'No, Fowler. Sealandings has a habit of forgetfulness, not mindfulness.' This truth had come late. Now he must act on it.

'Very well. Wait.'

Ven heard him leave, and pondered. It was an effort. How had he cured the sick ferment at the Donkey and Buskin? There had been some casual chat with John Weaver, he vaguely recalled. Something about the malt's cooling, the foolish prejudices against iron cooling pans or traditional wood. And the temperature. Or whether to beat in the crusting yest or leave it atop the gyle or fermenting tun . . . The inconstancy of brewing practices throughout England was notorious, no two counties doing alike. Far different from the Continent, where the 'double beer', the famous Brunswick mum, was so constant that its import had become a national scandal, leading to the prohibitive tax of fifteen shillings a barrel in old Queen Anne's reign. It was still talked of.

Some things were common knowledge, of course. They had entered everyday speech. The grist once ground, and stirred with hot water in the mashing tun, was called *the goods*, and 'delivering the goods' had become a commonplace. But such snippets did not help much, now Ben Fowler was begging for superior knowledge. Ignorance, always the enemy. If knighthoods were given for bewilderment . . .

'Doctor?' Fowler was back, breathing hard. 'I've got sure news. Mehala has left Sealandings. After the floods, she gained the gunsmith's help in finding you at the sea cottages, but you had gone from Raffin's. She and Miss Baring from the rectory seek you. Mehala stayed at Whitehanger – a carter, one Darling. She has gone out inland, on the Norwich road. She passed the tollgate afoot.'

Ven felt his eyes prick, and for a while said nothing.

'The floods? What was Mehala to the floods?' He vaguely remembered the two constables speaking of the sealands, but that part was all a haze. He put his ear close to the door while the taverner spoke long and fast. As he listened, his chest began to fill with a strange serenity. The landlord's whispered words tumbled out. There could be only one explanation for Mehala's actions: she was unaware of his capture, and had set out to follow him to St Albans. Bless her heart, her dear loyal, loving heart.

He found himself smiling, his eyes stinging.

Mary Prothero sent for the two women without delay when she became aware of their endless differences. Hobbes the chief servant was ordered to find out the reasons for their constant affrays, but reported failure. It was a housekeeping matter, of textures, purchases, colours, outside his competence.

Mary watched them approach her across the panelled room. She was no stranger to such disputes, and had often exercised her authority at Calling Farm in similar household battles. Reconciliation was always possible, but ever since arriving at Carradine she had felt this undercurrent of seething resentment. It was not so much against herself, oddly, but between Mrs Tyll and Miss Blaker.

The two women were strikingly different. Judith Blaker was dark, yet admirable of features, so aquiline and deliberate. She was not tall – it was her stance that seemed to make her compact form so. She possessed the curious attribute of seeming motionless whether gliding across a carpet or hurrying to complete some task. Barbara Tyll on the other hand was pale, somewhat taller, always trying to seem willing and even kindly. But whereas Tyll was simply quiet, Blaker was silent. What passed for frank agreeability in Barbara Tyll was opaque obedience in Judith Blaker. The newcomer had seemingly proved a godsend, according to Mr Greyburn, who as bailiff and head steward of the Carradine estates since they had passed to Jason had been responsible for finding the right workmen to repair the storm damage. She had been instrumental in somehow obtaining the services of many excellent artisans and maids.

More strikingly, the new skilled men and indoor servants, now numbering more than a dozen, had remained loyal to Carradine Manor in spite of the growing agitation about the outbreak of disease in Sealandings. These considerations only increased Mary Prothero's difficulties.

'Good day to you, Mrs Tyll, Miss Blaker.'

She had a set scheme: *never ask*. Taught her by her mother, a wise if otherwise ineffectual lady. Mary often sighed over her mother, God rest her, wishing she had passed a little resolution to her only daughter. 'There will be tea provided for you both in the garden withdrawing room, after we have spoken. I learned today of a complaint. Before inviting your accounts of the matter, I wish you both to learn of my disapproval of the manner in which the problem came to my notice. A travelling merchant draper's report is *not* the usual way for a lady to become apprised of a dispute in her own house.'

The silence told Mary she was dealing with experts. Neither wanted to speak first.

She had to prompt. 'I hear there is an argument about the purchase of a select scarlet silk.'

Judith Blaker could contain herself no longer and burst out, 'If you please, ma'am, I gave instructions that your orders were to be followed exactly. The scarlet silk is of excellent quality. You yourself decided the price was reasonable. I simply passed on your instructions. I asked the draper's assistant to re-measure his bolts, and found your orders suspended!'

'I see,' Mary said slowly. Still she would not bring herself to form a direct question. Barbara Tyll stood like a statue in dress.

Judith Blaker coursed on. 'I sent the maid Prettiance to keep check on the assistant. When I returned to Gaskell, Mrs Tyll had countermanded your order!'

'Those events seem clear, Blaker.' Mary turned to Barbara Tyll. 'I am sure there is some ready explanation, Mrs Tyll.'

The paler woman inclined her head. No ambition here, Mary thought, beyond those of a normal competency. She was sure this woman was honest, though Blaker was trying to hint of dark dealings. The commonest way of defrauding a household was for servants to come to a private arrangement with suppliers – drapers, haberdashers, vintners, carters, postmen even – whereby continued placement of a great family's custom depended on a secret bribe, usually a halfpenny in the shilling.

'I suggest that Gaskell be summoned and his word taken, ma'am!' Blaker shot in. 'I'm sure it won't be the first time he's been asked for Jew's portion, a fob, as bribe is called, ma'am.'

'Mrs Tyll has yet to speak, Blaker.'

'If you please, ma'am,' Tyll said quietly. 'I mistrust the scarlet silk shown.'

'On what grounds, madam?' Blaker said hotly. 'Ma'am, she dares contradict you!'

Barbara Tyll waited until the mistress' gesture to silence had taken effect.

'Silk cannot be dyed a full scarlet, ma'am. The material shown you is faulty.'

Mary felt her cheeks redden in embarrassment. She herself had seen the wonderful scarlet silk, among several bright colours, and been enthralled.

'On what grounds do you say this, Tyll?'

'If you please, ma'am. The small sample shown is not silk. It is finest cotton thread, which takes scarlet well – murio-sulphur salt of tin, then cochineal followed by quercitron bark, as used for silk proper.'

'The silks were genuine, Tyll.'

'Indeed, ma'am. But the single sample of scarlet silk shown you was not. It is a common deception practised by wandering drapers. The cotton, which takes such a dye well though fleetingly, is spun to the greatest degree of thinness, dyed and then oiled in some manner I do not know, to simulate the feel of silk's consistency.'

There was silence, during which Blaker made to speak but was quietened by the mistress' mute admonition.

'Go on, Tyll.'

The housekeeper had gone quite pale. 'Silk is dyed red, usually with cochineal, ma'am, but sometimes carthamus or Brazil wood. A trace of madder has been used in the trick sample. It has taken up the dye well enough, except pure silk will not take up madder to give a good enough colour.'

'That is where she is wrong, ma'am!' Blaker erupted. 'Archil is used to give silk a bloom, which shows how little this woman knows!'

'Archil *is* employed, ma'am,' Tyll spoke on. 'But never by itself, unless the desired colour be lilac.'

Mary was out of her depth. 'You are wondrously well informed, Mrs Tyll.'

'I am of a dyer's family, ma'am.'

'And of a vagabond's too, by her knowledge of trickery!'

Barbara Tyll refused to rise at the insult. 'I was told the trick of mimicking silk by the sea-girl Mehala, ma'am, in the town market, three weeks agone. She showed me several samples.'

Blaker's expression was murderous. Mary thought of the curious facility with which the darker woman had used Gaskell's name, how surely she had known what his statement would be when questioned, even though by her own account she was with the maid-of-all Prettiance when Tyll challenged the draper's assistant. And was it not Blaker who had brought in Prettiance for hire, an obscure relative?

'Mehala could be questioned, ma'am, and her opinion tried against samples. I admit I may be wrong,' Tyll quietly concluded, 'but felt obliged to ask that the order be reconsidered. If I am in error, I apologise, ma'am.'

'Who knows who this Mehala is?' Blaker cried in exasperation. 'Ma'am, she is nothing but a vagrant! Would Mr Prothero permit such a test, to hinge on the word of sea-brought flotsam?'

'Thank you both. You may go.'

Mary waited until both had left the room, then rang for Hobbes and told him to bring Gaskell.

The draper was a smiley, rotund man with a breezy manner, fresh and brisk, but now affecting a diffident frown as he entered.

'Please tell me the conversation between yourself and Mrs Tyll,' Mary asked, feeling angry at herself for weakness. She instinctively felt Barbara Tyll was speaking the truth, as surely as she knew Judith Blaker was not. Yet here she was, asking this wandering draper's account, simply because Blaker had mentioned Jason's name and hinted he would be furious at her handling of the dispute.

'Now, please, ma'am,' Gaskell said, rubbing his hands and clearing his throat. 'I have no argument with the two housekeeper ladies, I assure ma'am. But I have to say that one was, ah, most suggestively inviting me to make a contribution to her reticule, if you understand me . . .'

'No, sir,' Mary said sharply. 'I do not understand. Explain!'

'The taller lady said I could have the order, on payment of a tithe to her good self, ma'am.'

'Tyll? Asked for a bribe?'

'Most regrettable, ma'am. Such things do go on, even in the very best regulated households. Now, ma'am, if I could suggest a slight compromise, it might seem best if one lady was placed in complete charge – '

'That will do, Gaskell,' Mary said in quiet fury. There was no other way now. She would have to let Barbara Tyll go. 'The order is cancelled.'

'Cancelled, ma'am?' Gaskell cried in dismay. 'But the silks – '

'Hobbes?' Mary called, and Gaskell retreated, still protesting and calling discounts.

For some time Mary sat in solitary contemplation. This was hard, and more than a little disturbing. Barbara Tyll was reliable, firm and some kind of ally. Even before Carradine had lost his fortune, she had been a mainstay of the Manor, keeping the main house functioning as well as any of the great family homes in Sealandings. Now, on the word of a wandering merchant – whose presence in Sealandings at a time of cattle plague was more than a little curious – Tyll, whose husband kept the tollgate reliably enough, was to be bagged, leaving Judith Blaker as the housekeeper. It was an unpleasant duty, one Mary felt she had been forced into by trickery.

She sent for Hobbes, and told him to bring Mrs Tyll to her forthwith.

42

The man at the tollgate was inclined to talk, wanting to complain about the absence of herds on the Sealandings road, the paucity of his takings, the frightening dearth of waggons coming through. Mehala heard him out as she paused for a rest against the nearby stile. She had already gone past, so as not to be misunderstood, and observed that he must lead an active life.

'Indeed, Miss,' Tyll told her, pleased at the diversion. 'I had the Doctor through here, and constables appointed to chase him. Now, he's a gentleman of the Three Ins. He'd been sore beaten. I've never heard but good of the man.'

'Did they take him?' Mehala felt faint at the thought of being spared her journey, for the worst of reasons. The Three Ins were Tyll's commontalk. The chilling joke ran: in gaol, in debt, in danger of life imprisonment.

'They did truly. While yet dark, having caught him skulking – their word. But what man does not sleep by night, and travel by day?'

A tinker's tax cart came by, with a licence number and name painted on the side. Mehala took the opportunity to start off, bidding the toll-farmer a good day. The tinker called out to her as a gilflurt, but she walked on unheeding, hearing Tyll reprimand the man.

Her heart was beating fast as she stepped out, for it was important that she be thought to have left Sealandings. Others coming through would find Tyll as free with his chatter as every toll-piker ever was. Let foes, even friendly ones like Miss Euterpe, assume she had gone.

This part of the road was new to her, for she had never even been up to the tollpike hitherto, barely coming in sight of it from Two Cotts when brought in the carriage by Simple Tom.

Only when she was sure the toll-barrier had gone from view did she take stock. Tall trees hid her on one side, but on the Carradine Manor side, to seaward, the land fell away sharply behind a thick screen of hawthorn and sloe twined about with dog rose and bramble. That might be one way, except she would have to await a distraction before she could chance the detour. Unless she walked left, and followed some track between the tenant farms? All the Eastern Hundreds was crisscrossed by ancient cattle trackways, unseen from the turnpike roads, free to the foot traveller still in spite of the terrible enclosures of common land. Yes, that was the way.

In less than two miles she found such a track, and hurried on to it. It rose slowly for some hundreds of yards. She emerged on a slight tumulus, from where she could see out to sea. Down below was the town. The roof of the tollgate house was visible, but nothing of the road, until the gaggle of houses and their red tiled roofs and thatches showed about the slanted roof of the Corn Mart, near the squat tower of St Edmund the Martyr. Smoke from cottage fires hung on the air. The sky seemed to go on for ever into its own thin cloud mist. Far beyond, she could see to the south the curve of the bay of Sealandings, with Watermillock's bright blue-and-white exterior showing.

It was then, smiling with certainty that back there lay her man, that she became aware of a sour, acrid and offensive scent. It hung on the air, thick and ugly. She cast around searching for the origin, and saw over to her right, away from the shore and the ships riding at anchor between the Moles, dark palls of smoke rising slowly from the farms lying south-west of the town. She had met that hideous aroma once before, when the sweating sickness had afflicted cattle around Maldon. Then, the whole estuary there had been overhung by that same grievous death stink. They were burning dead cattle in Sealandings. In Calling Farm, from the location of the densest plumes, and its tenancies, seemingly Nelmes' tenancy among them. She raised herself on tiptoe to try to see, and found the skies over Lorne House's land evidently quite clear. Some farmers buried dead cattle, others burned, some left whole herds to rot, for no one knew what should be done. Others simply left their farms and ran to cities, spreading rumour. But it boded ill for the town, and all the Eastern Hundreds. No wonder Mr Tyll had grumbled and shaken his head. People were simply terrified of a murrain.

Squire Hunterfield was the man. There could be no more

questions of pride, purity of motive. He had offered his help freely. She had to accept it for Ven Carmichael's sake. If she had to run any gauntlets to reach Hunterfield, why, she would run them and take the consequences. If it was he who had ordered Ven's capture, she would throw herself on his mercy and beg for Ven to be given back to her. To herself. To be his. He had done nothing wrong, that she knew. She would swear it. If it was not the Squire's doing, then he must rescue Ven. She found herself walking quickly, almost at a run, between the hedges towards Sealandings. If this trackway led past the church on its way through the countryside, she would call at the rectory and tell Miss Euterpe what she now knew. Perhaps that lady had learned how Doctor Carmichael had come to be labelled a criminal. Find that, and he was on the way to being saved.

'Ticklish times,' Prothero told himself. He felt old today, deceived, betrayed. He had spent part of the day at Two Cotts in seclusion with one of the abbesses there, though he felt unsatisfied this time. Oh, the nun, as prostitutes were called, had plied him right enough, with Madeira wine and relief, but it was sawdust relish. And that gapstopper, the whoremistress, had been offensive when he settled his bill. She had grumbled openly about the blight on trade caused by the outbreak at Calling Farm, and the three deaths among the labourers. 'Nine milkmaids and four more booys now down with the ailment,' she preached. He flung the money at her, the poxed bitch, and threw himself out of the place.

He dismounted at the main steps, snapping abuse at the groom who came to take the gelding's bridle, when Carradine hallooed from the drive and rode up, sliding from the saddle without invitation and casting the reins to the now-smiling groom.

'Glad to happen on you, Prothero. We need exchange a word.'

'I am busy today, Carradine.' Prothero eyed the man. Here was a vestige of the old Carradine, the grand scion he had dispossessed.

'Not for me, Prothero, I think.'

'You have some new information?'

'A great deal.' Carradine started up the steps, talking over his shoulder as he went. Prothero had no option but to accompany him. 'I now see what a plight you are in. Terrible for one of your breeding, to suffer so. I am here with a little neighbourly advice in your hour of need.'

'I am not in need, sir!'

'No?' Carradine turned so swiftly Prothero thought for one moment he was about to strike him. Then he stared over the formal gardens, seeing the men at work among the shrubs and the mazes, and smiled. It was an owner's smile. 'No, Prothero? You know otherwise, sir. Am I to give you the benefit of my opinions, or am I to go, and never grace this doorstep again until such time as. . . ?'

'Until what time, sir?' Prothero demanded, his voice ugly with anger at Carradine's impertinence.

'Until such time as you are cast out from every rod, pole, perch, stetch, acre, copse you hold, sir. Until you wander the land in a state of destitution, with every man's hand raised to damn you, sir.'

Carradine stepped aside, bowing. For a moment Prothero was unable to see why, then saw Mary standing aghast in the main doorway. Judith Blaker stood in the shadows behind her.

'Ma'am, I apologise,' Carradine said smoothly to Mary. 'I spoke words unfit for a lady's hearing.'

'That will be all, Blaker.' Mary waited until the housekeeper had made a reluctant withdrawal, her tardiness almost bringing a laugh from Carradine. Now Blaker would depend on *him* for account of what was said. The spy unspied!

Mary explained to her husband, 'I came to welcome you with the household news.' She addressed Carradine, her face pale. 'May I ask what transpires with my husband's situation, sir?'

'I mislike to bring ill news, Mrs Prothero.' Carradine spoke with seeming reluctance. 'Somebody has informed on your husband's scheme to land contraband at the Carradine Manor jetties during the dark hours. The Excise night-riders have imposed a watch on Carradine lands – and a sea embargo. This has never happened before in our history, Mistress Prothero. I came here, at great cost to my own situation, simply in order to try to prevent any further damage – '

'This is utterly, damnably false, sir!' Prothero thundered, pacing the porch and gesticulating. 'I shall have the law on anyone who imputes – !'

'The law already takes its course, Prothero!' Carradine exclaimed harshly. 'Face it, man! Your scheme to land tobaccos and spiritous liquors from the Continent in defraud of Excise is known. The man Giffler is sought. Word is he has a rich accomplice at Carradine Manor. Who, Prothero? You cannot have been so foolish as to believe that it would have gone unnoticed, in a place like Sealandings? God, man! Every man, woman and infant knows everything that happens here! The news was passed to the Customs the minute you conceived the plan – I am sure of it!'

'Utterly false, Carradine!' Prothero was pale to his lips now.

'Who else but you stands in such need, Prothero? Nobody. I admit I, alone of the gentry hereabouts, formerly stood in your station, but I no longer live here. The jetties, land, the men, are yours. And the motive, Prothero.'

'Motive? To defraud the King?' Prothero almost whispered the words. Mary had drawn to her husband's side, white-faced.

'I visited Calling Farm. It is almost derelict. You passed no true information to the neighbouring gentry?'

'It was true.'

'It might have been true for one day, or even two. But now people have died, Prothero. Your tenants have the right of redress. As has Golding, now a magistrate. And Milton Hall. And God alone knows who else! All Sealandings is in the pillory. The magistracy is assembling at the Corn Mart, to make decisions about your conduct. I would not be surprised to see Customs officers attending.'

'This cannot be.' Prothero glanced at his wife, who gazed imploringly at him. 'It is prefabrication. A falsehood, start to finish.'

'The lights, man. Riding lights, placed on the jetties these past two centuries, were extinguished by your order.'

'That is untrue!' Prothero cried. 'Dear God, how many times must I tell you? I gave no such order! I was unaware until your words that any riding lights were ever hung out! I swear it!'

Carradine shook his head in rue. 'I dearly wish to help, Prothero. It was I who effected your rise, unwillingly of course, but now I feel it was to the good. It restored me, saved me from a life of dissipation. I mean this.'

'Help? Help how?' It was all suddenly so wrong. Prothero had no reason to believe Carradine, but it would do no harm to hear the man out. And no servants were in earshot.

'And why, Rad?' Mary asked quietly. 'You above all have no reason to support my husband.'

Prothero stifled an urge to reprimand her. She had a point.

'Look around, Mary,' Carradine said evenly. 'Look at the place. A thousand years, more, of tending and building, controlling, guiding. If your husband sinks to ruin, all will go with him. The law knows no limits to any man's purse save the stitches. This house will vanish. The Carradine name. Maps will be redrawn. Sealandings will have lost one of the noblest family crests ever borne. I shall survive, yes. My fortunes might rise again. But the shame of having seen Carradine Manor ruined, its great lands overgrown by scrub, its farms desolate heath, would damn me for ever. How could I face my ancestors? So I swallow my pride, and come with this offer.'

'What offer, Rad?' Mary asked before Prothero could speak. She linked her arm through her husband's.

'Return to Calling Farm, Mary. Leave here.'

Prothero inhaled with a hissing noise, ready for a hot denial. Mary managed to still him.

'Hear me out,' Carradine said. 'Leave. Cope with your epidemic of cattle plague as best you can. That one act would convince the magistracies that you have not simply run away.'

'A posture that seeks approval? Is that your suggestion?'

Carradine acknowledged the man's scorn. He had been ready for it, gone over the very words in long rehearsals with Judith Blaker.

'That, and more. You are a skilled farmer. It would restore confidence in Sealandings. It would give the lie to any who accused you of obfuscating, telling untruths about the murrain. Deny your own words!'

'That would be quite wrong!' Mary exclaimed.

Prothero was already nodding slowly, seeing the sense of Carradine's words. 'And the sea lights?'

'Once you are back to Calling Farm, who could say the reasons that caused the lights to be dowsed? When the . . . ' Carradine had difficulty for a moment. 'When the former master is departed, and the new master has not yet had time to install himself, who can cast blame? As tonight would be the second night without, so they say in the taverns – I happened to overhear a man speaking about it – who can point the finger at you, if you are at Calling Farm?'

'That is right.' Prothero stood motionless, staring past Carradine, thinking hard. 'Who could?'

He seemed to have shrunk, perhaps from the effect of the illness he had suffered, perhaps the worry. Carradine could hardly forbear laughing at the figure Prothero presented. To think that he had once been almost in awe of the oaf! And him raised on nothing more than tailor's ragout – bread soaked in the redundant oil-vinegar slop after slicing cucumber! Now look! A Chancery Lane comic show.

'There would be the stewardship of this Manor,' Prothero mused.

'I could offer my services,' Carradine said, frowning as if assessing possibilities. 'Except I am committed to wait on a family inland, though for one day only.' He added disarmingly, seeing the flash of distrust in Prothero's eye, 'I should promise in writing, before witnesses, to be here only as your accredited agent. And for any stated period you wish. I would hate to be thought wheedling my way into your residence!'

'Witnessed and signed?' Prothero pursed his lips.

'Drawn up legally,' Carradine said blandly. 'The lawyers could execute it in the next few weeks. Or have the agreement written and witnessed within the day, then pass it to the lawyers to register at their convenience. Whichever suits.'

'It would have to be done speedily, if at all.'

'One caution, if you please, Prothero.' Carradine spoke almost penitentially. 'Take other counsel. From your friends, relatives. Act only when you are sure, and then with circumspection.' He permitted himself a wistful smile. 'So much has happened to my own fortunes these past few months that I am loth to proffer advice.' He gave Prothero sign he was ready to leave, and Prothero rang the grooms' bell. Carradine was finding the new role of confidant hugely enjoyable, even though the consequences would be the instantaneous ruin of this low-born bumpkin. He was particularly pleased at having advised this dullard to take counter-advice from friends. As if a loon had any!

389

'I shall consider your advice, Carradine, and thank you for calling by.'

'My pleasure,' Carradine said. He was disappointed the idiot had not leaped instantly at his offer. 'I wish you and your lady good fortune.'

'How may I reach you, should I decide to accept?'

'I shall be calling at Milton Hall this evening, before I leave Sealandings. You could address a note to me in care of Thalia De Foe.'

Jason Prothero seemed to draw breath to speak, but stayed silent. The Protheros stood on the verandah as Carradine rode away on his hired mount, concealing his exultation. Soon he would be back in Carradine. Possession was nine parts of the law.

The rectory gate was ajar, Reverend Baring there bidding goodbyes to Mr Bettany the windmiller. Mehala avoided the risk of calling on Miss Euterpe, and moved quickly down the slope of Market Square. Parker the public stabler was walking on ahead of them, evidently just having left their company. Endercotte, as always carrying his Bible like a staff of office, stalking solitary in his black crow's garb, frowned to see a woman in haste. She gave him no greeting, knowing that gentleman's propensity for condemnation. Some gathering of religionists had taken place, a disturbing thought. More people were coming from the south-easterly corner of the Square, talking together. Bures House lay that way, a few furlongs along the trackway to Whitehanger. And Golding was now magistrate.

She was alongside the Corn Mart, thinking to knock at Hast's gunmaker shop, when she heard her name called. Euterpe Baring was standing under cover, almost lurking in the shadow.

'Miss Euterpe! Have you news? I heard that special constables have taken – '

'Quickly, Mehala.' Miss Baring surreptitiously watched the rectory gate, where her brother conversed with Bettany. 'I must not be seen. Bartholomew Hast called upon me but five minutes since. There was a meeting – '

'Ven,' Mehala interrupted, knowing her pallor was all-revealing, but beyond care. 'Where is he?'

'The Goat and Compass, taken by Rodway, a special constable.

He is locked there. A meeting will be held tonight. Mr Hast persuaded Sir Charles Golding to stay his hand until the Squire gives approval. Mr Hast has gone to see Doctor Carmichael, and will return to tell me.'

'Thank you, Miss Euterpe.' Mehala almost flew from beneath the shelter of the Corn Mart. She heard Euterpe Baring call something after, but could not wait.

The Goat and Compass lay beyond the sea cottages, inside the North Mole. Its coaching yard was the stand for the coastal coaches. Not a very lucrative trade, for they competed with small coastal craft that plied swifter, and a great deal cheaper in these turbulent times. Mehala crossed the front of the place, avoiding the flint-cobbled concourse, and went quickly round to the rear. Aggie, an enemy she knew well, raised her head from filling buckets at the yard pump, and stared after her, then ran in. Mehala ignored her.

She heard voices in the coachyard. Relief weakened her of a sudden, for one of the voices was Bartholomew Hast's. He was arguing in anger.

She entered under the coach arch, and stood appalled. Rodway and Ben Fowler held a dishevelled, crumpled figure upright between them. The features were so begrimed she hardly recognised Ven. His eyebrows were caked with old blood. The stubble on his chin was matted with dried blood and mud. His surtout was filthed and torn. His hands were ungloved, the knuckles bloody. The small finger of his left hand stuck out at an impossible angle. He had lost one boot and sock. He was hardly conscious, and would have fallen if it were not for the two men. The gunsmith was standing in their way on the path to the privy.

'This man is in custody for Squire Hunterfield!' Hast was saying loudly. 'You incur his wrath, I warn you!'

Mehala ran, almost weeping with impotent fury, and tried to put her hand to Carmichael. She was thrust away by Rodway.

'Stand clear in the name of the law!' the special constable yelled.

'This prisoner is in the protection of the Lord of Sealandings!' Hast yelled, even louder. 'Injury done to him will be answered for in the Squire's court! I shall bring testimony!'

Mehala heard a commotion behind, and saw several people emerge from the inn, curious to see the cause of the din. She realised Bartholomew's strategy, to raise enough noise to attract witnesses. She tried to reach Ven. He seemed delirious, bewildered. Ben Fowler rudely shoved her away.

'That's it, master!' Aggie rushed up to join the affray, mob cap askew and her stained apron caught up in its ties. 'Let me see to the harlot!'

Mehala caught her with a wide swing across the face and sent her sprawling, astonishment on the maid's face and blood spattering from her nose. It was lucky, but Mehala felt pure relish at the contact. She rounded on Rodway and Fowler.

'Gentlemen! Whatever crimes Doctor Carmichael has committed, they were at *my* instigation! Whatever guilt he stands accused of, it is mine. Let him go. I shall stand in his place.'

'His libber pleads for the traitor!' Aggie screeched from the ground, weeping, touching her face for blood.

The watching crowd muttered, started to withdraw at the feared accusation of treachery. Aggie's incoherent remark took away all the benefit of inquisitive spectators. Very well, Mehala thought, and stepped up to stand by the special constable while Bartholomew Hast tried to intervene.

'Please, Mehala. Come with me. I shall make a direct plea at Lorne House, and you along of me.'

'No, Mr Hast. I thank you.' She spoke directly to Rodway, ignoring the publican. 'Mr Rodway. You are charged by the law to apprehend Doctor Carmichael, I take it? Then you have no choice but to apprehend me also. For I serve him, and aid and abet all his work, good or bad.'

'Mehala.' The young gunmaker was distressed, and vainly looked about as if hoping assistance would come riding to the rescue any moment.

'No, Mr Hast.' Gently she reached across to touch Ven's face, tears blurring her vision at his swollen eyes and blood-rimmed lips. 'No. This is my place now. Beg aid for us if you will, with my gratitude. But I stay.'

She heard herself with a kind of wonderment. Us. At last and finally. No longer *me, he,* two separate people. Us.

'I surrender myself to Constable Rodway,' she said simply. 'I abide by the law.'

'There's no space for two in that place,' Rodway said. This was making him uncomfortable. Just his luck to be left in charge of this mayhem, with Moat sunning himself before grand admirers. 'The cellar, Mr Fowler?'

Fowler licked his lips. He too hated the difficulties he was saddled with.

'Very well.' He gauged the gunmaker's intentions, but Hast stood aside with a curt nod. The physician was almost beyond giving him any advice about the sick ale now, bad cess to the felon. That would have to wait. 'Adjoining the main cellar.'

'Bring the girl,' Rodway wheezed, taking the opportunity to mop his brow.

'Allow me to lead.' Mehala stepped ahead of them, pausing a fraction as she came alongside Aggie, who withdrew a pace. Then she continued on past. The gunsmith watched them go.

43

Fellows De Foe had ridden out to the shoot with Hunterfield, Percy Carmady and Sir Jeremy Pacton, and a few of the favoured tenant-farmers chosen from as far afield as Saltworth and Maidborough. The gentry's ladies brought hampers, and picnicked by the broughams and phaetons. Pacton, a friend of the De Foes, always saw himself as a gay blade, in spite of his father's increasing admonitions to 'settle down'. He dressed in the height of wrong fashion.

'So as to impair any chance of success!' he joked, eager to get the rustic pursuit over with and enjoy converse on the coloured rugs servants had laid for the food and drink.

The ladies were charmed, all except Thalia De Foe. She felt there on sufferance, and talked with the Hunterfield ladies as if at penance. Tabitha irritated her from the outset, by speaking of Carradine. Not that Tabitha could possibly know of her own preoccupation with him: she was too green and stupid. Thalia was meticulous about secrecy – what woman was not? So she listened, seemingly offhand but with mounting annoyance, as the ignorant little trollop bandied words about a man she knew nothing of. Thalia now understood love, whatever Carradine's character. Nobody else could understand.

'Carradine seeks the company of the Astells,' Tabitha Hunterfield informed the ladies confidentially. 'I cannot reveal my sources, but twice have had letters from Maidborough.'

'I remember meeting him,' Mercy Carmady said vaguely. Her eyes were on the distant figure of Hunterfield, signalling to his line of beaters on the valley shoulder. Tabitha noticed Mercy's prolonged stare, quite wanton in this company. She was beginning to dislike Mercy. La Carmady had shamelessly manipulated her brother to obtain invitation to today's shooting party. She could tolerate Olivia Maderley, who so far had contributed very little to the conversation, thankfully knowing her place as Letty's art teacher's sister.

'Carradine will perhaps seek the company of a *particular* Miss Astell!'

'Oh?' Lydia Vallance smiled tolerantly at her younger sister, who knew so little but tried to know so much. 'Brillianta, or Lorela?'

Tabitha grew excited, unaware of the effect the conversation was having on Mrs De Foe. 'Let's play a game!' she cried, clapping her hands. 'We decide the proposal of a gentleman to a lady, sparing no one! I shall start with Carradine!'

Thalia De Foe would have felt langorous today, but under these circumstances a purring repletion was clearly impossible. The revelation of the nature of her love for Carradine, transcendental and worth any risk, assuaged her soul. And there was a special fillip. Carradine's departure to see the Protheros at Carradine Manor, in response to an urgent letter for Carradine from those jumped-up peasants, maddened her beyond measure. Carradine had simply ridden furiously off without a word. She had stormed into her dressing room and thrashed Meg, accusing that sullen bitch of interrupting her summerhouse meeting with Carradine for no other purpose than self titillation. It had calmed her. Whipping a servant always did. The sheer physical exertion, the beautiful immediacy of the red weals appearing on Meg's back, the sound of the sharp crack with each fall of the crop, the stifled whimpers, were almost as thrilling as the savagery Carradine inflicted upon her own body. Afterwards, she had lowered herself on the bedside chair, dabbing her wrists and upper lip with lavender water, watching as the lines on the prone girl's flesh grew darker scarlet. This brought flavour to discipline, a relish that mere obedience spoiled. Once, after a shuddering love, Carradine idly asked if she did not punish her abigail too much. Thalia had laughed openly, chiding him for a simpleton. The peasant class expected it. They wanted their place in society reaffirmed. It gave them a sense of security, for it was ordained by God. He had shrugged, forgotten it when taking her a second time with rough impatience.

'. . . Mrs De Foe?'

She came to. Tabitha, asking her turn in the little cow's stupid game, evidently.

'What do you think, Mrs De Foe?' Tabitha was excited. 'I suggest Carradine and Letitia!'

'A fine match, Tabitha.'

Thalia was screamingly bored with this silliness, and with the Hunterfield ladies, and with dull Olivia Maderley. And with the rapacious Mercy Carmady, who so far had only ogled Henry Hunterfield. Thalia smirked inwardly. She herself had secretly used Hunterfield for many months to advance Carradine's ambitions. It had not come to anything, on account of Carradine's unlucky gambling streak. This time, with Cousin Charles now a Sealandings magistrate, all would be easy. The first exhibition of his new-got legal power was now due, with the trial of Doctor Carmichael and his doxy Mehala. She herself had stressed its importance to Charles. The few times Carradine had mentioned Mehala there had been something disturbing in his voice, though Carradine had hardly exchanged more than a few words with the wanton harlot. As far as she knew.

Olivia Maderley's cheeks coloured a little. She recognised the jibe. A hundred yards away, her brother William was at his easel, painting the landscape and, presumably, the shooters. Close by, Letitia was seated at a portable easel, making watercolour sketches.

'Miss Letitia's artistic skill goes far beyond my brother's expectations, Miss Tabitha,' Olivia told the other candidly. 'He is astonished at her aptitude.'

'Imagine how delighted we are to hear that, Olivia!' Tabitha responded brightly. 'Of course, I had no doubt but that Letitia would excel. Does she not at simply everything?'

Shots came in a ragged volley as the coveys rose. Tabitha clapped her hands and called congratulations. Sir Jeremy Pacton turned and waved to the ladies. Several dogs were sent on fetch. A rider approaching on a spent mount drew rein to avoid the activity. It was Simple Tom, her brother's personal groom. She realised she had not seen him attending Henry for some time. His absence had gone unnoticed in the furore of visitors.

'Such a pretty, moving sight!' Tabitha cried. 'Letitia will weep for the birds, you see!'

Lydia was cross with Tabby for implying criticism of Letitia this way, but could not say so in company. She checked the hampers. The drinks and liquors could have been better packed, she thought, but as the supervision had been left to Tabitha it was fortunate that any beverages were come at all.

'Could you please see to the crockery, Tabby dear?' she asked sweetly. It was a command. Tabitha obeyed with ill grace, but kept to her game.

'While we ready the picnic for the gentlemen, ladies, I insist we consider the next eligible: I nominate my brother Henry!'

Lydia interrupted briskly, 'Tabitha, your game can wait, please. First see the servants have set twelve courses and a sufficiency of drinking glasses. Otherwise we shall have to call some servants over, which will displease me.'

'Very well, Lydia dear!' Tabitha set to, kneeling on the travelling Wilton, the colours of which went rather well with her white and green riding-coat dress, trimmed as it was with brandenburgs. The contrary mock-severity of the bodice made Mercy Carmady's redingote and its falbalas look plainly silly, while Olivia Maderley's muted pastels vanished in comparison. Letitia had striven yet again for plainness. Sister Lydia was married, as was that vicious bitch Thalia De Foe, so that was that! She felt glorious, the most admirable among all the ladies present. 'I think Mr Maderley *must* consider Miss Carmady. What of it, Mercy?'

Mercy Carmady dragged her eyes from the line of sportsmen and tried to enter into the spirit of Tabitha's play.

'I am certain Mr Maderley's reputation will carry him far beyond myself, Miss Tabitha. He already has new works appearing in the London salons, has he not, Miss Olivia?'

'Yes.' Olivia was relieved as Mercy deflected the subject on to safer ground. 'His *Leaping Horse* has attracted notice, and recent landscapes have – '

'There!' Tabitha exclaimed, smiling. 'Two happy couples rejoicing in as many minutes! Which leaves – '

'You, Tabitha.' Mrs De Foe was all smiling innocence. 'We cannot allow you to escape! Who will it be?'

'Me?' Tabitha felt excitement stir. There was a brilliant glitter of malice in Mrs De Foe's eyes she had never seen before, and wondered why. Suddenly this was less of a game. She ignored Lydia's gesture to open the largest of the seven wicker hampers, and smiled in riposte at Thalia. 'I fear that all the truly wonderful gentlemen of the district are already taken, alas!'

'Always assuming your suggestions take place!'

Tabitha felt her mind spin of a sudden. *Mrs De Foe has an association with . . . someone!* Thalia's gleaming eyes, the incisive words, their meaning scarcely veiled, could only add up to one thing –

'Tabitha!' Lydia's sharp reprimand cut through her reverie. 'Miss! If I must tell you once again to stop daydreaming, I shall have to send you home with the servants!'

Tabitha stammered compliance and set to, hurrying to distribute the dishes. The revelation shocked her. Who? Surely not Henry? Unthinkable! Carradine! Lieutenant Percy Carmady, whose sister Mercy it seemed had returned to her distant eyeing of the shooters on the green incline below? But he was yet hardly in the district. And how did a married lady manage to have a clandestine relationship with a naval gentleman, forever at sea? Or was it spontaneous, during these past few days? Or Sir Jeremy Pacton, that rather foppish London aristocrat with high connections? His visits to Sealandings were surely too infrequent. The certainty struck her that . . . *Lydia knew*. Her elder sister was too waspish, speaking far too abruptly for her sudden mild asperity to ring true. She decided to risk further displeasure.

'I shall cast lots, Mrs De Foe,' she said with a gay smile. 'And trust to fortune.'

'Among whom, though, Tabitha?' Thalia would not let go. 'So many gentlemen! Surely your die must find a preference?'

'I shall decide today, Mrs De Foe!' Tabitha laughed at the facility of her escape. 'You will be the very first to know!'

'That will now do,' Lydia scolded. 'I rule the game done, since you have exhausted all possible contestants.'

'Except one, Lydia.' Tabitha smiled her sweetest at Olivia, who was helping to lay the cutlery.

Olivia smiled, shook her head. 'Alas, Miss Tabitha. I am not quite of the company!'

'There, then!' Lydia pronounced in relief. 'We *are* done! Not even Tabitha can start including the married ladies!'

Not before today, Tabitha thought. But now I have learned about Mrs De Foe. She looked speculatively at her eldest sister. If marriage did not exclude Thalia De Foe from such an innocent, not-so-innocent, pastime, must Mrs Lydia Vallance remain unconsidered?

'I think we are near to calling the party together,' Lydia announced, and said for the shooters to be summoned to the picnic. The gentlemen who smoked were to be seated to leeward, as was proper.

As the sporting group broke off, she noticed her brother wave his guests on, and stroll across to meet Simple Tom. Henry stood, intently watching the groom's signs, then came on smiling casually as if he had been bothered unnecessarily. But she knew her brother, and wondered what important news he had just received.

The place was no more than a cubicle in the cellars of the Goat and Compass. Brick-lined, rime crusting the mortar. The door was strong, double, arched, studded with metal. And empty, not even a pile of hempen rope or cordage, as would be the case in a ship's locker. The door slammed, steps receded, Ben Fowler grumbling and Rodway complaining. Nobody had said anything to him about the girl, or letting the prisoner out of the privy . . .

Mehala tried the door – bolted, of course. A little light seeped in from barred windows further along the cellar. Ven had been flung on to the floor and lay in a heap, his breathing stertorous. She went to him, raised him as gently as she could into a sitting position, and settled beside him. This was the closest she had ever been to him. She hesitated. This was no time to be absurd about propriety. They were fellow prisoners. She gloried in that terrible fact. Prisoners, yes, but together.

She had nothing to clean his face, nothing to wash him with. Nothing to cover his poor exposed foot – that more than anything moved her inexpressibly. She tried to align his legs, thinking it would be less uncomfortable for him after the cramped privy. Gingerly she raised her arm and embraced him, drawing the flaps of his surtout over his legs and trying to tug down her skirts to cover his bare foot. His forehead came against her cheek. She felt it there with wonder. His hair was damp, and he felt hot in spite of the cellar's chill. He was shivering. She drew her shawl over their shoulders, and with the end began to stroke his face, running her fingers through his hair in an attempt to comb it into a semblance of order. His hat was gone. He started muttering, incoherent and fitfully.

'There, there,' she said. 'Mehala's with you now.'

He fell silent, stilling like a child. Once, she felt his eyelids flicker open, then he seemed to sink into slumber, only to rouse and try to push her away, clutching at her arm a second later, then sinking into the same disturbed sleep.

'There,' she whispered into his face, her mouth almost on his. 'There, dearest.'

The word shocked her. She had not intended to speak so, to speak at all in fact. Dearest. She knew the common opinion in Sealandings, that she was more to Doctor Carmichael than his housekeeper, that they were . . . well, libbers, as that scrawny head servant Aggie had screamed in the tavern coachyard just now. Lyers together, as man and wife. She had stated her place. With him, wherever his place was to be. If it meant they were destined to be lovers, then let that be also. Life was fleeting; love should be a part of it, the only force capable of . . .

His poor hand. The finger was dislocated at the knuckle joint. She felt it as gently as possible, and entertained a sudden resolve. How often had he spoken of the need for all surgery to be done during sleep? She had seen him restore dislocated fingers. They were among the commonest accidents, to fisherman and farmer alike. He did it with a strong narrow cord, and a flat piece of wood, with holes.

The latchings of her bonnet would do. She tore them off and tied them end to end, twisting them for greater strength. A piece of firm thin board. Leather? She took one of her slippers and ripped its side with her teeth. It needed a line of holes for proper effect, but the strip's ragged edge would have to do, with the two gaps she had managed to bite away. As long as it held.

His finger was longer than the leather fragment. He had taught her that short was better than too long. She took his hand and talked gently to him, shushing him when he yelped in pain. She laid the leather along the finger's dorsum, then tied the string of brides tightly round and round. That took longest, with Ven restlessly trying to pull his hand away in his partial stupor, muttering. Done. She held the two ends after tying the knot. She felt tears start. It had to be done. Who else had he?

She lowered his hand to the floor. Then she knelt her full weight on his forearm. He stirred, moaned. She inhaled, held her breath, grasped the cords.

'I'm so sorry, darling.'

She sobbed the words. And pulled with all her strength.

His scream cut her to the heart. She heard the dull click, actually felt the slight jerk as the finger-joint was hauled into place. Weeping, she let go, gathering him to her.

'I'm so sorry, love. All done, dearest. Shhh . . .'

It was only after a sudden frightening drenching sweat that he began to settle, to her relief. She got him into a less twisted position to support him. She stayed that way for well over an hour. During his restless sleep she managed to remove the leather and her cord of chin stays from his finger. It felt alarmingly swollen, but she knew it would heal well enough in three days now it was reduced. He had shown her the course of a dislocated finger's recovery. Certain she knew she had done right, she dozed.

It was Ven's groaning that wakened her. His free arm came round, reaching her shoulder. His face sank further until it lay on her breast. Were he a babe, his position would be that of a suckling infant. She held him close with such sudden ferocity that he groaned involuntarily and she made a small reproving sound at herself for foolishly hurting him.

How long they lay like that, Ven in her arms, she did not know. The exertions of forwandering had tired her more than she realised. She must have slept again. She was roused by Ven's voice speaking clearly, though in snatches, as if making some formal announcement.

'You see, Father,' was the first she heard, 'it is not a question of knowing a person fully. You do see that, Father?'

She listened. He muttered fitfully, then fell silent, breathing quickly, somnolent.

'I determine to marry her, you see,' Ven explained in a voice so clear and sudden that she started. 'It is not the infatuation I had for . . .'

For whom? There had been a lady, she knew, of London gentry, and too grand for him. She had pieced slivers of his history together over the months at Shalamar.

'Love brings certainty, Father. Something I never knew . . . Am I importunate in having expectations? She is so far my superior that . . .' He was still dreaming of the woman he had known, Mehala thought, until he babbled restlessly, 'I could not forbear . . . Mehala will always be mine, Father . . . believe I have any man's right to speak, and ask for her hand.' Ven's hand left her breast for a moment and tapped her arm assuringly. His speech was firm, seemingly that of a reasoning, alert mind, but she knew better.

'I will find her family. A maid at Bettany's mill said Mehala was from the south, had grand possessions. Of course,' Ven said confidently, 'anyone could tell that. She is a queen. My status is only . . .'

He slept. Mehala felt unable to breathe for a few moments, thinking. His father had died some years before he qualified in London, that she knew. He was dreaming, back in time. He intended to ask for Mehala's hand. He was not speaking of the other woman at all.

Gently she let her hand touch his brow. She wet the end of her shawl at her lips and with soft strokes used it to clear the grime from part of his face. Then she gathered him close, and let him rest.

There had been a day once, long ago, when she had gone north along the coast with Old Abby on a peter boat. The vessel belonged to his relatives, from the lower Thames, and was in the Blackwater and Colne to be sold. Abby wanted help to crew her to buyers in Felixtow port.

They had set sail in the beamy, shallow vessel, enduring many jokes from the Colne fishers at its strange double-ended shape. Old Abraham shouted coarse abuse back.

'They be ignorant, gal,' he told her as the boat fought her tiller opposite the Fastness signal staff and beat awkwardly towards The Naze. 'These peters be old Thames boats, long before Lunnon itself ever were. Bootiful, they be.'

It was hardly a beautiful journey. It was the furthest Mehala had ever been from shore, or indeed from home. The boat rolled and swayed like a sick nag, yet made good progress. Abby took her close inshore across Harwich's mouth, skirting perilously close to the Andrews and Polleshead before beating inshore, along the line of Martello Towers that were built against the Tyrant Napoleon. And so to Felixtow where he had tied up on the old stones of the Roman wharf built in the days of the great Caesar.

402

It seemed an exhilarating adventure at the time, and the land journey back even more exciting. But the sea was different, lovely within itself in a way the land was not or ever could be. Perhaps, dreaming now of times gone when she was hardly more than a little girl, her mind was romancing, blowing bubbles of pretence. But that sea journey told her something about herself she never would have learned. She could decide. She had power to commit her own life to a purpose, without reference to others. The North Sea was a whole world, yet connected to other seas and oceans, other lives. It was like flying. The breeze came against her face, blew her hair, allayed, died, then came fresh again, living strong as before. Its simple presence was a call to life, to live.

The wind coughed, choked, settled, and she knew it for Ven's breathing. She was imprisoned again, with her man. She smiled, held him with a whisper.

A few sounds were audible. She noticed the daylight dwindling. The cressets along the shore would be stacked with oiled woods and torchings. People would be carrying them into place, as signal lights to mark the treacherous banks and shoals. Aye, and for grimmer purposes too, as at Salcott where the wreckers lay silent along the fleets and sea marshes ready for the ships that drove ashore and slewed on to their beam ends in a wreck's surrender. And Mersea Island. And Great Clacton Marsh, where contraband would be carried along tracks past St Osyth and the Bentleys and Bromleys, to appear magically free of Custom costs in Manningtree and Colchester and thence further inland still.

With the last of the daylight, Ven started muttering words she did not understand. Nosology, the arrangement of diseases according to Doctor Cullen, Doctor Sauvage . . . Then in a strangely lucid manner, he was suddenly lecturing somebody about yeast, brewing, the importance of having a cylindrical gyle, since the old fermenting tuns of rectangular shape accumulated dirt and old bad yest . . .

'Are you listening, Fowler?' Ven demanded weakly.

'Yes,' Mehala said. Not darling, dearest. 'Yes, Doctor.'

'If your casks be cleaned every time of using,' Ven said with great gravity, 'your sick ale will mend. Keep them, once filled brimful with the fermenting beer, in a stillion trough, so it catches the yest as it works from the orifice of each round or cask. You see? Thus you keep the new beer free of the spent yest . . .'

People were calling up above now. A trapdoor went back with a crash. A ladder ran down with a slither and a thump. Servants into the next cellar? The brewing cellar of this tavern? Somebody shouting almost inaudibly into another's echo about the two felons. Perhaps she and Ven would be taken out soon. She could ask for drink. Ven was parched. Had Bartholomew Hast kept faith, reached Squire Hunterfield? And would the Lord of Sealandings heed? Had Euterpe Baring managed to obtain some assistance? Surely she if anyone was still trying, for Mehala was convinced the Rector's sister loved Ven. As perhaps did Mary Prothero, did that lady but know it.

'You have but three sources of badness and spoilage, Fowler . . .' Ven was mumbling now. He stirred, groaning, coughed and winced with pain she felt for him.

'Shhh. Try to rest, dearest.'

The stern lecturer's intonation came. 'Think of cattle murrains in the same way, Fowler. Don't you see? Contamination from *contagion*. Touch spread. Simple as that. Never mind your fancy notions of miasmas and noxious vapours, not for this . . .'

Mehala was suddenly wide awake. She tried to lower her voice to a man's pitch, trying to become the taverner he was speaking to in his disordered mind. 'Yes, sir?'

'Don't you see? The sick and dying are probably those who ate the dead meat, like vagrants and the poor. Or who came in close contact with the sick beasts, like milkmaids . . . So with your beer. Spoilage through transferring the bad yeast. So the murrain goes from cattle to person by the same means of transfer. Nothing more complicated than that . . .'

'The murrain, the cattle plague?'

'Yes. Destroy the sources . . . fire, heat, anything to kill the living agent of the malady. Just as brewers have always expunged fouled ferments by fire, or by washing utensils in hot liquids, beer, anything . . .'

He subsided after that into fitful slumber, occasionally rousing to speak solemnly to one Doctor Arbuthnot, his old teacher, but sinking still more. Mehala stayed as motionless as possible to calm him, trying to see his face in the gloaming. When she was sure he was quietened, she slowly lowered her mouth on his, dizzying herself by the pure simplicity of the act, thrilled by the warmth of his lips. Astonishingly, she would have licked away the cacked blood there but for fear of waking him.

They were both huddled together in a doze, when much later Moat and Rodway finally came to extract them from the cell.

44

There had never been such a gathering in Sealandings. The commonalty mingled shyly with the gentry. Carriages started and backed in the driveways of Bures House. Servants rushed with benches and forms as the great hall rapidly filled with inhabitants of all classes. Fisherfolk mingled with farmers, labourers with masters. Hunterfield was pleased to see it, even warmed. He was casually standing in the main porchway, waiting to be received by Golding, talking with Letitia who alone of his household had elected to accompany him. The other two ladies were to come with the Carmadys.

'Like olden times, Letty,' Hunterfield was saying. 'Then, lords sat down with peasants at one board, all in the one hall. Children and all! After the Tudors, rules changed for reasons nobody can now remember. Was it wise, or unwise?'

'Hardly wise, Henry.'

'Yes.' He squeezed her hand and drew her arm through his. 'Your beliefs are so like mine. Even,' he joked straightfaced, 'in music and the other arts.'

She smiled, but her features were drawn. People jostled past, diffidently avoiding coming against the Squire as they recognised him. Some murmured greeting, others hurried past quickly. Greeting as a clue to fealty, Hunterfield guessed. Letitia had a quiet confidence, and spoke quickly. There would be no time once the trial began.

'Henry, please may I speak? I have had no opportunity to seek your favour in the matter of Doctor Carmichael. I am sure he is blameless. Most families here can testify to his zeal. Why, as far as . . .' She caught herself for foolishness in almost mentioning Whitehanger, where the Darlings had the little girl Clare, reputedly an illegitimate offspring of a local titled gentleman. She could not invoke her brother's emotions on that matter, not openly. 'He is esteemed – '

'Apologies, Hunterfield,' Charles Golding drawled, tapping the

Squire's shoulder in interruption and nodding to Letitia. 'Glad I caught you.'

'For what, Charles?'

'For insisting on holding this trial here.' Golding made sure the largest possible number of people heard him. 'I did not want it held in the Corn Mart. Ramshackle old building, that. Time you built Sealandings a fine new legal edifice.'

Hunterfield shrugged affably. Letitia stiffened in affront at Golding's offensive manner. 'The Corn Mart is traditional, Charles,' Henry said in mild reproof.

Golding was giving offhand acknowledgements to people arriving. 'Evening, Prothero, Mrs Prothero. And Reverend Baring, Miss Euterpe.' He turned back to the Squire condescendingly. 'Look, Hunterfield. It's no good protesting about tradition. I know you wanted the trial in the same old rubbish tip, but I wanted it here. You see?'

Letitia was baffled by her brother's meekness. She expected him to make some quiet countermand, use his authority to quell Golding's arrogance, but he only sighed. It was just like the other evening, when Milton Hall had been treated to a similar display.

'Very well, Charles. Do you insist?'

'I really do, old chap. You must learn to fadge along with me now.'

'Do take caution, Charles, I beg,' Hunterfield said with an air of tired resignation.

Golding was off, bowing to representatives of the great families, nodding curtly to underlings. His agent Lazard slid up, passed some discreet message which made his master smile. The gunmaker Bartholomew Hast paused by the Squire, clearly wanting to speak, but Hunterfield simply gave him an affable nod before moving aside.

It was Henry's caution that made Letitia pause. She did not like to discomfort him by looking directly into his eyes as if interrogating, but for the first time felt something approaching hope, if not quite relief. She too had seen Simple Tom arrive at the shooting party picnic, seen the exhausted state of his hack. And seen him pass a letter to Hunterfield, which the Squire had slipped into his pocket unread. She took her brother's proffered arm and together they moved with the press. There they encountered the

Maderleys. Hunterfield greeted the artist less warmly than he did Olivia Maderley, Letitia noticed, instantly guilty at having made so frank an appraisal of her brother. She would not have detected any change in Henry's manner were it not for her acute sensitivity to anything affecting the artist himself.

'I trust you will not be sketching all the way through the proceedings, Maderley,' Henry said bluntly. 'You have set Miss Hunterfield here squiggling at every opportunity. One dauber is sufficient.'

'No, Squire. I promise.'

'Miss Olivia.' Hunterfield made a slight bow. 'I trust you will sit with my party, if you can persuade your brother?'

Olivia looked her best, Letitia saw, in a purple pelisse with burano lace showing at the cuffs of her Caroline sleeve, and with matching clementine at the bonnet lining. Very commendable to appear so presentable in popular company, of course. But consider that Olivia Maderley had looked simply beautiful at the shooting tea. Was this a further sign? How ridiculous for society to rule against simply asking William's opinions on this important matter! All must be found out by cleverness, which was not quite proper. As well as almost impossible, which was even more irritating.

'I am honoured, Squire!'

'Then please do the honours for Miss Hunterfield, as I shall for Miss Olivia.'

Letitia's attentions were agonisingly divided as they processed into the great hall. She was conscious of William's arm pressing her hand tightly in unspoken comment, and strove to ignore the warmth of her cheeks. Following Henry, she felt unexpressed delight and thought *They look well together!* The Lord of Sealandings and the daughter of a widow? The Squire of the east shores and a tide-miller's family? That the Maderleys were wealthy was irrelevant. The Carmadys were of higher stock, almost as estimable as the Astells, and Brillianta's inclinations towards Henry were well-expressed, even if his preferences did lean towards Lorela. Letitia wished she could discuss it openly with Henry, Lydia, anyone.

The hubbub in the hall faded as people recognised the Hunterfields. The main body of seating was occupied by the tenant-farmers. The labourers and men from the fisher cottages remained standing in clusters against the walls at the rear. The religious leaders and their adherents were talking in the spaces between the benches, as if finding places quickly would somehow demean themselves. Reverend Baring however was already moving to the front, accompanying Euterpe with two of his churchwardens. Hunterfield bowed to the De Foes, seated close to where an imposing mahogany desk with extravagant lion monopodia had been placed. As Fellows made proper recognition, he murmured to Thalia and conducted her to a position at the front of the main body.

'This will do, Henry!' Fellows remarked jocularly. 'I have been trying to discover seats conveniently near the doors, that I may leave in time for the cockfight!'

Hunterfield smiled. Golding's chief servant Clark, today in the household livery, waited to usher Hunterfield into a tall joined armchair raised on a dais.

'Your chair is to one side of the court space tonight, Henry!' Thalia De Foe could not resist the taunt. 'How does it feel to play second to my Cousin Charles?'

'Apologies, Squire Henry!' Fellows interjected quickly. 'My lady is overcome by the occasion!'

'No offence taken, Fellows. I am consoled by not having to sit alone on the lower steps, however. I see my young friend Astell is here!'

The elderly Sir Edward came up to the company, a servant in Arminell livery helping him forward.

'What time d'you call this, Henry, for God's sake?' Sir Edward smiled and made his bows to the ladies. 'You had best have some decent Portugal claret, hawking me out on such a journey, or I shall set my daughters on you!'

'None of my doing, Sir Edward. Golding's prisoners, Golding's charge! A monstrous arena, for some trifling misdemeanour. We must humour him. Every boy wants his first cravat tight enough to throttle!'

Hunterfield made apologies to Olivia and Letitia before drawing Sir Edward aside. Letitia's hopes rose even further. For the first time for some days her brother seemed his former self, and was speaking intently to the aged judge. Clark and two servants

409

hurried another joined oak chair forward for Sir Edward. Thalia De Foe was casting glances round the audience, but was clearly disappointed at having only the Carmadys, the other Hunterfield ladies, and the Misses Astell to greet.

Lydia Vallance, Tabitha and Mercy Carmady were brought in to sit with William Maderley's charges, which spoiled Letitia's plans to become better acquainted with both sister and brother. Another fine opportunity wasted, she thought, smarting. Pleasant to have Percy Carmady's company, but irritating to have to suffer the usual asides about placing wagers on the outcome. She found herself next to Olivia, thank goodness, and unfortunately Tabby, who was swivelling round to look at everyone there. It came to Lydia's attention.

'Tabitha,' Lydia whispered with a frown. '*Stop using your eyes this instant!*'

Tabitha sat back pouting, a mutinous expression on her face. Thalia De Foe almost laughed aloud. And she had actually worried that this chit harboured designs on Carradine! As Letitia hastily coined some commonplace to cover Tabitha's annoyance, Thalia heard a murmur in the hall and turned to see Carradine himself enter, almost as if conjured by her very thought. She felt replete at the very sight of him, and with satisfaction gave her attention to the front. Golding had appeared.

The place quietened. Golding was now attired in sombre greys and blacks, against the fashion. Only the silver buckles on his gleaming black shoes, and his white cravat, showed any brightness. A theatrical exhibition of dress, Hunterfield noted dispassionately. Yet it made the point, contrasting sharply with the elegant dazzle of the gentry. Even his dark shirt had chitterlings of the same black silk. His aggravators, twists of hair brought round the temples to touch the corner of the eye, added a shrewd malevolent quality aimed to quell opposition. Hunterfield almost smiled, feeling Sir Edward's sardonic glance. He did not respond.

Golding strode to the centre and faced the people. Lazard beckoned to the local constable to step forward as people rose in acknowledgement then sat, footwear thundering on the boards and throats being cleared.

Hunterfield eyed the man carrying the constable's staff. Jod

Raynforth was a local man whose career was blighted by a succession of almosts. Sycophantic and weak, he had sought nomination as High Constable for Sealandings. Hunterfield had refused to appoint him. Then Raynforth had tried to become the workhouse master, turnpike trustee, then tollgate keeper. A vacillator, his nature was belied by his appearance. He was above average height, stalwart, brisk of manner. He was alleged to have stolen some church bells from a ruined church inland, but the suspicion had never been proved.

'My lords,' Lazard announced as Golding took his seat. 'People of Sealandings. This court is assembled for the purpose of trying one Ven Carmichael, Jod Raynforth the constable attending.'

'Bring in the prisoner.'

Sir Edward leant across to say something. Hunterfield gave a minimal shake of the head and the old man stayed quiet.

Into a shocked silence Ven Carmichael shuffled, limping, one foot bare. His clothes were torn and filthy. The caked body, the swollen eyes, the matted stubble, made Letitia exclaim in pity. Silently she implored her brother, but Hunterfield simply sat, his face set as stone. Mehala entered, and came forward beside Carmichael. He stood, swaying slightly, between Rodway and Moat. Lazard moved to his desk facing Carmichael, and took up his quill. Whispers began, instantly hushed.

'Who is the woman?' Lazard demanded.

Raynforth replied pompously, 'Mehala, sir. Surname unknown. Of no fixed abode. Likewise Doctor Ven Carmichael, vagrant and beggar unlicensed.'

Letitia saw Percy Carmady lean forward, his gaze on Mehala.

'State why she is here,' Golding intoned. Sombre in voice too, Hunterfield noted distantly. He stifled his rising anger and stayed silently casual, outwardly bored.

'She confessed to all the crimes committed by the prisoner, your honour. An abetting partner in his wrong.'

'Then let the charges serve the woman as they serve the man.'

Lazard rose, and read from a prepared script. 'The charges laid before this court are that Carmichael, with the collusion of Mehala his housekeeper, then resident at Shalamar in Sealandings, did set going a cattle plague on the lands of Jason Prothero, gentleman farmer of Calling Farm.'

Raynforth called for Jason Prothero to rise and be identified. Prothero obeyed uncertainly, hesitatingly sat.

'That the prisoner did seditiously spread noxious vapours, so as to cause the deaths and sickness of loyal subjects in Sealandings Hundred; that he did injure the property Shalamar, in the estate of Milton Hall; that he did incur debts not discharged . . .'

Lazard halted. Golding was idly toying with a desk knife, and looked up in annoyance.

Sir Edward Astell had risen. With the instincts of the jurist he swivelled to present his shoulder to the company.

'Sir Edward,' Golding asked sharply. 'Can you not wait until the proceedings are – ?'

'Proceedings? What proceedings?' Astell pointed with his stick at Carmichael. 'Is this man the accused?'

'Indeed.'

The old man looked down at Hunterfield, who pursed his lips in evident annoyance.

'Sir Henry? This is contrary to law as I know it. Is there any explanation?'

Golding clambered to his feet, his face darkening. 'This is my court, Sir Edward! I shall thank you to – '

'If you please, Sir Henry!' Astell interrupted with asperity. 'You had better explain. It is your district.'

'I want to hear your comments from your good self, sir!' Golding raised his voice, causing Sir Edward to pause.

'A serious miscarriage of justice seems about to occur, Golding.' Astell was unused to correction, and showed his displeasure by drawling his words, glaring. 'You would be unwise to continue with this . . . process.'

Golding leaned over his desk, quivering. 'And for why, sir? I demand your reasons!'

'I have no reasons, sir,' Astell rebuked with cold precision. 'The law has many. I advise you to listen! Sir Henry?' He sat, his manner glacial.

Hunterfield rose, seemingly apologetic. 'Sir Charles, the law cannot transcend the law. Legal processes cannot be sedition. It is a principle. From it follows the axiom that homemade law cannot transcend the laws of this Kingdom.'

'This is my court, sir! I have the legal right to accuse and

412

imprison anyone!' Golding raised his copy of the *Magistrate's Manual* and brought it down on the desk with a crash.

'Except. . . ?' Hunterfield paused to allow the prompt to sink in.

Golding glared at Hunterfield. Then at Sir Edward Astell, whispering explanations to Lydia Vallance. His gaze scanned the row, halting at Thalia De Foe's aghast features. She was white to the lips.

'Except what, sir?'

'Officers of the law, legally appointed, may not be prevented from executing their duty. Except *that*, sir.'

Golding pointed at Mehala. 'She tried to prevent my special constables from carrying out their own sworn duty, Hunterfield!'

The Squire sighed, regretfully shaking his head. 'Miss Mehala was simply doing her legal duty, Sir Charles. Being a frail and weak woman, she was unable to protect her senior legal officer from being wrongfully taken. I believe she tried.'

'Her senior legal officer?' Golding stared at Sir Edward, at Hunterfield, at the silent company.

'Sir Charles,' the Squire said, sadness in his voice. 'You have impeded the King's justice.' He sighed. 'I honestly do deplore my role here this evening. So prestigious a family as the Goldings, and for many centuries living with mine in neighbourly bond.' He sighed more graphically still. 'It hurts me more than I can say, to notice that you obstructed the King's law by private machinations. I have to inform you that your actions are treasonable. You, sir, are guilty.'

'Treason?' Golding sank into his chair, ashen. Murmurs of fear rose in the hall. Somebody, possibly Clark, banged a staff calling for order.

'Treason, Charles. I would give almost anything not to be the instrument of this sad news. You surely know that the High Constable of a Hundred must not be impeded from the proper exercise of his – '

'High Constable?' Golding was bewildered.

'Doctor Carmichael is legally appointed to that office, Charles.'

There was no sound. Mehala's head turned slowly. Her gaze set on Hunterfield, who was busy seeming most apologetic, opening his palms in regret, bowing to Astell.

413

'You appointed two special constables, Charles, to capture the High Constable of the Hundred of Sealandings and have him wrongfully imprisoned. Why?'

Hunterfield held the pauses deliberately, now taking a pace, now shrugging, now folding his arms and turning back to Golding.

'Doctor Carmichael's appointment was legally ratified *before* your magistracy, Sir Charles.' Hunterfield seemed overcome for a moment. Acting, Letitia thought. Henry is acting. This was his plan all along. 'I am heartbroken, to say this in such plentiful company. Yet perhaps it comes better from me than from a stranger.'

He took a step towards Lazard, imperious.

'Lazard! Did your master consult the list of officers of Sealandings?'

The agent licked his lips, glanced at Golding, back to Hunterfield.

'The answer will be easy to find,' Hunterfield said, merciless. 'Show me the list, Lazard – if you have it!'

'I have none, sir.' The agent was almost inaudible.

'None?' Hunterfield wagged his head in pretended pity. 'Sir Charles, it is a magistrate's first duty to identify the legal officers! Sir Edward Astell and I signed Doctor Carmichael's appointment as High Constable.'

'But this is – '

'Allow me, sir!' Hunterfield's sudden thunderous words made people start. He strode in an abrupt show of anger towards Rodway and Moat. 'Did either of you ask this alleged prisoner for his written legal authority? Did you?'

The two were bewildered. They stayed silent.

Hunterfield glowered at them. 'Then you are to share the treason! Unhand the High Constable! This instant!'

They stepped away under his glare. Mehala went to hold Ven's arm.

'This so-called *court* is a mockery. It shall be the subject of a special report. You two are dismissed forthwith. Do not leave Sealandings. Lazard, destroy the records, and the trumped-up charges against the High Constable.'

He calmed, strode slowly back to his seat. 'Sir Edward? Do you have anything to add?'

'Yes, Hunterfield. Golding's resignation from the magistracy is immediately acceptable.' Sir Edward stood, his servant hurrying to help. 'This is a sorry day, Henry.'

Hunterfield hesitated, as if remembering something. 'Oh, Lazard. See that the High Constable is given every facility to recover, then conduct him to my residence within the hour. I want his report.'

'Yes, Sir Henry.'

Hunterfield proffered his arm to Lydia, who signed to her sisters to rise and follow. With the Maderleys and Carmadys, the Hunterfield party left the hall at Sir Edward Astell's slow pace, in total silence. Mehala remained still, observing Hunterfield's retirement, almost disbelieving. She saw Letitia look back doubtfully into her eyes. Ven was bewildered, unable to take it all in.

'Mehala?' he asked dazedly. 'May we go home?'

'In a short while, dearest,' she said. 'Now, we rest.'

45

They were well treated at Bures House for that last hour, two serving maids being sent by Clark to act under Mehala's supervision. She was delighted to find Little Jane her friend still serving as under-housekeeper there. Always the chatterbox, Little Jane gave Mehala the youngest maid, Dora, for herself. Ven bathed in hot water carried into a guest bedroom. He was still bewildered, and needed help to dry and dress. Little Jane found an old bathing shirt for him. By the finish even Ven was laughing at his own clumsiness, though Mehala scolded Dora for being too amused. Little Jane asked Clark's permission to borrow some clothes for Carmichael, but Mehala refused. She sent his garments to be washed and dried in one of the drying ovens while Ven sat in a long nightshirt. They were fed in the kitchen by Mrs Glasse, who was delighted at the novelty but worried at the effect the master's sorry exhibition in the great hall would have on the household. Mehala accepted the meal for Ven's sake, and because Hunterfield himself had ordered that they be cared for before reporting to Lorne House. Little Jane was sad they could not stay, and wept, still chattering, as they finally left on the night walk to Lorne House.

They went slowly, both tired. Mehala could not remember so happy an end to any day. They walked apart, of course. Mehala was indignant at such an absurd degree of propriety, especially after all they had gone through. And after what Ven said. Admittedly it was in his derangement, but so? Truth outs at such a time. He loved her. Much was spoken of love, where it came from, how it could start. Was it that a man's nature was only to love a woman *back*, reflecting the love shone to him by the woman? If so, she need no longer doubt. He had talked with his dead father about his intention to marry her, though he might never remember.

Ven said hardly anything. The night was clement, a mild sea breeze shushing in the trees as they came slowly up to the first cottages. They turned right, taking care on the rutted track. The main coast road to Whitehanger was in poor repair. The moon gave some light, and the reflection from the sea added to the skyglow. To the left, the lanthorns of the Donkey and Buskin, always left burning the night through, showed gold among the dark cottages. The distant light of the North Mole could be seen, and beyond, the twin torches of Carradine's small jetty. And, across the small town along the rise of the Norwich road, a cluster of lanthorns. Carradine's pile itself? Such activity at this hour!

The road crossed the River Affon by a wooden bridge, lately mended. There, she remembered, she had stood one day, in hopes of seeing Doctor Carmichael return from Whitehanger when he had tended poor little Harry Darling. And William Maderley had, unbeknownst to her, been painting her as she stared down into the river. It seemed a lifetime ago. Now, she did the seacoast trick of moving her head from side to side, the better to see her way in the dark. Ven was walking slower. She insisted they rest a moment.

'I dreamed, Mehala,' he said, leaning on the bridge. 'Did I say anything?'

'Many things, Ven.'

'I was confused. The strangest analogy came to me – fermentation, and the cattle plague. We have long thought of some diseases as ferments. What did I say?'

'Beer – cooling processes. You said it was all so simple. Spoiled brews were the fault of filthy utensils. You spoke of washing things in hot liquors.'

'Mehala!' he exclaimed. 'I wonder if the source of the disease is nothing magical at all! It might simply be the products of the sick beasts. Coming from transmission. Touch, eating the bad meat. Perhaps even inhaling the very spotlets from the beasts dying of the murrain!'

He spoke on, becoming more excited, until she had to suggest they walk on, to calm him.

'It is no noxious vapour, Mehala. Not something brought on the wind, or by the seasons, conjunction of planets. No exotic theories. It is merely passed, as an evil *thing*. From the sick to the healthy. So it spreads!'

'Then how does it start?'

He fell silent. They travelled a furlong more before he replied, downcast.

'I don't know, Mehala. That is the flaw. Ignorance again. From where does a disease enter Sealandings? We know from the experience in the Derbyshire village of Eye that a whole habitation can be kept free of plague by diligence. And the Romans kept ships in quarantine – the very name means forty days.' He thought a moment. 'Which tells us how to end a cattle plague, Mehala.'

'That would be marvellous, Ven.'

'It *would* be so, yes – if Sealandings would accept my preventives, and if I reason right.'

She was shocked. 'Sealandings must, Ven! Nobody could be that foolish!'

'After what Sealandings has done to you, Mehala? To me? For no cause? No, this place will never take a suggestion from me.'

'Then it will from both of us.'

He sounded bitter. They were within sight of the lanthorns at Lorne House. 'Do you mean both? Or do you mean the influence you have over Squire Hunterfield?'

She halted, gently taking his arm. There was no one to see. 'What are you saying, Ven?'

'It's true, Mehala. The only time I seem to succeed is when you are by me.' She felt him shrug despondently. 'Think of my situation. Not a penny – nowhere to go. What shall I receive, beyond the gate lights of Lorne? I already know: charity, from the Lord of Sealandings. Not from merit, Mehala, nor from my surgery, my work as physician, but on account of your presence.'

'Is that wrong, Ven?'

'No.' She would have been gladder had he disagreed, instead of concurring with such despair in his voice. 'I suppose not. But help for the sick, by machinations, by scheming? Why not, just for once, by pure reason? Mehala, I am almost sure I could have prevented the deaths – how many now, six is it? And twenty more sick? Instead I let myself be driven out, beaten, taken by constables, imprisoned, put on trial. And simply went along, helplessly.'

'What else could you do?'

He cried out in anguish. '*I could have fought!* Can't you see, Mehala? *You* would have!'

She felt tears start. He was punishing himself for not being omnipotent.

'Wouldn't you, Mehala?' he asked, brokenly.

'Yes, Ven.' It was no good trying to evade. 'I did, in my way. And will again. As long as I draw breath.'

There. It was done. Said openly, on a lonely coast road, the uttered words hanging in the night air between them.

'I came back. I was following you to St Albans, guessing you might have started out to the relative you mentioned. I returned, when I heard you had been arrested. I don't know how much you remember from the Goat and Compass. There, I gave myself in custody, self-accused, to be by you.'

'It was true, then! I have been trying to remember . . .'

She was lost now, not knowing what to say. She continued lamely, 'If your work profits by my help, why not accept it?' Her voice trembled.

'Did I say anything else, Mehala?'

She hesitated. Even more dangerous ground. With others, it would be easy. With a man so wounded it could prove disastrous. In the pause, she felt rather than saw a fox slip across the road in the moon shadow.

'You . . . you seemed to speak with your parents, I think.'

'What did I say?'

'Please, Ven.' She tried to move away, but he caught and held her.

'Tell me, Mehala.'

'You spoke to your father. Explaining why you wanted to . . . to settle down.' He would not release her. 'You spoke of someone.'

His hand let go. 'You, Mehala. I remembered, when we were taken to stand trial. I must have been incoherent, from my *concussio*.'

'I did not hear everything,' she said desperately.

'You heard me say I wished to propose marriage, Mehala?'

'Yes.' It seemed suddenly vitally important to avoid making a claim on him. 'You were ill, Ven. That horrid Rodway must have beat you sorely before I arrived – '

'Will you, Mehala?'

'Will I . . . ?' She failed to understand for a moment.

'Give me your hand.' Quickly he spoke on, apologising. 'I admit

419

to few prospects. I have no wealth, no affluent relations. My situation here is fraught. After tonight I shall start inland, hoping to find a position in some surgical practice, but have no sure idea where. As to character, I want repair to several faults – '

'Shhh.' She stepped closer. 'Your faults are blessings, dearest.'

'You will?' He sounded astonished, the same tone as when she had explained the Flora's Ring of flowers at Shalamar. This was beyond his ken.

'Yes, Ven.'

'I shall write the minute I get established,' he started eagerly. 'With fortune, I could be in practice in a month, perhaps two. And could send for you, Mehala.'

'No. I shall come too, Ven. That is marriage. Together as one. To help howsoever I can.'

'Without a home? You don't understand – '

'No, dearest,' she said, half-laughing. 'It is you who doesn't. I understand enough for us both. Our real life's work together is about to begin.'

She moved towards him, inside his embrace. A man's hoarse voice called a challenge. They separated, embarrassed.

'Come within the light, whoe'er you be!'

'Doctor Carmichael and Mehala.' She resisted the urge to announce Ven as the High Constable of the Hundred.

Together they walked into the light's cast. The gatekeeper of Lorne House came slowly towards them, holding a flintlock short arm and his lanthorn. He scrutinised them, nodding in recognition.

'The great house for you, Mehala. Gamekeeper's lodging for you, Doctor.'

Mehala was about to make some retort, but stayed silent. A boy was sent with them as guide. Mehala was taken into the manor house by Rebecca, the chief maid, who was waiting by inside the servants' entrance. Ven was conducted to a gamekeeper's cottage just in the woods a half-mile distant, within sound of the small waterfall on the River Affon.

In spite of the pain from his finger and his bruises, he slept soundly until the morning came.

46

This homecoming was even more strange.

Carradine felt something had gone. Or perhaps had come in with Prothero, and like a ghost settled never to leave? A house has character, its own will ingrained in its walls. Windows too are living entities, eyes that should be looked through only by the master and mistress of the dwelling, and by no other. The furniture was the same. The costly Argand lamps burned just the same. Carpets, curtains, wall panellings, tapestries identical. The same portraits of his – *his* – ancestors stared imperiously out along the landings and staircases.

Carradine had to face it. For two hours he wandered the corridors and inspected the rooms, attended by Judith Blaker and Hobbes, with an entourage of six maids-of-all. Everybody smiled, seemed delighted he was back, paid him their best compliments, bowed, dropped curtseys . . . And yet there was something radically wrong at Carradine Manor.

He chided the cook, Mrs Chandler, carried her screaming about her kitchen, joked that he was going to rush her upstairs and bed her. The dogs Ranter and Bell were beside themselves. The footmen even forgot themselves so far as to applaud, and eight grooms were there to take his horse when he dismounted. The same as always, yet not. When finally he dismissed Hobbes and the entourage, he detained the housekeeper, saying he wanted to go over the housekeeping books in detail, his unvaried custom when returning: a foible to deceive the staff. This time it was not Mrs Tyll, but the dark-eyed Judith Blaker who lay with him on the great bed. She was competent, exciting, inventive even. Yet it was curiously dispassionate love-making, though the same gush of physical ecstasy came, the same relief sweated him to a sleep.

He leaned against the sellore afterwards, drinking thick red Portugal. Blaker was enticing, yes, but only as long as the physical excitement lasted. Was that the reason for this odd restlessness? Was it that he expected other events, along with triumph?

Or could it simply be that Tyll was gone?

Possibly. Before, Mrs Barbara Tyll would be frosty, all reproving at his antics and display of glee. She would scold any maid who as much as glanced his way. And when reporting to his private chambers she would painstakingly try to confine the encounter to a perusal of the housekeeping ledgers. To fail, of course. Her stern propriety was made for the breaking. She strove to cover his mouth at the climax to stay his final cry, for fear of giving scandal, but it was she as much as he who worked in the bed, labouring and sweating them both to a shared paradise. The shame she felt afterwards was beyond him, beyond any man's understanding. He often jeered at her, shaming her emotions, laughing openly and giving mocking reminders of her fevered wantonness, copying her crude cries in cruel falsetto, reducing her to tears. And he never restrained his amusement as she dressed in the dark hours, stealthily unlocking the door and descending the stairs to start the morning's duties as though the night had been passed in moral solitude.

Now, the stars were once more in their courses, the master back at Carradine. And Judith Blaker was in charge of the housekeeping, seemingly a model of propriety.

Or was it the events concerning Mehala? Indirectly she had been responsible for his loss of Carradine Manor, every stick, stitch and stone of his inheritance. Now, her adherence to that pock-picker Carmichael had somehow made Hunterfield ruin Golding's ambitions. Which would allow another member of the great families of the Eastern Hundreds to step in. It seemed that even the opportunity for his own advancement – as far as Parliament, even – was Mehala's doing. The girl was always there. From the first time he had come upon her, defiant in the dusk at Shalamar, she glided distantly through his consciousness. Raven hair, eyes brown, pale skin high of tone, gleams of russet in the locks, her very movements those of a creature more than a woman. Never pretty, always beautiful. Every man seemed to share this awareness. And even great ladies became conscious of threat in her presence.

At Carmichael's trial she had stepped forward with him. Steady, resolute, sure. How could that be? A wretch arriving well-nigh drowned, carried into a smoky tavern fug from the sopping decks of a Yorkshire lugger, penniless and friendless. Rising from there to be a poor quack's skivvy. It made no sense. How could she stand there before all Sealandings, hated by the religionists, condemned by magistrate and gentry alike, yet look through the lot of them with such startling serenity? Was there an understanding between her and Hunterfield? Such affairs were not impossible. Hunterfield was known to have sired one brat, a moppet at Whitehanger, and possibly others. And Thalia De Foe herself testified to the Squire's healthy lust. It was unlikely. Young she might be, but Mehala was no woman to love at distance. If she was Hunterfield's, she would already have displaced Mrs Lydia Vallance from Lorne.

'Lover,' Judith said. She was lying across the bedclothes, her weight on his legs. Her isabella-coloured satin nightdress had been torn away, and trailed on the carpet. 'I made sure the cressets were taken to the jetty tonight. And lit.'

'It was you?'

She laughed, low and feline. 'Who else? Not by my own hands, of course. Once you mentioned the conversation between Fowler, yourself and Prothero about contraband, the way was clear.'

He looked at her. How many other ways were 'clear' to this woman, Carradine wondered, that would only occur to him late or never? She sprawled naked and uncaring, almost as if nakedness was her natural state. Lucy, and even the three or four lesser whores he knew at Two Cotts, were more concerned, while Barbara Tyll would have quietly covered and even averted her eyes from his nakedness. Judith's mouth was only an inch from him. Judith was a woman of the wild, unused to living indoors. She almost seemed above possessions, which no woman could ever be.

'You did excellently,' he admitted. 'That tipped the scales and sent Prothero packing.'

'Do you miss that cold bitch Tyll?' she asked him suddenly, taking him by surprise.

'No. Should I?' he meant it, at that moment.

'You shagged her.' She laughed softly at the expression on his face. 'It matters nothing, lover. She is gone. You're the better for it.'

'Unless Prothero finds some way of recuperating his fortunes.' He was asking what further plans she had. It made her smile.

423

'He cannot.' She spoke candidly. She was already moving her palm across his thighs.

'He still legally owns Carradine, the Manor, estate.'

'Prothero will come a-begging soon, lover.' Her eyes held his.

'For what?'

'For you to relieve him of the terribly heavy burden of Carradine, and all its possessions.'

His throat dried as her fingers began to stroke. He could not take his eyes from her.

'Impossible. He need only stay at Calling Farm until the epidemic spends itself. These estates will stay free of the murrain. He can then reclaim it. My stay here is temporary. I must leave when Prothero commands. I signed to that effect. You were there – and three witnesses.'

She was smiling, her fingers stirring him, rousing, almost penetrating his flesh. They felt on fire. He wanted her anew, all problems gone.

'Are you sure, lover?'

'The document is in the bureau. Two copies were lodged with the lawyers.'

'They were *sent*, lover. From here. Two copies, by separate couriers, as Prothero ordered.' She was drawing down the sheet to expose him. The tip of her tongue moved slowly along her lower lip leaving a shining trail of moisture. 'Did they arrive?'

'They went under secure guard. I saw them leave.'

'And the riders?' She bent her head, let her tongue touch his thigh.

'Were my own men from Carradine. They can be trusted. If one fails to reach Maidborough, the other will. I've never known them fail.'

'You have never known me, lover.' She ran her tongue indolently along his skin, making the muscle beneath quiver and leap. 'Neither parchment will reach its destination. The couriers' bags will be empty.' Her dark eyes seemed to envelop him. He felt as if he was starting to fall into the widening darkness of her gaze.

'Empty?' he repeated thickly.

'Both. By morning the two copies of Prothero's agreement will have . . .' She smiled, showing her white teeth in a mock snarl, caressing and stroking. 'Shall we say . . . flown?'

424

'Prothero has them at Calling Farm. Under lock and key.'

'Had, lover.' She lowered her head, mouth open, the sensation making him gasp. He arched with a great groan of pleasure. Her head raised as if nothing had happened. '*Had*, lover.'

He stared, her meaning slowly seeping into his brain. 'You mean they will be . . . ?'

She slowly pulled herself along his length to straddle him, bending to look into his eyes. Her eyes glowed, luminous.

'By dawn there will be no trace of any agreement between you and Prothero.'

He gasped at the dazzling sensation as she stirred, her whole body swivelling on his pivot. He tried to speak, ask questions, demand to be told more, but could only marvel at the bliss she gave him. She smiled, whispering, goading.

'You want to know about the witnesses, lover? Go on, lover. Ask.'

'What. . . ?' He could only revel in the pleasure, and join her sweet work.

'There are no witnesses, lover. They too will be gone by dawn. Do you trust me, lover?'

'Yes,' he gasped.

'Wholly and completely? For ever and ever? Trust your lovely Judith?'

'Yes, yes.' His eyes were closed.

'That's my sweet lover,' she crooned, crushing herself down harder on him and moving faster. 'That's my darling man. Mine. All mine.'

In the final moments, he heard words he had never before heard. Beating savagely towards climax, she urged him on with a gutteral, '*Atch opray!*' and screeched a triumphant '*Ava-a-a-a!*' And his world and all its problems vanished into a place where all should have been rapture and peace, but now seemed a dark prison, with chains of passion heavier than any he had ever known.

47

Mehala wakened early. She looked out from the cellar lodging in the servants' quarters on to the Lorne House gardens. Exactly at eye level! Twisting, she could see the tall mulberries, the giant oaks, the beeches and holly trees. Beyond, the grounds sloped up from the vegetable and herb gardens into the wooded hillside beyond which lay Whitehanger. Somewhere, in a gamekeeper's cottage, Ven Carmichael was sleeping, she hoped restfully. Or was he lying awake, thinking of her? She had great hopes for today. Today Sealandings must say it wanted him back, to cure the cattle plague, apply his brilliant ideas.

St Luke's Little Summer had come to Sealandings. The autumn patch of brilliance, its very shadows lit by ambers, russets and deep scarlets below sap green, the sunshine casting a rich gold over all, would have been a welcome blessing and portent. Now, with the cattle plague, any return of the summer's heat was an affliction.

Lorne roused with vigour. Breakfast was being served to the early servants – estate men, footmen, maids-of-all, the cook's scullions. Mehala went to join them, was given a platter and bowl among the kitchen servants where she was interrogated by a thrilled audience about the previous day. She answered in monosyllables. A pressing bootboy she finally had to quell by saying the master was to send for her and Doctor Carmichael soon. She was allowed to sit and finish her porridge, cheese, bread and fish alone. She joined in the kitchen work until she was sent for and told by Crane that the Squire would see her at eight o'clock in his writing room. She wanted to ask after Ven, but stayed silent. At twenty minutes past seven she was taken by Rebecca, their housemaid, and made to stand in the grand marbled hallway until summoned.

The Squire had Carmichael fetched, instructing Crane to keep the man with the grooms for the while. Hunterfield had risen almost before the maids were tiptoeing about the landings, even before the first horses had left the stables for the pasture. He loved mornings, always went to the roof where some ancestor, loving the views as he, had built a belvedere from where almost the whole shore could be seen.

Quieter than ever, the vista seemed. No fishing vessels were standing out to sea, as they would normally. No heavy carts moving in towards the Square. Smudges of black on the azure from inland and across to the north-west terrain showed where desperate farmers were burning carcasses. Others believed burning was wrong, dangerous, seeing the smoke as a cause of new plagues, that the safest means was to let bluebottles infest the corpses with maggots. Or let carrion pick the bloated dead cattle bone-white. Or bury the dead beast. Or pray harder. Or draw them through the undergrowth of a night-time, and heave them into the River Affon or the sea. Or even butcher the beef and rush it secretly to market, to sell as from a clean-killed animal. As if any of these things did any good. Hopelessly haphazard, simply the erratic behaviour of frightened people. Sealandings was dying, sinking into a morass of poverty and disease.

He descended the turret steps, heavy at heart. Family problems had to wait. Lydia wanted to see him this morning, about something Tabitha had brought to her notice. And Golding also – a letter begging a meeting before eleven. And, most weird, one from Thalia De Foe. And a short courtesy note from Mary Prothero simply notifying the Squire of the Protheros' return to Calling Farm. But first Mehala, then Doctor Carmichael.

The writing room adjoined the library. Letitia had seen to its furnishing for him when he had taken charge of Lorne House. Not long ago, but seemed a generation. Then Lydia had arrived, and Letitia had stepped down for her older sister. There was no doubt; he had allies in his family, and loyal support. If only there was somebody among the gentry who could be relied upon. It had been Mary Prothero's family, once. And Fellows De Foe, once – until the South American Bubble burst and the De Foe fortunes went in the huge mercantile banking collapses in the Chilean and Peruvian loans, causing Fellows De Foe to all but abandon his local concerns and stay in London to recoup. He had made an excellent job of it, too, by all accounts, and was now as wealthy as before.

Hunterfield sent for Mehala, and tried not to watch too obviously as she entered. She was beautiful, there could be no question. Her inner serenity he found disturbing and delightful. Her attire was that of a humble woman, yet he found himself trying to match her like among his female acquaintances, and could not. Once, he had seen her in high dress, at the great occasion in Milton Hall. She had eclipsed that glittering occasion by mere presence.

'Good morning, sir.'

'Good morning.'

Crane closed the door. Mehala remained standing on the edge of the carpet. Motionless, he noticed, but not with the affrighted stillness of the anxious servant. Hers was the attitude of simple enquiry, awaiting decision. Once given, it would be swiftly received, and she would be off and away to Carmichael. Her man? He had no doubt of that. Whatever had happened, she loved her leech.

'Does Doctor Carmichael know, Mehala?'

'Know, sir?'

'Yes. How much have you told him?'

'Sir?' She paled even as he looked.

'Should I call you Mrs Rebow? Or Miss Sharland?' He rose, made an awkward gesture of apology, sat down again in the same chair, uncomfortable at the task. 'I am sorry, Mehala. Perhaps you have remembered nothing. Or perhaps you have?' He paused, then went on, 'No matter. I have good reason to thank you, for bringing help to the flood.'

'The names you call me, sir. I . . . I . . .'

He saw she knew her true identity, but waved her admission away.

'Mehala you are, Mehala you may remain. How you came lost at sea I need not know.'

'Thank you, sir.' Her words were almost inaudible.

'But there are others, Mehala.' He felt ashamed to press her. 'You have been recognised by a gentleman visitor. I believe you realise this.'

'Lieutenant Carmady.' Mehala spoke tonelessly.

'There may be others. I regret having to say this. Some in Sealandings may be displeased by recent events, and focus their dislike on you . . .' He gave a bleak smile. 'Me, among others.'

'I am aware of that, sir.'

'I say this not to threaten, Mehala. Or to demand that you reveal your identity. But to warn.'

Her head raised. 'To warn, sir? Against what?'

'You know the answer, Mehala. Two things. Your time has run out. You can no longer stay an unknown. This is not my doing; it is simply fact. Events here are talked of all along the coast. You know how swiftly word travels among the estuaries. I have to make report of your trial.'

'Need anything be written of me, sir?'

'I must do my duty. If magistrates do not uphold the law, who does?'

'Very well, sir. The second thing?'

He hesitated. Difficult it had been for him so far. This would be even harder.

'A girl rescued, well, she may find her place by her own endeavour. There is little enough tolerance in Sealandings, God knows, but its folk understand the sea. For a girl saved, they make certain allowances. You have had your share of adversity, but for all that have been accepted. And your position with Doctor Carmichael has been condoned. But once your identity becomes known, you lose the protection of anonymity. Your very position in Sealandings becomes questioned.'

'I must leave?'

'No, but the freedom you have been allowed will end.'

'I do not understand, Squire.'

He paused, not knowing how to say it. 'Your husband, Mehala. He was *reported* lost, I learned yesterday. There is yet no confirmation.'

She cried in despair, in sudden fright, 'But he drowned, sir. I alone was . . .'

'Rescued? How do you know, Mehala?'

She went white, whispering. 'He could not be alive. No. *No!*'

'Improbable. But he might well have been taken up by some ship leaving for deep seas, Mehala. Have you thought of that? He could be in the Indies, perhaps even now on his return voyage – '

'*No!* He can't be! He drowned. I felt us both go under . . .'

'Yet you were saved, Mehala. He too could have been.' He gave

429

her a moment. 'Until he is confirmed as dead, you are still Mrs Rebow.'

'Still married? To a. . . ?'

'You must not think in that way, Mehala.' He spoke harsher. 'Ask yourself the question. *Does he know*?'

'No, Sir Henry.' She was sure Ven knew nothing, or very little.

'Are you sure? My reason for asking is that his position too is doubtful. I have managed to protect him by a device, but he invited animosity from at least one of the great families, and perhaps more. I can promise his safety for a short while only.'

'No, sir. I am not sure.'

'Very well. I intend to give him a particular duty. You will assist him. I take it that is your wish. . . ?'

'It is, Sir Henry.'

'Wait with Rebecca. I will see Carmichael now.'

She left, and went to stand in the hall. Crane brought Ven in then. He looked across at Mehala, his face lighting up when he saw her. He would have started over to speak, but Crane ushered him towards the writing room door. He gave her an eager glance over his shoulder. She repaid him a smile in return, but it faded as the door closed on him.

He looked so much better for his night's rest. Still dishevelled and ill-kempt, and his bruised eyes and swollen lips were even more evident than previously, but he seemed himself at last. It was the Ven Carmichael she knew and loved, come back.

Except that Elijah Rebow, her husband, now haunted her in death – she *knew* he was drowned – as in their terrible brief life at Red Hall. And stood between her and Ven. Her heart ached. His glance had been full of hope, expectation even, brimming with happiness. How to tell him? Stupidly she had procrastinated. Like a little girl unwilling to face some scolding teacher, she had played truant. But this was no childish tantrum. The time of reckoning had come. She must pay the price for her brief respite. Most agonising was that Ven would have to pay for that short relief – and his price was the costlier. As always, for the innocent.

The door opened some five minutes later. Crane emerged, ushering Hunterfield and Ven.

'Crane, please send for Tayspill instantly, and have the

barouche brought round. The perch-high phaeton I ordered earlier will not serve.'

'Yes, Sir Henry.'

Hunterfield nodded to Ven. 'Doctor Carmichael and Mehala will accompany me round Sealandings this morning. See both are provided with writing materials. I want to see Tayspill for a few minutes apart before we leave.'

'And when will you require breakfast, Sir Henry?'

'Convey my compliments to Mrs Vallance. I shall have only half-a-dozen courses before my departure, to save time. Mrs Vallance can attend to visitors.'

'Very well, Sir Henry.'

Torn between Ven's evident pleasure at whatever the Squire had decided, and her own worry about how to tell him that she was legally still married, Mehala was distraught. She felt Hunterfield's attitude had hardened. He spoke brusquely, was almost dismissive. He strode off quickly, leaving herself and Ven in the servant's charge. It felt the end of any special concern he might have had. The sudden loss was startling. She felt exposed and vulnerable, as if he had announced a complete withdrawal of his protection. For as long as she had been in Sealandings she had been conscious of Hunterfield's awareness. It had grown rather than lessened. Was it that he suspected she had been cruel, self-seeking, in keeping secret the knowledge of her returning memory? Or was it something more? A feeling of desolation stole over her. Ven's response could be anything, were she to blurt out her legal status, so easily could he be wounded. Yet she dare not risk delay in telling him. Hunterfield was right: at any moment Ven might hear from someone else, which would be disastrous.

She looked across the hall, desperately wanting to speak, but it was not possible. He was standing by the window where Crane had left him, and she remained opposite him, the enormous expanse of the hall between. Rebecca was there, to guard against the gross impropriety of allowing an unmarried man and woman to be together unchaperoned. Rebecca was clearly not going to be the first to condone such indecency. They all three stood in silence, Ven occasionally trying to catch Mehala's eye to exchange a smile, Mehala with her gaze downcast, and Rebecca composedly watching the space between.

The barouche ran to two horses in pole gear, the box seat high above the bodywork, as with the landaus. Its body was partly covered by a half-hood. The choice of carriage showed Hunterfield's thoughtfulness, for the phaeton would have been too wearing for Ven who, close to, was fast tiring as the journey progressed round the farms of Sealandings.

Tayspill proved to be a thin middle-aged man with a ready expression, brisk but taciturn. He had come on loan from some Hunterfield relative in Gloucester, where he seemed to serve as land agent. Mehala noticed his acute looks, sharp and inquisitive. Several times he seemed on the point of asking the Squire to approve a detour, but never spoke.

Hunterfield himself was diligent, observant and shrewd in his questions to the tenant-farmers on his own lands, and gravely attentive when calling on the lesser holdings of other great estates. The latter he simply heard out, nodding after a greeting. Everybody seemed to expect his arrival. One small family, of the smallholding adjacent to Andrew Nelmes' farm, was standing waiting with infinite patience at the farmhouse door. Mehala was struck by their frankness when speaking to the Squire. Most others from the county families would have been met with a scared silence.

Ven Carmichael sat next to her, sometimes leaning over to ask a question of the farmers or wanting to be taken to see some sick beasts. On setting out from Lorne House, Hunterfield urged Ven to list the sick, but to leave attending them until later. Mehala's duty was to record addresses, numbers in each family and their health. Tayspill made quick notes of the livestock, using the old tally-stick method with a folding knife and a beech rod, and only once or twice taking a Borrowdale-graphite pencil from a pocket and laboriously setting initials beside the cuts.

The first visits were relatively mundane. Only two of the ten holdings had suffered. But as their visits led further afield, the afflicted herds became more numerous. One farm's herds had virtually been eradicated. It was then that Ven asked Mehala to keep a record of how the farmers were coping, what carts they had, the horses. He was worried to find that some farms shared porterage, in one area no fewer than six owning one set of horses and one Surrey waggon for common use. Sheep and pigs were dying in the farms abutting Calling Farm land. All the cattle herds had at least some sick cattle. It was a disaster affecting the whole district.

'Reverend Baring says he has buried six, attributed to the fever. Not counting the poor drowned girl.' It was Hunterfield's reply to Ven's audible musing.

'Six?' Ven glanced across at Mehala, whose head was bent in concentration over her paper and board.

'Two others were buried in the Maidborough Hundred, but the families deny they suffered from this same fever. Two certain at Wheatfen.'

'The ways they each cope might be of utmost importance, Squire. I mean in disposal.'

'Disposal of what?' Hunterfield asked, puzzled. 'Each farmer does as his own fathers did. All are different.'

'Squire.' Ven leaned forward, elbows on knees, eyes fervid with concentration. 'Long ago, in the time of the Great Plague, a man lived in London. He wrote a book, simply listing the numbers dead from plague. He paid streetwomen for the information. From his *Bills of Mortality* we know with some exactitude what actually happens to living beings in a plague.'

'Wait!' Hunterfield called to the coachman, and tapped Tayspill's knee to call his attention. 'Is this the plague?'

'No, Squire. We would have had far more deaths. Cattle are mostly spared in the Black Death. And pigs, sheep, dogs, cats. The sneezing, buboes, black patches on the skin – no, Squire. This is different. It is a cattle murrain.'

'But certain clues in the *Bills* can guide us, and possibly show us how to manage, when living things start to die in a plague. What actually to *do*.'

Hunterfield was disappointed. 'That might do for the future, Carmichael, but what of now?'

'We should think how the few instances of plague that were controlled achieved their object.'

'Tayspill?' Hunterfield invited the Gloucester man's opinion. It was grudgingly given.

'I hear some fancy new magic every time a beast stops belling, Squire. Coloured flannel at the throat, prayers at crossroads, laces from a hanged man's shoe. But nothing stops a murrain, that I know.'

433

'I admit ignorance, Squire,' Ven said doggedly. 'I confess to not knowing how to prevent this spreading sickness. But some means could guide us to an answer.'

'Such as?'

Ven felt his finger gingerly. He had told Mehala when entering the barouche that his gamekeeper host had lent him a glove to cover his swollen hand, and thanked her for reducing the dislocation the previous night.

'There was an account written of Tripoli, in North Africa. A maiden lady, sister to the British Consul at the Bashaw's court, left a detailed journal of her sojourn. The Black Death visited the city. For many months, the Consul kept his gates closed. Food was passed through the grille. Messengers were bathed in fluids if they had to visit, and kept in a closed gatehouse for long periods.'

'And they survived?'

'That is my point, Squire. *All* survived. No plague entered the consulate.'

'Food? Water?'

'They had their own well. Food they treated as bearing the disease, and kept it in sulphurous air, and similar treatments.'

'Tayspill?'

'Squire, this seems another vagueness. How can that be done to cattle? To herds of pigs? To sheep wandering in flocks over the Hundreds?'

Hunterfield nodded in regret. He seemed about to order the carriage's return, but Ven was already speaking, now more urgently than ever.

'Please, Sir Henry, I beg of you. Already we have some curious observations, do we not?' Eagerly he seized Mehala's writing board with a muted yelp of pain, ran his eyes down the lists. 'You see, Squire? We have been out barely an hour or two, and here are discrepancies! One farm has lost two calves, of twenty-four. One other has lost nine, of twenty! *And one has lost none!* Why is this?' He rounded on Mehala and demanded eagerly, 'How many have we been to so far? Eight? Nine? And what totals do we have?' Before she could answer he was off again. 'It *must* be important, Squire! Is it the water? Is it a different species of beast? Or some method of husbandry the sick farms avoid? We must examine the differences, surely to God, must we not? Please, Squire. Give me

434

one day, I beg. Let us inspect the township and its district. What harm can we do?'

'We can catch the sickness, Squire,' Tayspill interposed sourly.

'Then you shall avoid seeing the sick! And stay in the carriage! Most of the families seem well, and report no sickness.' Ven smiled at Mehala. 'I shall see the sick people on my own. The farms can be Mr Tayspill's assignment.'

Hunterfield pursed his lips, gave a small headshake to Tayspill. 'Continue,' he said eventually. It would convince the people he was concerned, if nothing else. The other great families, he thought drily, were notable by their absence.

The barouche returned to Lorne at four o'clock in the afternoon.

They came in chastened silence. It was far worse than Hunterfield had suspected. Tayspill was appalled. Ven sat, grey with fatigue and worry. Mehala was exhausted, her hand cramped by the effort of entering Ven's lists.

Of the ninety farms or holdings they had visited, only eighteen were spared the cattle sickness. Twelve people were dead, possibly from similar sickness. Most of the farmers buried the cattle carcasses. A few burned them. Some were not able to say, or would not. A few stared guiltily at the ground, saying nothing with a shrug. Some slaughtered beasts as soon as they fell sick, but some doing this had sent the meat to butchery, to minimise the money lost. Mehala was mostly worried by the long list of homes where one person or more lay sick a-bed. To these Ven had faithfully promised to visit soon.

'Doctor Carmichael?' Hunterfield disembarked on to the gravel curve before the balustrade. 'Can you give me an appraisal?'

'Tomorrow, Squire. It will take me some hours to assess.'

'At your earliest, if you please. Step with me a moment.'

Hunterfield drew away out of earshot, followed by Carmichael. The Squire examined the other's face before speaking.

'Doctor. For you – and for Mehala – all hangs on your success with this epidemic. You understand?'

'That need not follow, Squire,' Ven began eagerly.

Hunterfield wearily cut him short. 'In a perfect world, Doctor, it need not. But Sealandings is backward, a pit of superstition. Rid us of this murrain, and you will be reinstated. Sealandings will

435

have no choice but to condone your living with Mehala in an unmarried state – I impute nothing, Doctor; merely tell you how folk will respond.'

'And if my theories fail?'

Hunterfield waited for some time. This was the brunt. 'I shall be hard put to get you safely out of the Sealandings Hundred. There will be riots, talk of killing. You might lose your life, even. Make no mistake, Mehala shares the same risk. Or . . .'

'Or, Squire?'

'You can go now. I can get you to St Albans unscathed in two days, God willing.'

'Mehala too?'

Hunterfield felt his spirits sink. He acquiesced. 'Yes. Mehala too.'

Carmichael was surprised to recognise that Hunterfield was as deeply affected as he was himself. It was a revelation. Sir Henry wanted him to leave, so that Mehala would be safe inland. But the sick were here, in Sealandings. And here too lay the chance he had always longed for, to combat ignorance – and perhaps win.

'I shall stay, Squire. And try.'

'Thank you, sir,' Hunterfield said. Ven was unsure of the cause for his gratitude.

They rejoined the others, the Squire asking Carmichael what he would need.

'I want assistants, please. If a chaperone could be provided, might I have Mehala? She is skilled in medical lists, and has often done this for me.'

Hunterfield did not glance her way, nodded assent. 'Mehala can see Rebecca, who will attend to you. See Crane. He will find you a place to write, and materials.'

'Thank you, Squire.'

'Tayspill, if you please. Be on hand should I need you urgently for the home estates. And Doctor Carmichael will require you.'

Tayspill raised a hand. Mehala went to the servants' entrance with Ven and Tayspill. There had been no chance to say a private word to him all the livelong day.

48

Throughout the night Ven and Mehala studied the lists Mehala had made, and transcribed Ven's scrawls. During the dark hours, working in the astonishingly efficient illumination from new oil lamps, they produced a map of Sealandings. It was expanded from Captain William Mudge's systematic triangulation mapping under the Board of Ordnance in 1805. That only showed the district, so together they compiled a map of Sealandings itself, giving farms and estates and cottages. Mehala drew in the town and harbour, managing to get in every lane and giving the dwellings numbers.

It was nearing five o'clock in the morning when Ven exclaimed and pointed to the largest chart, now pinned to a wide board.

'Mehala! Don't you see? There are three farms which have not suffered at all!'

'They did, Ven. The blue colour signifies – '

'Yes, yes!' he cried excitedly. 'But they only suffered *once*! No recurrence! No spread to the rest! No sickness among the families either!'

She was almost dropping with weariness. She had tried persuading him to rest, stop for a meal, anything for respite.

'So? Does it not mean they were simply more fortunate?'

'Perhaps. But it may mean *they did something different!* Don't you see, Mehala? Let us assume these three farms had the same risks as the rest. What if they all three coped with their sickness the same way? *Then they have an answer!* And we must make all act the same!'

'And if not?'

His shoulders drooped. 'Then we know as little as before.'

'I have the lists.'

He read them swiftly, becoming more excited than ever. He raised his eyes to hers in awe.

'Mehala. All three farmlets are small – none has more than thirty beasts. All keep their herds separate, all confine their pigs – and all killed any sick beasts the instant they recognised the disease.'

'Yet they had the sickness, Ven.' She assumed the role of devil's advocate.

'Once. *Then no more!*' He fumbled for the lists, almost snatched them from her. 'You see? Some others had the same risks, but handled their beasts differently. These three farmers killed their beasts by striking the poor creatures on the head. No blood was spilled, no cuts. Then the beasts were burned where they lay, unmoved. And the farmer prevented any carrion animal from approaching until . . .' He sat in a chair, almost awed by sudden understanding. 'It fits, Mehala! A sequence of events, a chain of consequences!'

'But now the sickness strikes throughout Sealandings.'

'True! So let us try now to limit it, as if it were new!'

'How?' She was almost past caring, from wanting so badly to reveal what Hunterfield had said.

'By doing as the safe farms did. Even at this late stage!'

His eyes were brilliant with hope. It almost broke her heart. There was no avoiding telling him the truth about herself. And not many more hours were left. He was shaking her arm in excitement.

'Pen, Mehala, if you please. A new list!'

'Yes, Ven.' In a matter of moments, this would seem like a paradise lost.

Not long after, they became aware of a commotion. Squire Hunterfield was roused by a visitor, and strode past in a long flowing nightcoat of thick wool. He paused imperceptibly as he caught sight of the two of them and their mounds of papers and charts, then hurried on. Minutes later, Crane came to summon Ven. He was hurried off to see Meg, the maid of the lady at Milton Hall. She had been carried upstairs and laid in a maid's truckled bed in the dormitory.

Mehala worked on, partly aware of Fellows De Foe's gaze as he stood waiting in the corridor, watching her. He neither spoke nor moved, until some time later when Hunterfield descended the stairs, fully dressed for the day that had not yet dawned. Together they spoke some time in undertones before walking slowly off down the corridor leading to the main reception hall.

An hour, or perhaps only a few minutes later, Ven himself returned, eyes a-glow.

438

'Mehala,' he said, dazed by the good fortune. 'We are to return to Shalamar, come dawn. Both of us!'

'We are? That is . . . is . . .'

'I know, Mehala.' He misunderstood her inability to speak. 'Let us say nothing. Just resume work, and delight in Shalamar when morning comes.'

How did the high women of Ancient Rome feel when baulked? Loss has its own fury, Thalia discovered that morning. She should have been awakened at eight of the clock, and it was forty minutes later before any servant bothered to arrive. Fellows was absent from his bedroom. His dressing room was tidy, as if *he* had been served. But she, mistress of Milton Hall, was left unconsidered. It was a gross abuse of her leniency. They would pay: the whole of Milton Hall would pay. She rose in a blind fury, and set out to punish.

But there was something wrong. Meg was nowhere to be seen – some pathetic slut came as substitute with the bland message that the master had sent Meg on a special errand. Thalia was speechless. It was incomprehensible. A lady's abigail was her property. That was immutable, God-given. How dared the underlings transgress! She would have blood for this. Doubtless Meg, that whore of an abigail, had muttered all night long about the well-deserved whipping she had earned, and made the entire Hall a mass of sullen resentment. Well, the mistress had finally risen. Milton Hall would suffer a rude awakening!

She slapped the substituted maid-of-all – an incompetent bitch called Joanna she should never have accepted in the first place – and demanded to know where Meg was, threatening that she would thrash her again, the idle bitch. The maid sobbed all through Thalia's toilet, dropped combs, hairpins, made mistakes with her dresses, failed even to get the bath-water right. 'All it takes is twenty buckets of hot, you stupid whore!' Thalia shrieked, flinging her laburnum powder bowl at the girl's head. 'I shall not tolerate laziness!'

The house was stiller than she could ever remember. It *felt* wrong. This stillness held a core of malice. Calm was altogether different; so was quiet. Those two qualities were peaceable. Some mornings one actually wanted tranquility, to sail from dawn gently into day, into afternoon and reach evening untroubled. Not often, for excitement was the very soul of life. This morning, Milton Hall was ominously silent. Perhaps this was the reason she had always feared peace, for it often brought the feeling of being alone. And loneliness was the most terrible thing on earth.

As now.

It was all-pervading, bringing with it sundry cruelties: neglect, whisperings, spiteful gossip. Since girlhood, she had known there was nothing so wicked as even the most charitable smile. Innocence was a myth constructed by the weak to praise their own hopelessness, a smile a dagger's stab. Sweetness was trickery to deceive. She used them to the utmost. Why else was her brain given her?

As soon as she was dressed, she rushed downstairs to have it out with Fellows. Her temper was met with a worried ignorance from Mrs Randon, the housekeeper. Ennis the footman, idiot, could not put two words together. She had to rely on Prengle, lately the head servant on Willoughby's advice. He was supervising the breakfast room with four maids. She noticed with a frisson of alarm that only one place was set.

'Is the master abroad, Prengle?'

'Yes, m'lady. Since six of the clock.'

She controlled her anger. That she, mistress of so mighty an establishment, should be reduced to enquiring from servants for her husband's whereabouts!

'What message did he leave for me?'

'None, m'lady.'

The old dolt was parroting his replies. She swallowed her rage.

'Where is my abigail this morning? Who had the effrontery to – ?'

'Begging Your Ladyship's pardon, the master had Meg conveyed to see Doctor Carmichael.'

'Meg? *Conveyed?*' The world spun, came to rest. A *maid?* In a *carriage?* She gestured imperiously, and the four breakfast maids fled. 'Explain, Prengle!'

'The master rose at the fifth hour, m'lady. He sent Ennis to discover the whereabouts of the town leech, one Carmichael. The master then rode to Lorne House. Two grooms and a footman took Meg to Lorrie and thence on to Shalamar.'

'To Shalamar?' It was said in a whisper.

'The master placed Meg at Mrs Trenchard's cottage. I had Mrs Randon send Joanna to you, hoping for your approval,' Prengle hesitated. 'Meg was adjudged ailing, m'lady.'

'How came this *ailment* to the master's notice?'

'The master did not say, m'lady. Does Your Ladyship wish – ?'

'Quiet, Prengle.'

The words were intoned, level, quiet. She waited a moment, then ordered breakfast for herself.

It was served in monastic silence, the maids freezing in fright at the slightest sound of dish touching plate. Thalia felt only slight gratification from seeing one maid's hands tremble so badly she was unable to serve a simple tansy. Such ineptitude was good grounds for dismissal. That pleasure would be savoured later, when all this subterfuge was exposed for the malicious plot that it clearly was.

But behind the morning's disruptions lay the one single delight that shone throughout her whole existence, and would illuminate her life for ever. Carradine, her beacon, was back in Sealandings, and was wholly hers.

Very well. This curious message – Prengle was elderly, might have got things wrong – about the leech and his bitch returning to Shalamar against her express wish . . . And that catastrophic excursion of her stupid Cousin Charles into the magistracy had proved a damaging error. It could be rectified. The first thing was to assess the injury to Charles Golding's ambitions. He was expendable; Carradine was not. But why was Fellows at Lorne House? Only he could countermand her order to Willoughby that Shalamar should be restored. Admittedly work was proceeding slower than expected, owing to the storms, this cattle plague, supplies arriving ever slower. But Shalamar was still too grand a pile to hold only a blundering quack and his doxy.

She toyed with the food. Carmichael's doxy. Wherever that stray whore wandered, trouble followed. Always, since she was dragged ashore. What bliss, for Mehala to have gone back into the North Sea instead of that trollop lately drowned! Such wishes were fanciful. Cousin Charles had failed to eliminate her and the leech. She herself must take a hand.

The meal ended by Thalia rising suddenly, making the silver

coffee pot and its tray slide to the carpet with a fearsome crash. Coffee splashed gratifyingly. Her dress was ruined, of course. It was a semi-piedmonted pelisse-robe in ghastly pale green with hideous front bows down to the hem, therefore no great loss. She had already decided on a lavender dress instead. Green was unlucky for ladies to wear going a-visiting, as everyone knew – so why had that cow Joanna put her into this awful rag? More malice. She lashed at the maid who leapt forward as the silverware fell, and swept from the breakfast room. She would see the cost of the damage to her valuable dress and the carpet was paid for by a communal bating of wages throughout the Hall. That would turn the servants' sullen anger on the four breakfast maids. Serve the bitches right.

Prengle received her order for the phaeton to be fetched with a silent bow. Ennis was not to be seen, which was a pity. Thalia wanted that dullard's account of the events on the journey to Bures House. By the time she had finished dressing she had decided what to do: Charles would have to propose. Letitia Hunterfield would be better, more malleable than that empty-headed but restless bitch Tabitha. What sense had a woman who read all day long? And if the marriage proved too bothersome, Letitia was too retiring a character to challenge anyone threatening it. She could easily be dispensed with. Yes, Letitia Hunterfield would be the instrument of annealing Hunterfield's fortunes and those of Charles Golding. Charles must propose to Letitia today.

The sight of Shalamar moved Mehala almost to tears. Her Flora's Dial was ruined by mounds of builders' sand. The house itself was exposed, almost unclothed, with the vines and creepers pared away from most of the front aspect. Stone slabs leaned in ranks against the kitchen walling. Two windows of the second storey were boarded over. The interior was dusty, threadbare and ramshackle as always, but in four rooms the walls had been reconstructed. The plasterers had almost completed their work there. Old Mrs Trenchard and her husband were already waiting, the old lady beaming in tearful pleasure and proudly bearing a solemn message: the maid Meg from Milton Hall was lodged at the Trenchards' cottage, for propriety's sake, for her injuries to be treated once each day, a fee of thirteen pence daily being sent from Milton Hall for the purpose. Trenchard doffed his rough hat, revealing his soiled woollen underhat. Ven shook his hand. The old man quickly whistled his dog and left in embarrassment.

Tayspill had been ordered to come with them. All reconstruction work must cease until further notice. The agent Willoughby was nowhere in sight. No workmen appeared until long after ten o'clock, by which time Tayspill had lost all patience and ridden off on his hack to carry out Carmichael's first instructions.

Oddly, the one thing Mehala missed was having a trunk to unpack. They had nothing save their clothes.

'I feel more lost than ever,' she told Ven. She asked Mrs Trenchard to bring a hot drink of tea, using the provisions fetched with the cart that had brought them from Lorne.

'Lost?' Ven looked up, his eyes shining. 'Lost, when we are home again?'

The old deal table Mehala once found in the south corridor and re-polished for Ven's use was now in one of the redecorated withdrawing rooms, much the worse for wear. The plasterers had used it for laying out their implements. Ven quickly covered it with Mehala's notes and the large chart of Sealandings.

Mehala reached over and touched his hand. 'Houses have their loves and hates, Ven. Just like we people. Do you believe that?'

'Yes.' He seemed surprised. He straightened, looked around. 'Yes, I do. Shalamar feels . . . right. It is as if we have always been, well, living in a state of – '

She spoke to cover his stuttering. 'It gave us its blessing, when others would have denied us.'

'That's it, Mehala! Could anything be more auspicious?' He excitedly returned to his charts. 'And now we have a golden opportunity to stop this disease!'

'There is a matter I have to speak of, Ven. It – '

'Can it not wait, Mehala?' His eyes were already on the large chart. He had placed crosses, circles, dots, to depict their findings. 'Our residence here I can leave to you. I am famed for my clumsiness.'

'Have you made your decisions?'

'Yes. All of them, though we have only just started, Mehala! Look at the tasks to be done! Think how important our records might be for the future!'

'Does Tayspill have them?'

He showed her list, annotated now. 'He soon shall. We have the whisky, so are free to ride anywhere. You can drive: I can hang on the cane basket. First, copy these out, Mehala. This wretched hand has swelled to twice the size. A mortal cruel surgeon she was, who reduced my dislocation in the dark!'

Tell him, she thought, and with sudden resolve took his hand. He smiled, a little startled.

'I have some grave news, Ven dearest.' She could not go on for a moment. His expression altered.

'News?' He searched her face.

'News given me by Squire Hunterfield.'

'When he gave us separate audience?'

'Yes. Forgive me, Ven. I have been desperate to tell you. I forbore only to save you worry.'

They stood facing, holding each other's hands.

'Is it so serious, then?' he asked at last.

'I fear so.' Her voice had sunk to a whisper. 'I am from . . .'

'I heard you are the Lady from Red Hall.'

She almost recoiled in shock, letting his hands go. 'You know, then? But . . .' But he could know no more, or he would never have proposed.

Ven admitted. 'The maid at Bettany's windmill was very kind. She had once seen you in your carriage, in high-born company.'

'What else did she tell you?' Mehala felt herself go giddy, and managed to sit on a stool. This was more terrible than anything she had experienced.

'Nothing. She left the district immediately.' He came, put his arm on her shoulder. 'Your station deterred me from saying anything, Mehala. Once before, I was foolish enough to hope, against all sense. It came to grief – happily, as Fortune proved! I was young, ignorant beyond measure. Now I am a little more seasoned. And a thousand times more fortunate, in having found you.'

'I – I was once married, Ven.' She felt his hand start away, and caught his sleeve, looking up. 'Please, hear me out. I never doubted but that he was drowned. In the dim images of my mind, as it returned to me, I was sure I was alone. I still have that conviction.'

444

'Married?' He could hardly say the word. He stared at her as if he had never seen her before. She saw him inspect her mob cap, her hair, her shawl. He was a man trying to see.

'Not now. I am certain. But Squire cautioned me against expectation. In the eyes of the law I am not yet free.'

'Married.' He repeated the word dully. He turned to stare at the fire, look round at the walls, examine some chart as if his attention was suddenly caught.

'I can stay, Ven. Help you – live here as your housekeeper for as long as . . .'

'Until you are noticed. We can live here, in dread of some chance encounter?' He spoke without rancour, stood looking into the flames, one hand on the cornish.

She went to sit on the inglenook stool. This was worse than ever she had imagined. A thousand times she had gone over it, to cause him least injury. She wanted him to erupt in white-hot rage, strike her, cry out in anguish. Anything would do, instead of this quiet reason. His wound was so deep she bled with him.

'What will you do?'

'Do?' she asked, startled. All would depend on his decision, his response. She was fortunate that Ven did not ask how long she had stayed at Shalamar with her memory quite returned.

'You have . . . responsibilities at Red Hall.' He was wondering if she had children, a family, parents.

'I think I have not.'

'Can you be sure?'

'I call to most of my memory, Ven. I *am* alone. My parents are passed on. The same with *his* people.'

'So you knew.'

'I became more sure as the weeks went by.'

'And your place?'

'It is – was – a large residence, few servants, not as grand as Shalamar must once have been.'

He seemed to rouse. 'Did Hunterfield advise your best course?' He asked it in a tired, flat tone. It had been all too good to be true, his voice said.

'To admit my identity. To you, then to all.'

His listlessness dismayed her. She had seen him worried, unbearably saddened, moved to tears by the children, and the disease among poor familes, but this terrible apathy struck her.

'What must I do, Ven?' It was all she could do, bring it to him.

'Have I any say?'

Since her revelation he had not uttered her name. She wanted to hear him say it. 'Yes, Ven. You have the right. My being with you, before and still, is because my affection is returned to you as given.'

'Circumstances preach otherwise.' He took a deep breath, looked from the fire at the mass of documents. 'You have a right to know, of course. I shall see this through. By then you will have decided if you ought to return to Red Hall.'

'And ascertain my legal position, Ven,' she said eagerly, hope returning. 'There must be some way of making sure.'

'One way or the other.'

Dear Heaven, she thought, what if Elijah was alive? Hunterfield implied it was not impossible. Where one had been saved, so could another be.

'I have every confidence, Ven. My dear.' Her eyes filled. He was so stricken. 'A woman *knows*. I could not be more sure if I had seen . . .'

It was ghoulish to speak so, hoping that monster was dead so she could rejoice at Sealandings. Ven shook his head, staring blindly at the charts.

'You have already said the law is one thing, and unsupported beliefs another. No. We have to endure. I thank you for your assistance in this epidemic. I cannot cope without you. But for now, we must stay apart.'

'Apart?' She rose and stood before him, trying to take his hand. 'You mean, me to leave Shalamar? On the day we return to it?'

'I dearly wish you to stay,' he said with sudden harshness. 'But what would Sealandings say? They would see you as a betrayer of your class, a traitor to your station in life.'

'But I have known poverty, Ven. Before I became mistress of Red Hall, I was but a fishergirl on Ray Island.'

'You reason as I wish to reason.' He ran his uninjured hand through his hair. 'Sealandings – all society – will see it as sin. While you were a sea waif, you were accepted. You were assumed to be of lowly status because of your abilities. Good at everything, beautiful without artifice.'

'I am the same person, Ven.'

'To me, always. But to others? Never. To the great families you will instantly become a traitor to all gentry. To the folk you will be the lady who has sunk from position. Their world is set. Preaching and teaching tells how we are born into our stratum of society, there to remain for aye and a day.'

'The world is changing, dearest!' She cried the words, wringing her hands. 'The late wars against the Tyrant showed it! Armies greater than the world has ever seen, led by peasants' sons! Navies that covered oceans, captained by common men! And in the North the land itself is felled to industries' empire. The gentry are moving *with* the commonalty, or being left to one side! Can we not continue as we were? I promise I shall return to the Essex coast as soon as you declare Sealandings free from the plague!'

He looked at her. 'I simply fear for you. Can you not see? I am hopeless. Unable even to protect myself from bigots when I treat prostitutes. How can I protect you? We could have been hanged, transported, but for the Squire's clever deception.' Ven hesitated, thinking of the lengthy efforts the Lord of Sealandings had gone to, on Mehala's behalf, but said nothing of it. 'I prove poor company.'

'You are the company I want, dearest.'

'I will bring you ruination. That was the Squire's meaning. Work with me, if you wish. I shall be grateful. You are important to me. But public opinion is a vicious judge.'

'Until when?'

'Until the world changes. Or until we can change it, by some means.'

'So I must leave?'

He leant forward and placed his mouth gently on hers, withdrew as she moved towards him. A carriage sounded on the driveway.

'You have always helped me. Help me now, Mehala.'

When Tayspill and a coachman entered, they were at their former places, Ven poring over the lists and dictating to Mehala. She was writing, head bent.

447

49

Tayspill had twenty men assembled in the central yards of Lorne House's home estate. A sombre Hunterfield rode up on Betsy as the carriage bearing Mehala and Doctor Carmichael arrived. Lieutenant Carmady accompanied the Squire, riding a stable hack with unease and worrying the reins every few moments as if trying to convince himself that horseback was his usual means of progression. He caught Mehala's eye briefly, gave a slight bow. She looked away, concentrating on the men who would carry out Ven's instructions.

Three gamekeepers, a scatter of farm labourers, two cattle herdsmen. All were from Lorne House. The grand families had ignored the Squire's call, as usual. Simple Tom dismounted, waiting by a fence. He smiled at Mehala, touched his hat to Ven as they descended. Hunterfield nudged his mare to confront the men.

'Good morning,' he began. 'Your task begins today. You will visit all the farms, homesteads, smallholdings, tenancies, and the great estates too, in Sealandings Hundred. You will be guided by Doctor Carmichael here. He is High Constable. Mr Tayspill will serve as legal agent.'

He scanned the faces, gestured with his riding stock to indicate Mehala.

'You know Mehala. She will write down certain things, on my order.' He caught the shuffle of anxiety among the men. 'Those of you who do not write need not fear. She writes only what actions are decided upon, who is fallen sick, what cattle need be killed. She writes nothing that can tell against you. I promise you that.'

'Squire, sir!' A hersman raised a hand and stepped forward as he made the traditional call to be heard. 'What if the writings be not shown thee, sir?'

Hunterfield nodded. It was a fair question, from illiterate country folk who saw writing as the fearsome making of magic hieroglyphs. There was a dreaded symbolism in the sinister black marks that despoiled white virgin paper.

'Very well, Nodger. Name any one among you, then, who can read.'

The man reddened in pleasure at being named, and called, 'Doctor Carmichael, Squire!'

Several men said an, 'Aye!' To them there was no incongruity. A doctor kept his counsel, and in any case wrote letters for most of the illiterates in Sealandings.

'So it shall be,' Hunterfield pronounced. 'After each farmstead is dealt with, Doctor Carmichael shall read aloud what Mehala has writ. Doctor.'

Nervously Ven stepped forward. He had never addressed so large a number before.

'Good day, gentlemen. We will go in turn to every place where sickness might be evident, among cattle or man. Every beast, pig, sheep, cow and bullock must be looked at for signs of illness. If one such be found, it must be killed by the old country method of stunning – no blood-letting. It must be quick; the beast must then be burnt. One group must obtain wood sufficient for the purpose. The fire must be watched to its ash, so no part of the animal is left unburnt for carrion.'

He thought of the notes in his surtout pocket, but after the Squire's expert handling of the writing problem refrained from pulling them out to check.

'The numbers and disposal of sick beasts should be told to Mehala for writing down.'

'Doctor, what of dead meat? Some farms have cattle dead a-field. I seed 'em.'

'They too must be burnt as they lay. Even if they are partly crow-picked.'

'And in the brooks? We bain't be loightin' many fires in water this morn, Doctor!'

There was a general laugh, to Mehala's relief. Doctor Carmichael flushed at the good-natured jibe.

'Cattle already thrown into streams or ponds must be dragged out and burnt, even if partly decomposed. I shall be on hand at every farm to explain. Farmers must weed out their sick beasts immediately, separate them in open field, and send word to Shalamar.'

449

'We do this tomorrow if need be, Doctor?' The men were becoming interested.

'And tomorrow, and tomorrow,' Ven said firmly. 'Until the murrain is gone from Sealandings.'

'What if it keep coming back?'

Ven looked at the ground, cleared his throat. 'I believe it won't. After a few days of this, perhaps two weeks, we shall have no more murrain plague here.'

The men murmured, staring at him. Nodger spoke up.

'Doctor! What should a man refuse to let us take his sick beasts?' Nodger glanced apologetically at the Squire. 'Some farm folk be mortal strong resisters. We'm loike to get galdered for touching a man's mung, much less his cattle!'

Carmichael glanced helplessly at Hunterfield, who nodded Tayspill forward as he spoke.

'Let no man obstruct you this day, or any following. And inspect the mung fodder, that no offal from dead meat lies therein. You know Mr Tayspill. He carries my legal order. All cattle killed will be paid for at half market value. No farmer shall conceal – *all* beasts must be seen. Spare the healthy, kill the sick.' He smiled bleakly at the man Nodger. 'Now launch away, less it be time for Nodger's kickel.'

The men laughed. Nodger pulled out a piece of the sugared currant bread from under his smock and mock-offered it to the Squire, who averted his face with a grimace to general good humour. He turned his mare and cantered from the yards with Percy Carmady joggling along behind.

The men fell silent. Ven looked along the rows of faces, suddenly feeling lost with Hunterfield's departure. Mehala stepped beside him.

'We thank you for doing this work,' she announced in her clear voice, 'and for letting us be with you. The book will be here on the carriage for all to read who can. If any doubts, let him come to Mr Tayspill and thence to Doctor Carmichael. Victuals will be supplied daily: beef pressed in salt corns, cheeses, breads, and small beer to wash the corned beef down apace!'

Her levity amused only a few. A gamekeeper spoke up. From his manner Mehala guessed he was the one who had played host for Ven.

'Doctor, *will* the murrain plague end, by all this?'

Ven drew breath and Mehala tensed. He had promised to cut the plague short by these measures, yet he had admitted he did not know if they would work.

'Yes. In two weeks, Comber. Farms which disobey will suffer longer.'

Mehala broke the silence by stepping up to the cart. The men took up their two-pronged forks, Tayspill mounted his hack and with Simple Tom riding along, the procession moved out of the estate heading for Prothero's Calling Farm.

In the distance a carriage attended by three outriders approached the main gate to Lorne House. Mehala discerned the gold and blue of Bures House livery. Charles Golding would be the greater enemy now, after his débâcle and demotion. He would see his failed ambition as the fault of others, especially Ven and herself. And his cousin Thalia De Foe knew no forgiveness.

Coldly Thalia inspected the man seated opposite in the carriage. He had obeyed this morning. No drink, freshly presented, elegantly dressed. She sighed in exasperation. It was like having a bear, ignorant and hopelessly stupid.

Charles Golding was aware of her scrutiny and took offence. 'You wish to speak, ma'am?'

'Don't be pompous with me!' Thalia snapped each word out and sat thin-lipped as the carriage slowed to enter Lorne. 'I despair. You can't even follow instructions!'

'There are too many, Thal!' Golding smarted under her attack. She gestured for him to lower his voice lest the postillions heard. 'You are forever hectoring, badgering. Not a single day but what you hatch some plot.'

'That will *do*! I have to plan! You are beyond doing that for yourself, Charles – you always were. Somebody has to forward the family ambition!'

'It should be me, Thal! It is undignified for a gentleman. I am the head of our side of the family – I do not include your feckless husband. His family is gentry for a few generations only, mine since before the Conquest.'

She stared him down, ice in her expression and rage in her eyes. 'You forget, Charles. I too am of our family's blood – though God knows I deplore your being the notional head. You have not a tenth the acumen of Fellows.'

'Acumen?' Golding jeered. 'When he lost almost every penny mercantiling in the South American Bubble?'

'And recouped handsomely, by something called diligence! Would to God you did as well, with the ample fortunes my family bestowed on you!' Her words cut him like sleet. 'I am presenting you with a means of cobbling your tattered esteem. You will for once think with pride – *pride*, Charles Golding! – of our lineage. Remember the grand patrimony, nobles from whom we are sprung. Nobles that ruled empires, Charles.'

'I am sick of them,' he grumbled, fazed.

'Do as I tell you!' She leant across and tapped his knee. 'Today you propose to Letitia Hunterfield. I have gone to a great deal of trouble arranging this. Henry Hunterfield is no fool, for all his countryfied concern. Everyone looks up to him – fools they! Your status mends, the moment that meek little woman accepts. She will be delighted to receive your proposal, of course. You must act overcome with delight.'

'Have you arranged Hunterfield's acceptance?' her cousin asked, with sly innocence.

'That will do!'

He was pleased to have struck back. 'From the length of your past association with Hunterfield, you more than any have a right to enter closet agreements with that gentleman.'

She would have slapped him in anger, but he offered his cheek. It would show a mark, of course. Normally he withdrew and almost whimpered. He always had done as a child.

'No more, Charles Golding,' she whispered. 'Not one word more, or I shall wash my hands of you completely.'

'Yes, Thal,' he said miserably.

'Now compose yourself. Your purpose and actions, Charles?'

'I propose marriage. She accepts. I say how thrilled I am.'

'Very good.' She looked out of the curtained window. 'We are arriving. Remember; do not change one word of your rehearsed proposal speech. Attempt no humorous chatter – you always fall on your face.'

'Yes, Thal.'

'*Never call me Thal*. I shall not tell you again.' She inspected him

452

from head to toe. Her certainly looked the part. She sighed. Carradine could stand in rags and look fifty times the man, and for all his rectitude, Hunterfield asleep carried more authority. 'God help me,' she said, 'but within the hour, you will be the second mightiest gentleman in Sealandings.'

The Hunterfield ladies were waiting in the main hall of Lorne House. Thalia De Foe was pleased the day was here at last. Charles really ought to be settled, and a Hunterfield girl would be better than most. Hunterfield's support, Henry's wisdom and unflagging zeal in the Eastern Hundreds would carry the Goldings to the heights they had singularly failed to reach under Charles' drunken guidance. It would do Charles no harm to have a pliable obedient wife. And, who knows, Henry Hunterfield had been no bad plaything. Should Carradine travel occasionally, she herself would have proximity's excuse to perhaps take up Henry where she left off – assuming she could evade the eagle eyes of his bitch of a sister Lydia Vallance.

The welcome was somewhat less than effusive. Lydia herself emerged to receive them, with Tabitha holding back as befitted her station. Hunterfield was in the library, and came to join them once they were settled in the green withdrawing room. It had a small terraced walk outside the french windows, but the ladies agreed it was far too inclement to have them opened.

'No Lieutenant Carmady, Squire?' Thalia asked brightly. 'Is he afraid of so many ladies, then?'

It would have been improper for a male visitor to intrude in close family business. Hunterfield made some polite excuses for Carmady, and told of the efforts begun that day to counter the effects of the murrain.

'Percy Carmady has been of utmost help,' he invented generously. 'It is a pleasure to have him now come to stay at Lorne, together with Miss Carmady.'

'I know they are perfectly charming guests, Henry!' Thalia gushed. 'Miss Mercy is such a sweet conversationalist. So ingenious at inventing topics to discuss!'

'I am only sorry you cannot accept an invitation to take coffee,' Lydia said, equally gushing but vastly relieved the interview would not be prolonged. 'I have some grains from the Dutch colonies of St Eustatia which you should test – it is reputed to be the best imported! But,' she added quickly in case Thalia decided to change her mind, 'I see your purposes today are too compelling.'

'Indeed, Mrs Vallance.' Thalia smiled at Charles, then Tabitha. 'I am only here to witness, however. My dear Cousin Charles is the one who wishes to speak.'

'Tabitha,' Lydia said. 'Could you please find Letitia, and wait perhaps in the west corridor? I would be much obliged.'

'Leave, Lydia?' Tabitha looked imploringly at Henry, and received a look from him that made her rise and quickly absent herself. There was silence as she withdrew, not quite slamming the door.

Lydia smiled. 'High spirits are commendable, are they not,' she said in a level voice. 'Thank heavens youth is no prohibition to beauty and talent, or I should find many of the young tiresome indeed!'

Her nervous smile faded as Charles Golding rose. He was imposing enough in his short cape, worn Spanish fashion, cast back over the left shoulder. His spencer was highly embroidered, his shirt so ruffled it seemed nothing but chitterlings of pure white. He wore a shawl collar to his toilonette waistcoat, and elegant collegian boots of bottle green leather.

'Sir Henry,' he began deferentially. 'I notified you on an earlier day of my profound admiration for one of your sisters, an admiration that has endured. I come formally to ask your favourable response to my proposal. I request, sir, her hand in marriage.'

'Please proceed, Charles. I shall hear it.'

'Thank you, sir.' He cleared his throat and continued, growing in confidence. 'I have felt the deepest longing for Miss Letitia's company over the past year, from afar. I am unable to refrain from laying at her feet my possessions and myself. As any gentleman making this commitment has the right to ask, could you please see your way to conveying my proposal to the object of my admiration?'

'Do seat yourself, Charles. I am happy to.'

Hunterfield nodded while Lydia rang the bell and Crane appeared to take the summons for Miss Letitia. The old man's stately progress was watched surreptitiously from behind the pillars and curtains of the great hall. He paused crossly to catch the

454

chief maid Rebecca and scold her for allowing so many maids-of-all to be excitedly whispering about the place instead of getting about their duties. She curtseyed in apology and obediently banished the maids elsewhere, then herself silently returned to see Miss Letitia announced into the company. Of course the whole of Lorne House was agog, knowing a proposal was imminent.

Inside, Letitia crossed to sit on the Grecian squab, avoiding looking directly at Golding or Thalia De Foe as she greeted them formally. Her heart was beating so loudly she wondered if all could hear. She had been dismayed when the summons came, and Crane had given her the compliments and not Tabitha. She was desperate to look at Henry, see what he had decided, but was afraid of Lydia's response. She prayed there would be time to obfuscate, plead for a few months, anything. Lydia smiled as she made the announcement.

'Letitia, a great honour has been done to you by the gentleman visiting us this morning. You are well acquainted with him, as we. He has asked permission of our brother for your hand in marriage.'

Letitia lifted her eyes imploringly to Lydia, but saw only her older sister's concealed delight.

'I am honoured, ma'am,' she answered quietly.

'Charles Golding's eminence in the great families need not be stated, Letitia. Any girl will be proud to accede.'

Thalia De Foe was smiling in approval. It was predictable, of course, that the girl would – should! – be overcome at the honour. She probably was beginning to be afraid she might not attract any gentleman, and here was Golding himself, the very plum of the Sealandings gentry, calling to ask for her hand! If Letitia had been anything other than overwhelmed, she would have been furious at such a wanton display of immodesty!

'I am aware of that, ma'am,' Letitia told the carpet.

'And?' Lydia prompted, almost hugging herself with pleasure.

'I request time to consider my reply, ma'am.'

'Time. . . ?' Lydia fingered her amethyst necklet. She glanced at Henry, who was looking steadily at Letitia. 'Time, Letitia?' She carolled a nervous laugh. 'Come, Letitia! What need for time? I assure you there is nothing lacking in modesty, to give instantaneous acceptance!'

'Certainly not,' Thalia cooed. The girl was right to be meek, seemingly reticent. 'In fact, it is a lady's duty to acquiesce to such!'

'I . . . I request a little time, sir.' Letitia's voice had become all but inaudible.

'But . . .' Lydia was appalled. This was tantamount to a refusal. She dithered, wondering if Henry would blame her for this. Or was Letitia hiding some ghastly reason?

'Very well, my dear.' Henry's deep tone startled them all. He nodded at Thalia and Golding. 'It is a lady's prerogative to want a few moments of secret guesswork, is it not?' He was smiling. 'My sister has, what, a fortnight to consider.'

'To *consider*, sir?' Thalia bleated in affront.

'Henry, dear . . .' Lydia said faintly, feeling her face turn all colours at once.

'Yes.' Henry rose, sighing, extending a hand to Letitia so she could rise to him without giving offence. 'Heavens knows what these girls find to think about! Half the time I think they don't know themselves. Allow me to conduct you, Letitia.'

He led her out of the room, with apologies to the visitors, and gently into the great hall.

She turned tearfully to him as soon as the door closed. Crane withdrew quickly, driving the flustered Rebecca as she was discovered, leaving them alone.

'I am so sorry, Henry. I have disgraced you and the family. But I – '

'Shhhhh, Letty,' he said quietly. He rubbed a rough hand on her cheeks. 'Dry your eyes. I do not blame you in the slightest. I only hope that madman you prefer dresses half as well!'

She looked at him, blinking in amazement. 'Madman?'

'That lunatic artist.' He gave her a rough buss on her forehead. 'Get along, Letty. I shall have a hard time getting rid of this pair.'

She was astonished. 'Oh, Henry! Thank you! I shall be truly so very good, honestly – '

He watched her go, smiling, then turned ready to re-enter the room and face recriminations.

50

The visits of Brillianta and Lorela Astell to Sealandings had to be postponed. Coastal gentry ruefully cancelled proposed jaunts to relatives and friends inland. Others invented various pretexts, then fled.

The flight of great families from the murrain only served to spread the evil news through the Eastern Hundreds. As far as the Isle of Southwold and the Colne estuary, and inland beyond Wheatfen even to Cambridge and Rutlandshire, the ill-fame shot fear into the hearts of traders, merchants, drovers. The waggons of Sealandings were stoned on the highways, turned back from tollgates. The mail coaches made the muddier and costlier journey to Saltworth, and there refused to come the remaining three leagues as news worsened. No ships docked in the harbour. Only Sealandings folk frequented the two taverns, and they spent sparingly and less often. The market was not held, by common consent.

It was two days after Charles Golding's ill-received proposal that he received Letitia's letter. It was thoughtful, gracious, but declined his proposal. He was left in no doubt about the permanence of her feelings against continuance of such an offer. She expressed sympathy, good wishes, and deep appreciation of the signal honour done her by the affection he had expressed. It was not in her heart to return that fondness. She ended with felicitations to his cousin the Lady of Milton Hall. She had informed her brother the Squire.

Thalia was shown it by a bemused Charles, who brought it to her within an hour. She read it in total silence. He felt relieved, though partly outraged at the insult. He ranted before Thalia, declaiming a new hatred of the Hunterfields.

She heard him out, silently placing the letter on the social table – Charles was already at the bottles in its semicircular recess. He was pacing, agitated. Was he putting on a show, to conceal relief? Or was he genuinely drawn towards Letitia Hunterfield? She realised with a slight shock that she no longer cared.

'Charles. Please leave.'

'Leave? Leave what?' His eyes were bloodshot. He had been drinking heavily.

'Here, Charles. I am . . . busy.'

He left more puzzled than angry, but clearly glad she had not thrown a paroxysm of rage, his usual fare when his cousin's plans did not go right. She did not even accompany him to the porch. Instead, she went to her husband's smoking room. He was not there. For a moment she sat on a sally wood chair.

The furore raised by Hunterfield's assault on the farms afflicted by the cattle murrain had caused Fellows to make special rules for the household, insisting on their strict enforcement. She was compelled to apply them, for he continually questioned and inspected. She fretted at being unable to ride out. Learning that Carmichael and Mehala had come with a bailiff and a score of Hunterfield's men to confiscate, kill and burn Milton Hall's valuable cattle, made her speechless. Fellows simply ignored her fury, speaking past her to Prengle and Mrs Randon on more than one occasion. Everything seemed to be *wrong*.

Since Meg's removal, Fellows had seemed even more distant. Normally she would have welcomed this, but now, something cold was forming, a hideous conviction that authority was leaving her. Meg had been her source of Sealandings news – not the silly who-said-what gossip of parlours, but the more vital happenings. Like how it had come about that Carradine was now at Carradine Manor and the Protheros returned to Calling Farm. And what tavern talk said about Carradine's ominous change in house-keepers. Why no word from him? Each day she hoped to drive out to the lonely cottage where they had met before; each time she had been baulked. The night before, she had flown at Fellows in anger, saying Hunterfield was under the influence of that evil woman Mehala, who was using the outbreak of disease to get power for her pimp Carmichael. Her husband responded quite mildly, and strolled away.

Her mood since then had swung deliberately to one of sober conviction: disaster was imminent. She rose from the sally wood. The window looked away from the trees of Whitehanger, towards the north-west. The sky was black with smoke from burnings. You expected fires in autumn, yes, but this madness made her shudder.

All Sealandings was an inferno. Even this limited view showed several flickering red pinpoints, bonfires that had been going on through the night. Pillage, looting – that's what it was. Destruction on a scale worse than the disease itself. All caused by that malign Mehala. Without her, that cheap quack would have been successfully imprisoned by now, and forgotten. But Mehala swayed Hunterfield, Golding's advancement was despoiled, her own plans ruined. Any fool could see it: Mehala had Hunterfield.

She felt suddenly cold. A new spurt of flame showed on a tenant-farm less than a mile away. Fellows told her they were torching stores of animal foods – had there ever been such a thing? – digging new channels to quicken the water flow in brooks, and draining ponds. That might be the explanation for Carradine's delay: he too was being forced to undergo this mad inspection, and to stand impotently by while Hunterfield's despoiling army ravaged his herds, all in the name of a crazed leech and a whore. She rang for a shawl. The maid brought it, the wrong one of course, but Thalia accepted it without comment and stood watching the fires. She craved Carradine. Let Sealandings suffer its ordeal by fire. She would torch the whole world for him. Whatever Fellows decided to do on the morrow, she determined to ride out to Carradine Manor, unless she heard something today.

Prothero took the note, read it thunderstruck. Read it again. And again.

'. . . *reasons for debit sums on Calling Farm demanded from Carradine Manor estates. The liberty lately acceded, for you to sojourn at Carradine during your recent difficulties, should in no case, sir, be understood as an extension, of that freedom to larger purpose. I am accordingly instructed, sir, to return your statements of debit, with the information that no such notes will be honoured at Carradine . . .*'

Some ignorant clerk had signed it, with a million flourishes. Not even Carradine's hand.

'*My* recent difficulties?' Prothero asked the counting house. All Sealandings knew that he, Jason Prothero, had rightful possession. He had documents to prove it.

A sudden horrible suspicion struck. His hand was trembli

he unlocked the bureau for the two precious copies of the document appointing Carradine his – *his*, Jason Prothero's – resident agent. They were gone. He stared at the wall. He searched in silence for an hour, through the bureau, his other rooms, frightening his wife and servants by his silent obsessed progress. He then questioned Mary, Mrs Perrigo, then all. Finally, he went to sit alone and look at the bureau.

Would the theft – for such it was – matter? With two copies already lodged with inland lawyers? But no receipt had yet come. He stared at the letter, and smelled the smoke from more burnings.

The Prothero farm received its third visit from Ven and the men that afternoon.

Prothero was on hand. He spoke only to Tayspill, coldly ignoring Carmichael. He did not glance Mehala's way, but brusquely ordered his men to get her tax cart off his estate. Mehala was driving the compact one-horse vehicle. She complied, tethered the vehicle and walked back.

Ven was supervising the carnage. By now all of the dead beasts had been dealt with. Mounds of ash still smoked everywhere across the Calling Farm fields. Three whole lengths of hedgerows were lost, timber stacks being claimed for firewood. Copses had been drastically thinned for kindling. Five stands of trees had gone. The very landscape was changing.

For all his animosity, Ven gave the man his due. Prothero was as able a farmer as any in the Hundred. He was indefatigable, seeming to find in his refutation of blame a reason to carry out Hunterfield's commands with a frenzy approaching mania. He was the first to attack the trees, the first to reach for the stounding hammer to kill the next ailing cow, the last to pause for rest when sawing branches for a new fire. The farm was despoiled, almost a total ruin. Only one herd survived in any number. Milking was done to spare the cattle, but the valuable yield left to sour. Ven ordered that the barrels, bought at Prothero's expense, be covered and stored until the milk had fully curdled, then taken and ~~tied~~ from boats standing out to sea, and the barrels burnt. documented each cask, inventing a marking system to ~~day~~ of filling and the herd milked.

~~d~~ that the men leave work for meals. No drinks were

to be had during spells of labour. Small beer from the Donkey and Buskin and Lorne House itself was provided by a Surrey waggon, with food sent from Mrs Kitchiner at Lorne. The men were unhappy at their unpleasant tasks, grumbling about seeming trivia. One complained he wanted his dog along. Another was made to surrender his favourite sickle when it was inadvertently dropped where three sheep had earlier been found dead.

As the searches and burnings went on, Ven became more obsessed with avoiding touching the sick animals. It was on this same third visit to Calling Farm that he ordered all labouring men to replace their outer clothing at the end of the day's work. The soiled smocks and hats were steeped in beer fetched from the brewing vats of the Donkey and Buskin and heated in two huge coppers, drawn on a Suffolk waggon, and left to be heated to boiling at the last farm gate.

'I know it seems eccentric,' Ven argued with Tayspill when there were protests. 'But it has to be.'

'But *beer*? Everyone already thinks us mad, Doctor.'

'Let them. It stops the transfer of bad ferment. It succeeds for breweries, so it may for us.'

'The taverner wants to speak about payment, Doctor.'

Ven sobered at the news. He was buying six barrels of fresh beer every day. Mehala had already relayed the bafflement of the washerwoman at Lorne House at receiving a score of beer-boiled smocks each noon and the same again at dusk. He went to speak to Prothero, but the man bawled at Tayspill to get the idiot leech away from him or else. He walked up to the main house, where Mary came to the door with her maid Libby.

'I shall not allow myself to be invited in, Mrs Prothero,' he said without preamble, to Mary's unspoken relief. Libby withdrew, leaving him awkward on the steps.

'I understand, Doctor.' She glanced over her shoulder. Mrs Perrigo the housekeeper glided across the hall and from sight. 'My husband is in the fields.'

'I know, Mary. I tried to speak with him a moment since.'

She looked down the drive. Apart from two sawyers cutting a tumbled beech there was nobody.

'Oh, Ven. Is all this necessary?' To his dismay her eyes filled. 'I feel everybody blames Calling Farm, and this destruction worsens it so.'

'I don't know, Mary.' Ignorance sounded absurd. 'I see it as a cleaning operation. A debridement of a wound.'

She implored him. 'You could be wrong, Ven. Yet you order such killing! People already protest. Mr Prothero has petitioned the Squire that it all cease.'

This brought him up short. Mehala, who now slept at Lorne House, had said nothing. 'On what grounds?'

'That some sick beasts recover, and can be sold. It is money thrown away, for . . .' She hesitated. 'Crazed ideas.'

No word had come about this from Hunterfield, either. 'It must go on, Mary. Your husband loses only a fraction of his possessions. I . . .' He hesitated in turn, steeled himself instead to speak of money. If Prothero was trying to raise opinion against him, Hunterfield might lose conviction. Then all was lost.

Ven felt the press of exhaustion. Partly it was learning of Mehala – possibly widowed and thereby in mourning, or possibly still married and therefore beyond reach for ever – but part of his utter weariness was physical. He had not slept. At night he transcribed Mehala's lists, and produced plans for each successive day. Now this new threat from Prothero. Many in Sealandings would listen, and parrot Prothero's words to order. When Prothero's land alone had suffered the outbreak, all were against the man. Now, most were suffering the forcible loss of their livestock, irresponsible damage to their breeding herds, crops, fodder. They would be all too eager to yell assent with any man, Prothero included, who opposed the extreme measures.

'I come in urgency, Mary. I need assurances about money from Mr Prothero.'

'Money?'

He was puzzled at her expression of alarm, even fright? He felt he must have misunderstood the fleeting look in her eyes, for Prothero was now among the wealthiest men in Sealandings. Admittedly Calling Farm was suffering, but Carradine Manor so far had suffered little.

'I regret to ask. It is for supplies of . . . of liquor for cleaning the men's garments after work. Tayspill rules that your husband is liable. May I charge the bills to Carradine Manor? I am sorry, Mary.'

462

She was clearly struggling for composure. 'Ven. Please. I tell you in strict secrecy. Mr Prothero seems to be experiencing difficulty. He charged eighty barrels on Carradine Manor yesterday. The bill was refused.'

'*Refused?* That cannot be, Mary. He owns – '

'Carradine is now Mr Prothero's agent there.'

Ven's heart sank. 'Carradine? Back at Carradine Manor?'

'Yes. His appointment was signed, and copies lodged with solicitors. I don't know why problems have risen.'

No wonder Prothero had evaded him. Ven nodded slowly. He would have to tell Tayspill to take the matter up. Whatever else, the work had to continue. To change plans now would be disastrous. He would be lost on a wide sea of ignorance.

'You have my fondest thoughts, Mary. You know that.'

'Ven.' She tried to speak. The words came hesitantly. 'May I see you? I know Jason would forbid me, but I truly do need . . .'

He was moved by her pallor, shocked by her distress. 'My great pleasure, Mary. You know I am now at Shalamar?'

'Yes. Mr Perrigo keeps me . . . mentioned it.'

He left, wondering what occurred between man and wife. How could Mary enter marriage's happy and sacred state young and gay, and change into a distraught tortured soul, all her bright lustre vanished? He returned to the fields. The men were erecting enclosures for the few remaining healthy calves. The Donkey and Buskin would not refuse supplies, but money still had to be found.

During the day he asked Mehala for the news of Carradine Manor. He had sent Tayspill there on the previous day, while he himself had seen to the sick people on the tenant-farms. She gave him three pages. Carradine had suffered least among the great estates, its tenants likewise seemingly spared the devastation. It was almost as if it had been forewarned, and kept its interchanges with Sealandings at a standstill before the outbreak had begun. Or was it something to do with its relatively exposed position? Carradine's land ran along the shore for quite some distance beyond the North Mole.

He told Mehala that Carradine was now back at the Manor, and was refusing Prothero's debits. She said nothing, simply made a note on the top sheet. It was his opportunity.

'Mehala. Forgive me if I intrude, but your former life . . .'

463

'Yes, Ven?' She seemed prepared, laid aside her lists.

'Did you have a friend, a lady perhaps, to whom you could safely write?'

She shook her head. 'I thought of that, Ven. No. My . . .' She caught herself, toyed with the goosequill, replaced it in its wooden sleeve. 'I remember almost all. My existence was solitary, at that place. I lived – was kept – in seclusion.'

He saw a group of Tayspill's men approaching along a footpath. He would have to go.

'Is there no hope, then?' he asked, and could have kicked himself. It was a blunt request to replace a man he wanted declared dead.

'I shall find out, Ven. And soon. I promise.'

She watched him join Nodger's group. Squire Hunterfield could write to the King's Coroner for the Blackwater estuary, or the Deputy of Sandwich. All she wanted was legal proof she was now a widow, please God.

That noon, Hunterfield rode back to Lorne to bid goodbye to Mercy Carmady and her brother. Their decision to return to London had been made the evening before, to Lydia's relief. During dinner, she managed to hide her surprise when Henry himself gently introduced the topic. Sealandings was becoming a deucedly unpleasant place, and likely to remain so a while. Percy Carmady showed no sign of having been alerted to Henry's feelings, but jumped in with alacrity and suggested that, if there was no offence, he ought to think of an earlier departure. Mercy was upset, trying to argue him out of it, but her requests were easily disposed of despite a show of reluctance on the part of the Hunterfield ladies. Letitia was less grieved by the Carmadys' decision than Tabitha, who was starting to see the benefits of having the presentable young ex-lieutenant about the house. He had already taught her carpet bowls, and croquet was to be next. Now, she saw stretching before her a nun's existence, with Henry's ridiculous new rules on remaining at Lorne House making matters worse.

Mercy gave Henry a present of a special laburnum wood sovereign case. Its silver escutcheon was engraved with a sentiment to him in her brother's name, as was only proper, but her

464

sincerity was evident to all. Henry's fondness towards her was also frank. He promised to send her a full account of the progress of the repairs to the sea dykes, in which she had showed a surprising interest. Tabitha hated Mercy all the more, seeing a shrewd cunning where others detected only sentiment.

It was only after their carriage left, with Mercy tearful at leaving such dear friends as Letitia and Tabitha, and Percy being made to promise to return to Sealandings, that Henry's manner immediately became brisk. He announced a particular task he wanted completed, with all speed.

'You will accompany me to Watermillock, Letitia,' he said. 'We leave now.'

'Watermillock, Henry?' Lydia halted. They were not yet in the house, from waving the Carmadys goodbye. 'Should I not be the one to – '

'If you please, Lydia. I require an expert opinion on my portrait. Letitia knows art.' He smiled at them, to share the joke. 'I may let Maderley to ruin my ladies' features, but not mine. The Lord of Sealandings has his pride.'

'Now?' Letitia was shocked by the prospect. 'But – '

'In, miss. Out in ten minutes. I have one letter to pen, to a boring old Coroner at Colchester, then we shall be off!'

Letitia fled indoors, while Lydia inspected her brother candidly.

They walked slowly inside. 'It is not exactly a day to take Letty riding, Henry.'

'I do not intend to, Lyd.' He too glanced outside at the charred sky. It looked thunderous with smoke and soot. 'Matters have gone on long enough. Have you given any thought to Tabitha's position?'

'Yes, sir.' Lydia had her answer ready, though her brother would not be pleased. 'She is proving difficult. I have hopes of Percy Carmady. And Sir Jeremy Pacton has written of his desire to bring his friend Alex Waite. And Rodney Treggan. Though married to Harriet Ferlane as was, he has a brother, Bramston, whom we all rather liked. I can arrange a party as soon as . . .'

'The smoke clears, Lydia?'

And what of yourself, sir? she thought of asking with some asperity, but did not dare. Olivia Maderley was out of the question for her august brother. Mercy Carmady? Obviously smitten with admiration, as her little gift testified. And Henry seemed very inclined towards. Brillianta Astell was Lydia's own choice, though Henry spoke more often of the plainer but cleverer Lorela. Men were decidedly odd, she knew, no accounting for their waywardness. They simply had to be coped with, like extraordinary weather.

'It is cruel to joke, Henry. I have corresponded with several families of our acquaintanceship. I can make a full report of progress whenever you wish.'

'Not today, Lydia. Give me its quiddity by the week's end.'

'Very well, Henry.'

Half an hour later they left Lorne House, Henry driving the large cane whisky with Letitia seated beside him. Simple Tom followed, leading the Squire's mare Betsy. Word was sent ahead, so Mrs Maderley was waiting on the doorsteps of Watermillock ready to receive them. Olivia was busy in the withdrawing room overlooking the side reach of the tide-mill's seawater lake.

'My son will bring the portrait down, Squire,' Widow Maderley announced, flustering her way ahead. Prissie, the afternoon maid-of-all, was in position to take cloaks and gloves. 'Olivia? Squire Hunterfield would like to be seated facing the inner wall. The light is better.'

'Thank you, Mrs Maderley. I acknowledge the place of honour, but I admire the outer view.'

'Certainly! Prissie, the high wicker!'

Letitia noticed that arrangement would place Olivia directly opposite Henry, and waited to be offered the seat by his left hand. She remained there as William arrived in hasty disorder, aromas of oil of turpentine and walnut wafting in with him. He carried an unframed canvas. Olivia did not glance at Letitia.

'Good day, Squire! I do hope you'll be pleased. I have several touches to make to the sky – backgrounds are never finished first, as people believe – '

Letitia looked hopefully at her brother. 'I think it admirable, Mr Maderley.'

William held it up in full view, eagerly awaiting Hunterfield's opinion.

The portrait was unusual. No dark interior, only a lurid expanse of sky tormented by cloud and suggesting a surge of wind. The seas

466

seemed to be cresting under a louring storm. In the foreground was the Lord of Sealandings, looking past the viewer. His eyes were unfashionably wrinkled against the rising breeze, his hair in disarray. He wore a swirling cloak, a muted blue riding coat. His hands were ungloved. The scene was no simple portrait. This man was in harmony with the cruel shores, intelligent, a man of depth.

Widow Maderley laughed uncertainly and fanned herself. 'William! No hat! Is it fashionable to paint the Squire without gloves, though outside?'

Hunterfield said nothing. He was studying his own face. The portrait's eyes were judging, assessing something enthralling. His eyes . . . pierced, in the modern phrase. Did he really look like that?'

'Your opinion, please, Miss Olivia?'

'It is beautiful.' Olivia coloured as she spoke the quiet words. 'Mistrust me, sir. A loving sister, after all.'

'Well, I never heard such!' Mrs Maderley was almost overcome. 'Miss Letitia will give a more moderate view, I hope.'

'Miss Olivia is right, ma'am. It shows me more of Sir Henry than I would have believed possible.'

Hunterfield was still eyeing it quizzically. 'Then the verdict goes in your favour, Maderley. Your commission is ended satisfactorily. I should like to see it alone, outside.'

'Absolutely right, Squire!' The artist rushed excitedly to the door. 'Light bedevils art! We shall look at it facing north!'

Hunterfield followed him out to the paved walk by the herb garden. He watched rather than listened to the man as he placed the painting, scanning the skies, then rushed to move it.

He said finally, 'You have a considerable talent, Maderley, if a disturbing one. You have had success in London recently?'

'Of a minor kind, Squire.' William hesitated. 'Sir Henry. I have a request to make of you, if I may risk offence – '

'You offended me at the sea dykes, Maderley.' Hunterfield was smiling. William, momentarily startled, managed a worried smile in response.

'I apologise, sir. It was a marvellous artistic opportunity! The gales . . .'

'Indeed,' Hunterfield agreed drily as William petered out.

'It is . . . My affections for Miss Letitia, Sir Henry. I have come to so admire that lady that I am unable to withhold a frank statement. Though my position is far below that of Miss Letitia, sir, I can say that my family's lineage, though mercantile rather than landed, is unsullied, and is the object of approbation of some . . .'

Henry gave him an encouraging nod and stood in an attentive attitude, hands behind his back. He stopped listening, looked at his portrait.

Odd how a sheet of canvas, frayed would you believe, nailed to a square of wood then daubed with pigments in smelly oil, could be extraordinarily convincing, even moving the emotions. As much a gift as knowing the seasons, building bridges, handling horses, judging human conflicts. And how strange that a man, shirking duties at his valuable mill, should spontaneously show this amazing skill –

'Mmmmh?' The man had fallen silent. Had he finished? What on earth had the man being saying? 'Ah, well, Maderley. I understand the implications. Could you be more frank about your aims?'

'Sir Henry,' Maderley said solemnly. 'Were you to allow me to apprize Miss Letitia openly of my feelings for her, and she were to approve, I should hope for a marriage.'

He waited nervously. Hunterfield nodded. His attention seemed to have slipped somewhat at a crucial point. No matter.

'Very well, Mr Maderley. You may speak with Letitia.'

He saw the artist's expression light up. Instantly the man began babbling of his prospects for artistic advancement, how he also had every intention of taking his responsibilities at the tide-mill, of his plans for improving the Watermillock estate . . .

Hunterfield made approving grunts as they walked inside. A madman in the family was not such a dear price to pay for keeping Letty's sisterly love. And Olivia would be that much closer, which would be no bad thing. Lydia might prove difficult. He could easily remind her of Tabitha, now her main problem . . .

468

51

The man's breathing had changed. Overnight, Southman had sweated, then entered a parched delirium. He could not get his breath. His woman had sent one of her children running through the dark morning lanes to Shalamar for Doctor Carmichael. He reached the farm by four o'clock, before dawn.

Jode Southman's small tenancy stood behind Prothero's great expanse, bordering the farm of Andrew Nelmes. The farmhouse was in Suffolk pink, that curiously bright hue which in the light of early day always reminded Ven of the late-autumn colour of sloethorn. A lanthorn burned at an upstairs window, and one on the porch wall. The door was opened the instant Ven arrived.

He made a swift inspection of Jode Southman, telling the frightened wife to keep the six children away from where their father lay wheezing and struggling to speak. His throat seemed distended, thickened almost. The sheets were damp beneath his body, where he had voided urine, but not within the last few hours.

Southman was stocky, heavily built, his hands showing all the signs of a lifetime's toil on his smallholding. His features were dark, reddish, his breathing coming fast, gasping.

'Has he drunk anything?'

'No, Doctor. He does not know me. Sometimes he sleeps, but fitful, restless. Then he sinks.'

Ven looked helplessly down at the recumbent man. How marvellous, to have one of those instruments, newly invented, by which the chest could be listened to! Auscultation! Sheepishly he brought out of his pocket a crude cedarwood tube, twelve inches long, one end bell-shaped. It was his own design, cut with old Trenchard's help. The design was taken from a description he had read a year since.

'Can you uncover him, Mrs Southman? I will touch his chest with this instrument, and listen to his breaths.'

'Will it hurt him, Doctor? Only, he has suffered much worry lately, that . . .'

'No, Mrs Southman. It is a new instrument called a stethoscope.' He did not add that it was homemade, by guesswork based on nothing more than the imperfect memory of a casual description, and that he had never used it before.

He hesitated. Did you listen by putting the bell end on the naked chest? Or was that the end you put to your ear? The doctor to whom he had written had mentioned some metal tube thing that 'acted as a stopper', but Ven had no idea what that meant. Gingerly he put the bell end to his ear, and pressed the blunt end of the wooden cylinder to Southman's chest. The heartbeat was immediately audible, but came and went as the man breathed. It took him quite some time to realise his stupid mistake: the tube's angle of the device altered with each breath, so the sound escaped. Press it firmly to the skin, freeze motionless in position, and you could hear continuously.

Trying not to look as if he was proceeding by trial and error, he reversed the cedar cylinder, and put the bell end on the same place. He was immediately astonished at the almost deafening sound of the heart's beat. The bell end to the chest, that was it! Far better than the naked ear, the way some doctors did. How criminally wrong, for doctors to be so secretive with their learning, jealous lest other doctors used the knowledge to increase their earnings. He listened rapturously, overcome with the impression of some hugely sophisticated engine working away in the human body. It was . . . it was beautiful! He listened to the breathing, faint whistling and cracklings. What did they mean? Some patches of the lungs beneath seemed to transmit few sounds at all, the breath dull and distant. Others came through with a horrid rushing sound, as if the very windpipes leapt suddenly close to the surface. It was all beyond him. The poor man was in a terrible fever. Ven put aside the stethoscope and felt Southman's skin.

'Cover him, please. Come aside, Mrs Southman.'

In the parlour he consulted Mehala's notes of this farm and its vicinity. It was not yet dawn but, even opposed by the light of the pottery Norfolk lantern, the eastern sky showed a hint of morning.

'Have you had cattle deaths, Mrs Southman?'

The woman looked frightened, wringing her hands in her apron. 'No, Doctor. None. As God's my judge!'

470

'I didn't ask for a sworn oath, Mrs Southman. Only whether your husband has had contact with the cattle plague.'

'No, Doctor. None!'

Ven checked the notes again. Mehala never erred. One or two mistakes of interpretation, yes; they were natural. But for unrelenting accuracy she was unexcelled, better than he himself by a royal mile. He trusted as well as loved her. Yet the poor farmer upstairs was dying of the chest complication which was somehow acquired from sick cattle, if his theory was right.

'Mrs Southman, your man is very sick. It seems to be the malady which afflicts others in Sealandings. Do you understand?'

She nodded, her appalled eyes on him. He tried to find refuge in his handful of papers.

'Come dawn, Mrs Southman, I must bring Mr Tayspill's men back here, and search every inch for traces of missing cattle. My list says you have a few sheep, and six pigs. They too will be . . .'

The woman burst into tears. She started to speak, babbling. 'I said we should get in trouble with the Squire's men, Doctor, but Jode wouldn't listen. He said it was a golden opportunity, meat being so scarce with the murrain upon Sealandings, God save us.'

Ven listened, heartbroken. A cow had fallen sick. Her man had concealed it on the hedged border with Calling Farm, only bringing it out after Tayspill's men had left. He then slaughtered the beast, and alone prepared the meat for sale. But that was the night before this, and he had not risen at all. His eldest boy Thomas had helped.

'How is the boy? Was it he came to fetch me?' The lad had seemed well enough, having run most of the journey carrying an oil lantern.

She caught at his sleeve imploringly. 'Oh, please, Doctor. He's but a child. He sleeps yonder in the downstairs cot.'

Ven made her rouse the boy. He came blearily, seemingly in health. He confirmed his mother's story.

'Today I take the meat cart to Eldridge's. He has already paid Father.'

Eldridge was the butcher in Sealandings. His shop adjoined Bartholomew Hast's premises.

'Thomas. Today you will do nothing until Mr Tayspill says. The Squire's men will come with the dawn. Show them the place where

471

the cow stood in the hedgerow, and where Father prepared it for sale.'

He was thinking of Eldridge, an obsequious man of pious reputation. Mehala had called on the man the day before, and asked him to report each afternoon how many beasts he sold, and their origins. Ven had not brought that first list with him, but could not recall any mention of supplies from Southman's farm.

The inhalation he prescribed would do little, he knew. He left the small quantity of peppermint, cinnamon bark and lavender oil, but had nothing else. He thought wistfully of old Doctor Arbuthnot, who could easily afford so much of the Camphorasma plant from the Indies that he would occasionally chew a piece of it, absently spitting out the residue into his surgery's waste basket. He did not need to tell Mrs Southman how to prepare an inhalation bottle.

'Will it do him good, Doctor?'

There was no easy way. 'Very little, I fear. Prepare for the worst. We know of no cure. Hope is all we have.'

He left her weeping. Without a lantern, he stumbled towards the spreading light of dawn, cursing his ignorance. Wealth seemed to go hand-in-hand not only with pleasure but also a person's lifespan. Every great household in Sealandings had apothecary cabinets filled with costly medicaments. It seemed so unfair. Poor Jode Southman would not see another dawn.

The Landau Grande Daumont was one of the grandest carriages Milton Hall possessed, drawn by four greys, with two postillions. Fellows, readying himself for departure to London, expressed surprise at his wife's sudden desire for such ostentation in so confined a theatre as Sealandings.

'The whole area is dead as a doornail, my dear,' he observed, to Thalia's irritation. 'Yet you emerge like a queen in state!'

'I intend to call on Mrs Prothero, Fellows,' she told him, cleverly. Mary Prothero could be at Calling Farm or at Carradine Manor. She intended to find Carradine, from whom still not a word. 'Thereafter on my Cousin Charles. I need to make an impression for the good of the people's morale.'

'Do hasten back, my dear,' Fellows said mildly. 'I need some moments of your time, on a family matter.'

They parted amicably enough. Thalia took the offside facing seat, always the best in a landau, and even, it was said by the riffraff who had to travel by those conveyances, in a common post-chaise. She would not have to suffer the view of the postillion's rear bouncing up and down on the nearside grey, the subject of much vulgar ribaldry. She gave the leading postillion instructions to make immediately for Carradine Manor.

Her journey was literally clouded by the smoke rising from fires in a huge crescent round Sealandings. It now hung in a single pall, mercifully drifting slowly inland on today's cool easterly wind. She put aside her venomous thoughts about Henry Hunterfield. If the insipid fool was gullible enough to follow the dictates of a quack doctor intent on ruining the Eastern Hundreds, let him. Already rumours told of the Lord Lieutenant of the County demanding to know what calamities were being visited on the coasts. And now that lunatic dog-doctor was experimenting at Shalamar with brimstone and other hideous compounds! Yet still Hunterfield listened to the dolt! The Squire was heading for a fall, and his own ruin. The murrain was bound to worsen, with all this burning madness. It always did, in spite of all.

The vehicle's leather heads were drawn up, to make it a closed carriage for fear of soot falling on her dress. Her bibi capote was cream in colour, always wise for her lovely complexion, and her curricle pelisse was new, its three capes cunningly falling in shades to accentuate her figure. Carradine would admire her more than ever. And want her the same. Of course, the poor dear would be off in the estate somewhere, like as not. She smiled openly, imagining his joy. He would ride to the mansion, fling himself from his mount and come rushing in, bellowing his delight . . .

It was threatening a light drizzle when her landau came to a stand outside the main steps of the Manor. She alighted, adjusted her skirts to perfection, and glided in to be met by Hobbes, the elderly chief servant. He was accompanied by a plain maid-of-all, one in fact so ugly that Thalia could not help but stare. Oddly, the girl carried a half-chatelaine at her belt. Hobbes explained that the master was in the flower garden.

'Mistress Blaker has instructed that you be conducted there, m'lady.'

'Mistress . . . ?' *Mistress* Blaker? The serving woman who . . . ?

473

Thalia gave a curt nod, and was ushered through the house to the garden. A wide flagged terrace rimmed by a low stone wall was set with statues and ornaments – new, and hideous. Just like her Carradine to have indulged himself, with execrable bad taste. As ever! She smiled to herself as she glided winsomely across the paving. The gruesomely bad ornamentation was more evidence that Carradine needed a woman's touch, in every way! Like the sloppy message the chief servant had given her. And that extraordinarily ugly maid, wearing the chatelaine of an assistant-housekeeper, if you please! The sort of thing a man would never notice, but which to a woman told clearly of hopeless disorganisation in any household!

She stopped at the terrace wall. Four steps led down to the rose garden. Carradine was there, a woman on his arm, smiling and chatting to him. Her manner was possessive, intimate. She was deliberately looking away from the house, and thus away from Thalia and the accompanying servants, though she surely must have heard them arrive. Hobbes coughed behind his hand.

'If it please you, sir. I announce Lady De Foe.'

Judith Blaker looked up, bored to welcome. 'Ah. Thank you, Hobbes. Rad? Introduce us.'

'Good day, Thalia. Lady De Foe, may I present Mistress Judith Blaker. Judith, I present Lady De Foe.'

'Do come, Lady Thalia,' Judith Blaker gushed. 'Rad and I are having *such* an argument! I long for a lady to set him right! Assist me.'

As if in a trance, Thalia moved down the steps and stood staring at Carradine. She was speechless. This woman was the very one she herself had sent into custody some months ago. Who had embezzled the household moneys from her cousin Charles Golding's estate. Who had inveigled her own wandering kin into Bures House, to public scandal. Who had stolen, filched, and utterly exploited the Golding property. Her low-life enemy, no better than a trollop. Who now wore a lovely expensive dress of coral, made, Thalia saw as white-hot rage came to her aid, of that most costly material which folk called 'French' merino, though of English manufacture. And a small matching decorative shoulder cape of Florentina! When this ignorant cow was nothing more than a prison inmate, who deserved to wear nothing better than crude marry-muff.

'The question is these new plants, Lady Thalia,' the upstart bitch was saying airily. And Carradine mute. 'Oh, Cant. Come here.'

An old gardener approached, diffidently touching his hat to the bitch before acknowledging either the visitor or Carradine himself.

'Cant is most knowledgeable about things floral, Thalia. Tell this lady, Cant, about these new flowers.'

'Well, m'lady,' Cant began, while Thalia's mind screamed at the insult. *She! To call me 'this lady'!* 'The dahlia, it is called. Brung to the Continent from a place called Mexico in 1789, nigh thirty years agone. Royal Gardens, it were, in Madrid. Our ambassador sent seeds home. Since Wellington, God save him, saw Tyrant Napoleon safe off, it is fashionable in London.'

'You see, Lady Thalia?' Judith Blaker beamed. 'Isn't my old gardener a veritable mine of information?'

Thalia said nothing. She could feel Carradine's tension, his enveloping shame. And servants to see his mortification! *Yet he endured it and said nothing*. Thalia felt weak. The old gardener mistook the silence for an invitation to continue his rambling discourse.

'Frenchmen believed dahlias would be tasty, loike, m'lady. But what can you expect, from a Spaniard priest called Cavanilles, and a Paris professor? Enough to feed a county through the seasons, they thought. I tasted it. Inedible, it is!' He tutted at the folly of foreigners. 'Tastes nothing on earth!'

'Thank you, Cant. That suffices.' Judith Blaker smiled brilliantly at Thalia and invited her to join them in a walk. 'Isn't Cant absolutely marvellous? He worked for me once before, at Bures House. You may possibly remember him!'

'I do not,' Thalia ground out, glaring at Carradine. 'I have no wish to promenade in your company.'

Judith Blaker glanced at the darkening skies. 'I do agree. It seems most inclement. Isn't that odd? After such a promising start! Come indoors, Thalia, for some hot chocolate – no! I remember.' She gently steered Carradine round until they were heading back along the walk. 'It's *tea* you so much prefer, is it not?'

Thalia felt her face drain of colour. She had sacked this odious trollop from her cousin's employ for adulterating precious varieties of Singlo, Haisven and Campoi tea, that most valuable commodity, with various gums and leaves, and so stealing large sums of money. Judith Blaker prattled on.

'Rad, dear. Go on ahead and fetch my Aragonese. Thalia and I will not reach shelter before the drizzle catches us!' She turned confidingly to Thalia as Carradine strode off without a word. 'I have a new bonnet, made of macabre. I hate it! I want an excuse to spoil it, which this weather will provide! Rad is such a dear. He shall get me another, when we go to London . . .'

She looked at Thalia De Foe in sudden concern, placing her hand restrainingly on the other's arm.

'Why, Thalia, my dear! How very pale you look! Are you well? Have I said anything to upset you?'

Thalia struggled for composure. She faced the scheming bitch in a blind fury. Blaker had stolen into Carradine Manor, and somehow disaffected her lover, emasculating him by some sinister treachery she could not understand. It was a mistake to speak. She should have swept out immediately, keeping what shreds of dignity she could. But her rage drove.

'Have done with your effrontery, Blaker,' she heard herself say. 'Whores never change. All women know that. I don't know how you have seized authority here, but I shall never move aside. I rid a great house of you and your foul kin once before. I shall do it again.'

She marched away, up the steps and across the terrace, hearing the woman's mocking cry of regret.

'Oh, Thalia! *Must* you go? I have some wonderfully fresh Bohea tea! Come again!'

On the way Thalia passed Carradine. He was emerging from the double doors with a bonnet in his hands, staring straight ahead. She did not give him a glance.

The man Jode Southman died at four o'clock that day. Ven was at hand, impotent. In the sickroom there was evidence of Mrs Southman's ineffectual attempts to ease her husband's breathing. The towel, the earthenware jug in which she had made the infusion, the scraps of cinnamon bark. He died in a torment, hot as fire, his last breaths rasping, delirious, babbling incoherently.

Shamed, Ven said his few words of sympathy to the weeping woman. He tried to speak, say anything, to the appalled faces of the six children, but could not. He left, and caught Simple Tom on the road from Watermillock, his fourth attempt to catch up with Tayspill's men since morning. They were working vigorously, touring the farms ever faster now they knew the procedures. He reported the death to Tayspill, and sent Simple Tom to tell the Squire.

Hunterfield visited Shalamar an hour later, as Ven arrived intending to make notes about the dead farmer. Mehala was already there, seated at the deal table that was now the centre of all Ven's records. Hunterfield was asking after the conditions at Southman's place.

'I shall visit the family repeatedly, Squire,' Ven told him heavily. 'The man's son Thomas worked with the sick animal.'

'Could he too die?'

Ven squared up slowly. He felt like death himself. 'Yes, Sir Henry,' he said quietly. 'He may. Or not. I do not know.'

'And the family?'

'I am less sure still of them.'

Hunterfield nodded acquiescence when Mehala asked if they would take some small beer, all there was. He observed the house curiously, staring round at the wretchedness of the place. Some windows gaped badly and were patched with paper and rag. Floorboards in the porch were badly warped. Mrs Trenchard was sent for the drink. There was no fire, on such a cold damp day. He kept his cloak on, and wished he could have kept his beaver Wellington hat on also.

'How goes your scheme, Doctor?'

'Mehala. Give Sir Henry our progress.'

'Yes, Doctor.' She took a moment counting along a list of figures, then summed the numbers for him: the cattle sickening, removed, burnt, the people reported ill. She ended with a mention of Eldridge the butcher. 'Dead meat is evident in the butcher's shop, Squire.'

Hunterfield listened, glancing at Ven. 'Does it matter? Some country folk swear by dead meat.'

'They are the poor, Squire. They will always swear by what they can get.' Ven made a gesture of apology. 'I am not guilty of leveller talk, sir, but everyone would eat fresh food – if he could afford it.'

'Are the sick people . . . ?'

'Three bought the cheap meat, Squire. Eldridge says he has done nothing wrong.'

'He bought meat believing it was fresh,' Mehala explained. 'He lies, though.'

'Lies? How do you know?'

'The only beast we missed was Jode Southman's hidden animal. Tayspill says no other could have escaped counting. Doctor Carmichael ordered a new count today. Two animals are not accounted for, both from Calling Farm. They must have been sold to Eldridge.'

'Is this true?' Hunterfield asked Ven, who invited him to look at the chart.

'You see, Squire? The total gives all cattle, sheep, pigs, in Sealandings. Those we have destroyed, subtracted from that total, leaves those still alive. It falls short – '

'Of the two from Calling,' Mehala completed for him. 'And Eldridge's piety covers the omission.'

'You are very sure of yourself, miss!' Hunterfield spoke sharply at this new headache.

'No, an you please, sir. I am sure of Doctor Carmichael's belief.'

'Is *he* so sure, though, Mehala?' They spoke as if Ven was not present.

Mehala spoke quietly. 'No, Squire. I must be sure enough for us both.'

Mrs Trenchard brought the small beer. It was cold, in plain countryware.

'Thank you, Mrs Trenchard,' Hunterfield said courteously, taking one. He noticed Carmichael did not touch his but kept his eyes on Mehala's charts. Even as he watched, Ven pulled out from his pocket a piece of paper and gave it to her.

'Give me a time, Doctor,' Hunterfield said at last. 'When can we tell if your measures will succeed?'

'I *did* guess fourteen days.'

'A murrain usually wanes only after three months,' Hunterfield said heavily.

'You shall see me declared right or wrong, Squire, within the fortnight.'

Hunterfield thought with sudden surprise, why, he's a brave man! Such a revelation at this late stage! The quack could simply go his way, leaving Sealandings to its plight. Instead, he risks the superstitious hatred of uneducated folk, who mistrust a doctor's potions and medicines.

'Time passes at speed, Doctor,' he said kindly. 'I think you and Mehala need a pony trap of your own. Give Tayspill the tax cart.' If Carmichael's notions failed, and the murrain raged on unabated, at least they could escape the people's vengeance in a pony trap.

Ven was startled. Mehala concentrated on her charts without looking up.

'For me, Squire? I've . . .' He reddened.

Never ridden? 'Simple Tom will bring one across to you, Doctor. Thank you for keeping me informed.'

Ven caught him as he made to leave. 'Please, Squire. Keep the trap. Give me the money instead.'

Hunterfield looked his surprise. It was out of character.

'I have lately experimented. I need chemicals, expensive compounds in large quantity.'

'For what?'

'Contagion is the transmission of disease by touch or close habitation – or so we think. The strongest known destroyer of contagious miasmata is chlorium, a dangerous gas.'

'Gas? Can it be bought?' It was beyond Hunterfield.

'No, but it can be made with three parts of common salt added to one of black oxide of manganese. I would collect the gas in a water trough. Once, with my own eyes, I saw Sir Humphrey Davy conduct the very experiment.' Mehala gently gave his drink into his hand. He took it mechanically. 'The powerful gas, so trapped, is believed to destroy miasmata. I shall use it for instruments, clothes, dead animals, to kill the disease principle.'

Hunterfield sighed. The costs themselves were fleeing reality. Very soon, far more would depend on this Doctor's theories than mere reputations. If the plague came to a speedy end, his own coffers would feel relief at least equal to the people's.

'Very well. See my principal bailiff at dusk. And have the trap also.'

They thanked him, Mehala curtseying and Ven accompanying him to the porch. He rode out, glad to be heading home to Lorne House, where there would be a warm fire and dry clothes. He thought of Carmichael and Mehala at Shalamar. He had dispatched a groom to Colchester, bearing a letter to the King's Coroner there, asking after any local reported drowned around the date of Mehala's rescue by *The Jaunty*. He did not mention Mehala's name, nor give her description. Answer would not be long coming.

52

The drizzle remained steady on an onshore breeze. It troubled Ven. He said as much to Mehala when she remarked how unusual the thick warm moist air was instead of brisk autumn winds and squalls. The very trees seemed to be waiting. Folk began to mutter of yet more storms brewing in Sealandings Bay. The few drinkers in the taverns spoke ominously of past tragedies, and saw portents everywhere. The religious hinted darkly of the 'Doctor's smoke' causing unknowable dangers. There was even mention, where cliques gathered, of sinister powers forcing Squire Hunterfield to obey the whims of evil. Doctor Carmichael's name was on everybody's lips, and with him that of the strange girl Mehala.

The land became saturated, as it had been after the Sir Roger storm made the roads run rivers. But this wetness was somehow more penetrating. The very world seemed filled to brimming. Clothes never dried, even indoors. Fuel would not light. Cottages chilled. Draughts came unbidden. Polished furniture lost its shine under a faint clinging mist of damp that never went, even by afternoon. Of an evening, fogs held the air still as paint out in the harbour. No boats put to sea. Lanterns burned lower, though wicks were trimmed and oil reservoirs replenished as always. Candles appeared dim, on the point of quinkling. Children coughed all night long in the heavy air. Labourers began to default from work, staying home not to tend their own patches of land but to sit hunched before cold grates.

Church alone flourished. Churchwardens made folk sit in the aisles, and sent children running home to bring stools to cope with the crowds. Reverend Baring's sermons were his lengthiest and most sepulchral, on texts drawn from Old Testament prophets obsessed with doom. Misery, he lectured privately to Euterpe, is what religion needs among simple folk. He did not hear her replies. In his thunderings were references to a destructive God who rained disaster on the heads of the unheeding. One such miserable woman was the prostitute Bella of Two Cotts, swept away as punishment for her wickedness, and drowned in the harbour which gave Sealandings its life. She now lay buried outside the churchyard, in unconsecrated ground. A fate she richly deserved, to be shunned by the pious in death as in life. There she would remain until the Last Judgement, when her shame would be evident to the whole of Creation.

The death of Jode Southman brought most dismay. He had been popular, a tug-o'-war hero when younger, and one who had fought famously in the annual football free-for-all with White-hanger's battlers one May. People began to remember that Doctor Carmichael's secret ritual called vaccination was done in the farm next to Jode's – and wasn't it cows he used, those very cows now dying in their scores? And him now cunningly trying to rid Sealandings Hundred of the evidence by burnings, casting the remains overboard from boats that he sent night-stealing out over the dark sea?

The talk grew. Discontent and rumours fed on each other, especially when news came that Doctor Carmichael was now brewing potions in strange glass instruments of a night, working alone in the hours of darkness at his great gaunt house of Shalamar. Curious alchemical compounds, of unknown powers, were purchased from afar, to brew fluids he kept concealed, the evil fumes being discharged into the night sky. Only at dawn did he desist from his mad rites, and start the day in seeming normality. But what malevolence did his secrecy conceal? An innocent farmboy wandered into the grounds of Shalamar, for laths to make rabbit snares – and Doctor Carmichael had set about him, shouting in anger that he could be killed were he to come near the strange containers bubbling on a fire built right there, on Shalamar's old herb garden. He tried explaining that it was some evil gas, to be avoided at all costs. But why make more destruction, when Sealandings already suffered so?

A group of the religious leaders petitioned the Squire for an audience, were received and heard out. They wanted Doctor Carmichael's alarming nocturnal activities stopped. Also, how long were the burnings to go on? Could they not be halted, at least until the dreadful unending wet weather eased? Nobody could trade. All commerce and mercantile activity had now ceased. No ships arrived. The smoke signalled terror and disease to the passing coastal ships. Waggons avoided Sealandings. The post no longer came. Coaches now approached no nearer than Wheatfen. It was now no longer a question of what was right for Sealandings, it was a matter of how much longer the religious elders and churchwardens could hold the people's fear and anger in check.

Squire Hunterfield let them have their say. He said he had given Doctor Carmichael all the help he could, to curtail the cattle plague. The Doctor had promised that the plague would end soon – in less than three weeks, instead of as many months. Reverend Baring reminded the Lord of Sealandings that pain and suffering were sent from Heaven to punish mankind's wickednesses. As such, they were Divine. Retribution could neither be shortened nor eliminated. Heaven's punishment was sent for our instruction, and as reminder of our mortality ever since the first evil despoiled the Garden of Eden . . .

Squire Hunterfield said his decision had been made. God would judge, would He not? he ended drily. In a matter of days, now, the plague would end – if Doctor Carmichael was right. It would continue for two or three months more, if God saw fit to expose Doctor Carmichael as wrong. He ended by asking for their prayers. When they had gone he mopped his brow and called for some of Letitia's special cherry wine. She kept it back for him, for occasions of special trauma or delight. That day he stayed indoors, while Letty sang to the William Southwell Cabinet Pianoforte, an ingenious new device which she played admirably. And he listened without hearing a single word as Tabitha doggedly opposed Lydia's plans for the forthcoming wedding of Mr Maderley and Letitia. He drank the whole bottle and, surprised to find it empty, called for another.

53

A woman acquires a sure sense of her house far more telling than a man ever does. Thalia *knew* Milton Hall had gone awry. Not in the attitudes of the servants, no; they were as obsequious as ever – and they had better stay so. And Fellows was as blandly indifferent as ever. She had resorted to the woman's artifice, of inviting lovemaking. It was the evening of her dreadful visit to Carradine. She was satisfied Fellows felt exactly the same. Fellows always loved in a tumult, tumbling away into some sky like a delirious clown at the May 'outgoing', where even the gentry danced with milkmaids to fife and tabor. Simple, like the deluded fool that he was. That aspect was still secure.

No. The air in the house felt wrong. Oddly, it was the same in the grounds, along the rose arbors, the covered walks by the ornamental lake. Heavy alien air, difficult to breathe, hard to endure. Rest was beyond her. Fellows' conversation was inane as ever – about London, dealings, finance, the cost of some hideous estate he had acquired in the despicable Midlands. As if a gentleman should concern himself with such things! They should be left to hirelings, the under-folk, servants such as bailiffs, agents, stewards . . . and housekeepers?

The thought of that upstart bitch now queening over Carradine Manor was so galling that Thalia almost fainted. Fury kept her still, staring into space, seeing the trollop done out in finery like a magistrate's wife going to the Michaelmas Day appointings. Her fury would strike that woman from Sealandings forever. Obviously a lowly harlot, carriage-climbing to grandeur through schemery. It was no surprise, now Thalia had had time to think, that the evil cow ingratiated into a place with the aid of sundry subservients, then obtained employment for them. Her familiars. Thalia had indeed recognised the babbling old gardener and that ugly maid Prettiance also – hadn't she too been at Bures, got in by Whore Blaker, to spy out the land for yet more familiars?

Coming back to Milton Hall after that terrible defeat, Thalia's first impulse was to write to her elderly cousin Sir Philip Banks, who had tried and sentenced the thieving bitch, and demand an account of her conviction. How had she got free? Was it by devilment, or special influence? That was always a risk, friends in high places. Thalia had resisted that impulse, and instead went over every clue, every memory, however painful, of that humiliation. Carradine had fetched her bonnet! For Christ's sweet *sake*! Her passion-crazed lover who had once bludgeoned her to the carpet in some heated exchange, aye, here in her very own house, with Meg keeping a terrified watch on the stairs and Fellows due back from the capital any moment – and torn the clothes from her, to beat then take her as she was, almost stifled by being pressed against the bed valance as he slammed and thrust into her.

No. This was something new, outside her experience. Perhaps not new to Carradine, who had lately known humiliation, though now thank Heaven that was mercifully ended. *Or was it*?

This thought rankled, coming to her again and again during fitful sleep when she struggled for answer. She tried to direct Fellows' maddeningly dull conversation to Carradine, circuitously via Milton Hall estates, servant expenses, the sufferings of tenant-farmers, Hunterfield's hopelessly optimistic expectations about the epidemic, the deaths in Sealandings. But Fellows was either too clever – ridiculous to imagine! – or too stupid to be pinned down. She even tried a short visit to Lorne House, for nothing more than a coffee trial, hoping to draw out the Hunterfield ladies on affairs at Carradine Manor, but got no further than hearing them all declare that Isle of Bourbon coffee was far superior to Levant coffee, before they started on the forthcoming betrothal party of Letitia Hunterfield and that lunatic millwright-artist William Maderley. She had showed disapproval by her manner. If God intended the gentry to couple with brute artisans, He would have made everybody equal. God had, in His infinite wisdom, created nobility to rule, and serfs for work.

On the third night after that slum-bred slut had jeered her from Carradine's terrace, Thalia began to see a glimmer of light. Perhaps it was in this very notion that a germ of the concealed truth lay. How *had* the whore climbed from gutter to ladyland, from bare foot to fur slipper? It was a power that reversed positions. Blaker was mistress of Carradine; the master the servant.

Of course! It had happened once before, had it not? Thalia was so excited that she sat up in bed and exclaimed aloud. Carradine had lost all; now he was temporarily reinstated. But he behaved as if . . . *as if he was at Carradine on sufferance!* That was it! He had temporary mastership because of Prothero's insurmountable problems – but what if the whore and her brood of familiars somehow promised Carradine *permanent* repossession?

She lay back on the pillows, and pulled the bellcloth. Blaker had discovered some means of regaining Carradine Manor for Rad. Yet it must be something more. Blaker must have some power to undo her foul knitting at any time, and dispossess him anew – on her own whim! So as long as Carradine played lapdog, he could live in seeming authority. Resist, and he would be cast out penniless. But what of Prothero?

The maid came breathless and frightened at the night summons. Thalia ordered her to bring a drink of hot chocolate, and to be sure to test the solid nuts for electrical property before making the drink. As Thalia gave the order, she felt herself recover from her frantic period of uncertainty. It had quite unwomanned her.

'You understand?' she asked this hopeless abigail. 'I want fresh milled chocolate, newly turned out from the tin pan.'

'The pan, m'lady?' The maid dithered, still half asleep. 'The chocolate nuts are in pieces of paper – '

Thalia smiled with satisfaction, her old self again. 'Listen, idiot. Mrs Thornton made a new half-hundredweight on Tuesday last. I myself sent word to the Officer of Excise, as law requires. Newly milled chocolate stays electrical for some time. Has that lazy cook not taught you how to test for that sign of newness with a shred of paper?'

'No, m'lady. B-b-but Is'll – '

Thalia smiled her sweetest. The watch in its hanging bracket showed ten minutes short of three o'clock. 'Why, then, the solution is plain! Rouse Mrs Thornton, and Mrs Randon. They will be pleased to show you how. And have the six serving maids woken. I wish them also to learn. It is a very necessary art.'

'Now, m'lady?'

'Yes, now. Why not?' Thalia stretched luxuriously. 'Light me two lamps. And set a fire while you are about it.'

'Yes, m'lady.'

Thalia sank into her pillows, revelling in the pleasure of her new certainty. The answers of course lay at Calling Farm, with that other jack-a'back Prothero, and his mouse of a wife. A morning visit was due. She would wring the truth from them – and once she knew the truth, God help that whore Blaker.

An urgent visit to Calling? Or a slower, more carefully planned visit? The latter, she decided, in spite of the urge to rush out there practically before dawn. She had made a ghastly mistake in not investigating, by every means at her disposal, the circumstances at Carradine before driving there. And suffered for it. No, this time she would be meticulous. Send a card, perhaps a short note? That was it. Say how pleased she was to have her neighbours restored to her! That imbecile Prothero was ever conscious of social distinction – which he totally lacked, of course. It was quite comical, the way he grovelled. As if an ex-cowherd could ever enter the gentry's ranks! A card would take one full day. Then the receipt of Mary Prothero's reply – full of gratitude for being noticed by so fine a lady. Then her own answer, after another day to maintain propriety, and finally her grand descent on Calling Farm. That was the trouble. Neighbourliness ruled that a simple visit took four days to arrange. But she would have the answers she wanted. Meek little Mary Prothero and her obsequious peasant husband would be only too delighted to provide them. Ammunition, wherewith to destroy the Blaker woman.

Distantly, she heard sounds of the household begin – very gratifying. The servants would realise that their Mistress' recent abstraction was now ended. Milton Hall was back to happy normality. And if Bitch Blaker had any sixth sense, she would be lighting candles to St Mary Magdalene, patron saint of all trollops, for protection. Or perhaps instead to St Anthony, patron saint of swine? She smiled with satisfaction at her little game. For herself, whom should she choose? Perhaps St Gertrude, expeller of rats? Or St Roque, dispeller of plagues? No doubts for her own Carradine: for him she would invoke the mighty St Leonard – he who shatters prison doors, and breaks chains asunder. Once achieved, she would cast off her own manacles. She herself was the only patron saint Carradine would ever need.

The night rider reined in at the crossroads and drew his cloak tight against the rain. He sat, thinking.

Coming quickly from the south, he had changed horses at Ipswich, then at Wickham Market and Saxmundham. His last mount had been hopeless, a gelding that cast its offside fore shoe almost as soon as he resumed his journey. That caused him to ask at a common inn for a swap. It was only after much arguing, and invoking the name of his master Sir Henry Hunterfield, that the innkeeper grudgingly allowed him to shift his saddle and the letter pouch, against payment of the fee for the check ticket he would need for legally passing each tollgate. It was fortunate the incident happened so far north of Colchester – famous for its 'lovely roses, ugly women' as the famous writer Defoe once joked about that town of brooding suspicions – or he would be sleeping in some ditch until dawn brought hostelries to life. At least he made good time, and was now north of Saxmundham, well into Suffolk. Even so, he felt uneasy. He was tempted to opt for the coast road, instead of following the rough track that ran due north-east. It would be safer, for should this mount fall lame – no experienced rider trusted inns on any night journey – he would be easy prey for any footpads, now those blackguards lurked in threes ever since the French wars ended.

His horse fretted. The inn he had roused was one he usually avoided when carrying the Squire's private mails south from Sealandings. Fine in daylight, but uneasy in the owl hours. He scanned the sky. Rain still, without the racing moon he loved to ride by. Riders had a saying: a half moon is better than a full sun. And it was true. Any mount worth its salt also loved moonlight, but this poor beast was already windbroken, and felt swaybacked. If he 'asked it the question', as the racing Fancy now said to each other at the Squire's racing parties, and wanted it to go flat out – as when escaping from pursuing footpads – it might be too spent to raise a gallop. Then he would lose his precious letters from the Deputy of the Sandwich Cinque Port and Colchester town's Justice. He had primed his own pair of Segallas flintlock pistols himself, and knew their worth from previous confrontations. But two shots only . . . He hoped one day for an old pepperbox pistol –six shots! – like Twigg used to make in London, or a four-shot ducksfoot flintlock, the sort ship captains carried. More fangled, maybe, but daunting enough. He scanned the road behind, the road ahead. Hardly a distant glim of light, and only the nightglow to go by.

The innkeeper had, oddly, hung out a second lanthorn as he had seen the night rider away. A signal? These inland taverners were in league with rogues and high pads. On the seaward road, he would be in reach of coastal taverns. It would be more secure, though a deal slower. The Squire would approve, if the letter pouch arrived safely.

Directly ahead lay Blythburgh. To the right lay the coast road to Dunwich, Southwold and thence Sealandings. He would have to explain how came he to Lorne House through Whitehanger, but . . .

On impulse, he swung the poor beast on to the easterly path, and rode towards the sea. He could change horses at Dunwich by cockshout.

'You are unhappy, Euterpe?'

'Not particularly so, Josiah.'

Reverend Baring appraised his sister. She seemed worried. This was strange, for she was not given to swings of mood, or sudden sorrows. Since coming to Sealandings she had proved most reliable, except for one lapse from grace, over her ridiculous concern for that leech.

They were reading in the withdrawing room. The rectory was quiet, apart from the sounds Bridget made as she swept the stairs.

'I understand,' he said knowingly. 'The affliction. But there is good in all this, Euterpe.'

'Good? In plague?' To his astonishment she sounded bitter. He lowered his book.

'Indeed,' he chided. 'Tribulation is for our benefit. Divine Providence ensures that, Euterpe.'

She too laid aside her book. He noticed how pale she was. Or perhaps it was a trick of the oil lamplight.

'Sealandings has tribulation enough, Josiah, without your approval of the terrible effects of a murrain.'

He gave her a fond smile. 'Approval, Euterpe?' He chuckled, wagging his head. 'Divine Providence does not need *our* approval, my dear. We must simply endure.'

She appraised him in turn. He had grown in stature these past weeks, taking on a bishop's gravitas. Listening to his ponderous pronouncements from the pulpit, seeing his orator's tricks displayed in full, she was almost sickened. He was actually enjoying these events. His long-winded sonorous preaching over the drowned girl's burial nauseated and repelled her. This was the dear brother from whom she hid all her true feelings, whom she evaded as if he were her worst enemy. Doctor Carmichael had been in mortal need of aid, and she had not been on hand – on account of her loving brother. This same vicar who, pious to a fault, relished finding Biblical analogies between Old Testament ramblings and the problems of this little harbour town on a remote coast.

'Euterpe,' this dear brother was saying. 'Obedience is our lot. To bow under adversity in spite of all.'

'Why, Josiah?' She was suddenly calm, her anger quelled to fight all the harder.

He was astonished. 'Why? Why, as example!'

'So others will do the same, Josiah? Endure? Humble themselves to sorrow?'

'Of course! It is our bounden duty!'

'Tell me, Josiah. Was rabble-rousing, to have Doctor Carmichael set upon and battered to insensibility, a good example?'

'Certainly not, Euterpe!' He rose to stand before the fire, legs apart, hands clasped behind his back in the attitude she knew so well. 'That was simply unfortunate. But it showed the popular feeling against sin. A holy response, of people with deep-seated convictions – '

'Deep-seated prejudice, Josiah!' she cried. 'Stupidity kills!'

'Euterpe! That is a shocking allegation, unproven – '

'Ask Doctor Carmichael for proof, Josiah!' she gave back.

'I see!' He was almost triumphant. 'I realised as soon as you started this diatribe – Doctor Carmichael lies at the back of it! For some weeks I have suspected that your absurd predilection for this penniless leech has lingered. And now it ghosts to the surface. Euterpe, I want to clear this ail, restore the harmonious relations that used to exist.'

'Ail?' She gathered her composure. 'You see my concern for this poor man as a malaise, Josiah? He is one of the few people in Sealandings who honestly tries to better the lot of anyone.'

'Better the lot . . . ?' He gave a harsh laugh. 'Tell me, Euterpe.

Whose lot *has* he bettered? The town? The sick? When he goes about openly admitting he has no knowledge of diseases? That his vaunted medical education – ha! Are those two terms not mutual exclusives? – was a hopeless sham? That he is ignorant of treatments? His drugs and simples fraudulent? Is that betterment, Euterpe?' He was pacing now. He rounded on her, thunderous. 'Or is it that he believes medicaments transcend God's almighty law, and so blasphemes?'

She stayed outwardly tranquil. 'Don't use your orator's tricks on me, Josiah. I have seen them all. And been unutterably bored by them.'

'Euterpe!' He was appalled. She had never spoken like this to him, not even when they were children. She was always the moderate sister, the smiling background, the friendly vague presence in the family. He inspected the title of the book she had put down. *Pride and Prejudice*. He should have known it would be some scandalous tale filled with crime and deceits. No wonder the author chose to remain anonymous. Why, rumours said it was even written by a woman – one clearly taken leave of her senses. It was an outright disgrace. 'I am outraged! But I forgive your scamandering opinions. They can only come from the oppressive atmosphere of this place, since these mad burnings started – '

'You are so right, Josiah! Doctor Carmichael would never make a clergyman. He is too concerned with the sick. No wonder you see him as an enemy. He is simply trying to do his best.'

'His worst, Euterpe! Can't you see? His very *reasons* are devilish! He plans to end a plague. How can that be? Is he God? Heaven itself has ruled that plagues are unalterable.'

'Can't *you* see, Josiah?' She was calm, almost sure Ven was right. 'If he succeeds, your holy arguments are nothing more than mad delusion!'

'Euterpe! What would our dear parents think to hear you speak so outrageously? I thank the stars they rest in peace.'

'Think on't, Josiah.' She stood to confront him. 'Ven believes in his hopes, just as you do in yours.'

'Mine are not *hopes*, Euterpe! My beliefs are unshakeable convictions! They are all truth!'

'Cherish them, Josiah! For if the cattle plague is brought to an

491

end by Doctor Carmichael's mad burnings and weird fluids, it is your mind that is flawed, Josiah. And not his!'

He stared at her. 'You have gone mad, Euterpe. You have the effrontery to doubt? To deplore your very education, upright and decent as it was?'

'Decency is no longer religion's prerogative. Now, doubt reigns supreme.'

'Blasphemy, Euterpe!'

She watched him recoil with dispassion. 'I should have spoken like this long since, Josiah. Be prepared for a greater shock still: I would walk out from here this instant, if Doctor Carmichael would invite me to be his housekeeper. It almost happened once before, remember. I regret not having gone. I ought to have. Poor I would have been, and probably lost your brotherly affection, but at least I would have met my obligations to myself, Josiah.'

'And neglected your obligations to all others?'

Her tone was quieter, not even unkind. 'I see I would have fulfilled my obligations to everyone else far, far better.'

'See?' he cried, baffled. 'I see and hear only madness. The end of civilised life! You must change back –'

'As I speak now, Josiah, so shall I speak tomorrow and ever. Accept it or not, so I am.'

She swept from the room, leaving him staring at the closing door.

54

The question was, what sort of vehicle should she take to Calling Farm? For one long afternoon of crochet, Thalia imagined herself driving in this carriage, then that. Maddeningly, the problem resolved into a choice of extremes: a small whirligig, or the grand phaeton. The estate coach would be too overwhelming for Mary Mouse. But what if she drove up with, say, herself at the reins of a dennet gig? Two seats only, herself guiding with informal ease – just the sort of visit to inspire confidences! Would the grand phaeton seem intimidating? She asked her husband's opinion, her motive for the journey suitably disguised. Infuriatingly, Fellows offered immediate answer.

'The dennet is out of the question, my dear,' he told her. 'It is beautifully sprung, gives the more restful drive. But you may not be aware of the vulgar saying, that whoever rides in the dennet gig crushes the backs of three ladies.' He smiled at her alarm. 'No, nothing superstitious, Thalia. Its three springs – one cross, two lengthwise – have common nicknames, after the three Dennet sisters of the London stage. You should have seen them, my dear! Unmatched for their dancing, wit, beauty! The phaeton is more modest. Besides,' he added candidly, 'you are too unskilled. Managing the dennet on autumn's roads can be hell. That Mehala girl could. She can drive anything from oxen to – '

Thalia slammed out and left him to his correspondence. He seemed always to be writing letters these days. Some aftermath of Cousin Charles' fiasco? Fellows was partnering Sir Jeremy Pacton in some mercantiling venture. He had spoken of it over supper, but she was too distracted to pay real attention. It involved ships lying at Lowestoft and London, and boring talk of the Americas where Pacton had cousins.

The following Saturday she drove out to Calling Farm. She insisted that the head footman Ennis accompany her, knowing he was one on whom she could rely. The delay was justified, for the horrible thought had occurred: what if that slattern Blaker's hold over Carradine was so complete that she forced him to *marry* her? The thought made her so ill she took to bed. Carradine was wild, a free-living creature who would die in captivity. All lay on this last throw of the dice. She was finally so well prepared that she had left nothing to chance. Ennis, the footman she employed in bringing Sealandings gossip, had twice been sent to the Carradine estates on pretexts. His tales suggested all was as she had left it.

The Protheros were expecting her. She alighted from the phaeton, and swished indoors. Nobody could offer such charm as she, when she wanted. All morning she had rested, and now looked the part, a visiting lady calling on a vastly inferior neighbour. Noble families had these obligations.

Mary Prothero was in a muted blue circassian gown bodice, its cross-over folds really not too hideously formed in a slightly darker blue. Quite surprising how effective she looked, really, but the astute could put it all down to how very slender – practically wasted away – this ineffectual hostess was, having lost so much weight. The folds came from the shoulders and crossed at Mrs Prothero's slim waist. The circassian wrap-round matched the lighter blue. Even the wrapper's lace strips were of the same colour. Quite nice, on someone vivacious. Thalia had vaguely expected the hostess to be flapping about in some ancient trollopee or slammerkin inherited from her grandmother. Why, she looked almost presentable! Nothing to rival her own plum-coloured cavalier-sleeved dress, the half-tight forearms fashion-ably closed in a series of bows of darker shade, and the bodice almost – not quite! – carolined as for evening wear. She had been tempted to wear something dazzling, but instead had settled for modesty; well, as much modesty as a titled lady could allow herself. Obligations were serious matters, and could not be shunned.

The welcomes were effusive, she was pleased to note. Prothero fawned in a new red spencer and a fresh white stock pinned high, almost like a dandy's hunting-stock. The fool looked ridiculous. Tea was laid in the afternoon room. Thalia took her place, murmuring appreciation. Here again, she was quite surprised. Any other woman of Mary Prothero's station would have covered her entire house with edibles and elegant dishes. This was almost sparse, not to say frugal. A mere ten or so sorts of cake, though sensibly including cold beef cake, sundry biscuits, again wisely including four kinds of hot biscuits, and no more than two sorts of fashioned creams, quite cleverly decorated. There were of course macaroons, ratafias, and a selection of various breads and sandwiches. She was pleased to see the salmon, the foie gras, and the salads. No salmagundi to spoil the general air of care. Yes, this little woman had perhaps a trace of quality in her. The tea cakes were small, thank heavens, and the choice of marmalades sensibly kept down to eight. And Bohea, with a sweet-scented Imperial Bloom, were the only teas on offer. It was all so precise and planned that Thalia wondered whether Mary Calling did not have some inner breeding.

She praised her hostess' selection and arrangements, but not too effusively. Mary Prothero accepted this without seeming at all overwhelmed, which was slightly annoying considering the immense favour being shown her miserable household by this visit. And the mouse was only a farmer's daughter, after all, even if her acreage and lineage were extensive. But Thalia had a purpose here, and must be single-minded.

'Your staff have excelled, Mrs Prothero.' Thalia repeated the praise, as a test.

'Thank you, m'lady.'

Thalia sensed rather than saw Libby, the chief maid, stir, and guessed that Mrs Prothero herself was responsible for the provinder. A hostess who actually evaded fulsome admiration from her betters? Thalia wondered if she should not have cultivated this Mary Calling sooner.

'We have the very best servants in the Hundred, m'lady!' Prothero said pompously. He gave a chuckle, but his eyes were bleak and humourless. 'We Protheros don't want to let Sea-landings gentry down!'

'Indeed not.'

'Shall I cakate, my dear?' Prothero asked. 'Or shall you do the honours?'

'Thank you, Jason.' Mary's quiet voice sounded kindly, but nipped any more of her husband's archaic effusiveness in the bud and mercifully kept him in his chair. 'Would m'lady find the Bohea or the Imperial tea to her liking? Others can be sent for.'

'Oh, Imperial if you please – '

'We have a dozen sorts,' Prothero put in eagerly. 'Never mind the expense!'

'How thoughtful.' Thalia affected not to notice Mary Prothero's face blanch.

Mary stepped in. 'Your kind remark prompts me to thank you for your own generous condescension, m'lady. Not everyone would visit to Calling Farm in the present circumstances.'

'Think nothing of it.' Thalia watched the maid prepare the tea. No mistakes so far on the part of this hostess. Perhaps the maid would blunder? 'It was my intention to come as soon as I learned of your happy return.'

'Happy indeed, m'lady!' from Prothero.

'I trust the sojourn at Carradine was not too exacting, Mrs Prothero.' Thalia sighed, when nothing was said in reply. 'I know only too well the difficulties. Oh, the hardships one has to endure! They can be limitless, yet a lady carries on. And the adversities among servants!'

'Home is the heart's place, m'lady.'

'How very wise, Mrs Prothero!' Thalia cried. 'And how very astute of Mr Prothero to satisfy your longing for Calling Farm, when such advantage lay at Carradine!'

'Lay, m'lady?' Prothero's face darkened. 'Lies there still!'

Thalia smiled, now on the right road. 'It *does*, Mr Prothero! You will doubtless resume your position there, once this terrible murrain is done with. And I shall be overjoyed to see you occupy both Carradine Manor *and* Calling Farm.'

Prothero seemed about to speak out, but Mary interposed to ask if her guest was ready for tea. The business of serving occupied them immediately. Mary conducted the conversation into cuisine. Thalia could have wrung the silly little woman's neck for her plain domesticity. It was quite some time before she regained the subject.

'I envy you, Mrs Prothero,' she finally worked into the conversation. 'Being able to leave so splendid a household as Carradine in the hands of no less than *two* housekeepers! I forget who mentioned it. Possibly Miss Carmady, before she sadly had to leave Sealandings with her brother.' She sighed. 'Mine is the burdensome duty of trying to place Miss Carmady in correspondence with some lady who could recommend a trustworthy housekeeper. I think you know that Lieutenant Percy Carmady seeks a residence hereabouts?'

'Mrs Tyll has left Carradine Manor, m'lady.' Mary's expression was drawn and tense.

'Left?' With difficulty Thalia affected a mild puzzlement. Had this stupid woman managed things better in her brief reign at Carradine, that odious bitch Blaker and her evil spawn would never have dug in. 'You dismissed her, Mrs Prothero?'

'It is a complicated matter, m'lady.'

'I respect your reserve, Mrs Prothero.' Thalia felt Prothero almost desperate to explain, but kept her gaze on his wife. A long-pent dam gives more when it breaks. 'Might I ask only if the circumstances of Mrs Tyll's departure preclude any further employment? I am only anxious to offer Miss Carmady the best advice.'

'The lady was dismissed without a character, m'lady.' No wonder Mary Prothero looked concerned as she made the admission. 'Certain events at Carradine took place without my approval.'

'Without your. . . ?' Thalia hardly needed to pretend shock. Her hand rose to her throat. She whispered, 'That cannot be, Mrs Prothero! It goes against all . . .'

'You might well say!' Prothero interrupted belligerently, frowning in anger. He sent Libby off with a gesture. 'I was already on the point of approaching Sir Charles Golding, as a wise gentleman, for advice.'

'About a housekeeper's dismissal, Mr Prothero?'

'Not exactly, m'lady.' In spite of his wife's clear agitation the burly farmer went on. 'There have been anomalies since we left Carradine. Carradine himself is in authority there, with me lacking a single shred of proof of ownership.'

'I fail to understand, Mr Prothero.'

'Please, Jason,' Mary tried. He did not even look her way.

'You give me an opportunity to invite the great families' intervention,' Prothero said harshly. 'This must be brought into the open. It smacks of deceit!'

'You can't mean Carradine?' Thalia gasped.

'I signed over temporary possession. Carradine was my agent, m'lady.' Prothero paused to let the word sink in, only narrowly preventing himself from reaching across to tap her knee for emphasis. Thalia listened to the crude oaf in appalled fascination.

'I had copies, m'lady. The witnesses were new artisans, as a precaution against enthusiastic loyalty of Carradine Manor's resident staff. Supposedly,' Prothero said bitterly, 'to protect *me*! Do you see the perfidy?'

'Whose?' Thalia asked weakly. Her mind was drawn into dreadful contemplation. How vulnerable the great families were against treachery from the lower orders!

'Thieves stole my copies from Calling Farm, m'lady. The lawyers inland never received their copies. No copies exist at Carradine.'

'Then all is simple, Mr Prothero!' Thalia cried, pleased. 'Reclaim your rightful possession! Simply drive up and . . .' It did not sound quite right, but Thalia could only think of that thieving mare who had stolen Carradine.

'And what, m'lady?' Prothero said heavily. 'That housekeeper of his seems to . . .'

Thalia understood his sudden silence. Carradine had duelled several times, more than one death resulting. That duels were now illegal would mean nothing to him. She felt a sharp sting of pride. But how cunning Blaker had been! Were anyone to expose her fraud, Carradine would be dispossessed. Leave her untouched, and she remained queen of Carradine, man and estate.

'I do not understand, Mr Prothero,' she said innocently. 'How could so many copies of such a valuable agreement be lost?'

'Thieves, perhaps.' Prothero was uneasy even stating this conclusion.

'Surely Rad Carradine would leave, the instant he knew of the position, Mr Prothero?'

'I would have hoped so, m'lady.'

'I mean, a gentleman's honour is . . .' Thalia looked from Mary Prothero to her husband. Prothero was about to explode, his features suffused and dark.

A gentleman's honour is everything, she had been about to say. As vital as a woman's reputation. Without it, all fell as a house of cards. But Carradine, with his peculiar view, could behave with wild unpredictability that could stun and bewilder even herself. Desperately trying to murmur some equivocation to buy time, she

498

struggled to put her own mind in place of her lover's. He was destitute, or he was rich beyond comprehension. He was nothing, or a grand noble. Vagabond, or gentry.

He had friends in London, true, but only as a member of the titled aristocracy. His drunken reminiscences, she remembered, were of mad carousings, wassailings with high-born London ladies, cavorting, and even salon rape. Gambling too, fights, suicides of officers in despair at having lost their last on a single card. He had mumbled names too, in half-sleep. Isabella the most frequent, doubtless the infamous hostess Mrs Isabella Worthington. From fragments of gossip, Thalia could piece together Carradine's tempestuous affair with that notorious bitch: the headlong amour, that august whore's inevitable betrayal by Carradine – what woman could keep him chained for long, except herself, Thalia De Foe? And lastly Carradine's expulsion from London society when his dalliances were exposed by some oh-so-well-meaning friend. Thalia had long since stitched *that* tapestry into a picture: Isabella Worthington was a coquette of King and princes. Her hate banished greater nobles than Carradine.

So London was virtually closed. He had nowhere except Sealandings. And in any case London residences needed fortunes. She shivered. Fortuitously, her response was misunderstood as compassion.

'Please, m'lady. Don't distress yourself on our behalf.' Mary Prothero poured more tea. 'Your sympathy does you great credit.'

Thalia seized the opportunity, with convincing modesty. It was vitally important to keep close to the Protheros. 'Thank you, Mary. May I be allowed to use your given name? It seems so terribly *wrong*. Your husband satisfies Carradine's gambling debts – when Mr Prothero had certainly no need to!'

'Quite right!' Prothero exclaimed.

'And so owns Carradine Manor.' Thalia almost choked on the words. 'Now you are *illegally* dispossessed! Has this new housekeeper . . . ?'

'Anything to do with it?' Prothero ended for her. 'I suspect so!'

'Then your next step is quite clear, Mr Prothero,' Thalia said firmly. 'You must visit Carradine and discuss its return this instant!'

'Do you think so, m'lady?' Mary asked doubtfully.

'Indeed I do, Mary!' Thalia waxed indignant. 'Give Carradine the chance he surely needs, to act honourably! To serve the agreement he signed!'

She already knew the outcome. Carradine would be compelled, by Judith Blaker, to refute Prothero's claim. And possession was nine points. If that sinister woman who held Carradine in thrall was able to spirit away documents by the half-dozen, then she surely had lawyers crooked enough to serve her malign interests better than Prothero's. So Prothero's demand for return of Carradine Manor would achieve only one thing: it would prevent marriage between the Blaker woman and Carradine. For a noble to wed his housekeeper was one thing; for him to marry her when there was the slightest taint of scandal was altogether another. Prothero was obviously incapable of tact. Within an hour, his visit would be all over the Eastern Hundreds. Simplicity itself!

'Should Carradine wish to take offence, m'lady. . . ?' Prothero was thinking of being challenged to a duel.

'You obviate that, Mr Prothero, by explaining that you come to request the return of Carradine, at *my suggestion*! You are thus merely acceding to a lady's request, and not acting solely on your own behalf!' She smiled with apparent relief at Mary. 'No gentleman could possibly take umbrage! Is that not so, Mary dear?'

'I fear that matters have already gone too far for any withdrawal now.'

'*What* matters, my dear?' Thalia was feeling friendlier by the minute.

Mary was about to decline comment, but Prothero bulled in. 'The serious problem of finance, m'lady.' To her horror he seemed about to use her own given name, but forbore at the last moment. 'My funds drawable on Carradine Manor have been refused me. Illegally. I cannot afford the vast expense of this burning madness, this witchery brought down upon Sealandings by that insolent dog-doctor! I am being compelled to indemnify the entire Hundred against part of the total losses, simply because I kept a wise silence – from the pure and honest wish to spare everyone anxiety!'

Thalia tutted in sympathy. 'I shall approach Sir Fellows, Mr Prothero, and prevail on him to visit the Squire. There *has* to be some moderation of this disastrous policy, or Sealandings will be black as the North!'

'Thank you, m'lady,' Prothero said, almost wagging with relief. 'It is a delight to hear so grand a lady express support. We must all stay as one, together against the commonalty!'

'Too kind, Mr Prothero,' Thalia murmured, hiding her revulsion.

The instant this insolent peasant carried out her plan – stirred Blaker up to realise the outrage she had committed – he would have to be slapped down. *We*, indeed! She had been right all along, recognised how Blaker had seized power. Thievery, trickery, perjury, and blasphemy all in one. How very proper the little scene must have seemed, to this stupid couple! The reserved, grave witnesses at attention by the master's accounting table, ready to sign. Blaker the housekeeper marshalling quills and parchments. The Protheros, smiling approval even as they were duped, and Carradine going along, at first unsuspecting. The signing ritual taking place even as Blaker's own cutpurses were already lying in wait for the couriers at some inn along the night roads . . .

'Mary,' she said confidingly. 'If there is anything I can do, please call on me. Even if you need only a sympathetic friend to hear what develops, do not hesitate to visit Milton Hall. You will always find a ready welcome there.'

They parted a full hour later with protestations of regard. Prothero was almost jubilant. Mary curtseyed in the porch as the phaeton wheeled slowly away. She found herself wondering exactly why so grand a lady would visit her. She had heard servants' whispers of illicit 'conversation' between a certain titled lady and Carradine, but dismissed it as common tittle-tattle. Thalia De Foe's concern had seemed genuine – but so it would, if she was the lady in question, would it not? Events had proved that any approach from her husband to Carradine would serve no fruitful purpose, so why advise Jason to call there? She resolved to dissuade him from making the visit, but Jason was so desperate to enter elegant society he would do anything the gentry suggested . . .

At the entrance to the main drive at Milton Hall, Thalia ordered the carriage to pause for her to inspect the new bush-garden there. Ennis accompanied her. She made extravagant pointing gestures until the moment they were out of earshot of the postillions.

'Well, Ennis? What did you learn?'

He proved as laconic as ever. 'Libby the chief maid told me Calling Farm is mortal impoverished. Nine bills sent to draw Carradine Manor moneys have been returned. Mr Prothero has sent to lenders in St Edmundsbury. Nothing more, m'lady.'

Thalia smiled. Even more desperate than she had been led to believe! 'Forty shillings more for you anon, Ennis.'

'M'lady.'

That dusk, Ennis was summoned by the master to prepare a pouch for letter post. In the reading room Ennis delivered the same terse report he had given to the mistress.

'How much did she give you?' Fellows asked.

'Forty shillings promised, sir.'

Fellows was curious. 'Does she pay, Ennis?'

'No, sir. All depends on the outcome.'

De Foe smiled. That was Thalia; pay Dame Fortune but default on servants.

'Well done, Ennis. The account I have for you and Meg is sound. I hear Meg recovers. Doctor Carmichael says she may resume duties tomorrow.'

Ennis bowed and withdrew with the riding pouch. Fellows thought a moment. Before long, Ennis and Meg would want to leave, with the nest-egg he would provide for their valuable services. He would miss two such excellent spies – and Meg's humble but undeniably essential bedroom activities. He sighed. Well, all things pass. And times were hard.

Doctor Carmichael was discussing the request for supplies of alchemical fluids from the Goat and Compass with Tayspill when Mehala entered the room.

'We have an obligation, Mr Tayspill,' Ven was saying to the bailiff. 'These are the very people we are trying to help, are they not?'

Tayspill was unsure. 'Help is one thing, Doctor. Giving them license to exploit our reserves of alchemicals is altogether different.'

'But don't you see, Mr Tayspill?' Ven cried eagerly. 'We will show Mr Fowler and all Sealandings that we are on their side!' He drew Mehala into the argument. 'I am sure Mehala will agree!'

She smiled to see him so animated. The excitement of the new counts these past three days had brought him new life. The lines on her charts were falling ever lower. Since Southman's tragic demise, no new patients had been found. The remaining herds of cattle were restricted in movement, admittedly, but the proportion being found sick was less every day. The number of bonfires lit each morning was reduced to units rather than tens.

'The Goat and Compass has asked my help, Mehala, because of Fowler's spoiling brews!'

'We have little enough, Doctor,' Tayspill countered, appealing to Mehala. 'We bought all the black oxide of manganese available, and copious amounts of sulphur. Then liquid – what is it called? – muriatic acid. Then, as that expended, red oxide of mercury. Now we have little of that. And the men are complaining of the colour of that new puce-coloured powder – '

'Oxide of lead, Mr Tayspill. As long as they follow instructions and stay upwind, no harm will ensue. I myself collect of the green gas, and always by daylight so it can be seen.' He smiled at Mehala. 'They thought nothing happened at all in candlelight, for it fails to show.'

Tayspill doggedly held to his argument. 'The point is, Doctor, we are running short. We have bought all that the apothecaries and druggists can provide.'

'But to convince folk of our sincerity – !'

'Doctor. We are out there, scouring the farms for sick cattle. You comb the town district for ailing people, rich or poor, clean or filthy.' Tayspill stirred the carpet with the toe of his boot. 'They *see* our sincerity!'

'And they fear it, Ven,' Mehala added.

'All the more reason to offer help!' Ven cried. 'Goodness always repays goodness, Mehala.'

Tayspill was becoming agitated. 'Doctor, you are blind! You ignore people's greed. They would sell any principle!'

'No, Mr Tayspill. We must look to the innate good in Man, not the bad.'

It was becoming serious. Mehala quickly stepped in. 'Ven. Mr Tayspill. May I please cope with Mr Fowler's request?'

'Cope how?' Tayspill demanded, still worried. ''Tis I must face the Squire's accounting table.'

'Lives are at stake, and livelihoods,' Ven countered.

'I shall accomplish both aims, gentlemen,' Mehala offered. 'Say I can, and I shall.'

'Help him to end the spoiled brews? Yet *not* give him that help?' Tayspill looked at her, his face settling into a slow smile. 'Very well, Mehala. If Doctor says.'

'Ven?' She saw him hesitate, and made a promise. 'Mr Fowler will rejoice his tavern is saved, by what I will provide.'

'Go, then, Mehala. When you finish the new day's lists.' Ven's last doubt vanished in her lovely smile.

The Goat and Compass was quieter than Mehala had ever seen it when she arrived three hours later. Ben Fowler was in a sour mood, and looked beyond her to see if she was accompanied by anyone carrying containers of the compounds he desperately needed. She disabused him instantly, and remained on the doorstep, wanting to remind him of her previous visit.

'I call on Doctor Carmichael's behalf, to offer you what you asked.'

'Then where it is?' Fowler was suspicious.

'You need the chlorium vapour, Ben. Why?'

He snorted in derision. 'You'm thick as you look, girl! For to prevent the spoilage of my ale! The strong beer's working off, too. It's mortal bad fortune.'

'Can you not buy sweet ale, then?'

'You know I cannot. The cost be too huge.'

'Doctor Carmichael told you how to use the gas fluid, did he not?' She saw his hesitation, and said innocently, 'Only, he is worried you don't know how to use it safely.'

'Of course I do, girl! Didn't he explain it to me in detail, over and over? He was here in . . .'

'In your stinking privy, Ben?' She smiled, now not so innocent. 'I remember. And how you used his imprisonment for your own profit.'

'I need the fluid, girl! I face ruination.'

'Very well, Ben. I shall see the chemicals and fluids come to you this day.'

'You will?' He was astounded, hardly daring to hope. 'Is this some trick?'

'No. It is expense, Ben.' She saw his face settle into craftiness. 'Demur or refuse, and I walk away. Doctor Carmichael will accept what I say.'

'What's your arrangement?'

'You get the fluid, against a written agreement to restore our alchemical supplies. From London.'

He gasped. 'But the cost! You can't expect me to – '

Mehala turned away. 'I see I can't expect you to . . .'

'Wait!' Fowler fidgeted on the doorstep. 'Wait. I might be able to get a small amount from – '

'*All!*' Mehala spoke back with ferocious intensity. 'Say it, Ben Fowler. Or I shake your dust off my shoes!'

'Right! Right!' He wrung his hands. 'You've no idea how terrible it is, Mehala. Customers I have served these ten years go to the Donkey and Buskin. Not one coach . . . They're saying my small beer's afflicted by the cattle plague . . .'

Mehala's calm demeanour reclaimed his attention. 'That isn't all, Ben Fowler. That arrangement only exchanges our chemicals for your chemicals promised, does it not? With you standing to gain, and Doctor Carmichael to lose.'

'Lose?' he cried in anguish. 'Lose what, for God's sake?'

'Lose any chance of recompense, Ben.' She smiled, relishing the chance of forcing him to make restitution. 'A guinea an hour, for the time Doctor Carmichael was kept confined.'

'At the magistracy's command!'

'And half a guinea for the rudeness with which you treated him, Ben Fowler. Pay me.'

'Pay?' He literally staggered. '*Pay?* But that amounts to . . .'

Mehala smiled up into his eyes. 'I know, Ben. Is it not a terrible sum? So I propose repayment over a period of one year, to be delivered to Doctor Carmichael every month. Let it equal one twelfth of all the ale, small beer and strong, you sell for a twelvemonth.'

He groaned, his lips purple. 'Impossible! It is extortion, oppression of the very worst kind!'

'I know,' she said with mock sympathy. Then, briskly drawing her shawl about her. 'Good day, Ben. May your troubles end soon.'

'Mehala.' He was broken. 'One thirty-secondth?'

'My twelfth will become a tenth soon, Ben.' She saw him digest the warning. 'You see, I can't trust you. You will cheat Doctor Carmichael, lie that you have sold less than usual, that his fluids failed to cure the spoilage, that custom has fallen off – '

'I swear on the Good Book, Mehala!'

'The Good Book has let us down lately, Ben Fowler,' she said with asperity. 'As have its readers!'

'Then I offer a basic payment!'

She paused, pretending to think. 'Who will verify the barrelage to be paid in addition?'

'Whomsoever is Constable?'

Her laugh took even herself by surprise. 'Like Moat? No. Squire Hunterfield's bailiff.'

He swallowed, made to bargain, then crumpled as she took a step.

'Let it be so, then,' he said.

Mehala smiled. 'My felicitations, Fowler. You have just regained your livelihood.'

Meg was pleased. Fellows entered her cubicle, this once with Mrs Randon's foreknowledge. For the sake of propriety he carried an imposing ledger. Meg was waiting, sitting on her truckle bed.

'I knew you would come, masther.'

'You are recovered?'

'Doctor Carmichael saw me daily, masther.' She smiled shyly. 'Mrs Trenchard chaperoned.'

He slid the door bolt. 'Let me see.'

She was ready there, too, lowering her unlatched bodice and turning, her dress falling about her waist. The savage cuts of Thalia's whip hardly showed. He stroked the scars. 'Good, loyal Meg. Monies – yours, and your man Ennis' – are full accounted at Holt's in London. I've had Ennis taught to write his signature. I wish you all fortune.'

'I am grateful, masther.' Her eyes filled.

'The gratitude is mine, Meg. I want you every way, this last time. A lovers' farewell.'

506

Smiling she helped him free of his clothes, and knelt, his hands already tugging her hair.

55

Hunterfield's meeting took place at Lorne House's counting house in its main farm. Tayspill attended with two fore men, Carmichael and Mehala.

'Is this the good news we expected?' Hunterfield asked. The plans and charts meant nothing to him.

'Indeed it is, Squire!' Tayspill grinned with pleasure. 'Do you not see? This black pillar on Mehala's picture shows the numbers of livestock taking ail. One pillar each day. See how they lessen?'

Hunterfield inspected the paper quizzically. 'Fewer beasts will become sick?'

'No, Squire. It shows what has happened, since Doctor Carmichael's scheme started, the burnings, the alchemicals.'

Hunterfield pointed to the red crosses. 'And these?'

'People, Squire.' Ven spoke uncomfortably into the quiet. 'Crosses for dead. A circle means one sick person.'

'They too have ceased, Squire,' Mehala interjected quickly.

Hunterfield smiled. 'So many lists, Mehala. I swear the expense of paper will cripple me!'

The men laughed dutifully, shuffled as Hunterfield examined the charts.

'Doctor Carmichael. Why is the end pillar in dots only, not lines?'

Ven reddened. 'That is my way of showing the numbers of beasts due to fall sick. Tomorrow.'

Mehala finished the claim for him. 'It will not happen, Squire. If that number *should* succumb, yet do not, then . . .'

'Then?' Hunterfield asked.

'Then the epidemic is ended. As Doctor Carmichael predicted.'

The Squire looked at the skies through the window for some time. 'Tomorrow.' He said the word once or twice more. Then men cast glances at him, then at Tayspill's smiling face. Hunterfield turned back.

'Ahead of time! By how much?'

'Nigh on nine weeks, Squire.' Mehala was standing close to Ven, who nodded confirmation.

'Of course,' he added hesitatingly, 'there is always the possibility of some farmer transgressing the rules – '

'Tomorrow,' Hunterfield said. He tapped the large inked chart. 'These papers are proof?'

'No, Squire,' Ven said patiently. 'We use them to see how the disease progresses. Like in London's Great Plague.'

'It has been of utmost value, Squire,' Tayspill advised, wanting praise.

'I'm sure,' Hunterfield said politely. 'Doctor, you understand that this triumph ends your position as High Constable?'

'Oh. I had quite forgot . . .'

Hunterfield dismissed the grinning men, but beckoned Mehala. 'A moment.'

She walked with Hunterfield to stand outside the counting house as the men dispersed.

'I corresponded with officers in south East Anglia, Mehala,' Hunterfield said. 'I have definite news, from the Isle of Southwold.'

Mehala's mouth dried.

'Concerning one Elijah Rebow, of Red Hall. Are you prepared?'

She nodded in assent. Hunterfield watched Tayspill telling off the fore men to their duties for the day. The skies were almost clear of black smoke. A single streak of blue showed to the south-west.

'The body of one Elijah Rebow was washed ashore at Mill Bay, near to Harwich. It was discovered by soldiers from the Orwell and Stour coast batteries, three days after you were rescued by *The Jaunty*. Identification was by means of keys, clothing, and a wedding ring – '

' – of iron,' Mehala said dully. 'Inscribed with his name.'

'Just so.' Hunterfield looked at her expression, bleak enough to make a man shudder. 'The body lies buried in a common grave on the Isle of Southwold, at St Edmund's Church.'

She answered his unspoken question. 'No, Squire. I thank you. Nothing more.'

'As you wish, Mehala.' He remained curious. 'There will be

some inheritance . . .' He looked pointedly after Doctor Carmichael, who was with Tayspill. 'It would benefit you to assert your rights. I understand Red Hall is quite profitable.'

'Profitable?' She searched his face.

'Its sale could provide the purchase price for Shalamar, were Sir Fellows De Foe willing to sell. The sale could be conducted in secrecy.'

Mehala looked after Ven, striding along, his old surtout flapping as ever. He occasionally stopped to expound something to Tayspill, then hurried on. As she looked he stumbled over some stone, recovering his footing. He exasperated her a hundred times a day with his preoccupations, his incessant reading, his imaginings and fevered enthusiasms . . .

'In secrecy?' she echoed.

'Milton Hall might be prevailed upon to transfer Shalamar to some willing buyer. Though your moneys might not be sufficient to restore it fully.'

She considered this. Two years of mourning was not mandatory, but a lesser period would be reprehensible. Two years was endless. Ven could decide to move anywhere, do anything – unless he had good reason to stay. 'Thank you, Sir Henry,' she said at last.

'The Deputy will provide a separate certificate as widow, and of interment.'

He raised a glove to the counting house as she started to say her thanks. 'Get your documents, Mehala, lest they blow away. Sealandings will recover its breath now the skies are clean of your Doctor's damned smoke.'

At Lorne, Letitia was being told what arrangements she was to make for her wedding. Tabitha was dissatisfied with Lydia's choice of bridesmaids, but her opposition was overruled.

'Priscilla is quite unsuitable, Lydia. On the grounds that her colouring . . .'

Is the same as yours, Miss, Lydia said cryptically to herself. Tabitha fought on.

'Her cousins are the Misses Astell, Lydia,' she reminded. 'They will want to come, too. They are always troublesome.'

'Tabitha!' Lydia rebuked. 'I must remind you that family

discussions are no place for unfortunate opinion. Any more, you must retire to your room!'

'Yes, ma'am.' Tabitha tried to invoke Letitia's aid, but her sister failed even to notice her appealing glance. She had done nothing but moon lately. She even misplaced books, since accepting William Maderley's proposal. It was stupid. And now that horrible Priscilla Mortimer – though hadn't she a brother called, what, Rohan, something regimental? Tabitha brightened. 'I apologise. Has Letitia an opinion?'

'Letitia will accept mine, of course!' Lydia smiled fondly at her betrothed sister, who was reading absently in the window bay. 'I shall be happy to acquaint Mrs Maderley with my decisions, after I have informed my dear brother.'

Tabitha had to clench her hands to stop herself screaming in impotent rage. Why was it that Henry was always Lydia's own personal unshared brother, when he was being coerced Lydia's way? Such impudence! *My* dear brother, if you please! Any other time Henry became *our*.

'Beg pardon, ma'am.' Crane appeared with a silver tray bearing a letter.

'Let local correspondence wait, Crane,' Lydia said off-handedly, enraging Tabitha further.

'It is from oversea, ma'am. It bears Captain Vallance's regimental seal.'

Even Letitia came to at that, as Lydia accepted the letter and carefully broke the seal. Her husband always cross-wrote. Whole sentences were rendered indecipherable by clumsiness when opening.

'What does he – ?' Letitia gestured in time, to silence Tabitha's soft scream. So many letters from the Kingdom's overseas stations contained grim news that it was wise only to rejoice after a full reading.

'He is coming home!' Lydia raised her head in quiet astonishment. 'James is coming home!'

'Oh, Lydia!' Letitia's cheeks ran with tears. 'I am so happy for you!'

'Wonderful, Lyd!' Tabitha exclaimed.

'Yes!' Lydia said, a little too brightly. 'Marvellous news!'

'How soon?' Tabitha asked. 'If his letter accompanied dispatches from – '

'Yes, Lydia!' Letitia cried. 'Think! If Captain Vallance were to disembark at the Red Sea, proceed overland to Alexandria, and there embark for Marseilles, why, he should be – '.

'The thirtieth of this month.' Lydia maintained her joy with some difficulty, her mind racing.

'In time for the wedding!' Letitia exclaimed, still dabbing her cheeks. 'Oh, Lydia! How we rejoice with you! A month of happiness!'

Tabitha cried, 'You must open your own house at Wheatfen this instant, Lyd!'

'How could we forget that!' Lydia said, appalled. 'Heaven! There is so much to *do*!'

Tabitha clapped her hands. 'I want to be the first to tell *my* dear Henry the very second he returns from perambulating with Miss Olivia!'

Lydia was about to issue yet another sharp reprimand when she caught herself, and paused. Tabitha's features were composed in innocence.

With James returned, her own duties at Lorne House were ended. She would have to open Forreston immediately. That meant leaving Lorne, to Letitia's care. But Letitia's marriage was soon, for Henry disfavoured long periods of betrothal and had given firm instructions on the matter, to Letitia's delight.

Which meant the keys of Lorne House would be in Tabitha's hands. Lydia smiled brilliantly to cover her dismay. Tabitha, mistress of Lorne, its great estates and lands, with the immense authority of the Lord of Sealandings? Unthinkable! The girl was too wayward, in her sudden moods and pouting shows of temper. Inexperienced, though she of course considered herself the most knowledgeable woman on earth. It was utterly ridiculous. In fact, wholly unallowable.

'See, Letty!' Tabitha gushed, realising the implications as swiftly. 'Our dear sister is overcome!' She rose and crossed to pat Lydia fondly on the shoulder. 'Lydia dear, we rejoice more than words can tell!'

My very first decision, Tabitha thought sweetly, would be to send Miss Maderley off with a flea in her ear. Olivia was encroaching far too much on Henry's time lately, and indeed his preferences. She had said as much to Lydia, only to earn herself a stern reprimand. The days of being lowly in authority among the ladies of Lorne were fast ending. Olivia Maderley's time, like Lydia's, was over. She herself would find the right woman for the Squire of Sealandings.

Lydia forced a smile of happiness. 'I know how deeply you both share my joy,' she managed to say.

Letitia wept unrestrainedly at the pure family love. Tabitha borrowed a cream-coloured handkerchief, so much more flattering to her complexion than plain white, to dab her eyes, when her reflection was visible in the seeing-glass. Lydia watched her, and counted days.

The affront almost made him turn on his heel and walk out. Then he bethought himself, and stood his ground in the writing room.

'My appointment was with Carradine,' Prothero said.

'I am aware of that, Mr Prothero. Pray be seated.'

'I would rather stand.'

Judith Blaker was amused at his manner, but refrained from smiling. This dolt was a *gorgio* of some importance. Wealthy still, though unable to meet the payments dunned on to him by this murrain plague. She did not want his antogonism. After all, a simple man was just the sort a woman might need. Rustic plainness was easiest handled.

'As you will, Mr Prothero.' She frowned, as if some sentiment gave pain. 'I have a document here which will give you some solace, and some discomfort, sir. Please first read its contents.'

'First?' Prothero eyed her as he took the document. Not so long ago this woman had curtseyed and fawned on him with the best of them at Carradine Manor. Now, she addressed him as a mere visiting artisan. 'Please explain the three men waiting outside.'

'Mr Greyburn you know. And Hobbes. The third man is Foley, a journeyman joiner presently in Rad Carradine's employ.'

Rad Carradine, was it now? Not 'sir', nor yet 'the master'. 'Their purpose?'

'Witnesses, Mr Prothero. To your signature on the document you hold. I have five other copies.'

'So certain of the outcome?'

She seemed to reflect on that jibe for a moment, then returned her look at him, and said simply, 'Yes.' Her demeanour shocked him. Here, in this great mansion which he owned.

He read the copperplate handwriting, down to the last word. And a second time. He looked up. She was waiting with unnerving composure.

'Send for Carradine,' he said harshly.

'No, sir. Carradine does not concern himself with money matters.'

Prothero exploded. 'By God! He concerned himself enough with money matters when he tried to win fortunes on a rigged barefister! *And* he used my money to do it!'

'What do you accuse Carradine of, sir?' she asked calmly.

Prothero fell silent, fuming, the parchment clutched in his hand. His fear of the man's latent violence returned. 'Nothing,' he said with some difficulty. 'Nothing.'

'You will sign?' She was interested, honestly interested in the man's fight with himself. A woman would have no problems – she would sign and be off, retaining shreds of her dignity and vowing eternal hate for having been forced to yield. A man was entirely different. Hatred, yes. Never quite as durable as a woman's, it would anneal with other emotions as time passed, meld into something new, something usable. Look at the strange way that Fellows De Foe had come to accept Lady Thalia's infidelities with Hunterfield, with Carradine too for that matter. Though of course love had long since flown from Milton Hall.

'Eight hundred sovereigns is nothing,' Prothero got out.

'It is eight hundred gold pieces more than nothing, sir.'

'By accepting, I renounce all claims to Carradine estates?'

'Naturally. Seeing you have no claim upon Carradine.'

'Nothing provable,' he shot back.

'Sadly the same thing in law, sir.' A courtesy title was nothing, when the battle was already won. Politeness was the wisdom of victors.

'You arranged it all? The thefts, the cutpurses who stole the parchments from the couriers?'

She widened her eyes. 'La, sir! You affront a lady!'

'Is Carradine here?' The writing room adjoined the study with its reading room through double doors.

'I am not sure of Carradine's movements today, Mr Prothero. He wants this affair settled.'

Prothero nodded at the threat implicit in the word *affair*, the euphemism for a duel. She could easily relay his outburst to Carradine, which would be the end of all.

'Very well.'

She rose and looked about as if for eavesdroppers, lowering her voice. 'Mr Prothero. You have been quite scurrilously treated. Please do not blame me for my part. These events were none of my doing. I try hard to oppose Carradine, but I am in mortal fear of him. He is a fiend incarnate.'

Prothero too glanced about, infected by her surreptitious manner. 'What can I do?' he asked quietly. 'I am bound.'

She placed a hand on his arm, coming a step closer to look into his eyes. 'Just remember Judith Blaker, as one who would be a friend to trust, sir. Is'll be good to you, if you will allow.'

Prothero swallowed hard, glancing at the closed double door. 'Trust is hard come by. And costs mortal.'

Her voice was now a whisper. 'I want you to trust me, Mr Prothero. You will see exactly how trustworthy a friend I can be. I promise. You will not regret signing. Let it be our contract. Yours and mine.'

'For what purpose?' Her attractiveness drew him even in these circumstances.

'For *our* purpose, Jason. Yours. Mine. I shall prove it, when I can shed this Carradine for another master. With you in command of much, much more than Carradine Manor.'

Ten minutes later, before the three waiting witnesses, the documents were signed. Prothero renounced all claims on Carradine against a payment of eight hundred sovereigns. The sum was paid over that moment, and Prothero was ushered out of Carradine, a mere departing visitor.

For a few moments she stood at a window watching Prothero leave. An enemy, yes, but not quite. And not for long. She had sparked his eyes to a gleam, with her casual pressure of hand on arm, her hints. He was not a wicked man – she knew many. He was a simpleton, a *dinnelo*. Who so badly wanted to be gentry with the *gorgios* that he had littered the Eastern Hundreds with *mullo mas*, sick-dead meat, and thought himself justified. Ambition was a gift, or madness.

'*Keir-rakli?*' She spoke the word softly. Prettiance stepped into the room from the hall and silently closed the door.

'I hate you calling me "maid",' Prettiance said sulkily.

Judith took no notice, her eyes following Prothero as he rode away. 'Take the other parchments. Put them where I told you.'

'What are they?'

Judith smiled. '*Miri!* Mine.'

She waited until Prettiance gathered the documents and slipped away. Carradine was waiting in the reading room, pacing before the fire of sea coals. She entered, locked the double doors and approached him smiling.

'Well?' he demanded impatiently. 'Did he take it?'

'Like a lamb.' She gave him the one copy, and lied, 'Mr Greyburn keeps the others in the estate files, darling.'

He sank into an armchair, stared dazedly at the fireplace, the books lining the walls, the furniture. She lifted her skirts and stepped astride his extended legs. She lowered herself on him, pressing her face to his, whispering.

'Judith wants a pat, Rad, for being good. Undo our latchings, darling.' She relished the feel as his *churi* hardened. 'That's it, lover. Seal our bargain.'

56

The day seemed thick with a heavy mist, almost like a mid-winter fog. Ven was already awake when Mehala arrived from Lorne House at seven. Doctor had been walking the rough grounds of Shalamar, Mrs Trenchard told Mehala, since the third hour. She had glimpsed his lanthorn from her cottage.

Mehala made his thick milkless porridge, bread with cheese, and tea. A peasant's breakfast, he told her many times. She went out to meet him, and sat to share the meal. He told her, as he had done every day since the new arrangement, that she ought to have her first meal at Lorne with Mrs Kitchiner. She smiled refusal, as always.

'You don't understand, Ven.' This was the first time they had said anything more than generalities. 'I want to break fast here. Eating together was probably the first social thing ancient peoples ever did. It was a sign.'

'A sign?' He was puzzled. 'Breakfast is the most important meal of the day, Mehala. We doctors know little, but we do know that.'

The previous day's work had ended close on midnight, when he had accompanied her to the Lorne gatehouse.

'A sign of being together. It is worth the delay. And it pleases me.'

He tried to scan the sky through the thick mist. He asked her if she had seen any early activity from Tayspill's men. She had seen Nodger's group in the distance, but no new fires.

This morning he finished his meal slowly. Usually, he would be up and away, talking of possibilities, of the herds, the dangers. Today he sat with her.

'What will you do, Mehala?'

The question took her by surprise. It was the first time he had let optimism through. His eyes seemed hollow. She knew with sudden intuition that he had indeed not gone to bed, but stayed awake throughout the night, watching the sick town as he had watched by the recumbent sick. The epidemic was ended; he was telling her that he too believed it now.

'What will you, Ven?'

He inspected his spoon closely. 'Did you know there is a most useful bone gouge, based in design upon the Arabic spoon of the the Middle East?' She waited, knowing he would eventually answer. 'I am ashamed, Mehala.'

'Shame is for those who never try, Ven. We try. You most of all.'

He raised anguished eyes. 'To fail times without number, Mehala. My learning is mostly rubbish. My surgery that of hacking at injured bits, without rhyme or reason. It is not learning as such, merely practice based on hearsay. Folklore without understanding.'

'You won't surrender, Ven. I know it.' She put her hand on his. 'You will keep trying. Here or elsewhere.'

'Shalamar?' He gave a wry smile and shrugged. 'I cannot even provide for you, my dear. I need you. Not simply any woman. You, Mehala. I can't give you food, clothe you, keep a roof – even this leaking shelter – over your head.'

'There will be money, Ven. Some. Mr Fowler of the Goat and Compass will pay a fraction of his sales, once his beer comes through the spoilage.' She raised a hand to stay his protests. 'He agrees. He acknowledges the saving of his tavern.'

He brightened. 'It could be used for the workhouse.'

'Part, certainly,' she said firmly. 'But a little to stop you having to live on nothing, charity, scraps from Tayspill's men. You cannot go on this way. Then there is Shalamar.'

'We will be evicted once the murrain has gone. Soon. Today, perhaps.'

'Or we might stay.'

'You think we will be allowed?' he asked anxiously. 'There will be rent, upkeep. I never did get my finances in order – '

'Hunterfield might help us to an arrangement permitting us to stay here indefinitely.' She wanted to break the news the Squire had given her, that she would be free after the time of mourning was done. This was a man who would disbelieve any woman's leanings, even her obvious love. Tell him in so many words, he would still doubt. He would have to be taken by the hand like a child and shown the way into love. Was a woman attracted only towards extremes? As was Thalia De Foe, married into an established county family, yet said by servants to be mad for Carradine, rake and rioter, her husband's avowed opposite? As perhaps she herself, married by a madman's compelling force, and here loving Ven Carmichael, a soul so distressed by life's sorrows that he even avoided her eyes when close to, frightened by the love he might discover there. Extremes, in the complex range of men. What then of old Mrs Trenchard, over forty years with her one solid countryman? And did the same hold for men? If so, was that Harriet Ferlane woman Ven had once proposed to at some opposite pole to herself?

He could not meet her gaze. 'I see how Hunterfield looks at you, Mehala. I want no favours from him. Not for us. I understand, for I feel the same. He is a great noble. And you are a lady, above my station.'

'You are thinking of the lady you once loved, Ven.'

He smiled freely then, in easy denial. 'I didn't know what love was, until you came from the sea, Mehala.'

'I stay with you, Ven. If you go, I go with you.' She reached up and gently touched his face. 'I made the mistake once. I never shall again.'

'And Squire Hunterfield?'

'Is Squire Hunterfield, Ven. I am not for him, nor he for me. I am for you.' She was warmed by the look he gave her. 'Who knows? I may become the first-ever woman doctor, if you teach me right and I learn well!'

He became rueful. 'And do more good in one year than I in a lifetime, Mehala. You have an aptitude few possess. I watch you, with children, the sick.'

'I reflect you, Ven. As a mirror does a likeness, as stars concentrate the night's glim.'

A carriage sounded on the drive, and a whistle. They separated, Mehala hurrying for the accounts of farms to be visited and calling for Mrs Trenchard. Ven went for his notebook and quills, then outside to take the reins of the trap. Simple Tom tipped his hat, and wriggled his fingers to mimic fire.

'Any yet this morning, Tom?' Ven asked.

Simple Tom drew a flat hand levelly across his mount's mane.

None. He shivered to indicate the eerie stillness of all Sealandings now the epidemic was suppressed.

'Good news, eh, Tom?' Ven said.

The mute raised crossed fingers, and spat for luck.

That afternoon, Fellows De Foe sent for Thalia to join him before tea. She sent advice by her abigail that she was unable to come immediately, but would join him later when her headache had lessened. Fellows sent a note in reply, saying that her carriage would be sent for today, rather than tomorrow, if she insisted in procrastination.

She arrived then, pale and intent. He rose with every show of friendliness.

'How charming you look, my dear!' he exclaimed, dismissing the maid-of-all. 'You have always graced Milton Hall, better than any other lady could!'

'Have, Fellows?' She sank on to a walnut saddle-cheeked chair. 'Past tense?'

'Deliberately, my dear.' He was full of himself, always a dangerous mood.

They had made love the previous night, she distractedly, barely conscious of his threshings and moans. He had expressed gratitude afterwards, as he always did. Sometimes it was with a mere, 'Thank you, Thalia.' Other times it was with profoundly felt tender speech. Last night it had been, 'For that, much thanks, Thalia.' Unusual, but she had been too preoccupied to play the irritating game of trying to read meanings into his words any more.

'For what reason? And *what* carriage, Fellows?'

'Your carriage, my dear. To wing you away from this coast. Inland, to a better and more wholesome place.' He spun, catching her expression of dismay and deliberately misreading it. 'I see how delighted you are, Thalia!'

'Why now?' she whispered. She could not possibly quit Sealandings, leaving that harlot in charge at Carradine Manor.

'Why now?' He affected astonishment. 'Why, Thalia! Have you not noticed the terrible cattle plague? And counted the crosses in St Edmund's churchyard? Of course you have! I heard you complain bitterly of the dereliction of Sealandings, its remoteness from society.'

'But *now*, Fellows!'

'Now better than ever, my dear! I hear Captain Vallance is returning – probably landed by now, I shouldn't wonder. Which means the Vallances will open their homes near Wheatfen instantly! Other families are leaving – '

'The murrain is over, Fellows. It must be! There are no new fires . . .'

He spread his hands disparagingly. 'Dearest! What does one bonfire more or less tell us? That Hunterfield's men are making a late start? That the smoke is blowing inland, for once sparing us a blacking? No, dearest. You shall leave here. I have arranged it. A surprise!'

'To go where, Fellows?'

He was hugging himself with glee. 'I have ordered our house at St Albans opened. I knew you would be thrilled! Did you ever receive a more welcome present? You shall find everything exactly as you would have arranged it yourself!'

He smiled down at her. 'No! Don't say anything. No thanks are due! I love to give you these surprises, dearest. Remember the ruby pendant I brought from London on our last wedding anniversary? How delighted you were?'

She remembered. He had returned at a most inopportune moment, with Carradine rising half-dressed after she had enjoyed an exhilarating two hours of passion with him in her bedroom, with that slut Meg coming scampering in, squeaking that the master was come home of a sudden . . . Yes, Fellows could surprise.

She smiled at him and rose, extending her two hands. 'You are the most thoughtful of husbands, Fellows darling!' She let him kiss her. 'This very evening I shall set about making plans! Over the next few days, to furnish – '

Fellows was smiling. 'No, my dear. Tomorrow morning. Six of the clock, you depart in the high carriage for St Albans.'

'Tomorrow?' She trilled a laugh, unconvincing even to her own ears. 'But, darling! How can I possibly arrange – ?'

'All is arranged.' He relinquished her hands and stood away, now gazing at her with something less than adoration. 'You shall leave on the stroke. The grooms and servants have their orders.'

She strove to recover a semblance of her authority. 'But my maids, Fellows! There is Meg – '

'The maids work to the early departure. Meg is no longer in your employ, nor Ennis. They leave tomorrow. I have seen to their funding.'

'That is my task, Fellows!'

'Was, Thalia.' His wintry smile warmed at some inner humour. 'Past tense again. What a day for those!'

She sank into her chair, feeling pale as death. 'It is too soon, Fellows.'

'It is not a moment too soon, Thalia. As you well know.'

'Is there no means to – ?'

He smiled, his old self. 'No, Thalia. There are changes in Sealandings. New and terrible ones, I think. You must escape them. Think how thrilling St Albans will be!'

'St Albans.' She echoed the name dully. A small cramped town of soporific stupor, without society, a gillion miles from Carradine.

'I knew you would be overwhelmed!' He pulled her upright. 'Go and prepare for your journey.'

'Yes, Fellows,' she responded, and left defeated.

An hour before dusk, Hunterfield rode to Whitehanger along the coast road, taking the path past the sea dykes. They were holding, and the pumping long since stopped. A channel had been dug to run rainwater from the wooded slopes into the low-lying fields, though the land still showed signs of ravaging by salt waters. It would be a year in the recovery, but was at least rescued.

He dismounted at the Darling cottage, handing Betsy's reins to Simple Tom. Mrs Darling opened the door before he had chance to knock, and in a flutter admitted him.

'Emiline. Is your man at home?'

'No, Squire. He is in the south, carrying winter fodder, there being precious little . . .' She paused, scarlet with embarrassment. 'I mean no offence, Squire.'

'I understand.' No work, for a local waggonmaster. The cottage interior was almost a curiosity to him each time he called. The joinery chairs, the table, the sloping wattle-and-daub walls, the flagged flooring, the oven, hearth and inglenook. He sat as bidden. 'The murrain seems ended, Emiline.'

'Ended, Squire? Don't they take. . . . ?'

'Many months, with the Lord's aid.' He shrugged. 'Less, it seems, if we give Heaven some assistance.'

'Praise be!' Her eyes filled with tears of relief. 'Will the harbour be as before, now? The land? Markets?'

'God willing, Emiline. The first flock of Norfolk Black turkeys walked into town this very day.' He paused a moment. 'How fares my little Clare?'

She calmed. 'Well, thank you, Squire. She learns apace, can read and write. I follow your instructions.'

'I want to see her soon, Emiline. No,' he hastened to say as she took alarm. 'For my own satisfaction.'

She hesitated. 'I am ever grateful for your consideration, Squire.'

'My duty, Emiline.'

'No, sir, saving your pardon. Many evade. I could have suffered. Instead, you found me a good man, marriage, a home.' She smiled wistfully. 'It seems a lifetime since I was a young maid-of-all, and Shalamar ablaze with lanterns for great gatherings.'

He looked at her. Still appealing, her form endeared, her hair straying in wisps from her mob cap. Her face was unlined, though tanned from the coast weather.

'I promise your husband will not want for waggoner's work now, Emiline. Tell him that I will make up any deficit.' He cut short her thanks. 'There is something else. I think of marriage.'

She had remained standing by the inglenook. Now her hand went to her throat.

'Marriage? Does that mean Clare will – ?'

'No. I shall not take her. She is yours, as mine. I shall have a different household very soon. There will be opportunities. I will see her provided for.'

'But the ladies, sir. Your new . . .'

'Wife.' It sounded strange even to him. 'My sisters will be differently placed. Mrs Vallance rejoins her husband soon at Wheatfen. You will have heard of Mr Maderley and Miss Letitia's betrothal?'

Which, Emiline thought, left Miss Tabitha. No creature to cross. Why, even as a young moppet she had a ferocious temper worse than any village ragamuffin's. But Sir Henry was not given to guesses. There must be something in the wind for Miss Tabitha.

Something far away, please God. Clare was but a child still, and masters of great houses did not always know what cruelties happened below stairs.

'Indeed, Squire. One brightness in a dark month. That and Mehala.'

'Mehala?' The change in his voice surprised her. 'What of Mehala?'

'I – I – didn't mean to intrude, Squire, but 'tis said she is mind-mended, and will . . . stay with Doctor Carmichael at Shalamar.'

'Mrs Trenchard, I suppose,' Hunterfield sighed. 'Secrets are unknown along this damned coast.'

She coloured slightly, finding him looking at her. The day's light had drained fast. Only the flickering fireglow illuminated the interior, bringing an intimacy to the room. It must have been in front of this very grate that Carmichael had fought his terrible fight for Clare's life, Hunterfield supposed. Aided by Mehala. He shivered. Emiline Darling hurried to put more wood on the fire with a small cry of annoyance. He stayed her with a hand.

'No, Emiline. Not that.'

She stared, gasped, both hands at her cheeks. 'I could not! Not here, not with – '

'Where is Clare? With the Overtons?'

'Yes, sir. But – '

Winifred Overton, Emiline's cousin, would not allow Clare home until she saw the Lorne House groom and his master leave.

'Now, Emiline. As before.'

'But what if – ?'

'Nobody will,' he said. Protesting and worrying, she hurried to undo her dress, begging him not to be long in taking her.

Outside, Simple Tom saw Mrs Darling draw the curtains. He pulled his riding cloak tight round his shoulders, settled his hat brim-down, and nudgd his mount into the lee of the cottage, Betsy sidling after at a tug. The tide had turned, and a breeze freshened from the east. He estimated an hour's wait, about the usual, scanned the darkening skies to gauge the time. Clear and clean, all this livelong day. Perhaps at last a return to normal heavens above Sealandings.

57

The Sunday service was over. Reverend Baring was displeased, not least by the occasional spaces he discerned in the congregation. How soon did folk forget the benevolence of God! For over two weeks now, as autumn gave way to the creeping cold of winter frosts, there had been no new sickness. Sealandings was recovering its busy life. Ships were in harbour, and the waggons on the move again.

He stood in his thick cassock, his priest hat needing holding against the wind, greeting the people leaving the church. He wore kidskin gloves, as most Established clergy still did in spite of the damnable move to abolish the custom.

'Good morning, Squire,' he said to Hunterfield, smiling obsequiously and bowing low. 'Good morning, Miss Maderley.'

He had exchanged harsh words lately about gloves with that loathsome prelate at Chelmsford, sinisterly mad for change at any price. What, he remembered arguing in heated correspondence, of Honorius' opinions of the twelfth century? Were they to discount him? And the factual evidence of William of Wykeham's red silk pair preserved at New College, Oxford?

'Ah, indeed, good morning, Mrs Vallance! I do so regret hearing of your impending departure from Sealandings – though,' he was quick to fawn, 'rejoicing in its cause!'

'Thank you, Reverend.'

'I look forward all the more to your return for the happy occasion!'

Only a distant murmur as she swept out.

She seemed less than content. Was it the closeness of her brother to Olivia Maderley? Reverend Baring wondered if he ought to look up the rulings on degrees of kindred for marriage. A brother-in-law and sister-in-law could surely marry without impediment. . . ?

'The organist was somewhat less than musical, I found, Rector.'

'Good morning, Sir Fellows! Ah, yes. A slight indisposition in my sister. No, nothing untoward. I pray she will be back with us very soon.'

'I hope so. Though I shall be gone to London shortly. St Dunstans-in-the-West parish.'

'Not for long, I trust?'

'That depends on others, Reverend.'

Miss Matilda Gould had played in Euterpe's stead, whose absence was a cause of tattling among the parishioners. But then what was not? The return of Mehala to Shalamar with that odious sinner, that opposer of God's omnipotent goodness Doctor Carmichael, was proof enough that gossip sometimes selected its targets aright. And just as often chose them wrongly.

The worshippers thinned to a trickle. Letitia Hunterfield and her betrothed were among the last to leave. The lady accosted him, asking him after Euterpe's well-being. He found her scrutiny uncomfortable.

'Nothing doctrinal, Miss Hunterfield,' he assured her earnestly, as ever assuming that others too thought first of heresy. 'My sister's regrettable absence is more an opportunity for Miss Baring to make assessment of her own responsibilities than to signal discontent. Do not disturb yourself.'

'I would have Miss Baring call, at her convenience, Rector, should she wish to do so.'

He flushed with pleasure. 'Why, Miss Hunterfield! Such condescension! We are honoured!'

'I am dismayed that the distance between your sister and myself has increased, Rector. Please assure Miss Baring . . .'

William Maderley listened to the compliments. He was dismayed by something much more important than the mere lack of communication between two ladies. He deplored the absence of the plague fires, that constant billowing smoke, the wondrous effects, the staggering cattle dying in the meadows, the untended harvests. Opportunities such as those came so seldom. Like the tempestuous floods, the broaching of the sea dykes, now restored to a banal normality too mundane for any artist worth his salt.

Across the churchyard, through the dispersing congregation, he saw Doctor Carmichael. Same old battered beaver, same old flapping surtout. But new boots, he could tell even at this distance.

And was he not carrying some sort of new leather case? It looked for all the world like a –

'A gunsmith's box, William. Is that what you stare at?'

Maderley turned to greet his friend. 'Good day, Bartholomew. Your work?'

'My own fair hands!' Hast said with mock pride. 'Heaven alone knows what he has in it – nothing, probably, though I hear he sends to London for some instrument or other. I am making a piece for him. A screw, on a large key. To do with teeth. Horrible thought.'

Maderley was already miles away, speculating on whether he dare call at Shalamar and ask to witness some kitchen table operation. But Carmichael could be difficult on the sanctity of the sick. Another obstacle to true art! He began to wonder if Squire Hunterfield, when once his brother-in-law, might persuade Doctor Carmichael to see things in a less restrictive way, and allow him in to selected operations to paint the suffering.

'Oh, yes,' he said to Letitia, as she took his arm. 'Coming! See you soon, Bartholomew.'

The gunmaker stood watching as the artist and his betrothed walked together down the church path among the yews. He saw Mehala approaching from the Norwich road. The same instant, William Maderley also noticed her and seemed to pause, recollect himself, and walk on with Letitia.

Bartholomew sighed, batted his hat on his knee and donned it. His own fortunes had been less than well served lately. Over twenty years old now, he felt age wagging a warning finger. He had admired so many girls, and so often if truth be told, that he felt his intentions were as difficult for himself to discover as anyone else. For just a while, he had felt something stir between himself and Mehala. But now she wore black, and a black bonnet, and was outside anyone's orbit for many a moon.

'Yes, Mr Hast,' Reverend Baring's voice intoned ominously. 'Isn't it reprehensible? That woman a known widow but a few days, yet she has not the good grace – or penitence! – to come to church of a Sunday!'

'Perhaps she believes differently, Rector. Something . . . doctrinal, perhaps? The nonconformists are extending faster than – '

'Pah!' Reverend Baring shuffled angrily. He did not moderate his voice, not caring who overheard his unfavourable opinion of such dire enemies. 'She seemed to have sense, once. Too much, to lean towards such misguided anti-Christs!'

The gunsmith noticed several Sealandings folk acknowledging Doctor Carmichael as he threaded his way through the press in the Market Square. His success would hold – at least until the next rumour, malicious or otherwise, disaffected people again. His own trade was surer, dealing as it did only with death and the means of causing it. With the new percussion system spreading apace, the art of killing was nearer perfection than any doctor could bring the art of life. An irony that the one science could not embill the other, as one bird feeds another before it is powerful enough to fly. Or was it simply that lethality held the greater gain for mankind, and life was somehow valued the less? One thing was certain: the great families had become gentry by reason of their greater might, not by meekness. Humility was the profession of the lowly, not nobles.

He bade Reverend Baring a good day and went towards the Square. This week, the first market would begin. Already two or three licensed tinkers and pedlars had come to Sealandings, occasions for excitement, as if they heralded a return to prosperity for all. Stray pikers! With a few ribbons! To be welcomed as kings making royal progress throughout the Hundreds! It showed the depths of people's fears, and their apprehension that Sealandings would be long blamed for the disastrous murrain. He had work to do, behind his closed doors this Sunday. Orders for weapons were growing fast. He was already far behind.

The passage of Mary and Jason Prothero through the congregation was not as well received. Few made acknowledgement, though Doctor Carmichael doffed his hat and hesitated, to bow awkwardly to the gig they boarded. Only Mary responded, with a shy glance and an inclination of her calash hood. Prothero stared ahead, affecting not to notice the Doctor. Bartholomew gave a casual wave to Ven, who returned the greeting before continuing on his way to meet Mehala. Hast did not stay to watch.

Ven smiled as she approached. 'Mehala. I thought you had gone to Sunday service.'

She smiled impishly. 'My service is in my heart, Ven.'

'Shhh.' He reddened. Folk were almost close enough to hear. 'I

528

have been banned from St Edmund's. There is no need for you to earn the disapproval of everyone.'

'They do not disapprove, Ven. One or two admire. And I think some even envy.'

Ven glanced about. This was uncomfortable talk among the pious on a Sunday. Holiness came well armed, and in mobs, as he knew to his cost.

'Did you see the Nelmes family?'

'Yes, Ven darling. All are well. The cowpox has not come back, though.'

He coloured deeper at her endearment, but tutted in vexation at her news. Without a good staunch case of cowpox there was no source of vaccination for people.

'I shall call at the Goat and Compass, darling,' she told him, amused at his discomfiture. 'The first payments are due on Fowler's small beers, so we shall have enough for food again. And to pay Mrs Trenchard.'

'Yes,' he said, uneased. 'I am not at all sure of the morality of this, Mehala. It seems so . . . unfeeling to accept moneys one has not properly earned.'

She bobbed a curtsey to a passing family. They were accompanied by Veriker the clockmaker. He raised his hat. Ven returned the salutation thoughtfully.

'I wonder if Mr Veriker could manufacture an instrument, Mehala. I have one promised by Mr Hast, but the obstetric forceps I have heard of might well be more the sort of thing a clocksmith's skill would be inclined to produce.'

'I think he might fear for his trade, Ven. What if a babe should die in birth, and the stillbirthing be laid at his door?'

'Mmmh,' Ven concurred glumly. 'It is a danger. I am used to that animosity. Perhaps it is justified.'

'Gunsmiths are less sensitive to such considerations,' Mehala said. 'Perhaps we will do better to stick to Mr Hast. Or try to order some instruments from inland, when we have the money.'

'You are right, Mehala.' He was looking at St Edmund the Martyr's squat tower. 'We must come to some arrangement.'

Mehala gently drew him aside to let the last of the carriages pull out of the Square. He saw the verger close the church doors. He cleared his throat.

'Mehala. I have a small journey to make.'

'I know, Ven. To the workhouse. I shall accompany you. It will be better if –'

'Not yet awhile, Mehala. Perhaps in an hour or so?' He seemed uncomfortable, almost evasive.

She was worried. 'What is it, bonny? I will come. I dislike us going separately, ever since the religionists hurt you.'

'Please,' he asked. 'We shall meet . . . under the Corn Mart. I shall not go far, I promise.'

She scoured his face, and reluctantly gave ground. 'If you say, darling. I shall be there. Promise me you will be safe?'

'Too safe, Mehala!' He said it with a smile. She was only partly reassured, but stepped back to let him go.

He paused. 'One thing, Mehala. It is very charming, and pleasing, but do you think you might possibly be giving scandal, to such as overheard your use of endearments, in public places?'

'Why, darling?' She widened her eyes innocently.

'People might assume . . . They might start to think . . . You see, Mehala, some folk do condemn us for being, well, almost as if . . .'

'But we are, Ven.'

'Shhhh! Please. For me, Mehala. Be as circumspect as you can, in your mode of address.'

'If you say, my . . . Doctor.'

He was relieved, and nodded. 'One hour, then. At the Corn Mart.'

She waited until he was almost out of sight along the Norwich road, then followed at a discreet distance. She saw him enter Parker's common stables, and emerge a few minutes later carrying something coloured. By then she was standing by the hedgerow near Bettany's windmill. She watched as he walked past, his head down, towards town. Then she followed. Where he went, so would she go.

Ven felt he was being observed, but saw nobody except a few children playing and a few families out to visit others. The weather had turned too chill for walking, Sunday's common pursuit. He kept on, carrying his light burden and his instrument case, and entered the churchyard.

It was empty. The great yews were bending slightly in the wind.

How had they managed to last so long, with seemingly so little give in them? The wise tree bends before the gale, and survives.

The grave was apart from the rest. The graves were not quite in lines, but had a semblance of order. This one lay separate, an ungrassed mound without a headstone. No flowers. He tutted in irritation, then felt apologetic, when a thorn from his bunch of roses pricked his finger. Of course it would have to be the one injured in all that contumely. It was still somewhat swollen, but was at least usable now.

He stood at the foot of the grave and cleared his throat.

'Hello, Bella.' He coughed on to his wrist in preparation. 'It's me, Doctor Carmichael.'

He did not feel in the least foolish, standing there talking to the air above a grave destined to lie unmarked. The land was at the edge of the churchyard, outside the boundary proper. The grave was dug lying north-south, another cruelty undeserved.

'I'm sorry, Bella. I failed you. As I've failed Mehala. I could have fought, if I'd had the courage, but I trusted blindly in people. I should have *made* them listen. There would then be none of this. You dying alone, lost like . . . like Mehala might so easily have been.'

He had difficulty seeing for a moment, brushed a hand across his eyes. He held up his bunch of roses as if she could see them from where she lay in her grave.

'I got these from the common stables, Bella. You must have often seen the roses from Two Cotts. I think perhaps you liked them. I know nothing about you. But I should have seen you safely away from harm.'

He laid the roses down on the grave. There was no container. He tutted again, thinking, I never plan ahead. What is the matter with me, for heaven's sake?

'I don't know how to consecrate ground, Bella. Nor can I hold an arvill, a funeral feast. But I can read the burial service for you. For us people.'

The book was borrowed from Mrs Trenchard, her mother's. He began to read, haltingly at first, then gathering conviction. It started to rain, slowly at first in great drops, then settled to a steady drizzle. His beaver was in his hand, his leather case on the ground.

'. . . ever more,' he ended.

'Amen,' a voice said. He looked round, startled.

Mehala was standing beside him. She had approached unheard, and was shawled tightly.

'Heathens!' a voice boomed. 'Pagans!'

Reverend Baring stood at the edge of the churchyard, hand outstretched into the air in admonition.

'I'm sorry if I give offence, Rector,' Ven began. Mehala angrily stepped in front as if to shield him.

'Heathens, Reverend Baring? When it's you that despoils and damages, in the name of anything that takes your fancy?'

'Please, Mehala.' Ven tried to disengage her, but she would not heed.

'No, Ven! This odious man claims to be your enemy? Then let him be so!' She raised her voice to vent her rage. 'Know this, Reverend. My man and I are going to visit your precious parish workhouse, that stinking cramped prison of verminous filth you set aside for the poor! It's victory you want, is it not? It's power, subjection, is it? Well, you'll get none of that from Doctor Carmichael and his woman, now or forever! It's a battle you s'll get! That's God's truth!'

'I forbid – !'

'*You can't forbid*, you . . . you thump-cushion!' Mehala shouted. Ven tried to pull her away. 'Don't you understand? *We won't go away!* Not until your whole miserable carping crew are finished for good!'

'Leave this holy ground!' Baring shouted. 'I abjure you in the name of God – !'

'Abjure all you like, dolt!' Mehala brushed away a wisp of hair that had escaped in her fury. 'This is free common ground, remember? Unconsecrated, where you flung this poor girl. Too improper for the likes of you, but ideal for the likes of me and my man! And for poor Bella, God rest her!'

She fumbled for a moment, caught Ven's hand and struggled to force something on his finger, raising her head at last triumphantly.

'There! It's done! With this ring I thee wed, Ven Carmichael!' She seized him and kissed him fiercely on the mouth, rounding on the appalled priest who stood gazing down at her in horror.

532

'Isn't that the Church's own law, priest?' she yelled, beside herself. 'That it is the betrothed who do the marrying, while you priests only look on?'

'Blasphemy! Shamelessness!'

'Blaspheme yourself! It is the truth! Sibberidge is only church custom. We need no bans. So now I am his wife, he my husband. In the eyes of Heaven itself! So says the law of the land *and* of churches, Rector!'

She linked arms with Ven, and said mildly, 'Come, husband. Come home for a short while before we start our work at the poorhouses.'

Ven stared at his hand. An iron ring was on the third finger of the left hand, a new iron ring.

She smiled at him, ignoring Baring. 'I had it made for us, my darling, at Temple the blacksmith's forge. He did not know what it was for.'

'Married?' Ven was astonished. He glanced at Reverend Baring.

'It is true. All laws say so, Ven. Sibrit, what folk call the sibberidge bans here on the coasts, are as unnecessary as a church, and as that holy man yonder. People simply choose to forget, in the gaiety of marriage and their eagerness for ostentation.' She smiled, indicating the cleric and the grave. 'We even had our two witnesses.'

'It seems rather irregular, Mehala.'

'The service can wait two years. Our marriage starts now.'

'I mean, I ought to have given you a ring.'

He was scarlet as they left the graveyard and went by the hedgerow to the Market Square and started the uphill walk along the South Toll road.

'That too can follow.' She took his instrument case from him in spite of protests, and hugged his arm close. 'Tell me what we do at the workhouse this afternoon. I don't know what to expect, never having visited there.'

'Ah, yes. Until now, I have been reluctant for you to see the terrible things there, the dreadful plight of the children and inmates. Now, we must begin the truly hard part of our work.' He gathered himself a moment, began earnestly, 'The children are kept in the most sordid conditions. Several are gone blind, with purulent eyes. Now, we don't yet know the true cause of this, but I do believe that if we apply some kind of astringent – though how we can afford silver compounds I do not know – as a lotion to the eyes, we might be able to – '

'There might be some at home.'

He halted. She had used the term before the Rector himself. 'Home?'

'Home, darling. Shalamar. Our home.'

'Our home?' he repeated, astonished by the very sound of the word.

'Come home, husband. Let us see.'

He looked directly into her, took a slow breath, and assented with a curt nod. He let her carry the instrument case, and together they resumed the uphill walk to Shalamar. Hesitantly he started speaking again, giving her his sparse knowledge and little experience with many apologies and ifs and buts, even stammering once or twice, but gradually gathering conviction as his enthusiasm took over and his gestures began, until his vehemence was thrilling her through and through and her eyes were shining with visions of the world that lay ahead.